THE
Becker Brothers
BOXSET

THE Becker Brothers

BOXSET

KANDI STEINER

Published by Kandi Steiner
Edited by Elaine York/Allusion Publishing
www.allusionpublishing.com
Cover Photography by Perrywinkle Photography
Cover Design by Kandi Steiner
Formatting by Elaine York/Allusion Publishing
www.allusionpublishing.com

Table of Contents

On the Rocks

To those who love whiskey and sunshine,

long summer days and front porch sittin',

dips in the river and never taking life too seriously –

this one's for you.

Chapter One

Noah

When you hear the word *Tennessee*, what do you think of?

Maybe your first thought is country music. Maybe you can even see those bright lights of Nashville, hear the different bands as their sounds pour out of the bars and mingle in a symphony in the streets. Maybe you think of Elvis, of Graceland, of Dollywood and countless other musical landmarks. Maybe you feel the prestige of the Grand Ole Opry, or the wonder of the Country Music Hall of Fame. Maybe you feel the history radiating off Beale Street in Memphis.

Or maybe you think of the Great Smoky Mountains, of fresh air and hiking, of majestic sights and long weekends in cabins. Maybe you can close your eyes and see the tips of those mountains capped in white, can hear the call of the Tennessee Warbler, can smell the fresh pine and oak.

Maybe, when you think of Tennessee, all of this and more comes to mind.

But for me, it only conjured up one, two-syllable word.

Whiskey.

I saw the amber liquid gold every time I closed my eyes. I smelled its oaky finish with each breath I took. My taste buds were trained at a young age to detect every slight note within the bottle, and my heart was trained to love whiskey long before it ever learned how to love a woman.

Tennessee whiskey was a part of me. It was in my blood. I was born and raised on it, and at twenty-eight, it was no surprise to me that I was now part of the team that bred and raised the most famous Tennessee whiskey in the world.

It was always in the cards for me. And it was all I ever wanted.

At least, that's what I thought.

Until the day Ruby Grace came back into town.

My ears were plugged with bright, neon orange sponges, but I could still hear Chris Stapleton's raspy voice crooning behind the loud clamor of machines. I wiped sweat from my brow as I clamped the metal ring down on another whiskey barrel, sending it on down the line before beginning on the next one. Summer was just weeks away, and the distillery swelled with the Tennessee heat.

Being a barrel raiser at the Scooter Whiskey Distillery was a privilege. There were only four of us, a close-knit team, and we were paid well for doing a job they hadn't figured out how to train machines to do yet. Each barrel was hand-crafted, and I raised hundreds of them every single day. Our barrels were part of what made our whiskey so recognizable, part of what made our process so unique, and part of what made Scooter a household name.

My grandfather had started as a barrel raiser, too, when he was just four-teen years old. He'd been the one to set the standard, to hammer down the process and make it what it is today. It was how the founder, Robert J. Scoot-er, first noticed him. It was the beginning of their friendship, of their partner-ship, of their legacy.

But that legacy had been cut short for my grandfather, for my family. Even if I had moved away from this town, from the distillery that was as much a blessing to my family as it was a curse, I'd never forget that.

"Hey, Noah," Marty called over the sharp cutting of another barrel top. Sparks flew up around his protective goggles, his eyes on me instead of the wood, but his hands moved in a steady, knowledgeable rhythm. "Heard you made the walk of shame into work this morning."

The rest of the crew snickered, a few cat calls and whistles ringing out as I suppressed a grin.

"What's it to ya?"

Marty shrugged, running a hand over his burly beard. It was thick and dark, the tips peppered with gray just like his long hair that framed his large face. "I'm just saying, maybe you could at least shower next time. It's smelled like sex since five a.m."

"*That's* what that is?" PJ asked, pausing to adjust his real glasses under-neath the protective ones. His face screwed up, thick black frames rising on his crinkled nose as he shook his head. "I thought they were serving us fish sticks again in the cafeteria."

That earned a guffaw from the guys, and I slugged our youngest crew member on the arm. At twenty-one, PJ was the rookie, the young buck, and he was the smallest of us by far, too. His arms weren't toned from raising barrels day in and day out for years, though his hands were finally starting to callous under his work gloves.

"Nah, that's just your mama's panties, PJ. She gave them to me as a sou-venir. Here," I said, right hand diving into my pocket. I pulled out my handker-chief, flinging it up under his nose before he could pull away. "Get a better whiff."

"Fuck you, Noah." He shoved me away with a grimace as the guys burst into another fit of laughter.

I shook the handkerchief over his head again before tucking it away, hands moving for more staves of wood to build the next barrel. It took anywhere from thirty-one to thirty-three planks of wood to bring one to life, and I had it down to a science — mixing and matching the sizes, the width, until the perfect barrel was built. I hadn't had a barrel with a leak in more than seven years, since I first started making them when I was twenty-one. It only took me six months to get my process down, and by my twenty-second birthday, I was the fastest raiser on our team, even though I was the youngest at the time.

Mom always said Dad would have been proud, but I'd never know for sure.

"Seriously, though," Marty continued. "That's three times now you've creeped out of Daphne Swan's house with the cocks waking up the sun behind you. Gotta be a record for you."

"He'll be buying a ring soon," the last member of our team piped in. Eli was just a few years older than me, and he knew better than anyone that I didn't do relationships. But that was where his knowledge of me ended, because just like everyone else, he assumed it was because I was a playboy.

They all assumed I'd be single until the end of time, jumping from bed to bed, not caring whose heart was broken in the process.

But I wanted to settle down, to give a girl the Becker name and have a few kids to chase after — maybe more than anyone else in Stratford. Only, unlike all my friends, I wouldn't just do it with the first girl who baked me a pie. There were plenty of beautiful girls in our small town, but I was looking for more, for a love like the one my mom and dad had.

Anyone who knew my parents knew I would likely be looking for a while.

"Daphne and I are friends," I explained, stacking up the next barrel. "And we have an understanding. She wants to be held at night, and I want to be ridden like a rodeo bull." I shrugged. "Think of it as modern-day bartering."

"I need a friend like that," PJ murmured, and we all laughed just as the shop door swung open.

"Tour coming through," our manager, Gus, called. He kept his eyes on the papers he was shuffling through as his feet carried him toward his office. "Noah, come see me after they're gone."

"Yes, sir," I replied, and while the guys all made ominous *oooh's* at my expense, I wasn't nervous. Gus had nothing but respect for me, just as I had for him, and I knew maybe *too* confidently that I wasn't in trouble. He had a job that needed handling, and I was always his go-to.

The door swung open again, and the teasing died instantly, all of us focusing on the task at hand as my brother led a group of tourists inside.

"Alright, remember now, this is another area where no pictures are allowed. Please put your phones away until we venture back outside. Since we're one of the last breweries that still makes its own barrels, we don't want our secrets getting out. We know at least half of you were sent from Kentucky down here to spy on us."

The group laughed softly, all of their eyes wide as they filtered in to get a better look at us. Marty hated tours, and I could already hear his grunts of disapproval, like the group was sent with the sole purpose of ruining his day. But me? I loved them, not only because it meant Scooter Whiskey was still a household name, and therefore — job security — but also because it meant a chance to rag on my little brother.

I had three brothers — Logan, Michael, and Jordan.

Jordan was the oldest — my senior by four years. Mom and Dad had adopted him before I was born, and though he might not have *looked* like the rest of the Becker clan, he was one of us, through and through.

Michael was the youngest of us at just seventeen, only one summer standing between him and his senior year of high school.

And Logan, who just walked through the door with the tour, was the second youngest. He was two years younger than me, which meant he was my favorite to pick on.

He was my first little brother, after all.

Once the entire group was inside, Logan gestured to us with a wide smile.

"These are the fine gentleman known as our barrel raisers. You might remember learning about them from the video earlier. As it mentioned, each of our barrels is crafted by hand, by just four upstanding gentlemen — Marty, Eli, Noah, and PJ."

We all waved as Logan introduced us, and I chanced a smirk in the direction of the hottest girl in the tour. She was older, maybe mid-thirties, and looked like someone's mom. But her tits were as perky as I imagined they were on her twenty-first birthday, and she was looking at me like a hot piece of bread after a month of being on a no-carb diet.

She returned my smile as she twirled a strand of her bright blonde hair around her finger, whispering something to the group of girls she was with before they all giggled.

Logan continued on, talking about how the four of us as a team made more than five-hundred barrels every single day before sending them down the line for charring and toasting. He explained how Scooter Whiskey is actually clear when it's first put into our barrels, and it's the oak and charring process that brings out the amber color and sweet flavor they're accustomed to today.

Even though my hands worked along on autopilot, I watched my brother with a balloon of pride swelling in my chest. His hair was a sandy walnut brown, just like mine, though his curled over the edges of his ball cap and mine was cut short in a fade. He stood a few inches taller than me, which always irked me growing up, and he was lean from years of playing baseball where I was stout from years of football before I became a barrel raiser.

If you grew up as a boy in Stratford, you played at least one sport. That's just all there was to it.

Though we had our differences, anyone who stood in the same room with us could point us out as brothers. Logan was like my best friend, but he was also like my own son. At least, that's how I'd seen it after Dad died.

Just like there were only a handful of barrel raisers, the same was true for tour guides. They were the face of our distillery, and on top of being paid well for their knowledge and charisma, they were also tipped highly by the tourists passing through town. It was one of the most sought-after jobs, and Logan had landed it at eighteen — *after* Dad died, which meant he didn't get any help getting the position.

He got the job because he was the best at it, and so I was proud of him, the same way I knew our dad would have been.

It was no surprise to our family when he landed it, given his rapt attention to detail. He'd been that way since we were kids — nothing in his room was ever out of place, he ate his food in a specific order, and he always did his homework as soon as he was out of school, exactly as it was supposed to be done, and then did his chores before he even considered playing outside.

For Logan to be comfortable, everything needed to be in order.

The poor guy had almost made it through his entire spiel when I kicked the barrel I was working on and dropped the metal ring to the floor, creating a loud commotion.

"Ah! My finger!"

I gripped my right middle finger hard, grimacing in pain as the rest of the crew flew to my side. The tourists gasped in horror, watching helplessly as I grunted and cursed, applying pressure.

"What happened?"

"Is he okay?"

"Oh God, if there's blood, I'll pass out."

I had to strain against the urge to laugh at that last one, which I was almost positive came from the hot mom with the great rack.

Logan sprinted over, his face pale as he shoved PJ out of the way to get to me.

"Shit, Noah. What'd you do? Are you okay?" He thwacked PJ's shoulder. "Go get Gus!"

"Wait!" I called, still grimacing as I held up my hand. It was in a tight fist, and with everyone's eyes fixed on it, I slowly rolled my fingers of my free hand beside it like I was coaxing open a Jack in the Box, and I flipped my little brother off with a shit-eating grin.

The guys all laughed as my brother let out a frustrated sigh, rolling his eyes before grabbing my neck in a chokehold. I shoved him off me, stealing his hat and tossing it on my own head backward as I raced toward his tour group.

"Sorry about the scare, folks," I said, playing off the charm of the drawl I was given naturally from being born and raised in Stratford. "Couldn't pass up the opportunity to give my little brother here a hard time."

There were still some looks of confusion aimed our way, but slowly, they all smiled as relief washed over them.

"So, you're okay?" I heard a soft voice ask. "You're not hurt?"

It was the mom, and I leaned against one of the machines on one arm as I crooked a smile at her.

"Only by the fact that I've gone my whole life without knowing you, sweetheart."

Her friends all giggled, one of them wearing a BRIDE TO BE button that I hadn't noticed before. The mom was still blushing as Logan ripped his hat from my head, shoving me back toward the barrel I'd abandoned.

"Alright, Casanova. Leave my group alone."

"Just making their tour of Scooter Whiskey Distillery one they'll never forget, little bro," I chided, winking once more at the mom before I got back to work.

Logan was already continuing on with the next part of his tour as he walked the group out, and I held the mom's eyes the entire way until she was out the door.

I imagined I'd find her at the only bar in town later tonight.

Marty griped at me for being stupid, as PJ and Eli gave me subtle high fives. They were all used to my pranks, especially at my brothers' expense. When you grow up in the same town, with the same people, all working at the same place and doing the same damn job, you learn to make the most of what little fun you can slip into the everyday routine.

"Noah."

Gus's voice sobered me, and I dropped my cocky smirk, straightening at his call.

"My office. Now."

He hadn't even risen from his chair, but I knew he'd heard the commotion from the prank. My confidence in being untouchable as a Scooter employee slipped a little as I peeled off my work gloves and made my way to his office.

"Shut the door behind you," he said without looking up.

My ears rang a little at the sudden quietness, and I let the door latch shut before taking a seat in one of the two chairs across from him.

Gus eyed me over the papers he was still running over his hands, one brow arching before he sighed and dropped the papers to his desk. "First of all, even though I appreciate you bringing some laughter into this place, don't play around when it comes to job safety, okay?"

"Yes, sir."

"I know Logan is your brother, and I don't mind the occasional prank. But slicing a finger off is no laughing matter. Our founder is proof of that."

The story of our founder passing away from a minor finger injury was one we always told to the tours that passed through. Here was this healthy man, older but not suffering from any illnesses, and in the end, it was his pride that got him. He'd cut his middle finger right where it connected at the base of his hand, but rather than telling someone, he just wrapped it up and went about his normal routine.

Infection took his life well before it was time.

"I understand, sir. It won't happen again."

"Good." He kicked back in his chair, running a hand over his bald head as his eyes fell to the paper again. "We've got a potential buyer here who wants one of our single-barrels. But, the situation is a little precarious."

"How so?"

It wasn't strange for Gus to ask me to show one of our rare barrels to potential buyers, mostly older gentleman with too much money to know what to do with it anymore. Each barrel sold for upwards of fifteen-thousand dollars, most of that money going to good ol' Uncle Sam.

"Well, the buyer is only nineteen."

"That's illegal."

"Thanks for stating the obvious." Gus thumped a hand on the stack of papers he'd been staring at. "She's a Barnett."

I whistled. "Ah. So, we can't say no."

"We can't say no."

"But we also can't let it get out, especially since Briar County is just looking for a reason to shut us down again."

"You catch on fast."

I nodded, scratching at the scruff on my jaw. The Barnett's were one of the most influential families in the town, right next to the Scooters and, at one time, the Beckers. The Barnetts had a long line of mayors in their family line, and if they wanted a single-barrel of Scooter Whiskey, there was no saying no — regardless of the age.

"When's this girl coming in?"

"She's here now, actually. Which is why I called you in. I need you to show her the barrel, but keep it low key. Don't do our normal tasting, just to be safe. Show her the room, give her the fluffy breakdown of what her money's getting her, and get her out of here."

"Are her parents going to pick up the barrel at the ceremony?"

Every year, we hosted a big ceremony — better described as a backwoods party — to announce the different barrels, their distinct notes and flavors, and their new owners. We also cracked open one of the single-barrels for the town to indulge in. It was the only barrel not sold to the highest bidder.

"Apparently, her fiancé is. He's twenty-four, so he's legal."

"Why can't he be the one to check it out, then?"

Gus pinched his brow. "I don't know, the girl wants to give it to him as a wedding gift, I guess. She's waiting, by the way, and I just want this taken care of. Can you handle it?"

"I'm on it."

Without another word, Gus dismissed me, more than happy to let me do his dirty work.

I slipped into our one and only bathroom in our little share of the distillery, washing my hands and face the best I could with short notice. Not that it mattered. The kind of people who could afford to spend what I'd pay for a good car on a barrel of whiskey didn't give a shit what I looked like when I told them about it. They only cared about the liquid gold inside.

So, I dried my face and hands, rehearsing the words I'd said to hundreds of rich men and women before this one as Gus' sentiment rang true in my own mind.

"Let's get this over with."

Chapter Two

Noah

Anytime I had to go to the welcome center, I always garnered more than a few curious looks.

There were several small groups of tourists milling about the welcome center, taking pictures with our founder's statue and reading about the transition of our bottles throughout the years as they waited for their tour slot. As I made my way through, heads turned, brows arching as they took in my appearance. It made sense, seeing as how I was always dirty, and a little smelly. My mom would argue that the reason they stopped to stare was because I was "handsome enough to make a church choir stutter in unison."

She said I got that from my dad, too.

I still said it was the whole smelly thing.

I smiled at a pair of older women near the ticket desk who weren't the least bit ashamed as they ogled me. Their husbands, on the other hand, glared at me like I was a bug that needed to be squashed. I just smiled at them, too, and kept my head down.

"Noah Becker," a loud, boisterous, and familiar voice greeted as I neared the ticket desk. "To what do I owe the pleasure?"

"Came to beg you for a date, of course." I leaned over the desk casually, cocky smirk in place. "What'dya say, Lucy? Let me spin you around on the dance floor this Friday?"

She cackled, her bright eyes crinkling under her blushing cheeks. Her skin was a dark umber, but I always caught the hint of red when I flirted with Lucy. She was my mom's age, a sweet woman who had a reputation for fattening all of us at the distillery up with her homemade sweet potato pie.

"You couldn't handle me."

"Oh, don't I know it." I tapped a knuckle on the desk, looking around the seating area. "I'm looking for the potential barrel buyer. She was supposed to be waiting up here."

"Ah," Lucy said, her lips poking out as she tongued her cheek. "The Barnett."

"That bad, huh?"

Lucy nodded toward the front doors. "Too pretty for manners, I suppose. But then again, can't really blame her, considering who her mother is."

Lucy kept talking, but my gaze had drifted to the fiery-haired girl pacing outside. The sunlight reflected off her auburn hair like it was the red sea, her eyes shielded by sunglasses too big for her face as her all-white stilettos carried her from one edge of the sidewalk to the other. She had one arm crossed over her slim waistline, accented by the gold belt around her crisp white dress, and the other held a cell phone up to her ear. Her lips moved as fast as her feet, the swells painted the same crimson shade as her hair.

She was nineteen, dressed like she was at least thirty, with a walk that told me she didn't take any shit.

"She stepped outside to take a phone call a few minutes ago," Lucy said, bringing my attention back to her. "Want me to let her know you're ready?"

"No, no," I said quickly, my eyes traveling back to the girl. "I got it. Thanks, Lucy."

When I pushed out into the Tennessee heat, squinting against the glare of the sun, the first thing I noticed were her legs.

I'd seen them from inside, of course, but it wasn't until I was right up on her that I noticed the lean definition of them. They were cut by a line of muscle defining each slender calf, accented even more by the pointy-toed heels she wore. She was surprisingly tan, considering her hair color and the amount of freckles dotting her nose and cheeks, and that bronze skin contrasted with her white dress in a way that made it hard *not* to stare. The skirt of that dress was flowy and modest, but it revealed just a little sliver of her thigh, and I had to mentally slap myself for checking out a fucking teenager.

"Mama, I don't care if the flowers are dust pink or blush pink. That sounds like exactly the same shade to me." She paused, turning on one heel as she reached the far end of the sidewalk.

I kept watching her legs.

"Well, I'm not Mary Anne." Another pause. "Why don't you just call her, then? She'd be happy to argue with you about which shade of pink is better, I'm sure."

"Ms. Barnett?"

She stopped mid-stride, slipping her sunglasses down her nose just enough to flash her haunting, hazel eyes at me before the shades were back in place again.

"I have to go, Mama. I think the..." She hesitated, assessing my appearance. "I think the *fine gentleman* who will be showing me the barrel is here."

I smirked, crossing my arms over my chest. If she thought I was going to back down from her *I'm-better-than-you* attitude, she was mistaken.

"Yes, I'll come right home after. Right. Okay, okay." She sighed, tapping her foot before she pulled the phone away from her ear. "Okay, gotta go, BYE."

When the call was ended, she let out another long breath, pulling her shoulders back straight as if that breath had given her composure. She forced a smile in my direction, the phone slipping into her large handbag as she stepped toward me.

"Hi," she greeted, extending her left hand. It dangled limply from her dainty wrist, a diamond ring the size of a nickel glimmering in the sunlight on her ring finger as it hung between us. "I'm Ruby Grace Barnett. Are you showing me my barrel today?"

"I am." I took her hand in my own, her soft skin like silk in my calloused, dirty palm.

Her nose crinkled as she withdrew her hand, and she inspected it for dirt as she reached into her bag, pulling out a small tube of hand sanitizer.

"I've been waiting forever." She squirted a drop of the cleaner in her hand and rubbed it together with the other. "Can we move this along?"

I sniffed, tucking my hands in my pockets. "Of course. My apologies, ma'am."

I started off in the direction of the warehouse that stored our single barrels, not checking to see if she was following. I heard the click-clack of her heels behind me, her steps quickening to catch up.

"*Ma'am*," she repeated incredulously. "That's what people call my mother."

"I'm sorry," I said, not an ounce of actual apology in my voice. "Would you prefer *Miss*?"

"I would," she said, sidling up to my side. Her ankles wobbled a little when we hit the gravel road. "Is there... are we walking the entire way?"

I eyed her footwear. "We are. You going to make it?"

The truth was, we had a golf cart reserved specifically for showing our clients the single barrels. In the back of my mind, I knew I should grab it. Miss Barnett *was* a potential buyer. But the way Lucy had responded to my mention of her name, and the way she'd practically curled her lip at the sight of me was enough to make me conveniently forget about the cart.

Little Miss Ruby Grace could walk in those heels she loved to tap so much.

She narrowed her eyes at my assumption. "I'll make it just fine. I'm just surprised you don't have... *options* for your clients. Especially considering the price of the product I'm here to inquire about."

The words were strange as she spoke them, holding a level of arrogance but softened by the lilt of her Tennessee twang. It was like she was still a little girl, playing dress up in her mom's heels, trying to be older than she was.

I stopped abruptly, and Ruby Grace nearly ran into me before her heels dug into the gravel.

"I could carry you," I offered, holding my arms out.

Her little mouth popped open, her gaze slipping over my dirty t-shirt. Even though she was eyeing me like a mud puddle she had to maneuver around, I noted the slight tinge of pink on her cheeks, the bob of her throat as she swallowed.

"I don't need you to *carry* me, sir." She adjusted the bag on her shoulder. "What is your name, anyway?"

"Does it matter?"

I started walking again, and she huffed, hurrying to catch up.

"What's that supposed to mean?"

It means, I know you don't give a rat's ass what my name is and you'll forget it as soon as you walk out of this distillery and back into your little silver-spoon world.

I sighed, biting my tongue against the urge to be an asshole.

"Noah."

"Noah," she repeated, rubbing her lips together afterward, like she was tasting each syllable of my name. "Nice to meet you."

I didn't respond, reaching forward to unlock the warehouse door, instead. Once the lock clicked, I tugged it open, gesturing for Ruby Grace to enter.

She stepped through the doorframe, pushing her glasses up to rest on top of her head as her eyes adjusted to the dim lighting. The distinct smell of oak and yeast settled in around us, and when the door closed, Ruby Grace's eyes found me, wide and curious.

"Wait," she said as I flipped on a few more lights. "You're Noah *Becker*, aren't you?"

The skin on my neck prickled at the way she said my last name, as if it said more about me than my dirty clothes in her mind.

"What about it?" I turned on her, and she was so close, her chest nearly brushed mine. She was still a few inches shorter than me, even in her heels, but her eyes met mine confidently.

"Oh, I'm sorry," she said, taking a tentative step back. "I didn't mean it in any way. It's just, I used to sit behind you in church. When I was little." Her cheeks flamed. "We would play this game... oh gosh, never mind. I feel so silly."

She waved me off, stepping even farther away as her head dipped. She clasped her hands together at her waist, waiting for me to speak, to lead us through the towering rows of barrels, but I just stared at her.

It was like seeing her for the first time.

That one apology, that awareness of herself, it was genuine and true. It was the young girl she actually was, slipping through the façade she'd painted so well.

And I smiled.

Because I did remember.

I wasn't sure how I hadn't put two and two together, but then again, how could I recognize the stunning, classy woman before me as the same freckle-faced kid who used to kick the back of my pew? She'd been just a girl then, and I had been eighteen, fresh out of high school and just as bored in church as she was. I couldn't even remember what the game was that we played, only that it used to make her giggle so hard her mother would thump her on the wrist with her rolled-up program.

I smiled at the memory, and then it hit me.

I'd just checked out a woman who used to be the annoying little kid behind me in church.

New low, Becker.

"You were a little shit," I finally said.

Her eyes widened, a small smile painting her lips. "Says the Becker. You boys are notorious for causing trouble."

"We like to have fun."

She laughed. "That's one way to put it."

Her eyes twinkled a bit under the low lighting as she assessed me in a new way. She didn't look at me like I was dirty and beneath her, but rather like I was an old friend, one who reminded her of youth.

She was only nineteen, but the sadness in her eyes in that moment told me she lost her innocence a long time ago.

I didn't realize I was staring at her, that we'd gravitated toward each other just marginally until she cleared her throat and stepped an inch back.

"So," she said, eyes surveying the barrels. They were stacked thirty high and a hundred back, each of them aging to the perfect taste. "Which of these beauties is mine?"

"The single barrels are back here," I said, walking us down one of the long rows of barrels.

Ruby Grace's eyes scanned the wooden beasts as we walked, and I opened my mouth to spout off the usual selling points of a single barrel — how limited they are, how no one else would have a barrel of whiskey that tasted like hers, how each barrel was aged differently, for different time periods, and at different temperatures. But the words died in my mouth before they could come out, a question forming, instead.

"So, you're buying a barrel for your fiancé, huh?"

Her eyes were still on the barrels, the corners of them creasing a little as a breath escaped through her parted lips.

"That's right."

I eyed her ring again.

"When's the big day?"

"Six weeks from Sunday," she sighed the words, fingers reaching up to drag along the wood as her heels clicked along in the otherwise-silent warehouse.

I whistled. "That's pretty soon. You ready?"

Ruby Grace stopped, her fingers still on the wood as she eyed me under furrowed brows. "What?"

I arched a brow. *Did I say something wrong?*

"For the wedding? To be married? You know, commit yourself to someone for the rest of your life, that little thing you said yes to?"

She swallowed. "I... Well, no one has asked me that."

"No one asked you if you were ready to get married?"

She shook her head.

Somehow, the rows of barrels felt smaller, narrower, like they were moving in on either side of us, pushing us together centimeter by centimeter.

There was so much wrong with the fact that no one had asked her that pivotal question — at least, in my mind. Here was this young girl, not even twenty years old, not even *close* to her prime years, and she was settling down. It wasn't unheard of in Stratford, or anywhere else in Smalltown, USA. Plenty of my friends got married right out of high school. Most of them had kids before they could even have a legal drink.

But something told me that wasn't what Ruby Grace had pictured for herself.

"Well, I'm asking. Are you ready?"

She blinked, and it was as if that blink stirred her from the thoughts she'd been tossing around. She started walking again, folding her arms gently over her chest. I watched her try to slip on the same disguise she'd been wearing when she introduced herself to me. She wanted the world to believe she was poised — a polished woman, a dignified lady who didn't take shit.

But the truth was, she was still a girl, too. She was still nineteen. Who made her feel like that wasn't okay? To just be a nineteen-year-old girl who doesn't have it all figured out yet?

"Of course," she finally answered. "I mean, Anthony is great. He's older than me, twenty-five to be exact, and he's so mature. He just graduated with his master's in Political Science from North Carolina. That's where we met," she said, her head leaning toward me a bit on that note. "At a party on campus. He said the first time he saw me, he knew I'd be his wife one day. Which is so sweet. And he's on track to be in politics for life." She smiled, but it didn't mask the slight shake of her voice. "The engagement happened a little faster than I expected... I mean, we've only known each other a year. But I think when you know, you know. You know?"

I smirked in lieu of answering.

"And Mama was so excited when we announced our engagement, she wanted to do the wedding right away. It's crazy, knowing we have what usually is about a year's worth of work to do in six weeks. But, she's been taking care of a lot of it... Lord knows that woman loves a project." Her voice trailed off on a soft laugh before she spoke again. "And Anthony, he's exactly what my family had in mind for me. And we get along, you know? We have so much fun."

Why did it feel like she was trying to convince me? Or maybe, it was *herself* she was trying to convince.

"And you love him," I pointed out.

She paused, eyes flicking to mine as she tucked a strand of hair behind her ear. "Right. And I love him."

I could have stared at her all day, deciphering her like a riddle that had an obvious answer if I just thought about it long enough. But she shifted under my gaze, and one glance at the rock on her finger reminded me that she was someone else's puzzle to put together — not mine.

"Well, here they are," I said, tapping one of the barrels on the back wall. They were stacked just as high as the rest of the room, each barrel stamped with a batch number and an exclusive, gold-plated plaque that had all the details about when it was distilled, barreled, what rows it's been aged in over time, and more.

"There are so many," she said, eyes scanning up. "How do I choose? I mean, should I be looking for something specific?"

I scratched at my jaw. "I mean, there is incredible whiskey inside each and every one of these barrels. Part of what makes buying a single barrel so enticing is that you'll have a one-of-a-kind whiskey," I said, finally remembering to give her the spiel I'd put off before. "Usually, we let our potential buyers taste a few to compare but..." I smirked. "There is that whole legal drinking age debacle."

Ruby Grace laughed. "Oh. Yeah. That old thing."

She swayed from foot to foot, grimacing a little as she eyed the barrels.

"Are you okay?"

Her face twisted again as she shifted her body weight to her left foot. "Yes. Sorry, it's just these stupid shoes. I told my mom I didn't need to wear heels to inspect whiskey barrels, but she was *not* having it with me wearing boots."

For a split second, I pictured her in said boots. I wondered if the brown leather would cap off under her knee, if her thighs would have been even more exposed in the shorts she would have paired with those boots. Or would she have worn jeans, covering her legs altogether?

Stop thinking about her legs, Becker.

"Take them off."

Her brows shot up, eyes widening as they found mine.

"What?" She asked, laughing. "I can't just *take my shoes off*." She threw her arms up, gesturing to our surroundings. "We're in an old, dirty warehouse."

"You act like you weren't born and raised in an old, dirty town."

"Yeah, well," she said, crossing her arms. "I wasn't exactly working in the distillery or out raising cows on the outskirts, now was I? A little bit of a different setting when you're the Mayor's daughter."

She tried to smile, but a soft curse left her lips when she shifted her weight again.

Without hesitation, I reached back for the collar of my t-shirt and ripped it up over my head, laying it down on the ground at her feet.

"Here," I said, holding out my hand. "You can stand on that. It might not be a freshly polished marble floor, but your precious feet should survive."

Ruby Grace was gaping, her jaw completely unhinged as her eyes crawled over my abdomen and chest. "I..."

"Shoes. Off." I pointed at her feet. "You do that, and I'll let you taste a few barrels. Just don't tell anyone, least of all your parents."

She chuckled, but finally stepped out of her heels. They fell on their sides as a relieved sigh slipped through her lips, and I watched her polished toes curl on my t-shirt.

"*God*, that feels so much better."

I shook my head, reaching back behind the first row of barrels for the tasting glasses we housed there. "Are you always so stubborn?"

"I wasn't being stubborn."

"I guess that's my answer," I said, pouring a tiny splash from one of the barrels before holding the glass toward her. "Here. Take a sip."

"Oh, no," she said quickly, shaking her head. "It's okay. Like you said, I'm underage."

"So you've never had a sip of alcohol in your life?" I challenged.

She bit her lip. "I mean... I *have*, but not whiskey. That's a man's drink."

At that, I full on belly-laughed. "What the hell kind of talk is that? Whiskey is a *man's drink*?" I shook my head. "It's whiskey. It's *expensive* whiskey, at that. And I assure you, it's delicious — whether you have tits or not."

Ruby Grace blushed, biting her lip against a smile. "God, sorry. I sound like my mother. More and more every day now, actually," she mused, glancing down at her toes before her eyes found the glass in my hand again.

I pushed it toward her. "Just a sip. You're not even going to get *close* to feeling a buzz. But this way, you can taste the difference between a few barrels that were aged in different ways." I swallowed. "You can pick out the perfect one for your future husband."

She hesitated, but her hand reached forward, taking the other side of the glass. Our fingertips brushed just slightly, just enough to make me jerk my own hand away.

"And, hey, bonus," I continued, shaking off the awkward tension. "You can be as 'unladylike' as you want here. I won't judge. You can even burp, if you're really feeling frisky."

Ruby Grace laughed, eyeing the whiskey like she still wasn't sure before she shrugged and tilted the glass in my direction. "Oh, what the hell. Bottoms up."

She took a sip, and then promptly grimaced and stuck her tongue out as soon as she'd swallowed.

"*God,* that's awful." She shook her head, shoving the glass back in my direction. "Definitely not doing that again."

I laughed, rinsing the glass with a splash of water from the bottles we kept nearby before filling it with the same whiskey.

"Okay, that was my bad. Maybe I should have told you how to taste it first." I handed it to her again, though she eyed it like it was poison. "Smell it first."

She did as I said, uncertainty shading her face as she looked my way again. "I'm not sure I'm doing it right."

"You're not sure you're smelling right?"

She narrowed her eyes. "You know what I mean. I don't... I don't know anything about this stuff."

"It's okay, that's why I'm here." I stepped closer to her, taking the glass from her hand, and when I inhaled to demonstrate, it was her I smelled instead of the whiskey.

She smelled like lavender, like an open field in the heat of summer.

"Watch," I said, taking another breath, this time focusing on the whiskey. "You smell it first, and ask yourself what you smell. Oak? Vanilla? Honey? Maple? Every whiskey is different, depending on how it's aged, how the barrels are charred and toasted. See what notes you can detect first. And then," I continued, taking my first sip. I let it linger in my mouth, swirling it a round before swallowing gently. "Taste it. I mean, *really* taste it. Does it give you different flavors on the tip of your tongue than it does on the back? Does it burn going down, or is it just warm? And what's the aftertaste?"

Ruby Grace watched me, fascinated, her lips parted softly, eyes falling to my bare chest where a small drop of whiskey had landed. I thumbed it away, handing her the glass again.

"Now, you try."

She took a deep breath, like she needed to focus to really do it right, and then she repeated my steps. And this time, when she finished swallowing, she smiled.

"Wow," she said. "It's different when you don't just throw it back like a shot."

I chuckled. "Well, this isn't shooting whiskey. It's Tennessee Sippin' Whiskey," I said, tilting my imaginary hat. I tucked my hands in my pockets, nodding toward the next barrel. "Take a little from that one."

"I can pour it myself?"

I nodded. "Just twist that spout a little, not too much. You don't need a lot to taste it."

She was hesitant as she poured a sip into her glass, and her eyes lit up, a little squeal of joy popping from her mouth. "I did it!"

And for the next ten minutes, I watched Ruby Grace be a girl.

She was so far from the snotty woman who had offered me her hand like a prize when we first met. She was just a teenager, a soon-to-be sophomore in college, drinking whiskey, learning something new and having fun.

I wondered when the last time was that she had fun.

I wondered if she'd ever had fun at all.

The way she looked when she laughed, I hoped she had. I hoped it wasn't the first time that laugh had been genuine, the first time that sound had made its way into the airwaves. She laughed the way the wind blew — softly, and then all at once, without an ounce of shame for how that sound might permanently shift the atmosphere around it.

When she'd decided on the barrel she wanted, Ruby Grace regretfully slipped back into her heels, and I tugged my t-shirt on before leading us out of the warehouse and toward the welcome center.

"So," I said, walking slow so she didn't kill her feet in the process of getting back to her car. "What are Anthony's plans when you go back to school in the fall?"

"What do you mean?"

"I mean, are you guys moving in together and he's getting a job there? Or are you guys doing long distance for a while or what?"

She laughed, her hair falling over her face a little as she watched our feet. "I'm not going back to school."

"Oh..." I paused. "You don't want to?"

"I mean, I guess I do... but, there's no point. You know? I'm getting married. I'll be his wife now, and I'll have so much to do. He's already getting into the political arena, and he'll need me to be by his side, campaigning and networking and all that." She shrugged. "I don't really need a degree to do that."

"Is that what you want to do?"

"It doesn't matter if it's what I want to do," she said quickly. "It's what I was bred to do."

"*Bred*?" I frowned. "You're not a horse. You're a human."

Ruby Grace stopped with an abrupt click of her heels once we reached the welcome center entrance, and she crossed her arms defiantly as her eyes found mine. She didn't even have to say another word for me to know I'd pushed the wrong button, and I was about to get the same woman I met in this very spot an hour before.

"Look, you don't know anything about me, okay? Or my family, or what I want or what I *don't* want, so just stop trying to presume whatever it is you're presuming."

"Oh, look at you," I chided, stepping into her space. "Using big words again."

She scoffed. "They say nothing changes when you leave this town and come back, I guess you just proved them right."

"Well, that's my job," I fired back. "Proving the ominous *they* right. Glad I've still got it."

Our chests were close again, the stains on my off-white t-shirt highlighting the crisp cleanness of her dress.

"Lucy will take your money inside," I said, nodding to the doors behind her. "Congratulations on your engagement."

I turned just as her mouth popped open, but I didn't look back.

"Thanks for the *tasting*," she said, making sure her voice was loud and clear.

"Go ahead and say it louder, princess," I threw behind me. "You'd be in just as much shit as I would."

She didn't respond to that, and when I chanced a glance back in her direction, there was steam rolling off that cute face of hers as she ripped the door to the welcome center open.

And I couldn't help it — I chuckled.

I didn't mean to ruffle her feathers, but damn if I didn't like getting under that pretty bird's skin.

Chapter Three

Ruby Grace

"**E**rgh!"

I gripped the steering wheel on my convertible tighter, not even attempting to tame my hair as it blew around in the wind. Mama would be upset that I'd messed it up after she fixed it that morning, but I didn't care.

I needed the wind to blow away my anger.

"Look at you, using big words again," I mocked in my best Noah Becker voice.

I turned the wheel, making another tour through town. I wasn't ready to go home yet, wasn't ready for Mama to hit me with a thousand questions on what kind of flowers I wanted and whether I wanted ribbon or twine around the edges of the ceremony chairs. I hadn't even been home from college for two full days and she was already driving me mad.

My stomach sank at the thought of the University of North Carolina, of the university I'd wanted to attend ever since I took a road trip with my best friend there when we were sixteen. I'd gotten in, and my first year there had been everything I'd hoped it would be.

But I wouldn't be going back.

"Oh, you don't want to?"

Noah's voice hit me again, like it was the ping pong ball and I was the paddle beating it against the wall.

I sighed, another grunt of frustration rolling through me as I let my left hand hang over the edge of my door. I slowed the car down as I hit the Main Street drag, not wanting to give any of the small town cops a reason to give me a ticket.

Lord knows they were bored enough that it didn't take much.

I wasn't even sure *why* I was so annoyed and frustrated with Noah. He was just making conversation, just asking questions — but they were questions no one else had asked. And, to make it worse, they were questions I didn't have answers to — at least, not *reasonable* answers.

I had the ones I'd been told, the ones I'd rehearsed, the ones I'd repeated to myself night after night until they stuck, until I believed them, too.

But it wasn't just his questions that had thrown me, it was the man, himself.

I think I recognized him even before he told me his name. Maybe that was why I'd been so insistent that he tell me. It was hard to forget the boy I crushed on as a young girl, and continued to fantasize about up until the very day I left Stratford.

The first time I'd laid eyes on him, I was only nine years old, and he was the cute boy who sat in the pew in front of me in church.

The last time I'd seen him, he was a drunken mess, yelling at his older brother at a farm house party about who was man of the house now that their dad had passed away.

That was five years ago, when I was fourteen and sneaking into my first party. I remembered I didn't drink a drop that night because I was afraid I'd end up just like Noah Becker.

But five years had changed him.

He wasn't a mess anymore.

That pecan brown hair of his that used to curl around his ears was cut clean and short now, making his strong jaw stand out even more than it had when he was a boy. Those eyes that had tipped me off to who he was before he'd offered his last name were the same as they were the last time I'd seen him — cobalt blue, almost gray around the pupil — but now, they were a little less haunted, and a little more determined, like he had something to prove, just like I did. His arms and chest were fuller — a sight I got to inspect *quite* closely after he stripped his shirt off — and he was tan the way only a man who works outside can be.

He'd grown up, from a boy to a man, and everything about him was just *bigger*. His presence was larger than life.

More than anything, his confidence poured off him in waves, or maybe it was *cockiness*. Either way, he'd thrown me. I'd walked into that distillery with my head as high as my heels, and I was prepared to show this town that I was the *new* Ruby Grace Barnett — polished and poised just like my mother, ready to take on this town with my husband-to-be as the future State House Representative of North Carolina. I'd left that knobby-legged, freckle-faced little girl behind and come back as a well-to-do *woman*.

At least, that was the plan.

In reality, I'd stood barefoot on Noah's dirty old t-shirt and giggled as I poured whiskey from a barrel for the first time.

Classy. Mama would be proud.

And maybe *that* was the most frustrating part — that not only had I strayed from the plan, from the woman I wanted others to see me as, but that I'd also had fun in the process.

The truth was, I could have stayed in that old, grimy warehouse full of whiskey barrels with Noah Becker all day. He made me laugh, and for that one hour in time, I wasn't just Anthony Caldwell's future wife. I wasn't a smile and a handshake and a side kick.

I was just me.

But Noah's questions at the end of our tour had whipped me back into reality real fast, and here I was, finally making the turn toward home.

Back to the real world for Ruby Grace Barnett.

My phone rang as I pulled down our long driveway, the familiar white house stretching out before me. It was two stories, completely symmetrical, with a porch that wrapped all the way around. Like any southern belle's dream, there was a swing on the porch, and a garden Mama had cared for as her own pride and joy for my entire life. An American flag hung proudly from above our stairs, waving in the gentle, Tennessee breeze.

I kept my eyes on that flag until I dug my phone out of my bag, smiling at the picture on the screen. It was Anthony's smiling face, his arms around me in one of my favorite dresses, the picture one we snapped at his parents' lake house that spring.

"Hey, you," I answered.

"Hey, yourself. How's my beautiful fiancé today?"

"Tired," I answered on a sigh, putting the car in park. I held the button to bring the convertible top back up, the sun fading from my shoulders.

"More wedding planning?"

"*All* the wedding planning. But, the good news is, I have your wedding gift taken care of."

"Oh, is that so? What'dya get me?"

I smiled. "Well, I can't tell you, now can I? It wouldn't be a surprise, then."

Anthony laughed, and I let my head fall back against the head rest, picturing what he looked like then. I missed his laugh, his smile, his arms around me.

More than anything, I missed our conversations.

Before he proposed, we would talk for hours — about everything. We'd talk about our dreams, our plans for the future, our pasts, our families, our deepest fears. But after the proposal, all of our conversation shifted to the wedding, to me becoming his wife.

"Fair enough. I can't talk long, but I wanted to see how you were doing. Dad's got me working with this media crew covering my first run for State House Representative. It's been madness over here."

"I'm sure it has, but you've wanted this forever," I reminded him. "Your dreams are starting to come true."

"And you'll be there beside me when they do."

I smiled, but couldn't help but notice the way my stomach dropped at his words. I was happy for him, and a part of me couldn't wait to move back to

North Carolina after the wedding. Of course, I wished I was going back to the university, but I wasn't really sure why.

This was what I'd always wanted. It was what I'd always hoped would happen.

I was marrying someone with the same political heart as my father, and his father, and his father's father. It was what my family had always wanted for me. If anything, Anthony was *more* — he didn't just want to be mayor, he wanted to be president.

And I would be his first lady.

My smile grew a little more genuine at that, at being in a position where I could make a difference. That's what had always appealed to me about living in the political circuit. I could help children, or battered women, or the homeless. I would have a platform, a goal, and a voice to raise.

And a husband who would stand beside me, just as I would him.

"I miss you," Anthony said on a sigh, bringing me back to the moment.

"I miss you, too. But I'll see you soon. Six weeks."

"Six weeks," he repeated. "And then you walk down the aisle to me."

My stomach dropped again, and I placed a hand over it just as my mother appeared on the front porch. She hung her hands on her hips, her eyes hard on me.

"Well, the wedding planner is waiting on me," I said. "Good luck with the media circus over there."

"Thanks, babe. Talk to you soon. Tell your mom I said hi."

I laughed. "If I can get a word in edgewise, I'll do that."

Mama was already down the porch and en route to my car by the time I pushed the driver side door open. She held the handle, eyes wide as she took in my appearance.

"I cannot believe you put that top down after I spent all that time on your hair this morning, Ruby Grace," she tsked, but she offered a hand out to take my bag, anyway.

"I got it," I said, stepping out and shutting the door behind me.

Mama looped her arm through mine, the other hand picking at my tangled strands.

"How'd it go?"

"Fine," I answered as we climbed the porch stairs. "I still think it's way too much to spend on a barrel of liquor."

"It is," she agreed. "But, it's good to support the community, and your father has built a great relationship with the distillery over the years. Anthony will enjoy it, I'm sure."

"I don't even think he drinks whiskey."

"He will once he's in this family," Mama said with a chuckle. "Your father will make sure of that."

It was true. Anyone who married into the Barnett family, or *any* family in Stratford, for that matter, had to be a whiskey lover. Our town was built around the Scooter Whiskey Distillery, and it was our main source of income. It brought us tourism, fame, notoriety. If you lived in Stratford, you either worked at the distillery or had family who did. It was our livelihood.

Scooter Whiskey was known all over the world. You were hard pressed to find a bar that *didn't* carry it, and more than the whiskey itself, Scooter was a brand. Women wore the logo stretched across their breasts in tight little tank tops. Men wore it on their motorcycle jackets and tattooed it on their arms. There were houses all over that were decorated with Scooter Whiskey barrels and neon lights, with glasses and barware, with posters and branded chairs.

It wasn't just a whiskey, it was a lifestyle — and Stratford was where it was born.

"Speaking of which, where is Dad?"

Mom waved me off. "Oh, you know him. He'll be working until at least seven, and then I'm sure he'll find somewhere to play cards or bet on horses."

I nodded. Tennessee didn't have a single casino, but drive to any state border and you could find a way to gamble. Dad had always been big into cards and horses, sometimes sporting events, and if he wasn't at the casino on the Georgia state line, he was at one of the council members' houses, where they'd make a casino of their own.

I hung my purse on one of the hooks in our mud room, kicking off my heels and wincing as my feet adjusted to being flat on the hardwood floor. My toes ached, the balls of both feet on fire, my ankles screaming.

Mama bent to retrieve the shoes as soon as they were abandoned, shaking her head at me.

"These are designer heels, Ruby Grace. You don't just kick them off. Go put them away in your room."

If only she knew where I'd kicked them off less than an hour ago.

"Yes, Mama."

She handed them to me, but before I could make my way upstairs, her hands were in my hair again, trying to fix the mess the wind had made. I studied the faint lines on her face as she did, seeing so much of her features in my own reflection now that I was nineteen that it somewhat scared me.

Her hair was the same burnt orange as mine, though hers was cut just above her shoulders, and our noses were identical, the tips of them rounding in a little button. Her eyes were mocha brown where mine mirrored the hazel of my father's, and her freckles were more pronounced, her skin as pale as Snow White's, where mine was easily bronzed in the summer sun. She was rail-thin and just barely over five feet, where my curves were slight but still present.

We were different in so many ways, and yet in so many others, exactly the same.

I wondered if I was looking at my future, at the woman I would become —
a wife, a mother, a last name known all over town.

Or maybe all over the nation.

She sighed, giving up on my hair and hanging her hands on her hips
again. "Well, why don't you go up and get changed. Your father will be home
in an hour or so. Come help me with supper and we can talk about the photog-
raphers again. I talked Mr. Gentry down on his price. And we need to make a
decision between ribbon or—"

"Ribbon or twine on the chairs," I finished for her, fighting back a sigh.
"I know."

I made my way upstairs, my feet aching with every step, but Mama kept
talking.

"Yes, and your sister said we can video call her after dinner to talk about
the shades of pink for the flowers." Her voice grew louder when I hit the top
stair, making my way down the hall toward my old room. "Can you bring that
book down here? Oh, and—"

"The seating chart," I said at the same time as her. "I've got it, Mama. Be
right down."

When my bedroom door closed behind me, I pressed my back against the
wood, closing my eyes and reveling in the momentary silence.

If my older sister, Mary Anne, were here, she would be in heaven. She was
older than me by four years, and as soon as she graduated college, she ran off
to Europe, hell bent on chasing her dreams of being a fashion designer. So far,
Dad had said about all she'd done was blow through his money and kiss foreign boys. I didn't know if that was true, but I did know three things for sure.

One, she would have loved this wedding stuff more than I do. And she
would have known what decision to make, what colors to choose, where to sit
who at what table.

Two, I envied her a bit, that she got away from this town, from her responsibility as a Barnett daughter.

And three, she wasn't here — and even if she was, she could never save me
from the mile-long wedding to-do list I was faced with.

I sighed, letting my head fall back against my door. I was supposed to be
excited about all of this, wasn't I? Shouldn't I *want* to plan the seating chart,
and care about the color of the flowers, and get excited about the photographs
and the cake cutting and the first dance? It was my wedding. It would only
happen once, and it felt more like a chore to me than the big day I'd dreamed
of since I was a little girl.

I loved the man I was marrying, and I loved the town we were getting
married in.

I had the dress of my dreams, my best friend to stand by my side, and the
honeymoon of a lifetime planned in the Bahamas.

Everything was perfect, and if you asked any of my friends, they'd say I was the luckiest girl in Tennessee.

So then why did it feel like I was drowning?

• • •

"Why, that can't *possibly* be *the* Miss Ruby Grace, can it?"

My best friend, Annie, flourished her thickest Tennessee accent from behind the front desk at Stratford's only nursing home, her gap-toothed smile wide and welcoming as I let the door shut behind me. When I unwrapped the mint spring scarf from around my neck, she gasped, pressing her hand to her chest.

"Why, it *is*. Oh, heavens. Someone give old Mr. Buchanon his blood pressure medicine before she walks through the halls."

I chuckled, hanging my purse and scarf behind the desk before I lifted a brow. "Haven't seen you since Christmas, and that's the welcome I get?"

"Well, I'd jump up and hug you, but it's a little more difficult these days," Annie said, gesturing to the watermelon of a belly she had blooming under her oversized scrubs.

"How about I assist?"

I reached down, and when Annie's hands were in mine, I pulled her up, both of us laughing as she leaned back to balance out the weight of her belly. It was hard to believe she was the same girl I'd road tripped to North Carolina with just two summers ago, the same blonde, giggly girl I'd stayed up too late with on countless nights, laughing and dreaming and making plans for our future husbands, our future families. I was so sure we'd room together at UNC, or chase our dreams of traveling the country and helping others in AmeriCorps. It didn't matter what we did — I just *knew* we'd do it together.

But when Annie fell in love with Travis, everything changed.

It wasn't out of place for a nineteen-year-old to be pregnant in Stratford. Half my graduating class was already married and popping out babies. But, seeing my best friend with a stomach the size of Texas was new for me. It was proof that we were older now, that life had changed, that all those dreams we'd had on the days we'd played house as kids were coming true.

She was a wife. Soon, she'd be a mother.

And I wasn't far behind her.

"Annie, you look…"

"Fat? Sweaty? Like I did our freshman year with all this acne?"

I laughed. "You look *beautiful*. You're glowing."

"Why does everyone say that?" she asked, hugging me as best she could with her belly between us. "There is positively no glow going on here. Unless the fluorescent light is hitting my sweat sheen in some magical way."

That sent both of us into a fit of laughter, and when it settled, Annie shook her head, eyes sweeping over me. They widened a little when they took in the kitten heels Mama had insisted I wear, even though I'd be on my feet all day. "*You* look incredible. I swear, I'm going to blink and have your mother as a best friend one day."

I grimaced. "Please don't say that."

She chuckled, waddling back into her chair. "I didn't think I'd see you here so soon. Didn't you just get into town Sunday night?"

"Yep," I said on a sigh, flopping down in the chair next to her. "It's been a hundred miles a minute on wedding planning since I got here. I just needed a break, to do something for myself."

Annie nodded in understanding, patting my hand just as a visitor approached the desk. While she checked them in, I let out a long exhale, taking in the familiar surroundings of the nursing home.

I'd first volunteered as a fourteen-year-old my freshman year of high school. My dad had been the one to suggest it — more as a way for me to give back to the community than anything else — but he never could have known the love it would spark inside my heart.

I still remembered that first day, losing hours with people seven times my age who had the best stories to tell. I remembered the scent of Mrs. Jeannie's perfume, the collage of photographs she hung on her wall from her time as a nurse in the Vietnam War. I remembered Ms. Barbara's lemon cake, the way it melted in our mouths that afternoon after she gave me the recipe to try to make it since she couldn't anymore.

She'd nearly cried when that first bite hit her tongue.

I remembered the soft velvet of Mrs. Hamilton's hands in mine as we gently danced in her room, and the euphoria I felt when I turned on an old record from the fifties and saw a room of faces light up, and the incomparable joy I experienced when I was the one who made grumpy Mr. Tavos laugh for the first time in years.

It was the first time I felt the high of my own personal drug — helping others. It was the spark that gave way to a flame that burned brightly in me ever since. I loved to volunteer, to give my time to people, organizations, causes that mattered to me.

I'd dragged Annie with me, and though she hadn't taken to it quite as quickly, she'd made it her home just as much as I had. And now, she was a full-time employee.

"Well, do you want me to give you the run down or do you just want to frolic on your own?" Annie asked when the young family she'd checked in made their way down the hall to their mother's room.

"I'll meander, make myself useful."

She leaned back in her chair, one hand soothing her stomach. "Okay. Well, when you're done meandering, you owe me a lunch and a thorough run down of all the wedding planning I know your mother has you doing."

I chuffed. "We'll need more than one lunch break for that."

"I can't believe it's so soon."

"Six weeks from Sunday," I murmured, rocking in my own chair.

Annie watched me. "That's not the best reaction to have when you're six weeks from getting hitched."

I sighed, shaking my head before I let it fall back against the head rest of the chair. "I really *am* excited — to be married, to start a family, to be by Anthony's side as he makes his dreams come true. I just…"

My words faded, because it felt selfish and ungrateful to follow them up with something as petty as *I just wish I could travel or get my degree before I get married.* This was what so many girls in this town dreamed of, it was what *I* had dreamed of — I'd just found it sooner than I imagined.

And I loved Anthony. I was lucky to have found him at all.

I sighed in lieu of finishing my sentence, and Annie just continued rubbing her stomach.

"I know," she said. "I'm sure wedding planning with a family like yours is a lot of pressure and a lot of stress."

I lifted my head again and nodded rather than telling her my true feelings on the subject. "Yeah. But, I'm lucky to have parents who are paying for such an extravagant wedding, and to have a fiancé like Anthony. I couldn't have dreamed up a better match for me, for my family."

"Mm-hmm," Annie agreed, but the way she watched me, I knew I'd let my façade slip. She saw it, what I was trying to hide — not just from her, but from myself. "Speaking of wedding planning, I heard you got Anthony the classic wedding gift."

I frowned. "How did you possibly hear about that? I was at the distillery for all of an hour."

Annie scoffed. "Come on, like you don't already know this town is filled with bored old women who have nothing better to do than gab." She paused, biting back a smirk before she waggled her brows at me. "I heard something else, too."

"What? That I tasted the whiskey? Like no one in Stratford has ever had a drink underage."

"Oh no, it wasn't the barrel tasting making the gossip rounds," she said. "It was the certain barrel *raiser* who hosted the tasting that everyone wanted to talk about."

My jaw dropped, foot stopping where it had been rocking me gently in the office chair. "*Noah*? What were they saying?"

"Oh, not much," Annie said, glancing at her cuticles before she peeked at me again. "Just that he was looking hot as sin when he walked you into that warehouse, and that you looked a little flustered when the two of you came out."

My cheeks burned, the memory of Monday afternoon with Noah making my skin crawl in a way I wasn't sure how to decipher.

Annie shot up, eyes widening. "Wait, is there a little *truth* behind this rumor?"

"There's no *truth* in this town, period." I stood abruptly, making myself a volunteer name tag and smacking it on my blouse. "People are ridiculous."

"What happened? Did he get all up in your space? Did he give you that sexy Becker smirk?" She gasped. "Oh, my God. If he kissed you I will *die*."

"He didn't kiss me, for Christ's sake. He showed me the barrel, and the most scandalous thing that happened was he let me taste a single drop of whiskey."

"Off his tongue?"

"I'm *engaged,* Annie!"

She threw her hands up. "You say that like a Becker brother would even pause at that fact before they planted a hot one on you."

I rolled my eyes. "And on that note, I'm going to make the rounds."

"Don't leave me hanging!" she hollered at my back as I made my way down the hallway. I flitted my hands above my head, waving her off as she groaned. "That's just *cruel*, Ruby Grace."

I chuckled, shaking my head as I dipped into the first room and introduced myself to a new resident who hadn't been there before I left for college. His name was Richard, and it wasn't long after our introductions that he was telling me stories about his days in the distillery and showing me pictures of his late wife.

And just like that, all my wedding planning stress was forgotten.

I lost myself within those walls, surrendering my thoughts and energy to others. I asked to hear about the decades I hadn't been alive to experience, administered medicine, played board games, fixed hair, applied makeup, told jokes, crocheted, danced — and before I knew it, an entire morning had passed.

It was just the release I'd needed.

"Hey," Annie said after lunch, eyes softening as she watched me pull a stack of magazines out of my leather Kate Spade bag. "Remember what I told you."

"I remember."

She frowned more. "I just don't want you to be disappointed. She might not even recognize you."

"I won't be disappointed, even if she doesn't," I promised, balancing the magazines in the crook of my elbow as I smiled. "But, I talked with Jesus this morning, and I think she will."

Annie smiled, too. "I'm not sure how this place survives without you."

"Easy," I said, tapping her nose with my index finger. "They have you."

I was still smiling and confident as I turned, making my way down to the last room in the left hallway. My eyes scanned the names and decorations on the closed doors, and I nodded to those who peeked out at me from where they watched the TVs in their room or read in their beds. When I reached the door at the very end, the one that had donned a red and white wreath since I was a freshman in high school, I let out a shaky breath, eyes washing over the familiar name in gold above the wreath.

Betty Collins.

A smile touched my lips, memories of the spunky old woman I'd first met years ago resurfacing. Betty was an eighty-nine-year-old woman with a loud, genuine laugh and a birthmark that sprawled across her forehead. She covered it with white, whispy bangs that she'd constantly run her freckled fingertips over as she told me stories about her favorite movie stars.

She was a forgetful old woman, and though half the staff thought she was showing signs of dementia, I knew better. Betty was more in her right mind than half the people my age were. She just had *selective* memory — and also approximately zero patience when it came to people she didn't care for.

Annie worried that with me being gone so long, she might not remember me.

Again, I knew better.

We'd kept in touch while I'd been gone, writing letters and having the occasional phone call. She'd remembered me just fine when I came back for Christmas break, and I had a feeling she'd never forget me — even if she ever *was* diagnosed with dementia.

And I also knew I'd never forget her.

Betty was the first one to ever open my eyes to a world outside of Stratford, to challenge me to take risks, to move passionately and unapologetically through life. *"Anyone can lead an ordinary life, child,"* she'd said to me one lazy afternoon. *"But the best adventures are reserved for the ones brave enough to be extraordinary."*

I inhaled a deep breath, knocking gently before I pushed through the door and into her room.

Betty sat in the same rocking chair she'd been in the last time I left her to go back to UNC. She faced the window, though the curtains were drawn, and she rocked gently, humming the melody of "Good Morning" from *Singing in the Rain.* I smiled at the sight of her long, white hair, her magazine collages hung on each and every wall, old movie posters filling any space left between them. When the door latched behind me, Betty stopped rocking, ears perking up.

"Who's there?"

"Why don't you turn around and find out, old lady," I sassed.

Betty's head snapped around, her eyebrows drawn in like she was offended, but when her eyes settled on me, everything softened as a smile slid into place. "Well, I'll be damned. Look what the wind blew in."

I returned her smile, rounding the bed until I could sit on the edge closest to her chair. I leaned forward, folding one hand over hers as her eyes glistened with unshed tears. "You need to stop frowning so much," I said, squeezing her wrist. "You're getting wrinkles."

"Ha!" she guffawed, squeezing my hand where it rested on her arm. "I smiled too much when I was younger. I'm just trying to reverse the damage."

I chuckled as her eyes fell to the magazines in my arm.

"Are those for me?"

"Hmm... that depends. When's the last time you stole someone's pudding?"

"Last week," she confessed, her gray eyes almost a silver as she leaned in conspiratorially. "But it was a vanilla one, so does it even count?"

I smirked, handing her the stack of magazines. She took them with a smile that doubled the one she'd greeted me with, already flipping through the pages as I settled back on her bed. It only took a few pages before she started telling me how Anne Hathaway was named after Shakespeare's wife, and I nodded and listened intently as she continued flipping, pausing on each page to tell me a new story about a different celebrity.

Betty was born and raised in Stratford, and she'd never been farther than two counties from the town that she called home. Though she'd never physically traveled, her imagination wandered all the time, and she loved to escape into movies and books, to live the lives of spies and queens and young college students. The collages that decorated her walls brought her favorite adventures to life, and in her mind, she'd seen the world.

She'd seen everything.

"I'm getting married," I told her after an hour had passed, and she paused where she was reading about Chris Pratt's hobbies, a strange shadow passing over her features.

"That so?"

I nodded.

"How did he propose?"

"We were at a party with all his friends and family," I said. "He'd just announced he was running for state representative."

"A political man," Betty mused. "Your father must love him."

"He very much does."

"And do you?"

I smiled, throat thickening in a way it never had when I was asked that question — not until it was asked by Noah Becker, anyway. "I do," I said through the unfamiliar discomfort.

"Well," she mused, nodding as her eyes lost focus somewhere on the page. "I'd like to meet him. Will you bring him by?"

"He's coming into town in six weeks for the wedding," I told her. "I'll try to sneak him away."

"And where will you sneak away to once the knot is tied?" She looked at me then, brows tugging inward.

I leaned forward, folding my hand over hers. "Not too far. I'll never be too far."

I knew she didn't understand how much time had passed since she'd last seen me, but I also knew she could sense that it had been a while. I squeezed her hand, falling quiet as she flipped through the pages of the second magazine before a yawn stretched between us. I reached for the magazines, and once I deposited them on her bedside table, I helped her under the covers.

"This man you'll marry," she said as I pulled the knit blanket up to her shoulders. "Does he make you feel the way Richard Gere made Julia Roberts feel in *Pretty Woman?*"

I smiled, tucking the blanket around her arms as I considered the question. Did Anthony make me feel like that — special, desired, beautiful in a way that he can't resist? Not necessarily. But did he make me feel safe, comfortable, cared for? Yes.

"I think so," I whispered, but then I raised both brows as my eyes found hers. "He's not quite as handsome, though."

"Well, no one is as handsome as Richard Gere, my dear," she said on an exaggerated sigh, as if that were obvious. "Don't be so hard on yourself."

I laughed, and Betty smiled before her eyes fluttered closed. Within minutes, her soft breathing turned to a light snore, and I found myself staring at her favorite scene from *Pretty Woman* that hung above her bedpost. I imagined the scene, wondering what Anthony would look like if he swept in to save me the way Richard Gere did — a white knight in a limo instead of on a horse.

I was sure he would act out a grand gesture if he ever needed to. I was sure he would take care of me, that I'd be comfortable as I stood by his side on his race to his political dreams. And I was sure he was just as handsome as Richard Gere, regardless of what I'd told Betty.

But as I stared at Julia Roberts's wide smile, the one thing I *didn't* know for sure was if I wanted to be the princess he saved.

In the back of my mind, I heard a voice I'd been trying to forget since Monday afternoon.

"No one asked you if you were ready to get married?"

And I wondered why it never occurred to me that I had a say in the matter.

Chapter Four

Noah

On Friday night, I sat at the table my father built with my three brothers and the woman who raised us, drinking a cold Budweiser after another long week at the distillery. I'd had family dinner with my friends, with a few girlfriends in the past, and I'd always been disappointed. Because where most families were quiet and orderly and respectful at the dinner table, my family was the exact opposite.

In the Becker household, it was always madness at dinner time.

Complete and utter chaos.

"God, you're disgusting," Logan said, tossing a green bean at our youngest brother, Michael, who had just belched so loud even I was impressed.

Mom swatted Michael's arm to show her own disapproval, but couldn't hide her smirk. "Manners, Mikey."

"What? Better out than in, right?" Michael grinned at all of us before burping again.

"Feet off the table, Logan," Mom said next, as soon as she finished plating the last of his meatloaf. She set it in front of him where his feet had been, smacking his hand away when he tried to dig into the mashed potatoes. "Not until we pray."

"Yeah, Logan. Not until we pray," I said, sneaking my own bite. He narrowed his eyes at me, and Mom smacked my hand next.

"Gray hairs," she murmured, shaking her head. "Every single one of you are giving me gray hairs."

She took her seat, hands reaching out — one for mine, one for my older brother, Jordan's — and the rest of us linked hands and bowed our heads.

"Heavenly Father, thank you for this meal, and for these boys, though they drive me insane. Please bless this food and this day, and be with those who need you most. Amen."

"Amen," we all echoed, and it was the quietest that house would be all night as we each stuffed our faces with the first bite.

Even though we liked to rag on each other, my brothers and I were close. We were like a well-oiled machine, and Mom and Dad were the grease that kept us in working order. After Dad died, Mom took on that job as a solo party, and that was the only time I ever remember the machine breaking down.

Our dad was well known in the town, especially since *his* dad was best friends with the founder of Scooter Whiskey. They had built the brand together, essentially built the town together, and anyone who watched the Scooter Whiskey brand take over the world knew my grandfather was a pivotal member in the team that made it happen.

But when Robert J. Scooter passed away, he left no will behind, and his family inherited everything — leaving our family cut dry. It wasn't long after that that our grandmother passed away, our grandfather following quickly after. Dad always said it was from a broken heart, but he never clarified if it was Grandma who'd broken it or the Scooter family.

I always thought it was a little of both.

Dad had never given up on our family, though, and he'd already established himself as an integral part of the Scooter Whiskey Distillery before the founder passed away. He was young, ambitious, and the Scooter family was happy to keep him around. He worked his way up the ladder, eventually becoming part of the board, and that's where the trouble started.

Somewhere along the line, my dad pushed the wrong buttons.

He wanted to stay true to the Scooter brand, to the company his dad had helped build, but the ones who inherited the distillery had other plans. Where dad wanted to keep the tradition, the "old ways" of making whiskey, the Scooter family wanted to lean more toward innovation. The more Dad fought them on it, the more they did to silence him, and sooner or later, Dad learned to just comply to get by.

But his pay suffered, and so did his job duties.

He went from essentially running the company to pushing papers, taking care of remedial tasks that were better suited for a secretary. One of his last tasks was cleaning out Robert J. Scooter's old office, and though Mom was upset when they assigned it to him, Dad took it in stride. He was always so optimistic, and used to always say that, *"Every experience is an opportunity, no matter how trivial it may seem. Some of my best ideas and most memorable achievements began from a seemingly ordinary day."*

Little did we know that that "seemingly ordinary" day, that "seemingly ordinary" task, would be the literal death of him.

There had only been one fire in the Scooter Whiskey Distillery, and my father was the only one who perished in it.

To this day, no one in our family believed the story the Scooter family fed to us. The fire department claimed the fire was started by a cigarette, and our dad didn't smoke. I would never forget when Patrick Scooter, Robert's oldest son, tried arguing with my mother that he'd seen Dad smoke plenty of times.

Maybe he just never told you, Patrick had said, and I'd seen murder in my Mom's eyes when she stepped up to that fully grown man, chest to chest, mascara streaked down her face, and told him no one knew her husband like she did, and she dared him to try to tell her otherwise again.

We'd never been given the truth, not in all the years we'd looked for it.

And that one time in our life was the only time I ever remember the machine breaking down.

We fought. And cried. And asked for answers when we didn't even know what questions to ask. Mom drank for the first time in her life, and Jordan and I struggled to hold the family together, all the while fighting for who was the *man of the house.*

I wanted that title so badly, and Jordan tried to take it simply because he was the oldest. So, we fought one night — literally, punched and kicked until we were both bruised, bloody messes — and then, we came together.

Jordan was the one who made me realize that we were *all* the man of the house — and we were all in this battle together.

Ever since that day, the machine seemed to work even better together than it did when Dad was alive. We were in sync, tuned into each other's needs, and forever protecting each wheel and axle.

God help any man or woman who ever tried to break down a Becker.

"What are you boys getting into tonight?" Mom asked, taking advantage of all of our mouths being full.

It was Friday night, which was like a weekly holiday in Stratford. Other than the tour guides, the weekends were slower for most employees at the distillery, and that meant less time spent working and more time spent living. We always did family dinners on Friday night before dispersing to whatever weekend plans lay ahead.

Michael was the only one of us who still lived at home with Mom, and he had just turned seventeen. He was going into his senior year after the summer, and we were all just waiting for the day he said he was moving out of the house and into a place with his high school sweetheart. They'd dated for two years now, and he was the only one of us I could ever imagine actually settling down.

I worried about when he moved out, though — and part of me wondered if I should move back *in* at that point. The thought of Mom living alone in a house that once fit a family of six was hard to stomach.

"There's a party out at the Black Hole," Logan answered, grinning at Mom. "Wanna come?"

"And have to bear witness to whatever debauchery lands one of you in jail tonight?" She shook her head. "Just bail each other out and I'll see you for dinner next week."

Logan's smile mirrored Mom's, the resemblance uncanny. He and Michael favored her — hazel gold eyes, olive skin, lean and fit, a smile that stretched across their entire faces. I looked more like our dad — stout, tan skin with a reddish tone that he attributed to the Native American in our blood, striking blue eyes that almost took on a silver hue in the sunlight. Mom said sometimes when she looked at me, she saw Dad when *he* was a boy, when they first met.

I'd always worn that like a badge of honor.

Jordan, who was the quietest at the table, didn't look a thing like any of us. His skin was a light umber, his hair black and cut in a short fade. He was the tallest, the largest, the one who always stood out in family photographs.

And yet, he was our brother just the same.

"Bailey and I are heading up to Nashville for the weekend," Mikey announced, and judging by Mom's widened eyes, it was the first she'd heard of the plan.

"Oh?"

He nodded, stuffing his mouth with more mashed potatoes and speaking around them. "Her label is doing a showcase at one of the bars on Broadway. It'll be kind of like Nashville's first taste of her as part of their team."

"I thought she hadn't signed with anyone yet?" Jordan asked, speaking for the first time since we'd dived into our dinner.

"She hasn't."

"And when she does?" Mom asked, brows pulling together.

Mikey was quiet, pushing green beans around on his plate before stacking a few on his fork with a shrug. "I don't know. I guess we talk about it then — where we'll move, what our next steps will be."

An uneasy silence fell over all of us then. We knew the day would come that he would move out, but what worried all of us — though no one said it — was that he was so sure his future was with Bailey.

And we couldn't be sure she felt the same.

She *seemed* to love him, to care for him the way he cared for her, and we all knew he was like me in the sense that he wanted what Mom and Dad had. They had met in high school, and I knew Mikey felt like Bailey must be *it* for him because she was his high school sweetheart, too.

But anyone who knew her could see that music was her first love. And we weren't sure where that would leave Mikey.

"Well," Mom finally said, forcing a smile. "Be careful. And don't get into too much trouble."

All of us scoffed at that, because just *being* a Becker meant trouble was never too far off.

After dinner, Logan and I helped Mom clear the table — Logan's favorite job — while Jordan helped Mikey pack up his car. I walked out onto our old wooden porch just in time to see Mikey's taillights pull away, the sun setting over the hills in the distance. I sidled up next to Jordan, draping my arms over the railing and cracking open the two beers I'd brought while he stood with his arms crossed hard over his chest.

"Your worry is showing, big bro."

He humphed, taking the beer I offered him and popping the lid open. "Kid pretends to be so tough, but if that girl leaves him behind…"

"It'll break his heart," I finished for him. "I know. He'll be okay. He's a Becker."

Jordan nodded, shoulders relaxing a little, as if that one fact was all the reassurance he needed that everything would be alright.

"How's the team looking?" I asked after a moment, taking the first swig from my beer.

"Better than last year. The seniors are strong, and we have some good freshman blood rolling in, some sophomores who got tougher while on JV." He shook his head. "But, still too early to tell how they'll all work together. It'll be a long summer of conditioning."

"And the parents?"

He rolled his eyes. "Still assholes."

I chuckled, sipping from the can in my hand before letting it drape over the railing again. Jordan was the head coach of the Stratford High School football team and had been for four years now. He was the only man in the family who didn't work at the distillery, who never had, who never *wanted* to. Part of me wished he were there with us, carrying on Dad's legacy and helping solidify the Becker name in the Scooter Whiskey history book. But, I couldn't blame him for not wanting to work in a dirty warehouse all day — and I couldn't do anything but support him when I saw him on that field.

Football was his everything.

He'd played his entire life, and where my brothers and I took our aggression out on each other or enemies in the town or even strangers at a bar, he took his out on the field.

And now, he was teaching other boys to do the same.

He was one hell of a coach, and the parents knew it — whether they wanted to argue about who started and who rode the bench or not. And the single moms in Scooterton?

Well, let's just say they were more than happy with Jordan's *coaching*.

The married ones didn't seem to mind much, either.

"So, I heard you caused a bit of a scene at the distillery this week?"

I cocked a brow. "*You* heard?"

"Look, I try as hard as I can to ignore the football moms chattering behind me in the stands, but sometimes I swear they speak louder just so they can be sure I hear them."

"Like when they talk about how tight your ass looks?"

"Or when they talk about you pushing your luck giving whiskey to a minor."

It was my turn to roll my eyes. "They have no proof."

"Do they need any? You know as well as I do that the people who run this town can find evidence for anything they want."

We both fell silent at that, each of us taking a swig of our beer as memories of our father filled the space between us. Crickets chirped to life, the sky taking on a purple glow.

"It was the Barnett daughter," I said, breaking the silence.

"Mary Anne?"

"Ruby Grace."

He balked. "She's like sixteen, Noah."

"Nineteen," I corrected, swallowing down another gulp of beer. "And she's getting married. She was buying one of the single barrels as a wedding gift."

"Wonder who the lucky guy is."

"Some young buck in politics she met at UNC."

"Politics, huh?" Jordan's gaze drifted somewhere beyond the horizon. "Guess he'll fit right in, then."

I nodded, but my stomach tightened as I pictured Ruby Grace's eyes — wide and taken aback when I asked her if she was ready to get married. I still couldn't believe I was the first to ask her.

I still didn't believe she knew the answer herself.

It made no sense, that I harbored some kind of sympathy for a girl who had looked at me like I was the mud staining her designer shoes. She and her family had never wanted for anything, and yet I felt sorry for her, because I knew without being around her for more than even three minutes that she wasn't happy.

She didn't know who she was.

Then again, did *I* at nineteen?

A familiar tune sparked to life from inside the house, shaking me from my thoughts of Ruby Grace as a smile stretched on my face. I glanced at Jordan, who was smiling, too, and he looked back into the house as a long exhale left his chest.

"I used to think she'd remarry, find someone else eventually. But, after the first full year of her playing this song every night, I knew I was wrong."

I followed his gaze, throat tightening at the sight of Mom and Logan dancing around the living room to Eric Clapton's "Wonderful Tonight." It was the song she'd danced to the night she and Dad got married, and I'd watched them dance to it so many times in that living room that I'd lost count.

But it was her son who held her now, swaying and smiling and acting like that song didn't hurt a little for all of us. Logan exaggerated a dip with Mom in his arms before spinning her around the coffee table, and she laughed and laughed, her messy pony tail swinging with the motion.

"I don't think there ever could be anyone else," I mused.

Jordan nodded, each of us finishing off our beers, and I wondered what it felt like to love someone that much.

I wondered if I'd ever know for sure.

Chapter Five

Ruby Grace

"You've got to be kidding me."

I crossed my arms, deadpan expression on my face as I glared at my best friend — though I was debating the title at the moment.

The bonfire the Jensen twins had started was high and warm behind her, dozens of Stratford's residents littering the space around it, as well as stretching into the barn and beyond. There were five kegs, an entire table dedicated to liquor bottles and mixers, and every single person held a red plastic cup that housed either beer or a mixed drink. Ages ranged from sixteen to fifty-five, though everyone seemed to have their own little sections of the Jensen property marked off for their clique. The last time I was here, I was with the high schoolers who liked to party in the barn next to the resident DJ. Now, I was somewhere in the in-between, not sure where to stand or where I fit in.

The Black Hole was the main party spot in town, especially on Friday nights, and Annie had begged me to come with her since it was my first week back in town.

And now, she was bailing.

Annie cringed, forcing a smile through it as she gestured to her belly. "I know, I'm sorry. I really did want to come, but little man is rolling around so much tonight. I just want to go lie on the couch."

"I think that sounds pretty perfect," her husband, Travis, said, wrapping his arm around her. He pulled her into him, kissing her temple as she melted into his side. When she looked up at him, they shared a longing look before he kissed her nose.

And as cute as they were together, they weren't cute enough to bail on me.

"I didn't even want to come here," I reminded her, an almost whine in my voice. "You *begged* me, Annie. And now we've been here for an hour and you want to leave?"

She apologized again, going on about how she'd make it up to me, she'd take me out for ice cream at my favorite little diner in town later this week, and she'd come over and help me and Mom with wedding planning, too. The longer she rambled, her little belly bouncing with her as she pleaded, the less I could hold my anger.

My best friend was too cute for her own good.

I sighed, running a hand back through my lightly curled hair — hair that had taken an hour to fix — before I conceded. "Fine. Let's go."

Annie blanched. "Wait, I meant *we* would like to leave," she said, gesturing between her and Travis. "As in, the two of us. You should stay. Have some drinks, catch up with people."

"Catch up with *who*, exactly?" I probed. "The girls I thought were my friends in high school before you and I both found out the hard way that they only hung out with us for our money? Or how about the boys who, even after graduating, are *still* boys, and are already tripping over themselves with the urge to ask me out... even though they *know* I'm engaged?"

I glanced over at a group of guys I recognized from high school — some of them graduated, some of them seniors now — and they all looked away simultaneously, sipping on their beers and pretending like they hadn't been staring.

Annie chuckled. "Okay. Fair point," she said, but then her eyes flicked somewhere behind me. "Well, would you look at that. It's your buddy from the distillery."

I turned, following her gaze over my shoulder, and immediately locked eyes with Noah Becker.

He was standing with his younger brother, Logan, as they filled their cups from the keg. He smirked when I saw him, saying something to Logan before he started toward me, and I whipped back around, eyes wide.

"He's walking over here," Annie whispered as Travis pulled to the side, saying goodbye to his buddies.

"I noticed. Come on, let's head out," I murmured through clenched teeth, but before I could take even one step, Noah Becker was standing in the space in front of us.

"Ruby Grace," he mused, holding one of the red cups in his hands toward me.

"Noah," I nearly seethed. I didn't take the cup he offered. "We were just leaving."

"*We* were just leaving," Annie corrected, gesturing to her and Travis, who was a few yards away with his buddies now. "But, Ruby Grace, you were thinking of staying, weren't you?"

"No, I wasn't."

Noah smirked, first at Annie, then at me. "I saw you were empty handed. Thought I'd be a gentleman and bring you another beer."

"That was so nice of you," Annie said, practically melting in a cartoonish swoon.

I glared at her.

"I don't drink beer," I told Noah, my glare still on Annie.

"Oh, I didn't realize. Is it a *man's drink*, too?"

I rolled my eyes. "Honestly, yes. And it's carby. I have a wedding dress to fit into."

Noah kept his gaze on me, but the corner of his mouth twitched a little at that comment. "Suit yourself," he said on a shrug. Then, he lifted the cup he'd been offering me to his lips and drained it in three clean swallows before he stacked the other full one inside the now empty one.

"Classy," I mumbled.

"Thanks. One of my many party tricks."

I waited for him to walk away, but he didn't. He just stood there, one hand wrapped around that cup as his free one dipped inside the pocket of his faded blue jeans. I hated that I noticed the way they fit him, the way they hung off his hips, the edge of his brown belt just barely visible under the navy blue t-shirt he wore. It had a logo on it that I wasn't familiar with, but combined with the low orange light of the fire, that shirt set off the cobalt in his blue-gray eyes in a mesmerizing way. His thick biceps strained against the fabric of the sleeves, and when I glanced at his face again, I realized he was checking me out, too.

His gaze was fixed on my legs.

I cleared my throat, crossing my arms over my chest as I shifted my weight. "Aren't you a little old to be here?"

"Aren't you a little young?" he countered, taking a sip of his beer as his eyes scanned the scene behind me like he was suddenly bored.

I scowled. "Look, if you came over here to berate me, feel free to leave."

At that, his eyes snapped back to me. He pinned me with that gaze, like I was a child or his next target — which one, I couldn't be sure.

"I came over here to bring you a beer," he reminded me. "I was trying to be a gentleman, and I was going to apologize for upsetting you earlier this week at the distillery. But now, I'm not sure why I bothered."

Noah shook his head, his shoulder brushing mine a bit as he walked past me with my mouth hanging open like a fish. I blinked several times, digesting what he'd said before my cheeks flushed with embarrassment.

Annie cringed. "I don't think he's being a creep, Ruby Grace," she said as Noah walked away. "It seemed like he was trying to apologize. Maybe you should let him."

I closed my eyes, letting out a long exhale before I turned, jogging after him. "Wait!"

He paused where he was, turning as I caught up to him. I swallowed when our eyes met again.

"I'm sorry," I said, running my hands back through my hair before I let them hit my exposed thighs with a slap. "I didn't mean to be so rude. It's just..." My voice faded, and I had a laundry list of excuses I wanted to spew — about the stress of the wedding, the fact that my best friend had toted me to a party I didn't even want to go to and then wanted to leave an hour in — but, I knew Noah Becker didn't want to hear my problems, so I stopped there. "It's just been a hell of a week."

Noah nodded, waiting.

"Anyway," I continued. "Thank you for the beer, even though I didn't take it. And for apologizing for the distillery." I paused again. "I guess I should probably apologize for that day, too."

Noah tilted his head a little, his eyes curious. "So, are you going to?"

I rolled my eyes. "Can't you just *not* be a brat?"

He chuckled at that, sipping from his cup. "I don't think anyone has ever called me a brat, outside of my mom."

"Mom's always right."

"Touché," he said, tapping his cup with one of the fingers that held it before he nodded over his shoulder. "Come on. Let's ditch this place for a while."

My eyes widened. "What?"

"You don't want to be here," he reminded me. "And honestly, I'm bored out of my mind. There are some stables down by the creek. Let's go for a midnight ride."

"We can't just ride someone else's horses."

"One of them is mine."

That shut me up.

I shifted, tucking my hair behind my ears as I looked around us. People were already watching, whispering, wondering what in the world Ruby Grace Barnett was doing talking to a Becker boy.

"We can't leave together," I said, lowering my voice as I folded my arms back over my chest. "People will see."

Noah furrowed his brows like he didn't understand it, but when he followed my gaze, noticing the group of girls around my age with their eyes on us, he nodded in understanding.

"Ah," he said, sliding his free hand back into his pocket as he took another drink of his beer. "I see. You still give a fuck what other people think of you."

"No," I said quickly, too quickly, blowing my faint attempt at nonchalance.

Yeah. Clearly he'll believe that.

The truth was I *did* care — more than I wanted to admit. Our town loved to talk, and the last thing I wanted was to be the subject of anyone's gossip.

"No, that's not it," I said again, voice more steady, though it was still a lie.

"Mm-hmm."

"It's not," I argued again, like a child. "I don't care what anyone in this town thinks of me."

"Okay. Prove it, then," he said, draining what was left of his beer before he tossed the cups in one of the trash cans nearby. He didn't look over his shoulder to see if I was following him, just started off in the direction of the stables in the distance.

I bit my lip, looking back where Annie and Travis were — *were* being the big key word. They were gone, and when my phone pinged, I looked down to a text from her.

We're heading out. Seriously, stay and have fun. Don't let the old married couple drag down your night. Call me if you need a ride later. Love you!

I groaned, sliding my phone back in my pocket as I glanced back at Noah. He was already on the other side of the bonfire.

"*Prove it*," I mocked, crossing my arms. "Whatever. I'm not a kid, I don't need to prove anything to him."

But even as the words rolled off my tongue, I knew they didn't reflect what I actually felt. I *wanted* to prove him wrong, to prove to him and everyone watching and maybe even to myself that I could do whatever I wanted and it didn't matter what anyone had to say about it.

Plus... I hadn't gone riding since before I left for college. I used to love riding. That would be way more fun than sitting around drinking with a bunch of people I didn't really care about... right?

I told myself *that* was the reason I went jogging after Noah, telling him to wait up. It wasn't because I was being stubborn, or defiant, or because I wanted desperately to put my money where my mouth was and prove to Noah that he didn't know everything about me like he thought he did. And it wasn't because it was him, or because I wanted to be near him.

It was because I wanted an excuse to ditch that party and ride horses.

Noah chuckled when I caught up to him, my breath labored. He didn't say a thing as we walked, and when the voices and music from the party were out of range, the familiar sound of the creek and the crickets chirping came to life, instead. I sighed, my breath steadying, tension seeping out of me like water through a leaky faucet.

"Better?" he asked when the sound from the party was completely muted by the sounds of Tennessee, instead.

I smiled, shoving him in lieu of admitting he was right. I blushed a little when my hand wrapped around his bicep before I pushed him away, because even that brief contact reminded me how stout he was, years of raising barrels building him into a specimen unlike any other.

He smirked, bouncing back from my shove easily before his eyes trailed down my legs. "Now, let's see if you can ride in those boots."

• • •

Noah

I didn't know what made me do it.

I didn't know what made me fill a second cup up with beer after my own was full and walk it across the Black Hole to Ruby Grace Barnett. Part of me really did want to apologize for whatever I'd said that had upset her after the tasting at the distillery, but part of me also just wanted to talk to her — period. I didn't have a reason, so I'd brought that beer, thinking it'd be an ice breaker.

For a less stubborn woman, it might have been.

But, whatever the reason, I was glad I'd gone over to talk to her, because regardless of her being feisty and acting like she didn't want to give me more than two minutes of her time, she'd let that same part of her slip that she had at the distillery — the young girl inside. She'd let her guard down, confessed her anxiety over being back home, over being at the Black Hole. I didn't know the complete reason why, but she'd needed someone in that moment.

And I was that someone.

I smiled as Ruby Grace ran her hands over the smooth, white and black tobiano pattern of Tank's neck, her polished fingernails scratching a little as she did. Tank leaned into the touch, neighing softly, tail swishing back and forth in his stall.

"I never knew you rode horses," she said after a long moment, wide eyes glancing at me before she focused on the horse again. "No offense, but it's not exactly something I pictured a Becker doing."

I scoffed. "What, you think we just drink and fight all day, every day?"

She didn't respond, but her apologetic glance told me she actually *did* think that.

I chuckled, kicking off where I'd been leaning against the stable watching her. "My mom taught me how to ride when I was a kid. My other brothers never really got into it, but it's always been a release for me. Dad bought me Tank when I turned fourteen. He was just a year old, then." My heart ached a little at the mention of my father, just like it always did. "We keep him out here at the Jensen's because they have everything they need to take care of him. I pay them a monthly fee, and I can come out here and ride him whenever I want."

"And do you often?"

"At least once a week, sometimes more."

Ruby Grace smiled, both of us falling silent again as she ran her fingers through Tank's mane. He was an American Paint Horse, strong and muscular, his spotted coat and multi-colored mane the most eye-catching elements about him. Tank was fifteen years old now, and though he didn't show signs of becoming a senior horse anytime soon, I still went easier on him now than I had when I was younger. We used to jump logs and round barrels, dredge through the creek, gallop as fast as I could get him going. Now, I usually took him for long, easy rides, letting him stretch his legs as I got lost in my thoughts for an evening. Sometimes we'd go out to the old tree house Dad built for me and my brothers, other times we'd just walk the trails, along the river, or wherever Tank's hooves wanted to take us.

Watching Ruby Grace pet him made my pulse quicken. She wasn't the first girl I'd used that line on. I'd used it plenty of times, bringing whatever girl was into me that night down to the stable to watch them pet Tank and fuss over how cute he was before I laid them down in the straw bales and fucked them until the sun came up. But Ruby Grace was the first one I brought here because I knew she needed to get away, she needed to escape.

And this is where I came to do just that.

I knew I wasn't going to fuck Ruby Grace. For one thing, she was nineteen. For another, she was engaged. She was also the most infuriating girl I'd met, stubborn and judgmental, and nowhere near my type. I liked my women wild, little spitfires who could give me a run for my money in the sack. But none of that changed the fact that she was very, *very* nice to look at.

I'd wondered that day at the distillery what she would look like in boots instead of heels, and I'd gotten my wish. Her brown and turquoise buckaroo boots covered her calves, spanning up to just below her knees where her smooth, tan skin was exposed. That skin was mesmerizing, her toned thighs seeming somehow longer in those boots and the tiny, ripped-up white shorts she'd paired them with. The outfit was nothing like what I'd seen her in that first day, no fancy dress or belt or designer heels. She was just a girl in a tank top and shorts and boots.

A country girl.

And I hated what seeing her that way did to me.

I swallowed, shoving those thoughts aside and tearing my eyes from her legs as I crossed the space between us. I reached up to pet Tank right under where she did, debating if I was really ready to offer my next statement, because I never had before.

"Wanna ride him?"

Ruby Grace lit up, smile as wide as her face as she turned to me. "Really? You'd let me?"

My chest tightened again, because I'd never let *anyone* ride Tank — save for the Jensen family who cared for him. But, this was the most relaxed I'd seen Ruby Grace since she barreled back into town, and for some reason, I wanted to keep her like that.

"Yes, really," I said on a chuckle. "Hang on, let me get her suited up."

Ruby Grace looked around the barn as I brushed Tank, strapping him up with his riding pad, saddle, girth and bridle next. I checked everything twice, including each and every hoof. I'd been out earlier that week to trim his hooves, but I wanted to be sure they were in good shape to ride. Once I was satisfied with my inspection, I guided Tank out of the barn and into the warm summer night.

"Alright," I said, patting the saddle before I turned to Ruby Grace, reins still in my hands. "Hop on up."

I expected her to whine, or scoff, or ask *how in the world to you expect me to do that in these shorts*? But to my surprise, little miss Ruby Grace didn't say a single word. She put the toe of her boot in the stirrup, reached one hand up to grab the horn, and heaved her opposite leg up and over, shifting her weight a bit until she was comfortably seated.

She smirked when she saw my face, tossing her long red locks behind her shoulder as she shrugged. "What? Did you think I was too prissy to know how to ride a horse, Noah Becker?"

I put my hands up in a surrendering gesture. "I didn't say a word."

"You didn't have to. That trout mouth of yours said it all," she said.

"Alright, watch your foot for a second," I said, ignoring her last remark. She frowned as I handed her the reins, confusion rolling over her as I put my own foot in the stirrup and heaved myself up to sit behind her. When I edged forward, the zipper of my jeans hitting the back pockets of hers, I inhaled a steep breath, looking up to the moon like it would somehow save me from getting a boner once we started riding and that sweet ass was rubbing up against me.

"Oh," she said, and even from where I sat behind her, I could see her cheeks flushing in the moonlight. "I... I didn't realize you would be up here, too."

"You think I was just going to walk alongside while you rode, princess?"

She frowned. "Don't call me that."

"Whatever you say, ma'am."

She growled a little at that, elbowing me in the ribs as I laughed. Then, I grabbed hold of the reins, and away we went.

The moon was full and bright that night, reflecting off the creek as we rode along its edges. For a while, we were both quiet, soaking in the dampness of the night's humidity, the sounds of the water and insects around us, the smell of the country. I closed my eyes and inhaled a deep breath, finding that peace and comfort I always did on Tank's back, mixed with a little of something unfamiliar with Ruby Grace being there, too. I wondered what she was thinking, if she was happy to be there, if she was still anxious about what people would say tomorrow.

And they *would* have something to say.

I couldn't remember how old I was when I realized that would never change, but that I changed *my* perspective on it, not giving people the power they wanted with their gossip. I knew I was older than Ruby Grace when it happened, and I knew it was after my father had passed. At first, I'd been so triggered by the rumors, by the way that whole town talked about my father like they knew him when they didn't. But after a while, I started to care less, and less, until I didn't give a single fuck about anyone but my family.

We trotted along my favorite trail, ducking our heads when the branches of the trees dipped a little too low. I was right about Ruby Grace's ass rubbing against me, and when she edged back, adjusting her weight for what I assumed was comfort, the fabric of her jean shorts rubbed over the length of my cock in a way that made me bite my lip to keep from groaning out loud.

"So," I said, trying to spark up conversation that would get my mind off her body touching mine. "What's got you so stressed out that you're biting off a nice guy's head when he offers you a beer?"

I expected her to pop off back at me, but she just chuckled, letting out a sigh on a shrug before she spoke. "I don't know. Being back home, I guess. UNC felt like my new home, and now I'm back in this place where I'm not sure where I fit in. And my mom is all over me about the wedding, which I know we still have a lot to do with it being only six weeks away. But... I don't know. It's summer, it's supposed to be fun, and I just feel..."

"Smothered," I finished for her.

She turned a little over her shoulder, and though our eyes couldn't meet, I knew I'd struck a nerve. "Yes," she agreed, turning back forward. "Exactly that."

I nodded. "I'm sure it's a lot of pressure, being the Mayor's daughter. And now, getting married." I debated my next words carefully before speaking them out loud. "Don't take this the wrong way, because I don't mean anything by it, but... you're young. I was surprised when my boss told me I was showing a barrel to an engaged nineteen-year-old."

"Plenty of people get married at nineteen," she spouted back. "Especially in Stratford."

"I know," I said, soothingly, calming my voice so she could see I wasn't picking a fight. "I guess it's just that when *I* was that age, I didn't even know who I was, let alone who the person was who I wanted to spend the rest of my life with."

Ruby Grace fell quiet at that, and for a while, it was just the sounds of the night around us. I thought I'd overstepped again, and I waited for her to push me off the horse or demand that I take her back, but instead, after a long pause, she just sighed.

"I think they just expect me to be like my sister," she murmured. "Mary Anne loves this kind of stuff — picking colors of flowers, choosing between ribbon or twine, finding the perfect dress."

I remembered her older sister, especially because she was only a couple years younger than Logan. They'd run in similar crowds, been in similar parties. But, after college, Mary Anne had made her way over to Europe to study fashion design. The town hadn't seen much of her since.

I wondered if that was part of Ruby Grace's sense of obligation — the fact that her older sister was gone, and she was here, waiting to fulfill her family's legacy.

"And I guess a part of me always thought *she'd* be the one to get married first," Ruby Grace continued. "That she'd be the one to find a husband like our father and make the grandkids I know my parents want."

I was nodding, realizing my instinct had been true until she mentioned the word *grandkids*.

I stiffened. "Are you already thinking about kids?"

"I mean... not *immediately*, but, Anthony wants to have them sooner rather than later."

My blood boiled a bit at her statement. "And do *you* want to have them sooner rather than later? Or at all?"

"Of course, I want children," she defended. "But, I admit, I thought I'd be much older when I had them. I thought... well, it doesn't matter."

Tank neighed, as if he spoke my thoughts before I got the chance. "It does matter, Ruby Grace. What did you think?"

She fiddled with the reins that I'd let her take over. "I don't know... I just always thought I'd graduate, maybe do a year or two in AmeriCorps before I settled down."

"AmeriCorps?"

"Yeah, it's like the Peace Corp, but specifically here in the states. You can be a teacher or camp counselor or even work in wetland restoration." She shrugged. "I've always loved to help others, to volunteer my time, and I thought it'd be a great way to do that before I got married and had kids of my own."

I gritted my teeth against the urge to tell her she still *could* do those things — married or not. Just because she was committing to this man as his wife didn't mean she had to lose her identity, surrender what she wanted for all that *he* wanted, but I knew it wasn't my place to say any of that.

Then again, it probably wasn't my place to have her ass rubbing against me, but I wasn't doing anything to change that at the moment.

"But," she said after a long, awkward pause. "That's what's so great about marrying Anthony. He's a politician, and as his wife, I'll have so many opportunities to help the communities we serve in. And when he's president, I'll be the first lady. I'll be able to create and manage whatever charities and organizations I want. I'll be able to make a difference."

I nodded, but I still didn't agree with it. "Well, that's good, then."

"Yeah," she said, and for a moment, she seemed lost in her own thoughts before she came back to the moment with me just as I grabbed the reins from her, turning Tank around to head back toward the stables. "What about you?" she asked.

"What about me?"

"Do you want a wife, kids?"

"I do," I answered.

She waited, and when I said nothing more, a soft laugh escaped her lips. "Well, please don't tell me too much. After all, I didn't share anything personal with you."

I smirked, shrugging. "There's nothing more to really say, is there? I do want to get married and have kids one day."

"You're twenty-eight," she pointed out. "What are you waiting for?"

"The right woman."

The answer rolled off my tongue so easily, but it shocked both of us. I stiffened behind her, aware of the space of vulnerability I'd put myself in, and Ruby Grace glanced over her shoulder, like she wished she could see my eyes after saying that.

"Oh," she said after a while. "Well, that's nice, Noah. That's really nice. And I'm sure you'll find her."

I cleared my throat, ready to change the subject, but she beat me to it.

"What else?" she asked. "What else do you want in life?"

I shifted. "Honestly, not much. I just want to make whiskey barrels. I'm a pretty simple guy."

"Why do I feel like that's the first time you've lied to me?"

Her question surprised me, and I swallowed down the discomfort building more and more rapidly the more the conversation was focused on me.

"It's not a lie. I'm a family man, I want to be here for my brothers, my mom, and, someday, my future family, too."

I paused, and she waited, wanting me to keep going even when I didn't know what else to say.

"I guess I kind of feel like a dad already, in a way," I confessed. "Jordan and I really stepped up after my father died, and we've been taking care of Mom and the house and our younger brothers ever since. And now, Mikey is going into his senior year. He's going to move out of the house soon after he graduates, and then Mom will be on her own, and I'm not sure what she'll do then. If we sell it, put her in a smaller place, it'd probably be better for her. But then again, I can't imagine us not having that house to go home to."

Ruby Grace pulled Tank to a stop, turning enough so she could look at me. "So, it seems that where I feel smothered, you feel a little lost, huh, Noah Becker?"

I smirked. "I guess so, Ruby Grace."

"Well, I've heard some of the best adventures come from finding yourself a little lost," she offered.

"Oh, who told you that?"

"The wise Betty Collins, of course." She smiled, shrugging. "This older woman I care for down at the nursing home. We've become good friends over the years."

Looking at Ruby Grace in that moment, I didn't see a girl. Her fair, young skin and wide, innocent eyes glowing in the moonlight told me she was still a girl, but her heart that volunteered her time to the elderly told me she was more of a woman than most I'd slept with.

"Well, if she's got more wisdom like that, you'll have to introduce me to her sometime."

Ruby Grace smiled at that. "I just might."

We were quiet the rest of the way back to the stable, and when we both hopped down and I took all the riding equipment off Tank, I gave him a treat, patting his butt affectionately before Ruby Grace and I made our way back toward the party.

"Thank you," she said, tucking her hands in the back pockets of her shorts. "For tonight. I haven't felt that kind of peace in a long time."

"No problem," I said, coming to a stop. She turned, brows furrowed. "Figured I'd let you walk up first, go find your friends. I'll come up in a bit, that way no one thinks we were together."

She rose one brow. "I'm pretty sure they already know."

"Well, then, let's fuck with them," I said. "Give them something to make them doubt it all when they're gossiping in the morning."

Ruby Grace smiled even wider at that, and before I knew what she was doing, she crossed the space between us and threw her arms around my neck. I opened my own just in time to catch her, to feel her tight little body pressed against me as she gave me a hug.

"Stay out of trouble, Noah Becker."

"Never."

She chuckled, letting me go and waving at me over her shoulder as she strutted back up the hill toward the bonfire.

Chapter Six

Ruby Grace

My first thought was that my skirt was too short.

It was Sunday afternoon, and church had let out on a beautiful day where Dad had some time blocked off for his daughter being back in town. He'd insisted we go golfing — much to his delight and my disdain — and so here we were at the Stratford Country Club golf course.

The Stratford Country Club golf course only existed because Dad had insisted the town needed a proper country club back when he was running for his first term as mayor. He'd worked with the wealthiest families in the town to bring it to life, and then they'd made the requirements to get in so specific and the spots available so limited that it was pretty much just a place for him and his friends to hang out and play golf.

Daddy was lining up his shot on the fourth hole, his pot belly stretching the light pink fabric of his polo as he tightened his grip on the club. He'd picked that shirt so he could match me — a daddy-daughter-duo. Dad was a big man, standing six-foot-three and close to two-hundred-and-fifty pounds. He had a smile that took up his entire face — one that Mama called his "mega-watt" smile. She swore it was how he won elections.

I favored my mother, but I did have my dad's hazel eyes.

It was a gorgeous day, mid-seventies with big, puffy white clouds rolling over us, giving us a brief reprieve from the sun before it'd beat down on us again. For all intents and purposes, it was the perfect day to be on the course.

But, I hated golf.

I respected it for the tradition it had in the sports world, and I figured that, had I been raised differently, I might have found joy in watching it or playing from time to time. But, as it was, Daddy had taught me as soon as I could *hold* a golf club that business deals were made on golf courses, and I needed a strong game to represent the family — especially once I was a politician's wife.

Or, a politician myself — which Daddy had said he'd have been just fine with, too.

So, golf for me had always been a chore. It started with the pressure of learning, then, the pressure to be *good*. And once I'd achieved that, once I could hold my own with Dad and his buddies on the course? Well, by that time I was just so tired of golf I didn't want to be there at all.

I hated golf.

But, I loved my dad.

So, when he'd asked me to spend the afternoon with him, I was excited — even if it *was* to play golf. Daddy was always busy, running around the town of Stratford and making sure every wheel and axle was in place. Any time I could steal him for more than a twenty-minute conversation at dinner, I was thrilled.

"How come your ears are steaming over there when *I'm* the one lining up a shot?" Dad asked, glancing at me with a quirked brow before he took a practice swing, stopping the club right before it hit the ball.

I tugged on the hem of my skirt — which was *plenty* long enough, by the way — with my eyes on the group of four older women eyeing me and whispering from the seventh hole.

"Mrs. Landish and her gaggle of geese are looking at me like I'm not a member," I said. "Or like my skirt is so high my tush is showing."

Dad followed my gaze, smirking as he turned back toward the ball. "Well," he said, squaring up his feet and lining up the club with the ball. "You know they're always looking for something to talk about — and you skipping off with Noah Becker in the middle of the night is worthy gossip."

He swung, smacking the ball down the green. It flew high and arched, about two-hundred feet before it came back to Earth, and Daddy turned, a toothy grin of pride on his face.

My jaw was hanging — and not from his shot.

"What do you *mean* that I 'skipped off with Noah Becker'," I scoffed, neck heating.

"I don't know," Dad said on a shrug. "I just heard them saying something about you and Noah Becker at the Black Hole when we were checking in for our tee times earlier."

"We were at the same bonfire party, yeah. But, so was half the town."

I glanced at Mrs. Landish again, who shook her head with pursed lips, saying something to her passenger seat rider before cruising off in her golf cart of gossip.

I rolled my eyes. "Honestly. And Mrs. Landish wasn't even *there*."

"She doesn't have to be — not with the way news travels in this town."

"*News*," I spat, plucking my driver from my bag and stepping up to the tee. "Stratford needs a craft fair or something to keep them entertained."

Dad chuckled at that, putting his own driver away before he leaned an elbow on our golf cart, watching me line up my shot. "Don't worry about them.

Someone else will do something equally as innocent and have them drawing other dramatic conclusions in no time."

I smirked.

"But, just to be clear... you *didn't* skip off with Noah Becker in the middle of the night... right?"

I stopped where I was lining up my shot, leaning one hand on the butt of my driver as I leveled my face at my father. "Dad."

He put his hands up. "I was just checking. You know the reputation those boys have. Gotta make sure my little girl is safe."

I smiled, shaking my head as I got back to my shot.

My pulse ticked up a bit at the lie I'd told my father as I took a practice swing. Daddy was right — the Becker boys *did* have quite the reputation. But, if I was judging only by the Noah I was with Friday night, I would never understand why.

He was kind. And patient. And funny.

My smile widened remembering how focused he looked as he brushed his horse down and got him ready to ride. But, as soon as he'd popped into my mind, I shoved him back out.

Smack.

My own ball went flying down the green, landing about twenty-five yards shy of where Dad's had. He cheered, clapping me on the shoulder as we watched the ball roll a bit.

"That's my girl! Come on, you drive."

The rest of the afternoon slid by easily, but I didn't miss how Daddy was checking the time on his watch often. If I knew him, he'd likely scheduled out the *precise* amount of time it would take to get in a round of golf before he had somewhere else to run.

I was his daughter on *his* time, but it didn't bother me. I knew I wasn't the only one who needed him. When you're the mayor of a small town in Tennessee, you're pulled a million different directions. And, if I was being honest, he inspired me. He was the reason I'd gotten involved with volunteering, the reason I hadn't stopped at just showing up there, but took it into my own hands to make our nursing home the nicest in the county.

Dad was a doer, and he'd raised me to be one, too.

"So, how is my little girl?" he asked when we were riding out to the ninth hole later that day. "Ah, I don't even know if I can call you that anymore, now that you're an engaged *woman*."

I smiled, taking my sunglasses off to wipe the lenses as he drove. "I'm alright, Daddy. And I'm still your little girl — even after you walk me down the aisle."

"Wow," he breathed, and if he wasn't wearing his own sunglasses, I'd have bet those hazel eyes of his were glossy. "It sounds so real when you say it like that."

"It's pretty real," I mused, putting my glasses back on. "I bet you're tickled pink that your baby girl is marrying a politician, just like you always wanted."

Something in Dad's demeanor changed then, and he cleared his throat, switching hands on the steering wheel. "Yes. Anthony is a good man. He'll do right by you."

I nodded. "Yes."

We both fell silent again, and I watched him carefully, wondering why the sudden shift in his mood. But, as soon as he parked the cart, he was out and lining up his last shot. He glanced at his watch as soon as he'd hit the ball, turning back to me with a smile that told me he was cutting it close.

"Daddy, it's okay," I said, plucking my driver out of my bag again. "We're almost done here, anyway. If you need to go, go."

His brows folded together. "Are you sure?"

"Of course." I smiled, leaning my club against the cart before walking over to give him a hug. "I'll see you at dinner sometime this week."

He sighed when I was in his arms, wrapping me in a bear hug with a gentle kiss pressed to my hair. "You're the best kid ever."

"I love you, too, Daddy."

I insisted Dad take the cart so he could get back faster, assuring him I wanted the walk. We weren't far from the club house the way the course was lined up, anyway. And once he was gone, I swung my driver a few times behind where the tee was set up, preparing for the last long shot of the day.

As I lined it up, my thoughts drifted first to Dad, to his reaction when I'd brought up Anthony. He *loved* Anthony — he and Mama had both made that very clear just after one dinner with him. And, provided that he'd just asked me to marry him a month ago and we were six weeks out from the big day, it was safe to say they both approved.

So, then, why the odd response?

I shook it off, cracking my neck and focusing on the ball. But as I squared my shoulders, my thoughts drifted again, this time back to Mrs. Landish and her cackling crew.

Which then led my thoughts to Friday night.

To Noah.

I wondered if he saw it that night at the bonfire — the stress I swore I was wearing like a choker. Annie didn't seem to, nor did anyone else. But Noah... it was like he saw right through me.

I swallowed, let out a long breath as I cleared my mind once more, and hammered the ball down the green.

...

Noah

Everyone knew not to talk to me that Wednesday.

I showed up to work an hour early, desperate to get my hands dirty, my muscles fired up, my mind on anything other than the anniversary of my father's death. That day marked nine years of him being gone, and I thought with time, that sting would fade. I thought I'd become immune to the pain, to the anger, to the aching emptiness I felt that no justice had ever been served in his honor.

But I'd been wrong.

Most of the week, I'd been fine. It was a normal weekend, a little partying and a little relaxing with the family. Church happened on Sunday, just like always. Once Monday arrived, I was back in work gear. And through all of that, my thoughts had been occupied by the Mayor's daughter.

I didn't like that Ruby Grace was on my mind, that when I was playing cards with my brothers on Saturday evening, I thought about the way her hair smelled as she sat on that saddle in front of me. I didn't like that when I saw her at church, prim and proper in her lavender dress, I thought about how much I liked her better in the jean shorts and tank top she'd worn. And I definitely didn't like that when I woke up on Monday morning, I had a hard-on the size of a sledge hammer after having a dream about her.

I wanted her off my mind. She was someone else's fiancé. She was also nearly ten years younger than I was.

But now that my mind was taken over by thoughts of my father's untimely death, I wished it was just her in my head again. I wished I could think about anything other than how badly this day would always hurt, for the rest of my life.

Marty, Eli, and PJ worked alongside me without saying a word that day. They didn't even joke around with each other, sensing the mood I was in, the somberness that settled over the entire distillery.

The Scooter family and the board always glorified this day. The morning announcements asked for a moment of silence for the only employee to ever perish at Scooter Whiskey. They praised the safety plans they'd had in place, attributing the fact that there weren't *more* deaths because of that plan they'd had in place. They praised the firemen, too, that they arrived so "quickly." Then, they would read off my father's accomplishments like a grocery list, have that one minute of silence, and then everything was back to normal.

Even though Logan was across the distillery preparing for his first tour when that morning announcement came, and even though Mikey was in the welcome center, getting the gift shop ready to open, I still felt them in that moment those announcements were read. I felt their hearts squeezing in pain the same way mine did, felt their anger, their hostility toward the company that paid their bills, that our grandfather had helped build, that we both loved and cherished but were also bound to in some sick, sadistic way.

I thought of them, of our family, all day long as I kept my head down, focusing on the task at hand. I built more barrels than my daily quota called for, but I didn't care. As long as I was busy, I was okay. I just needed to get through the day.

I just needed to survive.

It was well after lunch when Patrick Scooter swung through the doors that led to the barrel raising warehouse. I hadn't even noticed, hadn't stopped working until I felt a number of eyes on me. I looked up at Marty first, who warned me with a stern brow fold, like he was worried I'd do something irrational. PJ and Eli watched me, too — their eyes flicking back and forth between the door and me. When I followed their gaze and saw Patrick talking to Gus, a clipboard in his hand, dressed like he was in an office in New York City rather than a distillery in Stratford, Tennessee, I clenched my jaw.

Patrick Scooter was a few years older than my father would have been if he were still alive. They grew up around the distillery together, almost like brothers until Patrick's dad passed away, leaving the distillery to him.

Everything changed then.

I didn't have any certified or blatant reason not to like Patrick, other than the fact that something in my gut told me he was a shit guy. Something in my gut told me he didn't like my family.

Something in my gut told me he had something to do with my father's death.

I didn't know why, and it wasn't ever something I'd speak out loud, but it was there, deep in my belly like an ache I'd never be rid of. And I'd learned as a young country boy that you trust that gut feeling.

Patrick signed something on Gus's clipboard before his eyes scanned the warehouse, finding mine after one sweep. He gave a grim smile, saying something to Gus before making his way toward me.

I ground my teeth, lowering my head to the barrel I was raising in an effort to school my breaths and the rage I felt boiling inside me. If he knew what was best for him, he'd stay away from me today. But of course, he didn't care. Part of me thought he actually reveled in the fact that he still had my father's kids working for him, like somehow that meant he'd won.

But we weren't here for him. We were here for my father, for the legacy *he* built — that my grandfather built. Patrick and his family may have wanted to erase us from their history books, but my brothers and I would make sure that never happened.

I had just shoved the last stave of wood into the barrel I was working on when I felt a clammy hand clap me on the shoulder, squeezing and staying there until I was forced to lift my head and take the orange sponges out of my ears. Patrick met me with sympathetic eyes, a sorrowful smile, like he knew my pain, spread on his face.

"Hey, Noah. How ya hanging in today?"

Do not punch him. Do not give him a reaction at all.

Patrick stood there in his suit, eyes surveying his surroundings like he was well above the men working for him. And I knew he thought that to be true. He was so much like my father — tall, stout, tan — but his hair was gray, where my father never had the chance to get there, and his eyes were smaller, beady and evil, his face too long, nose too big. He looked almost like a live action Frankenstein.

I wished I could put the bolts through his head to bring the whole look together.

"I'm well, thanks for asking," I responded as politely as I could. "How are you, Patrick?"

"Oh, you know me. Just rocking and rolling through every new day," he said, his smile showing his too-white teeth now. It slipped again in the next instant. "Although, this particular day is always a rough one on all of us."

I swallowed down my pride, forcing the best smile I could muster. "Indeed."

"He would have been proud of you, you know," Patrick said, squeezing my shoulder where he held it. "Your father was such a close friend of mine, and my heart aches every day that he's gone. But his boys are serving him well here at Scooter Whiskey." His lip twitched a little. "We're so lucky to have you."

Liar.

It was all lies, all bullshit — and we both knew it. But this was the game we played. The Scooter family kept us around as to not stir up more trouble or gossip than they already had with the fire, and we stayed to avenge our father's death, to ensure the Scooter family didn't get what they wanted by erasing the Becker name from their history.

I simply nodded, lips in a flat line. I reached out my hand for his, shaking it once before I put my ear plugs back in and got back to work on the barrel. Patrick stood awkwardly at my side for a moment longer before he made his rounds to the other men, then he waved goodbye to Gus through the window of his office, and he was gone.

I tried to keep my head down, tried to breathe through the rage, tried to forget he was even there, but once he left the room, everything I'd been fighting down all day rose to the surface. I reared back, kicking the barrel I'd just built and splintering the wood everywhere. I hadn't tied it down with the metal rings yet, and the time I'd spent putting it together went to waste with one heavy heave of my boot.

No one tried to stop me as I continued kicking, hitting wood, equipment, whatever was near. The only thing that stopped me was when Marty placed a gentle hand on my shoulder, and when I looked at him, he nodded toward the tour group that had just walked in.

I locked eyes with Logan, his brows bent together in an understanding sympathy, and I felt shame wash over me.

I was his *older* brother, and I was acting like a child. I'd let Patrick get under my skin, and I hated it.

The tour group was still watching me, murmuring as Logan pulled their attention back to him, listing off his usual spiel. Gus came over to join Marty and me, excusing Marty before he pulled me to the side.

"I think you should take the rest of the day off, Noah."

I just nodded, yanking off my work gloves and powering toward the door that led to our little locker room. My blood was still red hot as I grabbed my shit, and then I slammed my locker closed and barreled through the back warehouse door with only one destination in mind.

• • •

Eric Church blared from the jukebox, and I bobbed my head, singing along a little between sips of my whiskey. I'd had way too many for it to be only eight o'clock, but it was numbing my body, and my mind, which was exactly what I needed it to do.

"Noah, I love you, kid. But I'm cutting you off after this one," Buck said. He was the bartender at my favorite watering hole in town — namely because it was the *only* watering hole in town — the neon sign outside flashing his name in a simple manner. He was also a longtime friend, and he'd saved me from my own drunk ass too many nights for me to count.

"Alright," I said on a nod, not willing to argue. I was getting tired anyway, and was ready for the godforsaken day to be over already. I had half a glass of whiskey left and then I'd roll my ass home, crawl into bed, and wake up to a new day tomorrow.

A day that wouldn't be the anniversary of Dad's death.

I pulled out my wallet to pay Buck, and once my cash was on the bar, my thumb hovered over the corner of the only photo I carried with me. I pulled it out slowly, eyes scanning the younger faces of my brothers, of Mom, and of Dad. It was the year before Dad had died, when we'd taken a fishing trip to the lake, and we were all grouped together in front of one of our tents, sunburnt and smiling. Mikey was missing a front tooth, his adult one yet to replace the one that had fallen out. Logan and Jordan had their arms slung around each other, Mom standing behind Logan with her hands on his head.

And then there was me and Dad.

I had jumped on his back for the photo, giving him a noogie as the picture was shot. He was full-on laughing, looking up at me, and when I looked at that picture, all I felt was happiness. All I felt was indescribable joy for a family that didn't know what hardship lay ahead, that had everything they ever wanted or needed.

If I could go back in time, I'd go back to that exact moment and live there forever.

"Two beers, Buck. Whatever you got that's cold and wet," someone said from beside me, knocking their knuckles on the bar. I was fine to ignore them, just like I'd ignored everyone else that night, but then I felt eyes on me, and I turned, meeting the gaze of Patrick's youngest son.

Malcolm was a scrawny kid, just a few years older than Mikey. His older sister was Logan's age, and she was about the only Scooter that I didn't hate — maybe because she was sort of the black sheep in their family, acting out in every way possible, down to getting her septum pierced her senior year of high school.

I liked a girl who ruffled feathers.

Malcolm, on the other hand, was long-faced just like his dad, with skin that somehow always looked dirty. He was scrawny, liked to wear his ball caps a little to the left like it was still the 90s, and had a knack for getting under my skin, too.

"Well, if it isn't the oldest Becker boy," he spat — literally, *spat*, the words coming out of his mouth just as a thick wad of chewing tobacco did. He spit it into an empty Mountain Dew bottle, grinning at me with pieces still in his gums, and already, he was trying to push my buttons by calling me the oldest.

It was Malcolm's way of saying that he didn't recognize Jordan as a proper part of our family, because his skin wasn't the same color as ours and some bullshit paperwork said he wasn't blood.

My pulse kicked up a notch.

"Rough day at the office?" Malcolm asked when he didn't get a rise out of me.

I blinked. "Fuck off, Malcolm."

"Ohhh," he said, raising both hands in a mock surrender as he elbowed his buddy next to him. I didn't know his name, but recognized him from around town. "Someone's on their rag."

His eyes dropped to the photo still in my hand as he rested his elbows back on the bar.

"Ah," he mused. "I see. You're crying into your whiskey over your daddy, huh?" He framed his chin with his thumb and forefinger. "Was it today's date that that fire happened?" He shrugged, smiling at his buddy. "Guess I forgot."

Buck slid Malcolm the beers he asked for, eyeing me with a warning and a slight shake of his head. "Here are your drinks. Now go play pool or sit at a table far away from here, understand?"

"Aw, come on, Buck," Malcolm said. "We're just kidding around. Noah and I go way back. We're buds." He clapped me on the shoulder, and every nerve came to life at his touch. "Ain't that right, Becker?"

"Get your hand off me."

"Or what?" he seethed.

And I should have let it go. I should have slammed back my whiskey and walked out that damn door. But instead, I slammed my hand into his chest, gripping his shirt and yanking hard until his back hit the bar. He yelped a little as I stood, lowering my nose to his, steam rolling off me as I poked a finger in his face.

"I told you to fuck off, Malcolm. You should have listened to me."

I reared back, ready to plow my fist into his smug smile, when Buck intervened, jumping over the bar and grabbing me from behind. He yanked me away, my fist still twisted in Malcolm's shirt until his buddy tore it away from me, ushering Malcolm to the other side of the bar.

He was laughing.

I charged after him again, which only made him laugh harder as Buck caught me around the chest, spinning me around to face him.

"Hey!" he said, voice loud and firm.

I had no idea if he'd said anything to me before that moment. I couldn't hear anything but that asshole's laughter.

"Listen to me," he warned. "You know that pussy will call the cops and have charges pressed against you. You don't need to spend any more nights in jail. Okay? So finish your whiskey and get the hell out of here."

I tried twisting out of his grip, but he held me more firmly, and my breath singed my nose with every exhale. Finally, I growled, shaking him off and reaching for my whiskey. I tilted the glass back, finishing what was left, and then plowed through the bar door just as I had the one leaving the warehouse earlier that day.

My vision was half red, half black as I barreled through town, walking the short distance to my house that was a few blocks behind the main drug store. I stayed on Main Street until I hit that street, and as soon as I turned, I nearly ran over Ruby Grace Barnett.

"*Oof.*" She gasped as I plowed over her, both of us spinning and her nearly toppling over before I caught her by the upper arms, righting her again. The paper bag she'd been carrying out of the drug store fell in the process, toilet paper and toothpaste and other miscellaneous girly shit that I didn't recognize spilling out onto the concrete.

"Shit," I murmured, bending to help her retrieve it all.

Ruby Grace bent down as much as she could in her skirt, and once everything was back in the paper bag, we both stood, an awkward, heavy silence passing between us.

"Sorry about that," I murmured, scratching the back of my head. Then, I turned, ready to close the distance between me and my house that was just a couple of blocks away now.

"Wait," she called, and I paused, forcing a breath before I turned to face her. "Are you okay?"

"I'm fine."

"You almost ran me over," she said, smiling a little. "And you look like you're ready to kill the next person who looks at you."

"Not far from the truth."

She crossed her arms over the bag, balancing it on her hip as she cocked a brow. "Want to talk about it?"

"No," I answered definitively. I made to turn again, but she spoke before I could.

"Someone's particularly moody tonight."

My nose flared, head aching with how tightly I gritted my teeth. I needed to get home. *Now.* "And someone else is particularly nosey."

Her face fell at that. "Noah..."

"Look, why don't you stop prying into my life and get back to your own? I'm sure you've got cake to taste or ribbons to tie or something."

Ruby Grace's mouth popped open. "Why are you being so mean to me? I was just making sure you're okay."

"Oh, is that right?" I asked, seething as I stepped into her space. Our chests were an inch apart, my breath hot on her nose as I looked down on her shocked expression. "You want to go back to the Black Hole, sit on my horse and rub your ass on me while we ride? Pretend like you don't have a fiancé who would mind while I tell you all my fucking problems?"

Her brows folded together, eyes narrowing into slits. "Fuck you, Noah Becker."

"I'm sure you'd like to, sweetheart. But, not tonight." I somehow managed a smirk before I turned on my boot, shoving my hands in my pockets and picking up my pace to get back to my house.

It was out of line. It was nowhere near what I felt about Ruby Grace, but she'd been in the wrong place at the wrong time, and my fury needed a friend to call home.

She was the lucky winner.

I heard a cross between a huff and a growl behind me, but I didn't turn around to see the face of the girl I'd just insulted. I couldn't bear to see her anger, just as I couldn't be bothered to apologize for my own. I didn't owe Ruby Grace anything, anyway. What did it matter if I upset her?

I shoved it out of my head as I walked, hell bent on getting home, into a hot shower, and then into my bed.

I'd had enough bullshit for one day.

Chapter Seven

Ruby Grace

That Sunday at church, I was everything I was supposed to be.

I was dressed prim and proper, thanks to Mama picking out a gorgeous, sunshine yellow dress that hugged my waist and flared at the hips, cutting off just below my knees. It was covered with lace, and she'd paired it with a large white hat with a yellow ribbon that matched the dress, as well as white designer heels — the same ones I'd worn to the barrel tasting my first week back in town. My hair was curled and smoothed to perfection, makeup classy and well done.

I was on time, in the third-row pew where Mama always liked to sit, and sitting like the young lady I was.

I was smiling, shaking hands with the congregation as they chatted before taking their own seats.

I was proudly and properly representing the Barnett name, the town of Stratford, the mayor everyone knew and loved.

And I was happy.

I am happy, I told myself, over and over and over.

This is me. This is my family. This is everything I'm supposed to do and know and *be* on a Sunday morning.

But right in the center of my chest there was an ache. A tight, unfamiliar pressure, like I was in a glass box sinking deeper and deeper into unmarked waters, sipping air as casually as I could and ignoring the feeling that there would soon be none left to sip.

I felt marginally better when the congregation was fully seated, our pastor taking to the podium on stage to open service with a prayer. Soon, we'd sing and praise the Lord, witness a few baptisms, hear the message of God through our pastor, and then I'd be set free for the afternoon.

At least for the next hour, the attention would be off me.

I hadn't realized what I'd been feeling until Noah Becker pinpointed it with the perfect word.

Smothered.

And ever since he'd said it, I couldn't shake it.

When Mama wanted to plan, to spend hours and hours every single day working on the tiniest details of the wedding, I wanted to crawl out of my skin. I felt the collar to any dress or shirt I wore growing tighter as the days grew longer, summer in full swing. The only bit of relief I got was when Anthony would call and talk to me at night, calming my breaths and easing my mind by assuring me he would be there soon, that he'd help, that no matter what, it would all be okay.

No matter what, we would be married in five weeks. And that was what mattered.

Those conversations with him that drifted into late night laughter were the only things that saved me.

That, and the night with Noah.

But that had been tarnished.

I found him one section over in the front row, sitting with all his brothers and his mom. Last Sunday, I'd watched him with a curious smile, thinking about our night at the Black Hole together.

Today, I wanted to shoot laser beams through the back of his head with my eyeballs.

I frowned, narrowing my eyes as I stared at his perfectly styled hair, the collar of his olive green button up, the tan skin of his neck. I'd been naïve to think Noah Becker could be anything less than an asshole. I thought he'd shown me a softer side of him that night at the Black Hole — he listened to me, saw that I was anxious before I did, and even opened up to me a little. All week, I'd caught myself thinking about that night, about the way it felt to ride Tank in the moonlight, to have the heat of a man behind me, the ear of the last person on Earth I expected bent to listen to every word I had to say.

But it was just an act, or a drunken game, or some way for him to mess with me.

He'd shown his true colors again when I'd run into him Wednesday night.

First, he'd nearly run me over. And as if that wasn't enough, he'd *yelled* at me — speaking to me like I was just another nosey, gossiping bitty in town. Add in the fact that he'd practically accused me of wanting to cheat on my fiancé, and I knew one thing for sure.

I was *done* with Noah Becker, and I never wanted to talk to him again.

But I still wanted to knock him upside the head.

I was still staring at that head of his when I heard my name flow from the pastor's mouth.

I blinked, turning my gaze to the stage as the congregation applauded. My heart rate ticked up a notch as I tried to dig through the haze to see if I'd heard anything that had just been said.

"Stand *up*," Mama said under her breath, keeping her smile as she clapped.

I did as she said, tucking a strand of hair behind my ear as I offered the warmest smile I could to the pastor.

"There she is," he said, hands outstretched.

Pastor Morris had been the pastor for Stratford's Baptist Church since before I was born. He was a jolly man, average height with a belly built on all the church baking fundraisers. He was pale as snow, with hair that he dyed the black it was in his youth — though the gray peppered it now.

"Ruby Grace," he said, shaking his head as the applause died down. "I remember when you were just a young girl, singing for us up here during Vacation Bible School. Hasn't she grown into a lovely young lady?"

The congregation applauded again, Mama dabbing at the corner of her eyes with her handkerchief as my cheeks burned.

"Ruby Grace has been such a woman of God, giving her time to those in need by volunteering all over our town, namely at our nursing home, and she's continued to help spread the word during her time attending the University of North Carolina. And five weeks from today, right here in this church, our lovely Ruby Grace Barnett will become Mrs. Anthony Caldwell."

The applause was deafening at that, whistles ringing out as I fought the urge to curl into a ball under the nearest pew.

"There will be an open reception at our house after!" Mama called out, standing long enough to say her peace before curtsying and sitting back down. Everyone laughed at that, a few hollers about free champagne echoing before it was silent again.

"Now, for those of you who don't know Anthony, he is a good Christian man. I had the pleasure of meeting him when I sat them down for their pre-marriage interview, and he absolutely blew me away," Pastor Morris said. "And, much to Ruby Grace's father's delight, I'm sure — Anthony is running for State Representative of North Carolina!"

A mixture of *ooh's* and *ahh's* touched my burning ears, and I smiled as widely as I could, waiting to be dismissed, to sit back down, to blend in again.

"Ruby Grace, we are all so very proud of you," Pastor Morris said, his eyes shining as he placed a hand over his heart. "And we honor your choice to forego your education and follow your mother and father's footsteps. Lord knows they have done so much for us in this town, and we know you and Anthony will do the same for North Carolina, and someday, the United States of America as a whole."

Daddy's chest swelled at that, pride rolling off him in waves as he beamed up at me from where he sat next to Mama. I wasn't very close with my father, but in that moment, he looked at me like I was the only thing that mattered in the world.

"Congratulations, Ruby Grace," Pastor Morris finished. "May God bless you and your union."

Amens rang out in unison across the congregation, and I finally sat with the applause fading as Pastor Morris continued with service. Mama squeezed my hand, still smiling, and I smiled back as much as I could before turning my attention to the program in my hand.

Once the attention was firmly off me, I looked up again, watching Pastor for a while before I scanned the stage absent-mindedly, my thoughts drifting. I was ready to send more laser beams into the back of Noah's head, but this time, when I looked at him, he was staring back at me.

I blinked, surveying the bend in his brows, the sympathetic line of his lips pressed together in understanding. He was the only one I'd opened up to about the pressure I felt, about the wedding, in general.

And now, it was like he was the only one in the world who truly saw me.

I tore my eyes away.

• • •

After the service, Mama insisted that I stand with her near the door to shake hands with everyone as they passed. It felt like we were practicing for the receiving line at my wedding, and all I could think about was how badly my feet hurt, and how much I couldn't wait to get away from that church.

I was in a daze, smiling and repeating the same sentiment with each hand I shook, until Noah Becker stepped into view.

I paused, my smile slipping into a frown as I met his hand with mine. "Have a blessed day," I said flatly, ignoring the warmth I felt from his calloused hand.

He chuckled, cocking one brow. "That sounded more like a curse than a blessing."

"Take whatever you want from it," I said, pulling my hand away to shake his mother's and the rest of his brothers'.

He still stood there, waiting.

They were the last ones out of the church, and though Mama was caught up talking to the pastor, I excused myself, making my way to our car. Daddy had already left, saying he had business to attend to, and I was more than ready to join him in that escape.

"Hey," Noah said, jogging to catch up to me even though I'd made it clear I had nothing more to say to him.

"Mm?" I asked nonchalantly, not stopping. In fact, I took my phone out of my pocket, instead, proving my disinterest as I typed out a reply text to one I'd missed from Anthony.

"Giving me the cold shoulder now?"

"You're lucky that's *all* I'm giving you," I mouthed back, still looking at my phone.

His rough hand caught the crook of my elbow, pulling me to a stop when I was just a few feet from Mama's car.

"I deserve that," he said as I finally lifted my eyes to his. They were strikingly blue against the dark hue of his shirt, the clear sky behind him highlighting them even more. "And I wanted to apologize."

"Wanted to? Or are you actually *going* to?"

He smirked. "I'm going to. I am, if you'll let me speak."

I narrowed my eyes, tucking my phone in my purse and crossing my arms before leaning on one hip to wait.

Noah bit his lip against a bigger smile, glancing at our shoes before he met my gaze again. "I'm sorry for nearly knocking you over, and for taking out my anger on you. I shouldn't have said those things I said."

"You're damn straight, you shouldn't have."

"I know. It was uncalled for. I also know it doesn't make up for anything, to feed you an excuse, but..." He sniffed, glancing around us as if to make sure no one was close enough to hear before he spoke again. "It was the anniversary of my dad's death, and that's always a really tough day for me. Even nine years later."

My cocky glare slipped from my face, heart aching in my chest as Noah softened like butter in the warm summer sun.

There he is again, I thought. *There's the man from last Friday night.*

"Anyway, I want to make it up to you," he said, grabbing the back of his neck with one hand. "Just tell me how."

I chewed my lip, watching him as if I was looking for anything other than sincerity in his steel gaze. When I found nothing, I smirked, standing straight as I uncrossed my arms. "Fine. You can make it up to me by meeting me somewhere in a couple hours. Bring your swim trunks."

He cocked a brow. "Swim trunks? Where exactly am I meeting you?"

I smiled wider. "I'll text you the address. Be there at two, sharp."

Noah checked his watch, nodding with an amused smile before he tucked his hands into his pockets. "Alright, then."

"Alright," I repeated.

We watched each other for a long moment, until someone clearing their throat brought our attention to my left.

"Ruby Grace," Mama said, smiling at Noah before she eyed me cautiously. "Why don't you hop in, now. We better get going."

"Yes, Mama," I said before turning back to Noah. "See you around."

"See you," he said, catching on to the fact that I didn't say *see you in a couple of hours.*

Some things Mama didn't need to know.

She smiled politely at Noah, wishing him a blessed day, but her smile faded when he turned to walk back toward the church. She eyed him until he was around the corner of the building before sliding into the driver seat next to me.

"What were you talking to Noah Becker about?" she probed.

I shrugged, pulling out my phone to text Anthony. "Nothing. Just the barrel for Anthony. He wanted to know which one I'd decided on."

"Oh," Mama said, a mix of doubt and relief in her voice.

I thought she'd say more, but she just put the car into reverse, backing out of the parking spot as I let my gaze float out the window.

Chapter Eight

Ruby Grace

"No, no, no," Betty said, shaking her head — which was quite comical, considering her long, silver hair was wrapped up in a hot pink swim cap. "You've got to really get your hips into it. Channel Mr. Swayze, son."

I covered my smile with one hand, and Noah cocked a brow at me as if to say *are you enjoying yourself* before he grinned at Betty. That grin was deadly on any occasion, but when he was shirtless and slick, the pool cutting him off right at the hem of his board shorts, it was absolutely lethal. His arms were a little more tan than his abdomen, but the way his skin was already bronzing, I knew it wouldn't take much time outside for him to even the lines.

My eyes slipped to the ridges of abs that lined his stomach, smaller at the top and growing larger toward the bottom.

I wondered what those ridges felt like.

"Yes, ma'am," Noah said, hanging his hands on his hips as he caught his breath. "I'm sorry, it's just that you're so much better at this than I am."

She waved him off. "Years of practice. Don't worry, you'll catch on. Now, let's get through this. Lord knows we're going to need more time to work on the lift."

Betty winked at Noah then, and I couldn't help the chuckle that escaped me. He eyed me again, fighting against a smile of his own as Betty sidled up beside him once more. Noah took her hands in his, listening carefully as she walked him through the dance at the end of *Dirty Dancing* for about the seventh time.

It was a hot afternoon — a warning that summer was here to stay. I relished it, leaning back on my hands and angling my face toward the sun as I swung my feet in the pool. Summer was Betty's favorite time of year for this exact reason — pool days. The other residents generally skipped out, or if they did come outside, they'd stay under the umbrellas and watch the pool rather than get in it.

But not Betty.

She moved best when she was in the pool, like she hadn't had a hip replacement a few years before, and like her body wasn't failing her just as quickly as her mind. In the pool, she was free to move, to dance, to laugh.

And she did all three that afternoon.

She was having a good day — a day when she remembered everything, when she wasn't too tired to leave the bed, when she was the same, sassy old woman I'd met when I was fourteen. I'd been spoiled by her good days, lately, and I was thankful. Annie said it was the most she'd had in a row since Christmas.

She also said it was because I was back in town.

I couldn't know that for sure, but I took whatever time I could to be there with her — just in case.

I watched from the sidelines as Betty schooled Noah on the final dance scene from the classic movie — and one of her favorites. Noah, bless his heart, took it in stride. He held her hands, spun her gently, even went under water completely to give Betty some sort of "lift" that made her feel like Jennifer Grey.

That was when her smile was the largest — her eyes closed, face cast upward, arms out in the same iconic flight stance that the actress had done.

If I wasn't laughing so hard, I might have cried at the sentiment.

After a dozen more run throughs, Betty called for a break, and the two of them swam up to the side of the pool where I sat. Betty took the lemonade I offered her, sipping and hollering across the pool at Mr. Buchanan — who was seated under the umbrellas. Noah rested his arms on the concrete edge, crossing them and resting his head on his forearm before he peered up at me through lashes still dripping with water.

His eyes were an endless blue, the light from the pool reflecting off them like a tropical dream.

"Enjoying your entertainment this afternoon, Miss. Barnett?"

I bit my lip against a smile. "Very much so, Mr. Becker. I never knew you were such a great dancer."

"Oh, you should see me on the actual dance floor. I can two step and waltz and cha cha with the best of them. And don't even get me started on what happens when 'Watermelon Crawl' comes on."

"I'm sure it's quite entertaining," I mused, still dangling my feet in the cool water.

"When do I get to see your dance moves?"

I barked out a laugh at that. "Um, that would be approximately... never."

"Never?" he asked, popping his head up off his arms with a look of injustice. "But you've seen all my moves, now. I show you mine, you show me yours. Isn't that the deal?"

"I never agreed to that."

He narrowed his eyes, running his forefinger and thumb over the stubble on his chin before he nodded. "I see..." Then, a wicked gleam came over those blue steel eyes, and before I could so much as scream, his hand wrapped around my wrist, tugging forward until I was off the ledge and under water.

I popped up instantly, not even able to open my eyes against the chlorine yet before I was swinging at him. "Noah!"

He laughed, catching my advances easily and pulling me into him. I blinked several times, shaking the drops from my eyes before I glared up at him.

"You jerk. Mama's going to kill me for ruining my hair."

"Mama will live," he said, and then one arm wrapped around my waist, the other taking my hand in a leading position. "Now, let's dance, little lady."

With one pull of my hand and push of my hip, I spun away from him, reeling back in like a yo-yo and falling in line with his steps before I realized what was happening. Surprise ripped through me, brows shooting up to my hairline as he somehow managed to smoothly twirl me around that metaphorical dance floor even with water hitting us waist deep. My feet felt sluggish, the moves slower than if we were in boots on a hardwood floor, but somehow, that made it even more fun.

I laughed and laughed as he danced me around — until he had the bright idea to flip me like a swing dancer. I emerged from the water beating on his chest again, which just made him laugh harder. And when we were breathless, Noah tugged me to the side of the pool again.

"Thank you for the dance," he said, both of us still breathing heavily as he wrapped his strong, rugged hands around my waist. For a moment, he just held them there, the rough pad of his thumbs smoothing over my exposed hip bones. My smile fell, chest still heaving as my eyes slipped to his lips.

I didn't know why I looked at them.

I didn't know why I couldn't look away.

Noah swallowed, tightening his grip on my hips before he lowered in the water a little and helped push me back up onto the edge of the pool where I'd been seated before. Once I was steady, he released his hold on me, backing away with a distant look in his eyes that I couldn't decipher before he tore them from me and looked at Betty, instead.

"Now, how come you don't move with *me* like that?" Betty teased, hanging her hands on her hips.

"I did!" he defended. "You just out-dance me. Hard to realize how great I am when you're out there showing me up."

Betty smirked, taking a sip of her lemonade before she leaned against the edge. "I knew your father, you know?"

Those words sucked the air out of my lungs, and judging by the way Noah's smile slipped off his face, they did the same to him. He glanced up at me, a question in his eyes, but I just shook my head slightly.

I hadn't told her anything about him, not before we got here. And all I'd said was, "*Betty, this is Noah.*"

I shrugged, an apology in my eyes as Noah cleared his throat, turning to Betty once more. "*My* father?"

"Oh, yes," she said, nodding with a knowing smile. "You're Noah Becker. I'd know those eyes and that mischievous grin anywhere."

At that, my mouth popped open, and Noah stilled completely.

"Your father took a liking to my Leroy," she explained, her eyes growing misty as she watched the water from the pool lap the sides. "And my Leroy sure did appreciate having a friend, especially there toward the end."

I swallowed. "Leroy was Betty's husband," I explained. "He passed away about twenty years ago."

"I'm sorry to hear that," Noah said in a hushed voice, and the confusion in his eyes shifted to sympathy as he put a hand on Betty's shoulder.

"It was a hard time," she said. "But, honestly, it's him I feel sorry for. Poor bastard has been waiting at Heaven's gates for me all this time. He had to know I'd take a while, but I'm sure if he could, he'd holler down at me just like he used to holler up the stairs." She chuckled, brows folding together as she did her best impression. "*Woman, get your cute behind down here. Ain't no makeup or hair curlers gonna make you look any more beautiful than you already are.*"

My heart swelled, and Noah smirked up at me before he dropped his hand from Betty's shoulder. "He sounds like quite the guy."

"He was," she agreed. "But, then again, so was your father. It seems we lose all the best ones too young."

Noah sobered at that, nodding just once. "Yes, ma'am."

"Your father would come see us every Good Friday," Betty explained, which was the nickname the distillery had given to the last Friday of every month, when they would give each of their employees a free bottle of whiskey with their paycheck. "Every single one for about four years, right up until the time the good Lord took my Leroy. They had met down at Buck's one night, and I don't know what transpired there, but boy, did those two take a liking to each other." She smiled. "So, every Good Friday, your father would come by with his bottle of Scooter Whiskey and a bag full of fried chicken. We'd all sit out on the porch and eat and drink and laugh until it was way too late for two old folks to be up. Sometimes your mom would join, sometimes not. But John? Well... Johnny was always there."

Noah swallowed, looking down at the water for a long moment before he met her gaze once more. "Sounds like a wonderful friendship."

"It was," she agreed. "And your father, he was a good man. When I met you today, I almost swore a ghost had come back to life. You look just like him, you know?" She beamed. "Same eyes, same hair, same Becker Trouble Grin."

She pinched his cheek at that, and Noah smirked.

"You've got his spirit," she said, her voice softer now as she watched

Noah. "You're a good man, too, Noah Becker. And I'm glad I got to spend the afternoon with you."

I watched what I would have sworn was Noah's bottom lip trembling, but as soon as I thought I'd seen it shake, it was steady again. He smiled through whatever he was feeling — and I knew he was feeling *something* — as he reached forward to pull Betty in for a soft hug.

"Me, too, Miss Betty. Even if you did show me up on the dance floor."

She chuckled, her little shoulders shaking in his broad arms.

When he pulled back, he cleared his throat. "If you'll excuse me, I'm going to go get a shower and dry off. I've got this thing I've got to get to."

"What thing?" I probed.

He grabbed the back of his neck. "Oh, it's nothing, really. Me and my brothers try to get together every weekend to play cards. I usually host, and they'll be heading over in about an hour." He shrugged, giving me a soft smile, though he still seemed caught up in his thoughts. "Someone's gotta order the pizza."

I nodded, but my stomach sank at the realization that the day was nearly over. Noah would go hang out with his brothers, and I'd go home...

To wedding planning.

And Mama.

And all the stress I'd forgotten about over the last few hours.

I chewed my lip, eyes bouncing back and forth between Noah's before I swallowed. "I like cards..."

He blinked, the tiniest smirk climbing at the corner of his lips. "Yeah?"

I nodded. "I used to play blackjack and Texas hold 'em with my dad and his friends sometimes. Just for fun, but... yeah."

Noah smiled wider. "You want to come over? We could use some fresh blood at the table."

"Are you sure?" I asked, a little too quickly. "I don't want to impose."

Please say yes.

He shook his head. "We'd love to have you. I'm just going to go change and we can head out, grab the pizza and beer on our way. Meet you out front?"

"I'll be right behind you."

Noah placed his palms flat on the edge next to me, lifting his body out easily and saying one last goodbye to Betty before he made his way inside. Betty and I both watched him go, the water spilling down his back like water falling over the strongest side of a mountain, carved carefully over thousands of years.

When he disappeared through the doors, I turned back to Betty, and she was smirking at me.

"What?" I asked.

Betty's smile climbed higher. "You sly devil. You didn't tell me you were engaged to a *Becker*."

The color drained from my face.

"You lied about him not being as handsome as Richard Gere, my dear," she said, wagging her finger at me. "But, hell, I suppose I would have done the same. If that boy was mine, I wouldn't want a single other woman coming onto him."

"Betty…"

"I like him," she said, not letting me interrupt. "He's a good man, from a good family. He'll treat you right, Ruby Grace." She smiled wider, squeezing my knee where it hung off the edge. "You did good, my girl."

My cheeks burned, because somewhere under my haste to tell her she had the wrong guy, I felt something else, something stronger.

Longing, I realized distantly.

And then I stamped it down in the same breath.

"Noah's not my fiancé," I explained with a gentle smile. "We're just friends."

Betty frowned. "*Friends?*"

I nodded, but Betty's eyes drifted over my shoulder. When I followed her gaze, I saw Noah through the pool fence waiting for me in the parking lot, his hands shoved in his pockets, back leaned against his old, beat-up truck. I felt Betty watching me, but I couldn't hide the blush on my cheeks, the bob of my throat as I swallowed.

A few feet from the pool, my phone vibrated on my towel, screen lighting up with Anthony's name — with the picture of us that I loved so much.

Betty eyed it with me, and when I turned back to her, she just lifted one silver eyebrow. "Are you sure about that?"

● ● ●

Noah

Dad was still on my mind as I watched Ruby Grace hustle my brothers in poker that night.

We were all gathered around my folding table in the middle of my modest home, Sturgill Simpson on the stereo, two half-eaten boxes of pizza propped open on the kitchen counter behind us. My house was the one most "in town" between me and my brothers, just a few blocks off the Main Street drag on the south side. Jordan's house was ten minutes out of town, to the west, and Logan's was northeast, a little farther out than Mom's.

I still couldn't be sure if we'd meant to surround Mom's house the way we did, flanking her on all sides, or if we'd done it subconsciously. Either way, none of us were more than twenty minutes from each other, and we were all less than ten from Mom's.

My house was the closest to beer and pizza, however, which meant it was the prime choice for poker night.

It was pretty standard for my brothers and me to get together sometime during the weekend to play cards.

Ruby Grace, however, was a new addition.

"That's bullshit!" Logan yelled, thrusting his cards forward. They fluttered over the massive pot he and Ruby Grace had built up during the hand, and he sulked further when she reached forward with a grin to rake it all in.

"Don't hate the player, Logan."

"I hate the *cheater*," he said, folding his arms over his chest.

"I don't even have sleeves to hide cards," she pointed out, gesturing to her toned, tanned arms. "Come on, now. Beckers aren't sore losers, are they?"

"Don't let his little boy actions speak for all of us," Jordan chimed in. He was being a good sport with our new guest at the table, but I didn't miss the questioning glances he shot me over his cards the whole night.

Logan stuck his tongue out, but then smirked, shaking his head and gathering the cards for his turn to deal. "You didn't warn us that you were bringing a shark to the table tonight, Noah."

I shrugged. "Ruby Grace is full of surprises."

Her eyes caught mine, then, my brothers picking up the conversation around us as we stared. Her smile was soft and sweet, the blush on her cheeks just barely visible now that her tan from the day was setting in. She held my gaze for a long while before tucking a strand of red hair behind her ear and picking up her cards for the next hand.

I kicked back in my chair, checking out my own cards as the day floated through my mind. I couldn't believe Betty knew my father, and the way she'd talked about him made my chest tighten. She was right — he was a good man. He was the *best* man, and it was a knife to my gut every time I realized that he wasn't here anymore, that he didn't get to see us boys grow into men, that he wouldn't be there to stand next to Mikey when Bailey walked down the aisle to him.

Or next to me, if I ever found a woman who would do the same.

The next dozen rounds of poker flew by, and after Ruby Grace knocked all the guys out once again in a bigger hand, Mikey groaned, tossing his cards in and standing. "I need a root beer float. Anyone else?"

Logan scoffed. "Uh, no thanks, Mikey. We're all old enough to drink *actual* beer. But thank you."

"She's not," he pointed out, gesturing to Ruby Grace.

That fact soured my gut a little.

"And besides, you're telling me that just because you're old enough to drink beer, you don't want a delicious root beer topped off with creamy vanilla ice cream right now?"

Logan's mouth pulled to the side, his eyes glancing around the table, to his cards from the last game, and back up again.

"Alright, I give. That does sound fucking delicious."

Mikey smirked triumphantly. "That's what I thought. One round of root beer floats coming up."

"You better not spill it down the sides," Logan called after him. "I swear, if my glass is sticky, I'll thwomp you!"

"Extra sticky glass, you got it, big bro!"

Logan humphed, pushing back in his chair before trotting after Mikey into the kitchen.

"I better help," Jordan said, standing. "If Logan goes into an OCD attack, no one is safe."

Ruby Grace chuckled lightly as Jordan tipped his imaginary hat at us, leaving us alone at the table. She leaned back in her chair, then, gathering her hair in one fist before letting it fall behind her. It exposed the delicate lines of her collar bone, the lean muscles of her neck, and I hated that I wanted to taste her so bad I had to physically hold onto the edge of the table to keep me from getting up and doing just that.

Seeing her with Betty and the rest of the residents at the nursing home today hit me in a way I didn't expect. She wasn't anything like the girl in church. No, at the nursing home, she was boisterous, playful, entertaining. She was everyone's highlight of the day, and she shone as bright as the sun did at that pool.

They loved her, it was easy to see.

And it was also easy to see *why*.

When she came back to my place for dinner and to play cards, I'd sat on the opposite side of the table from her. I needed to put space between us — especially after being skin to skin in the pool, her toned stomach pressed against mine, her surprisingly ample breasts exposed in her little bikini top.

But getting away from her didn't prove to be helpful.

If anything, it only gave me a better view of her hazel eyes, the freckles dotting her cheeks, her smooth, plump lips. I was thankful I couldn't see her legs under the table, because I already knew what those did to me.

And watching her with my brothers, handing out shit just as well as she was taking it from them, it made me feel something I never had before. I couldn't even put my finger on it, what that warmth in my chest was, that sinking in my gut.

As her phone lit up yet again with her fiancé's name on my folding table, I realized it was a longing, a sense of loss.

Because no matter how I tried to deny it, I wanted her to be mine.

It was silly to even think it when we hadn't so much as held hands, but I felt it — some sort of deep possessiveness over a girl I'd never have. She was going to marry another man, entertain *his* brothers, or family or friends. She would cook for him, hold him when shit got rough, be his rock when he needed to lean. She would wrap those pretty little legs around *him* at night, and I'd never get to touch them.

Jealousy ripped through me, and I knew it was the wrong move, I *knew* I shouldn't have, but I couldn't stop myself. When she reached for her phone like she was finally going to answer him, I called out her name.

"Ruby Grace."

She paused, frowning at the phone before she looked up at me.

"Want to get some fresh air with me on the porch while Mikey makes those floats?"

I expected her to hesitate, to say, *"Yes, but let me answer this call first."* Or to just flat out deny me. But, she smiled almost instantly, her cheeks high and rosy as she nodded, tucking her phone away in the purse she had hanging on her chair. "Sure."

Jordan eyed me suspiciously from the kitchen as I rose from my chair, meeting Ruby Grace on the other side of the table. I didn't meet his gaze for long, though — maybe because I knew what facts he wanted to point out.

I knew them very well.

The night was pleasantly cool, considering how hot the day had been. That was what I loved about June in Tennessee. The days were long and hot, but the nights were cool — perfect for a bonfire or to get close to someone for a little warmth.

"It's beautiful out," Ruby Grace commented, leaning her arms on the wooden railing of my porch. It had been old and rotted when I moved in, but it was my first project — fixing up the exterior. Now, the porch was maybe the best part of the entire house, rebuilt and painted white with a couple of rocking chairs Mom had gifted me when the project was done.

I considered asking Ruby Grace to sit, but she looked so comfortable against the railing, her eyes scanning the yard and the houses across the street, that I just slid up next to her, instead.

"It is. It was a nice day at the pool, too."

She smiled. "Thanks for coming with me today."

I shrugged. "Hey, there are much worse ways you could have made me pay for being such an asshole to you."

"Betty adored you."

"Oh, we're totally getting married," I joked.

"Funny. She said the same thing."

I chuckled, letting the sounds of the crickets settle between us before I spoke again. "You were really in your element there."

Another smile bloomed on her lips, but this one fell a little too quickly. "Yeah."

"I liked you like that today."

She frowned, turning to me, then. "Like what?"

"I don't know," I started with a shrug. "Carefree. Young. Unrestrained. You're always so put together." I paused. "I like it better when you're just a girl being a girl."

I could see the warmth in her eyes under the porch light as I spoke, but when I finished, she stood taller, shoulders back. "I'm a *woman*, thank you very much."

"Oh, trust me," I said, eyes trailing down her legs. "I know that, too."

When I met her gaze again, she was biting her lip against a smile, and she turned back toward the yard, draping her arms over the railing once more. "I really do love it there," she said after a while. "It was my favorite thing to do when I was in high school, spend a day volunteering at the home. My best friend, Annie, works there full time now."

"Did you think you would, too?"

She considered that. "No, I don't think so. I always pictured Annie and I going to UNC together, and then..." Her voice faded, and she glanced down at her hands hanging over the railing.

At her ring, maybe?

"And then?" I prompted her.

"Oh, it's silly. Anyway, I suppose nothing turns out how we imagined, right?"

I frowned, turning toward her. I chanced touching the soft skin of the inside of her elbow, getting her to face me, too. "Hey, don't do that."

"Do what?"

"Don't act like what you want doesn't matter."

She swallowed, looking at the porch beneath us. "It's just like I told you that night we went riding. Annie and I always had dreams of joining AmeriCorps. We wanted to give back, to travel and help others for a while after we graduated." She smiled. "I just thought it'd be so fun, you know? I'd be with my best friend, we'd see new places, meet new people. I'd get to do what makes my heart happy."

"I remember you talking about that," I said, also remembering how frustrated I'd been that she didn't see that as an option anymore. That night, I had left it alone. But tonight, I wanted to probe. "What happened?"

She sighed, finally pulling away from where I held her and leaning her hip against the railing. "Well, Annie found Trav. They got married, she's pregnant now. She never did go to UNC. And I... well..." She held up her left hand, pointing to the rock on the third finger.

I nodded. "Yeah. I mean, I know it'd be a little different without Annie, but you could still go. Right?"

She scoffed. "Of course not. I'm getting married."

"I guess I just don't understand what that has to do with anything."

"It has *everything* to do with all of it," she said, flustered. "I'll be a wife. A *politician's* wife. I have new duties now, new things expected of me."

"And would your new husband not understand if you wanted to chase your own dreams for a while?" I countered. "It wouldn't be forever. Why can't you have what you want while giving him what he wants, too?"

She shook her head. "You don't understand."

"Oh, I think I understand just fine."

I stepped into her space, and before I could think better of it, my hand touched her arm, sliding up to her neck, her jaw, until I slipped my fingers in the soft strands of her hair and framed her face, tilting her gaze toward me again.

"You deserve to have the things you've dreamed about, Ruby Grace," I said. "And when you marry someone, you become a *team*. It's not all about him and his dreams and his achievements. You are not just a sidekick."

I paused, licking my bottom lip as I considered my next words. Ruby Grace's eyes were soft, wide, almost a little scared as she watched me.

"You are the heroine just as much as he is the hero," I reminded her. "And if he loves you, he will support you and your dreams just as you've supported his and will continue to in the future."

She leaned into my touch, eyes fluttering shut before they opened slowly again. "You make it all sound so easy," she whispered. "So simple."

"With the right person, it is," I told her. I swallowed, glancing at her lips before I found her gaze again. "If you were mine, Ruby Grace, your dreams wouldn't come second to anything."

It was an overstep I didn't mean to make.

The words came out before I even realized what I was saying, and now, it was too late to go back. There was a line between us, one we never had to draw because that ring on her finger had drawn it for us the first day she came back into town. But there on my porch, in the soft, cool, Tennessee summer night, those rules didn't seem to apply.

We were in another universe altogether, and in this one, that ring on her finger didn't exist.

I hadn't even realized her hands were on me, not until they fisted in my t-shirt at my abdomen, pulling me closer. My hand in her hair gripped a little harder, her eyes on my lips, mine on hers until we were so close I couldn't even see them anymore. Our breaths met in the space between, hot and heavy with words we wouldn't say.

Her lips parted.

Mine grazed hers, eliciting the sweetest gasp.

But before I could connect the kiss, before I could pull her in, feel her melt into my arms, the front door swung open.

Ruby Grace jumped back, folding her arms over the railing and looking out over the yard like she had been before. I looked up at the awning over my porch, suppressing a groan as Mikey bounded out, completely oblivious.

"Two root beer floats," he announced proudly, handing me two Mason jars filled to the top with the frothy vanilla ice cream and soda mixture. "And Ruby Grace, we demand a double-or-nothing rematch."

She finally turned toward us, her smile weak.

She wouldn't look at me at all.

"Thank you, Mikey, but I actually have to run. I didn't realize how late it was. Would you mind grabbing my purse?"

He shrugged — again, completely oblivious. "Sure! Be right back."

When Mikey dipped inside, I sat the floats down on the table by the rocking chairs before turning back to her. "You're leaving?"

She still wouldn't look at me.

"I think we both know it's for the best."

Her words twisted like a knife in my chest, but I didn't have any words to say to make her stay.

She was right.

I hated it, but it didn't change the fact that she was right.

Mikey came out moments later with her purse, and the guys met her at the door, giving her a hug and a little more shit for taking their money. She was all gracious smiles and warm thank you's until the door shut, my brothers back inside, leaving us alone on the porch again.

I opened my arms. "Thank you for today. For tonight."

But she just stared at me, her eyes filling with tears that wouldn't shed. "Why did you have to do this?"

I frowned, letting my arms fall. "I—"

"No," she said, shaking her head, hands clinging to the strap of her purse like a lifeline. "Everything was fine. I was *fine* until I met you. You've messed everything up."

My brows furrowed more. "What, by reminding you that you have a choice? That you don't have to marry someone who makes you feel this way?"

"I *love* him," she spat.

"Fine. But does he love you?"

She scoffed. "Of course he does. How dare you even insinuate otherwise."

I smirked at the word *insinuate*, sensing the well-to-do woman she was raised to be slipping back into place just like she always did.

Shaking my head, I put my arms up in a mock surrender. "You're right. I'm sorry. Just forget about AmeriCorps, about school, about anything that doesn't revolve around Anthony and *his* career. Clearly, you're very happy and I was mistaken by saying anything at all. I sincerely apologize."

I was being an asshole. I knew it, but just like I'd overstepped earlier, I couldn't stop myself from doing so now.

I wanted her to wake up, to see what I saw.

Even if it hurt.

Ruby Grace's bottom lip trembled a bit as she pressed it to the top, adjusting her purse on her shoulder before she growled and stormed off my porch.

"See you around?" I called after her.

My only response was one middle finger thrown my way over her shoulder.

• • •

Ruby Grace

Once again, I found myself speeding through town with the top down on my convertible, cursing Noah Becker's name.

"Oh, the *nerve* of that man!" I growled, punching the gas again once I made the turn down the old road that led to my parents' house. The warm night air whipped through my hair, little tendrils of fire red invading my vision as I drove. The radio was silent, the only noise the revving of my engine and the revving of my temper.

Noah had crossed a line. He shouldn't have held me the way he did in the pool, with his hands on my hips, his chest so close to mine. And then on his porch, he'd stepped into my space like he owned it, like I was *his* and not Anthony's.

And he'd even said it.

"If you were mine, Ruby Grace, your dreams wouldn't come second to anything."

My cheeks heated, a rush of blood flowing through me at the memory of my hands in his shirt, his in my hair, our lips touching just long enough to send a zip of desire through me.

I'd nearly cheated on my fiancé.

I shook my head, letting out another frustrated growl as I took the turn into my driveway.

"It wasn't even a kiss," I reminded myself out loud. "We got a little too close, but that was it. It was a mistake. We were just caught up in the moment."

It would never happen again.

And I promised myself I'd stay far away from Noah Becker to ensure it.

By the time I put my car in park, punching the buttons on the consul to put the convertible top back in place, I'd made my decision. Noah was nothing more than the guy who showed me the barrel I purchased for *Anthony*. He wasn't my friend, and he wasn't someone I should lean on the way I had been.

It didn't matter how I felt around him, or how I found myself already caring about him and his family.

He was a lightning storm, fun to watch from afar but dangerous to dance with.

I wasn't going to toy with that line of danger.

I dragged myself out of the car, exhausted and ready for a hot shower and my bed, but the sight of a familiar car next to my dad's truck in the driveway made me pause.

Before I could even register what that car meant, the voice that belonged to it spoke in the darkness.

"There she is."

Anthony trotted down the steps of the front porch, his wide and brilliantly white smile visible even in the dim light of the night. He held his arms open, but my feet remained glued to the spot I stood.

"Come here, beautiful," he said, taking my hesitance for shock as he chuckled and pulled me into his chest. He wrapped his arms around me, swaying me in a hug before he pulled back and framed my face with his hands. "*God,* I've missed you."

His lips were on me in the next second, kissing me with the longing of the last few weeks we'd been apart. I didn't come to until halfway through it, and when I did, I wrapped my arms around his waist, kissing him in return as my mind reeled.

And I couldn't figure out why when his lips were on me, I was still thinking about Noah.

When Anthony pulled back, he wrapped me in his arms again, threading his hands on the small of my back as he smiled down at me. He was tall, body built like a brick wall from playing lacrosse his entire life. His bicep muscles were the size of my thighs, and with them encompassing me like that, I felt an equal measure of warmth and confinement.

"Shocked?" he asked with an amused smile when I still didn't say anything. His blond hair was styled in a neat wave, his hazel eyes matching the hue of mine. He reminded me a little of a Ken doll, or Superman, or a combination of the two with his cleft chin and strong jaw line, his face freshly shaved and smooth, his skin a perfect shade of bronze.

I nodded, forcing a smile.

He chuckled. "I thought you'd be. Where have you been? I've been waiting all night to see this look on your face."

Panic zipped through me, but I swallowed it down, running my hands over his chest. "Oh, just at the nursing home. I didn't know I had such a surprise waiting for me."

Warmth touched his eyes. "My girl, always the giving heart." He shook his head, leaning down to peck my lips before he pulled back again. "One of the things I love most about you."

My smile was genuine this time, and I mentally slapped the guilt I felt away. I hadn't done anything wrong with Noah. We hadn't actually kissed. It was a mistake, a weak moment where I was too close to him, too close to my feelings of anxiety surrounding the wedding.

It could happen to anyone.

But it wouldn't happen again.

I pulled Anthony in for another kiss to seal that promise to myself, and when I pulled back, he threaded his hand in mine, tugging me toward the house.

"What are you doing here, anyway?" I asked. "And how long are you here?"

"Well..." he said, and before he could answer, he swung the door open and Mama bounded toward me, wrapping me in her arms in an excited hug.

"Oh, Ruby Grace! You're home!" She squeezed me tight before pulling back and framing my arms in her hands. "Can you believe it? Anthony surprised us all this afternoon. And he's staying until the wedding! I'm just so thrilled!"

My brows shot up. "You are?" I asked Anthony.

"I am," he said, a soft grin on his perfect lips. "We've been getting a lot of media attention with me running for state representative, and it seems that marrying you is everyone's favorite topic. Can't say that I blame them," he said, chucking my chin. "Anyway, Dad thought it would be good to capitalize on all the attention. He sent me out here with a small film crew. They're going to film us preparing for the wedding, capture our love story for the media outlets and possibly some campaign commercials. Don't worry," he said when he saw the worry in my eyes. "They won't be with us all the time. And we'll have a say in what they can use."

I nodded through my discomfort, especially since I couldn't quite place its origin. Was it the thought of cameras following me that made my stomach lurch like that, or the fact that Anthony was in my hometown to stay for the next five weeks?

And if that was the case, *why* did it make me uncomfortable?

"Oh, I just can't believe it!" Mama said, clapping her hands together. "I'll have to plan a dinner this week for the crew. We can all get to know each other and I'll make my famous lemon bar cookies. We're just so thrilled to have you, Anthony!"

She wrapped him up in her arms before scurrying off, calling down the hallway for Dad to come join us in the living room for a night cap.

I stood in the foyer in a daze, blinking repeatedly, sensing the disarray of my hair as if it were the only sense I could focus on in that moment. I smoothed my hands over the frizzy curls, over and over, staring at the family photo that greeted all our guests who entered the house.

"Hey," Anthony said, taking my face in his hands. He leveled his gaze with mine. "I know this is a lot, and surprises aren't really your thing. Why don't you run up and take a shower, get changed, take some time for yourself. I'll handle entertaining your parents until you feel ready to come down and join us. Okay?"

My heart squeezed painfully in my chest. He was so aware of my needs, of who I was, and I'd just been in the arms of another man. I wanted to cry, to throw myself into his arms and beg for forgiveness, but I didn't even know what to apologize for.

Or, maybe part of that came from the fact that I wasn't sorry, not the way I should have been.

"Okay," I said, eyes watering a little as I nodded.

Anthony kissed my forehead in understanding, and once he let me go, I dragged myself up the stairs and to my room. Anthony's stuff was in the guest room down the hall, and I passed it, eyeing the luggage before I swept into my own room and locked the door behind me.

I ran the shower water as hot as I could stand, hoping it would scald away my guilt, my confusion, my warring thoughts.

My fiancé was in town. He would be here to help with planning, with all the decisions. We'd be able to spend time together, celebrate this time leading up to our wedding like a normal couple.

The man I loved was here, and I wanted to find relief in that, to wrap myself up in the comfort of his arms.

I just had to fight through the feeling of suffocation, first.

Chapter Nine

Noah

Against my strongest urges, I left Ruby Grace alone after that night at my house.

I told myself it was because I was respecting her claim that she loved Anthony, and that he loved her, but the truth was probably somewhere more along the lines that I knew I'd see her later that week. I fought the urge to text or call her Monday through Wednesday because I knew on Thursday, I'd get to see her in person.

And I always did my best work in person.

I needed to apologize, that much I knew fairly clearly. I didn't necessarily *want* to, because the bigger part of me wasn't sorry for pulling her close on my porch, for nearly kissing her, for calling her out on the bullshit rules of the marriage she was about to enter into. I didn't want her to give up *her* dreams for his.

There should have been balance, and room for both.

I didn't know why I felt so passionately about it, why it irked me so much that she was so willing to push everything she wanted aside for him. More sane people might have seen it as an honorable sacrifice. But me? I thought of my parents, of how Mom supported Dad in all his aspirations at the brewery while he supported her dreams when it came to building our family. They respected each other, and not one part of the team was more important than the other.

I wanted that for me.

And for some unbeknownst reason, I wanted it for Ruby Grace, too.

So, on Thursday, the night of the annual Scooter Whiskey Single Barrel Soirée, I went over everything I'd say to her while my hands worked on auto-pilot getting the event ready.

"Can you even imagine what it would be like," PJ spoke through grunts as he unloaded another barrel from the truck. "To have enough money to just blow fifteen grand on a barrel of whiskey?"

I smirked, reading the name inscribed on the golden plate of the barrel he'd just pulled off the truck. I scribbled a check next to the one on my sheet, nodding to Marty, who loaded it onto a dolly and took it on down the line to the buyer's VIP tent.

"Trust me, if I had money like that, I wouldn't be blowing it on alcohol," he continued.

"Oh, yeah? What *would* you spend it on, PJ?" Eli teased, leaning one elbow on a barrel. "Let me guess. Hookers."

The guys snickered while PJ turned a bright red. "*No*," he answered quickly. "I get plenty of sex. For *free.*"

"Right," Eli said. "And Noah is celibate."

"Hey, don't drag the innocent bystander into this," I said, chuckling as I checked off another barrel before sending it down the line.

"I don't, nor would I ever, pay for sex," PJ insisted again. When no one answered with more than a lifted brow, he threw his hands up in the air before letting them hit his thighs with a slap and a groan. "You guys suck."

We all laughed at that, me ruffling his hair before telling him we were just teasing. He was the youngest, just like a little brother to us, and we couldn't help it. He didn't seem appeased, but he got back to work, each of us falling into the groove as Eli rambled on about what *he* would buy if he had stupid money.

They didn't ask me what I would do, and I was glad for it. I probably would have lost a few of my man points if I told them the truth. All I'd want is a modest house, big enough for my family and my horse. I'd want to spend our time traveling or farming or building memories together, never working another day in my life and making it so my wife wouldn't have to, either. Not unless she *wanted* to.

That thought was still in my mind when Ruby Grace's barrel stopped at my feet.

I stared at the cursive loops of her name on the gold plate, tracing them a little longer than necessary before I checked the box next to her name and sent the barrel on. My eyes followed it halfway to the buyer's tent, pulse picking up speed at the thought of talking to her tonight.

It made no sense. I didn't know what I expected to get out of any of it. She was getting married — in less than five weeks, no less. I had nothing to offer her that she didn't already have and she couldn't give me a single thing more than what she already had.

And yet, there was some part of me that desired her, that needed her in whatever way I could get her.

I didn't really give a fuck if it was right or wrong.

I was still analyzing it all, trying to pinpoint what it was about that girl that got under my skin, when the rest of the guys and I retreated to the staff tent to freshen up before the opening speech from Patrick Scooter. In less than an hour, the entire Scooter estate would be littered with people from Stratford and the surrounding area. It was the biggest party of the year, a time when no matter where you lived or how much money you made, you got to come together with the rich and the fabulous and drink the same whiskey as them. For one night, our town was united — though everyone would likely still stay in their little circles.

The band was already playing when I emerged from the staff tent, dressed in my good blue jeans and white, button-up shirt. I left the top button unfastened, rolled the sleeves up to just under my elbows, and topped the whole look off with my best cowboy boots and my favorite cowboy hat. It was a Stetson, made of premium wool that matched the dark mocha brown of my boots, and before it was mine, it had been my father's.

Gus had me running around, greeting the barrel buyers I'd worked with throughout the season, making sure they knew where their barrel was to take home after the event and getting them set up in the VIP area with whatever they needed. I'd take pictures of them with their barrels, introduce them to the rest of the barrel raising team as well as the scientists behind the creation of their unique whiskey, and answer any questions they had before moving on to the next.

This was my element.

I knew whiskey. I knew Scooter Whiskey. I knew the barrel raising process, the science behind our whiskey, what we could and what we *couldn't* tell the buyers about the product they'd paid top dollar for. I knew how to charm a crowd, how to impress someone and make them feel good about blowing all that money, and how to represent our company the same way my father had.

What I *didn't* know was what to do when Ruby Grace walked into the VIP tent hanging on her fiancé's arm.

I knew he was Anthony without needing an introduction. He just *looked* like a politician — all navy suit, complete with tie and pocket square, dress shoes shined to perfection, hair styled in an immaculate wave like one you'd see on the red carpet at a Hollywood award show. He carried himself with a mixture of arrogance and confidence, a balance not many men could pull off. He was both welcoming and threatening all at once, and I found myself hating him before I even had reason to.

Maybe it was because of the girl he held by the waist.

A small crew of cameras and microphones followed them around, staying back just enough to give them space while capturing every interaction they had. I assumed it was something he was doing while running for office, some sort of propaganda. Anthony seemed to shine with those cameras on him.

Ruby Grace seemed to want to disappear.

She didn't even notice me, not with Anthony toting her around from group to group, a politician's smile on his face while she wore a more subdued smile of her own. I watched her for a long while, and I noticed she did nothing more than shake the hand of whomever they were talking to before Anthony would take over, commanding all the attention, leading the conversation.

She was a sidekick, a wallflower, and it made absolutely no sense to me.

If he would let her speak, she'd steal the show. It would be *her* everyone wanted to know. It would be Ruby Grace who would light up the room with her smile, knock men on their asses with the modest yet somehow classically sexy emerald dress she wore. The collar was high, the sleeves covering her shoulders and upper arms, but the hem of the skirt cut just above her knees, showing her deadliest weapons — those killer legs.

But it wasn't just the way she dressed, or her body, or her smile or her fire-red hair. It was her passionate and giving heart, her quick and witty banter, her *intelligence* that made her stand out.

No one would know that, though. Not if he never let her speak.

I tore my eyes away from her long enough to toast a glass of whiskey with two buyers I'd met in the winter. They had traveled all the way from California to pick up their barrel and spend a week in Tennessee. The barrel they'd selected had high notes of vanilla and nutmeg, giving it a holiday feel that captured their hearts since they had visited during Christmas break when they bought it. The whiskey warmed its way down my throat, settling in my stomach along with the dozen other ounces of whiskey I'd tried when welcoming our guests.

It was a perk of the job, and right now, it was also the liquid courage I needed.

"Enjoy the rest of your evening, Mr. and Mrs. Wheeland. I'll be around if you need anything at all." I shook their hands, offering a tip of my hat before I excused myself.

And then I made a beeline for Ruby Grace.

Her eyes were distant, a little glossed as she listened to the woman Anthony had engaged in conversation with. She stood with her husband, too, both of their gazes fixed on Anthony while Ruby Grace stood there like his shadow.

Those hazel eyes popped to life when they saw me.

At first, she didn't register me. But on a double take, her eyes widened, brows rising just marginally as I made my way toward her. I was confident in my walk, slow and purposeful, letting her drink me in as I crossed the space between us. She'd never seen me dressed up like this, and the flush of her cheeks told me she was affected. I wondered if she was thinking about us standing together on my porch, of my hands in her hair, my lips grazing hers before my brother forced us to tear apart.

The way her ruby lips parted, I would have bet money that she was.

It shouldn't have brought me satisfaction, not with my intention of apologizing to her and setting everything straight between us. I knew I needed to fall into the friend zone, that that was all we could be.

But damnit if seeing her there with him didn't light the *other* fire inside of me, the one that said a feverous *mine*, over and over and over again.

Her eyes shifted from something between desire and shock to warning and anger the closer I got. She didn't want me there. She was likely still pissed about what had transpired between us Sunday night, and she likely didn't want me bringing it up in front of her fiancé.

And I wouldn't. I was a gentleman, after all.

But I was still going to talk to her.

I slid my hands into the pockets of my jeans, sidling up next to Ruby Grace with my eyes on her fiancé as I waited for him to finish his conversation with the couple. I could feel Ruby Grace staring holes into the side of my face, but I just kept my smile, waiting patiently.

Anthony glanced at me quickly before turning his attention back to the couple, acknowledging my presence with a hint of annoyance. When the conversation was wrapped up between him and the couple, he shook their hands — and then they shook Ruby Grace's, of course — before finally turning to me.

"I'm so sorry to interrupt, Mr. Caldwell," I said, the most southern and welcoming smile on my face as I stretched a hand toward him. "I'm Noah Becker, one of the barrel raisers here at Scooter Whiskey. I helped your fiancé pick out her barrel, and I'm at your service tonight."

Understanding shaded the annoyance, and Anthony returned my smile in the most genuine way I imagined he could before taking my hand and shaking it firmly. "Ah, yes. Of course. How do you do, Noah?"

"Oh, I'm fantastic. It's our Academy Awards, after all, and I'm akin to the host of the show." I grinned wider, squeezing his hand a little too hard before I dropped it and offered my calloused palm to the girl he still held possessively by the waist. "Ruby Grace, always a pleasure to see you. And might I say you look beautiful this evening."

Her eyes narrowed into slits as she let me take her hand, and I lowered my lips to the back of it, pressing an appropriate kiss to the soft skin before turning back to Anthony.

"I thought I might show you to your barrel, let you taste it, since you weren't there for the original purchase?"

Anthony eyed me, his gaze flicking to his blushing bride-to-be — who pretended not to be affected by our embrace — before it pinned me again. "Of course."

"Wonderful," I said. "Right this way."

I gestured to the rows of barrels lining the far side of the tent, falling into step beside Ruby Grace as we made our way. Her jaw was clenched tight, skin pale as she watched me from the corner of her eyes. She seemed to be warning me, begging me for something, but I kept my attention on the man who demanded it so much.

"Ruby Grace surprised us all with her very generous wedding gift to you, Mr. Caldwell," I said, stopping when we reached their barrel. "She surprised me even further with her impeccable knowledge of our whiskey. It's such a rare sight to behold, a woman who knows how to detect the special flavors and notes, to pick out a fine whiskey. Your fiancé has great taste," I said, watching his expression the entire time.

Anthony sized Ruby Grace up, like he was seeing her for the first time, and his brows lowered as he found me again. "I wasn't aware there was a tasting involved."

"Oh, only a small one. No more than an ounce or two," I assured him. I leaned in closer, whispering conspiratorially. "Of course, that's between us three. Wouldn't want anyone getting wind of an underage tasting. But, hey, when the mayor's daughter is getting married to such a prestigious, up-and-coming politician?" I shrugged. "The rules can be bent."

I saw the war in his eyes, the struggle between wanting to feel threatened battling with the base level of my words that were flattering him. He cleared his throat, adjusting the lapels of his suit jacket before he gestured to the barrel. "Well, let's have a taste, then, shall we?"

I poured each of us a one-ounce pour, handing them their glasses first before I lifted mine in a toast. "To a beautiful and happy marriage," I said, smiling at Anthony. My gaze fell to Ruby Grace, then, eyes pinning hers. "And to the *team* you two will become. May you always love and *respect* the other."

Anthony mumbled some sort of acknowledgement before throwing his whiskey back like a shot.

Ruby Grace, on the other hand, watched me with murder in her eyes.

I just smiled, tilting my glass toward her before I took a sip, tasting it in the same way I'd shown Ruby Grace. She followed suit, and she couldn't hide the smile on her face when she tasted it the right way, indulging on all the notes of the fine alcohol while her husband-to-be grimaced against the shot he'd taken.

"Wow," he said, face still twisted up. His eyes watered a bit as he handed his empty glass back to me. "She really does have great taste." He sniffed, putting his arm around her and tugging her close. "Such a thoughtful wedding gift. I'm glad I got to be here to taste it at the unveiling. Thank you, sweetheart."

She smiled, but before she could answer with a *you're welcome*, Anthony dipped her back, kissing her possessively.

Ruby Grace was stiff as a board in his arms, and when he slipped his tongue inside her mouth, she pressed against his chest, breaking the kiss with a glare of disapproval masked by a forced smile.

"My parents are right over there," she whispered, not bothering to look at exactly *where* her parents were to make her point clear. She cleared her throat, instead, turning to me with the same tight smile. "Thank you for the tasting, Noah. Now, if you'll excuse us, we have to get back to the party." She rested her hand on Anthony's chest — the hand that shone with the diamond he'd given her. "So many people to introduce Anthony to. You understand."

I swallowed past the thick knot in my throat, forcing a smile that was just as tight as hers. "Of course," I said, waving my hand toward the rest of the crowd. "Enjoy your evening, and let me know if I can be of service to either of you."

Ruby Grace rolled her eyes, though Anthony didn't see, and I smirked a little at that.

"Will do," Anthony said, shaking my hand. He held it in his vise grip a little too long, letting Ruby Grace walk a few steps away before he lowered his voice. "You enjoy your evening, too. Somewhere far away from my fiancé, preferably."

I tilted my head to the side, smile not wavering. "I'm sure I don't understand what you're implying, Mr. Caldwell."

"And I'm sure I don't need to repeat myself to make my point clear."

He dropped my hand, wiping his palm on his jacket like I'd given him some sort of disease before he turned, offering his arm to Ruby Grace and toting her off to the next victim.

I tucked my hands back in my pockets, watching them go with a sense of jealousy settling over my chest like a hot, wet, suffocating blanket.

And I knew I wouldn't find relief until I kicked my way out from under it.

•••

Ruby Grace

The Scooter Whiskey Single Barrel Soirée had always been a grand event in Stratford. I remembered attending as a child with my parents, hanging out in the kiddie area where there were endless games and blow-up slides to crawl all over. As I got older, I'd come with my friends in high school to dance and sneak illegal sips of whiskey — of course, *I* never drank the whiskey, because I had always been told by Mama that it was a man's drink.

I hadn't tasted it at all until the day Noah Becker showed me the barrel I'd purchased for my fiancé.

He was still on my mind as Patrick Scooter gave his welcoming speech, relaying a short history of the distillery and his family's legacy before he launched into the details that made all the barrels in our presence tonight so special. While those of us who purchased barrels were the only ones who could taste those specific ones, there were three barrels of single-barrel whiskey that were cracked open for the town to indulge in. Considering how poor most of Stratford's residents were, this was a special occasion. Everyone was dressed up, smiling, and celebrating.

And somehow, on our town's most joyous night, with my fiancé's hand on the small of my back, I felt more numb than I had in my entire life.

"You okay over there, sweetheart?" Daddy asked in between one of his conversations.

I smiled, assuring him with a squeeze on his upper arm. I knew it wouldn't be long before someone else would pull him aside and need his ear, whether to pitch an idea for the town or to lobby for his support on an issue. "I'm fine, Daddy. Just a little tired."

His eyes softened. "I know this can be a lot. I've got my truck keys, if you want to escape for a while."

Even though my father and I didn't talk much, he understood me in a way Mama didn't. She was an extrovert, outgoing and social in every way. Daddy was more like me — he preferred to be with his close circle of friends. We both struggled in big settings like this, and I had a feeling it was *him* who was thinking about escaping in that truck.

"Thank you, but I think we're both stuck here for a few hours. Might as well make the most of it." I held up my glass, which held a tonic and lime, and cheersed it with his whiskey tumbler just as the Parkers approached him.

It was always like that for Dad — just a constant revolving door of people.

I leaned in closer. "And, hey, if you really need to escape, give me the signal and I'll fake an extreme illness."

Dad chuckled at that, squeezing my shoulder with eyes that said, *Okay, here we go*, before turning to the Parkers and greeting them.

The night passed in a sort of daze after that, a blur of names and *how do ya do's* and dances with strangers. I ate the little hors d'oeuvres as they passed by on the silver trays, sipped on the tonic and lime I'd ordered to not be the only one without a drink in my hand, laughed at the jokes Anthony told — the same ones over and over to new people — and when asked, I danced with whoever wanted to dance. That was what was expected, after all. Whether it was my father's business partners or someone Anthony had just introduced me to, my job was to entertain, to charm and dazzle and impress.

And while I sparkled on the outside, I felt dead on the inside.

"Ruby Grace, could I trouble you for a spin on the dance floor?"

I blinked out of the daydream I'd been in, plastering on my best smile to turn and accept the invitation from whoever had asked. But when I spun on my heel and found Noah Becker's cobalt steel eyes, I frowned.

"No, thanks," I spat.

Noah tilted his head. "Come on, now. That's no way to speak to a gentleman."

"I see no gentleman here."

He chuckled, stepping into my space with his hands sliding easily into the pockets of his dark blue jeans. They were so tight they might as well have been painted on, and I hated that I noticed. I hated that every girl ogled him as he walked around, eyeing his ass through the fabric — me included. He was every country girl's dream tonight — crisp, white button-up, dark, lethal jeans, smooth, tan skin, boots and a hat that matched and topped off the look.

My grandmother would say he looked "sharp," if she were here. And I agreed.

He was a blade, and I knew I needed to stay away or I'd end up shredded.

"Hey," he said when he was closer, lowering his voice. "Look, I'd really like the chance to properly apologize to you. And I *know* you'd love a break from all of... *this*." He looked around us for a moment before he found my gaze again. "So, please, Ruby Grace — dance with me."

Noah pulled one hand from his pocket, extending it to me with a gentle smile. Something in my chest loosened at the sight, at someone seeing me without me saying a word. To everyone else, I was the charming, entertaining Ruby Grace tonight. But Noah saw what no one else did.

It seemed he had since that first day at the distillery.

A long sigh left my chest as I nodded, slipping my hand into his and letting him lead the way. Anthony had disappeared to go to the restroom about twenty minutes prior — the cameras from his media crew disappearing with him — and I imagined he'd been wrangled into conversation with someone else on his way back. And besides, I had danced with countless men that night. Noah was just one more, and it wasn't frowned upon for the barrel buyers to dance with the raisers.

Logic and explanation aside, I *wanted* to dance with Noah.

And maybe that was all that mattered to me in that moment.

I stared at my hand in his as he guided me to the dance floor in front of the band. His hand was so large, hard and calloused, his wrist thick and fore-arms lined with muscles and veins. My hand disappeared inside his grasp, my dainty wrist sparkling with the tennis bracelet I wore. He was all down-home country, and I was refined country royalty.

Still, I marveled at how well my hand fit in his.

When we made it to the dance floor, he stopped, pulling me into him until his hand was on my waist, the other still holding my hand. For a long, stretched moment in time, he just watched me, his eyes dancing between mine. A small smile found his lips, and he nodded once before taking the first step, leading the way and guiding me along with his movements.

And then, we were dancing.

The song was a familiar one in Tennessee, "I Cross My Heart" by George Strait. The lead singer of the band crooned out the lyrics as everyone on the floor gently swayed or two-stepped.

But Noah?

Noah guided me in a beautiful waltz.

"How do you know this?" I asked, smile breaking on my face despite my urge to be angry with him after Sunday night.

"What? Waltz?"

I nodded.

Noah smiled, stepping with me into a soft turn before pulling me back into his arms. "My mom. She and Dad used to dance after dinner every single night — in the living room, the kitchen, wherever. And after Dad passed, the tradition didn't stop. My brothers and I take turns dancing with her. And bless her, she taught us all with patience."

My heart squeezed. "I bet that means so much to her."

"Yeah," he said, and I waited for him to continue, but he just swallowed, forcing a bit of a smile before he changed the subject. "I'm sorry about what I said Sunday night, Ruby Grace. I was out of line."

He twirled me again, and I was thankful for the break in eye contact before we spun back together. Of course, that break in eye contact was long enough for me to realize how many *other* pairs of eyes were locked on us at the moment.

"Thank you," I said, glaring right back at one of Mama's friends until she tore her gaze away before I looked back at Noah. "Seems like half our conversations are apologies."

"Well, I'm an asshole," he offered honestly. "And you're stubborn."

I narrowed my eyes. "Am not."

Noah just smirked, falling back into step as the song's chorus flowed around us. His smile leveled out the longer he watched me. "So, why didn't you tell me Anthony was coming into town?"

"I didn't know he was," I shot, and I couldn't stop the defensiveness from breaking through. "And even if I did, I don't see why I would owe it to you to tell you."

Noah lifted his brows. "I was just trying to make conversation."

"Mm-hmm."

"Why are you so defensive?"

"I'm not," I said quickly. "I just know how you feel about him, and I don't want to play into it anymore."

"I don't even know him," he responded. "I don't feel anything toward him."

"Sure," I said, twirling out twice before I slipped into his arms again. "I totally got that vibe with the barrel tasting earlier. And with everything you said to me on Sunday."

"I told you I was sorry for that."

"Yeah, but did you mean it?"

His jaw clenched at that, and he watched me for a long moment before his eyes cast up to the top of the tent and back down. "You're infuriating, you know that?"

"Well, then, it's a good thing you're not the one marrying me, isn't it?"

Noah slowed, his hand on my waist squeezing a little tighter. He opened his mouth to say something, but then his eyes skirted behind me, and he cleared his throat, forcing a smile as Anthony slid up beside us.

"Mind if I cut in?" Anthony asked. His threatening tone wasn't lost on me.

Noah swallowed, his Adam's apple bobbing hard in his throat before he released me, offering my hand to Anthony like I was some sort of prize. "Of course not. She is your bride-to-be, after all." He looked at me with those words, and I felt those eyes like the hot blade of a knife. "Thank you for the dance, Ruby Grace."

Without another word, he dropped my hand, tipped his hat at Anthony, and walked calmly off the dance floor.

A flurry of girls chased after him — ones who'd been watching us dance from the sidelines — and when he granted one of them her wish of completing the dance with him, my stomach twisted.

Daphne McCormick.

No one could keep a secret in this town — and it was *far* from a secret that Daphne and Noah had hooked up a few times, that she had had him in her bed more consecutive nights than any other woman in town could say. And the way her long fingers curled around his bicep possessively as she dragged him back to the dance floor, she knew it.

His smile was tight as he took her in his arms, but then she said something to make him laugh — *really* laugh — and seconds later, he was spinning her around the same way he had me.

I tore my eyes away, ignoring the sinking in my stomach and smiling at Anthony as he wrapped me in his arms. I started to waltz, but Anthony's face screwed up in confusion before he slowed us into a gentle sway like the rest of the patrons.

Except for Noah and Daphne.

"What's up with that Noah guy, anyway?" Anthony asked, noticing that my gaze had shifted again.

I snapped my attention to him, frowning in confusion. "What do you mean?"

"Did you two used to date or something?" He was eyeing Noah menacingly, like he could somehow squash him like a bug with that look.

"Of course not," I assured him, shaking my head. "We're just friends."

"Friends," Anthony murmured, watching Noah a long moment before he turned his gaze to me. "Before, he was just the guy who showed you the barrel. Now you're best buds."

"Don't be like that," I said, voice low. "I'm *yours*, okay?" I held up my hand with the Harry Winston diamond on it to prove my point. "Yours. No one else's."

Anthony let out a long breath, nodding as a smile bloomed on his face. "I'm sorry. I guess you just bring out the possessive side in me."

I smiled at that. "Guess that means you like me, huh?"

Anthony kissed me long and slow, stopping our dance altogether so he could frame my face.

And somewhere across the room, I felt another pair of eyes on me.

Later that night, when we were back at my parents' house, Anthony strengthened a kiss between us, turning that sweet and romantic one from the dance floor into one heated with passion. He peppered my neck with hot, sucking kisses, his hands roaming, breath picking up speed in the hallway outside my bedroom.

"Anthony…" I sighed, pressing my hands into his chest to stop his advances. "I think we should wait."

"Wait?" he asked, one brow cocking. "I took your virginity a month after we met, Ruby Grace. I think we're past waiting."

He moved in again, and though I chuckled, I felt a shade of embarrassment leak into my gut at his words. "I mean that we're sleeping in my parents' house, and we get married in five weeks." I shrugged, running my finger over his chest. "I don't know, it might be kind of fun to pretend. Go the traditional route. Wait until our wedding night."

Anthony's face screwed up like he thought that was the most ridiculous thing he'd ever heard, but as his eyes searched mine, he blew out a long sigh, dropping his forehead to my shoulder with a groan. "Fine."

I chuckled, patting his head like he was a child.

"I'd do anything for you," he said, lifting his head. He ran the pad of his thumb over my chin, pulling me in for a long, sweet kiss. "And you're worth the wait."

I swallowed, smiling through the unfamiliar discomfort I felt. He was my fiancé, I used to squirm under his touch, anticipating more.

Now, I wanted to crawl out of my skin.

"Thank you," I whispered, kissing him again, this time with my hands in his hair and pulling him closer. I wanted to erase the discomfort, convince myself it was just pre-wedding jitters, or the overstimulation of the day.

I love him, I told myself as we kissed. And I knew it was true.

I just couldn't place the *other* emotion that I felt.

"Okay, okay," he said, breaking our kiss and smacking my butt playfully. "Stop kissing me like that if you're not going to put out, little lady."

I giggled, pecking his cheek once more before I let him go. "I'm going to take a shower and get some sleep. See you at breakfast in the morning?"

"See you then. And, hey," he said, sweeping my hair from my face. "You were wonderful tonight. I'm so lucky to have a woman like you standing behind me."

My throat tightened again at the phrasing he used. I knew what he meant, that I was by his side, his partner in crime — but the thought of me only standing *behind* him made my stomach turn.

And Noah's words popped into my mind.

I smiled, running my hand over his arm until I held his hand in mine. I squeezed it once, excusing myself in the next breath and escaping to my bedroom.

As I showered and got ready for bed, I tried to decompress from the night. I ran through everything I loved about it, and chose to acknowledge the things I didn't love so much without judging them. I let those thoughts pass almost like clouds in the sky, touching each of them before I let them pass without another thought.

I had a tendency to overthink, and I knew in my heart that was what was happening now. I still loved Anthony. I still wanted to marry him. I still wanted to be the woman next to him when he was sworn into office as State Representative, and one day, as the President of the United States.

This was the life I wanted. This was the life I was always meant to live.

I crawled into bed with a renewed sense of ease and excitement for the weekend. I had wedding planning to do, and Anthony would be there with me. I wasn't alone anymore, and I took comfort in that as my eyelids grew heavy, the gentle breeze outside lulling me into a peaceful sleep.

Until around three in the morning, when I woke from a dream with a sheen of sweat on my forehead and Noah Becker's name on my lips.

Chapter Ten

Noah

The next night, my brothers and I sat on Mom's porch, drinking beer and decompressing from work while Mom made her famous pork chops inside. She had Fleetwood Mac's *Rumors* album blasting as she sang and danced along, moving around the kitchen, occasionally popping outside to see if any of us needed another beer. Family dinner night was always the happiest I saw Mom. It was when she had all her boys home, a meal to cook, a purpose.

I kicked back in one of the rocking chairs on the porch, one boot propped on the porch railing as I cracked open a new beer. I was still dirty from raising barrels all day, my muscles aching from the additional lifting I'd done loading up the single barrels the night before into buyer vehicles after the Soirée.

The sun was beginning its slow descent over our sleepy Tennessee town, casting Mom's small garden in an evening glow as I took in the sight of my brothers. Jordan was still in his coaching gear, fresh off a day of summer training with Stratford High's football team hopefuls. Logan wore his Scooter Whiskey tour guide polo and faded denim jeans, his face as worn as mine from working the night before at the Soirée and then an entire Friday shift, too. And though Mikey didn't have to work the Soirée, he had still been there all night, dancing with Bailey before having to report for an all-day shift at the Scooter Whiskey gift shop.

It'd been a long Friday for all of us, and the normally rowdy Becker brothers were almost completely silent as we watched the sun set, sipping on our beers, rocking in our chairs, just existing together. We'd talk for a little bit before falling silent again, until someone else felt enough energy to pipe up.

"The boys looked good out on the field today when I drove by," Logan commented to Jordan.

My older brother nodded. "Glad that's what you saw. It was a mess from where I was standing."

I chuckled. "You say that every year, and then you make it to state or damn near."

He humphed. "Sometimes we get lucky. Sometimes we don't."

"Luck has nothing to do with it," Logan said. "A hard-working team and the best coach in Tennessee does, though."

"We lost half of that hard-working team when this year's seniors graduated," Jordan pointed out.

"I wish Dad was here."

The words came from Mikey, who had been silent up until that point, and they sliced through the quiet evening like the screeching tires of a car seconds away from slamming into a tree. Every single one of us paused where we were rocking in our chairs or taking a sip of our beers, a heavy silence falling over the entire family like a weighted fog.

Jordan cleared his throat first, clamping a hand on Mikey's shoulder with an understanding, soft smile. "We all do, buddy."

Mikey nodded, working the tab on his root beer back and forth before it broke off and he dropped it inside the can. "I think it's different for me, though."

"Why do you think that?" Logan asked.

Mikey shrugged. "Because I was only eight when he died. You guys were all older, teenagers, at least. You had all this time with him." His voice faded, eyes still on his can. "He won't be at my graduation."

Logan and I exchanged a glance, then, realizing why the topic had been brought up. Mikey was seventeen, heading into his senior year — and Jordan had just mentioned graduation. I remembered that time of my life so well — the excitement of being at the top of the school, of finally finishing, mixed with the worry of what would happen next, where life would take me.

I had so many questions when I was that age — a teenager, becoming a new adult.

And I had Dad to answer them.

So did Jordan.

So did Logan, though Dad died just weeks after his graduation.

We'd all had him there, and once again, Mikey was left out of that equation.

"We'll be there," I finally said to Mikey, breaking the silence. "Mom, too. And Dad *will* be there, even if you can't see him."

Mikey sighed. "It's not the same."

"It's not," Jordan agreed. "And it's okay to be sad that he's not here anymore. We all have days. We will for the rest of our lives. He was our father."

He paused at that, swallowing hard, and I could see it in his eyes, that sad truth like a ghost in his pupils. He *was* Jordan's father — no matter what anyone in the town had to say about it. But, I still knew he wondered who his *biological* one was.

I wondered if any of us would ever know.

"It happens to me more in the small moments than the big ones," Logan chimed in, finger tapping on the koozie wrapped around his beer can. "Like,

I didn't really think about him when I got the tour guide job at such a young age. But, when I'm fishing out at the lake, or when I catch a whiff of cologne that smells like the one he used to wear... that's when it hits me. That's when I have that *I wish he was here* moment."

My stomach twisted. "For me, it's always when I dance with Mom."

We all glanced over our shoulders and inside the house, watching Mom bop around the kitchen with a soft smile on her face.

"I can take your turn tonight," Logan offered. "If you want."

I shook my head. "Nah, I don't mind missing him, or thinking about him." I shrugged. "Like Jordan said, it's just become a permanent part of my life now."

We were all silent for a long moment, facing the garden again, sipping from our drinks.

"I think it's the unresolved part of it all that gets to me most," Mikey said after a while. "Do you think Mom will ever stop looking for answers?"

None of us responded. None of us had to. We all knew she'd never stop asking, stop looking for holes in the reports, for foul play at the distillery. No matter how many years passed, she would never believe that fire was started by a cigarette.

"Hey, how was Nashville with Bailey?" Logan asked, effectively changing the subject.

Mikey seemed a little hesitant to let the topic of Dad go, but after a moment, a grin spread across his face, his eyes sparking with the kind of love-sick look only Bailey brought out in him. "It was so crazy. Seeing her on stage, the crowds going wild for her?" Mikey shook his head. "I'll never forget it. She told the label she wants to finish high school, but that she'll sign the contract as soon as we walk across the stage. Can you believe that?" He just kept shaking his head. "She's going to do it. She's going to be the next country music star. A hometown girl from Stratford, Tennessee."

"And are you ready for all that comes with that?" I asked.

"As long as I'm with her, I'm ready for anything."

I opened my mouth to point out every flaw I saw in this potential plan, starting with the fact that Bailey's entire life would change when she signed that contract, but Jordan locked eyes with me, shaking his head almost imperceptibly to warn me off the subject. It didn't matter right now, and just because I was a pessimist didn't mean I had to drag my little brother down with me.

He had hope. And love. And a bright-eyed view of what the world could be for him.

I just hoped he could keep all of it.

"The Soirée was fun last night," Logan said, changing the subject yet again. One thick eyebrow ticked up as he appraised me. "Seemed like you found yourself in some drama, big bro."

Jordan narrowed his eyes. "What drama?"

"My thoughts exactly," I said to Jordan before giving Logan an incredulous look. "I showed up and did my job just like I do every year."

"You also ticked off the future State Representative of North Carolina," Logan shot.

I scoffed, draining the last of my beer before slamming the empty can on the table between us. "That guy's a douche. And I was nothing but polite to him, even though he didn't deserve it. I treated him just like all the other buyer's."

"Did you dance with all the other buyer's *fiancé's*, too?"

Logan waggled his brows, and I glared at him before thumping his arm.

"Ah," Mikey said, a shit-eating grin spreading on his face. "Ruby Grace's fiancé is in town, huh? Does he know about that close call you two had on your front porch after poker last weekend?"

"Shut it, Mikey," I warned, at the same time Jordan asked, "What close call?"

"Did you kiss her?" Logan asked immediately after, a grin sliding over his face. "You sly dog. You kissed her, didn't you?"

"I didn't kiss her," I growled, letting my feet drop off the porch railing and onto the wood below my chair.

"But you *wanted* to," Mikey said. "I saw you two. If I hadn't shown up with that root beer float, there would have been some lip lock action and you know it."

Logan and Mikey chuckled. Jordan just watched me, waiting. I leaned forward, elbows balanced on my knees as I tried to school my breaths, tried to think of anything I could say to get them off my back, but I knew it was useless.

I could deny it all day long, but these were my brothers. They'd see right through me.

I shook my head, letting it hang between my shoulders a moment before I lifted it again, eyes scanning the fading sun over Mom's yard. "Yeah, okay. Maybe I did want to kiss her."

"I knew it," Mikey chimed.

"But I didn't," I pointed out again, glaring at my youngest brother before I acknowledged the other two. "And it doesn't matter anyway, because she's getting married in less than five weeks."

"If she's so set on marrying that guy, why has she been spending so much time with you?" Mikey asked.

I shrugged, eyes falling to the porch. "I don't think she actually *does* want to marry him, to be honest. She's young, under pressure from her family. From what I know about her, this isn't the life she wants at all. But I think she feels... stuck."

Logan frowned. "That's sad."

I nodded. "It is. You know, when I first met her, I thought she was just another prissy, privileged rich girl. But she's so much more than what her family portrays her as. She's smart, and caring, and funny. She volunteers down at the nursing home, did you know that?" I shook my head. "That whole place lights up when she's there. And she had dreams of finishing college, going into AmeriCorps. But she's dropping out of school to be Mr. Asshole's wife — all because that's what she's expected to do."

My brothers were quiet for a long moment before Mikey spoke again. "I've never seen you like this before. You usually have girls lined up who want your attention, and you can never be bothered."

"Not for more than a one-night stand, anyway," Logan chuffed.

Mikey grinned, but it slipped when he faced me again. "You really like her, don't you?"

My stomach clenched, and I wished I hadn't drained my beer. I needed something to do, something to hold or drink or *anything* to keep my hands from tightening into anxious fists.

I couldn't answer that question.

I guessed I didn't really have to.

"Of course, she's under pressure from her family. She's a Barnett," Jordan reminded me after a long pause, as if that was a fact I could ever forget. "And that's even more reason for you to stay away from her."

"I disagree."

We all looked at Logan, then, who was never one to speak out against Jordan.

"I'm just saying, if there's something between you two, maybe she needs more time to see what you already see — that she's making a mistake. If you were around her more, showing her what it could be like if she was with someone who really gave a shit about her, someone who cared what *her* dreams were..." Logan shrugged. "I don't know. Maybe you could save her from making a mistake."

"That's not his job to do," Jordan fired back.

"Isn't it?" Logan kicked back in his chair, leveling eyes with our oldest brother. "We're Beckers. We always stand up for what's right. And Ruby Grace being auctioned off like an eighteenth-century bride isn't right. Her marrying someone she doesn't want to isn't right. And if Noah can stop her, if he can show her something more?" Logan looked at me, then. "I say, why not?"

"Because it's wrong," Jordan chimed in again before I could answer. "She's engaged to someone else. Whether she made that decision the right way or not is not Noah's or anyone else's business. As long as she has that ring on her finger, she's off limits."

"They could just be friends."

It was Mikey who spoke, then, and we all turned to him as he shrank under our gazes.

"I mean, I'm just saying, you don't have to do anything inappropriate," he clarified. "Just be there for her. Give her someone to talk to, someone to work through what she's feeling with."

We were all silent at that, and I mulled it over, tossing the thought around in my mind like a poker chip between my fingers. Ruby Grace and I hadn't crossed any lines, we hadn't done anything that she needed to feel guilty about. I didn't want to leave her alone. I missed her. And I wanted to be around her — in whatever way I could be.

But could I *just* be her friend?

It seemed impossible, knowing the way I felt about her now, the way I couldn't stop thinking of her, the way my blood boiled when I imagined that douchebag going home to her at night, putting his hands on her, touching her, kissing her.

My fists tightened.

"You'll just get yourself hurt," Jordan said after a while. "If you're her friend, if you're *more* than that — regardless, she's marrying that guy this summer. And the closer you get to her, the more that is going to gut you in the end."

"He's probably right," Logan agreed.

My heart sank, realizing how futile it all was.

"But," Logan continued. "I'm just saying, I know I wouldn't want to give up on it without knowing I tried. I'd rather be fucked up in the end and know I tried to get the girl than to just let her go without ever showing her what her options are."

Mikey nodded. "Same. I know I couldn't walk away from Bailey, even if there was another guy in the picture. She's the kind of girl you fight for. And it seems like Ruby Grace is, too."

Jordan stood, throwing his hands up. "Do what you want, Noah. But just know I don't approve of this. She's nearly a decade younger than you, she's the Mayor's daughter, and she's engaged. If you won't hit the brakes with all those road blocks in your view, then don't be surprised when you crash at the end of it all."

He walked inside, the screen door slamming shut behind him as he joined Mom in the kitchen. When he was gone, Logan and Mikey watched me carefully, both chewing the inside of their cheeks.

"This is idiotic," I finally said.

"Completely," Logan agreed.

"Jordan's right. I'll probably just end up even more messed up than I am now."

Mikey nodded. "Most likely."

I sighed, head bobbing between my shoulders as I ran over all the reasons I should stay away from Ruby Grace, all the reasons I should walk away and wish her luck and forget she ever came back to town at all. I ticked off each warning sign like a mental checklist, but while my chest should have been tight with dread, it was floating on the smallest ounce of hope.

I knew Logan was right.

I couldn't walk away from her. Not without fighting for her first.

I let out another long breath, eyeing Mikey before my gaze landed on Logan. "Will you help me make a plan?"

Chapter Eleven

Ruby Grace

The weekend passed in a blur of chiffon and cake frosting.

Mama packed every waking minute of my days with dress alterations, cake tasting, seating chart adjustments, wedding photography pose research, and more. By the time I made it to church Sunday morning, I was so thankful for an hour of sitting down with nothing to do but listen to the preacher, that I nearly started crying.

When I saw Noah walk through the door, that urge to cry doubled.

I'd been so busy over the weekend, I hadn't had much time to think about anything other than whatever wedding task was at hand. Still, when my mind *did* wander, it frustratingly wandered to those cobalt blue eyes.

Noah took his usual seat in the front row of the left pew section, alongside his mother and three brothers. I was still fixated on the back of his head when Anthony's hand reached over, squeezing my knee over the turquoise fabric of my dress.

"I'm so excited to spend the day with you," he whispered, leaning in close.

I frowned, turning toward him. "I'm volunteering at the nursing home today. Remember?"

"Oh," he said, confirming that he, in fact, did *not* remember. "Can't you just cancel?"

"Anthony, you know how important this is to me."

Disappointment sank into my every feature. I'd been telling Anthony all weekend that I had plans after church, just like I did every Sunday, and it was like he'd listened the way a child does to its mother.

"I know, babe. I know," he said quickly, squeezing where he held my knee. "I'm sorry. I just miss you. I've been here a week now and we've barely spent any time together."

My neck heated, because I was *very* aware of the fact I hadn't seen him much. Anthony conveniently had something to do with the media crew anytime Mama came running at me with a wedding task. He hadn't helped with a single thing since he'd been in town, and if anything, I felt *more* pressure with him here.

Pressure to make the wedding perfect. Pressure to be available to him when he needed me.

Pressure to be everywhere and everything to everyone.

"Why don't you help me register for our gifts on Thursday?" I asked. "We could spend the whole day together, pick out our future serving dishes and napkin holders." I leaned into him on a nudge. "You know, super thrilling stuff."

Anthony smiled, running the back of his knuckles over my cheek. "You know I wish I could, but we're going to shoot a little *around the town* short to air on our YouTube channel that day. I was actually hoping you'd be a part of it, if you have time?"

I sighed, fighting off the sinking of my heart. This was Anthony's life. This was how he'd always been, ever since I met him. He was dedicated to his dream, to his passion to hold office. It was something I loved about him, and I didn't know why I was suddenly annoyed by it just because he couldn't help with stupid wedding stuff.

In four weeks, we'd be married, and none of this stuff would matter, anyway.

"I understand. I have to get that registration done, but when it's over, I'll give you a call and see if I can come help out," I offered.

Anthony smiled wider, shaking his head before he leaned in and pressed his lips to my forehead. "I'm such a lucky man."

We were quiet as the service got started, and I reveled in the peaceful bliss of not needing to answer to anyone or be anywhere. If anything, the service didn't last long enough, and before I knew it, we were outside the church, Mama shaking hands and sending blessings with everyone as they left. Anthony joined in beside her and Dad, and I pulled up the end of the line, a numb smile on my face.

I was so fixated on counting down the minutes until I'd be away from everyone and in my safe place that I almost didn't notice when Noah Becker darted away from the receiving line, kissing his mother on the cheek before he climbed into his truck without so much of a look over his shoulder at me. Not that he owed me a look, or a handshake, or a Sunday greeting. But, we hadn't spoken a single word to each other since the Soirée, and part of me wondered if he'd ever speak to me again.

Part of me wondered why I cared if he did or not.

His truck peeled out of the church parking lot as Anthony put his arm around me, pressing a kiss into my hair.

"Are you *sure* I can't convince you to ditch on the nursing home?" he asked.

I tried my best to smile, turning in his arms to thread mine around his neck. "I'll see you for supper."

"It's my only free day," he pointed out again.

"I understand that. But *I'm* not free."

"But you *could* be."

My shoulders sagged. "Anthony..."

"I'm kidding, I'm kidding," he said, kissing my forehead again before steering us toward Daddy's truck. "I'll find something to do, maybe go check out the casino with your dad or something. He's been begging me to go."

I smiled as much as I could, aiming for lightness in my voice. "Well, that's not at all surprising. Hope you're ready to lose all of your Sunday in that dungeon of bells and flashing lights."

Anthony held the back door of Dad's truck open for me, closing it gently once I was inside.

In that moment of silence, I took my first real breath in days.

I couldn't wait to get home, get changed, and get away.

• • •

"You look like hell," Annie greeted, still somehow cheerful even with the insult flying from her lips.

"Happy Sunday to you, too," I replied on a chuckle. I flopped down into the chair next to her, sighing as the cushion gave into my weight in a familiar, soft *whoosh*. "Can I just... can I just nap right here?"

Annie snickered. "Mama Barnett pushing you that hard, huh?"

"You were there for the seating arrangement fiasco," I reminded her, referring to our Friday morning spent with my mom. "Now, just imagine that same frenzy... All. Weekend. Long."

She cringed, sliding her coffee toward me. "Here. You need this more than I do."

I took the hot mug gratefully, tilting it toward her in thanks before taking a sip. I hummed as the mocha-flavored magic made its way into my stomach, reaching forward to flip through the events calendar for the day. I'd only been inside the building for five minutes and I already felt my muscles relaxing, the tension leaving that spot between my eyebrows, my breaths coming easier. These walls and the people who lived within them were comfortable to me, safe, familiar. It was the one steady thing in my currently chaotic life.

"Everyone already at the pool?" I asked, noting that water aerobics had been added to the schedule for the day.

"Mm-hmm," Annie said, biting against a smile.

"Betty having a good day?"

"Oh, she's having the *best* day," Annie said, still with the weird smile.

I cocked a brow.

"She's out there with our newest volunteer — hell, the entire nursing home is out there. No one has been able to teach water aerobics since the summer started, so it was a welcome surprise for us to have some help."

"I could have done water aerobics," I offered.

"You still can," Annie said. "I'm sure the new guy would love the help. Those old ladies were practically ripping his swim trunks off when he made his way through the halls to the pool. I swear, in the five years I've worked here, I've never seen Mrs. Hollenbeck go swimming. Until today."

I frowned. "Interesting. We haven't had any new volunteers in a while, either — aside from those completing community service. Who is this guy?"

Annie's grin widened. "Oh, you know him."

My best friend had that look in her eyes, the one she used to get when she was about to ask me for a huge favor or to go to a party I didn't want to go to.

"Annie..." I warned. "Who is it?"

She just did a little shoulder dance, fishing one of the volunteer pool keys out of the desk and tossing it my way. "Why don't you go find out?"

I frowned deeper, clutching the key in hand as I stood. "You're a brat."

"You love me, anyway."

"Debatable."

She was still chuckling as I made my way down the hall to the bathroom, changing into the swim suit I'd brought with me. For some reason, my stomach was fluttery as I changed, mind swirling with the possibilities of who it could be. I wondered if it was Tanner, the guy I'd dated sophomore year. Or maybe Annie was joking about the guy being hot. Maybe it was someone weird, like the scrawny, perverted kid who delivered newspapers and always liked to stare a little too long into the windows of whichever girl didn't leave their curtains drawn enough.

My heart thumped even harder when I realized Anthony had left to go to the casino with Dad before I left for the nursing home. Dad hadn't even left yet, saying he had a few stops to make along the way and he'd meet him at the main bar.

Maybe it's him. Maybe he's surprising me.

I couldn't fight back my smile at the thought. It was a classic Anthony move, to surprise me and make a show of himself in the process. He loved to be the center of attention, and I knew him volunteering at a nursing home on a Sunday would be candy for the film crew.

With that thought in mind, I practically skipped to the pool, ditching my backpack at the front desk on my way out. Annie was still smiling like a loon, and I thought I finally understood why. She was in on the whole thing, the whole surprise.

But when I scanned my key card at the pool gate and flung it open, I stopped dead in my tracks, the smile sliding off my face like a limp noodle off a wall.

Noah Becker stood in the shallow end of the pool, leading a group of women and one brave man in a charade of water aerobics to an old 70's disco song.

His smile was blinding, hair wet and glistening in the sun as he pumped his arms and legs to the music. He shouted out instructions, laughing at all the women who were attempting to follow and giggling like a bunch of school girls in the process.

Betty was front row.

Noah threw his head back on one particularly loud laugh, elicited by something Betty had said that I couldn't hear, and when he was facing her again, his eyes flicked up to me.

Everything muted in that moment — the splash of the water, the bass of the music, the laughter of the women and the men lined up on the sides watching them. Noah watched me for what felt like an eternity — but was actually only a second — before he smiled.

That smile turned my knees to putty.

"Alright, take a break, ladies. Grab water, lather on some sunscreen, and meet me back here in fifteen."

Everyone let out various sounds of disappointment as Noah climbed out of the water, turning the music down on the pool stereo and swiping a towel off the back of one of the lounge chairs before he jogged over to me.

It was like a stupid scene out of a *Baywatch* episode, the way his pecs bounced as he ran, the water dripping slowly down every lean, toned, tanned muscle of his body. He shook the water out of his short hair right before he reached me, and when he did, his grin doubled.

"Hey there, Legs."

"Noah," I seethed, crossing my arms and ignoring his attempt at an adorable nickname. "*What* are you doing here?"

He just smiled wider, toweling his hair and a little of his abdomen before hanging the towel over his shoulders. He held it at each end, letting his arms hang in a way that accented his biceps.

Asshole.

"I volunteer here," he offered innocently.

I narrowed my eyes.

At that, Noah barked out a laugh, the hands holding his towel lifting as he shrugged. "Look, I came here to call a truce."

"I didn't realize we were at war."

"Oh, didn't you?" he countered, one thick eyebrow climbing.

I didn't respond, just shifted weight onto my other hip, keeping my arms crossed as I waited for him to continue.

"I know I crossed some lines, and I know I said some things that upset you."

"You already apologized for that."

"And clearly, all is forgiven," he shot back, still eyeing me with a cocked brow. "Would you just let me talk, Miss Stubborn?"

I pursed my lips. "I liked *Legs* better."

Noah chuckled, taking a step toward me, and the way his smile was shadowed with sincerity as he spoke his next words softened my heart. "I like having you as a friend, Ruby Grace."

I swallowed, eyes searching his as the sun above danced in the ocean blue waters of his pupils.

"I have to admit, my life was pretty boring before you showed up. It was work and family dinner and cards with my brothers and some random girl in my bed Saturday night. Wash, rinse, repeat."

I tried not to be affected by the mention of a woman in his bed. I had no right to be, but it still made my neck hot at the thought. I wondered if he'd taken Daphne home after the Soirée, and as soon as I thought it, my chest tightened painfully.

"I have fun with you," he said on a shrug. "And I think you have fun with me, too. I know you're not in town much longer, so what if we just... put all the bickering and bullshit behind us and be friends?"

"Friends," I deadpanned.

The corner of Noah's mouth lifted. "Yes. Friends. As in, let's volunteer together, and maybe hang out when you're free." He shrugged. "I can help you with wedding shit, take some of the pressure off. I'll even put up with your crazy mother and whatever task she needs handled."

A breath of a laugh escaped me at that, and I watched Noah carefully, looking for some sign of crossed fingers or a trick that I wasn't seeing. "You'd do that?"

"I'd do just about anything for you, it seems."

I smirked, chest fluttering at the mixture of excitement and warning blending in my gut. Part of me knew it was better to stay away from Noah Becker — especially with how much he'd been on my mind. I knew I had a crush on him, some sort of feelings that were beyond the friend zone he was proposing.

But the bigger part of me? She didn't care.

The bigger part of me felt the same way Noah did. I had fun with him. I liked being around him.

I missed him.

So, against every nerve in my body that warned me not to, I sighed, extending one hand toward him.

"Fine. Friends."

Noah glanced at my hand, a wicked smile on his face as he took it in his and gave it a firm, mock handshake with a serious business look on his face. "Friends."

"On one condition."

"And that is?"

I cringed. "We can't let my mom find out."

Noah full-on belly laughed at that. "What, Princess Barnett can't be seen with a Becker ruffian?"

"Not when the whole town has been whispering about us and it's been making its way back to my dad… and therefore, my mom."

Noah nodded. "Fair enough. An on-the-low friendship, it is."

He was still staring at me like he'd won some sort of prize when I rolled my eyes and shoved him back toward the pool. "Stop looking at me all goofy and get back in that water before these women lose their damn minds."

Noah laughed, wrapping his hands around my wrists where I was pushing against his chest. "Fine. But you're coming with me."

I blanched. "Noah… don't you dare."

In the next second, I was tossed over his shoulder like a bag of sugar, and he ran, jumping into the deep end with a splash that earned us applause from the entire nursing home once we emerged.

I swatted at him, splashing water in his face as he laughed at me catching my breath. As much as I wanted to, I couldn't even pretend to be annoyed. I laughed, too, tossing my head back and letting the sun warm my face.

And for the first time all weekend, I was happy.

Chapter Twelve

Noah

Ididn't know if my plan was working, or if I was just setting myself up for a massive fail.

Logan had high-fived me when all of my brothers and I got together to play cards at my place Sunday night. I told him how it went at the nursing home, how Ruby Grace had agreed to be friends, to let me help her with the wedding, and how we'd spent the entire afternoon together.

I had to admit, at the time I high-fived my little brother and simultaneously got a glare from my older one, I was on a high. It'd been easier than I thought to get her to agree to still spend time with me — even with her fiancé in town — and I'd spent an entire afternoon with her. Even better, I'd spent an entire afternoon with her *in her element*. She thrived at that nursing home, and everyone there loved her. They could tell she was different. She cared. She gave a shit.

I was convinced that people like her made up not even one percent of the entire population. She was just too good, too kind, too giving. It was like she'd strip herself bare if it meant she could shelter even one other person.

So, yes, that first night had felt great.

But now, five days later, I was beginning to wonder if I was the biggest idiot to ever exist.

On Monday, I worked all day at the distillery and then met Ruby Grace for dinner. Her mother had tasked her with booking the rehearsal dinner venue, and Ruby Grace looked like she was about to have a complete meltdown trying to decide on a place that would fit and please everyone.

Then, on Tuesday, I'd been half asleep on my couch after a long day at work when she called me and asked if she could come over. She showed up with chalkboard signs in hand and an apologetic shrug. We stayed up until almost one in the morning making *welcome* signs and *seat yourself* signs and *cocktail hour this way* signs and *gifts here* signs. Chalk dust clouded my living room by the end of the night, but hugging a sleepy Ruby Grace goodbye on my front porch made up for it.

I'd thought I'd be relieved to hear I wouldn't see her Wednesday, but instead, I was gutted when I saw her at the nicest restaurant in town on my walk home from the gym — seated next to Anthony in a cozy little booth, him feeding her a fork full of decadent dessert while she giggled and the cameras around them flashed.

And now it was Thursday, and here I was, circling yet another rack of expensive dinnerware at some fancy department store I couldn't pronounce the name of. I had a register gun in my hand, a fake smile on my face, and a knack for pretending like I had any shot in hell of waking up the girl holding the gun next to me and convincing her she was making the wrong choice.

The gun beeped in my hand each time I scanned a potential gift, and it was like those beeps were tied to my frustration.

Sure, I'd played in the pool with her all day long on Sunday, but she'd gone home to him.

Beep.

And sure, it'd been me who helped her with the signs, with the rehearsal dinner, but it'd been him who got to kiss chocolate off her lips.

Beep.

And fucking *sure*, she told me over and over how much she appreciated me being here with her today, told me how much it upset her that Anthony hadn't been able to make it, told me how much it meant to her that she didn't have to do it alone.

But it would be *him* she'd tell she loved in less than four weeks. It would be him she'd vow to love forever, that she'd promise to be faithful to, that she'd build a life with.

And I would still be here.

The friend.

The fool.

Beep-beep-beep.

"You okay over there?" Ruby Grace asked, smirking at my aggressive scanning.

I blew out a breath, cracking my neck before I resumed a more casual pace. "Just wondering why one couple needs so many plates and bowls, I guess."

Ruby Grace mirrored my sigh at that, holding up the gun to scan a set of wine glasses. "Honestly, I thought this would be my favorite part. I've always imagined hosting dinner parties the way Mama does, entertaining a house full of guests, making a four-course dinner and custom cocktails." Her hand dropped, the gun loose between her fingertips. "Now, I just wish I could fast-forward a few weeks and have it all over with."

I watched her for a long moment, a sickening wave of nausea settling in at her words.

Weeks.

I had *weeks*, and only a few of them, to show this girl what her life could be if she'd only open her eyes.

Ruby Grace went back to scanning, running her fingertips along some tablecloth fabric before checking the price tag and giving it a scan.

Beep.

The farther she walked away from me, the more urgency I felt. And before I could think better of it, I rounded the other side of the table she was circling, meeting her in the middle.

"Let me take you on a date."

She nearly ran into me, and when my words spilled into the atmosphere, they might as well have been hands shoving her backward. She stumbled a bit, and I reached out, my hand finding the small of her back and steadying her before she crashed into a rack of crystalware.

Her eyes were big, golden suns as they flicked between mine, her plump ruby lips popping open, closing again, popping open, closing.

"Uh…" she finally managed.

My brain snapped into damage-control mode. "A friend date."

At that, one of her manicured eyebrows rose, the corner of her lips curving into an amused smile. "A friend date," she repeated.

"Look at you," I said, stepping back as if to hammer home the fact that I had completely innocent intentions.

Even if that was a lie.

"You're so stressed out with all the wedding planning. It's been consuming your every waking minute of every single day. Hell, I've only been helping for a few days and even *I* am overwhelmed."

"I'm okay," she insisted. "A little tired, I admit. But, this is all part of the process."

"Ruby Grace, you can't even make a decision on which stupid plates you want." I held up the gun, clicking through a few screens until I could see everything we'd scanned. "As of now, if everything on this registry is purchased, you'll have two-hundred-and-seventy-three of them. And I'm pretty sure you don't plan on hosting any parties *that* big."

Her face screwed up like she was certain I couldn't possibly be right. She snagged the gun out of my hand, studying the screen before she let out a long sigh, pressing one of her delicate hands to her forehead. She held it there for a moment before dragging it over her face on a groan.

"Okay. You win."

I smiled. "My favorite words to hear."

Ruby Grace shoved my gun back into my chest. "The problem is *when* are we going to go anywhere or do anything when I have so much to get done?"

"That's easy. We go now."

"*Now?!*" She gaped. "We still have so much to register. We have two more floors to cover."

"So?" I shrugged. "We'll get it done. We have time."

"My bridal shower is next Saturday. And the wedding is in less than four weeks."

I huffed, dropping my gun on an empty part of the table next to us before I grabbed her upper arms in my hands. "Ruby Grace, there is nothing that needs to be done in this moment. Everything will be okay. Everything will get done — and in time. I promise."

"But I can't go anywhere right now. I'm not dressed for anything, unless we're registering for wedding gifts at a department store or going to church," she pointed out, gesturing to her knee-length sun dress and wedges.

"That's half the fun. We'll figure out what we want to do and then buy the clothes we need to do it."

"But—"

"You are spreading yourself so thin, you're going to disappear completely by the time your wedding day gets here if you don't take a moment to just *live* a little."

Her little bottom lip poked out at that, and I had to fight against the urge to pull her into me, frame that beautiful face, suck that lip between my teeth…

"You're tired. You need a break. We *both* do." I paused, searching her worried gaze. "Trust me?"

"No."

I laughed. "Liar."

She smiled a little at that, and then let out another long breath, her little shoulders giving way with it. "Okay. I trust you."

My heart did a little flip at that victory. "Good."

"But… Noah?"

"Yeah?"

"Before we go, we have to at least eliminate these plates down to less than one hundred."

She held up her gun, cringing at the screen.

I chuckled, swiping my gun off the table and spinning it in my hand a few times before tucking it in the band of my jeans like a cowboy. "Lead the way, Bonnie."

"Does that make you Clyde?"

"Of course."

"You know that story didn't end very well, right?"

I smirked, stepping into her space and lowering my voice so only she could hear. "I guess we'll have to re-write an ending of our own."

I stood there a little too close, a little too long, eyes falling to her lips for the tiniest second before I caught her gaze again. And she didn't say a word, didn't swallow or step back. She just stood there, staring back at me, letting those words linger in the space between.

She still hadn't taken a breath when I finally walked away.

...

Ruby Grace

"No."

I crossed my arms, covering the new bathing suit top Noah had purchased me at the lake shop for our spontaneous "friend date." It was all I wore — that new swim suit — but Noah was sitting on a beast of a machine, holding up a lifejacket he wanted me to put on over it.

"Come on," he said on a laugh, holding up the bright pink jacket again. "You're wasting daylight, and I have more planned for this friend date."

"I'm not getting on that thing."

"It's a jet ski," he reminded me.

"I know what it is, and I'm not getting on it." I crossed my arms harder.

"It's just like riding a horse."

"No," I argued, eyeing the beast. "On Tank, I knew you wouldn't purposefully throw me off or do donuts or go sixty miles per hour."

"It tops out at forty-five."

I gave him a flat stare.

"Fine," he said on another laugh. "I'll keep it under twenty until you're comfortable. And trust me, by the end of the day, you'll be begging me to let *you* drive. It's fun. And it's safe. Wear the life jacket and pay attention to other vessels on the water. It's that simple."

I blew out a breath through my flat lips, making the same noise Tank made the night I met him as I stared at Noah, debating. It was a beautiful summer day, the sun high in the sky and beating down on my shoulders as a cool breeze drifted lazily over the blue water of Lake Stratford. It was only a half hour outside of town, and a resident favorite getaway — especially in the summer. Other boaters and jet skiers were already out enjoying the water, sunbathers lining the beach, fishermen dotting the rocky shores.

When I finally uncrossed my arms and swiped the life jacket out of Noah's hands, a victorious grin spread on his face.

"You better not try to throw me off this thing, Noah Becker, or so help me."

He laughed, scooting up on the jet ski as I fastened the belts of the jacket around my waist. When I was all buckled in, I hopped on behind him, the tops of my thighs lining up with the backs of his, my chest to his back — which was bare, since he elected *not* to wear a lifejacket.

I swallowed at the heat of him, the tanned, toned muscles of his back already glistening with water from when he jumped in the water before climbing onboard. His hair was a little longer than when I first met him, the ends of it dripping water down his neck, and I watched those little droplets of water with something similar to envy as I wrapped my hands around his middle, scooting a little closer.

"You ready?" he asked over his shoulder, pressing the red button on the jet ski that fired the engine to life. It rumbled softly underneath us, and my heart picked up speed at the noise.

"No."

He chuckled. "Hold on tight."

Without another word or warning, Noah pressed his thumb on the throttle, and we shot away from the shore.

I yelped, nearly falling off backward before I gripped his abdomen tighter. "Noah!"

I watched the speed climb the same way the grin on his face did. The numbers on the little screen increased too quickly — ten, fifteen, twenty, twenty-five. We flew over the soft waves of Lake Stratford, slicing through the water like a viper, and my heart threatened to leap out of my chest with each new acceleration.

"I changed my mind. I want off. I want off!"

Noah just laughed, his head tilting back a little before he reached with the hand not on the gas behind him. He squeezed my knee once reassuringly, glancing over his shoulder quickly before he turned back to the lake ahead.

"It's okay. I promise. Just trust me."

I stared at his hand on my knee, the warmth of it spreading over my entire leg before it dipped somewhere under the bottoms of my swim suit. He removed it just as fast as he had placed it there, and my heart raced in my chest for a completely different reason.

I tried to calm my breathing, to find assurance in his promise that it would all be okay as my hair whipped in the wind behind me. But when a large boat crossed in front of us, leaving a massive wake, and Noah didn't steer away from it, my eyes bulged.

"Noah," I said as a warning.

He kept going, aimed straight for the large waves the boat had made when it passed.

"Noah, don't you dare."

"Hang on!"

"Noah!"

But it was too late. We hit the first wave made by the boat, the nose of the jet ski skipping up a few inches off the water. I screamed, gripping onto Noah so tight I thought I'd cut off his breathing. The next wave was even bigger, and the jet ski flew into the air, the roar of the engine ebbing a little at the loss of water pressure as we went airborne.

I was still screaming, gripping, fearing for my life when we landed again, and this time Noah cut the wheel right, turning us along the edge of the waves instead of straight over them. We rode them fast and furious, catching another fit of air before we were out of the waves and back on the glassy water.

I was pretty sure my stomach was still somewhere back behind us.

Noah slowed down until we were stopped, floating in the middle of the lake to the tune of the soft, rumbling engine. He turned to look at me over his shoulder with a shit-eating grin.

"That was fun."

I smacked his shoulder, shoving like I was going to push him off while I fought against a smile. "That was *not* fun! That was terrifying!"

"Yeah? Why you smiling, then?"

"I'm not smiling!" I insisted, but even as the words fell from my lips, I couldn't fight the grin. I laughed, softly at first before it took over completely, and I laughed so hard I had to wrap my hands over my stomach, my forehead hitting the place between his shoulders as I tried to catch my breath.

When I looked up again, Noah just quirked one brow in victory.

I shook my head. "You're infuriating, Noah Becker."

"I believe I was the first one to say that about *you*, Ruby Grace Barnett."

I smiled wider, blowing out a breath before running my hands back through my damp hair. "Okay. Fine. I admit it. That was fun."

"Told you."

"What now?"

He grinned, thumb hovering over the throttle as he faced forward again. "Better wrap those beautiful arms around me again, sweetheart."

And I did, just in time for him to cut the wheel and floor it, spinning us in a donut circle that made huge, billowing waves around us. I was laughing and squealing, leaning into the turn with him when he cut the wheel again, and we went flying over the waves we'd made.

I didn't know how much time passed with him doing donuts and figure-eights and making waves bigger than the jet ski before he'd send us barreling over them, but I *did* know that the huge smile didn't leave my face the entire time. My cheeks hurt by the time we finally slowed again, and we were both breathing hard, chests heaving with the adrenaline and excitement.

"You're wild," I whispered on a laugh, trying to catch my breath.

"What's that?" he asked, grinning at me over his shoulder.

"You're wild!" I said louder, throwing my hands up in the air and turning my face to the sun. I closed my eyes, basking in the rays and the feeling of euphoria for a long moment. When I looked at Noah again, he was watching me, throat thick with a swallow as his eyes searched mine.

The sun that had felt so light and airy just moments before seemed to beat down on us then, the heat unbearable, our lips so close where he tilted his head toward me, where I leaned into him.

My hands slipped around his waist again, shaking a little as they settled over the ribs and valleys of his abdomen. I licked my lips, eyes falling to his before I caught his steel gaze once more.

There were so many words I wanted to say in that moment, so many words that would have completely annihilated our *friends only* agreement.

Kiss me.

Touch me.

I don't feel this way with anyone else.

Each new thought shocked me more than the last, and my lips parted, the effort to catch my breath lost somewhere in the wind that swept over us. I should have been thinking about Anthony, about our wedding, about everything I needed to get done for it, about everything we would do as a married couple in our life together.

I should have been thinking about *anything* other than how much I wished Noah would cross the line we drew between us and capture my lips with his.

He wanted me. I knew he wanted me. And I knew if I leaned in even another inch, he'd take me.

So, with every ounce of willpower I had, I backed away, eyes floating down to the seat between us before I looked at him again, wearing a fake, *everything's okay* smile.

And instead of saying all the words whirring through my mind, I settled on three safe ones, instead.

"Can I drive?"

• • •

Noah

The sun was a lazy ball of fire riding on the evening clouds later that day when Ruby Grace and I spread out a large blanket on the beach. She was lying on her stomach, her legs slowly kicking in the air as she popped another strawberry between her lips. Her focus was on the lake, on the jet skis and boats and fishermen and tubers and swimmers.

Mine was on her.

The back of her swim suit top had shifted, showing me the lines the sun had already made on her skin that day. Her hips were narrow, her small ass curved and toned, her legs still the epitome of every man's fantasy as she swung them gently in the air — back and forth, back and forth, ten manicured toes skating the sky.

I would have been perfectly content to stare at her, just like that, for as long as I lived.

Even if I couldn't have her, if I couldn't kiss her or touch her or pull her into me and shield her from every unwanted harm — just *looking* at her was a blessing. I felt her presence swell into my chest, filling me up in some way that I never would have realized before.

Because I didn't know I was empty.

Not until she poured into my life.

Ruby Grace's content sigh brought me back to the moment as she shifted, rolling onto her side and propping her chin up with one hand. "So, what made you think of Stratford Lake for our friend date?"

I took another bite of the sandwiches we'd bought from the lake's convenient store, speaking around the mass of meat and bread in my mouth. "My dad used to bring all of us out here. It's one of my favorite places."

Her face sobered. "And you brought me?"

I shrugged. "I thought maybe it could become one of your favorite places, too."

A soft breeze rolled over us, brushing Ruby Grace's wild hair back over her shoulders as a soft smile found her face. I marveled at the deep blue water of the lake behind her, the beige sand, the warm glow of the sun drifting in and out of the clouds. It was the kind of view an artist would stop time for, pulling out their easel or camera or pen and paper to capture the moment in whatever way they could.

"What was he like?" Ruby Grace asked. "Your dad?"

I smiled, stealing a strawberry from her plate and popping it in my mouth. "He was the original trouble maker. I remember Mom always yelling at him for something. But, not in a way that they were *actually* fighting. It was more like this adorable, *you annoy me but I love you anyway* kind of yelling."

Ruby Grace smiled, running her fingers over the sand at the edge of the blanket. "So, I guess we have him to thank for the notorious Becker brothers running amok, huh?"

"Oh, definitely. But, it's not like we go *looking* for trouble," I pointed out. "We were just taught from a young age not to put up with anything that's wrong. So, whether that means sticking up for ourselves or for our brothers or a friend or even a complete stranger, that's what we did. It's what we *do*." I shrugged. "Dad never raised hell unless there was something to raise hell about."

"Like the way Patrick Scooter was running the distillery?"

I blanched, heart stopping in my chest as I watched Ruby Grace in a new way. She was the mayor's daughter — young, affluent, *far* removed from the distillery. I knew everyone in the town had some sort of tie to Scooter Whiskey, but it surprised me that she knew anything about the inner workings of the place.

"Yeah," I finally managed. "Exactly like that."

"My dad hated it, too," she said, dragging her index finger in a heart shape over the sand before she erased it with her palm. "He said Patrick was tarnishing the brand, taking out all the honesty and down-home history that made the whiskey special. He said Patrick was going too mainstream, trying to be something Scooter Whiskey wasn't."

"That's how my dad felt, too. And he had all these ideas about how to keep the same traditions, but liven up the brand, too. He was smart. He had research and industry surveys. He knew what he was talking about."

"But Patrick wouldn't listen."

I nodded. "He seems to still have that problem."

Ruby Grace watched me for a long moment, her fingers paused in their current doodle in the sand. "The fire your dad died in... your family doesn't believe it was an accident, do they?"

I swallowed, watching a boat in the distance as I tried to figure out how to respond. The answer was easy — no, we didn't believe it was an accident. But, admitting that was admitting that we had conjured some conspiracy theory, that we thought the Scooters were crooked, that someone had it out for our dad. It was essentially admitting insanity, and I didn't want to do that — especially when Mom's reputation and heart was on the line.

"We believe there's a lot we don't know about that day," I decided on, and before she could respond, I changed the subject to her. "What's *your* dad like? It had to be kind of hard, growing up as the Mayor's daughter."

A sarcastic smile spread over Ruby Grace's face, and she rolled, splaying out on her back with her eyes on the sky above. "Let's just say my dad felt more like a father *figure* than he ever did a father."

I frowned. "Wasn't around much, I take it."

She shook her head, eyes tracing the clouds. "Don't get me wrong, he's a great dad to me and my sister. He provides for us, tells us how proud he is of us and how much he loves us. He's like me in a way that Mom and Mary Anne don't understand. He gets it when I need to hide away, when my anxiety spikes in a crowd. And if Mom ever needs help with parenting, he steps in, no questions asked. He helped me with my college application and essay, told me he would support me no matter what I decided to major in. And thanks to him, I've got the best golf game of any woman in Stratford, I'd bet."

She paused, regaling his *great dad* qualities like there was some list and as long as he had checked those boxes, she couldn't say otherwise.

"But," she continued. "Sometimes it just felt like he was this mostly silent bystander and Mom was both parents. Dad's *real* kid is this town, and everything that goes along with nurturing it. That's where his time goes. That's where his energy is spent." She chuckled. "Well, that and the casino or any gambling event he can con the council members into."

"And that doesn't bother you?"

"No," she answered quickly, biting her bottom lip before releasing it again. "I understand it, feeling so passionate about something that you'd want to dedicate your life to it. He really looked up to Grandpa, too, and I think he always wanted to take his place. This is just what makes him happy. And I love him, I want him happy." She rolled onto her side again. "Now, do I wish we had more time together growing up? Sure. But, I get him. And he gets me. At least, for the most part."

"For the most part," I mused. "Meaning, he probably wouldn't be cool with you going back to college after the wedding either."

A shadow passed over her face, and I internally cursed at myself, knowing I'd crossed over in the territory that always made her clam up and run away. She didn't like talking about *her* dreams, about sacrificing those for her soon-to-be husband.

And it seemed to be my favorite button to push.

I was surprised when she didn't yell at me or tell me to mind my own business as she stormed across the beach and away from me. Instead, she let out a long breath, eyes falling to the blanket we sat on before they found mine again. "I'm sure he wouldn't exactly be thrilled, no. But, it's more Mama than it is him. She knows what it takes to be a politician's wife, and she's been more than open with me about it."

"What exactly does it take?"

She shrugged. "Selflessness. Passion. Love and understanding that I won't always be the priority in his life. But, that was part of the reason I was so attracted to Anthony when we first met. He knows what he wants, and he's driven, and smart. I love that about him."

My chest tightened the more she talked about him. It was the first time she'd said it — that she loved him — where I actually believed it was true.

I hated it.

"I think it's amazing that you found a man like that," I finally offered, swallowing my pride like a jagged pill. "I really do. But, and I don't mean to say anything out of line, but I wonder if he wouldn't support *you* the same — if you told him you wanted to go back to school or volunteer with AmeriCorps. You could be there for him and still be there for yourself, too."

Ruby Grace nodded, but she wouldn't meet my eyes. "Yeah. I suppose."

"Can I ask you something?"

Another nod.

"If you could look twenty years down the road on a blissfully perfect day in your future life, what would it look like?"

She smiled, finally looking at me again. Her eyes were filled with wonder and curiosity, like I was some project she was assigned to but didn't know where to start.

"Hmmm..." she said, lying back again. She crossed her long legs, folding her hands over her bare navel as she watched the clouds. "It would be Sunday. After church. I'd have a huge, delicious supper spread, the table set for a family of five. My three kids would be out in the yard playing, and as I watched them from the kitchen window, my husband would come up behind me, wrap his arms around me, and ask me to dance."

I swallowed past the thick knot in my throat, visions of my own parents flooding my mind. And it wasn't lost on me that in her vision, she didn't mention *Anthony*, specifically.

"What else?" I asked.

She smiled wider. "We'd have a dog — a big one. One that would slobber everywhere and knock our toddlers down when he played with them. And our house would be country, but not like the *classic* southern style. It'd be eclectic, with art from all over the world, and bright colors and funky designs."

The more she talked, the more she lit up.

"I think I'd like a big entertaining space in the back yard, a place to host parties and barbecues, and I'd want a little vegetable garden that I could grow my own tomatoes and squash." She paused, her smile falling a little. "And I'd have a charity, one that supported something I cared about... maybe earth conservation, or education in rural locations, or quality of life for senior citizens, or mental illness support for our veterans. A way to give back. A way to save someone..."

I smirked. "I bet it'd be the most efficiently run charity in the world. Probably the most well-known, too."

She rolled onto her side. "Why do you say that?"

"Because it's you."

She watched me for a long moment, like she was waiting for me to continue, but I didn't feel the need. That was all there was to say. It was her, Ruby Grace, and we both knew that anything she set her mind to, she'd not only achieve it — she'd break records, too.

"Noah?" she whispered.

"Mm?"

"Can I say something... and you not ask questions when I do?"

I considered it, curiosity overpowering any hesitation I had. "Okay."

Ruby Grace sat up, then, sitting on her knees as she tucked her hair behind both ears. Those kneecaps brushed the tops of my thighs where I was lying on my side in front of her, nothing between us but a half-empty container of strawberries and two bottles of water.

She chewed her cheek, like she wasn't sure what to say or how to say it, and her eyes watched her hand — the one braced on the blanket just a few inches from mine.

"I don't know if this is stupid or... I don't know, pointless to say, but..." She blew out a breath, lifting her eyes to mine. "Thank you, for talking to me, for being my friend when you didn't have to be." Her brows bent together, a shade of pink tinging her cheeks. "I never feel more like my *real* self than I do when I'm with you."

My next breath lodged somewhere in my throat, stuck and swelling with every new inhale I tried to take. Her words broke me as much as they filled me with longing and hope. It should be Anthony she felt most like herself with, since he was the man responsible for the diamond glittering on her finger.

But it was me.

Her eyes searched mine, her body leaning forward, down, toward mine. She was so slight that even on her knees, we were nearly face to face with my head propped up on one elbow. The closer she got, the more I saw the strawberry juice stained on her lips, smelled the sweet scent of her breath as her lips parted, saw the sunburst in her hazel eyes under the glow of the sun.

I knew in that moment that all I had to do was move toward her even an *inch*, and I could kiss her. I knew that if I reached out a hand, wrapped my fingers up in her red hair and pulled her into me, she would submit.

But I didn't.

I *couldn't*.

I'd promised her — just friends. And I would respect those boundaries until the day she didn't belong to another man.

Until the day she was actually mine.

"We should go," I whispered with her mouth inches from mine, her lids fluttering shut.

She popped them back open, blinking several times before she pulled back, clearing her throat on a nervous nod of acknowledgement. "Yeah. Yeah, we probably should."

But before she could stand, I reached out, covering her hand with mine.

I smoothed the pad of my thumb over her wrist, the smooth palm of her hand, the shiny skin over her knuckles. I hoped the touch would say everything I couldn't.

I feel the same way.

I want you, too.

I'm here, whenever you're ready.

I stood, wrapping her hand in mine to help her up before I released her and put the space between us again, packing up our picnic without another glance in her direction.

The ride home in my truck was quiet, only the soft melody of my playlist and the wind whipping in from the windows the only sounds between us. Ruby Grace looked out the window the entire time, her eyes distant, mind somewhere far away.

I let her be.

When I pulled into the department store parking lot, parking next to where we'd left her convertible, she finally pulled her gaze inside the truck.

"We didn't get a thing done today," she said, unfastening her seat belt.

I smirked. "But do you feel better?"

At that, she sighed, a genuine smile coloring her lips before she nodded. "I do. I really do."

"Then it was a successful day."

The sun had already set, the department store long closed, and the light from the moon above and my headlights seemed to be the only ones in the world.

Ruby Grace reached for the door handle, but paused, looking back at me over her shoulder. "Thank you for today, Noah."

"Anytime, Legs."

She shook her head, pushing the door open and sliding out before she closed it behind her. She leaned her elbows on the edge of the window, her hair a mess, skin sun-kissed, smile lazy and sated.

"I'll see you around."

I nodded. "See you around."

Her smile slipped, eyes searching mine for something that I was sure she didn't find because she tore them away too quickly, crossing her arms over her chest and walking across the lot to her own car. She slipped inside, offering me one last wave before she pulled away, turning left down the main drag that would take her all the way home.

And I just sat there, hands on the steering wheel, eyes on my passenger seat, and heart somewhere down the road with a girl who didn't even realize she had it.

Chapter Thirteen

Ruby Grace

"I call bullshit."

I smirked, holding my cell phone between my ear and shoulder Saturday afternoon as I packed up all the supplies for the centerpieces Annie and I were going to make that day. Photos of Anthony and me throughout the year had been printed, frames of the same size waiting to be filled, flowers and jars that would hold floating candles rounding out the look.

We had a lot of crafting to do.

And apparently, a lot of talking, too.

"There is absolutely no way you spent an entire day in a bathing suit with Noah Becker and he didn't put his hands on you."

"Not even once," I assured her, hiding my own disappointment at that fact. I folded the top on one box before working on filling the next. "He's my friend, Annie."

"Friend, shmriend. He wants you. And the way you talk about him, I think you want him, too."

"This is literally the first time I've talked to you about him, other than when you *forcibly* left me alone with him that night at the Black Hole."

"Exactly. You don't talk about him, but you spend at least four days a week with him and have been since you got back into town. You never talked to him *before* you went to college."

"Yes, I did," I argued. "I sat behind him in church, remember?"

"Right. Must have been thrilling conversations between a nine-year-old and a senior in high school," she deadpanned.

I sighed, plopping down on my bed and surveying the half-packed boxes around me. I didn't know why I was trying to hide it from Annie. She was my best friend. She could see through me like a jelly fish.

But admitting I had feelings for Noah to her — to *anyone* — was dangerous.

It was impossible.

If I admitted it, I'd have to *do* something about it — and that something was either give *him* up, or give Anthony up.

I couldn't do the latter.

I didn't *want* to do the first.

It was like white water rafting. I was in the raft — cold, wet, terrified. Worst case scenario, I'd get dumped, hit my head on a rock and life as I know it would be over. *Best* case scenario, I'd make it to the end of the river.

Still cold and wet, but alive.

There *was* no easy way out of the situation I'd found myself in, and the best way I knew how to handle it was to just avoid making a decision at all.

Noah and I were friends. No lines had been crossed.

Everything was fine.

"He's just my friend, Annie," I told my best friend, and myself, keeping my voice low. Mama and Daddy were gone, but Anthony was downstairs, working in Daddy's home office.

Not that I was talking about anything he couldn't hear.

At least, that's what I told myself as I lowered my voice even more. "We haven't done anything wrong."

"The fact that you have to say that…"

"I know," I said, sighing again. "I know. But, he makes me feel… like *me*. This summer has been so stressful with all the wedding planning, and when I'm with him, everything feels easier, lighter, more manageable. We have *fun*, even if we're just making stupid chalkboard signs."

"Do you feel that way when you're with Anthony?"

I didn't answer.

A long exhale came from the other end of the phone. "Alright. Just get over here so we can talk about this, okay?"

"I really would rather *not* talk about it and just make centerpieces."

"Well, you're going to have to do both. Text me when you're on your way."

I groaned. "Fine."

"I love you."

"Love you, too."

"Ruby Grace?"

"Yeah?"

Annie paused. "Everything is going to be okay. Okay?"

I nodded, ignoring the way my throat tightened at her words. "Okay," I whispered back.

When we ended the call, I finished packing up the last of the centerpiece ingredients, heaving the first box into my arms and carefully walking it downstairs. It was heavy, and I stumbled on a step, nearly crashing to the floor and taking the fragile contents of the box along with me.

"Shit," I murmured, balancing the box on the railing.

I was on the middle plateau between the two flights, and I didn't want to chance a tumble.

"Anthony?" I called out, still balancing the box on the railing. "Can you help me with these boxes for a second?"

No answer.

I frowned, looking around at my options. I didn't want to go back *up* the stairs, either, so I deposited the box on the floor of the square landing, trotting down the second flight of stairs and making my way back to Daddy's office.

"Anthony?" I called again.

No answer.

I heard his voice when I rounded the corner past the kitchen, making my way down the hall.

Of course, he's on the phone.

I hung my hands on my hips, pausing in the hallway to debate my options. I decided to just get a glass of sweet tea and wait for him to get off the phone so he could help me load up the car. I was in no hurry, anyway.

But before I could turn back toward the kitchen, I heard my name.

"Yes, it's been hectic being out here, but Ruby Grace has been great about it all. The crew filmed our dinner earlier this week, and she looked ravishing. She's everything I could have ever asked for in a wife."

I smiled, a mixture of guilt and love swirling in my stomach as I leaned my back against the wall, folding my hands over my heart. It was rude to listen in, and I knew it, but truth be told, I *needed* to hear that kind of thing from Anthony.

I needed to hear what I meant to him.

"I know, Dad. Yeah. Right. Ha! I know, you should have seen us at the barrel tasting event. I swear, this town lives and dies by that distillery."

I smiled. That was Stratford, alright.

"Oh, trust me, I can handle her father. With what we're doing for him, I don't think he could even pretend to not love me — even if that were the case," Anthony said, lowering his voice.

My stomach somersaulted, and I slid my back quietly along the wall, getting closer.

"It's not the only reason, Dad," he said after a long pause. "No. I know. I understand. Listen, being a politician is all I needed to do in his eyes. We golf, shoot the shit, gamble at the casino, talk about how the extremists are taking the country to hell in a hand basket. He dragged me to the casino last week." A pause. "I know. You think he would have learned after that, but... anyway. Her mom is a little tougher, but I play the perfect gentleman and she eats it up. Just have to open a few doors and call her ma'am and she lights up like a Christmas tree."

A pause.

An exaggerated sigh from Anthony.

"Dad, trust me, I get it. I know they're not exactly what we had in mind for the perfect in-laws. They're country bumpkins, *but*, they're in the political circuit — even if it's in a small way. This is what you wanted, right? The Barnett name is known in this town, and when we did the background check on Ruby Grace, we didn't find a single thing that could come up and bite us in the ass during the elections. She's clean. She's poised. She has no aspirations of her own." He paused again. "And, she's pretty, which is a bonus."

Another chuckle.

Another roll of my stomach.

"Her mom has trained her well to be the perfect politician's wife," he continued. "Her family isn't exactly the premier picture we had in mind, but they're pretty clean cut. They're reputable. And they need us to play our part, just like we need Ruby Grace to play hers."

I bit my lip against the tears stinging my eyes, confusion rolling over me and mixing with the betrayal. I didn't understand it — any of it. He loved me. He loved my family.

What part was he playing in our life?

What part was I supposed to play in his?

This can't be Anthony. He wouldn't talk about me like this. It's all a misunderstanding.

I tried to convince myself, fighting against the urge to hyperventilate as I pressed myself against the cold wall in our hallway.

But I couldn't lie to myself, not when I was hearing everything I needed to hear to know the truth.

"This was always our plan, Dad," Anthony said. "She's perfect."

A pause.

"I know," Anthony said. "The way I see it, Ruby Grace will be more than happy to take on the community projects. It'll be a good look for the campaign. And, hey." He lowered his voice even more. "Having her tied up in all of that will leave me plenty of free time for a little fun on the side... know what I mean?"

He full-on laughed at that, and even from where I stood in the hallway, I could hear the gusto laugh of his father.

His father, who had kissed the back of my hand when we met and told me how beautiful I was, how smart I was, how lucky Anthony was to have me.

And it was all a show.

It was all a lie.

They need us to play our part, and we need Ruby Grace to play hers.

A sob broke through my throat before I felt it coming, and I clamped my hand over my mouth, squeezing my eyes shut to force the tears back in.

"I gotta go, Dad, I think she's downstairs." A chuckle. "Okay, I'll call you later to discuss the speech."

I needed to move. I needed to get away from Dad's office, from Anthony, from this house and this entire town. But I couldn't move. The hardwood floor was quicksand, sucking me in, making it impossible to take even one step.

Anthony rounded out of the office on a sigh, running one hand back through his hair before he paused, eyes lighting up at the sight of me. "Ah, there's my beautiful wife-to-be. I was just coming to check on you." He smiled, pulling the shell-shocked board of my body into him and pressing a kiss to my forehead. "Need help with anything?"

I couldn't speak.

I just stared at him, at his hazel eyes — the ones I'd lost myself in for hours over the last year — at his perfect blond hair, his perfectly sculpted body, his perfect Superman chin.

And here I was, his perfect little abiding bride-to-be.

Anthony frowned, searching my face. "Baby? Are you okay?"

My stomach rolled violently at the nickname, and I blinked several times, awareness flooding back. "I'm fine. I just almost fell trying to get the boxes with the centerpiece stuff downstairs. Could you help me with them?"

Anthony smiled, thumbing my chin before he kissed my nose. "Of course, my little do-it-all-by-herself. You should have just asked me in the first place."

I faked the best smile I could, snaking my way out of his hold. "One of them is on the stairs. There are three more in my room. Can you load them into the car for me? I'm feeling a little lightheaded, think I need some water."

Anthony swept my hair away from my face, still wearing that stupid, sympathetic smile. "Of course. You go hydrate and rest. I'll be back."

He walked me to the kitchen, pouring me a glass of water before he disappeared up the stairs to retrieve the first box. As soon as he was gone, I took my first inhale, gulping down the entire glass of water before refilling it.

My mind was spinning, heart racing, rib cage closing in on my lungs. Every second that passed, my hands shook more, and the tears I'd managed to hold back flooded my eyes over and over before I'd blink and clear them away.

"All set," Anthony said, bounding back into the kitchen.

I didn't realize how much time had passed. Everything felt like a dream.

"Want me to come help? I can take a break from work. It is Saturday, after all."

"No," I said quickly.

Anthony frowned.

I swallowed, shaking my head and forcing another smile as I placed my hands on his chest. I wanted to beat my fists on it, scream at him, cry and kick him out and throw the ring on my finger in his face.

But even in my frantic state, I knew that wasn't the right thing to do.

I needed time. I needed space. I needed to think, to process, to figure out what to do.

Who to trust.

"Sorry," I said, still smiling. "I just, I haven't had much time with Annie since I got home, what with her being pregnant and me doing all the wedding stuff. I need some girl time."

Anthony returned my smile in understanding. "Of course. Well, you two don't get into too much trouble, okay?"

My smile was shaky, but I held it as long as I could, closing my eyes against the urge to vomit when Anthony leaned in for a kiss. I turned my head, offering him my cheek, and he kissed it sweetly before pulling back, still framing me in his arms.

"See you later this evening?"

I nodded. "Mm-hmm."

As soon as his hands were off me, I swiped my purse off the kitchen counter, bolting for the door. I practically sprinted across the drive to my car, hands shaking as I pulled the handle and climbed inside. The engine roared to life when I pushed the ignition button, and I threw it into reverse, kicking up gravel with my tires as I flipped it around and sped off down the old dirt road.

My heart kicked hard in my chest, picking up more and more speed with every inch I put between Anthony and myself. My eyes flooded with tears, ones I couldn't hold back any longer. They slid down my cheeks, hot and searing, my hands tight on the steering wheel, stomach lodged somewhere in my throat.

Halfway down the road to the Main Street drag, I pulled over, trying to calm my breaths before I had an all-out panic attack.

I needed to breathe. I needed an explanation. I needed someone to hold me and tell me it was all going to be okay.

I needed Noah.

The thought hit me as quickly and as unsuspectedly as everything else had that day, but it didn't make me panic more. If anything, the realization soothed me, blanketing me like a silky sheet of reassurance.

My heart rate slowed.

My breathing evened out.

My hands stabilized, the tears on my cheeks drying, no more falling from my eyes to join them.

For a long time, I just sat there with my hands on the steering wheel, staring at the swirling dust from the road between me and Main Street.

Then, I fished my cell phone out of my purse and texted Annie.

Mom sprung something on me, we'll have to reschedule our super fun centerpiece building day. See you at church tomorrow.

As soon as the text went through, I turned my phone off, put the car in drive, and floored it across town.

* * *

Noah

"Just a minute!" I called from the bathroom, cursing under my breath as I ended my shower prematurely and yanked a towel off the rack. I'd debated ignoring the knock at my door altogether — mostly because I was pretty sure it was someone trying to sell something or convince me to switch religions. But, there was a chance it was one of my brothers, or my mom, since all of them liked to stop by unannounced.

The knock came again, a little louder this time, as I swiped a pair of sweatpants from my bed.

"Yeah, yeah, I'm coming! Hold your horses."

I grumbled, putting on the first white t-shirt I saw hanging in my closet, even though I was still a little damp. As soon as I was dressed, I stormed across my house to answer the door, frustration boiling even more when yet *another* knock came. I frowned, blowing out a hot breath and ready to let whoever it was on the other side have it — unless it was Mom, of course.

When I swung the door open and saw Ruby Grace standing on my front porch, all the frustration died.

And was immediately replaced by the most powerful sense of protectiveness I'd ever experienced in my life.

Her fiery red hair was tied in a messy bun for the first time since I'd met her, little tendrils falling from the hair tie and framing her long, worn face. Her eyes were puffy and red, mascara smudged beneath them, bottom lip trembling as she watched me.

She looked so small — her arms folded over her middle, shoulders slumped, head hanging.

Someone had hurt her.

I swallowed, fists tightening at my sides, before I slowly pushed open the screen door between us. I didn't chance a single word when she stepped inside, and as soon as she was in my house, I shut both doors behind her, folding my arms over her like I could protect her from whatever or whoever had hurt her.

Ruby Grace melted into me, a little sob muffled by my t-shirt as she buried her face in my chest and twisted her hands in the fabric covering my abdomen. She pulled me closer, trying to fold in on herself as I surrounded her, hugging her tight, one hand finding the back of her head. I ran my fingers through her hair, pressed her closer to my chest, my lips finding the crown of her head as I forced a calming breath.

"It's okay," I assured her without knowing what *it* even was. "I'm here. I'm right here."

She cried harder at that, pulling at my shirt again like she needed me closer. There wasn't an inch of us that wasn't touching, but I tried, anyway. I tightened my grip, pulled long, calming breaths through my nose before gently releasing them, helping her to do the same.

It felt like hours that we stood there, just inside my front door, her wrapped up in my arms as I rocked her. With each passing minute, her sobs softened, her breathing quieted, and finally, she pressed her hands into my chest, lifting her head from that spot to lock her eyes on mine.

Her devastated, tear-glossed, achingly beautiful golden eyes.

"I'm sorry," she whispered, her bottom lip trembling with the apology. "I... I didn't know where else to go."

I ran the pad of my thumbs over her cheeks, wiping away the salty streams there before I framed her face in my hands. "You never have to apologize for coming to me. Ever. No matter what."

She closed her eyes, releasing two more parallel tears before she buried her head in my chest again.

I had so many questions — namely, who the fuck did I need to kill — but, I knew she'd tell me what happened when she was ready. So, instead, I held her, walking her over to my couch and pulling her down into the cushions with me. She curled up in a ball in my lap, and I covered us with a blanket, rocking her gently in my arms until her breathing quieted again.

"Do you want some water?" I asked after a while.

She nodded, sniffing and running the back of her wrist under her nose before crawling off me. I squeezed her knee before I stood, making my way into the kitchen.

Once I was alone, I cracked my neck, forcing a calming breath that was more for me than for her. I had the bad habit of jumping to conclusions, of letting my temper get the best of me, and I knew it was going to take every ounce of willpower I had to be calm and cool and collected when she finally did tell me what happened.

If it was Anthony, if he had cheated on her or broken her heart in any way, I *also* knew that "staying calm" would be a nearly impossible goal to accomplish.

With two glasses of water in hand, I made my way back to the living room. Ruby Grace hadn't moved an inch. Her eyes were blank, bottomless holes as she stared at my coffee table.

"Here," I whispered, handing one glass to her and setting the other on the table. She wrapped her hands around the glass, taking one small sip before resting it in her lap, her eyes focused on the liquid inside.

"Anthony doesn't love me."

She whispered the words, and not a single shadow of emotion passed over her face when she released them.

I didn't know how to respond. Half of me wanted to say *I fucking know that, I've been trying to tell you.* But, the other half of me knew there was a reason she thought he did before this moment, and there was a reason she thought he didn't *now.*

"That's not true," I finally offered, against the internal rolling of my eyes.

"No," she said, shaking her head. "It is. I heard him…"

I frowned, not understanding.

She closed her eyes, forcing a long breath before she spoke again. "He was talking to his dad on the phone, he didn't know I could hear him. And he… he said some *awful* things about me, about my family."

My throat tightened, and I reached for the other glass of water, taking a sip to cool myself down before I spoke. "What did he say?"

"That I was right for their *plan*. That I was pretty and I don't have any aspirations of my own and I've been *trained well* to be a politician's wife." She scoffed, eyes floating up to the ceiling as she rolled her lips together. "He doesn't want to marry me because he loves me, he wants to marry me because I fit the role." Her eyes fluttered shut again. "I'm a pawn in a game I didn't even know I was playing."

"He didn't say that."

Ruby Grace's eyebrows bent together in confusion, her gaze leveling with mine. "What?"

My jaw clenched along with my fists at my side. "Please, tell me he didn't say any of that. Tell me, so I don't get in my truck and drive across town and beat in his fucking face until no one recognizes him."

"Noah," she gasped, reaching out for me. "Please, don't. Don't hurt him." She swallowed. "Don't leave *me*."

The breath I blew out through my nose felt like fire and smoke, black invading my vision. That son of a bitch didn't deserve her in the first place, and now?

Now, he didn't deserve to breathe.

"Please," she said again, scooting closer to me. She placed her water on the coffee table, leaning into me, her small arms wrapping around my middle as she rested her head on my chest. "Please."

I blew out another breath, but this time, I let it out slower, wrapping my arms around her in return. There was nothing I wanted more than to drive across town and give that motherfucker exactly what he had coming.

Nothing, except to hold Ruby Grace and be the one who made her feel better, the one who showed her that what he did to her did not define who she was.

"I feel so stupid," she said after a while, her head still on my chest. "All this time, I thought I'd hit the jackpot. I had the perfect guy, the perfect ring, the perfect future. I didn't mind sacrificing my own dreams for his, because I knew he loved me. I knew that I'd be his partner, standing by his side, and he'd bend for *my* wants in the future." She paused. "I thought I'd found what my parents had. And that was all I'd ever wanted."

My heart broke with that admission, because I knew the feeling all too well. Ruby Grace had watched her parents grow in love just as I'd watched mine, and it was what we had pictured for *our* futures.

Now, her picture had been shattered.

I tilted her chin up, leveling my eyes with hers. "He's an idiot," I stated simply. "And I know that doesn't fix anything. It probably doesn't make you feel better, either. But, he is. And he's going to regret the day he lost you. He's going to regret that he didn't realize what he had when he had it."

She sighed, leaning into my hand. "I doubt he'll even care. He'll find someone else who can play the part, and he'll run for office just the same."

"He'll care," I promised her. "Trust me. And he'll regret it. There isn't a man alive who could be loved by you and not kick himself every single day for fucking it up."

A steady silence fell over us, her eyes on mine, those words between us.

"I don't even know how to *begin* telling my mom," she finally said, and those eyes watching mine welled up with tears again. "It'll break her heart."

"She'll understand. She loves you."

Ruby Grace shook her head, letting out a long, heavy breath. "Everyone is going to be talking about this, Noah. *Everyone.* Forever."

"Let them talk. They don't know you or the situation, and their judgment doesn't affect who you are." I held her gaze, running my thumb down the line of her jaw. "Do you hear me? What they think of you is not who you actually are. They do not have that power over you." I smirked. "Plus, someone else will fuck up and give them a change of subject. I mean, just leave it to me and my brothers. We've been doing it all our lives."

She chuckled, but it died quickly, sadness washing over her again. "I feel like a fool."

"It's *him* who's the fool," I assured her, searching her eyes with my own. "You are, without a doubt, the most caring, loving, passionate, intelligent, and classy woman I have ever met. You walk with a confidence unparalleled by anyone in this town, and you give without ever expecting anything in return, and you're brave." I shook my head. "You are *so* fucking brave."

Her eyes softened, her voice just a whisper again. "You didn't mention the way I look in any of those bullet points."

"You're beautiful," I said easily. "But that's not what makes you the woman I l—" I swallowed, throat constricting like her eyes held it in a vise grip. "That's not what makes you the woman you are. You are more than your eyes, and your hair, and your strawberry smoothie lips and long, lean legs. You're not meant to be a puppet in some man's sideshow, Ruby Grace. You're meant to be his entire world."

Ruby Grace let her eyes wander over every inch of my face, as if she was just noticing me for the first time.

And maybe she was.

"I love the way you see me," she whispered.

I swallowed, heart picking up speed as she leaned in closer, her hands fisted in my shirt, her eyes on my lips.

"I just see you with my eyes."

"No," she argued, her lips centimeters from mine, her sweet breath invading my senses. "No, you see me with your soul." She swallowed, eyes flicking up to mine before they fell back to my mouth. "And I feel you with mine."

Her lips touched mine tentatively at first — feather light, each of us releasing a shaky, anxious breath. I felt that tiny, almost non-existent touch in every inch of my body. A wave of chills rushed through me, our lips hovering, breaths hard and heavy with want.

With *need*.

Then, my hands slid into her hair, and I pulled her into me, claiming her mouth like it had never touched another man.

She moaned, melting into me as I deepened the kiss, my lips hard and hot on hers. Her hands twisted in my shirt before she let it go completely, sliding the warmth of her palms beneath the fabric and over my stomach. I shivered at the touch, groaning against her kiss and pulling her closer.

I felt stupid for ever thinking I could know, could fathom, what it would be like to kiss her, to have her in my arms like this.

Kissing Ruby Grace wasn't like kissing a normal girl. It was like kissing royalty, like kissing a goddess, like being hand-picked by the heavens to surrender your heart forever in exchange for just one, tender, earth-shattering moment.

I surrendered to that moment, to that sacrifice, letting my hands wander her curves, my lips savoring the pressure of hers, my tongue tasting the sweet taste buds of her own. I pulled her closer — tugging, reaching — until she straddled me on the couch.

But when the heat of her center rubbed against my hard-on, I bit her bottom lip, sucking in a groan and releasing her mouth on a panting breath that felt like I'd been sucked back down to Earth and landed flat on my back.

"Stop," I breathed, pressing my forehead against hers.

Ruby Grace's chest heaved, her hands still under my shirt, lips parted.

I swallowed. "I don't want you."

Her face crumbled at that, brows bending together as she pulled back to look at me.

"Not like this," I clarified. I reached under my shirt for her hands, folding them in mine and bringing her knuckles to my lips. "I have thought about kissing you since the day you showed up at the distillery, Ruby Grace. And I'd be lying if I said I'd never thought of doing more. But, I... I *can't*. Not now. Not when you're torn up over another man."

The level of hurt on her face in that moment was enough to make me wish

I'd never opened my door in the first place. I knew that kind of hurt — it was rejection. And *God*, it killed me that I'd been the one to put it there.

But I couldn't lie to myself, or to her. I wanted her more than I could say, but that didn't change the fact that she still wore another man's ring on her finger.

I waited for her to curse, to slap me, to crawl off my lap and slam my door in my face as she stormed out of my house and maybe even out of my life completely.

Instead, she let out a relieved breath, shoulders folding forward as she squeezed my hands that held hers.

"Tonight has nothing to do with him and you know it," she breathed.

My heart was a stallion in my rib cage, thunderous and powerful, steady and strong.

"We've *both* known it," she continued. "And I've tried to fight it, tried to convince myself that what I felt when I was with you was wrong, that it wasn't real." She shook her head. "But it *is* real. I'm just sorry it took me so long, that it took *this,* for me to finally admit that to myself."

I searched her eyes, and when I found nothing but sincerity there, I didn't know if I wanted to jump and throw my fist in the air or curl into her and fucking sob.

Because I felt it — right then and there on my couch on a normal, summer, Saturday afternoon in Stratford, Tennessee — I felt it and I knew.

The ring on her finger didn't matter anymore.

She was *mine*.

And I was hers.

As if to hammer that point home, she kept her eyes locked on mine as she reached down, slipping the ring off her finger and leaning back to deposit it somewhere on the coffee table before she slipped her hands back beneath my shirt.

"Now," she said, rolling her hips just enough to elicit a stiff breath from me. "I'm going to ask you to kiss me again, Noah Becker. And I won't ask you twice."

My lips were on hers before she could even say the words.

Chapter Fourteen

Ruby Grace

Dark.

Everything was dark.

Outside, the sun was shining, another bright summer day in Tennessee. But inside Noah's bedroom, where he was currently kissing me and backing me up — slowly, step by step — it was all dark.

Dark walls. Dark comforter. Dark curtains covering the window and blocking the sun's light from sneaking through. Blind caresses in the black space between us — lips and necks and hands and sighs. Dark intentions, dark promises waiting to be fulfilled.

His dark hair in my hands, my dark heart in his.

He was just a shadow as he held me, his kisses touching me like a sweet, soft, summer midnight on a tropical island.

I didn't realize how much a kiss could feel like a vacation.

I didn't realize how much a person could feel like home.

"I've wanted to kiss you for so long," he breathed against my lips, breaking contact just long enough to whisper the words before his mouth claimed mine again. "And now, I don't think I'll ever be able to stop."

Every breath was a trembling, shallow sip of air. My body didn't know how to react with new hands on me, with new lips, a new tongue, a new feeling. I didn't want to think about another man in that moment, but I couldn't help it. Because I remembered my first kiss with Anthony.

And it was *nothing* like this.

Noah's hands held my face like I was the treasure he'd hunted for his entire life and finally found. He peppered me with kisses before holding me to him longer, slowing it all down, caressing my lips with passionate, silky kisses. He'd slip his tongue inside my mouth, taste me, draw my bottom lip between his teeth and release it on a groan that I felt all the way to my toes.

This wasn't just a kiss.

This was a dream, a fantasy — and every part of my body surrendered to the impossible realism of it all.

Noah backed me up farther, his hands sliding down to the small of my back to guide me, and when the back of my legs hit the edge of his bed, he stopped, holding me steady.

"Ruby Grace," he whispered, kissing me again before I could answer.

"Yes," I barely breathed in return.

"Can I take this dress off you?"

"*Yes.*"

The word was a longing sigh falling from my lips, and as soon as it had, Noah trailed his fingertips down my arms, hands rolling into fists at my sides and bunching the fabric of my dress up with it. He captured my mouth even harder, sucking in a breath on a passionate kiss before he broke away and lifted the dress up and over my head.

My arms were still in the air when he threw my dress somewhere behind him, and he reached up, meeting my hands with his own as he kissed me again. He wound his fingertips with mine, and somehow, what his hands did to mine was even more sensual than the kiss, than his t-shirt on my half-naked body, than his hard-on pressing through the fabric of his black sweatpants.

I didn't ask to take his clothes off. Instead, I trailed my hands down, his fingers following mine until I slipped them between us. His hands found my waist as mine dove beneath the band of his sweatpants. I trailed my fingertips from hip bone to hip bone, just under the band, and I groaned when I realized he didn't have briefs on beneath.

"You surprised me," he mused with a smirk. "Didn't have time for underwear."

"Would have just gotten in the way," I breathed. Then, I gathered the hem of his shirt in my hands and tugged.

Noah lifted his arms, letting me strip him before he reached around me and unhooked my bra.

I inhaled a stiff breath when he slipped the straps of it over my shoulders, the fabric eliciting a wave of chills as he dragged it down my arms and let it fall on the floor between us. His eyes dipped to my exposed breasts for just the smallest moment before he found my eyes again, his Adam's apple bobbing hard in his throat.

Then, his lips were on mine again.

My knees buckled when he pressed me back farther, and I fell into his sheets. His lips never left mine as he helped guide me up, crawling over me, every part of him towering over every part of me as he settled between my legs. I sighed when the warmth of his bare chest brushed my nipples, and the heat of him lined up with the heat of me, only his sweatpants and my tiny strap of a thong separating us.

Noah pulled back, balancing on his elbows above me as he searched my eyes, my hair, every centimeter of my face. He seemed to be tracing lines between my freckles — first with his eyes, and then with the tender tip of his finger.

"God, Ruby Grace," he whispered, shaking his head. "What are you doing to me? I feel like I'm under your spell."

I smirked, rolling my hips against his. "The real question is, what should I do to you *next*?"

Noah groaned at the contact, biting his lower lip and kissing me hard before he pulled back again, this time peppering my collarbone with kisses and shifting his weight.

"*You* aren't going to do anything to me. Not yet. Not before I get my turn."

The chuckle I meant to give in response was lost in my throat, kidnapped by a gasp that ripped through me at the shock of his mouth on my sensitive nipple. He sucked gently, rolling his tongue over the puckered tip before trailing over to the other. He massaged the weight of each breast in his hands, his mouth devouring me like I was the sweetest dessert.

And then, he trailed down.

His lips wandered like lost travelers over the hills and valleys of my rib cage, sliding down the middle of my abdomen, traipsing the freckles between my hips before he settled on his elbows between my thighs. His eyes were dark and hooded as he gazed up at me, and with that look of sin holding me captive, he pressed one, feather-light kiss to the wet center of my panties.

I moaned, back arching up off the bed as my fists twisted in the sheets. When he slipped his thumbs under the straps of my thong and slowly trailed it down my thighs, I couldn't help but watch, and I loved the way his eyes darkened even more when I was bare beneath him.

I'd never had anyone that up close and personal to my vagina.

Anthony never went down on me, and as far as I was concerned, it was just something that happened in the romance movies Betty loved to force me to watch. But the second Noah had my panties off my ankles and dropped somewhere off the bed, he dragged his tongue up the inside of each of my thighs, and then, he pressed that same brush of a kiss to the same spot.

But nothing was between us this time.

Every inch of me trembled at the warmth of that kiss, and even more so at the loss of it. I gripped onto the sheets again, like they could ground me, like somehow they could steady my shaking nerves.

"You're trembling, Legs," Noah whispered against the spot he'd just kissed, his breath hot and wet and sending another wave of chills over me.

"I'm so nervous I feel like I'm about to pass out."

The words flew out before I thought better of them, and Noah laughed, pulling away long enough to look up at me. "Why nervous? It's just me. It's just us."

"I know," I said, shifting until I was on my elbows and could meet his gaze. "I just... I've never..." I didn't even want to say it, so I just nodded to where he was between my legs. "You know."

His face sobered. "A man has never eaten your pussy before?"

A fierce blush shaded my cheeks at the *p* word.

What, am I twelve?

"Never," I think I said. I wasn't sure if I just moved my lips or if an actual sound came out.

"Not even your *fiancé?*"

I shook my head.

For a moment, anger flashed in his eyes, and he shook his head again, jaw muscles ebbing and flowing in tense little pops. Then, he let out a long breath and met my gaze again. "Well, just proves to me once again that he's a fucking idiot. And now I'm hell bent on devouring your pussy until you have the best orgasm of your goddamn life."

I swallowed, the blush on my cheeks paling immediately as my fists twisted in the sheets. Noah glanced at my hands, and a devilish smirk spread on his handsome-as-hell face.

"Hold on tight."

Without another tease, or so much as a warning, his mouth was on me.

On me — as in, his lips surrounded my clit, his tongue tracing the sensitive bud in a circular rhythm before he dragged it back and forth in slow, long rolls.

I fell back into the sheets, my entire body convulsing at the feel of his expert tongue. I couldn't wrap my head around anything he was doing, and as soon as I felt like I was used to the sensation, his tongue would start a new pattern, or he'd suck my clit between his teeth, or drag his tongue between my lips and dive inside me before returning to my clit.

Every second was a new feeling, a new reason to shake, a new thief of breath.

"Yep," Noah said, kissing the inside of my thigh as he ran his hand up over my knee. "He's a fucking idiot. Because you have the sweetest pussy, Ruby Grace."

I didn't have time to blush or moan or bite my lip because in the next breath, he slid one finger inside me, right up to the knuckle.

I was so wet, he slid right in, but I still felt every inch of him stretching me open. I gasped, head rolling back in the pillow, fists abandoning the sheets to fly back and hang onto the top of his headboard. I needed friction. I needed grounding. I needed *something* to keep me from flying out of this universe entirely at the feel of him inside me *and* sucking me at the same time.

My mind raced, trying to piece it all together as Noah worked between my legs. I'd never felt so cherished, so worshipped. Having a man between my legs was somehow the most powerful experience, and I reveled in it, letting every time I'd ever wanted to touch him or kiss him build up in my memory before I'd remind myself that it was happening. That time was now.

Noah Becker had his face between my legs, and I was like a prisoner surrendering willingly to whatever consequence lay before us after this moment.

It didn't matter. *Nothing* mattered.

Nothing but this man and this moment.

Noah stayed between my thighs for hours. I was certain of it. It *had* to be hours. After working me open, he slipped another finger inside me, his tongue rolling in a new way as he curled his fingers inside me. And I felt it building, like a slow, glowing ember that caught oxygen and exploded into flames with another flick of his tongue.

"Noah," I breathed, heart racing, legs trembling. "Oh, God. Noah. *Noah.*"

His free hand gripped my ass, pulling me even more into him, the other working its magic inside me. And when he circled my clit faster, faster, giving me the friction I needed, I completely spiraled.

Sheets and headboard be damned. I flew into the atmosphere, every part of me alive and burning, stars invading my vision as I succumbed to the darkness and panted out each rolling, euphoric wave of my orgasm.

I was floating.

I was soaring.

I was nothing at all and everything I'd ever wanted to be.

My heart was still racing in my chest, breaths loud and heavy in the space between us as Noah slowly climbed his way back up, trailing kisses along the way. When he settled between my already sore legs again, he smirked, brushing my wild hair away from my face and kissing me.

I tasted me on him, tangy and sweet.

"That was hot," he said, his words reverberating through me. "*You* are hot."

"Noah," I breathed, threading my fingers through his hair and pulling his mouth to mine. I kissed him long and hard, feverishly, like my next breath had to be syphoned from that kiss. "I want you inside me."

He let out a shaky breath, pressing his forehead to mine. "Are you sure?"

I nodded, pulling at him again, nails on his back and in his hair and everywhere I could grab until he pushed off me, standing at the edge of the bed. He kept his eyes on mine, a hard swallow marking his throat as he reached for the band of his sweatpants. He bent, taking them down with the motion, and when he stood again, I forgot my next breath.

I just stared, mouth open, heart stopping along with my lungs before they both kicked back to life.

Oh, God.

I'd felt him against me when he was on top, his erection pressed into my stomach, but even that couldn't have prepared me for what I was face to face with now.

"Don't be scared," he said, worry etched in his brows as he stepped toward me. The monster between his legs was hard and thick in his hand, and he stroked it once, twice, three times before he rounded the bed and sat down next to me. His back was against the headboard, his legs out in front of him, and I edged my way up until my back was against the headboard, too.

He was pumping, swallowing, watching my expression.

I was still staring between his legs.

"Come here," he said, voice low and raspy. He reached for my hand, and when I met his fingertips with my own, he locked eyes with me, moving us both until my hand was on his shaft.

His eyes closed at the touch. My mouth fell open again.

And slowly, carefully, I wrapped my hand around him and slid it down, down, all the way to the base before I rolled it back up.

A heavy breath broke through his nose, and his hand left mine, reaching for my thigh, instead. He squeezed, letting me explore, letting me stroke him — gently, slowly, his erection growing harder and harder with each pump.

I wanted him inside me.

I knew it would hurt. I knew I likely wasn't ready to fit all of him in me. But, I wanted to try. I *needed* to know what it felt like to be connected with him in that way — nothing between us, no beginning of him or ending of me — just one, blissful being.

I swallowed past the knot in my throat as I released his shaft, his eyes creaking open at the loss of my hand. He watched me with that heated stare as I crawled into his lap, my hands balancing on the headboard behind him as I lowered down.

His thick shaft slipped between my lips, and I rolled my hips, sliding my wet core up and down his erection. Each time I rolled, the tip of his shaft would rub my clit as the rest of him floated between my soaked lips, and I moaned, letting my head fall back at the sensation and gripping the headboard even tighter.

"Jesus Christ," he cursed. Prayed? "That feels so good. I'm not even inside you yet. How does that feel *so* fucking good?"

I moaned in response, still rolling my hips, coating him with my orgasm and feeling another one building in the process. When he was nice and wet, I reached down, bringing my gaze to his as I wrapped my hand around his cock.

"Condom?" I breathed.

Noah wrapped one arm around me, holding me in his lap as he leaned over and dug in the drawer of his bedside table. His hands disappeared behind my back when we were righted, and I heard the tear of the wrapper, felt him pull his shaft from my grip and cover it with the latex, and then, his hands were on my hips again, his eyes on mine, all the control in my hands.

I swallowed, forcing a shaky breath before I reached back again. He pulsed in my hand, hard and ready, and when I lined up the tip of him with my entrance, we both stopped.

Our breathing stopped.

Time stopped.

And I lowered, just an inch, just enough for everything in the universe to snap back into action.

We breathed a sigh of ecstasy in sync, and I lifted my hips before sliding down even farther, taking him a little more. Each time I lifted, each time I sank down on him a little more, our breathing accelerated. Noah groaned when I swallowed him whole, feeling the stretching burn from the inside out, and for a moment I just stayed there — him completely inside me, his hands bruising my hips, the moment branding my heart.

I lifted, sank back down.

Rolled my hips.

Rubbed my clit against his pelvis.

"*Fuuuuck,*" he groaned, wrapping his arms around me as he sat up a little more. We were chest to chest, and he held one strong arm around me while the other slid up my back, his hand cradling my head and pulling it into him. He pressed his forehead to mine, closing his eyes as he flexed his hips, and I whimpered, feeling the extra inch of him I couldn't reach on my own.

I didn't know sex could feel like this.

I didn't know anything in the *world* could feel like this.

It wasn't a hard, pounding fuck, the way Anthony loved to take me. It wasn't minutes of panting and then a heady, quick release and roll off of me.

This was art.

This was Noah, the painter, his hands the brushes, me the canvas.

This was me, the muse, feeling every breath of his like the fire that fueled my existence.

We were slick with sweat, rolling and slipping over each other as I rocked and he flexed, his mouth finding mine, kissing me with reverence as sighs and moans mingled between us. They seemed to dance in time with our movements — a thrust, a sigh, a flex, a kiss, a roll, a moan.

It was a beautiful waltz.

And we danced for hours.

I came again, rolling my clit against him as he flexed into me, and then he rolled us until I was on my stomach, my face in the pillows, back arched up off the bed and ass up in the air — waiting. He entered me from behind, and the sheer sensation of that new depth of penetration shocked both of us.

I sucked in a breath.

He groaned out my name.

And in the next breath, he came, pulsing his release inside the condom as he pumped in and out of me, over and over, until every drop was expelled.

For a long moment, he stayed there, balanced on his hands above me as I released my grip on the sheets. Our breaths slowed, chests aching with the release of air, and he gently withdrew, discarding the condom in the trashcan by his bed before he collapsed back onto the bed.

I didn't have time to even reach for my panties before he pulled me into him, surrounding me with his arms, his legs, hands weaving into my hair, breath skating over the skin of my neck.

And I didn't know how to fight what happened next.

My eyes welled with tears, nose stinging as the dam broke loose, and as soon as those tears hit Noah's chest, he pulled back, worried eyes searching mine.

"I'm sorry," I whispered, wiping at one before Noah took my place, his thumbs brushing over my wet cheeks. "I don't know why I'm crying."

"It's okay," he responded, voice just as low. "I do."

My brows pulled together, eyes flicking back and forth between his. "You do?"

He nodded. "I felt it, too, Ruby Grace," he said, pulling me back into him and surrounding me with his heat, with his weight. "I felt it, too."

I closed my eyes, two more tears slipping free as I pulled him closer, wanting more, needing to seam us together in every way possible. It didn't feel real, the whole experience morphing in my mind like a dream I was suddenly aware of, a dream I was about to wake up from.

So, I held on tight, willing it to be true, willing *him* to be real.

My body succumbed to the darkness, my mind following quickly, every part of me slipping into the promising black space around us like it was the open arms of a long-lost friend.

If he was a dream, I would sleep, just so I could keep him a little longer.

I'd sleep, and maybe — just maybe — I'd wake on a day where I got to keep him forever.

• • •

Noah

God, I don't want to wake her.

It was all I could think the next morning as I sat on the edge of my bed, watching Ruby Grace sleep. Her hair had fallen out of the tie she'd fastened it in at some point in the night, and wild, red tendrils splayed over my pillow like flower petals. Her mouth was open just a bit, one leg kicked out of the sheets, eyes fluttering a bit behind her lids.

She was dreaming.

I hoped it was of me.

I sighed, watching her with a sinking feeling in my gut. She hadn't stirred since we fell asleep together, which was late afternoon yesterday, other than when I'd woken her up somewhere around midnight because her sweet ass was rubbing against my erection. We'd slowly made love, both of us on our sides, our eyes still closed, and as soon as we'd both reached our climax, she'd passed out again.

But my body woke me again at five — craving her, craving so, *so* much more of her.

So, I crawled out of bed — begrudgingly — and got a workout in.

I needed to do *something* with all the pent-up energy.

And the entire time I did my calisthenics, I thought about the girl in my bed. I ran over my memories of the night, searing into my mind what it felt like to touch her so I'd never forget it. And beneath all of that, I worked through the heavier feeling in my chest, the one that was as foreign as it was somehow familiar.

It was deeper than sex.

Now that I'd had her, I knew I couldn't live in a world where I *didn't*.

I wanted to let her in, let her see all of me, and I wanted to see all of her, in return.

While I'd spent the morning working out and planning every word I wanted to say to her, and knowing exactly *where* I wanted to take her to say it all, she'd been here, in my bed, sleeping. Knocked out. Completely exhausted.

After everything that had happened yesterday, I knew she needed rest, and I didn't want to take that from her.

But it was Sunday in Stratford, and there wasn't an excuse outside of being dead that could get Ruby Grace Barnett out of going to church.

I was still a little sweaty from my workout as I swept a strand of her hair from her face, running my fingertip down the line of her jaw. She stirred a little, stretching her arms up above her head and pointing her toes before her eyes fluttered open.

The moment they locked with mine, she smiled.

And my heart nearly burst at the sight of that sleepy smile.

"Well, good morning," she said, voice raspy. "You're sweaty."

I chuckled. "And you're sleepy."

She groaned, rubbing her eyes. "I really am. I feel like I could sleep for years."

"Here," I said, offering her the cup of hot tea I'd made her. "Earl Grey. Just a little bit of caffeine, but it should help."

She took it in thanks, scooting up until she was seated against the headboard, and after her first sip, she hummed.

"That's good," she said, wrapping her hands around the warm mug.

My sheets pooled at her waist, but her breasts were bare, exposed, just sitting there right in front of me in all their perky glory. Ruby Grace followed my gaze and gave me a knowing smirk.

"Whatcha thinking about, Noah Becker?"

"Just you, Ruby Grace," I mused, meeting her gaze again. "Always you."

Her eyes softened, one hand leaving the mug and reaching out for mine. She folded her palm over my knuckles, lacing her fingers with mine, a thumb brushing my wrist.

"Tell me last night was real," she whispered.

I swallowed, squeezing her hand in mine. "It was real," I promised her. "It was perfect."

She nodded, closing her eyes on a smile before she took another sip of her tea. For a while, we just sat there, eyes wandering over the other, gentle smiles on our lips. There was so much I wanted to tell her in that moment, so much I wanted to make known, but I knew it wasn't the right time. Or the right place. There were things I needed to do before I made my big gesture, before I showed her the way it could be, if she were to choose me.

If she were to give me the honor of being the next man she called her own.

"I want to take you somewhere," I said after a while, smoothing my thumb over her palm. "Will you go somewhere with me?"

"Where?"

I shook my head. "I don't want to tell you. Not yet. But... will you go with me?"

She leaned up, placing her mug on the bedside table before she took my face in her hands. "Anywhere."

I smiled.

"But, not today," she said next. "Today, I need to deal with... all of *this*." She gestured to the space around us, as if her former fiancé and her family and the rest of the town were right there in my bedroom with us. Then, she turned my hand over, checking the time on my heart monitor watch with another groan. "Starting with church. In like an hour."

I chuckled. "I understand."

Reaching for her hand again, I squeezed it in mine, frowning as I watched her. She was so young — *too* young to be faced with the hardship she was about to endure. It wasn't going to be easy to break off an engagement, espe-cially not in this town.

And *especially* not with her family.

"Why don't you take a few days?" I offered. "I'll be right here, but you do what you have to do. Okay?"

Her lips formed a brief smile before it fell again. "Okay. Yeah. I think that's best."

"Do you want me to come with you? To be with you for any of it?"

She sighed at that. "No," she said, rubbing her free hand down her face. "As much as I know it'd be easier that way, this is something I need to handle on my own."

"I get that," I said, lacing our fingertips together. "How about you save Friday for me, then?"

"Friday," she mused.

I nodded. "Gives me some time to get everything together."

At that, she cocked a beautiful eyebrow. "What are you planning, Noah Becker?"

"That's for me to know and you to find out, Ruby Grace Barnett," I retorted, kissing her nose, her cheeks, and then capturing her lips. She inhaled at the connection, breathing into me, a sigh leaving her lips when I finally pulled back.

Her mouth curved into a playful smile. "Last night, you said I have strawberry smoothie lips."

"You do," I said, running my thumb over said lips. The bottom one stuck to my skin, pulling down to expose her teeth before it popped back up.

That sight shot electricity straight down to my cock.

I groaned, shaking my head and readjusting myself in my shorts as I slid my hand back into her hair. "I thought that the first time I saw you back in town. And every day since, I wondered if they tasted like a strawberry smoothie, too."

"And do they?"

I shook my head, leaning in to kiss her and elicit another breathy sigh.

I decided it was my new favorite sound.

"Better," I murmured against her lips. "They taste even better."

Chapter Fifteen

Ruby Grace

Church felt like the Gravitron from the Tennessee State Fair that morning. One minute, I was smiling like a loon, stomach flipping as I replayed every moment with Noah the night before.

The next, that stomach flip would turn into more of a roll, and I'd lurch forward, feeling like I was going to vomit any minute.

In the course of twenty-four hours, everything had changed.

I glanced down at the ring on my finger — the one I'd put back on before leaving Noah's — and bile rose in my throat again. I couldn't wait to take it off. I couldn't wait to shake off the weight of the wedding to a man who didn't love me, who didn't care about anything other than what I would look like on his arm, what my family could do for his campaign.

I felt like the biggest fool, but soon, it would be *him* who felt that way.

Still, I knew my stomach wouldn't stop turning — not until it was all said and done, and maybe even then, too. I didn't know where to start, who to tell first, and I didn't have any way of knowing what to expect once our house of cards crumbled.

Our friends would be shocked.

The town would gossip.

Mama's heart would be broken, no doubt.

And Daddy? I had no idea how he would take the news. Part of me wondered if he'd disown me, if I'd even be able to call myself a Barnett by the end of the week.

Part of me didn't care, as long as I was free of the man who had lied to me for the past year.

And maybe that was what upset me most — that under all the anxiety over what was to come, I was still heartbroken over what had happened. The man I had promised my forever to wasn't the man I thought I knew at all, and as much as I wished I didn't hurt over that fact, as much as I wished Noah being with me the night before fixed everything, it didn't.

I had still been betrayed.

My heart fluttered at the thought of Noah, a small smile curving on my lips. I reached up, smoothing my fingertips over the bottom one, remembering how it felt when his tongue swept across the sensitive skin.

The way he touched me, the way he made love to me…

It was unlike anything I'd ever experienced.

How could I feel more passion and care in one night with that man than I felt in an entire year with the one I promised to marry?

As if he could sense I was thinking of him, Noah stretched his arms up over his head, resting them on the back of the pew before he did a casual scan of the congregation like he wasn't just trying to look back at me.

But he did.

When our eyes locked, every shred of doubt, every fear faded.

He smiled.

I smiled.

And then I counted down the minutes until I could be in his arms again.

• • •

"Mama, can we talk?"

She was in the kitchen, baking her famous lemon squares for her meeting with the women's circle at church the next day. Her auburn hair was up in a messy bun — which Mama never did, unless she was stressed, cleaning, or baking.

Sometimes, it was a combination of the three.

"Sure, sweetie. Just let me get these in the oven and we can pull up the seating chart again."

I shifted. "It's actually not about the seating chart."

"Oh," she said, opening the oven and sliding the baking sheet of squares inside before she popped it closed again. "Is it the registry? I know we're a little behind, but we can get it all done before next Sunday. Most people wait until the last minute to buy gifts for the shower, anyway."

"Mama," I said, taking a seat at the kitchen island. "It's important."

I set the ring Anthony had given me on the counter with a gentle *clink*, metal hitting granite, and it was as if that sound alone stopped Mama in her tracks.

She stopped right in front of the sink, one hand under the faucet and the other ready to turn it on, but she never did. Instead, she just stood like that, glancing at the ring, at me, back at the ring, at me again.

Her face paled, and she turned back to the sink, kicking on the faucet with her wrist before running her hands under the water. "We still need to decide what readings you want to do during the ceremony. I was thinking we should do something fresh. Corinthians is so overdone."

My heart squeezed.

"Mama."

"And you know, maybe we *should* do the twine like you wanted. Instead of the coral ribbon." She dried her hands haphazardly on one of the towels hanging from the oven, immediately launching into clean up. "You were right, that would look so much classier."

"Mama."

"And we need to go in for your final fitting on Friday. Don't forget that."

"Mama!"

She winced, shutting her eyes and hanging her head between her shoulders with the sponge in her hand. She shook her head, eyes still closed, and I knew in her mind she was praying to God that I hadn't actually taken my ring off.

"Please," I begged her, my own throat tightening. "Can you please sit down?"

She sniffed, dropping the sponge on the counter and sitting at the stool across from me. She wouldn't look at me. She kept her eyes on her hands, which were folded now, her right fingers playing with the ring that adorned her left.

I inhaled a deep breath once she was seated, once the ball was in my court. Dad and Anthony had gone out for the evening, back to the casino, and after talking to Annie first, she'd helped me decide that Mom was the first person I should tell in the family. From there, I could make a plan to talk to Anthony, to Dad, and figure out how to break the news to our close friends and family — and to the town.

If there was one thing Mama excelled at, it was damage control.

"I need your help," I finally said.

She lifted her head a little, her worried eyes finding mine.

"I overheard Anthony on the phone yesterday," I explained, and tears flooded my eyes, the shivers too much as I tried to steady my shaking hands by stuffing them between my thighs and the barstool. "He said some really awful things."

"Men say awful things all the time," she replied quickly. "They're stupid. And half the time, drunk."

"He was sober."

"Whatever he said, I'm sure he didn't mean it."

"I'm calling off the wedding."

Her eyes closed, and she shook her head, inhaling a deep breath before she opened her eyes again. This time, she held her shoulders back, her chin high, eyes locking with mine. "No, you most certainly are not, young lady."

"I am. And I need your help, because we both know this is going to take a lot of damage control."

"You're not calling off the wedding!" she hissed, whispering as if someone might overhear. "You can't," she said, voice calmer.

"He said he fully intends on cheating on me," I said, as gently as I could with those being the words coming from my mouth. "He said I'm perfect to fit the *role* he needs his dutiful wife to play. He said I was *bred for this*."

"And you were."

My mouth fell open. "I'm not a horse, Mother."

"No, but you *are* the daughter of the Mayor of Stratford, and you *are* a Barnett. Do you understand the implications of what you're saying? If you called off this wedding, the entire town would have something to say about it. You'd make our family a laughingstock. You'd bring us *shame*."

"And if I *don't* call off this wedding, I will be miserable for the rest of my life."

Mom threw her hands up, rolling her eyes. "Oh, for heaven's sake. So what, he wants to have some girls on the side. You think he's the only husband to ever have that thought? Your father has had many a secretary in his day, and you know what? It never mattered to me. Because it was *me* who had the house, and the kids, and the life I always wanted. Those girls, those *hussies*?" She shook her head. "They were just sex, sweetheart. It means nothing."

My mouth fell open wider. "Dad cheated on you?"

She waved me off. "Don't be so dramatic. It's not a big deal. And neither is any of that stuff Anthony said. He cares about you, Ruby Grace. He wants to provide for you, give you a home and a place to raise your children. He'll make sure you never want for anything."

"He doesn't love me, Mama," I whispered.

"What does love have to do with marriage?"

My heart broke again, this time by the realization that the love I thought my parents had was a sham. My father had cheated. My mother had stayed anyway. They weren't in love, they were in a business agreement.

But I would not do the same.

"Everything," I said. "It has *everything* to do with marriage. I refuse to marry a man who doesn't love me, who sees me as a prize or another tick on his list of things to get done in order to make it to a run for president someday. I'm a human being. I'm a woman. I deserve a man who will love and honor and cherish me, just as I do him."

"Anthony will do all those things."

"While he cheats on me? While he tells his father that I have no ambitions and I'm *pretty, so that's a bonus*?" I scoffed. "Mother, do you hear yourself?"

"You are not calling off this wedding," she said, ignoring me and shaking her head. She stood again, crossing to the sponge and picking up where she left off cleaning.

"I am."

"You are not."

"Mama, I—"

"You can't!" she screamed, turning in place. The sponge fell to the floor and her hands flew to her face, sobs racking through her in the next instant.

It was just like I'd thought

I broke her heart.

"Oh, Mama," I said, rounding the island and sweeping her into my arms. I held her tight, holding back my own tears. "I'm so sorry."

"No, no," she said, sniffing and swiping at the tears on her face as she pulled back from my embrace. "You don't understand. You *can't* call off the wedding." Her eyes found mine. "We made a deal, Ruby Grace. With Anthony and his father."

My blood ran cold. "A deal?"

Anthony's words swam in my head.

They need us to play our part, just like we need Ruby Grace to play hers.

Mom winced, her face screwing up before a few more tears were let loose. She swiped them away. "Honey, your father was in trouble."

"Trouble?" I asked. "What kind of trouble?"

"Well," she said on a sigh. "You know him and his card games. At the casino, he's fine. Once he runs out of the money he came to play with, that's it. And I keep a tight leash on what he's allowed to piss away." She let out a breath, brows quivering again. "But, I didn't know. I didn't know he'd been playing at the underground casino, the one the Scooters run out of their basement. I knew he went sometimes, just to show face, network, but I never thought..."

"Mom," I interrupted. "What kind of trouble?"

She sniffed, running the back of her hand under her nose. "He was taking loans from them at the casino for cards, sure he would win and pay them back. But he kept coming up in the red. Over and over again." She shook her head. "He didn't even tell me until the Scooters threatened to expose everything if we didn't pay up."

I covered my mouth.

No.

"We were going to lose *everything*, Ruby Grace," Mom said, reaching forward to grab my free hand in hers. "The house. The cars. *Everything*. He was in an amount of debt we couldn't even dream of repaying."

"But, he's the mayor," I said, lip trembling. "He's always made good money. We're fine."

Mom shook her head. "He never made money like this."

I dropped my hand from my mouth, shaking my head. "I don't understand."

"We were in deep, trying to figure out what our options were, when Anthony came to your father to ask for your hand," she explained. "And... well... we saw an out. We saw a way to make our problem disappear, and Anthony saw a way to get what he needed, too."

My blood ran cold.

It couldn't be.

It couldn't possibly be my mother standing across from me, speaking about me as if I was some old antique china cabinet or a prized hog to be bartered with.

But it was.

And suddenly, the betrayal I *thought* I'd felt from Anthony was nothing.

"How could you?" I whispered, shaking my head as tears flooded my eyes.

"I'm so sorry, baby," she said, reaching for me.

I yanked away.

"It was our only choice. We would have lost everything."

"Yeah? Well, now you lose *me*," I spat, turning on my heels. "I'm calling off the wedding."

"Ruby Grace! Please!"

She grabbed me from behind, spinning me around to see the devastation in her eyes — the *desperation* in her eyes.

"This is your family," she said through her tears. "This is your father, and your mother, and your sister. This is your family's legacy, the Barnett name, our entire reputation. This is more than just a wedding. This is the only way to save our family from complete and utter wreckage." She stood taller. "And I understand it isn't fair. I do. And I am so, *so* sorry that you are in the middle of this." Mama swallowed, like she didn't like the taste of the next words she was about to speak. "But, you are a part of this family. And that means that when a fire happens, you do whatever you have to do to put it out."

My next breath felt like the fire she spoke of. It was hot in my lungs, searing every fiber of muscle and organ around it. I whimpered at the feel, at my mother's hands on my arms, at the plea she was giving.

"You cannot walk out on this family," she said, tears building in her eyes once more. "We are a unit. We stay together — *always* — and we will get through this together. But we need you, Ruby Grace. Your father needs you. Your sister needs you. *I* need you."

I couldn't speak, couldn't think, couldn't *breathe*. Every muscle in my body was locked in place, heart racing, pulse heavy in my ears.

"You can call off the wedding," she finally said. "But if you do, you're calling off this family, too."

My mother's eyes searched mine in a way they never had before, in a way I never knew they could. I'd never seen my strong, commanding mother look so broken, so desperate, so on the verge of losing it. She looked at me like I was the key to everything, and I realized in that moment that I was.

She was right.

This wasn't just about me anymore.

And bile rose in my throat at what that meant.

We both jumped a little when the front door opened, Dad calling in from the foyer that he and Anthony were home. Mom's eyes doubled in size when they looked back at me, her pupils dilating as they flicked back and forth.

She needed an answer.

She needed to know what I would do.

She needed to know if she was safe, if our family was okay, or if everything was about to be blown to smithereens.

"Mmm, are those lemon squares I smell?" Dad asked, his voice closer now. He and Anthony would round into the kitchen at any moment, and either everything would be exactly as they left it, or nothing would be the same again.

Time was up.

And I had to make the hardest decision of my life.

Mom sucked in a breath when I pulled out of her grasp, but I didn't meet her eyes again as I made my way to the island.

Just as Dad and Anthony swung into the kitchen, I slipped the ring back on my finger.

Chapter Sixteen

Noah

I could barely contain my excitement when Friday finally came around.

All week long, my thoughts had been tied up in Ruby Grace.

When I was working, I'd watch my hands make whiskey barrels, but in my head, I remembered the way they looked like making Ruby Grace squirm in my bed. When I was at home, I saw her everywhere — on my couch, in my bed, in my shower. When I visited Mom in the middle of the week for a surprise dinner, I thought of Ruby Grace, of how one day I would dance with *her* in *our* kitchen.

I was in too deep, too fast. I knew it. I tried to hold myself back, but it was pointless.

I'd had a taste of her, and now, I wouldn't rest until I had all of her, too.

To pass the time that work didn't take up, I worked on my surprise for Ruby Grace. I knew exactly what I would say to tell her what I'd done, and where I'd take her to do it.

That's why, on Friday night, I asked her to meet me at Tank's stable at dusk.

I was getting him ready, brushing him and giving him a snack before I got him saddled up, when I saw a pair of familiar legs making their way down the hill.

The sun was setting, the clouds turning orange and pink and purple, casting a fairytale glow over the field of wildflowers Ruby Grace walked through to get to me. I paused where I was petting Tank, breath catching in my throat at the sight of her. She had her hands in the back pockets of the tiny jean shorts she wore, her long hair an illuminated orange and floating on the breeze behind her as she walked. She was so tanned from the summer, and the white, flowy tank top she wore just accentuated that bronze glow even more.

I swallowed, watching her take each step.

The closer she got, the more my heart raced.

I let out a whistle when she was close enough to hear, and as soon as I did, a grin split her face.

"Damn, Legs," I said, crossing my arms and not bothering to hide my eyes as they scanned her. "You should come with a warning label, you know that? *Warning: this woman will knock any unsuspecting man dead upon first glance. Proceed with caution.*"

She chuckled, shaking her head and stopping a few feet away from me. She crossed her arms to mirror mine. "You say that like you would have heeded the warning."

"Oh, I one-hundred percent would have disregarded it entirely," I said. Then, I opened my arms. "C'mere."

A tinge of sadness touched her eyes as she stepped into me. When I wrapped my arms around her, she rested her head on my chest, a deep sigh leaving her lips.

"Long day?" I asked.

"Long week," she answered, and her hands fisted at my back, twisting my flannel shirt in her grasp like she was in danger of me floating away. "Can you just hug me for a while?"

"For as long as you want," I answered easily.

She sighed again, turning her face until her forehead was buried in my chest. She held me tight, and I held her tighter, gently swaying us as the sun set. And though she seemed content there, *happy*, even — I couldn't shake the feeling that something was wrong.

It wasn't until Tank neighed, annoyed at the lack of attention, that Ruby Grace finally let me go.

"I see you, too, Tank," she said, voice soft as the smile on her face as she slipped out of my arms and over to him. She ran her hand over his neck, fingers touching his mane. "You look like you're ready for an adventure."

"I think he knows where we're going," I said. "It's one of his favorite places, too."

"And where exactly is it that we're going?"

I smiled, patting Tank's saddle. "Hop up and you'll find out."

We were both quiet on the trail, the only sound the rhythmic, soothing sound of Tank's hooves hitting the dirt and the soft buzzing of the insects coming alive as the sun set. I let my eyes wash over the lake, the tall weeds and flowers in the fields, the tall trees, their branches hanging over and shading the trail from time to time. And Ruby Grace rested her cheek between my shoulder blades, her arms wrapped around me, breathing soft.

Something was on her mind.

We hadn't talked much all week — mostly because I was honoring my promise to let her have her time to sort everything out. I had no idea what had happened since we parted, how she had broken the news to her family, to Anthony. I imagined they were still figuring out how to handle the fall out, since I hadn't heard anyone gossiping about it yet.

I knew that time would come. And I'd be there for her when it did.

"I think there's a storm coming," she mused, pointing to some building clouds in the distance. As if on cue, a soft roll of thunder made its way over the lake.

"Don't worry. We'll have shelter."

The sun had just dipped below the horizon when we reached our destination, and I pulled Tank to a stop, hopping down before tying him up to his favorite tree. It was right by the edge of the lake, and he could graze the grass next to it and get as much water as he wanted.

"Good boy," I said, rubbing his neck as I fished out an apple from my saddle pack.

"A treehouse?" Ruby Grace asked as I helped her down. She slid her hands in her back pockets as soon as her boots were on the ground, and I inhaled a stiff breath.

I was so jealous of those goddamn hands...

"This isn't just *a* treehouse," I told her. "This is *the* treehouse. It's in the best location, made from the sturdiest wood, and it has the absolute coolest hangout inside. It's award-winning. And usually, girls aren't allowed. But, you know, I'll make an exception just this once."

She smirked, nudging me with her shoulder as she scanned the treehouse.

It was nestled in an old, sturdy oak, with planks of wood hammered to the trunk that led all the way up to the door. It wasn't a luxurious treehouse, like the fancy ones that had plumbing and a bed. There were folks in town who built those kinds, mostly with the purpose of renting them out to tourists. But no, this was a *true* treehouse — built by a father with love for his sons.

Ruby Grace seemed to be taking in every corner of it, from the different-colored wood to the small windows and tin roof. Her hazel eyes swept over every inch.

And my eyes stayed on her.

"Can we go inside?"

I scoffed. "Of course. Why do you think we're here?" I unhooked my saddle bag, tossing it over my shoulder before I held my hand out for hers. "M'lady."

I helped Ruby Grace up the stairs first, popping the latch on the bottom door and keeping my hand on the small of her back as she climbed inside. When she plopped down on the floor and looked around, I reached up and to the right, flicking on the generator, and with it, all the string lights hanging inside.

And that's when Ruby Grace gasped.

"Wow," she breathed as I climbed the rest of the way up. I still couldn't take my eyes off her, not with her eyes wide like that, her mouth hanging open.

The inside of the treehouse was where the real magic lived.

There were eclectic rugs covering every space of the floor, collected over the years from places Mom and Dad traveled together. Four, giant bean bags large enough for at least two people each sat in every corner, and the corners were decorated to fit different styles — one for each brother.

Michael's had his old guitar leaned up against the wood, posters of his favorite southern rock bands taped to the walls. His corner used to be a lot younger, since he was only four when the house was first built. Over the years, he'd added to it, decorating it to fit his style the more he came into himself.

Logan's corner was two walls of very neatly organized bookshelves — his favorites and others that Dad bought for him to read throughout the years. They were ordered by author last name and then by color.

Jordan's had football legends ranging from last year all the way back to the early fifties, complete with a shelf of limited edition trading cards and a signed Tom Brady pig skin on a gold holder.

And mine was decorated with sailboats and constellations, with globes of all shapes and sizes, and a world map that spanned the entire wall behind my bean bag.

In the center was a large, square table where we would play board games, do puzzles, and have arm wrestling competitions. And above it all was a giant skylight window, revealing small branches of the tree and the now dark purple sky above.

"This is yours?"

I nodded. "Mine. And my brothers'. We all share it."

"I never knew this was out here," she mused, still taking it all in.

"Most people don't, not unless we bring them out here. And trust me when I say we don't bring many people out here. In fact, you're only the third guest outside of the family. At least, that I know of."

A smile bloomed over her face, eyes shining as they met mine. "Really?"

"Really."

"I feel special."

Her smile was sad, eyes worn.

I couldn't wait to get her mind off everything that put that sadness there.

"Good," I said, standing before I offered my hand down to her. "You are."

I helped her stand, and when she did, we were chest to chest, breath to breath, eyes dancing over lips. She swallowed, and that sadness she'd worn before crept back in, shading her eyes as she watched me.

I stamped down the feeling that something was off, choosing instead to slide my hands into her back pockets and pull her into me. She took a deep breath as my palms slid against the denim, and I cupped her gently, tugging her close.

"I'd like to kiss you, Ruby Grace," I whispered. My eyes flicked between hers, but her gaze was locked on my lips, her hands resting on my chest.

She didn't answer, just nodded, hands fisting in my shirt and pulling me closer as her chin angled up. I slipped my hands from her pockets, trailing my fingertips up over her arms before I slid my hands into her hair, cradling the bottom of her head, thumbs framing her jaw. She closed her eyes, a soft breath escaping her parted lips and touching mine before I closed the distance and kissed her.

Part of me wondered if the magic would fade, if now that we'd crossed the lines between us and taken each other when we knew it was wrong, if the chemistry would die. Maybe it was just lust. Maybe it was just me wanting someone I couldn't have.

The moment our lips touched, I knew it was more.

We both inhaled, like we'd been under water until our lips locked, and that was our first breath of oxygen in days. We drank each other in, hands roaming, pulling, touching, pleading. The kiss was gentle at first, just one long press of her lips to mine, but then we moved, lips opening and closing, tongues sweeping, teeth grazing the flesh tenderly.

She was shaking.

I was, too.

And when I pulled back, pressing my forehead to hers, we both let out a trembling exhale.

"I've wanted to do that all week," I confessed.

I thought she'd smile, or laugh, but if anything, her face seemed to crumple more. "Noah…"

"It's okay," I told her, pulling her into me. I wrapped my arms around her, resting my chin on the crown of her head. "I know it's been a long week. We don't have to get heavy yet. Here, let me show you something."

I grabbed her hand, leading her over to the aqua blue bean bag that was mine.

"Sit," I said, patting the giant chair. "You have to sit to get the full effect."

Ruby Grace obliged, a curious smile on her face once her cute butt was in the chair and her eyes were on me again. "Okay. Now what?"

I smiled. "Look up."

When she did, she gasped, eyes widening. "Whoa."

I plopped down in the chair next to her, shifting us until she was under my arm and we were both reclined back, our eyes on the tin ceiling. It was covered in pin-hole-sized dots that mirrored stars, building constellations that were illuminated by a light hanging outside the treehouse. The holes were covered by glass, shielding any outside weather, and Dad had painted the tin roof above my section a dark, navy blue to make it look like the night sky.

"Is that the Big Dipper?" she asked, pointing to the constellation.

I nodded. "Mm-hmm. And Orion's Belt, Scorpius, Lyra," I said, pointing to them as I called out their names. "There are more, but I can't remember them. Dad knew them all."

"Why are they only in this corner?"

"This is my corner of the tree house," I explained. "Dad built this for me and my brothers, and when he did, he tried to put a little bit of each of us in our own sections. At the time that he built it, I was hell bent on sailing around the world one day, and I had a big fascination with space and the constellations."

She smiled, eyes tracing the man-made stars. "Do you still want to? Sail around the world?"

I shrugged. "I mean, I think it'd be cool, but I think that desire shifted more to just traveling, in general. I'm so tied to this town, to the distillery, that I never leave. I want to change that in the coming years, get out and see the country, the world."

"I get that," Ruby Grace whispered. She opened her mouth to say something more, but paused, closing it again, instead.

I swallowed.

"My dad built this for us with the intention of us always having a safe place to run to. He never got upset if we wanted to take time out here, and he told us whenever we got angry, to come here and think it all through first before acting. And I mean, it wasn't *all* for angsty teenage boys," I said on a smirk. "We came out here just to have fun and hang out, too. But, it's been a safe place. For all of us. And I knew one day I'd bring someone out here, that I'd share it with them, I just didn't know who. Or when." I shifted, looking down at her in my arm. "I wanted to wait until it was the right time, the right person."

She pulled her gaze to mine, then, and her brows bent together. "Noah..."

"I know this has probably been one of the hardest weeks of your life," I said. "I can't even imagine what you've gone through in the days since I last held you. But, I'm so glad you came tonight."

Thunder rolled deep and heavy through the treehouse, and gentle rain began tapping on the tin roof, giving me the background music for the declaration I'd been preparing all week.

"Noah, we need to talk."

"I know," I said, thumbing her chin. "I know we do. But, can I go first?"

She frowned, but nodded in concession.

My stomach flipped a little as I sat up, turning until I could face her completely. "You aren't the first girl to come into my life, Ruby Grace, but you are the first girl to come into my life and leave a mark." I swallowed, searching her eyes with mine. "I've never experienced this kind of... feeling. It's selfless. I can't stop thinking about you, about all that you are, all that you *will* be. My thoughts are consumed with the way you make me feel, with the sound of your laugh, with the colors of your eyes, with the passion flowing from your heart for everyone you care about." I shook my head, taking both her hands in mine. "I thought it was impossible to ever make you mine... *truly* mine. And I would have settled on being your friend if I had to, but *God*, I'm so glad I don't have to."

Her eyes watered, and she bit her bottom lip, shaking her head and letting her gaze fall to my chest. "Noah..."

"I did something this week," I said, heart racing a little faster now. "And I know it's going to probably be a lot to take in, and you have time to consider everything, but..." My smile was so wide, I could barely speak through it. "I applied to AmeriCorps for you."

Her eyes snapped back to mine. "You... you *what?*"

"I only did it for two positions," I said quickly. "And only for two that I thought you would be perfect for, two that I knew you'd love. They're both out west. One of them is working in a center focused on mental health and substance abuse victims, and the other is on a Native American reservation working with senior citizens." My hands started shaking the more I spoke, my excitement growing. "I had to do some digging for your community service history, and I wrote a motivational statement on your behalf, but... well... yeah. I applied for you."

She gaped at me, and my heart raced more.

"Obviously, you don't have to go," I said, trying to gauge her reaction. I thought maybe she was in shock, or maybe she didn't think it was possible, that this was something she could do. I aimed to show her that it was. "And you can apply to different ones if those don't interest you. I just... I wanted you to know that you can do whatever you want. If you want to go into the Corp, you can. If you want to go back to school, you can. Because even if your parents cut you off, AmeriCorps will help pay for your education. And I'll go with you," I said, but as soon as the words left my lips, I paled. "I mean, if you want me to. Or I can stay here and wait, whatever you want. But what I'm trying to say is... we're a team, Ruby Grace." I smiled, smoothing my thumbs over her wrists. "We're in this together, and it's not just about me and my dreams. It's about you and yours, too."

The rain picked up, the *ting ting* on the roof the only sound between us as Ruby Grace opened her mouth, shut it again, opened it, shut it. She searched my eyes with a look I couldn't decipher — something between awe, love, shock, and hurt. All of those emotions existed in equal measure in those hazel eyes, and my stomach knotted tighter, my thumbs still rubbing her wrists.

"Can you say something, please?" I said on a soft laugh.

Ruby Grace rolled her lips together before closing her eyes, and she shook her head, as if the next words she was about to speak were burning her tongue but she was holding her mouth closed to try to keep them in anyway.

And when she finally spoke, I understood why.

• • •

Ruby Grace

My throat burned as I tried to sort through the thoughts in my head.

Every fiber of my heart urged me to throw myself into Noah's arms, to wrap myself up in him and cry tears of thankfulness. Here he was, the man I'd always dreamed of, showing me the kind of love I'd wanted all my life — the kind of love my fiancé would never give me.

And I had to walk away from it.

I had to walk away from *him*.

Tears stung my eyes when I finally opened them. Noah stared back at me, hope lit up in his cobalt blue irises, and he waited for me to speak.

You're amazing.

No one has ever cared for me this way.

I feel more like myself when I'm with you than I ever have before.

You're everything I want.

I love you.

"How could you?" I said, instead, and all the color drained from Noah's face when the words were in the air between us.

"I..." He closed his mouth, swallowing. "What?"

The tears I'd been holding at bay broke free, sliding down each cheek in parallel lines as I formulated the lie I had to tell him.

It didn't matter that I felt the same about him that he felt for me.

It didn't matter that I wanted him, that I wished more than anything in the entire world that I could kiss him and hold him and say, "*Of course, I want to go, and of course, I want you to go with me!*" I wished I could leave this town behind, leave my family obligations and expectations in the dust and just take on the world with him at my side.

But this wasn't a movie.

This was my life.

And in *my* life, there was more to think about than just my own selfish wants. I had a mother depending on me, a father in trouble he couldn't get out of on his own, a sister who was oblivious to the peril — and I wanted to keep it that way.

I came here tonight to give myself one last evening with Noah, one last time in his arms, one last kiss... and then, I knew I'd have to let him go. I knew I'd have to tell him something — *anything* — to get him to stay away from me.

If I told him the truth, he'd tell me it wasn't my problem. I already knew he would. But, he couldn't possibly understand. This was my family at stake — our name, our reputation. Generations of Barnetts were watching me from above, expecting me to do what was right to save the family name.

And I wouldn't let them down.

I couldn't let them down.

"I can't believe you would do this," I said, sniffing back tears as I stood, leaving Noah in the bean bag. He scrambled up after me. "You applied for a *job* without asking me, Noah. A job that requires years of commitment."

He gaped. "But... this is what you said you wanted."

"No," I corrected, even though my heart screamed *yes*. "It's what I *used* to want."

Noah furrowed his brows, taking a step toward me. "Baby, please. Come here."

He held his arms out wide, and my heart squeezed tight at the sound of the nickname rolling from his lips. I wanted to be his baby. I wanted to be *his*, period — and I cried harder at the cold reality that I never would be.

Life wasn't fair.

This was one lesson I'd never forget.

"You're treating me like a child," I said against the sobs. "Like you know what's best for me."

"That's not what I—"

"Stop trying to save me when I didn't ask to be saved."

His mouth popped shut at that, and he blinked several times, digesting my words as he watched me like I was someone else entirely.

In that moment, I was.

"Don't do this," he finally whispered, shaking his head. "Please. Don't do this."

"I'm not doing anything," I said, crying harder. "*You* did this." I shook my head, swiping the tears from my face as I made my way toward the treehouse door. "This was all a mistake. I stepped out on my fiancé after one stupid mis-understanding without even talking to him. And I'm sorry I did that, I'm sorry I went to you, but this?" I gestured to the air between us. "This *thing* that you're trying to make happen between us? It's just a fantasy. It's not the real world."

"Stop it!" Noah said, crossing the treehouse and stepping in my pathway to the door. "Stop pushing me away because I'm the first person in your life to actually give a damn about you."

I covered my mouth with my hands, closing my eyes and willing myself to calm down, to stop crying — but I couldn't.

"Look at me," he said, framing my arms, but I kept my eyes shut. "This isn't a fantasy and you know it. This? What *we* have? It's real. It's that bullshit man who only wants you to play a part that's not real. It's your parents who want you to be a prop in their life instead of an actual daughter that's not real."

I couldn't respond, not with my heart ripping itself to shreds inside my rib cage with every word he spoke. All I wanted was to wrap my arms around him, bury my face in his neck and tell him everything. I wanted to hear him say I didn't owe them a thing, that this wasn't my mess, and more than anything, I wanted to believe that myself.

But as much as I wanted those things, I wanted to be there for my family more.

I loved them, no matter what had transpired between us, and I couldn't let them go down in flames. Not when I knew I held the fire extinguisher in my hands.

"Look at you," he said, squeezing my arms as another sob ripped through me. "You feel it, too. You don't want to leave right now. You don't want to fight with me."

I shook my head, pressing my hands into my face more to soak up the tears as they fell.

"What are you not telling me, Ruby Grace?"

Another wave of sobs tore through me, and when I could finally force a breath, I let my hands fall, creaking my eyes open to look up at him through my damp lashes.

I still couldn't speak.

"What is it?" he whispered, hands framing my face as he searched my eyes.

I shook my head. "You don't understand," I whispered.

"So help me," he begged.

My face twisted, more tears breaking loose as I shook my head over and over again. "But, that's just it," I said, pulling free from his grasp. "You don't understand. And you never could."

"Ruby—"

"I have to go," I said, sniffing back the last of my tears with a new resolve. I skirted around him, flinging the door open and climbing down the ladder on the tree without another glance in his direction.

Noah called out to me the entire way down, calling my name and telling me to wait — *begging* me to wait. I swore my chest would explode any moment if I didn't put distance between us, and the cool rain splattering against my hot skin was the only welcome relief I found in the meantime.

"Wait," he said again when we reached the bottom. His hand caught the inside of my elbow and he spun me around, his eyes wild now, frantically searching mine. "Please. Don't do this. Don't leave, don't walk away from this, from…" He swallowed. "Don't walk away from me."

I let out an audible sob at that, ripping away from his grasp.

"You can't walk all the way back," he said when I turned. "It's raining. It's at least a mile."

"I'm fine," I said through my tears, through the rain, through the rolling thunder. I took out my phone, using the flashlight app on it to light my way.

"Damn it, Ruby Grace!"

Noah ran to catch up to me, blocking my path as the rain pelted down on us. His hair stuck to his forehead, his eyes transitioning to my favorite steel color as a crack of lightning sprawled across the sky.

"I love you."

The words knocked the breath from my chest, and I shook my head, trying to move around him.

"You love me, too," he said. "And you don't have to say it for me to know it. But what you do have to do is stay. Right now. You have to be brave, and you have to *stay*."

"I can't," I whimpered.

"Why not?" He stepped into me, hands reaching forward, and this time, I didn't rip away when his hands found my arms. "Just tell me why. Tell me the *real* reason why, and I swear, I'll leave you alone." His hands trailed up, framing my face. "If that's what you want."

Noah swallowed at that, like the words tasted as bad as they sounded. He lowered his forehead to mine, and both of us inhaled a breath that sounded like a roar of thunder.

"I promise I will," he said again, this time softer. "But I don't want to. I want you to stay. Please, Ruby Grace. *Stay*."

His lips found mine, hard and pleading, and I melted into him, my hands tugging at his wet shirt as another crack of lightning split the sky. I took that kiss selfishly, eagerly, opening my mouth and letting him slide his tongue inside as I moaned and leaned into him even more.

I wanted him to brand me.

I wanted to brand *him*.

For as long as I lived, I knew I'd never forget that last kiss with Noah Becker.

But when the lightning was gone, the thunder rolling behind it, I broke free, panting, and I didn't meet his eyes when I said the last words I'd ever say to him.

"Don't follow me."

With that, I was gone.

Chapter Seventeen

Noah

Two weeks.

Those words were on repeat in my head Sunday evening as I sat with all my brothers on Mom's front porch, holding a full beer in my hand, knowing I couldn't stomach even one sip of it. I hadn't touched anything Mom had made us for dinner, either.

Two weeks.

I counted the days, the hours, the minutes and seconds that fit inside that time period.

It was only fourteen days. Three-hundred-and-thirty-six hours. Twenty-thousand-one-hundred-and-sixty minutes. One-point-two-million seconds.

And then, she would be Ruby Grace Caldwell.

My fist tightened around the can, a bit of the beer spilling over the side as I fumed at that fact. I knew I shouldn't have gone to church, shouldn't have put myself in her vicinity where I could stare at her and sit in my misery like a masochist.

But I *had* to see her.

After she left that night, I followed her even though she told me not to. I had to make sure she made it back to her car okay. But, I stayed back, gave her space, and once she was in her car, I did as she asked me to.

I left her alone.

I thought she'd call, or text, or send a fucking smoke signal. *Anything.* Something to tell me that she'd just had a moment, but she was okay now.

But it never came.

And earlier, at church, our pastor announced that the wedding was just two weeks away.

Which meant it was still happening.

Which meant I didn't mean *shit* to Ruby Grace.

I sighed, releasing my grip on the can a bit as my eyes wandered over Mom's garden. I felt so many things in equal measure — betrayal, longing, confusion, anger, heartbreak. But more than anything, I felt foolish.

I was the biggest fool.

I'd chased a woman who had another man's ring on her finger, a woman out of my league by any standard, a woman younger than me, a woman who, in reality, was still just a girl in so many ways. I'd wanted to save her, to be her partner in everything, to fill the emptiness in my life with her and be the one to do the same in her life.

I'd ignored all the warning signs.

And now, I was paying the price.

"You okay over there?" Mikey asked from where he was strumming on his guitar at the opposite corner of the porch. He kept his eyes on the strings, plucking away. "You sound like a dragon with all that huffing."

"Fuck off, Mikey."

His head popped up at that, brows tugging together. "Hey…"

"Oh, don't mind him, Mikey," Logan said. "He's got his panties in a wad over Ruby Grace and clearly he just wants to sulk *around* us, but not actually get our advice."

"You don't know what you're talking about," I spat.

"I know I don't. None of us do. And we *won't* until you tell us."

"Leave him alone," Jordan said from his rocking chair, sipping on the old fashioned he'd made. It was like his word was final, Mikey giving me one last look before he started strumming again, and Logan sighing before he drained his beer and stood, walking inside to be with Mom.

Jordan didn't look at me, but I silently thanked him, anyway.

I had so many questions running through my mind, so many things I wanted to talk about and work through. But at the end of the day, I knew it was pointless.

It didn't matter *why* she'd run from me, or why she was still marrying Anthony.

All that mattered was that she *did*. And she was.

End of story.

I felt her hands on my shoulders before I even realized she'd joined us on the porch. Mom gave my traps a gentle squeeze, holding me in place while she spoke to my brothers. "Can you guys give us a minute?"

Mikey stopped playing abruptly, hopping up before trotting down the stairs to his car. "I'm going to Bailey's. I'll be back in a bit."

Jordan stood next. "I'll go see what Logan is up to." He paused, finally looking at me. "For what it's worth, I'm here. If you need anything."

Just saying that was hard for Jordan. I knew, because he hadn't approved of my plan to try to get Ruby Grace in the first place. But as he passed, he put a hand on my shoulder next to Mom's, squeezing once and leaning in to kiss her cheek before he left us alone.

That was a brother's love. It was resilient, and always there — even when we didn't deserve it.

When it was just me and Mom, she rounded my chair, sitting in the empty one next to me. For a long while, she was silent, just rocking next to me with her eyes on the yard.

It was crazy sometimes, looking at Mom. She'd aged in the years since Dad had passed, and I wondered what he would look like now. Would his hair be gray? Would the wrinkles around his eyes and lips be deeper? Would he still be stout as ever, or would he be thin, with a beer belly and a balding head?

Mom was still the same woman I remembered from being a toddler, even though her hair was shorter, a little grayer, her eyes a little more worn. She was still the same superhero I'd always seen when I looked at her.

"So," she said after a long moment, still rocking gently. "You better have a reason for not touching your brussel sprouts tonight. Those have been your favorite since you were a teenager. And your brothers hate them, so you know I made them just for you."

I tried to smile. "And you know I love you for it. I'll take some home, reheat them for lunch tomorrow."

"I'll pack them up for you. But that doesn't get you off the hook for telling me why you can't even drink your beer right now."

I glanced at the offending can, like it'd given away my secret even though I knew I was doing that well enough on my own.

I'd always sucked at hiding my emotions. Jordan was the best at that, Mikey was perhaps the worst. But, I wasn't much better than him. When I was angry, I lashed out. I got into too many fights. I shut out those who tried to help me. I would brood and sulk in my thoughts, but never share them with anyone.

Maybe because I knew no one could help.

Maybe because I was too scared to admit I needed it.

"Ah," Mom said after a long pause. "It's a girl, isn't it?"

I sighed, running my finger along the edge of my beer can. "That obvious, huh?"

She chuckled. "Well, I've seen you bent out of shape about many things over the years, Noah. But this... that misery on your face... it's the kind only a broken heart can bring."

When I didn't say anything more, Mom rolled her lips together, considering her next words before she spoke again.

"You know, I always knew that when you did fall for someone, you'd fall hard. You used to watch me and your dad so closely, and I had a feeling that you'd be the one who held out for the right one. Now, don't get me wrong," she added with a wry smile. "I'm not naïve enough to think you've never dated and broken a few hearts of your own. But, I guess I just knew that you wouldn't really give your heart away. Not until you felt like it was right."

I shook my head. "How do you do that? Do all moms have some sort of superpower where they can just see right through their children?"

She laughed. "Oh, I wish. I think you were just a little easier for me to read," she said on a shrug. "You're like me, in a lot of ways. And I think we've had a special connection ever since you were born." She chuckled again. "Your dad was always jealous of it. He wanted you to be a daddy's boy, but you were always on my hip when you were sick or down about something."

I smiled, heart aching at the mention of Dad.

"Now," she said, patting my knee. "Tell me about her."

I sighed. "You'll be disappointed in me if I do."

"Try me."

"She's engaged," I said first, ripping the Band-Aid off.

Just like I thought, Mom's face paled. "Noah Emmanuel."

"I know, I know," I said, pinching the bridge of my nose. "Trust me. I tried to stay away, to keep a boundary between us. But, I swear to God, Mom — she was like a magnet. The harder I tried to stay away, the more she pulled me in. And I have no idea why or how. I just know that I was powerless to resist when it came to her."

Her eyes softened at that. "Well, if I've learned anything when it comes to love, it's that it rarely follows all the rules we set in place for it." She sighed. "It's Ruby Grace Barnett, isn't it?"

I didn't answer.

I didn't have to.

"You know, when you were younger, I used to have to wait days for you to finally open up to me about what you were upset about," she said. "I mean, your younger brothers would break in minutes, and Jordan would take it to the grave. But you?" She smiled. "All you needed was time."

I nodded, knowing it to be true.

"And I understand if that's what you want now. I just hate seeing you like this, and I want to help." Mom reached over and squeezed my forearm. "But, I can't if you don't tell me what happened."

I sighed, looking up to the sky before I met her eyes. "I don't even know where to begin. I don't know how we ended up here, or how it all started. It just... happened."

"When did she stop being the annoying girl who kicked the back of your pew?"

I scoffed. "When she showed up at the distillery wearing a dress that made her look more grown than me, and heels that made her legs stretch on for days, and lips painted as red as the paint on Dad's old Camaro."

Mom smiled. "How about you start there, then."

So I did.

And before I knew it, the sun had set, the half moon and stars above our only light as Mom and I rocked side by side. I talked, and she listened, nodding her head and chiming in from time to time. But, for the most part, she was silent, and the night was silent — other than the faint sound of music coming from inside, where I assumed my brothers were eavesdropping and pretending to be busy.

When I'd finished, telling her about the treehouse and how Ruby Grace had left, I fell quiet.

I had nothing more to say.

Mom reached over, squeezing my hand where it rested on the arm of my rocking chair before she folded her hands in her lap again. She rocked, eyes on the stars, and a long moment passed before she finally spoke.

"There was another man before your father."

I cocked a brow. "What do you mean?"

She sighed. "I mean, before I fell in love with your father, there was another man who had my interest. And I had his. I would say we were in love... but, it's not the same love I had with your father. It was younger, wilder, not as steady."

"Did Dad know?"

She smiled. "He did. He didn't want to know much, to be honest. But I told him, just because I wanted to be honest with him."

I nodded, wondering why she was telling me this after all these years.

"When your father and I announced our engagement, that other man came back into my life. It had been years," she said, her eyes distant, a sad smile on her face. "And he'd been dating someone else... someone I was close with before. But, when he heard about your Dad and me, he came to me. He confessed his love, and he begged me not to get married."

My jaw fell slack. "Wow. Did Dad know about *that*?"

She chuckled. "He did. I told him when it happened, but again, he didn't want to know much. That was the special thing about your father. I was always open with him, and he was always trusting of me. I think that's how I knew our love was real. There was no jealousy, no fear of being betrayed. We just... we just *knew*. We were a fact, you know?"

My heart squeezed. "Yeah. I know."

Mom smiled my way. "Anyway, the reason I'm telling you this is that... there was a part of me — a very, *very* small part — that still had feelings for that man. I did. And I knew it was wrong, but when he came to me, I was faced with all those old emotions that we'd had together. And if I weren't stronger, if the love between your father and me wasn't as it was, I might have fallen. I might have given into him and done something I would have regretted." She paused. "But, as it was, I told him I was happy with your father and that he should leave me alone. Not just for now, but forever."

I swallowed. "Which is exactly what Ruby Grace said to me."

Mom sighed, gently nodding. "Yes. And I know it hurts to hear, Son. I know it does. And maybe she really *is* your first love. But, our first love doesn't usually tend to be our last. We learn from it, grow from it, and move forward. And I think that's what you have to do here."

My chest twisted, head shaking involuntarily. I didn't want that. It was the absolute last thing I felt like I could do — walk away from her — even if it was the right thing to do.

"I know you don't want to hear that," Mom said. "But, the way I see it, whether she cares about you or not, she obviously cares about Anthony more. She's still engaged to him, regardless of what happened between them. That tells me she wants to work on it with him. She wants to see this through. And if you love her — if you *truly* love her — you will respect that wish, and you will leave her be."

"If you love them, let them fly, huh?"

Mom's smile was soft, apologizing. "Something like that."

She reached over to grab my hand again, squeezing it once before she stood and clapped her hands together. "Now, I have peach cobbler inside, and you're not allowed to leave until you eat at least one piece."

"Mom..."

"Ah!" she said, holding up one finger as she turned her back to me. "No excuses, Noah Emmanuel. Inside. Now."

I smirked, shaking my head as I stood. And before Mom could open the screen door, I called out to her.

She turned, and in that moment, I swore I saw Dad standing next to her — maybe as a memory from long ago.

"Thank you," I said, holding my arms open.

She smiled, eyes glossing over as she stepped into my embrace. She rocked me like she had all my life, and I kissed her forehead, releasing her on a sigh.

"Always, baby boy," she said, reaching up to pinch my cheek. "Always. Now, come on. Pie awaits."

Jordan watched me a little too carefully as we ate pie at the dinner table, Logan filling Mom in on the latest from the distillery. I gave him what I could in terms of a reassuring smile, and he just nodded in understanding.

I'm here, he was saying.

I know, I said back.

As much as my stomach protested, I choked down Mom's pie — along with the advice she'd given me. It was the absolute last thing I wanted to hear, and part of me hoped she'd say something else.

Fight for her!

Object at the wedding!

Steal the bride!

But that wasn't who my mother was. She was sound, peaceful, logical, and patient. She was the most nurturing and intelligent woman I knew — and what she'd told me to do was the right thing.

I had to let Ruby Grace go.

Now, I only had to figure out how.

•••

Ruby Grace

I wondered if I should just stay there at the bottom of the pool.

It was quiet down there — peaceful. The sun's rays only barely reached me, and the water was thick and blue, my hair floating around me like a red tide. My chest was burning, thirsty for air, but I starved it a little longer.

I could just stay there.

I could stay there until I ran out of air, and then I'd never have to get married. I'd never have to rise to the surface and face the life I had cornered myself into.

I'd never have to look into Noah Becker's devastated blue eyes again.

It had been the absolute worst week of my entire life.

At home, everything went on as it would have. Mom made last-minute wedding adjustments, Dad worked all day and told me each night how excited he was for me, and Anthony held me like he loved me, kissed me like he cared — and remained completely oblivious to what I knew about his true feelings.

And I hadn't seen Noah.

In so many ways, he felt like a ghost to me now. I wondered sometimes if he was even real at all, if I'd imagined the events of the entire summer. But the bruises were there on my heart, the scars on my lips where his had burned mine — I felt him everywhere, like he was a permanent part of me, though I'd never see or speak to him again.

I closed my eyes, my heart all but convinced to succumb to drowning. But, my feet kicked without permission, forcing me toward the top of the pool as my lungs set a fire inside my rib cage. When I broke the surface of the water and inhaled, my body rejoiced while my heart cried out against the injustice.

I opened my eyes.

"Trying to break your third-grade record?" Annie asked, swinging her feet in the water and rubbing sunscreen on her exposed belly.

"Looked more like a poor suicide attempt to me," Betty chimed in, floating her arms up overhead before leaning to one side. It was part of the warm-up in Noah's water aerobics routine he'd been teaching there, and my heart squeezed at the memory, urging me to go back down for another try.

"Ding-ding-ding," I said, pointing at Betty. "We have a winner."

Annie frowned, exchanging a glance with Betty before she let out a sigh. "Okay, you're not even allowed to joke about that."

"I'm sorry," I said, swimming to the edge where she sat. I laid my head on my arms, letting the sun warm my back. "I must be so miserable to be around right now."

"You're not," she assured me. "But, I do hate this for you. It's four days before your wedding. You should be glowing, and happy, and have literal heart eyes popping out of your head like a cartoon."

I nodded. "I know."

"She also shouldn't be marrying that no-good, two-timing prissy son of a dirty politician."

Annie laughed at Betty's remark, and I tried to smile, but it felt like trying to run fast under water — impossible.

"Seriously," she said when I didn't respond. "What exactly is your plan here? You're just going to marry this man and then... what? Divorce him after your father's debt is paid?"

I shook my head.

"Annul the marriage?"

I shook my head again.

Betty was adjusting her swim cap, and she let it snap against her forehead, lowering her goggles and blinking several times as she watched me. "Wait... you're not actually planning on *staying* with him... are you? As in, marrying him, having his babies, being the dutiful politician's wife he wants you to be?"

When I didn't answer, Annie cringed and Betty fumed, shaking her head and holding up one old, wagging finger. "Oh, hell no."

"What would you have me do?" I asked.

"Call off the wedding like you were planning to," she said, as if it were that easy. "And run to that boy who *really* loves you."

"Betty..." Annie tried to warn, but I was already pulled into the argument.

"My hands are tied," I said, standing to face her. "My father's reputation, his job, our house, our entire *life* depends on me marrying this man. I can't just feed my father to the wolves."

"So, you'll feed *yourself* to one, instead?"

I opened my mouth to respond, but no words came. So, I just shut it again, eyes falling down to where my fingers skated over the water.

Betty sighed, making her way to the ladder at the edge of the pool before she slowly climbed out, Annie holding one hand behind her just in case. "Come," she said, not even looking back at me. "Walk with an old woman, would you?"

Water was still dripping off each of us as we walked in our towels, first around the tennis court and then back to the garden, where a path wound through each little corner of it like a snake. It was shaded, a nice reprieve from the sun, and it wasn't until we were within those garden walls that Betty finally spoke.

"I want to start by saying that no matter what you choose to do, I will love you through it," she started, tugging off her swim cap and pushing her goggles up on her head. "Because you are like a daughter to me, Ruby Grace. Like the daughter we never had."

Her eyes shined at that, and I knew she was thinking about Leroy.

I reached over, threading my arm through hers.

"And maybe that's why I feel compelled to say this to you. I know you already have a mother, but, the way I see it, you can never have too many moms in your life. And, if I'm being honest, I don't agree with the guidance your true mother is giving you right now."

I swallowed.

"I know it's complicated. I know it feels like your hands are tied, like there's no choice for you in this matter — but I want to be the one to tell you that there is. You're young, Ruby Grace. Right now, it feels like you have to do what is expected of you, that there is a standard you must meet, that in order to be happy, you have to follow this list of rules and guidelines and you have to marry a certain kind of man and live in a certain kind of house and raise certain kinds of kids." She sort of laughed, sort of scoffed. "But, honey? That's all bullshit."

I smirked.

"Can we sit?" she asked, a little out of breath as she pointed to a bench near the bed of Indian blanket sunflowers.

When we were both seated, she took a few breaths, dabbing at the sheen of sweat on her forehead with her towel before she sat back.

"There comes a time in your life when you look around you and you realize that you don't want to play the game anymore," she said. "You realize you don't want the fake friends, or the toxic relationships, or the people telling you how you should live *your* life when they can't even run their own. Some find it in their thirties. Some in their forties. Some, like the old woman beside you, not until most of their life has passed."

I frowned, reaching over to hold her hand. "You've had an amazing life," I argued. "A man who loved you, a town that cherishes you."

"That's just it, though," she said. "Leroy wanted to stay in this town, whereas I wanted to flee from it. I wanted to travel, to see the world, to talk to strangers from other cultures and learn more than just what's here in Tennessee. But I never did." She held up a finger. "Now, I don't want you thinking I wasn't happy, because I was. I loved Leroy. I *still* love that man — even though he broke our pact to let me die first, the bastard."

I chuckled, eyes glossing over.

"But, aside from his love, I never fulfilled *myself*. And that's one area where Leroy couldn't help me. He would have supported me, if I would have stood up for *myself* and said out loud what I wanted. But, I never did. Instead, I found my adventure by watching movies and living through *other* people — through celebrities. I waited until Leroy was gone from my life, until my legs were too old and tired, my lungs not capable of feeding me enough oxygen, my heart not steady enough to pump enough blood into my brain. It took me too long to speak up for myself, and I regret it. Truly, I do. I could have seen the world, could have experienced so much more with the man I loved, if I only would have stood up and spoke."

I sighed. "And that's what you want me to do."

"No," she said, shaking her head. "*I* want you to do what you want to do — regardless of if I agree with it or not. Like I said, you're my daughter in my eyes, and I will support you through anything." She paused, running her bony, silky finger over my wrist. "But, let's just say I'm speaking to you on behalf of future Ruby Grace. I'm speaking as Ruby Grace at seventy-four, in a nursing home of her own."

My heart kicked up a notch as I tried to imagine it — an older version of me, looking back on my life, on what I'd built, what I'd leave behind.

What hurt the most was that I couldn't even picture it.

"All I'm saying is that I know it feels like you're tied to a railroad track with a train coming straight at you. It feels like it's this or nothing. But, I'm telling you, you have a giant pair of scissors in your hands that you can cut that rope with."

"Betty..."

"It may be difficult," she said, cutting me off. "You might get rope burn and you may cut yourself and bleed a little. You may let some people down. Hell, you may uproot everything you knew about your life before, about what you thought it'd be, and you may walk into something completely different, something you never expected." A smile bloomed on her pale lips, then. "But, my dear, isn't that the best part of being young? The possibilities are endless, the paths limitless, and you have so many different directions you can walk." She shrugged. "You just have to decide if you want to walk the path of least resistance, the one where you are merely another traveler on the road. Or, if you want to forge a new path with those scissors, bit by bit, limb by limb, and discover something you never could have imagined."

"It sounds selfish."

She scoffed. "Selfish. What a silly word. Should you give to the ones you love? Absolutely. But should you lose yourself in order to better *their* lives at the expense of your own? Never."

With that, she stood, stretching her arms above her head with a yawn before she started walking.

I frowned. "You're leaving?"

"I'm going to take a nap, like an old woman should," she said, glancing back at me over her shoulder. "And I'm going to leave you alone to think. To *really* think — without your mom in your ear, or your sister, or Noah, or Annie, or me. I just want you to sit here, on this bench, in this garden, and I want you to ask yourself the tough questions."

"I know the questions," I said on a sigh. "It's the answers I'm having trouble with."

She smiled knowingly. "Well, then, sit here until they come."

"And if they don't?"

"Then you didn't sit long enough," she tossed over her shoulder.

Then she rounded an old oak tree, and she was gone.

• • •

Later that night, I knocked on my father's office door before letting myself inside.

He looked up at me from where he sat at his desk, his reading glasses low on his nose and hands still typing away on his keyboard. "Hey, pumpkin."

I swallowed, letting myself in and closing the door behind me with trembling hands. Anthony and Mom were out on the front porch, drinking sweet tea like Mama loved to do after dinner, but just in case, I wanted another barrier between us.

"I need to talk to you," I said when I was inside.

"Okay," he answered, but his eyes were back on his screen now, fingers flying over the keys. "I'll be out in an hour or so, just have to finish this up."

I ignored his request and sat down in one of the chairs on the opposite side of his desk, folding my hands in my lap.

Dad glanced up at me, and I watched the concern wash over his face when he saw me — when he really *saw* me.

I had to look as tired as I felt. I knew it. I knew there were bags under my eyes, that my blotchy skin had to be betraying the fact that I'd cried all evening after leaving the nursing home. I had barely eaten at dinner, which Mama covered up by saying I was worried about fitting into my wedding dress.

Ever the damage control.

But now, sitting across from my father, I didn't want to hide it anymore. I didn't want to pretend like everything was fine.

Dad swallowed, pulling his hands from the keyboard and steepling them together as he sat back in his chair. "Or we can talk now."

My next breath was a shaky one, one that burned as much as it brought relief in the form of fresh oxygen. I looked down at my hands, at my manicured nails, at the engagement ring on my finger.

"I know about the deal you made with Anthony and his father."

I couldn't look at my father, then.

I couldn't glance up from my nails and see the man I'd admired my entire life paling at the realization that his little girl knew about the debt he owed, about the way he planned to pay it.

My gaze stayed fixed in my lap, and that was the only way I had the courage to keep talking.

"I want you to know that I understand why you did it. I understand that, sometimes, sacrifices have to be made to keep a family afloat. You and Mom have taught me that." Tears flooded my eyes, and the next words choked out of me with less steadiness. "But, I also want you to know that I have never been so hurt in my entire life. And I never thought my father would ever be capable of selling me to the highest bidder."

"Pumpkin..."

"No," I said, shaking my head, effectively letting the first two tear drops fall into my lap. "I'm not finished."

Silence.

I sniffed, wiping the back of my hand against my nose with my heart thundering hard in my chest now. "Anthony doesn't love me. I know that now, and I also know that it doesn't matter. You and I both know that at the core of my heart, of who I am — I am a giver. Just like you. Just like Mom. We sacrifice for others, and more than anything, we put this family first."

My heart ached, Noah's face the only thing I could see as I shut my eyes and freed another set of tears.

"I will do this for you," I whispered, breaking with the admission. "For our family. Because it would kill me to do anything that would ever hurt you, or Mom, or Mary Anne." I sniffed, finally pulling my gaze up to meet my father's.

When I saw the tears on his cheeks, his eyes red and glossy, I broke again.

"But, you will do something for me in return," I choked out on a sob. "You have to get help, Daddy. You can't keep doing this — not at this expense. You have to go to Gamblers Anonymous. You have to stop with the casinos, and the card nights, and the horse tracks. It may have been all fun and games at one point, a way to pass the time and wheel and deal with the good ol' boys in this town, but now, it has affected not just your life, and not just my life, but our entire family's."

Dad rolled his lips together, two tears streaming parallel down his cheeks as he watched me. He was quiet for a long while, the air in his office stuffy and suffocating.

"I'm so sorry," he finally whispered. "I know... I know I'm sick. I know I have a problem. I... I never thought it would get to this point, I never thought..."

He paused, face crumpling as a sob broke through. In all the years I'd been alive, I'd never seen my father cry.

Not once.

But that night in his office, he broke, reaching for a tissue on his desk and wiping the tears away, wiping his nose before his gaze sat miserably somewhere in the distance between us.

Now, it was *him* who couldn't look at me.

"I don't know when it got this bad," he said. "I used to have a hold on it. I'd walk into the casino with what I was okay to lose, and if I lost it, I left. But, when I started going to Pat's club... I don't know. Everything changed."

Pat was my father's affectionate pet name for Patrick Scooter.

The man he now owed so much money to that he couldn't pay his own debt.

"When my money ran out, I'd just hang around, drink, smoke cigars with the other city council members. But, Patrick would entice me, tell me to get in on the next hand, that he had me, he'd lend me the bet. It was innocent at first, and I easily paid him back. Somewhere along the way, though..." Dad shook his head. "I don't know. I got pulled into something I didn't even realize. It was bigger than I could have ever known. And when I started losing more, I would ask for more — small, at first, but bigger and bigger as time went on. I just thought *one more hand, and I'll win it all back.*" A shadow passed over his face, like he was trying to pinpoint the exact moment it all happened.

Like if he could, he could go back and change it all.

His mouth hung open for a long pause before he continued. "Before I knew it, I was in over my head in a debt I couldn't even wrap my head around."

I swallowed, trying my best to find sympathy somewhere in my heart for my father, for the man who raised me.

I came up empty handed.

"Your mom didn't even know until it was too late," he said, his voice low and cracking. "We were going to lose everything... and then... Anthony came to ask for your hand."

Just the sound of his name made my stomach roll so violently I nearly vomited what little bit of dinner I could choke down. Tears flooded my eyes again, so fast I couldn't even try to stop them before they rolled down my cheeks.

"That's enough," I whispered, voice shaking through the shallow breaths I managed to sip. "It doesn't matter. What's done is done."

Dad opened his mouth, but after one look at me, he shut it again.

"I just needed you to know," I said definitively. "I needed you to know that I'm aware of what you did, and I needed you to know that as much as it hurts *me*, I will do what needs to be done for this family." I shook my head. "Even if I wasn't given the opportunity to make my own choice in the first place."

Dad didn't say anything else, which was wise, because I was in perhaps the most unstable state I'd ever been in in my entire life.

I nodded, the conversation over, and then I stood and walked to his office door, taking a moment to wipe my face before I opened the door. I glanced back at the big, broken man at that desk, and in that moment, I didn't recognize him at all.

"For the record," I said, standing tall. "Even if you do get help — and you will — I will never forgive you for this."

And with the most painful decision of my life made, I turned my back on my father and shut the door on everything I ever thought my life would be.

Chapter Eighteen

Noah

I wasn't going to go.

I swore on my father's grave, on the *Bible* that I was not going to go to the wedding.

There was no reason to go. My mom was right — I needed to walk away from Ruby Grace, from what we had, what we could *never* have, and leave her behind. I had to let her start her new life with another man, because that was the decision she had made.

It was set in stone.

I was set in my resolve.

And for the past two weeks, I'd told myself I wasn't going to go to that wedding — no matter what.

But all of that changed last night.

I had stayed late at the distillery, working overtime for as long as Gus would let me before he finally kicked me out and made me go home. I'd been at the distillery more than anywhere, trying to throw myself into work so I could take my mind off the impending wedding. I couldn't go ride Tank, couldn't go to the treehouse, couldn't go *anywhere* I used to find solace — because now, all I found in those places were memories of her.

When I finally made it home, it was well past sunset, and I noticed a white envelope half tucked under my front door as I twisted my key in the lock.

I bent to retrieve it with a frown, and that frown had deepened when I read in small, neat script on the front of it:

Read this before tomorrow. It's important.

My heart had leapt into my throat, and I instantly thought it was a letter from Ruby Grace.

I'd flown inside, thrown my shit haphazardly on whatever surface was nearby, and torn into the envelope with greedy hands, greedy eyes, a greedy heart. But, the letter wasn't from Ruby Grace at all.

It was from Betty.

And in that letter, she'd revealed the missing piece to the puzzle I'd been trying to solve since the moment Ruby Grace left me in the rain at the tree-house my father built.

That letter was tucked into the inside pocket of my tuxedo, and as if it possessed the courage I needed to walk through the church doors, I brushed a hand over my chest where it was hidden, taking a deep breath. My eyes scanned the large wooden doors of the church — the ones I had walked through nearly every Sunday morning since I was born — and I wondered how they could look so foreign.

Inside those doors, there was an aisle lined with flowers and twine — both of which I'd helped Ruby Grace pick out.

Inside those doors, there were hundreds of people, nearly the entire town of Stratford, and then some.

Inside those doors, there was a man waiting at the end of the aisle for the woman I loved.

And inside those doors was the woman I couldn't let go of.

My breath was surprisingly steady as I finally found the will to open those doors, like I knew what I was going to do when the reality was I didn't have a fucking clue. But, I extended one steady hand for the wedding program being offered to me, took my seat at the end of the back left pew, and I waited.

I was practically invisible to everyone inside, and in that moment, I was thankful my entire family had declined the open invitation to the wedding. I knew they had done so on my behalf.

None of them knew I was here today.

The other wedding guests were all chattering with their friends or fami-lies or dates, commenting on the beautiful decorations or the stunning music coming from a harp player near the organ at the front. It was a shushed sort of chatter as we all waited for the ceremony to begin.

And it would.

In less than ten minutes.

It's too late, the realistic part of my brain warned me as I sat there, both hands on the wedding program, eyes cast toward the altar. *She's marrying him. Today. There's nothing you can do.*

But, there was something more powerful floating inside my chest, calm-ing my breaths, easing my racing heart. It fluttered and filled me from the inside out with an inexplicable anticipation, like something epic was about to happen.

Hope.

I recognized it faintly as time warped and faded. I couldn't even be sure I was truly in the church — that's how detached I felt from my being. It wasn't until the moment I noticed a familiar pair of eyes watching me from the third pew that I came back to the moment.

Betty smiled, casting me a wink. I returned her smile, and it was as if that notion alone brought on all the jitters I'd been surpassing. My heart thundered to life in my chest, my hands shaking where they held the program, and I swore my feet were about to move without permission from my brain to hightail us out of there just as the harp died and the organ began to play.

The same camera crew that had followed Anthony and Ruby Grace around the Soirée was scattered throughout the church, cameras pointed in all different directions, with one free moving around the church and capturing the chatter before the ceremony. That camera moved to the center of the aisle, crouched low and out of view once the familiar hymn filled the air.

Pastor Morris stood at the altar now, smiling, his eyes scanning the crowd as he nodded silent hello's. Ruby Grace's mother was escorted down the aisle by an usher, but Anthony's parents were nowhere to be found. I frowned, wondering where they were, but didn't have time to process it much before a door opened to the right.

Anthony walked through it, along with some guy I didn't recognize. He stood next to Anthony and Pastor Morris at the altar, which told me he was the best man, but I couldn't keep my focus there for very long.

Because it took every ounce of willpower I possessed not to fly down the aisle right then and pummel Anthony's grinning face with my fist.

He stood tall and confident at the altar, wearing a light gray tuxedo with a coral pocket square and bow tie. His hair was neat and styled, his jaw freshly shaved, and to anyone else in that church, he looked like the perfect groom. He looked like what every girl had ever dreamed of when they pictured their wedding day.

But I knew the truth.

I knew the evil things he'd said about the best woman in the world, knew the pain he'd caused her, the way he'd treated her like some pawn in his game of life.

And now, thanks to Betty, I knew about the deal he and his father had made with Ruby Grace's parents.

That was what upset me the most. Anthony may not have owed Ruby Grace anything, but the fact that her parents could trade her hand in marriage in exchange for some debt to be paid off made me physically ill.

My fists tightened around the wedding program, all but crushing it. A couple I didn't recognize in the same pew as me eyed the crumpled up piece of paper in my hands before casting me a worried glance, to which I just offered a tight smile, relaxing my shoulders a bit.

Breathe, Noah.

A flower girl was the first down the aisle, and she sprinkled daisy petals behind her, smiling shyly at everyone in the pews.

Next was Mary Anne. Even though she'd been gone for a few years, it was impossible not to recognize her. She had the same red hair as her mother and sister, the same button nose, the same freckles dotting her cheeks. She was taller than Ruby Grace, though, and her features were less bold, somehow.

She looked older than she actually was, but when she smiled, I saw the resemblance like they were twins.

The last one down the aisle before the bride was Annie, the flowers in her hands balanced on the swell of her belly in the creamy, coral dress that she wore. Her smile was sad, though she tried to brighten it as much as she possibly could as she scanned the pews. I kept my eyes on her, heart thundering as I realized who would be the next down the aisle.

When Annie reached the altar, she turned.

And her eyes locked on me.

She paled, her pink-painted mouth popping open just as the organ changed tune and the congregation stood.

All the blood rushed to my face before draining completely as I numbly rose to my feet, turning to face the back of the aisle along with everyone else. The organ played, and I adjusted my tie, forcing one calm, cooling breath as the doors to the church swung open.

The first thing I saw was a long, slender hand clutching the grey fabric of a tuxedo-clad arm. Her nails were painted a neutral pink, the tips white, and she held onto that arm like it was the only thing holding her to the Earth.

One step, and then I saw the long, flowy, cream skirt of her dress, outlined by the leg she'd taken the step with.

Another step, and the bouquet I'd helped her decide on came into view — a brilliant gathering of daisies and roses, surrounded by fresh baby's breath and dusty miller.

Three steps.

That was how long I was able to keep breath flowing into my lungs.

That was how long I was able to keep blood pumping to my organs.

Because on the fourth step, Ruby Grace came completely into view, and everything stopped.

The time that had stretched and warped as I waited in the church before the wedding began paused altogether, the music fading, lights dimming except where they shone on her. I didn't even notice her father, the arm that she clung to — not when she was in full view. It was all I could do to take all of her in, every inch of her glowing beauty wrapped in that silky, cream wedding dress. Her cheeks were high and rosy, her lips painted a dusty rose, the freckles from our days in the sun breaking through the foundation that powdered her face. Her long, copper hair was braided on each side, the length of it twisted and tied in a knot at the back just below where her veil sat like a halo. Those hazel eyes I'd loved to stare into all summer were as bright and golden as the sun that peaked in behind her before the church doors shut again, and it was as if that sound slammed me back to reality, slammed time back into motion, slammed my heart back into its race within my rib cage.

I didn't even notice her dress.

I didn't care.

Because it was that woman I was here for, not the dress she wore — and if I had it my way, if everything worked the way I hoped, that dress wouldn't mean anything after today, anyway.

Ruby Grace wore the same solemn smile as Annie had as she walked down the aisle, slowly, her father rubbing his hand over where she held his arm in assurance. With his face ashen and long, I wasn't sure it was assuring her or himself.

Ruby Grace didn't notice me as she walked by. In fact, she seemed to be in some sort of daze, some sort of dream.

Or nightmare.

The crowd *ooooh'd* and *awww'd* as she passed them, women dabbing at their eyes with handkerchiefs as the men smiled in wonder and awe.

I had no doubt she was the most beautiful bride to ever walk down that church aisle.

When she reached the end, Pastor Morris asked who gave her hand in marriage, to which her father responded that he did. He kissed her cheek, made an attempt at a smile that fell flat, and then, carefully, he passed her hand to Anthony.

Ruby Grace handed her bouquet to Annie, and Annie whispered something, nodding back toward me. My heart fell to my stomach as Ruby Grace turned, and just as Pastor Morris told the congregation they may be seated, she found me.

She blinked.

I blinked.

Her lips parted.

I smiled.

And then, I sat along with the rest of the crowd, and her eyes stayed glued on me.

Pastor Morris was already speaking, launching into what a beautiful day it was for such an occasion, but Ruby Grace couldn't take her eyes off the back pew. She blinked, over and over and over, her bottom lip trembling, and it wasn't until Pastor Morris said her name that she tore her eyes away, swallowing as she turned her focus to Anthony.

"Anthony," Pastor Morris said, smiling at the groom before he turned his eyes to the bride. "Ruby Grace. It is with great joy that I stand here with you today, surrounded by your loved ones as we celebrate the unity of two hearts becoming one."

Anthony smiled at Ruby Grace, but she couldn't muster so much as a grin. Her eyes floated back to me once more. She blinked. Then, she faced Anthony again.

"Marriage is an honorable sanction, instituted by God," Pastor Morris continued, but his words faded out when Ruby Grace looked at me.

Again.

Annie nudged her from the back, but she kept her eyes on mine, her brows folding together, lips parting.

Anthony frowned when she took too long to look back at him, and he followed her gaze. When he saw me in the back pew, he scowled, lips flattening into a tight line. He cleared his throat, squeezing Ruby Grace's hand in his own to pull her attention back to him.

She seemed to do so reluctantly, and even when she was facing him again, she wore the same worried look.

Come on, Noah, I silently pleaded with myself. *Stand up. Say what you came to say.*

I didn't know what I was waiting for — a sign, perhaps. Or maybe the classic line from Pastor Morris — *Should anyone have just cause why these two should not be wed, let them speak now, or forever hold their peace.*

But those words never came.

Because in the next breath, Ruby Grace shook her head, pulled her hands from Anthony's, and whispered something that looked a lot like *"I can't do this"* from where I was sitting at the back of the church. She looked at her father in the front pew, words no one could hear exchanged between them in that weighted gaze.

Then, she reached down, bunched her dress in her hands, and turned to face the congregation.

She locked her gaze on mine, and my heart kicked hard and painful in my chest.

She took a step.

I stood.

Then, amidst the gasps and murmurs of four-hundred Stratford residents, Ruby Grace Barnett was a runaway bride.

And I was her getaway car.

• • •

Ruby Grace

Chaos.

It was all chaos as I ran down the aisle, as best I could in my designer heels, with my veil flowing behind me and my eyes locked on Noah Becker in the back pew.

Somewhere in the distance, I heard my mother scream out my name. I heard Anthony call out for me. I heard the gasps, the *oh my's*, and, somewhere through it all, the distinct melody of Betty's signature laugh.

None of it mattered.

The only thing that *did* matter was the man, now moving out of his pew to stand at the opposite end of the aisle, with a smirk on his face and his hands tucked into the pockets of his navy blue suit. Those hands slipped out of his pockets just in time to catch me as I threw myself into his arms, and then my hands were in his hair, and my mouth was on his.

And everything went silent.

Somewhere in my consciousness, I knew there was still chaos all around us. There had to be a flurry of gasps and screams coming from every which way. The Mayor's daughter was kissing Noah Becker at the back of the church she was supposed to be marrying another man in. But in that moment, all I could hear was the drumming of my heart in my chest, the relieved sigh from Noah's lips as they met mine, the steadying of my own breath. I wrapped myself around him tighter, and he pulled me in closer, as if to tell me it was all okay now, that we were safe, that it was all over.

But it was far from the truth.

"Noah," I whispered, pulling back and pressing my forehead to his. "I'm so sorry. I'm so sorry. I never should have left, I never should have done that to you. I was lost. I was confused and scared," I explained, shaking my head as my eyes glossed over, the tears breaking loose before I had the chance to stop them. "I didn't know what to do. And there was so much I couldn't tell you, or at least, I *thought* I couldn't tell you. But I can't walk away from you. I can't walk away from us."

Noah quieted my words with another kiss, sliding his hands up to frame my face before he locked his eyes on mine. "You never have to."

I smiled, but the tears kept coming, and I leaned into Noah's touch as he thumbed them away. "I can explain," I said pathetically. "My father..."

"I know," he interrupted, searching my eyes. "It's okay. I know."

I frowned. "You do?"

He nodded.

"How?"

Noah smirked, looking somewhere over my shoulder, and when I followed his gaze, Betty smiled at me from the crowd of horrified faces.

Sneaky old woman.

I turned back to Noah, eyes glossing over again. "I'm sorry it took me this long to be brave."

He scoffed. "Please. I'm sorry it took *me* so long to stand up and say what I needed to say here. You beat me to the punch. Didn't even let them get to the part where they ask if anyone objects to the marriage so I could stand up and steal you away like they do in the movies."

"Betty would have loved that," I said, one tear slipping free. "But you can't steal something that's already yours."

Noah wiped that tear with his thumb before it could fall past the apple of my cheek. With a gentle smile, he slid his hands back into my hair as he angled my chin up. But, before he could press his lips to mine again, he was ripped away from me as a fist crashed violently into his jaw.

"Noah!" I screamed, covering my mouth in horror as he fell backwards into the pew. People scattered away from him, from where Anthony now stood towering over him, chest heaving, eyes wide and terrifying.

"You sonofabitch," he seethed, pointing one hard finger down at Noah. "How *dare* you kiss my fiancé on our wedding day? Are you insane, or do you just want me to kick your ass in front of this entire town?"

"Now, now," my father said, joining us all at the end of the aisle. He placed his hands on Anthony's shoulders. "Language, son."

Anthony shrugged him off, his eyes wild, but he blinked several times, then, as if he remembered we were the center of attention for the entire town.

He turned to me, then, straightening his bowtie before he reached for my hands. "Come on, sweetheart. Let's get back to the altar."

"No," I said, tugging my hands away.

His eye twitched, but he smiled, looking around us nervously. "Baby, this is madness. Come on. Everyone came here for a wedding today."

"Well, they won't be getting one from us."

Anthony's eyes narrowed, his voice a low whisper as he stepped into my space. "Ruby Grace, you're embarrassing yourself."

"No, I'm embarrassing *you*," I corrected. "But, I don't care anymore."

"Get your ass back up to that altar," he seethed, pointing to Pastor Morris, who was watching us like we were all demons personified.

Dad's brows rose at that, and Mom reached for me from behind, tugging me close to her and Mary Anne. She said something under her breath, something that sounded a lot like *what did you do?*

"Alright now, that's enough. I think we all need to go our own way for now, cool down, catch our breaths."

"No, what we *need* to do is get your ungrateful daughter back up on that altar," Anthony seethed once more, stepping into Dad's space until they were nose to nose. "This family has been nothing but a pain in my ass since this wedding was announced. Now, I've had enough of this. We can edit this all out of the tapes, but your daughter is marrying me today." He turned on Noah again. "And *this* sonofabitch will be kindly escorted out by my team."

The security that traveled with Anthony as he filmed his documentary stepped forward from the back on that cue, grabbing Noah by the lapels of his jacket where he still laid sprawled on the ground and ripping him up to stand again.

"Leave him alone!" I cried.

I heard the flurry of gasps and murmurs as Anthony exposed himself to the congregation. He couldn't keep his cool any longer, and I didn't have it in me to care about keeping his cover anymore, either.

"He'll be fine," Anthony murmured, smoothing out his tuxedo as Noah struggled against the security. "Now, let me escort you back down the aisle."

The entire town of Stratford watched with rapt attention as the scene unfolded. I was surprised no one had popped popcorn and started passing it out.

Of course, no one had left, no one had done *anything* but stare and hold their hands over their mouths, some even had their camera phones out filming this shit show.

They loved the scandal — no matter the cost.

"You don't even love me, Anthony!" I tried to reason, shaking my head and pleading with him. "I heard you say so yourself on the phone with your father. I'm a trophy, a piece of your perfect political puzzle. Please," I said on a whimper. "Just let me go."

"That's absurd," he said, shaking his head like I'd made it all up. "I would never say any of that."

I stood taller. "I'm not marrying you."

"Oh, yes, you are," he said, grabbing my arm.

"Don't touch my daughter," my father interjected, stepping between us and peeling Anthony's fingers off my arm. "I think she's made her decision very clear."

"Oh, has she now?" Anthony asked, lowering his voice. "And what about our deal? What about the debt you can't pay, Mayor Barnett? Maybe you should fill her in on *that* before you let her make a decision."

"She already knows," Dad answered.

His voice was strong, loud and steady, as if he didn't hear the growing murmur of the congregation over what Anthony had just revealed. My father looked at me, then, his eyes determined, and he nodded.

That nod told me more than any words could.

"What's he talking about?" Mary Anne asked from somewhere behind me. I turned, seeing the confusion on her face, and my heart broke for my older sister. She'd been in the dark, living in Europe with no clue of the chaos going on back home.

I'd explain everything to her later.

For now, I had a dad who needed me.

Anthony's face was unreadable as I reached forward, threading my arm through my father's. "I do," I reiterated. "I know everything — including your plans to cheat on me as soon as this whole wedding was over, if you haven't already," I spat. "Classy, by the way."

He narrowed his eyes.

"And as far as my father's business goes, we'll handle that together. As a family," I said, squeezing my father's arm. "*Without* your help."

Anthony scoffed. "You daft woman. Clearly you don't understand anything about the amount of money your father owes to some very important people. There's no way you'll ever be able to pay it without us."

"That's where you're wrong."

The voice came from the front of the church, and Betty stood slowly, balancing herself with one hand on the back of the pew in front of her. She leaned against it, a victorious smile on her face.

"This old lady's got some savings that she can't take with her when she goes. I'll gladly contribute to the cause, if it saves Ruby Grace from marrying the likes of you."

The church was silent, every person inside it so still I wasn't sure any of us were breathing.

Anthony chuckled. "You clearly have no idea the amount of shit he's in."

That earned a gasp, and a flurry of whispers began again.

My poor father stood there like he'd seen a ghost.

"I'll help," Noah said, shaking the men off him as he readjusted his tuxedo jacket and tie. He stepped toward me, reaching out for my hands, and when I placed them in his, he squeezed tight. "I don't care how long it takes or what we have to do to settle it, we'll handle it without you," he said, eyes hard on Anthony. "But, let me make this crystal clear. There is no way I'm letting the woman I love marry a monster — especially not to pay a debt that was never hers to begin with."

A collective sigh rang out, and I swore I heard some girl cry out her injustice that Noah Becker was in love with someone who wasn't her.

I smiled at that.

"This has gone on long enough," my father said, standing between me and Anthony once more. "The debt is *mine*, and *I* will pay it. If you haven't noticed, I have a house and cars and plenty of equity to figure out my own solution." He swallowed, turning to face me then. "I'm just sorry I ever put you through this, Ruby Grace. I'm sorry I didn't step up sooner."

My heart squeezed, and I nodded in thanks. It was a wound I knew wouldn't heal for a long, long time.

But my father showed up for me in that church.

And for that, I was thankful.

Anthony growled, launching his fist into the side of a pew before he pointed one finger straight at me. "This is ridiculous. Get your ass back to that altar. *Now.*"

Noah's face hardened as he turned, guarding me from Anthony. "What aren't you getting here, buddy?" he asked. "It's over. And you can leave now."

"*Excuse me?*" Anthony stepped into Noah's space, but not before my father laid a hand hard on his chest.

"You heard him, son," he said. "I think you should leave now, before you do something you regret."

Anthony's mouth popped open, and he watched my father incredulously before turning to me, and then to my mother. He pointed at her next. "You're really going to let this happen?"

Everyone looked at Mom, then — who was pale, her eyes wide as a doe's, lips trembling. I waited for her to cry, or yell at me, or scream for everyone to look away so they could start the whole ceremony over. I waited for her to kick into crisis mode, to say it was all one big show, that it was a joke. *Haha, we got you!*

Instead, she swallowed, pulled her shoulders back, and lifted her chin up high as she stared directly at Anthony. "I don't think my husband stuttered when he said it's time for you to leave."

A few whistles rang out at that, some laughter and some clapping, and Mom fought back a smirk as Anthony's mouth fell open wider.

"No," he shook his head, running to the men holding the cameras. "No, no, no. Turn them off. Cut the tapes. Turn them *off.*" He was spiraling, raking his hands back through his full head of hair as he shook his head. "My father... he'll kill me... he'll disown me... I can't..."

And suddenly, it all made sense.

The man who had gotten down on one knee and asked for my hand in marriage was under pressure from his *own* father. Did he even want to be in politics at all? Or was *he* just a pawn in his father's game, the way he wanted me to be one in his?

His father wasn't even there, on his son's wedding day. That told me more than words how important he was in his life.

Just like he wanted me to play a part, that's what he wanted Anthony to do, too.

My heart ached for him, for the man I thought I knew, for the friend I'd found in him over the year we'd spent together. I stepped forward, wanting to comfort him, but the instinct died as soon as he leveled his cold, hard eyes on me again.

He shook his head, a disgusted look on his face. "After all I did for you, all I *could* have done for you... you ungrateful bi—"

The curse didn't even leave his mouth before Noah got his chance to return the favor from Anthony's sucker punch earlier. His fist landed hard against Anthony's eye, busting it open as he flew backward, the crowd gasping in horror again.

"Sorry, your warnings are up," Noah said, shaking out his hand. "Now, if you won't leave, then we will." He turned to me, then, offering his arm out for me with a smirk. "I've got your getaway car parked out front. What'dya say, Ruby Grace? Want to give this town something to talk about?"

My heart swelled in my chest, and I stepped forward, threading my arm through his as I leaned up and pressed my lips to his.

"Bonnie and Clyde," I whispered.

"Except a way better ending," he replied, and then he kissed me again — this time to the tune of four-hundred clapping hands and a frenzy of cheers.

Noah broke the kiss long enough to bend down and scoop me up into his arms, which earned us another loud cheer as I laughed, head back, eyes cast up to the church ceiling. I looked back at the congregation as Noah walked us toward the doors — at my parents, who both had tears in their eyes; my sister, who smiled at me reassuringly, though I knew she was hurt in her own way by what had happened that day; my best friend, who threw her fists into the air in victory; my town, who wore expressions ranging from excitement and scandal to confusion and anger.

And when I found Betty, I smiled, waving and blowing her a kiss.

Thank you, I mouthed.

She just winked, waving me off as the church doors swung open and Noah carried me out into the Tennessee heat.

I didn't know what came next.

I didn't know how my father's debt would be paid, or how Anthony would react once the dust had settled, or where Noah and I would go from here. I didn't know if my mother would ever forgive me, or if I would ever forgive *her*. I didn't know what the future held, but there were two things I knew for sure.

Everything would be okay as long as I had Noah.

And that day was a day that the town of Stratford, Tennessee, would never forget.

Chapter Nineteen

Noah

Staring up at the stars my father had made in the tin roof of our treehouse with the weight of Ruby Grace's head on my chest, I decided there wasn't a single moment in my life that anything had felt more perfect than it did right now.

I ran my fingers through her long, silky hair, still wavy from the braids I'd unfolded slowly before I slipped her out of her wedding dress. That dress now hung from a limb outside the tree house, and her bare chest rested against my rib cage, her arms wrapped around my middle, legs tangled with mine under the flannel blanket that covered us both where we lay.

The crickets sang a song outside the house, the sound mixing with the smooth, steady breaths Ruby Grace and I exchanged. She drew lazy circles on my chest with her manicured nails, and I could feel the curl of her smile against my chest as I let her hair fall from my fingertips before reaching back down for her scalp to start the trail all over again.

It was a dream.

It had to be.

It didn't seem real — the church, the wedding — or rather, the *not* wedding. I wondered if I'd imagined Ruby Grace running toward me in her dress, if I'd dreamed her into my arms now.

But the soreness of my jaw told me that sucker punch from her former fiancé was real. The dozens of missed calls from my family and half the town on my now-dead cell phone told me it had all really happened. Ruby Grace's hair in my hands, her breasts against my skin, the sweet, sated euphoria we both bathed in after spending the entire evening making love told me it was far, far from a dream.

It was the best reality I'd ever existed in.

I sighed, wrapping her in my arms tightly before pressing a kiss to her hair. She squeezed back, and after a moment of silence, she chuckled.

I felt the vibration of it through my chest, and I smirked, cocking one brow as I looked down at her mess of red hair. "What's so funny, Legs?"

She shook her head. "Just thinking about the look on Pastor Morris's face when you scooped me up and high-tailed me out of the church."

A short exhale of a laugh hit my chest. "I think he might need therapy after today."

"I think the whole *town* might."

"Any regrets?"

She leaned up on one elbow, then, resting her other arm over my chest as she faced me with bent brows. "Not a single one. You?"

I pressed my lips together. "Come on, now."

Ruby Grace smiled, leaning her cheek down on top of where her hand rested. Her golden eyes searched mine before they trailed over every inch of my face, like she was about to paint it, or like she was memorizing every detail.

"I feel like there's so much to talk about, but I don't know where to start."

I twirled her hair around my knuckle, letting one strand fall before I picked up the next. "Why don't you start with the first thing on your mind."

"How did you find out about the real reason I left that night we were here?"

"Oh, that's easy. Betty."

She rolled her eyes. "Well, I know *that* — at least, now I do. But I don't understand how, or when."

"She wrote me a letter," I explained. "Slipped it under my screen door while I was at work."

"How in the world did she get away from the nursing home... and did she *walk* to your house? How did she even know where you live?"

"She said something about having *a little helper*," I offered.

Recognition lit up in her eyes, then. "Annie."

"Maybe," I said. "Anyway, she — or *they* — left it the night before the wedding. Otherwise, I would have come a lot sooner."

"Why do I have a feeling she did that on purpose," Ruby Grace said, smirking as she shook her head. "That woman lives for the movie-like drama."

I chuckled. "Yeah, well, she got some today."

"That she did." Ruby Grace was still smiling, but it slipped as another moment passed between us, her fingers trailing up and down my chest. "I wish I could tell you all the hell I've been through these past three weeks, from the moment my mother told me about my father's debt. I know it probably doesn't make any sense to you, but... I felt this obligation to my family, to my father. I couldn't abandon them, couldn't walk out on them when it seemed I was the only way we could save our home, our possessions, our reputation, our... everything." She sighed. "I feel foolish saying it out loud, but, it's who I've always been. It's the way I was raised."

"Hey," I said, tapping her chin until she looked at me. "I understand. I promise, I really do."

"How can you, when I don't even understand myself?"

"That's easy," I offered with a shrug. "I would have done the same for my family."

Her brows rose. "You would have?"

"I understand that family tie. Blood is thicker than anything. And no matter what knucklehead in my family gets in trouble, we all rally behind them to make it okay again. There is no judgment, no pointed fingers — only love and understanding and, like you demonstrated, sacrifice."

She smiled. "I'm thankful you understand... but I think you and I both know what my parents did goes a little past what's acceptable."

I swallowed. "Yeah... it does." I paused, heart stopping on my next question. "Do you think you could have really gone through with it? Marrying him?"

"No," she answered immediately. "I thought I could. I had the decision made, solidified, and I was walking to the grave of what I thought my life could be as I walked down that aisle. But when I saw you... I knew I couldn't. I knew there was no path I could take that didn't lead to you in the end." Ruby Grace bit her lip. "And, honestly, I knew even before I saw you. I was walking down that aisle in a fog, trying to figure out what to say, when to say it, how to get myself out of that church and that dress and that whole situation. When I saw you... well, it was just the last kick of courage I needed."

I smoothed my knuckles down her cheek, over her jaw. "You surprised the shit out of me when you came barreling back down that aisle."

She chuckled. "I think I surprised *everyone*. Well, except for maybe Betty, who seemed to be plotting it this entire time." She shook her head. "I can't believe she stood up like that and offered to pay part of my father's debt."

"She loves you," I explained. "Plus, according to the letter she wrote me, she insisted that she couldn't take it with her when she goes, anyway. And she doesn't have any kids... other than you." I smiled when Ruby Grace's brows bent together. "Those were her exact words."

She frowned. "Wait... so you were both talking about paying off my father's debt even before today?"

I shrugged. "We didn't have a plan or anything... but, I think both of us knew we would do anything to keep you from having to be responsible for a debt that wasn't yours. Like I said, Betty loves you." I paused, eyes searching hers. "And so do I."

Ruby Grace melted into me, and my heart galloped and stuttered as she swept a hand through my hair, wiggling her way up my chest until her face hovered over mine.

"I never said it back," she whispered, hazel eyes dancing in the light from the makeshift stars. "And I'm sorry I didn't. Because you were right, when you said it the first night you brought me here. I love you, too."

Her eyes watered as I swallowed down the lump in my throat.

"I do, Noah," she said, shaking her head. "I'm so sorry it took all this for me to admit it out loud. I was scared. I was... *lost*. As much as the wedding planning and pressure from my family was smothering me, I chose to hide under that rubble instead of trying to break free. I think a part of me was worried about what I'd find on the other side..."

I nodded, understanding completely. I knew what it was like to have the town talk about you, to have your entire life uprooted in one single day. And I was sure that if I'd had a choice in the matter, I would have avoided it at all costs.

"But, that worry was unfounded," she continued, her plump lips spreading into a gentle smile. "Because I should have known from the very start that as long as it was you, as long as it was *us*, together?" She shook her head again. "There's no way life could be anything but perfect."

I smirked, capturing her chin in my hand. "It's okay," I whispered. "I'd be embarrassed to love me, too."

That earned me a laugh and a swat on the chest, but I killed her laughter when I pressed my lips to hers.

We both breathed into the kiss, inhaling each other, and when she let out a soft, longing moan, all the blood rushed to where her leg rested between my legs.

I groaned, rolling my hips to let her feel me. "It hasn't even been twenty minutes, and I want to bury myself in you again."

She bit her lip on a smile. "What are you waiting for?"

"Energy," I confessed honestly.

Ruby Grace laughed, kissing my nose before she balanced over me again. For a while we just stared at each other, listening to the insects, fingers trailing lightly over each other's skin.

"I think I want to do it," she whispered after a while.

I groaned. "Me, too, woman, but I need water. And a protein bar. And, like, at least thirty more minutes."

"Not that," Ruby Grace said, wide grin splitting her face. I counted the freckles that dotted her cheeks as she shook her head. "I mean AmeriCorps."

My heart stopped at that. "Yeah?"

She nodded. "Yeah. I can't believe you applied for me. I was so overcome with emotion when you told me... I just wanted to throw myself into your arms and thank you and thank *God* for sending you into my life. It was the first moment I realized you loved me... before you even told me. Because no one had ever done anything like that for me before. Ever."

I ran my hand down her cheek. "So, you want to go?"

"I do."

"Good," I said, smirking. "Because an email came through to my inbox yesterday. They want a phone interview for the position in Utah."

Her lips parted. "What?"

"They want—"

"AN INTERVIEW!" Ruby Grace screeched, throwing her arms around me and rolling until she was on top, surrounding me in every way with every limb as she squeezed and squealed. "Oh, my God. Noah!"

I laughed. "If this is the reaction I get, I'm going to apply for every job that exists in AmeriCorps."

Ruby Grace just squeezed me more before sitting up. She straddled me now, her legs around my waist as she pressed her hands to my chest. Her eyes searched mine, worry etched in the creases. "And you'll wait for me? If I go?"

"Are you kidding?" I asked, maneuvering until I was sitting up, too. We were chest to chest, then, and I wrapped my arms around her, pulling her close. "Anything, Ruby Grace. I'd do anything for you."

She kissed me, long and slow, our bodies melding together again before she fluttered her eyes open once more.

"I'll go, if they hire me. But only on one condition."

"And what's that?"

"Well, *two* conditions."

I chuckled. "Okay. You going to tell me what they are or just keep adding on?"

"One, you have to come visit me. Every chance you get. And I'll come home when I can, too."

"That's a given."

"And two," she said, trailing her finger down my chest and tapping it once. "When I'm done, we sail around the world together."

I threw my head back on a laugh. "It takes a lot of money to do that, Ruby Grace. And a sailboat."

She frowned. "Fine. Then when I'm done, we go sailing. Period. We can drive down to Florida, or up to Maine. Charter a boat. Whatever we have to do to get you on the open seas."

I smiled. "Why is this a condition?"

She shrugged, adjusting herself in my lap. "Because you're making one of my dreams come true," she whispered. "I want to make one of yours come true, too."

I swore, if any of my brothers could feel the way my heart melted at her words, they'd punch me in the arm and call me the biggest wuss in the world.

But I didn't care.

When it came to Ruby Grace, I *was* the biggest wuss in the world.

"You already did," I whispered back, brushing her hair from her face. "I dreamed of finding a woman like you, of finding a love like this." I smirked. "And here you are."

"Here I am," she said, giggling. Then, she rolled her hips, eliciting a sharp inhale from me as she painted on a face of innocence. "So, what do we do now?"

"Oh, I can think of a few things," I said, devouring her lips and pulling her back down into the bean bag.

"I thought you needed water. And a protein bar. And *at least thirty minutes*," she teased.

"Shut up and let me make love to you."

She giggled louder when I flipped her over, kissing her neck and pinning her arms above her head. And for the rest of the night, and well into the morning, we sealed our promises with every inch of our bodies, with every ounce of our souls, with every beat of our hearts.

When you hear the word *Tennessee*, what do you think of?

Maybe your first thought is country music. Maybe you can even see those bright lights of Nashville, hear the different bands as their sounds pour out of the bars and mingle in a symphony in the streets. Maybe you think of Elvis, of Graceland, of Dollywood and countless other musical landmarks. Maybe you feel the prestige of the Grand Ole Opry, or the wonder of the Country Music Hall of Fame. Maybe you feel the history radiating off Beale Street in Memphis.

Or maybe you think of the Great Smoky Mountains, of fresh air and hiking, of majestic sights and long weekends in cabins. Maybe you can close your eyes and see the tips of those mountains capped in white, can hear the call of the Tennessee Warbler, can smell the fresh pine and oak.

Maybe, like I used to, you think of whiskey.

But after that summer, Tennessee only conjured up one thing in my mind.

A girl.

No, a *woman*.

One who flipped my entire world upside down in just six weeks' time. One who gave Stratford the biggest scandal they'd seen since the distillery fire. One who would change the world — because she was destined to do so.

And one I knew I'd spend my forever with.

What a lucky sonofabitch.

Epilogue

Noah - Four Months Later

"**T**hank you again for having me over for Thanksgiving," Ruby Grace said to Mom as she helped clear the table. "And for having it a little earlier in the day on my behalf."

"Are you kidding?" Mom asked, stacking plates. "I've been the only woman at this table for years. It was a blessing to have someone else to help wrangle these heathens."

"Hey," Logan said with mock offense.

"Besides, you're family now," Mom continued, pausing long enough to smile at Ruby Grace genuinely. "And we're all so proud of you for chasing your dream."

My heart swelled at that, because it was true. My brothers had adopted Ruby Grace like she was the sister they never had, and Mom was happier than I had seen her in years when Ruby Grace was around — even if it was just for dinner or an after-church lunch. She hadn't just filled *my* life with light and love, but my entire family's. And now, on my favorite holiday, it was almost impossible to fend off emotions watching her clear the table with my mom.

Today was the day Ruby Grace would start her drive across the country to serve her first full-year term in AmeriCorps.

It was hard to believe the day had finally come, that in less than an hour, my girl would slide into the driver seat of her loaded-up convertible and head out west to Utah. My chest had been tight all day with the effort it took to fight off tears, but I swore to myself that I wouldn't cry — no matter how much I would miss her.

Because this was her dream, and I stood by my word that I'd help her achieve it.

"Are we excused?" Mikey asked from the end of the table.

An uncomfortable hush fell over the family, and Mom glanced at me and Jordan before she smiled at her youngest son. "I was going to get the pie."

"I don't want any."

Mom nodded, her eyes worried and sad. "Oh. Okay, then. Yes, you're excused."

Mikey didn't say another word, just shoved back from the table, the legs of his chair scraping against the wood before he stood and pushed it back in. He was down the hall and shutting the door to his bedroom before any of us even looked up again, and he didn't say a word to any of us — not even Ruby Grace, who he knew was leaving.

He hadn't said a word all day.

I sighed, reaching over to squeeze her hand. "Forgive him. He's still not okay after the whole Bailey thing…"

"It's okay," she assured me, squeezing my hand back.

Just like we had all feared, Bailey ended up taking the record label in Nashville up on their offer earlier than she'd promised. And, along with that change, she'd also broken up with Mikey. She'd told them it wasn't forever, it was just for a while, so she could focus on her music.

But to Mikey, it was the ultimate betrayal.

He hadn't been the same since then, and where he usually showed his emotions willingly, opened up to us and let us help, he had shut down completely at this. Since that cold, rainy day in October when she landed the blow, my little brother had been a zombie version of the kid who existed before.

I hoped we'd get him back soon.

Jordan and Logan finished clearing the table as Ruby Grace and I did the dishes, and once the chores were done, we all gathered one last time for pie and wine. The time passed too quickly, and before I was ready, we were all standing on the porch saying our goodbyes to the woman I loved.

Jordan gave Ruby Grace the first hug — along with a AAA card he'd set up without telling any of us. "For emergencies," he told her gruffly. She smiled and thanked him, giving him one last hug before he moved out of the way to let Logan in next.

"Stay safe, and have fun," he said, wrapping her up in a hug. "And for God's sake, try to call home at least once a day so I don't have to watch my brother mope around without you here."

I punched his arm.

Ruby Grace chuckled, giving me a knowing smirk. "I promise, I'll text him an annoying amount in an effort to avoid that very thing."

"Thank you," Logan said, pressing his hands together in mock prayer as his eyes floated up.

"And you have fun with your new trainee," she said, lifting one brow at Logan. "I heard she's quite the firecracker."

"Ugh, don't remind me," Logan murmured. "The only reason she got the job at *all* is because of her father."

"Doesn't change the fact that you're responsible for her now," I pointed out.

"Who knows, maybe they'll have you train her just so she can take your place as the lead tour guide," Jordan chimed in.

Logan paled at that, mouth gaping like a fish as he looked at Mom first, then at me and Ruby Grace, and finally back at Jordan. "Don't even joke about that."

We all chuckled, but I knew there was a part of Logan that might actually be scared that could happen. After all, Mallory Scooter was the black sheep of the Scooter family. She had tattoos and piercings and purple hair and a bad attitude that had tainted her family's image for years. It seemed her father had finally put his foot down, forcing her to be the distillery's latest tour guide addition. It was an extremely valued job, and one that other employees fought hard for. No one was happy she'd been the one to be hired — least of all her.

Her first day was Monday, and Logan had just found out he would be her trainer.

"You'll be alright, little bro," I assured him, clapping him hard on the shoulder.

Mom stepped up next, her eyes glossy as she folded her arms around Ruby Grace. She held her tight, swaying a little. "I know I said it before, but we are all so proud of you," she said, pulling back and holding Ruby Grace's arms in her hands. "I know you'll call Noah, but don't forget to call me from time to time, too. Okay?"

"Of course. And you promise to check in on Betty from time to time?"

Mom waved her off with a smile. "Are you kidding? Visiting that wild old woman is the highlight of my week, now."

We all laughed at that. Mom had started volunteering at the nursing home with Ruby Grace to get to know her better, and in the process, she'd fallen under the same magical spell Betty weaved on all of us. Now that Ruby Grace was leaving, I had a feeling they'd become even closer.

"Alright," Mom said, dabbing at the corner of her eyes. "Come on, boys. Let's leave these two alone. Drive safe, dear, and let us know when you make it. Okay?"

"Will do," Ruby Grace assured her, and with one last wave from each of them, my Mom and brothers went back inside, leaving just the two of us on the porch.

Ruby Grace turned to me with a sad smile. "I guess this is it, huh?"

"I guess so."

My heart squeezed violently in my chest as I reached for her hand, walking with her in silence off the porch and out to her car. It was loaded up with boxes and piles of clothes still on the hanger. I didn't think she'd be able to fit everything she wanted in that little convertible, but she'd surprised me.

We both stopped next to her driver side door, and tears flooded Ruby Grace's eyes as soon as she faced me.

"Hey," I said, pretending like I wasn't on the verge of crying myself as I pulled her into me. I wrapped my arms around her tight, resting my chin on her head as I felt her tears dampen my long-sleeve shirt. "None of that now. It's not permanent, okay? Plus, this is your dream, this is what you've wanted for *so* long. You're doing it, Ruby Grace," I said, pulling back to look into her shining eyes. "You're going to *AmeriCorps*."

"I know," she whispered, sniffing back more tears. "But, I'm leaving *you* in the process."

"Just for a little while," I reminded her. "I'll come visit for Christmas, and every other chance I get."

"And I'll be back after the summer."

"Exactly."

"And then?"

I smiled. "And then, we find some poor sucker willing to let us on their sailboat for a month."

Ruby Grace laughed through her tears, burying her face in my chest again with a little whimper. "I'm going to miss you so much, Noah." She lifted her head again. "I love you. You know that?"

I chucked her chin. "I do. And I love you. You know that?"

"I do."

Silence fell over us, and for a while, I just held her there in that quiet space, the sun above breaking through the crisp fall air.

"So, any other stops on your way out of town?"

She shook her head. "Nope. My family did our dinner last night, and I can't go through Mom holding me in a vise grip and sobbing all over me again," she joked, but I didn't miss the underlying stress in her voice.

She and her parents had been working on their relationship since the not-wedding day, but I knew she was still far from forgiving and forgetting.

"And I said goodbye to Annie, Travis, and baby Bethany earlier this week."

"I bet they're all going to miss you."

"They will," she agreed. "And I'll miss all of them. But, I'm ready." A genuine smile bloomed on my favorite strawberry smoothie lips, then. "This is it, isn't it? I'm going. I'm really going."

I returned her smile. "You're really going, Legs." I pulled her closer, sweeping her hair from her face before lowering my voice to a whisper. "I am so proud of you."

My fingertips found her chin, and I tilted it up, pressing my lips to hers. It was a kiss I never wanted to end, one that was slow and easy and felt like the most natural thing in the world. That's how it had been for us since that night in the treehouse — effortless.

"Don't find another girl while I'm gone," she said when we finally broke the kiss.

"Yeah, right. More like you finding a hot AmeriCorps hippie with long hair and hemp clothes."

She snorted. "You're ridiculous."

"And you're amazing." I framed her face, kissing her again. "This isn't goodbye. It's see you soon. Okay?"

Her eyes glossed again. "Okay," she whispered.

I could have held her forever, kissed her over and over and over until she missed her check-in time for her new job in Utah. But, I forced a heavy sigh, breaking away from her hold and opening the driver side door for her to climb inside. Once she was seated, she rolled the window down, leaning out of it and pulling my mouth to hers once more.

"Woman," I chuckled between kisses. "Go. Now. You've got a long drive to Kansas City and it's already noon. I don't want you driving when you're tired tonight."

She sighed, pulling back and pressing her forehead to mine. "Okay. Okay. I'm going." She ran her hand over my jaw, like she was memorizing my stubble. "I'll call you when I stop for gas and food."

"And I'll call you every morning to remind you how much I love you."

She smiled at that. "You better."

With one last, longing kiss, she let me go, and I stepped back, sliding my hands in my pockets as she fired the car up. She checked the directions on her GPS, set her phone on the dash, and waved at me with tears in her eyes before pulling out of Mom's driveway.

I watched her take the left, watched her stop at the stop sign down the road, watched her take the left that led out of town. And when I couldn't see her taillights anymore and she was really gone, I let the first tear fall.

I cried because I'd miss her. I cried because I'd never wanted to let someone go as much as I'd wanted to keep them forever. But I didn't cry because I was sad.

I cried because I was thankful.

I was thankful I could finally show her what I'd wanted to all along — that she could be in love and *be* loved while she had a life and dreams of her own. I was thankful for the two-week vacation I had coming up in a month so I could fly to Utah and spend Christmas with her. I was thankful for my family inside the house behind me, for the group I had to support me while Ruby Grace was gone.

And more than anything, I was thankful I'd found the woman I was sure didn't exist.

More than a thousand miles couldn't separate us — not really. She was still here with me, and I knew she took me with her, too.

For now, I wiped my tears and headed back inside to celebrate Thanksgiving with football and leftovers and time with my family. After all, I had one little brother stressed over his new trainee at work and the other holed up in his room over a girl we all knew was trouble.

I was needed in Stratford, and she was needed in Salt Lake.

So, I counted down the days until she'd be in my arms again, until she'd be back in Stratford, until we'd make our plans for where we'd go next.

Until I'd get down on one knee and give her the ring stashed in my bedside dresser drawer.

And though my ring wouldn't be the first to don her delicate finger, I had no doubt it would be the last.

Neat

Here's to the ones who don't have it all figured out,

to the ones focused on the journey,

and not the destination.

To the messes —

because life's too short to always be put together, anyway.

Chapter One

Logan

I was made to be a tour guide.

I know, it sounds crazy, right? What little kid looks at the endless list of possible career choices and thinks, "When I grow up, I want to walk tourists around an old, dusty whiskey distillery in perhaps the smallest town in Tennessee and tell them stories about how the Scooter brand came to be."

The likely answer? Not a single kid — except for me.

I could blame it on a number of factors — like that my dad worked at the distillery, and he was nothing short of Superman in my eyes. Or how my grandfather was a founding member of the distillery, of the Scooter Whiskey brand, of the distinct taste known around the world. Maybe I could attribute it to my weird fascination with history that developed at a young age, or my consistent need to learn something new every day and stash that information away to relay to someone else.

I loved reading books — especially biographies or history recollections. I loved watching documentaries, primarily centered around modern-day luxuries that we all take for granted and never wonder about how they came to exist. And, I loved checking the newspaper — every morning — for the latest technological advancement or forecasted "next big thing."

Essentially, I was a nerd — through and through — though I'd never portray that on the outside.

To everyone in my small town of Stratford, Tennessee, I was a Becker boy. I was trouble, never too far from a fight. I was the third oldest son of the late John Becker, a legend in our town, one taken too soon from all of us by a devastating fire at the distillery. And, I was a player, a man destined to never settle down, to hop from bed to bed for as long as the girls in town would let me.

That's what everyone saw me as on the outside, and only my brothers knew the real me.

I had three brothers — Michael, Noah, and Jordan.

Mikey was the youngest, a senior in high school, and he worked at the distillery with my older brother, Noah, and I. Mikey was in the gift shop for now, but I had a feeling that would change once he graduated. He was smart, and talented as hell on the guitar. Something told me he'd be moving on to an entertainment position of some kind, and that the distillery would be lucky to have him if he stuck around past graduation.

And Noah? Noah was the most well-known barrel raiser at the Scooter Whiskey distillery. He could put a barrel together faster than anyone I knew, and it'd been years since he'd had one that sprung a leak. He started as the youngest, and quickly moved his way up to a leader on the team. He loved to push my buttons when I brought a tour through his part of the warehouse, almost always pulling some sort of prank — like a sawed-off finger.

And I fell for it. Every single time.

Jordan was our oldest brother, and the only one who didn't work at the distillery. He was adopted before I was born, and though his skin was a darker shade than that of mine and my brothers, his hair coarse and black as night, he had always been our brother through and through — no "adopted" necessary to put before that title. He was the Stratford High football coach, and in my opinion, the best damn one our town had ever seen.

My brothers had quite the reputation around town — especially after our father died in the distillery fire when I was seventeen. No matter what we did, it seemed trouble always found us. Sometimes it was just a small bar brawl, other times it was stealing the mayor's daughter away on her wedding day — which was our latest scandal, thanks to Noah.

The town could say whatever they wanted about my brothers, but at the end of the day, they were the ones who knew the truth about who I was — and who I *wasn't*.

They knew that when those fights everyone loved to talk about happened, the only reason I was involved at all was because I was trying to play referee, to break it all up before anything even started. I only jumped in when I absolutely had to — which, sadly, with my brothers, happened to be a lot of the time. And yes, it was true that I hadn't held a single, long-term relationship in my life, but that wasn't because I didn't want to — it was because there wasn't a single woman in Stratford who could keep my attention.

My mind craved stimulation — late night talks about deep and unexplored topics, book discussions and conspiracy theories, questions I'd never been asked and beliefs I'd never been introduced to.

I was waiting for a woman to surprise me, and thus far, there had been none.

Well... there may have been *one*.

I tugged at the collar of my Scooter Whiskey Carhartt jacket at the thought of her, gripping the handle on the large door that led to the barrel-raising area of our distillery. I held the door open for the tour group following behind me, forcing a smile in spite of the turning in my gut at the thought of the one girl I was trying *not* to think about.

"Right this way, folks," I said, ushering our guests out of the cold and giving each of them an encouraging nod as they filed in. "Remember, this is an area where photos aren't allowed. Go ahead and stow those phones away now. And if I see any of you sneaking a picture, my suspicions about you being sent by those posers in Kentucky will be confirmed and I'll have no choice but to yank you out by your ear."

Several chuckles rang out at that, group after group squeezing past me and lining up against the wall inside to wait for me to continue.

I found Noah as soon as the metal door clanged shut behind me. He had bright orange ear plugs stuffed in each canal and protective eyewear over his eyes as he worked on situating the staves of wood in the metal ring to make a barrel come to life. He glanced up at me, a mischievous grin on his face, but he looked back down at his work before I could give him a warning glare not to fuck with me.

He knew that today of all days was *not* the time to give me shit.

"Alright, folks," I said, turning to face the group as they looked around. "Take it all in — *this* is where the real magic happens. If you recall the video we watched earlier, you'll recognize these fine gentlemen behind me as our Scooter Whiskey barrel raisers. Every single day, this small team of four bring five-hundred Scooter Whiskey barrels to life."

Noah, Marty, Eli, and PJ all waved from where they were working, offering the group welcoming smiles before their heads were down again, and they were back to work.

"Why can't you take pictures in here?" one of the men in the group asked. From chatting with him on the walk over from the gift shop, I discovered that he was passing through with his wife and sister-in-law on their way home from a Thanksgiving visit to Illinois.

"Good question," I said, pointing directly at him before I addressed the group. "We're one of the last distilleries that still make their own barrels, and we don't want our secrets getting out. Most get theirs from wineries nowadays, but we still take pride in making and charring our own — which is why with every bottle of Scooter Whiskey you drink, you get those familiar notes of vanilla and oak."

Murmurs rang out, each family within the group leaning in to talk to each other as they looked around at the barrels with more admiration.

"And these four guys are the ones responsible for every single barrel?" a woman asked.

I opened my mouth to answer, but before I could, a hand clapped down on my shoulder, and my brother took over. "Yep. My team and I are here five days a week, and we each raise anywhere from one-hundred-and-twenty-five barrels to one-hundred-and-fifty barrels every single day. Which means we get about twenty-five-hundred barrels out every week."

The crowd buzzed with a mix of *ooh's* and *ahh's*.

Noah grinned, and I couldn't help but smile, too. I loved that I got to work with my brothers, that they were a part of my every day. Noah was older than me, but just a smidge shorter — which always ticked him off. I was lean where he was stout, and our hair was the same sandy brown — though mine was a bit longer. And Noah had Dad's blue eyes, whereas I favored the hazel gold of our mother's.

"That's amazing," the woman breathed, and her eyes fell over my brother, from his arms to his midriff and lower. "Explains why you're built like an ox."

She said that last part almost so softly that I couldn't hear it, but I had — and I knew Noah had, too. If the poor girl had been a year earlier, she might have had a shot at ending her tour through town in my brother's bed. But, as it was, his heart was tied up in a redhead currently stationed across the country in Utah doing her first year in AmeriCorps.

Ruby Grace Barnett — the mayor's daughter who was supposed to marry someone else this past summer, but had ran way with my brother, instead.

Like I said.

Trouble.

Noah smiled, tipping his hat at the group before he turned. He squeezed my shoulder. "No pranks today, promise," he said. "I know you've got plenty on your plate."

My lips flattened. "Yeah."

"Has she come in yet?"

"Right after this tour."

He whistled. "Well, good luck. Come by my place later if you need a drink to decompress." He squeezed my shoulder one last time before letting it go and heading back toward his station, and though my stomach was twisting violently again, I turned to the group, continuing on with the rest of my spiel about the barrels before I led them through the door again and back out into the cold November air.

We were just a few days past Thanksgiving, and Stratford was well into the holiday spirit. Christmas lights were strung from every building at the distillery, and the entire town was dressed in lights and garland to match. The tree in the center of town was large enough to see from the end of Main Street no matter which way you were coming, and with all that around me, I waited and waited for the holiday spirit to find me.

It hadn't — not in years — not since my father passed away.

I inhaled the cool Tennessee air, the familiar scent of oak and honey wafting in on the breeze, but it did nothing to calm my nerves as I led the tour toward our final stop — the tasting. For the next twenty minutes, I'd be helping that group taste whiskey for what was likely the first time in their lives. Sure, they'd taken *shots* of whiskey, but they'd never stopped to smell it, inhale the special aromas, taste each flavorful note, and enjoy that familiar whiskey burn on the way down.

Twenty minutes.

That's how long the tasting would last.

That's how long I'd have before I'd be faced with the girl I'd been trying to avoid all morning, and for most of my life, if I was being honest.

Mallory Scooter.

Scooter — as in the name on the jacket I wore, the one in large letters on the building we walked inside, the one sprawled in the top right-hand corner of my paycheck each week.

And the one my family had been at war with for decades.

• • •

To fully explain my jitters as I waited in my office for Mallory Scooter to arrive for her first day on the job, we have to go back in time a bit.

You see, Robert J. Scooter was the founder of the Scooter Whiskey distillery. And though it's *his* name on the bottles and the building alike, he had a pivotal partner in crime — my grandfather, Richard Becker.

Granddad was the first barrel raiser at the distillery, the one who fine-tuned the process and made it the instrumental one it is today. It was the beginning of the partnership and, more importantly, the *friendship* between Robert J. Scooter and my grandfather, and it was one that lasted all the way up until the founder's death.

And that's when shit hit the fan.

There was nothing in Robert J. Scooter's will about my grandfather, about leaving any part of the company to him — even though it was Grandpa who had helped build and establish the Scooter brand.

The distillery and brand as a whole was left to Robert's family, namely to his oldest son, Patrick — who is the CEO of the distillery today. It wasn't long after Robert passed that my grandmother died, and my grandfather right after. We'd always been told he'd died of a broken heart, and while most would argue it was because of grandma, we all knew a big part of it was the Scooters.

After Granddad's death, my dad stepped up and kept the Becker name alive and well at the distillery. He had been young when he started, and not too long after the changing of the hands, he was made a member of the board.

That's when the real trouble started.

While the Scooter family wanted to blow full-steam ahead toward innovation, my father was hell bent on keeping tradition. He wanted to remember and honor what had made Scooter a household name to begin with. The more he pushed, the more they pulled his reins. Eventually, he was reduced to nothing more than a glorified paper pusher — and when they assigned him to clean out Robert J. Scooter's office, it wasn't only a hit to his ego.

It was a hit on his life.

There had only ever been one fire at the Scooter Whiskey distillery. It happened in that office.

And my father had been the only one to perish in it.

To this day, my mom, brothers, and I have had to live with the mysterious death of my father and no viable explanation as to why it happened. The town buzzed about it — some wondering if foul play was involved, others tsking him for the bad habit of smoking — which the Stratford Fire Department swore was the cause, and which my mom insisted wasn't possible because he didn't smoke.

It was a mess — a giant, steaming pile of mess.

It was also another stave of wood hammered between the Becker family and the Scooter family.

Noah, Mikey, and I worked at the distillery for many reasons — but the main one was to keep our family legacy alive. And though Patrick Scooter and his family played along, there was always an underlying tension, like we were some kind of infection they couldn't be rid of.

But to fire us would be to stir the pot of rumors that they had something to do with our father's death, and for us to quit would be turning our backs on the distillery our family had a rightful hand in owning and operating.

Even with all that being said, I shouldn't have been so worked up over the fact that Patrick's youngest — Mallory Scooter — would be walking through my door any minute now. I shouldn't have been working my stress ball overtime, tapping one foot under my desk, biting the inside of my cheek as I ran over the words I would say when she got there.

Sure, she was the founder's granddaughter and the current CEO's daughter.

Sure, she beared the last name of the family I couldn't escape.

And sure, she hadn't *earned* this job — not the way I had. It'd been handed to her, just because of the blood flowing in her veins.

But it wasn't even any of that that mattered.

What *did* matter was that I was the lead tour guide, and rightfully next in line to be manager — and I had a sneaky suspicion she was hired to thwart that.

Another thing that mattered — perhaps what mattered *most* — was that I'd had a secret crush on Mallory Scooter since I was fourteen years old.

No one knew that last part — not even my brothers, who knew *everything* about me. I'd never told a soul that I found her outspoken sass and open rebellion against her family and this entire town a huge turn on. I'd never once stared at her longer than appropriate, never showed the fact that my palms were sweaty every time she came around.

We were the son and daughter of a bitter rival sparked to life decades ago and still burning hot today.

There was no option for me to entertain my infatuation with her, and I'd known that. I'd steered clear of her with little effort over the years. It was easy to do in high school and even easier to do once she left for college. The few times she had come back home made it more challenging, since I knew she liked to hang out at the same places I did. Still, I'd avoided her in every way possible, shoving down any and every urge I had to get to know the blue-eyed girl with the septum piercing who I'd watched scribble in her sketch book from afar all through high school.

But now, I would be working with her every single day.

What was worse, I'd be training her — and likely to take the job *I* was rightfully owed.

That was why I couldn't sit still, why frustration and giddiness battled inside me as I waited for her to show.

I wanted to see her.

I *hated* that I had to see her.

I couldn't wait to talk to her after all this time.

I couldn't bear the fact that I had to talk to her *at all*.

Not a single emotion made sense as they fought that war within me, and logic didn't have enough time to show up and calm them all down before there was a knock at my office door.

I dropped the stress ball in my hand just before it swung open, and I followed that bright yellow, spongey ball as it rolled all the way across the office and knocked gently against the toe of dirty, white, high-top Chucks.

I'm not sure how long I stared at those shoes, only that it was a little *too* long. Because by the time my brain finally processed that I should stand and clear my throat and make my way around my desk to greet my guest, she was watching me with an arched brow and flat, beautifully painted lips.

"Logan Becker?"

I forced a smile, ignoring the way my name sounded rolling off her tongue. I couldn't remember if I'd ever heard her say it before, though I was almost certain I hadn't.

I'd have remembered.

She had a slight Tennessee lilt, which seemed a little out of place, given her appearance. She paired those high-top white Chucks with jeans that had more holes than fabric, revealing slivers of the tattoos on her thighs. Her t-shirt was black, with a band name I didn't recognize, and more tattoos peeked out from under each sleeve. She had a blue and green flannel tied around her waist, accentuating a waist I wagered was just right for me to fit my hands around. Her hair — which had been purple just last week — was now a platinum blonde, parted down the middle and framing her face in a tight, shoulder-length bob. Her lips were painted a dusty rose, her blue eyes lined and shaped like a cat's, and that septum piercing she was so famous for around town glittered in the fluorescent light of my office.

She was everything that every other girl in this town wasn't.

And I *loathed* that it made me want her so fiercely.

Mallory arched her perfectly drawn eyebrow even higher as the silence stretched between us without me answering.

"Uh, yes," I finally said, stepping away from my desk and extending a hand for hers. "That's me. And you must be Mallory."

She popped the gum inside her mouth in lieu of an answer, which made my eye twitch before she took my hand and gave it a firm shake.

"You changed your hair."

The idiotic statement flew from my mouth just as she pulled her hand from my grasp. She still had that one eyebrow cocked up to her forehead, and she tucked her hands in her back pockets, watching me. "And you know that... how?"

I fought against the heat rising up my neck, praying it didn't show on my cheeks. "They provided a headshot with your file," I lied. "Your hair was purple in it."

The corner of her mouth quirked up, drawing my attention to the overly plump shape of them. She eyed me like she knew I'd lied, but thankfully, didn't call me on it.

"It was," she finally admitted. "But *Daddy* said the Scooter Whiskey tour guides had an appearance to uphold, and I was forced to dye it."

I didn't miss the sarcasm laced in the word *daddy*, and if I'd had any question as to whether or not she was here of her own accord or by the force of his hand, I'd just found my answer.

Mallory twirled a strand of her platinum hair around her finger to illustrate the new color, tilting her head to the side as she took a step closer to me. "What do you think?" she asked, lips rolling into a pout. "Do I look as good as a blonde as I did with purple hair?"

My next breath left my chest mid-inhale, which just made Mallory smirk more. She *knew* what she was doing — which meant I was doing a piss-poor job of hiding the fact that I found her attractive.

But with another pop of that damn gum inside her mouth, I snapped back into business mode.

My breath found me again, and with it, my common sense. I turned my back on her without a response, crossing to my desk and casually sitting in my chair before I pulled her file from where I'd placed it on the corner of my desk.

"Please, take a seat, Miss Scooter," I said, my expression leveled, my demeanor cool once more. "We have a lot to discuss before your training commences."

Chapter Two

Mallory

L ogan Becker's office was my own personal hell of a jail cell.

Not only was it a symbol of my surrender to my father and the first day at a job I had been trying to avoid my entire life, but it also *felt* like a jail cell — or, at the very most, an uptight library.

The walls were cream, the wood flooring dark and warm — but all that warmth was offset by the blinding fluorescent lights lining the ceiling. Not a single piece of art hung on the walls. In fact, the closest thing to art was the impressive wall of bookshelves behind his desk. They would have been beautiful, had they not been so meticulously organized that they felt more like a farce of comfort in a doctor's office than a display of stories worth reading. The books were lined up by height order, and then by color, and then, I was sure, without even looking closely, by author last name.

His actual desk was the same dark wood as the floor, held up by black, metal legs. His monitor sat on it, along with the file he'd just pulled — that I assumed had something about me inside — and a swinging ball pendulum that tick-tacked back and forth slowly.

The entire office was colorless.

I sighed, taking a seat in the chair across from him at his desk like he'd asked. He was still filtering through the file in his hands, so I looked around for something — *anything* — that wasn't boring and bland. My eyes settled on a photo of a family at a lake — four young boys, a father, and a mother. One of the boys rode on the father's back, ruffling his hair with his knuckles as they both laughed. The youngest boy was missing a front tooth, and the other two stood with their arms around each other's shoulders, and their mother's hands resting on their necks.

I smiled, thankful there was a human hiding somewhere under that robotic façade.

I knew Logan Becker.

Well, I knew *of* him. It was hard not to hear the gossip mill churning about the Becker family, no matter how hard I tried to avoid it — and I did.

Logan had been in the same grade as I had growing up, but of course, he'd never talked to me. He was too busy dating every girl who'd look his way before dumping her and moving on to the next. And when he wasn't with a girl, he was with his brothers — probably getting into a fight or finding some other sort of trouble.

I also knew that ever since his father's death, he and his family didn't exactly favor mine.

My younger brother, Malcolm, caught on to that fact just as quickly as I did. But where I kept my distance and made it a point not to get caught up in the drama, Malcolm chose to thrive in it, instead. He'd been the root cause of more than a couple Becker brother fights — and honestly, I couldn't say I blamed any of them for wanting to punch my brother in the nose after some of the comments I'd heard him make.

But that wasn't me.

I got out of Stratford as soon as I turned eighteen, and if it were up to me, I would have never returned.

Too bad life didn't work like that.

I stared at Logan's young face, smirking as I recalled the fact that he'd called me *miss*, like I was ten years younger than him, rather than his same age. Then again, the way he was dressed in his dark, slim-fitting dress pants and Scooter Whiskey polo, he certainly looked a lot more grown up than I did.

We were both the ripe ol' age of twenty-six, which — when I was younger — I assumed was the age where you had all your shit together. It took years of struggling through school only to discover that the amount of jobs waiting on the other side of that diploma were abysmal for me to figure out I was wrong.

So, yes, I could admit that I looked younger than him in the current moment, but part of that was on purpose — because I knew showing up for my first day of work at the distillery in what I wore every day would irk my father. The other part was just that I found no reason to dress in a way I didn't want to. I didn't care to impress my father or Logan or anyone else.

I had a job to do for my father, one that would give me my own dream in return. *That* was the only reason I was even in that stuffy office to begin with.

I popped the gum in my mouth, a bad habit I'd picked up after I quit smoking a few years back, as I waited for Logan to say something. At that sound, his eyes flicked to me, to my mouth, and back to the file in his hands again.

His hands gripped it a little tighter.

"So, before we get started, I'll tell you a little about me and then I'd love to hear a little more about you," he said, his eyes still on the file. "Then, we can go over your training plan and I'll take you for a spin around the distillery."

I had to fight the urge to roll my eyes at that last statement.

My father *owned* the distillery, and every single member of my family worked there — save for my mother, who wouldn't be caught dead doing anything even close to work a day in her life.

"I'm Logan Becker, as you know," he started, and I smirked, sitting back in my chair and folding my arms over my chest as he recited what I was sure was a speech he'd been practicing. "I'm the Lead Tour Guide for Scooter Whiskey, and I'll be the one training you over the next few weeks. I started at the distillery when I was eighteen and I've been working my way up the ranks ever since. I'm very knowledgeable when it comes to our distillery, to our whiskey, and to our process, so I think you'll find I'll be a great teacher."

I raised my brows. "I'm sure."

"Why don't you tell me a little about you?" he asked, dropping the file to the desk.

"Wait," I said. "Is that it? You didn't tell me anything about you. You told me how long you've worked here, and your job title."

"I think that's all that needs to be said right now."

"Are those your books?" I asked, ignoring his attempt to avoid telling me more.

Logan followed my gaze to where it rested behind him, then faced me once more. "They are."

"They're so... *organized.*"

"I've been told I have a touch of OCD," he offered, picking up the file again. "So, it says here you attended the Tennessee School of Arts for seven years."

His brows shot up at that, and I knew he was thinking what everyone else did — *why so long?* But when you're in no rush to go back home, have nowhere *else* to go, and art has been your only escape your entire life? Well... seven years doesn't seem like a long time, at all. In fact, I'd argue it wasn't long *enough.*

"You have your Masters in Arts Management, with distinctions in photography and drawing." He frowned, eyeing me over the pages. "That's impressive. What brought you back here?"

"Did you miss it in all your research about me that the school I attended is in severe financial trouble and is no longer accepting new students because they're closing their doors soon?"

Logan didn't answer.

I shook my head. "Well, it's a fortune telling for my entire career, I think. Finding a job as an artist when you don't do graphic design or something similar is difficult. And so, here I am," I said, sweeping my hands over our surrounding area before I folded my arms over my chest again.

Logan opened his mouth like he wanted to ask me more, but thought better of it. He reached deeper inside the folder, instead, pulling out two copies of a very colorful sheet of paper.

"Alright, then," he murmured. "We'll get to know each other better at a later time. For now, let's go over your training schedule."

The Becker brothers were known for being as devastatingly handsome as they were mischievous, and I couldn't help but appreciate that fact as Logan started pointing out the various sections of my schedule. His skin was a mixture of olive and bronze, his hair a sandy brown shade that reminded me of the bark of an oak tree. His eyes were a bright hazel, almost like the golden yellow of a cat's, and ringed with a darker shade of olive around the rim. He was considerably taller than I was, which I noticed when he stood to greet me, and his body was lean and fit. I found myself wondering if he got up to run every morning, or if he spent his evenings doing calisthenics workouts in his back yard.

But of all his physical features that demanded a second look, it was his smile that was the most mesmerizing.

He'd only flashed it at me once since I'd walked in that office, but it'd been genuine enough for me to see the slight pinch of a dimple in his left cheek, to note the way those pearly whites of his spread across his entire face. His mouth was large, his jaw broad and sharp.

It was no surprise to me that he didn't let a girl tie him down. Why would you with a face like that?

"… and the yellow indicates lunch, which you'll see I've paired you with a different lunch buddy each day of the week for the first two weeks. I figured it's a good way for you to get to know some of the people who work here."

I chuckled, snapping back to the moment and finally noting the — impressive? crazy? — amount of colors on the spreadsheet in front of me. Every minute of my day over the next few weeks was mapped out in blues and oranges and yellows and greens and purples.

Logan paused. "Is something funny?"

I popped my gum, giving him a smile. "Just you. You're interesting, Logan Becker."

"Why, because I have an organized schedule for you as a new employee? Because I have my books in order?" The muscle in his jaw clenched when I popped my gum again. "I'm not naïve to the fact that you're making fun of me, Miss Scooter, and I'll have you know that I don't appreciate it."

I laughed harder at that, but it was cut short when Logan's fists landed hard against the desk.

Everything on it rattled and shook, the little ball pendulum being thrown off track before it slowly swung back into rhythm. My eyes widened, and Logan's narrowed, his next breath coming hard through his nostrils like that of a dragon.

"Why are you even here?" he asked, furrowing his brows. "You're not taking me seriously, you clearly don't want to be here, you're dressed like a teenager and you have the manners of one, too. So, before you waste any more of my time, tell me — why are you here?"

It was the first time I'd seen Logan Becker's backbone since I walked in that office, and I'd be lying if I said it didn't turn me on in the strangest way.

I'm here because I fucking have to be, I wanted to say. *I'm here because if I do what my father wants, then I get what I want. I'm here because life isn't fair and the starving artist life sucks.*

"It's none of your business why I'm here," I said instead, leaning toward him over the desk. "And I wasn't making fun of you. I think it's endearing that you took so much time to create a color-coded training schedule. I apologize if I offended you."

Logan narrowed his eyes even more, searching my gaze like he was looking for some sign of sarcasm. When he didn't find it, he sighed, sitting back in his chair and pinching the bridge of his nose. "Look, I don't want to do this anymore than you do, okay? Training the new employee isn't exactly high on my list of things I'd like to do, just like I'm sure working as a tour guide when you have a Masters in Art isn't high on yours."

My gut twisted.

"But, this is where we're at. Okay? So, are you going to cooperate and let me show you the ropes or not?"

I just stared at him, wondering why I liked the severity of his expression now more than I liked the friendly one he offered before.

Something about that scowl...

"Good," he said when I didn't answer, tucking his copy of my training schedule back in the file and slamming it shut before he stood. "Come on, it's time for the tour."

He didn't look behind him to see if I was following, and before I could stand, he offered one last remark over his shoulder.

"And for God's sake, lose the gum before I have an aneurysm."

• • •

"So, this is another area where photos are forbidden," Logan said as we walked through the barrel-raising area. I noticed him give a slight head nod to his older brother, Noah, who eyed me with a scowl that told me he didn't like that I was there.

You and me both, buddy.

"Because—"

"Because we're one of the only whiskey distilleries who still makes their own barrels," I finished for him. "I know. You forget that my father owns this place."

"Trust me, I didn't forget," he murmured, and then continued on with his spiel.

I listened — or at least, pretended to — as I watched the team of four arrange staves of wood in perfect order within a metal ring to make a barrel.

Noah slid the top ring down on a barrel he'd just put together, sending it down the line before he started the next, and I hated how much he looked like he loved his job.

Because I had a feeling it wouldn't be there much longer.

My father was all about innovation, about being the best of the best, being ahead of the times. Other members on the board had been fighting for tradition for years, urging him to keep the staples that made Scooter Whiskey a household name in the first place. But, those members of the board were thinning out, and slowly, Dad was turning the tides and showing why innovation should be at the forefront of their mind — especially with more and more craft distilleries popping up.

The team of four in front of me were some of the most important people in this distillery and had been for years.

And I couldn't be sure they'd have a job in six months' time.

Logan snapped his fingers beside me, and when I turned to face him, he cocked one brow. "Well?"

Oh, shit. Did he ask me something?

I smiled. "Uh... I'm sorry, could you repeat the question?"

Logan sighed at that, shaking his head slightly before making his way toward the back door of the warehouse. "Try to at least *pretend* you give a shit on this tour, could you?"

"I'm sorry," I said, jogging a bit to catch up with him. "Really, I am. It's just that I know this distillery like it's the house I grew up in... because, honestly, it practically was. This tour seems like a waste of time to me."

"You know the layout," Logan agreed, holding the back door open for me before we both slipped back out into the cold. Logan zipped up his jacket while I flipped up the hood on mine, tucking my hands in my pockets against the chilly wind. "You know the name and the processes. But, do you know the history? The selling points? The fun facts and figures that tourists will want to hear? The stories that will stick with them and have them telling their friends about the amazing tour they had when they get home?"

"Like that my grandfather died from an infection of a finger injury that he never told anyone about? Or how we use the fresh spring water on our property and that's why our whiskey has a distinct taste that no one can emulate?" I challenged.

Logan paused where we were walking, facing me for the first time since we left the warehouse. "Those are both great examples. But, they're also facts that can be found online. Tell me something no one can find with a quick Google search."

I opened my mouth, paused, and shut it again.

I couldn't think of a single thing.

The truth was that I *should* have known more stories than Logan Becker — being that I was the daughter of the owner and the granddaughter of the founder. But, I'd been trying to get away from this town and the legacy my family had built in it since I was fourteen.

I'd blocked out almost every story I'd ever heard my father tell, and any time someone asked me about my last name, about this town and the whiskey distilled in it, I gave them base-level information that anyone could find out on their own — simply because I didn't *want* to talk about it.

I didn't want to be a part of any of it.

Logan nodded. "I'll take your silence as an admission that you don't have an answer. Come on," he said, steering us in a new direction. "We're almost done, and then we can end your torture for the day."

We walked through various warehouses — where the single barrels are held, where the tasting takes place at the end of tours — before he gave me a quick overview of the gift shop and lobby area. His younger brother, Michael, was in the gift shop when we passed through.

He looked just as miserable to be there as I was.

"Is something wrong with your brother?" I asked when we left the gift shop, making our way through the back halls that led to the tour guide offices.

"Noah?"

"Michael," I clarified. "I've been in the gift shop a few times with friends who visited from out of town, and he'd always been so cheerful. But today... I don't know. He kind of seemed like he was going to bite the head off the next tourist who asked him how to order a Scooter barrel."

Logan's face soured. "He's just going through a rough time. But... you're right. He wasn't being the friendliest. I'll talk to him."

I blanched. "Oh, I didn't mean..."

I was mid-apology when Logan stopped, glancing down the hallway at an office door I knew all too well. It was Grandpa's office, the first one to ever grace this old building. For years, it had been unoccupied. Then, it had been damaged from the fire that took place inside its walls. Now, the door that had been closed since that day, other than to clean out the fire damage and make sure it was safe again, was open.

There were men walking in and out of it, carrying old, damaged furniture out and bringing in new furniture that looked similar to it. I noticed them removing a large canvas art print that I used to love, one I stared at when I visited Grandpa. It was of a young girl in a bright yellow dress dancing on the beach, her dress mid-twirl, golden hair spinning around her.

It was burnt, and the only reason I could even tell it was that painting was from a bright splash of yellow in the middle that had escaped charring.

"What are they doing?" I asked.

Logan's face was long and pale as we watched the workers. "I guess they're finally cleaning it out..."

"They're moving stuff in, too. I wonder if they're going to build it how it used to be, make it part of the tour?"

Logan stiffened at that, and he didn't respond to my question before he continued walking down the hall toward his office.

My throat tightened as I realized what that would mean for him, if what I suspected were true. That was the office where his father perished. It had to be hard enough to be in the same building with it, let alone walk a group of tourists into it every day and tell them about the man who used to work there… *without* mentioning the man who died there, too.

I caught up to him, unzipping my jacket and slinging it over my arm. "I really do like your bookcase," I said, trying to lighten the subject.

Logan raised a brow, eyeing me from his peripheral. "You like to read?"

He didn't ask in a sarcastic way, more in a way that he doubted I actually liked his bookcase and was instead wondering if I was making fun of him.

"Not particularly," I admitted. "But, I love anything that brightens up a room. And in your office, that bookcase is about as bright as it gets."

Logan actually smirked at that, and I noted the dimple on his cheek before it disappeared again. "Ah, right. As an artist, I'm sure my office is too bland for your taste."

I wrinkled my nose. "You have no idea. You need to hit up a craft market in Nashville or something, get something other than cream paint on those walls."

"I thought about it," he said, which surprised me. "But, I'm kind of banking on a promotion soon, so I was going to wait until I got into the new office."

He swallowed once those words were between us, glancing at me with a touch of discomfort before he opened the door that led to the tour guide quarters for me.

The promotion he was referring to was one he obviously knew I wasn't oblivious to. My Uncle Mac was his manager, and had been very vocal that he planned to retire within the next year. Logan being the Lead Tour Guide now, it made sense that he assumed the position would be his.

And now that he'd said it out loud, I wondered if there was more to my father's deal than dear ol' Dad had let on. Was it a coincidence that he wanted me here, in this department, right when a Scooter was about to retire and a Becker was possibly to be promoted?

"Well, I think I've submitted you to enough torture for one day," Logan said as we passed through the tour guide lobby.

It was a small area, with two large tables where Logan told me earlier that they ate lunch and had team meetings. It was also a bland room, and he and my uncle were the only ones who had offices to themselves. Everyone else had a locker and a small area to place their belongings — which made sense, since they were all out giving tours each day and didn't need an office to do the planning and behind-the-scenes work like Logan and my uncle did.

"You'll have the standard orientation for the next two days, so I won't see you much. You'll be watching a lot of videos and doing the mound of paperwork Scooter likes to dish out to new employees," he said as we walked back into his office. "But, on Thursday, we'll reconvene and pick up with your training plan."

I nodded. "Sounds thrilling."

Logan chuckled, but the small smile fell as he looked me over. It was like he'd been trying to avoid actually looking at me all day, but in that moment, he watched me like he didn't give a damn if it made me uncomfortable.

And it didn't.

I liked the way his pupils dilated the longer he looked at me, and the way his breathing shallowed, his jaw tightening. He didn't look at me like I was a pain in his ass then — more like I was a temptation he didn't want to fight against any longer.

I smirked when his eyes flicked to my lips — lips I'd painted a dusty rose with my favorite tube of lipstick that morning — but he pulled his gaze away quickly, filtering through some papers on his desk as he cleared his throat.

"You'll get your uniform tomorrow, too — which I'm sure you'll be equally as thrilled about. Other than that and the orientation, I don't think there's anything else to go over before we meet again on Thursday." He tucked the papers inside the folder with my name on it, but still didn't look up at me. "Do you have any questions for me before you go?"

For as much as I didn't want to be there earlier, for some reason, I now found I didn't want to leave.

I walked to the bookcase behind him, and he avoided looking at me again until my shoulder brushed his as I passed him. "Which one should I read?"

I glanced at the wall of color before looking back at him, and he looked more confused than I'd seen him all day.

"That is, if you can part with one piece of your perfectly put together puzzle here," I added with a smile.

Logan blinked. "You want to read one of my books?"

"I do. In fact, I want to read your favorite one. You said we should get to know each other better, right?" I shrugged. "I imagine reading your favorite book is a good place to start."

The corner of Logan's mouth tilted up marginally, and he took a step, reaching for a leather-bound book with gold letters on the spine.

"Wait," I said, wrapping my fingers around his forearm. He paused as soon as I touched him, the book hovering halfway off the shelf. "Something written in the last century, please," I amended. "I haven't read anything outside of required textbooks. Go easy on me."

I smiled, but Logan's face was completely blank as he stared at where my hand touched his arm. I pulled it back tentatively, not realizing how warm he was until I felt the brush of cold over me once we were no longer touching.

He replaced the book he had originally grabbed, reaching across the shelf in front of me for a hardback wrapped in a paper sleeve, instead.

"Try this," he offered, and as soon as I had the book in my hands, he took a step back.

"*All the Light We Cannot See* by Anthony Doerr," I mused, running the pad of my thumb over the beautiful cover. It was a blue-tinted photo of what looked like a coastal town in Europe somewhere, and a shiny, gold emblem boasted that the book was the winner of a Pulitzer Prize. "What's it about?"

Logan finally smiled again. "That's the point of reading it, Mallory — to find out."

I bit my lip against my own smile, and I wasn't sure if it was because he was joking around with me, rather than looking at me like I was a mosquito, or if it was because he'd said my name in a way that only a long-time friend would.

I wondered if it could be possible — a Scooter and a Becker being friends.

"Thanks for the tour. I guess I'll see you Thursday?"

He nodded, taking another step back so I could pass between him and the desk behind us. "See you Thursday."

His eyes darted to a space beside me, and I followed, chuckling when I noticed the now-blank space where the book had been.

"You're going to fix that before you leave, aren't you?"

"As soon as you're out the door."

I laughed, shaking my head as I slipped past him. "I'll leave you to it, then." I paused at the door, and couldn't help but smile at the difference in how I felt leaving as opposed to when I'd arrived. "Bye, Logan."

"Bye, Mallory."

Before I'd even made it out of the tour guide lobby, I heard him shuffling the books on the shelf.

Chapter Three

Logan

"That was one hell of a game tonight," I told my older brother, Jordan, Friday night as I heated up leftovers from dinner for him in our mother's kitchen. I opened the fridge and offered him a beer as soon as the microwave was started, but he shook his head, reaching into the cabinet behind him for a whiskey glass, instead.

I smiled, putting the beer back and opting for the bottle of Scooter's Winter Whiskey Mom had on the counter. It was a special release we did each fall that went away again in January, and it was one of Jordan's favorites. I poured him two fingers in his glass, and cheersed my own to his before he took a sip.

"It was more fun to watch than to coach, I assure you," he said, sucking in a breath through his teeth as the whiskey settled in his stomach. "We had too many errors. It shouldn't have been that close."

"Ah, but that's what makes it a good game," I offered, clapping my hand on his shoulder. "Have them run some drills on Monday, but tonight, we celebrate a win."

He tipped his glass toward me. "Hear, hear."

It was tradition for my brothers and I to get together at Mom's every week for family dinner, but during the fall, when dinner fell on a Friday, Jordan was always absent. He was the head coach of the town's high school football team, and that meant a game every Friday night for him. So, we'd have an early dinner, and then head to the field to watch the game. And after, we'd all meet at Mom's again, heat up some food for Jordan, and have family dinner round two.

Noah and Mom were at the table when Jordan and I made our way back to the dining room. Mom sipped on her sweet tea while the rest of us enjoyed our whiskey, and Jordan shoveled food into his gullet like he hadn't eaten in years.

"Careful," Mom warned with an amused smile. "The plate isn't edible."

Jordan made some noise that could have been a chuckle, if his mouth wasn't full, before shoving another bite in.

"Where's Mikey?" Noah asked.

Mom shifted, sliding her finger over the rim of her glass with a sad look in her eyes. "Back in his room. He was playing guitar for a while, but he's been silent for about an hour now... think he might be asleep."

My brothers and I exchanged worried glances of our own, wondering how long our youngest sibling would wallow in misery. His high school sweetheart had broken up with him last month, leaving school to chase her music dreams in Nashville. It had always been their plan to go after school ended... *together*. But, like we all feared, Bailey changed her mind and asked Michael for time and space to do her own thing.

It'd been the biggest betrayal to my little brother, who'd put Bailey above everything else — including his own dreams. Now, he was single for the first time in years, and just a half-a-year away from graduating high school with all the plans he *thought* he had thrown out the window.

"He'll be alright," I assured my mom, reaching over the table to squeeze her hand in mine. "He's heartbroken, but he'll bounce back. Just give him a little time."

Mom nodded, squeezing my hand in return and smiling as much as she could. Mom was a beautiful woman — always had been — and even in that moment, with her eyes rimmed with dark circles and her face long, tired, and worn, she was stunning. I loved how much of her I saw in me when I looked in the mirror — same hazel eyes, same full-faced smile. Noah was a spitting image of Dad, and sometimes I envied that he got so much of him, but I was proud to take after the strong woman who had raised us — when Dad was here, and after he passed.

"So, how did it go with Mallory this week?" Noah asked me, kicking his feet up in the empty chair Michael usually sat in. "Seemed like you two were ten seconds away from ripping each other's throats open in that tour run through on Monday."

Mom's face screwed up with worry, but she didn't speak, just sipped on her tea while she waited for me to answer. Something told me she was just as concerned as my brothers and I were that I was training a Scooter — especially one with a reputation like Mallory's.

Still, just the mention of her made my blood warm — and not in the way that my brother thought. From the moment she walked into my office that first day, I'd been fascinated by her. Hell, I'd been fascinated by her my entire life. But, that fascination was balanced out by my need to protect myself, by the fear that crept in every time I had a second to think and realized I could very likely be training the woman who would take the job I was rightfully owed in the end.

She infuriated me with her gum popping, her sarcastic remarks, her blasé attitude about being at the distillery — and yet, she still made my pulse race, made my hands ache with the desire to reach out and feel that silky, platinum blonde hair between my fingers.

"It was... fine," I said, deciding that was the best word to describe it. "She definitely had an attitude the first day, but by the time she left, she was playing nice. She was in orientation the rest of the week. I saw her briefly yesterday, and took her around for her first shadow tour earlier today." I shrugged. "It's weird. It doesn't seem like she wants to be there, but Mallory Scooter has never been one to do something she doesn't want to do. So, I can't really figure out why she's all of a sudden starting a career at the place it seemed like she'd been avoiding her whole life."

Jordan leaned back from his now-empty plate, his hand resting on his stomach now that he was up for his first breath of air since he started eating. "I saw her and her father checking out that empty shop at the edge of the Main Street shopping center on my way to the field today," he said. "I wonder if that has something to do with it."

"The spot where Rita's dress store used to be?" Noah asked.

Jordan nodded, reaching for his whiskey. "That's the one. They were walking around with Tracy from the real estate firm in town."

I frowned. "That doesn't make sense. Why would she be buying a store when she just started this new job?"

"Maybe it's Patrick who's buying it, and she was just hanging out with him?" Mom suggested.

"I don't know. She doesn't strike me as the kind of girl who would just hang out with her father willingly," I mused, running my fingers over the stubble on my chin. "Anyway, I feel like she's going to give me some trouble, but she's nothing I can't handle."

Mom laughed bitterly. "Oh, I have more than a feeling she's going to give you trouble. That whole family is just... just..." She shook her head, lips pursed together and face turning red. Mom was always a lady first, and I knew she was biting her tongue to keep from saying a whole string of curse words and other foul things about the Scooters.

Jordan reached over and squeezed her wrist, which brought her a new breath. She smiled, patting his hand and sipping her tea again without another word said.

"I'm sorry you have to work with her," Noah offered, sipping on his own glass of whiskey on the rocks. "I wouldn't be able to do it, work so closely with a Scooter. I get amped up enough when Patrick walks through the warehouse. I can't even imagine if I had to train Malcolm or something."

Malcolm was Mallory's younger brother, and a giant pain in our entire family's ass. Whereas most of the Scooter family held it together around us, playing nice and pretending like we all still got along after the death of my grandpa and Robert J. Scooter, Malcolm thrived in the drama. He loved to push our buttons — especially Noah's.

He was one stupid remark away from having his nose broken, if he didn't watch it.

"I agree," Mom said, her face souring. My mother didn't speak ill on any-one, but with the Scooters, even *she* had a grudge. "Honestly, I wouldn't be upset if both you *and* your little brother got out of that distillery altogether."

"We can't do that, Mom," Noah said gently, reaching over to squeeze her wrist. "Dad helped build that distillery, that brand... hell, *this* entire town. We're honoring him by keeping the Becker name alive in this company's history."

"I know," she said, brows folding together as sadness creeped in. "I know. And I know he's looking down on every single one of you, and he's so proud." She patted Noah's hand where it held her. "I just worry, is all."

"That's your job as our mother," Noah said.

"And we make it an easy job to do," Jordan added.

We all chuckled at that.

"Thanks, guys. But no need to worry. I've got it under control." I said the words as if I, too, was bothered by the fact that I had to be around Mallory Scooter. I'd avoided her my entire life, knowing I couldn't get caught up in a girl who was so off-limits it wasn't even comical to consider a world where I could try my luck with her. I still lived in that world, and I knew there was still no way in hell I'd ever have a chance... but being forced to spend time with her, to get to know more about the girl who'd always been a mystery to me?

It wasn't the *worst* thing I could think of.

It would, however, have been easier if she was as rude all the time as she was when she first walked into my office that Monday. Part of me wished we could live there — in the place where I annoyed her and she infuriated me. Be-cause when she asked about my books, about my family, about *me*... I liked it.

And I wanted to know about her, too.

"Well," Mom said, smoothing her hands over the napkin in her lap before she placed it on the table and stood. "I think it's about time for a dance."

Noah and Jordan smiled as I stood, rounding the table and offering my hand to Mom. "I think you're right, Momma. May I have the honor?"

She placed her hand in mine with a warm smile, and Noah crossed the liv-ing room to the old record player Dad had bought before we were even born. There was a moment of fuzz and static, and then the first notes of Eric Clap-ton's "Wonderful Tonight" sparked to life, and Mom released a breath, closing her eyes a moment before we both began to dance.

I wasn't even a thought in the universe on the night my mom danced with my dad to this song, her in her long, cream wedding dress and dad in his blue jeans and white button-up shirt. But, I'd seen the video, the photographs, and I knew that the smile my mom wore each time one of my brothers or I danced with her was the same one she wore that night.

She and Dad used to dance every night in our kitchen while she cooked, or in the living room after dinner. It wasn't always to this song, though it was a favorite. After Dad passed, my brothers and I decided to keep the tradition alive.

Not just for her, but for us, too.

In the months that first followed Dad's death, our entire family fell apart. Mom had taken to drinking herself numb, my older brothers were fighting over who was the new man of the house, and Mikey and I were retreating into the things that brought us most comfort — me into books, him into music. It was the first and only time I'd ever seen our family machine break down.

The night I asked Mom to dance after dinner was the first night we started to come back together.

It'd been nine years since my father's death, nearly a decade without him being here with us, and yet I still felt his presence as if he'd never left at all when we were all inside that house.

That's the thing about losing a loved one. In one way or another, they stay with us forever. They're never truly lost, never truly gone — as long as we choose to keep them alive in our hearts.

Still, the mystery of his death was one that haunted every member of my family. Almost a decade had passed, and we still didn't have answers for the flurry of questions we asked ourselves every night.

Part of me hoped we would find those answers one day.

The bigger part of me knew we never would.

So, I shut those thoughts out, focusing instead on the music filling our home as I spun Mom out before dropping her down in a dramatic dip. And in the back of my mind, I wondered what it would be like to dance with my own wife to a song that we'd call our own, one we'd lean on in the good times and the bad as we went through life together.

Then, for some odd reason, I wondered if Mallory Scooter liked to dance.

The thought was gone with the next spin.

$$\cdot \ \cdot \ \cdot$$

Mallory

Mine.

All my life, I'd wanted to look at something — *anything* — and feel that one, possessive, all-empowering word ringing true to my bones.

When I was younger, I'd wanted a dog — and we'd gotten one. But it wasn't *mine*, it was ours — my brother's, my dad's, my mom's. I'd had a room to myself growing up, but it had been decorated carefully by my mother, without a single representation of who I was. When I got my car, it was the one my father had driven for five years and then handed down to me. Even when I was at college, I shared an apartment with three girls I didn't know, and the space never felt like mine.

Now, standing in the middle of the gutted retail space that I would transform into an art studio, I looked around and tried to feel it.

Mine.

This place is mine.

I should have felt it, because for all intents and purposes, it *was* mine — along with the small studio apartment above it. It was free for me to do what I wanted with it, to bring my dream of owning my own studio to life.

I could look around and picture it all.

I saw the windows, floor to ceiling, letting in natural light and giving passerby's a view of the art being made inside. I saw the back room that I'd convert into a dark room, where photographs would slowly materialize. I saw the stage for live models, the easels surrounding it, imagined artists of all ages gazing up at their subject before dipping their paint brush to begin. I saw craft classes for children, saw date night painting projects for couples, saw wine night sketch classes for girls' outings. I envisioned students taking classes with me for years, honing their craft, becoming stronger and more creative as the years passed.

The options for what would happen inside that empty room were endless.

And still, it didn't feel like mine.

Because it came at a price.

It was my father's name on the check that secured that piece of real estate for me. It was because of him that I had a place to live on my own, and a business to bring to life.

And in order to keep it, I had to play by his rules.

Every time the thought assaulted me, my fists would clench, my nose would flare, and I'd close my eyes and try to find a breath that didn't burn on the way down. There was nothing I could imagine being worse than being in debt to my father, than being under his thumb again like I had been before I turned eighteen.

And yet, here I was.

I was still looking around, trying to find a sense of ownership when my best friend plowed through the front door with a bottle of champagne in his hand.

"I brought the bubbly!" Chris exclaimed, floating into the vacant shop with the same grace that he made an entrance everywhere he went. He was dressed impeccably in his beige cable knit sweater, accented by a thick, plaid scarf that hugged his neck and the tweed jacket shielding him from the Tennessee winter wind outside. I'd never seen my best friend in jeans, not in all the years I'd known him, so it was no surprise that he was in navy dress pants and brown leather ankle boots. His blonde hair was parted to the left, styled neatly, and his face clean shaven — which accented what I referred to as his Superman Jaw. His chocolate eyes were warm and inviting as always, accented by the flurry of freckles that dotted the apples of his cheeks.

I lifted one eyebrow at the bottle in his hands. "I'm sure you brought that bottle to celebrate the shop, and not at all because it's Saturday and you love brunch more than the cast of *Friends* loves coffee."

"Think of it as two birds, one bottle," he said with a mischievous smile. "Now, we just need two champagne flutes and a—"

Chris stopped mid-stride on his way over to where I stood in the middle of the room, his eyes dropping to the mound of matted fur in my arms.

"Mallory... what in the ever living *hell* is that?"

I glanced down at the subject of his disdain with a smile, running a hand over the little fur ball until I found an ear. I scratched behind it, and a soft purr rumbled against my chest.

"This is Dalí," I explained, and as if he already knew his new name, he peered up at me with green, glowing eyes that then turned to Chris.

"What the fuck is a *Dalí?*"

I rolled my eyes. "He's a cat, silly. Here," I said, holding Dalí out toward him. "You can hold him. He's really docile."

"*Why* do you have a cat?" he asked, leaning away with one brow climbing higher and higher on his forehead as he assessed the creature in my hands. "And *how* do you have a cat?"

"He was a stray. He wandered up when I was moving my stuff upstairs last night. I gave him some food, a place to sleep that wasn't freezing... isn't he cute? He reminds me of Salvador Dalí with his little mustache," I said, running my fingertips over the fur around the cat's mouth. "I thought he could be a sort of Shop Cat."

Chris blinked. "Only you, Mallory. Only you."

He rounded to stand on the other side of me, still watching Dalí like he was a dragon and not an adorable, fluffy, calico cat.

"*Anyway*," he said, unwrapping his scarf and letting it hang over his shoulders. "Can you put Mr. Dalí down and go grab us some glasses? We have celebrating to do!"

I sighed. "I can, though I'm not sure I'm much in the mood to celebrate."

"How could you not be? You have an *art studio*, Mallory. This has been your dream since you were in high school."

"But it's not mine," I reminded him, placing Dalí on the floor. I gave him one last pet before he sauntered off, finding a spot by the window where he could soak up the sunshine streaming in. "It's my father's."

Chris waved me off. "Logistics. His name was on the check, but it'll be *your* name on the door. And besides, you only had to sell him five years of your soul in exchange for something that you can build and enjoy for a lifetime." He pointed the bottle at me. "I'd say that's a deal worth making. Now, glasses. Stat." He started peeling back the gold paper around the cork. "Mama needs some champs."

I chuckled, jogging up the stairs that led to my small studio apartment above the shop. It was almost as vacant as the shop below, aside from my art from over the years that laid against the walls, waiting to be hung, the new bed I'd splurged on, and a random pile of shit I'd picked up from the local thrift shop. Mom had offered to take me shopping for furniture and essentials, but I'd declined.

I was already in enough debt to them as it was.

Because I knew my best friend was coming over, I'd been sure to make two champagne glasses first on my list at the thrift store. I plucked them free from one of the boxes, unwrapping the brown paper around them and rinsing them off in the sink. I glanced around at the assortment of boxes waiting for me to unpack them before my eyes landed on the one and only book in the entire place.

I paused, smiling as I thought of the boy who'd given it to me. I'd only read thirty pages so far, but already, I could tell there was more to Logan Becker than I ever imagined before.

You could tell a lot about a person by reading their favorite book.

I made a mental note to pick it back up before bed tonight, so I'd have something to talk to my new, grumpy boss about on Monday. Then, I made my way back downstairs.

"Two champagne flutes, as requested," I announced, setting them on the folding table left behind by the previous owner. It was the only piece of furniture in the shop, save for the metal folding chair beside it.

Chris popped the bottle of champagne open, both of us smiling at the familiar sound. He poured me a glass first, and then one for him before setting the bottle down and holding his glass in the air.

"To my amazing, hard-working, talented-as-fuck best friend and her dream becoming a reality," he said. "May this studio be everything you've ever wanted and more."

I touched my chest. "You're so sweet. But no, you can't host a grand opening."

He was just about to take a sip, but he paused, poking his bottom lip out. "Oh, come on. *Please?* You have to get the word out somehow. Just let me throw one, eensie-weensie grand-opening party with some glitter and booze and then I swear, I'll never ask to host an event again. I'll let you make the studio as boring and emo as you want."

I chuckled, rolling my eyes before I clinked my glass to his. "Fine. But no glitter, and *no* techno music."

"Your loss," he said on a shrug, taking his first sip before he did a little twirl, taking in the studio in all its naked glory. "So, work at the distillery five days a week, and you get to run this bad boy on the evenings and weekends. That was the deal you made with good ol' Patrick Scooter, am I right?"

"Yep," the word rolled over my lips with a pop. "Which basically means I'll be doing what I loathe more than anything for seventy percent of my life, and what I love for the other thirty."

"Life is about balance," Chris offered with a teasing grin. He leaned a hip against the folding table, watching me over the rim of his glass before he took another sip. "How was your first week at the glorious Scooter Whiskey distillery?"

"Annoying. I have a stupid uniform, and had a two-day orientation that I'll never for the life of me understand why I didn't get to skip, considering who I am." I sighed. "Oh, and, you'll never guess who's training me."

"Logan Becker."

I opened my mouth to tell him who, only to pop it closed again. "How could you possibly know that?"

Chris cocked a brow. "It's Stratford, honey. Not like this town doesn't know everything about everyone. Logan has been the Lead Tour Guide for two years now. Of course, he's training you."

"Huh," I mused. "Well, then you can also imagine how awkward it is."

"Oh, you mean because your families used to be best buds back in the day and now loathe each other?"

"Don't be cute."

"Impossible not to be," he said with a wink. "But honestly, it can't be that bad. You are both far removed from your parents' drama, aren't you? Logan Becker always struck me as the most level-headed of those brothers. He was always the one trying to stop them from fighting."

"But he never backed down from one, either."

"Touché." Chris took a drink of champagne. "Was he an asshole to you?"

I thought that question over, battling with whether the answer was yes or no. He *was* a bit rude, especially when he asked me why I was even there at all. Then again, with the way I dressed that first day and the prissy *better than everyone* attitude I walked in with, I couldn't blame him.

"No?" I finally said, taking my own sip. "I mean, I can tell he doesn't want me there — but I think it's just because of who I am, and the fact that my uncle is retiring soon, and he's had his eye on that job for years."

"You think they'll make you manager over him?" Chris shook his head. "That doesn't seem right. You're just starting."

"I don't know," I answered honestly. "Dad never said anything about that in his deal, but..."

We both fell silent, because I didn't need to say it out loud for Chris to know that my father wasn't known for playing clean or fair. He knew what he wanted, and he stopped at nothing to get it.

If me being manager was in his plan, it didn't matter if I knew about it or not — it would happen.

"Logan Becker," Chris mused. "*God*, I had the biggest crush on him in high school. He was always so broody, in like... a nerdy kind of way. You know? Like, he was always reading in a corner, being mysterious and shit." He sighed. "There's just something about a boy with a book in his hands."

I chuckled.

"What?" Chris said, crossing his arms, the top hand still dangling his champagne flute like a charm bracelet. "Like you don't recognize how down-home hot that boy is."

I shrugged, pushing off from where I was leaning against the table next to him to pace. "He's not hard to look at."

"Bullshit."

"Fine," I huffed. "Yes, he's hot. But, he's *Logan Becker*. That boy has had more girls in his bed than I've had pairs of Chucks — and that's saying something. It's not like he's anywhere near my type, or that I'm anywhere near his. We were in the same grade and never said more than two words to each other."

An amused grin split my best friend's face as he took another sip of champagne. "I never said anything about dating him, Mallory... but apparently that's a subject that's been on *your* mind."

He cocked a brow as I stood there like a guppy, mouth open, catching flies.

I rolled my eyes, trying to play it off. "I was just making a statement."

"Mm-hmm. You know, this actually would be kind of perfect." He gasped. "Oh, my God. It'd be like a modern-day *Romeo and Juliet*! Oh, *please*, can you do it? Date Romeo, Mallory. It'd be so fun!"

"You do realize that play is not romantic in the slightest, and that both Romeo and Juliet die in the end."

He waved me off just like he had when he first arrived. "Logistics."

"Logan Becker will never be my Romeo," I said definitively. "Now, can we get back to the subject of how the hell I'm going to survive the deal I made with the devil that is my father?"

Chris chuckled, standing straight and wrapping me in a bear hug with his glass of champagne still firmly in hand before he rested his chin on the crown of my head. "Oh, darling. Don't think of it that way, okay? This is a trigger for you. You hate to feel manipulated or controlled in any way, and that's what this feels like. The one man you've been trying to establish your independence from is the one man you can't seem to escape."

I sighed.

"But, that's not what this is," he continued. "You're a bad ass business woman, and you made a *business* deal. It's five years of sacrifice, and then?" He pulled back with a supportive smile. "Then, you're free — and this place really *will* be yours."

I swallowed, looking around as emotion threatened to surface. I didn't *do* emotions — but standing there inside of a blank canvas I'd been painting in my imagination since I was a little girl, I couldn't help but tear up.

"So, first thing's first, show me your uniform so we can make it cuter. If you *look* good, you'll feel good," he said, releasing me and draining the last of his champagne before he refilled it to the top. He spun, looking around at the empty space with a mix between an optimistic smile and a timid grimace. "And then, we start on this mess."

Chapter Four

Logan

On a normal Monday morning at the distillery, I'd be happy to be back at work. Of course, I'd be missing the weekend just like anyone else, but for the most part, being at work never bothered me. Even when I was a newbie and had to work tours on the weekends, I never complained. I was in my element when I was talking about history, and I was always happy to do it.

But today wasn't a normal Monday.

Today was the day Mallory would shadow me, which meant I'd be spending all day long with her. And as much as I'd spent the weekend pretending like that didn't faze me, like she was just another new guide and it would be business as usual, the unease in my stomach that Monday morning proved it'd all been bullshit.

Still, I schooled myself as much as I could, revisiting her training plan and making notes on important things I wanted to cover. That was my M.O. — throw myself into what I could control to avoid what I couldn't.

I couldn't control the fact that I should have hated Mallory Scooter, but I was intrigued by her, instead.

I couldn't control the fact that I had to train her when she didn't even want to be here.

And I couldn't control the fact that she was most likely here to take the job I'd been working my ass off for years... no matter how much that fact killed me.

All I *could* control was how well I trained her, how well I demonstrated that it was *me* who was made for the management job, who was destined to lead this team of tour guides — not her. It wasn't much, but it was something I could throw my all into.

If they gave that job to her instead of me, I wanted everyone in this company to know the wrong decision had been made — including the ones who made it.

I was still making notes in the margins of the day's agenda when there was a knock on my doorframe, and I looked up to find Mallory leaning against it, arms folded and an amused smirk on her face as she eyed my stack of highlighters.

"Mornin'," she said. "I see you're already color coding the day."

"And I see you're already making a habit of being late," I countered, checking the time on my watch. She was supposed to be in my office at eight, and it was eight twenty-two. "Have a seat, I'm just finishing up my thoughts here and we can go over the plan for the day."

"Can't wait," she muttered, and it wasn't until she unfolded her arms and made her way into my office to the chair across from me that I realized what she was wearing.

My eyes bulged — so much so that I knew there was no use in trying to hide the reaction. Her tight midriff was exposed by the tour guide polo that she'd maimed with scissors, cutting it into a crop top. A belly button ring glittered under the fluorescent light as she took a seat, and she crossed her right leg over the left, looking around my office like there was nothing out of the ordinary. She'd cut the hem of the sleeves, too, which caused them to roll slightly and show more of her toned arms. Tattoos crawled around the bicep of her left arm, and black script lined the skin of her right forearm. There was even the tail end of something peeking out from under her top, something that appeared to line her ribs and dip down to the top of her navel.

Feathers, I realized.

And for a split second, all I could think about was lifting that shirt to see the rest.

I blinked, clearing my throat and turning my attention back to my notes as I shot that thought down like a skeet disc.

"How was your weekend?" I asked.

"Oh, as thrilling as it can be in Stratford," she joked, still looking around my office. "How about you? You get into any trouble?"

"I'm a Becker," I answered, finishing my last thought on the agenda. "Trouble finds *me*."

"I did hear you all made an appearance at The Black Hole Saturday night."

The Black Hole was the pet name for one of the more popular party spots in town, an old barn with a huge fire pit that was always crawling on the weekends.

"Did you now?" I mused. "And what is the rumor mill saying my brothers and I did this time? Rode a wild hog? Got in a fist fight with twenty, full-grown men? Drove a car into the creek?"

"Actually, they're saying Mikey threw his guitar in the bonfire, and that you took Sadie Hollenbeck home with you... for the fourth time in three weeks." She lifted a brow at that. "That's like a record for you, isn't it?"

I frowned. "Mikey's going through a rough time... and that guitar is old, anyway. Maybe he just wanted to give the fire something more to keep burning."

"Right. Because the mound of firewood wasn't enough." Mallory rolled her lips together. "And what about the part about Sadie? That true, too?"

The way she watched me, I would have sworn she was a little jealous that rumor had it I'd taken a girl home from The Black Hole on Saturday night. I would have sworn it — had I been naïve and ignorant of the kind of girl Mallory was. She'd never had a boyfriend in Stratford — not since middle school, anyway. I'd heard she'd dated someone in college, but he'd never come home for holidays or made an appearance at any of the hometown hangouts.

I didn't think there was a man interesting enough for Mallory Scooter, and I knew for a fact that she didn't give a fuck who was warming my bed at night — which, though the town gossip would apparently argue otherwise, was no one. I didn't invite women back to my place, though I was never opposed to going back to *theirs.*

Sadie was a good girl, and she was going through a tough break-up with her high school sweetheart — who everyone now knew had been cheating on her for years. He'd already moved on, but Sadie was a mess. So, last month, I listened to her cry at The Black Hole and convinced her that he needed a dose of his own medicine.

I then offered to *be* that medicine.

So, yes, I'd gone home with Sadie a few times — but we hadn't done anything we couldn't do in church. Mostly, it was her testing out her baking recipes on me and me playing shrink, trying to help her heal and move on from her asshole ex.

Still — Mallory didn't need to know all that.

"Maybe." I shrugged. "But a gentleman doesn't kiss and tell."

She snorted. "Right. And you're the gentleman in this case, I presume?"

I pressed a hand to my chest, leaning back in my office chair with feigned offense. "I can't believe you'd insinuate otherwise."

Mallory just rolled her eyes, nodding at the agenda I'd just finished. "So, what am I in for today, boss?"

My smirk climbed higher when she called me *boss,* but I subdued it, picking up the piece of paper and reviewing it with her. "You're shadowing me today, so we're going to do two tour groups together. The first one, I'll lead, and you can take notes and follow like you're part of the group. The second one, I'll give you a little more of a hands-on role, let you pour the whiskey at the tasting and answer some of the questions."

Her smile tightened. "Oh, joy."

"But, before we get started... you're going to have to change," I said, eyeing her midriff before I met her eyes again.

"Why?"

"Because it appears a bear got ahold of your uniform."

She glanced down at her shirt, lifting a brow at me like I was seeing something she wasn't. "I made it look better. I made it *fit,* honestly, because it was like a bag on me before."

"We have smaller sizes in the back," I told her. "And, it's pretty chilly today. Let's go back to the supply closet and get you a long sleeve, and we can see if there are any jackets, too."

"I'm not changing." She set both feet on the ground, crossing her arms in defiance. "I look fine. Just because you're offended by a woman's stomach doesn't mean I have to cover it."

"I'm not *offended*," I said flatly. "You're a tour guide, Mallory. You're representing the company, the brand, and you're meeting with tourists from all over. Plus, like I said, it's forty-degrees outside. You really want to walk around like that?"

"Like *what*?" she probed.

I threw my hands up. "You know what, fine. Wear whatever you want. You are Mallory *Scooter*, after all, aren't you? I guess the rules don't apply to the princess of Stratford."

A shadow of something passed over her face then, her expression unreadable.

I stood, snatching my clipboard off my desk and heading for the door without another look in her direction. "Come on. First tour is in ten minutes, it's time to greet our guests."

· · ·

I was going to strangle her.

I was going to strangle Mallory Scooter.

And not in the sexy, playful way like I did my first girlfriend after high school, who used to love to be choked and fucked from behind. That was just a light pressure, a hand around the throat, gentle squeeze to get the adrenaline pumping and send a spike of pleasure through her bloodstream.

No, this was a different kind of urge — one that rang true somewhere right around *throttle her*.

We were nearing the end of the tour, and with every new stop along the way, the urge had grown larger. Mallory was a sideshow, popping her gum loudly and texting away on her cell phone — all the while wearing our company's logo on her chest with her fucking belly ring showing. She didn't pay attention, didn't take any notes, and whenever I asked her to assist with something, she rolled her eyes for everyone to see before obliging.

At least she was shivering whenever we were outside. Staying out there a little longer just to watch her suffer was about the only revenge I could get.

It was almost impossible to keep the group's attention on me with all her gum noises and incessant texting — not to mention her barely there uniform. I'd introduced her as our newest tour guide at the beginning of the tour, and everyone watched her like they were wondering if the money they'd paid was for nothing.

We were the face of the company, and Mallory made us look like a disaster on ice.

She was still chewing away on her gum, gaze fixed on her screen, when the tour group followed me to the building where we had the whiskey tasting at the end of each tour. I held the door open, smiling at each of them as they passed, but before Mallory could follow them, I hooked her by the elbow, swinging her outside and letting the door shut, effectively putting a barrier between us and our guests.

"Are you *trying* to look like an idiot, or is that just your natural state today?"

Mallory cocked a brow, blowing a small bubble with her gum before it popped on her lips.

I blew out a breath through my nose like a dragon.

"Careful there, might pop a blood vessel," she remarked.

"You're making a fool of yourself."

"I'm just acting like the *princess* that I am," she smarted off.

I released her arm with a scoff. "If there's a point you're trying to make, you can just go ahead and make it so we can all move on."

"My *point* is that a woman should be able to dress how she wants without someone trying to make her conform."

I pinched the bridge of my nose. "Mallory, that's not why I asked you to change. I agree, women *and* men should dress how they want to — on their own time. But when you work for a company, and that company has a uniform, you just have to suck it up like the rest of us and wear it when you're on the clock. That's all I was asking of you."

"Well, that's not how you said it. And besides, this entire training plan of yours is bogus. You're treating me like someone who just discovered Scooter Whiskey a week ago instead of someone who grew up living and breathing every aspect of this distillery. I don't need to shadow you to know how to give a fucking tour of my *father's* company," she reminded me, as if there was any way for me to forget. "You're a tour guide, Logan — not a brain surgeon. So stop treating this job like it's difficult, or special, or whatever else you think it is, and for the love of *God*, stop acting like I don't already know everything you can tell me about Scooter Whiskey."

My blood boiled so hot under my skin, I was sure I'd turned the color of a beet.

"I can do this tour in my sleep," she continued. "And honestly, I'm annoyed that I'm wasting my day following you around when I could be doing better things with my time."

I clenched my jaw, lips flat as I stared down at those icy blue cat eyes of hers. She was so tiny, and yet so fierce as she stared back up at me, chest puffed, not backing down.

I'd have found her cute if she wasn't being such a brat.

"You know what, you're right."

She narrowed her eyes, ready to fire back when my response hit her, and everything on her face fell slack. "What?"

"You're right," I repeated. "I don't know what I was thinking. Of course, Mallory Scooter doesn't need my help. Tell you what, you can lead the next tour."

She blinked. "Wait, really?"

"Of course," I said, glancing down at my clipboard and flipping through to check the times. "Let's just wrap up this tasting, and the next group should be here within an hour. We'll take a short break for lunch, and then you can lead the tour, and I'll shadow *you*. How's that sound?"

Mallory opened her mouth, shut it again, and finally gave a firm nod. "That sounds great. Thank you."

"Mm-hmm."

I didn't say another word, just left her standing there shivering in the cold while I made my way into the tasting building. I finished that tour with the smuggest smile on my face — one I was sure Mallory couldn't decipher, and for that, I was glad.

She thought my training plan was bullshit, that this job was easy and she didn't need any help? Fine. Time to show her the ropes the way my grandfather showed me how to swim — by tossing her into the pool without a floaty.

Sink or swim, Mallory Scooter.

Which will it be?

Chapter Five

Mallory

I couldn't wait to knock that smug smile off his stupid, too-handsome-for-his-own-good face.

It didn't take me long to figure out why Logan was so quick to let me lead the next tour. When he idled in the back of the group, arms folded, clipboard hanging from one hand and cocky smirk on his stupid face while I gathered everyone together, he might as well have been wearing a flashing neon sign that gave him away.

He thought I would fail.

No — he was *certain* I would fail, and that I'd eat crow and apologize.

Well, he was mistaken.

His first mistake was commenting on what I wore. I'd rebelled against my father for the same reason when I was younger. He wanted me to dress conservatively, professionally, *"like a lady"* — and I'd told him to shove his opinion on what *I* wore right up his ass — especially when dressing conservatively didn't stop his piece of shit friends from ogling me once I had tits.

If my own father couldn't get away with it, there was no way in hell a Becker would.

His next mistake was calling me the princess of Stratford. I was no stranger to that nickname, and he knew before he said it that it'd push all the wrong buttons.

So, I gave him the *princess* he asked for. I'll admit, it was a little immature, being on my phone and chewing my gum purposefully loud to make my point. But, I was already annoyed that I had to be here, and while I was perfectly content to do like Chris had told me and just bite my tongue to get through it in order to keep my studio, Logan had soured my mood instantly with his comments.

Now, I didn't just want to get through it.

I wanted to annoy *him* as much as this entire situation annoyed *me* — by showing him that I could do his job with both hands tied behind my back.

"Alright, everyone. Thank you for visiting the Scooter Whiskey distillery. Can everyone hear me okay?"

The group nodded in unison, though everyone was watching me with somewhat confused faces. I noticed a few of them looking at my shirt, whispering to each other.

Okay, maybe slicing off half my shirt wasn't the most professional thing.

Fine, Logan — you win that point.

"I'm Mallory Scooter," I said. "Yes, as in the daughter of the owner, granddaughter of the founder. I'll be your guide today."

The faces of the tourists in our group lit up, a few of them exchanging excited glances. I looked back at Logan to see if he was bothered, but he still watched me with an amused smirk.

Asshole.

"So, if you'll follow me right this way, we're going to load up on that bus over there that will take us down to the first stop on our tour — the spring — which is where we get the fresh, delicious water that we make your favorite whiskey with."

Everyone smiled, chatter picking up as they followed me down to the bus. I smiled proudly at Logan, but he just jotted something down on his clipboard, piling onto the bus after the group and taking a seat in the back.

And from there, the tour went perfectly.

For about ten minutes.

Talking about the spring was easy. I'd heard my grandfather tell stories about how he'd first came upon it, how it had been on the land of a pastor — a pastor who, funny enough, had a hankering for good whiskey. It was actually the two of them who made the first batch of what would become known as the distinctly flavored Scooter Whiskey.

I told that story with pride, adding in a few fun jokes my grandfather had told me about the spring, and then we were off to the next stop on the tour.

And that's when things went downhill.

We were outside for longer than I expected — mostly due to me chatting more than was needed — and I was shivering so much from the cold, my teeth were chattering as I tried to explain the distilling process, and how the yeast from our process combined with the microcosms near the freshwater spring to form the Baudoinia mold they saw covering the trees around the distillery.

One of the women on the tour asked me if I wanted her jacket.

To add insult to injury, I completely bypassed a part of the tour in my effort to get warm, skipping the warehouse with our limited-edition single barrels inside, and going straight to the warehouse with the pot stills that initiate the distilling process. Logan had to remind me, and we had to turn back, making an unnecessarily long trek back to where we'd just left before circling around again.

The more that went wrong, the more wired I became — and the worse the tour got.

To his credit, Logan's snarky know-it-all smirk had softened, and where he was quick and happy to point out that I'd missed part of the tour earlier, his voice was gentler as he filled in the blanks for stuff I missed as the tour continued.

Still, I was proving his point.

And I hated it.

"This is one of my favorite parts of the tour," I explained when we made it to the barrel-raising warehouse. I schooled my nerves, reminding myself that I knew more about this place than almost anyone, and not to let a few hiccups rattle me. "Scooter Whiskey is one of the few distilleries that still makes and chars our own barrels. And this team of four is the incredible team that brings those barrels to life."

I gestured behind me to the boys, and they all waved before getting back to work. I didn't miss the questioning glance Noah gave Logan, but Logan just shook his head, as if to say *I'll explain later.*

"Now, you might remember them from the video earlier. If—"

"What video?"

I stopped, searching for the source of the question. It was an older woman, the one who had offered me her jacket.

"I'm sorry?"

"You said we should remember them from the video. What video?"

"I—" I paused, realizing I'd skipped over the small museum of history put together over the years. It included all the versions of our bottle, label, and the first blueprints for the distillery.

It also included the video I'd just referenced — that no one had seen, thanks to me.

"I'm sorry," I said with a smile, shaking my head. "I must have forgotten that stop. We'll circle around after this."

"So, you forgot that stop, and the stop earlier, and, apparently, the other half of your shirt," she said, eyeing my midriff disapprovingly before she looked at her husband. "You'd think the owner's daughter would be better prepared to give a tour — especially one we paid for."

There were murmurs of agreement from the rest of the group, and a few people looked away with discomfort.

I swallowed. "I'm very sorry about missing that, but I assure you, we'll go—"

"I don't need your assurance, dear. I need you to give us the tour we paid for. Yelp reviews said this was an amazing experience, and so far, it's fallen pretty flat. I don't know about these folks, but I'd like a refund."

There were more nods, more agreements, and something that felt a lot like embarrassment settled low in my stomach. If I'd have been a more emotional woman, I might have teared up, but as it was, I just stood there, frozen like a stupid deer in headlights, not knowing what to do or say to make it right.

My eyes found Logan, and he frowned, tucking his clipboard under his arm as he made his way to the front to stand next to me.

"I apologize for the mishaps in today's tour, ladies and gentlemen. Mallory is a new tour guide, and this is her first tour she's led by herself. As you can imagine, it can be a little nerve-wracking."

He touched my arm — just for a second — but it was the only source of warmth I felt in that moment.

"We'd be happy to provide refunds," he continued. "But first, let me tell you a little more about these barrel-raisers, and then we'll get to the best part — the tasting. Sound like a fair deal?"

There were some chuckles and murmurs of approval at the mention of the tasting, and as if it was the most natural thing in the world, Logan slipped on his charm and took over, doing his best to turn the tour around.

And I couldn't even stay to watch it.

I smiled as best I could at the group, letting them all pass me before I escaped out the back door of the warehouse and practically ran back to the main building. I crossed my arms over my exposed stomach, shaking my head as the disaster of a tour replayed over and over in my mind. By the time I made it back to the tour guide lobby, I felt something so close to what I remembered crying feeling like that I locked myself in the bathroom so I could get my shit together.

I wasn't sure how long I sat there, fully clothed on the toilet, elbows on my knees and face in my hands as I focused on breathing. In and out, inhale and exhale. No matter how I tried, I couldn't calm down, and it didn't take me long to realize why.

I had made a fool of myself, just like Logan had said.

It was time to eat crow, to apologize to him and take back everything I'd said. Suddenly, my shirt felt idiotic. It was my sad attempt to rebel in whatever little way I could against my father and the deal we'd struck, and it'd been the catalyst for this whole disastrous day.

I had acted like a child, and what was worse, I'd lived up to the nickname I loathed so much.

I sighed, taking a moment to splash water on my face before I left the bathroom in search of Logan. He was just setting his clipboard down in his office from returning from the tour, and when he turned and found me standing in his doorway just as I had that morning, he gave me a soft, sympathetic smile.

"You okay?"

He could have gloated — God knows if it were me in his shoes, I would have — but instead, he stood there with his hands in his pockets, his shoulders folded, eyes sad like he'd just kicked a bunny.

Like *I* was said bunny.

I shook my head, swallowing down what was left of my pride before my eyes met his again. "Logan, I—"

"WHAT THE HELL WAS THAT?!"

My words were cut off by my Uncle Mac blowing past me into Logan's office, eyes murderous, face red and puffy as he slapped a thick stack of papers down on Logan's desk.

"A tour of twenty-five, and every single one of them demanding a refund. I had to give out free shot glasses from the gift shop in an effort to stop them from ripping our distillery a new asshole on Yelp reviews," he fumed, pointing a finger directly at Logan. "I need an explanation, and I need it *now*."

Logan stood straight, chin high and chest broad as he addressed my uncle. "Mac, this was all my fault. I thought Mallory was ready, and I let her lead the tour. I th—"

"It's her sixth day on the job, and three of those days were spent in orientation, for Christ's sake. What were you thinking?" He didn't wait for Logan's response before he continued his rant. "Of *course* she wasn't ready, and you knew better than to let her do more than pour the whiskey at the tasting, let alone lead a full tour."

"Yes, sir," Logan agreed. "I thou—"

"I don't need any more excuses," Mac said, holding up a hand to silence him.

"Uncle Mac," I said, stepping in to defend Logan. It was my mess, after all. "This wasn't his fault. I insisted on leading the tour. I know more about this place than almost anyone, and I didn't want to shadow. I was bored."

"Oh *no*," my uncle cried dramatically, hands framing his face. "You were *bored*? Well, we can't have that."

"You've made your point," I deadpanned.

"Have I?" He took a step toward me then, and his eyes slipped to my navel, brows screwing together. "What in the hell are you wearing?" He turned on Logan again. "You let her lead a tour dressed like *this*?"

Logan opened his mouth, but just shut it again without responding.

I knew it was taking everything he had to not throw me under the bus.

I knew it was taking everything in him to take that verbal scolding from my uncle without standing up for himself.

"Look, I don't have time to listen to whatever it is that's going on here," Uncle Mac continued, gesturing between me and Logan. "But you just lost us money, and I have zero tolerance for that. Get your shit together and don't *ever* let me hear about someone in your group requesting a refund ever again. Understood?"

Logan and I both nodded, Logan's eyes on the floor and mine on his, begging him to look at me.

"Good." Mac glanced at Logan once more before heading toward the door, and he shook his head at me as he passed. "And for fuck's sake, get her a proper uniform."

I flinched when Mac left the office, slamming the door behind him and leaving me and Logan alone. I let out a long breath, shaking my head as I crossed the space between us.

"I'm so sorry, Logan. You were right, I wasn't ready to—"

"I think we're done for the day, Mallory," he said, not giving me so much as a glance as he rounded his desk and took a seat, a frustrating sigh leaving his lips.

I should have left it alone, but I just stood there, waiting.

Logan picked a pen out of the cylinder on his desk, writing something on his clipboard and effectively ignoring the fact that I was still there.

"Logan, please. Talk to me."

"About what?"

I scoffed. "Come on. I know what I did was immature, and I'm sorry. I just thou—"

"I know what you thought," he said, slamming his pen down. He stood, finally meeting my gaze, and when he did, I wished he hadn't.

His warm, hazel eyes were gone, replaced by a cool steel that I felt piercing me to my bones.

"You thought you knew everything. You thought my training plan was stupid, and that there was nothing I could teach you that you didn't already know. You thought I took my job too seriously, and that you were too good to be here."

My heart sank at my words being thrown back at me. "I didn't mean—"

"You know, all this time I thought you were this intriguing girl," he said, rolling his lips together before he continued. "I thought Mallory Scooter was an enigma. You were always this fascinating creature to me, because you were unlike anyone else in this town. I thought you were different, elevated, just... I don't know. I couldn't ever put my finger on it, but you were something I'd never experienced."

Something happened then, a flip of my stomach, a flood of something warm and dizzying settling deep in my chest.

"Really?" I whispered.

"Really," he said. His eyes searched mine, like he'd lost his train of thought, but in the next exhale, he flattened his lips and shook his head. "But after today, I know I was wrong. You're just like everyone else. You have no regard for the people around you, you only think about Mallory and what serves *her*. So, thank you. Thank you for shattering the illusion I had of the mysterious Mallory Scooter. The veil has been lifted, along with the spell, and now I see you for exactly who you are."

That sting I felt earlier tripled, and my eyes glossed over — not enough to leak actual tears, but enough for me to feel a cool rush of wind all the way down to my toes.

I swallowed, trying to hold my head high as Logan waited for me to respond.

But I didn't.

What could I possibly say to that?

"Like I said, I think we're done for the day," he echoed, sitting back down and snatching his pen off the desk.

He started writing again, and I stood there — numb, ashamed — like a little kid put in her place. I wanted to apologize, but saying I was sorry felt just as foolish as my shirt did now. I'd gotten him in trouble, and he was pissed — he deserved to be. I wanted to make it right, but I didn't even know where to start.

So, I left, tucking my tail between my legs like the dog I was, without another word.

There were too many emotions flooding through me as I made my way out of that distillery like a zombie. I barely remembered the drive home — only that I could barely breathe, could barely think, could barely remember why I'd been so set on leading that damn tour in the first place.

I needed to calm down, to go to the place where I could be alone, where I could work through what had happened and get a lasso around what the hell was happening to my emotions.

I needed a pencil and a blank sketch pad.

I needed a camera and a sunset in the mountains.

I needed a canvas and a palette of paint.

And I needed to find a way to make it up to Logan Becker — and prove to him I wasn't the girl he thought I was.

. . .

Nothing cleared my mind and brought me peace as much as sketching did.

My left hand was covered in gray dust, fingers guiding the pencil over the page in my sketch pad as I kicked back in the corner of my very messy, soon-to-be art studio. More and more boxes of supplies I'd ordered had started to arrive, but I hadn't found the time or energy to go through anything yet.

My dream was in mountains all around me, and yet something was stopping me from unboxing it.

I couldn't think about that, though — not when my thoughts were consumed with Logan Becker and the hellish day I'd had at the distillery. And to escape *those* thoughts, I'd picked up a fresh new pencil, a blank sketch pad that I'd plucked from one of the boxes, and I'd turned my worries loose.

Sometimes my mind wandered while I sketched, but most of the time, it was just me and whatever I was creating — that image I was bringing to life. I'd lose myself in the comforting sounds of pencil against paper, of my hand skating across the page with each dark line or light shading. I had a soft indie playlist playing in the background, and the setting sun streaming in through the Main Street windows as my light.

A rush of cool wind blew my hair back off my shoulders, and it brought me out of my daze. I blinked, looking up at the front door, the first time my eyes had left the page since I'd sat down.

And then I sighed.

My parents were just inside the studio, looking around at the mess — Dad with his hands in the pockets of his dark jeans, Mom with her hands folded over her purse hanging off her shoulder.

Dad wore a cream cowboy hat over his white hair, his skin somehow tan even in the middle of winter. Wrinkles lined his long face, revealing more about the life he'd lived than any words could. He was tall and lean, a picturesque cowboy from an old western film. I half expected the sound of spurs clinking on his boots when he started making his way toward me, scanning the piles of boxes and yet-to-be-built furniture and supplies before his gaze found me.

"Looks like things are coming along," he said, a sympathetic smile touching his leather lips.

I closed my sketch pad, letting it fall on the folding table I'd had my feet kicked up on before I scrubbed my hands over my face. "I know it's a mess. I've been tired after work," I said that last part pointedly. "But I'll get started unpacking this weekend."

"I wasn't judging," he assured me, though his eyes told me otherwise.

I'd learned long ago that though my father always had the sweetest words for me, though he acted as if I was the pride and joy of his life — I was far from it. It was the same with my mother, who loved him unconditionally. And with my brother, who looked up to him like he was a superhero who could do no wrong. They thought they were his everything, that he'd go to war for them — just like I'd used to think.

But I'd learned better.

My father's main priorities were money, and that distillery, and this town of old men he had wrapped so tightly around his little finger.

That I was sure of.

"I bet it will be beautiful when you're all done with it," Mom chimed in, trying and failing to hide the wrinkle of her nose as she looked around the space. She wore a rose-colored pea coat that wrapped her up from shin to neck, and a fashion hat the same color hid her short, brunette-dyed hair. Her nude kitten heels tapped on the floor when she crossed to where Dad and I were. She smiled, folding her gloved hands in front of her and not saying another word.

That was what I'd come to know my mother as — a silent sidekick. Agreeable, polite, and ever the dutiful wife.

"I heard you had a rough day at the distillery," Dad offered, resting his elbow on one of the tall boxes that held shelves I needed to put together. "Everything okay?"

I waved him off, standing and making my way over to the one box I *had* unpacked — the one with the booze.

"I had a lapse in judgment," I murmured, grabbing the neck of a bottle of gin. I lifted it to my father to ask if he wanted some, but he just shook his head. I didn't even bother asking Mom before I shrugged, pouring a finger into a red Dixie cup. "I just tried giving a tour when I wasn't ready to. Classic Scooter know-it-all-gene biting me in the ass."

Dad smirked at that, folding his arms over his chest. "Ah. I've been struck by that a time or two."

Didn't I know it.

"Well, I didn't come here to make you feel worse about what happened," he said. "I just... I know you don't want to be there. But, remember, we have a deal."

I slammed back the alcohol I'd poured, my eyes landing on his with the swallow. "I didn't do this on purpose."

"And I believe you," he said, putting his hands up. "I just had to check. I know you have some sort of... *vendetta* against me."

I scoffed. "Dad. Please."

"Well, what other reason would you have to... to..." He gestured to me, as if I as an entire entity was a problem. "To dress like that, and ruin the temple of your body with those tattoos and piercings. And God knows you never *wanted* to work at the distillery."

"So you *did* come here to berate me."

"No," he said, a sigh of his own leaving his chest. "I just wanted to remind you that the reason you have this place is because we made a deal. And I don't want you to think that you can half-ass your part of it without me noticing."

"I'm not." I paused. "At least, I didn't mean to. And trust me, I ate a big helping of humble pie today."

Dad watched me, like he wasn't sure if he could trust me to be telling the truth.

That made two of us.

"I'll turn it around," I promised him. "Okay? I was just about to head out, actually. To go apologize to Logan."

Dad's face leveled at the mention of the name, and Mom snapped out of her daydream.

"Logan Becker?" she asked.

I nodded.

"Ugh," she huffed, shaking her head. "Those boys are such a menace. I don't understand why we put up with having them at the distillery at all, anymore."

"You know *exactly* why we do," Dad murmured to her, softly, but with a look stern enough to have her buttoning her lips. He turned his attention to me next. "Why are you apologizing to him?"

"Because he's the one I was a brat to today," I admitted. "And I got him in trouble with Uncle Mac. I need to apologize and make things right." I paused, lifting one brow at my father's unreadable expression. "You did know he's the one training me, right?"

Dad cleared his throat. "Of course." But the way he said it, I knew he didn't.

I smirked, crossing my own arms.

Uncle Mac must have left that part out.

"He's good at his job," I said. "Really good. And from what I can tell, every single one of the other tour guides thinks he'll be the one taking Mac's spot when he retires." I swallowed. "You think that's what will happen?"

My father shrugged noncommittally, already turning for the door, my mother on his heels. "We'll cross that bridge when we get to it. Anyway, I just wanted to check on you, but it seems like you're doing alright. Just... honor your promise to turn it around up there, okay?" He paused at the door, opening his arms. "Come give your old man a hug before you go out."

I crossed the room with heavy lead legs, hugging the man who had helped give me life like he was an acquaintance I was dropping off at an airport.

"Love you, kiddo," he said into my hair, placing a kiss there.

My heart squeezed, the young child inside me who had been Daddy's Little Girl longing for that connection again. But the woman who stood wrapped in that man's arms now knew his true colors.

Daddy's Little Girl would never exist again.

"Love you, too," I murmured.

Mom hugged me, too, before they were both gone, and as soon as they were, I jogged upstairs to get dressed and put on a fresh coat of makeup. Dad might have said every one of those words with a smile, but I read the threat beneath it all.

That was a warning to get my shit together before I lost the dream I hadn't even had the chance to unpack yet.

It was time to take the first step in turning it all around, just like I'd promised — starting with apologizing to Logan.

And I knew just where to find him.

Chapter Six

Logan

"And then, I actually started to feel *sorry* for her," I said, gripping the tumbler of whiskey in my hand a little too tightly as I recounted the day's disaster to my older brothers. "She almost looked ready to cry, so I stepped in, took over the tour to get her out of the hot seat. And when I got back to the tour guide lobby, I was checking on her, asking if she was alright." I shook my head. "Of course, that was *before* Mac came in and ripped me a new asshole big enough to shit a brick out of."

Jordan chuckled. "Well, feeling bad for her doesn't make you an idiot. It makes you a good human being."

I made a noncommittal noise, taking a larger sip of whiskey than necessary just to feel the burn.

"She's a Scooter," Noah reminded me from the bar stool next to Jordan. "Does it really surprise you that she acted like a know-it-all asshole? I mean, isn't that like on her family crest or something?"

I sighed, not wanting to admit that I thought Mallory was more, that she was different. "I guess."

Jordan clapped me on the shoulder. "Don't sweat it, okay? So what, Mac got a little pissed. I know you hate conflict, but to be fair, that old man is always grumpy about something. He'll get over it, probably tonight, and things will move on."

"But I still have to train her," I reminded him. "And there's that whole thing about her most likely taking his job when he leaves."

Noah slammed his glass down. "If they give her that manager job that you've been lined up for for years, they're going to have an entire distillery full of people to explain their actions to. Everyone in that place *knows* you're the best tour guide. You have been for years. And she just started, for Christ's sake. And obviously doesn't even want to be there."

"But that's just the thing, they don't *have* to answer to anyone," Jordan chimed in.

"Yep. They own the place — literally." I sighed. "It doesn't matter if I'm the best. What matters is that if they want her to take that job, it's hers. Period."

Silence fell over us, long enough for me to take the last sip of my whiskey. I held the empty glass in my hands like it was a lifeline.

"Hey, we still don't know that that's what they have in mind," Noah said gently. "For all we know, they could just want her to be a part of the company, finally live up to the Scooter name she seems to have been running from all this time."

"Yeah, I don't think anything points to them making her manager. Not yet, at least," Jordan agreed.

"Nothing pointed to them murdering our father, either. But..." My voice trailed off, a sticky and uncomfortable knot forming in my throat at the words. Because the truth was, we didn't have proof that our father's death was the result of foul play — only suspicion. We knew our father didn't smoke, and that's what the fire was blamed on. We also knew he'd been causing waves on the board, and that Patrick didn't like it, so he'd shoved him into the founder's old office to sift through paperwork. And maybe those two things together didn't sound like enough to get suspicious over, but even if it couldn't be explained, we all felt it — my entire family — that something was off about that fire that took my father's life.

Jordan swallowed down the knot in his own throat, not commenting on what I'd said and choosing to try to comfort me, instead. "Just try to get through her training, and then you won't have to deal with her as much. She can do her tours, you do yours. You'll only have to see each other at meetings and at lunch. You can survive that."

I nodded, but didn't have a response. The truth was I may not have had a reason to believe they wanted her to be manager, but I had a gut feeling — and if Dad had taught me anything as a boy, it was to trust that.

Still, there was no point in dwelling on it now. If it was going to happen, it was going to happen — and I'd deal with it then.

For now, I was more upset at the shattering of the illusion of a girl I'd crushed on secretly for years — not that I could tell my brothers that. But seeing Mallory act the way she had — childish, combative, entitled — it was like a sign from God that there wasn't a woman out there who fit the image I had in mind for what I wanted in a partner.

Not that Mallory Scooter ever could have been *that* for me.

But she was a beacon of light, one that showed me there were gems out there, women who were different, unique, fascinating. There were women I could talk to about something other than the town gossip or the latest country song. There were women out there who didn't care what people thought, who danced to the beat of their own drum, who were *above* the bullshit.

That's what Mallory Scooter had been for me — hope.

And now, that hope had been reduced to ashes.

Maybe it was silly to put so much stock in her in the first place. Hell, I hadn't been around the girl in years. I didn't actually *know* her. I'd created this image of what I *thought* she was in my head and clung to it like a naïve teenage boy with a crush on a movie star.

Now, I'd seen the real human behind the image I'd painted.

Now, I knew the truth.

"Unrelated, but before this whole shit show went down, Mallory told me that Mikey threw his guitar into the bonfire at The Black Hole on Saturday night," I said, effectively changing the subject.

"He *what*?" Noah shook his head. "Dad bought him that guitar. He's had it forever."

"I know," I said. "Bailey fucked that kid up. *Bad*. Worse than I thought, for sure."

"He'll be okay," Jordan said — which was his response to practically everything. I swore nothing ever fazed him. The zombie apocalypse could be happening and he'd be cool, calm, and collected as he loaded his shot gun and assured everyone around him that everything was fine. "Besides, you'll never guess who came by Mom's earlier when I stopped by to bring her some groceries."

Noah and I exchanged looks before he spoke. "Bailey's back?"

"No, no," Jordan said quickly, then he smirked. "*Kylie.*"

"Ky?!" Noah and I asked simultaneously. I shook my head, recalling the girl who used to practically be a little sister to us. "They haven't hung out in a long time... like, since he and Bailey started dating."

"I know. I mean, I'm sure they talked at school and stuff, but maybe Bailey had a problem with them being so close?" Jordan shrugged. "I'm not sure, but she was there helping Mom with dinner when I showed up. Mikey was in his room, and when he did come out, he didn't seem any more cheerful than he has been. But... she was there."

"Hmm," Noah mused, circling the ice in his whiskey. "Well, if we can't pull him out of this slump, maybe she can. They were best friends before Bailey came along."

Jordan nodded. "I guess we'll see."

The jukebox cut out just as the local band that played almost every night at Buck's bar started their mic check, tuning their instruments and getting ready to play. Buck's was the only bar *in* town — though there were a few just outside of city limits on both the north and south sides. Still, it was the watering hole of Stratford, and even though it was a Monday night, the place was packed.

I stared at the empty glass in my hand, debating if I wanted another one. I was slightly buzzed, and part of me wanted to go home, watch the space documentary I'd bookmarked on Netflix and forget about the shitty day I'd had.

But, the other part realized that the days of hanging with my brothers at a bar likely wouldn't last forever, and I was enjoying my time with them.

That thought won out, and I lifted my glass to signal to Buck that I was ready for another. As soon as my hand was in the air, another smaller, more delicate hand with black nail polish donning each nail was on top of it.

"Let me get this round."

I stiffened at the sound of her voice, face flat as I turned to look over my shoulder.

Mallory smiled, though it was a weak one — tinged with an apology she'd tried to give me earlier. Her platinum blonde hair was tied up in a messy bun that somehow looked perfectly designed, with little tendrils falling down to frame her face. Those cat eyes of hers were winged, her lips painted that dusty rose color I'd come to both love and loathe. The piercing in her septum moved a little as her smile widened.

"Please," she added.

Her eyes searched mine, and too many emotions warred inside me for me to decipher. I hated her. I wanted her. I needed her to leave. I longed for her to stay. The longer I watched her, the more I wondered if she could see right through me, if she could read every little thought.

Buck knocked on the bar, calling my attention back to him.

"Another?" he asked.

Buck was the owner of the little watering hole, his name painted on the brick outside. He wasn't just the bartender, though — he was everyone's friend, therapist, referee, and liquid pharmacist.

I nodded, sliding my glass toward him. "Scooter Signature. Neat." I tilted my head toward where Mallory stood behind me then. "Put it on her tab."

Buck lifted one thick, caterpillar eyebrow at Mallory. "Okay… and for you?"

"Gin and tonic, please."

He gave something close to a smile, still eyeing us like a Scooter and Becker together couldn't be trusted — he wasn't wrong — before he finally turned to make our drinks.

Jordan and Noah had been in their own side conversation, but I saw Noah nudge Jordan out of my peripheral, and they were both staring at Mallory now.

"Mallory, you know my brothers?" I leaned away from the bar so she could get a better view of them on the other side of me. "Jordan, Noah."

Mallory beamed, a smile bigger than I ever remembered seeing on her. "Of course. Hey, guys, how's it going?"

They murmured something that sounded like *fine*, offering strange smiles that did nothing to hide the fact that they were questioning why the hell she was here.

"I made an ass of myself and got your brother in trouble today," she explained. "Figured a drink or two might help make up for it."

Noah smiled a little more genuinely then, but Jordan's brows furrowed, and he offered nothing more before turning toward the shelves of alcohol behind the bar and sipping on his whiskey.

"How do you like working at the distillery so far?" Noah asked, aiming for amiability.

"It's... well, it's not what I expected." Mallory looked at me then. "I thought I knew what I was walking into, but I was wrong."

Noah nodded. "I'm not used to hearing those words come from a Scooter."

It was meant as a joke, but his voice didn't hide the fact that he was mostly serious with that statement.

Mallory chuckled. "No, I suppose you wouldn't be." Buck placed our fresh drinks on the bar in front of us, telling us to let him know if we needed anything else. Before I could take the first sip, Mallory grabbed both drinks in her hands and stood. "Play a round of pool with me?" she asked, her eyes pleading for a yes.

Everything in my chest tightened — but not in the way it should have. I told myself it was because I didn't want to play pool with her, that I was annoyed she was here, that I hated her and was still furious for what she'd done.

The truth lay more somewhere around me being giddy at the prospect of getting some one-on-one time with her — *outside* of work.

I stood in lieu of an answer, which had her smiling again as she turned and made her way toward the free pool table in the back. I didn't dare glance over my shoulder at my brothers — who were no doubt watching us walk away — because I knew what I'd find.

Questions.

Concern.

Opposition.

And I didn't want to answer to any of it.

Mallory handed me my drink once we made it to the table, taking a sip of her own before she sat it down and started racking up the balls for us to play. She was silent for a long while, and I just watched her fill the triangle with stripes and solids, moving the balls around until she had the order she wanted.

"So, obviously I owe you an apology," she finally said, removing the triangle frame. She glanced at me through her lashes, stowing the frame away and grabbing a cue stick from the rack behind her. "You want to break?"

"Go ahead."

She nodded, chalking the tip before she lowered her chest toward the table, lining up the shot. She steadied her aim, sliding the wood between her fingers a few times before she fired the shot, sending the white cue ball down the green felt to bust up the balls at the other end. They scattered, landing one solid and one stripe in opposite side pockets.

"Stripes," she called, lining up for the next shot.

She missed, and when she was standing again and it was my turn, she leaned on her cue stick, picking up her drink for another sip.

"I *am* truly sorry for what happened today, Logan," she said as I picked out my own cue stick, chalking the tip. "I acted like a fool — like a know-it-all — and this is me eating crow. You were right, I was wrong. And I'm sorry I had to act out like that to learn the lesson." She paused. "I'm doubly sorry that I got you in trouble with my uncle."

I nodded, lining up my first shot. I sank the four ball in the corner pocket, finally looking at her as I rounded the table for the next shot. "Thank you."

Mallory smiled, and silence fell over us as I took the next few shots. When it was her turn again, she passed by where I stood against the wall, her arm brushing mine before she paused in front of me.

"I've been thinking," she said, voice a little lower now. "About what you said earlier. About me."

She was so close, just another inch and her chest would touch mine. Of course — the top of hers would hit the bottom of mine. She was at least a foot-and-a-half shorter than me.

I swallowed, looking down the bridge of my nose at her glowing eyes. "Yeah?"

"Yes," she answered. "I like that you think I'm different." Her eyebrows folded in. "Well, that you *thought* I was different. And I was hoping we could start over, that we could go back to when you thought I was this intriguing minx and not just the princess of Stratford — like everyone else in this town."

I smirked. "I never said I thought you were a minx."

"But you did," she fired back with a smirk of her own. Her eyes glowed a little fiercer then. "You still do."

I rolled my lips between my teeth, looking up at the ceiling like God himself was up there to help me resist this woman in some way. When I looked at her again, her smile had climbed, eyes dancing in the low light of the bar as she waited for my answer.

"We can start over," I told her, avoiding the minx assessment altogether.

She opened her mouth to respond just as the lead singer of the band came over the microphone to introduce himself and the rest of the crew. Mallory immediately cringed, plugging her ears with her fingers as she glanced up at the speaker that hung right above us.

We were both silent as the band talked on, and when they started playing, Mallory unplugged her ears, saying something I couldn't make out — no matter how hard I stared at her lips.

And trust me — I was staring.

"What?" I yelled over the music.

She said it again, but I shook my head, still not able to make it out.

Then, she grabbed the collar of my button-up plaid shirt and pulled my ear down to her lips. The soft, warm, velvet flesh of them brushed my ear lobe when she spoke.

"Wanna get out of here? Take a walk?"

Chills broke out over every inch of me — which thankfully was covered by the sleeves of my flannel shirt and the denim of my dark jeans. Mallory released my shirt, stepping back with a hopeful smile.

Do not say yes.

Do not go on a walk with that girl.

Do not entertain whatever fantasy you have — not now, not ever.

But I ignored every warning firing off in my head, nodding instead as I hung my cue stick on the rack and drained what was left of my whiskey. Mallory sucked her drink down, too, nodding toward the bathroom. "Just give me a minute," she screamed. "I'll meet you outside."

I nodded again, apparently speechless now that I'd agreed to leave Buck's bar with Mallory Scooter. When she was inside the bathroom, I made my way over to the bar stool I'd abandoned next to my brothers, tugging my jacket off the back of it.

"Where are you going?" Jordan asked.

"On a walk."

"Alone?" Noah probed.

"Why don't you mind your own business?"

Noah laughed, while Jordan's brows folded over his eyes so hard I didn't think he could see me when his hand caught the sleeve of my jacket in a fist.

"She's a Scooter," he reminded me. "Watch yourself."

"She just wants to apologize," I said, ripping my arm away from his grasp. "Besides, we work together. We need to get along."

Both of my older brothers watched me like I was a kid walking into a snake pit I didn't even realize was there. What they didn't know was that I *saw* the pit, I just didn't care.

Maybe the snakes weren't the venomous type.

Maybe they were garter snakes, like the ones Dad used to find in our yard all the time.

Neither of them offered another word, and neither did I. I slapped some cash down on the bar for Buck for the tab I'd run up before Mallory paid for my last drink, nodding a goodbye to him before I made my way toward the door. Mallory was just outside, and when I pushed through the door, she turned, smiling as a puff of white left her mouth with her first breath.

She was wrapped up in a black leather jacket and thick, burnt orange scarf. Her hands were in her pockets, eyes somehow different than they'd ever been before as she offered me a smile.

"Should I lead the way, or am I following you?"

...

Mallory

Stratford was quiet, as it always was this late on a Monday night. Logan and I walked side by side, our steps in line, the only sound between us being the soft thumps of his boots on the sidewalk and the click-clacking from the heels of mine. Christmas lights were strung all along Main Street — curling up the light posts, adorning the limbs of each little naked tree, highlighting the storefront windows. Gold and garnet garland accompanied the lights on the posts, along with little signs that said things like *Merry Christmas* and *'Tis the Season*.

Even from where we walked at the north end of Main, you could see the lights from the big tree set up in our small town square at the south end of the main drag. That tree was erected every year on the Friday after Thanksgiving, Stratford residents always being more excited about seeing the ornaments and lights hung on that evergreen than they ever were about catching a Black Friday deal.

The holidays in this small town weren't just celebrated — they were honored like a sacred tradition.

I smiled, eyes trailing over the enthusiastic display the little boutique in town had put together in their storefront. It was like looking into a snow globe at the North Pole — complete with elves, Santa and Mrs. Claus, and all the reindeer.

"Do you like Christmas, Logan Becker?" I asked, pulling my gaze from the window back to the quiet man walking next to me. The same Scooter Whiskey Carhartt jacket he wore every day at work was warming him now, the hem of his blue and green flannel peeking out at the bottom. He wore an old baseball cap that I swore I'd seen him wear in high school, and his chestnut hair curled around the edges of it, giving him a young, boyish look.

A soft smile touched his lips, but he kept his gaze on the sidewalk. "Are you insinuating that I'm the Grinch?"

"No." I chuckled. "Although, now that you say it, I could see you painted green and slipping down chimneys to steal presents."

Logan glanced at me with a smirk before he let his gaze wander up and over my head, trailing the lights around us. "I used to love it," he said. "When I was younger. I always had this... I don't know, this indescribable feeling of excitement that would come over me around Thanksgiving. I remember putting up the tree with Dad, making cookies with Mom, wearing matching pajamas with all three of my brothers and watching all the classic Christmas cartoons on Christmas Eve." His eyes glistened under the lights, twinkling like stars. "I guess it's that Christmas Spirit everyone talks about. But... I haven't felt that in a long time." He frowned. "Honestly, Christmas just kind of floats by for me now. I see the decorations everywhere, I hear the songs, I see the movies on TV, but... it's just not the same. I don't feel it anymore."

"Since your Dad passed?"

His frown deepened on a nod.

We fell silent again, and I did the math in my head, trying to remember the details of an event the entire town was always trying to forget — my family, especially. There had only been one death at the Scooter Whiskey distillery — and it was John Becker. I was eighteen, and we had just graduated high school. Mr. Becker was at the ceremony, and died weeks later.

Logan was seventeen, I realized. I remembered he was always one of the young ones, and one of the only ones who couldn't join the senior ditch day when we went to Nashville to bar hop all the places that let you in at eighteen.

My heart lurched in my chest. I wasn't close with my parents — not my weak, spineless mother and certainly not my greedy, pretentious father — but even so, I couldn't imagine losing either one of them.

"What about you?" Logan asked when the silence had stretched into awkwardness. "Are you a Christmas fanatic, Mallory Scooter?"

I smiled a sour smile at the mention of my full name, a name I'd tried to escape my entire life, a name I realized I'd never be rid of.

"I'm not a fanatic about anything," I admitted. "Save for art. All those feelings you had around Christmas? I never experienced any of that. For me, Christmas meant Mom hosting lots of grown-up parties with the town's richest assholes, and Dad handing us gift cards of outrageous amounts on Christmas morning. Mom would decorate the house, but more for the town than for us kids. And I don't believe in the 'reason for the season', as they say." I shrugged. "But, I do love how magical it all can be, and I love to illustrate it, photograph it. Honestly, I was just thinking how this is the first time I've walked this town's streets and seen anything close to beauty. I kind of wish I had my camera with me."

"You're talking about me, aren't you?"

I scoffed. "I mean the *lights* are pretty." I paused. "I just never thought that before — not here, anyway."

We were quiet again, but I felt Logan watching me, his eyes dancing over my profile as I kept my gaze on the glowing Main Street tree in the distance.

"You seemed close with your family," he commented. "Until high school. It was like something switched over the summer between eighth and ninth grade, and you were a completely different person when you came back to school."

A chill rolled over me at the thought of that summer, but I smirked to hide it. "Everyone changes before high school," I commented. "I mean, you came back with muscles the size of my head."

"First you call me beautiful, now you're commenting on my muscles?" He tsked. "Feels like some real not-safe-for-work territory we're crossing into here, Minx."

I rolled my eyes, thinking the subject would change, but Logan still watched me, waiting.

"Let's just say I had an eye-opening experience that summer, one that showed me my family's true colors."

"And you didn't like them?"

I stopped walking, and Logan followed my lead, facing me in the middle of the sidewalk at the corner of Main and Ivy.

"Your entire family hates mine," I reminded him. "Is it really so hard to believe that I share the sentiment?"

The comment came out more of a bite than I intended, and Logan softened, his eyes searching mine.

"I'm sorry, I feel like I overstepped."

"It's okay," I assured him on a long exhale and a gentle shake of my head. "It's been a long day, as you well know. I think it might be time for me to get some sleep."

He nodded. "Yeah, I think that'd probably be best for both of us." I watched the thick Adam's apple in his throat bob on a swallow, and I wondered how I never realized how hot his neck was before.

Wait — did I just think his neck *was sexy?*

"Let me walk you home?" he asked.

I smiled. "Alright." We took three more steps, and I stopped again. "Welp, this is me. Thank you."

Logan's brows bent together, and he looked up at the last shop in the brick building behind me. I didn't have signage up yet, and when his gaze fell to the windows — to the empty space *inside* those windows — his eyes doubled in size.

"You live *here*?"

I chuckled. "I live upstairs, above the shop." Following his gaze, I smiled at the empty building behind me — a blank canvas — before I turned back to him with a beam of pride. "This is going to be my art studio — the first one in town."

"Wait, really?" He stepped past me, framing his eyes with his hands and pressing them to the windows to see more inside before he turned to face me again. "This is *yours*?"

"Mm-hmm. Well, *technically*, it's in my father's name for now... but we have a deal and..." I shook my head. "Anyway, yes — it's mine." I swallowed, not sure why my stomach sank to my feet when the next words rolled off my lips. "Want to see it?"

"Like, go inside?"

I nodded.

Logan smiled enough to show that little dimple in his left cheek, which somehow made my stomach flip even more. "I'd love that."

It was definitely the cold Tennessee night that had my hands trembling as I unlocked the doors. It was absolutely the fact that my leather jacket was more of a fashion statement than anything that could actually keep me warm. That's what I assured myself as the bolt unlocked and I pushed inside, Logan following close behind me.

It definitely *wasn't* because I was nervous, or because I hadn't shown my studio to anyone other than my parents and my best friend, and surely it wasn't because showing someone my naked studio felt a lot like showing them my naked body.

Which meant I was stripping down bare for Logan Becker.

I kept my jacket on, hoping it would calm my tremors as I pulled off to the side once we were in the studio, Logan walking past me, his eyes wide as he looked around the space. I tucked myself into the corner, as if I could hide, as if I could disappear and not watch him dissect the space.

Does he hate it?

Is it stupid?

Is he thinking no one will ever pay to take classes here?

Is he thinking art is a waste of time, just like my father?

I shouldn't have cared. I didn't *want* to care, but thoughts like those raced through my mind as I watched Logan from the corner of the room. He traveled the space quietly, slowly, eyes roaming, hands reaching out to trace the walls, the windows, the exposed brick on the back wall. Not much had changed since Chris was there on Saturday. We'd painted the walls, cleaned the brick, swept and mopped the tile floor, and cleaned out what was left in the back storage. Where it was a dusty blank slate before, at least now it was a clean one.

But it was still blank, and I wasn't sure anyone could see the vision except for me.

"Mallory..." Logan whispered, like speaking too loud in the space would disrupt it somehow. He stopped in the middle of the room, eyes scanning the ceiling before his gaze found me. "This is incredible."

I blew out a breath. "Really?"

"Are you kidding?" He smirked. "You have your own *art studio,* your own business. I'm so impressed." Logan shook his head, looking around again. "I can't wait to see what you do with it."

"Right?" I said, excitement bubbling over the anxiety as I pushed out of my corner and flew across the room. "I want it to be a multi-channel visual arts studio, with more than just one thing to offer. Like, over here, we'll have painting classes, with live models and still life and scenery inspiration, with all mediums — watercolor, oil, pastel, maybe even spray painting to jazz it up from time to time. And over here, sketch classes." I pointed to the far corner. "I want to transform that little office back there into a dark room to develop photographs, and do some walking tours around town where I can teach the photography essentials, help those who are interested in the art. Oh!" I skipped to the other side of the room. "And, over here, I thought I could put in an electric kiln, offer some pottery and ceramic classes. I think it'd be great for kids, and I could have more advanced classes for the adults — like vases and other things they'd love to decorate their homes with. And of course, I could host parties, do a sort of paint-by-numbers fun class like they do at those little drink and paint places in Nashville."

I whipped back around, smile nearly splitting my face — because though we were standing in an empty studio, it wasn't empty to me anymore. I could see it — *all* of it — every little picture I'd just painted verbally coming alive as if I'd dreamed it into reality in that dark space.

When my eyes found Logan again, he was watching me in a way I'd never been watched before. One brow was slightly quirked, his eyes wide and curious, the corner of his mouth lifted. It was like I was a street performer he'd just stumbled upon, like he was trying to figure out what I was doing, where the act was going, how much he should leave in my tip jar.

"What?" I asked, breathless.

His smile climbed. "I just love seeing people talk about what they're most passionate about," he said simply. "And I'm excited. For you, for this place. It's going to be great, Mallory."

I blushed, and as soon as I realized that was what was happening, that the heat in my cheeks was a visible sign of being a mixture of embarrassed and flattered, I wanted to slap myself — I probably *would* have, if that wouldn't have made me look like even more of a weirdo.

Suddenly, a dark figure scurried out from the back office, little legs carrying it straight toward me. But before I could bend to scratch behind Dalí's ear, Logan wrapped his arms around my waist, swinging me behind him and standing like a brick wall between me and the ball of fluff like it was a bear instead of a cat. One hand held me in place behind him as the other splayed in front of him, like a shield or a weapon.

If it wasn't somehow so fucking endearing that he was trying to protect me from something, I would have laughed.

"Wait!" I said, grabbing his shoulders to hold him back from killing my furry friend. "It's just Dalí."

Logan relaxed — though only marginally, and he still stood in front of me. "Who?"

I chuckled, releasing my grip on his shoulders as I made my way around him and bent to pick up the cat. "Dalí," I repeated. "He was a stray, and I adopted him. Thought he'd make a pretty cute shop cat."

Dalí croaked out an old meow when he was in my arms, his signature motorboat purr sparking to life. He was warm, like he'd been wrapped in a ball sleeping somewhere in the back, but I couldn't shake the fact that I missed another warmth I'd had just moments before.

Logan's body against mine, his hand on my waist…

"He is pretty cute," Logan said, relaxing even more now. He took a step toward us, reaching one finger under Dalí's chin to rub the patch of white there. Dalí leaned into the touch, which earned a chuckle from Logan and a smile from me.

When Dalí had enough petting for his liking, he wormed around in my arms until I lowered him back to the ground. He meowed once more before skipping off somewhere in the back, and then it was just Logan and me again.

His eyes bounced between mine. "Sorry I grabbed you," he said, reaching for the back of his neck with an embarrassed shrug. "Acting like a big bad knight in shining armor, protecting you from a *cat*."

I let out a soft laugh, folding my hands in front of me. "I appreciate the gesture. Glad to know I'd have some help if small, furry animals tried to over-run the shop."

Logan smirked.

"Anyway, thanks for indulging me," I said on an awkward laugh, covering my face when I remembered how I'd pranced around the empty shop like an idiot as I explained my vision for what it would become. I let my hands fall to my thighs with a slap, letting out a long breath. "It really has been a long day."

He straightened at that, his face leveling. "Yeah, let me get out of your hair, let you get some sleep," he said, his feet moving toward the door — toward me. He stopped with just a foot between us, and I felt that distance like it was a live wire, buzzing and sparking and warning of danger. "But, thank you for showing me... and for the apology for today."

I flushed again.

Stupid traitorous cheeks.

"Thank you for forgiving me," I replied. "And for letting us start over, so I can show you I'm not a *complete* brat."

"Just a somewhat brat."

"Right."

He smiled. "I'm looking forward to the new beginning."

"Me, too."

Logan stood there a moment longer, eyes flicking back and forth between mine, and if it wasn't so dark in the shop, I would have sworn I saw those hazel wells fall to my lips before he finally stepped away.

"Goodnight, Mallory Scooter."

And with that, he was gone — as was the man I thought he was before that night.

Chapter Seven

Logan

When I wasn't having dinner at Mom's or going out to the bar with my brothers, my normal night routine went like this:

Make a protein shake. Read the newspaper while I drank said protein shake, followed by a thirty-minute, high-intensity workout that mostly involved calisthenics in my back yard, and thirty minutes of yoga and meditation. Then, I'd shower, shave, and cook dinner — which was the same thing every night — chicken breast, baby carrots, zucchini, and squash — all baked in the same seasoning in the oven at three-hundred-and-fifty degrees for one hour. I ate at my small dining table alone, without the television on and without looking at a screen of any kind. After dinner, I either picked up the book I was currently reading — which almost always was a historical biography or a psychological thriller of some kind — or, on the nights I was feeling lazy, I'd plop down on the couch and indulge in a documentary.

Tonight, I wasn't necessarily in the *lazy* category, but I was very firmly in the *distracted* one — therefore, reading had proven nearly impossible and I was on the couch, trying (and failing) to watch the space documentary I'd been wanting to watch for weeks. Still, even though I was very interested in Apollo 11 and the countless people and thousands of hours that went into getting the first man on the moon, I couldn't focus long enough to actually learn anything. Instead, I watched the television as if from a distance, with the words jumbling together, the images blurred.

My workout — which usually got me out of my head for a while — seemed more difficult than usual tonight because I couldn't clear my head, couldn't submit to my body and just let it do the work for a while. I couldn't relax enough to successfully meditate, couldn't shower or cook or eat or do *anything* without all my thoughts drifting back to one thing.

To one *person.*

Mallory Scooter.

It'd been more than a week since our walk down Main Street, the Christmas lights glowing around us as the girl I'd always been curious about showed me a little more of who she was. I could still close my eyes and see the excitement on her face as she bounced around her empty art studio, showing me where things would be, illustrating her vision so clearly that I could see it, too.

It was a new beginning, a restart — and I'd found that it also might have been a mistake.

The next day at the distillery, we'd established a new sort of friendship. She was more serious about her training, and insisted on starting over — including getting another solo tour with me where I described all the points of interest on the tour we gave to guests before she even agreed to shadow me again. The rest of the week, she'd followed all my tours, bringing up the back and taking notes as we went along. By Friday, she was chiming in from time to time, telling our guests little stories about her grandfather or dad that I didn't know.

And we were getting along.

Gone was the combative girl who seemed hell bent on making my job training her miserable. She was replaced with someone determined to learn, determined to get along with everyone, determined to succeed in her role. I wasn't sure if it was Mac chewing us out that had changed her mind, or if her father had come down on her, or if maybe — just maybe — it was that she really did feel bad for what happened and she wanted to make it up to me. Whatever the reason, Mallory Scooter and I were finally getting along, and falling into a groove I never would have guessed we could find.

The problem was that the more time I spent with her, the more she drifted from hating me to tolerating me — the more I wanted to be around her.

I found myself making excuses to have lunch with her — even though I'd assigned her a different lunch buddy each day to help her get to know more people at the distillery. I'd somehow always be there, at the same table, inserting myself in their conversation so I could hang out with her. She always shadowed *my* tours — even though I could have easily assigned her to other tour guides — and after the last tour was done, I was always finding some reason to keep her around in my office a little longer.

And now, she'd invaded my thoughts *after* I clocked out, too.

I couldn't stop thinking about her studio, about the fact that she'd struck up some deal with her father that she didn't seem too keen to talk about. I wondered if *that* was why she was at the distillery — if he'd agreed to buy the studio for her in exchange for her working at the distillery. It seemed contradictory, but at the same time, I knew Patrick had wanted Mallory to be a part of the family legacy for years, and she'd always been absent.

Maybe this was his way of exerting power over her.

I wanted to know more, wanted to know what she'd decided not to tell me that night. I also wanted to see her art — her drawings, her photographs, the pottery brought to life by her hands. Sometimes, she'd walk into the distillery with paint on her jeans or a smatter of clay on her cheek, and I was so desperate to know what she created, what inspired her, what she brought to life.

I wanted to hate her. And if I'd left things alone after that day she'd gotten us in trouble — I think I could have. But no, she had to apologize, and she had to take me on that walk, and she had to remind me why I had always felt some magnetic attraction toward her.

Mallory Scooter was unlike any woman I knew, and I couldn't shake her from my thoughts.

I sighed when I realized I'd zoned out — again — thus missing the part of the documentary I'd rewinded to twice now because I couldn't focus. I clicked the television off with a huff, resting my elbows on my knees as I looked around my small living room.

My house wasn't much, but it was perfect for me. I'd embraced the minimalist life as soon as I'd moved out of Mom's, opting for an old farm house built in the late eighteen-hundreds on the northeast side of town. I was about five minutes farther out than Mom, which made it easy to get to her and yet still far enough away from town that I had peace and quiet.

I'd done my best to fix up what I could when I moved in, keep the original wood and structure alive and well. Everything that existed in that little home had a purpose, and there wasn't anything unnecessary — no décor, no expensive rugs or plants or pieces of art, no furniture that served more than a person or two. My home wasn't made to entertain, it was made to live in.

My books had a home on the two shelves I'd built against the wall where the largest window was, the one that gave me a great view into my front yard and a way to see any cars coming down my long, dirt driveway. There was a television, a two-seat love sofa — where I sat now, and a coffee table that Dad and I had built at my camp's father-son day when I was younger. There were a few family photos on the wall near the front door, and between the kitchen and the living room was a small dining table that sat four people max. The kitchen was small, too — with older appliances that barely got the job done anymore. I knew I'd have to upgrade them soon, but fought against it as long as I could. And in the bedroom was a simple bed frame, box spring, and mattress — plus one bedside table that was home to whatever book I was reading each night before I turned out the lights to sleep.

There were no curtains, no embellishments, no frills. It was a home, a place to live.

And it was *always* clean.

I'd been accused of being a neat freak my entire life — mostly by my brothers. Still, I didn't realize the full extent of my need to have everything in order and tidy until I moved out on my own. At Mom's, I'd had no say in décor or organization other than what lived inside the four walls of my bedroom.

But here, everything was mine.

And it was always, *always* clean.

Another minute or two passed with me looking around, and my eyes caught on my bookshelf, remembering how Mallory had teased me about the organization of the one in my office. The one at home was the same — organized by book height, color, and author last name.

I wondered if she'd started reading the book I'd loaned her.

You could always text her to find out...

I shook the thought off, leaning back into the couch on a sigh. But the longer I sat there, the more the idea sounded like a good one.

It wouldn't be *weird* to text her, I convinced myself. We were friends.

Ish.

We worked together, and we were friend-*ly*. There was nothing that said I couldn't text her, ask her about the book, see if she was ready for her first tour tomorrow.

Well, her first tour since the disaster one she'd had last week.

She was actually ready this time, and I'd be shadowing her first thing in the morning. Hell, I kind of owed it to her as her supervisor, didn't I? To check in and make sure she was ready?

I chewed my lip, considering it for all of two seconds before my phone was in my hands, fingers flying over the screen.

> **Me:** *So, are you ready for your first tour tomorrow?*

> **Me:** *Don't forget to wear an actual shirt this time.*

I smirked at the second text I sent, and before I could lock my screen and go do something to fill my time until she answered, I saw the bouncing dots that told me she was typing back.

> **Mallory:** *Ha, ha. I have my outfit planned out — full shirt and all, thank you very much.*

> **Mallory:** *Are YOU ready to lose your job after they realize what a kick ass tour guide I am?*

My smile fell, along with the food still digesting in my stomach. She'd meant it as a joke, I knew that, but the sickening reality that it could actually happen made it impossible to laugh.

> **Me:** *We'll see. You might be so distracted by the hot guy in the back that you forget your lines.*

> **Mallory:** *Ooooh, who's the guy? Do I know him? ;)*

> **Me:** *You know his favorite book. Have you started reading that, by the way?*

> **Mallory:** *I have. So far, no crying. You better pray it stays that way, or else.*

I smiled, laying my phone back down on the coffee table before I decided to try the documentary again. Maybe now that I'd talked to her, I could focus a little more.

Before I hit play, my phone lit up again.

Mallory: *By the way, if you want to text me, you don't have to make up a work excuse to do so.*

A jolt of anxiety danced with one of excitement low in my gut at her words, and I read them over and over, fingers hovering over the keys as I tried to think of what to say. I toyed with something close to a joke, trying to feign innocence and pure professionalism, but she texted again before I had the chance.

Mallory: *Goodnight, Logan Becker. ;)*

I smiled, shaking my head as I leaned back on the couch.

She really is a little minx.

I sent a goodnight text of my own, avoiding the fact that she'd called me out on my lame attempt at finding an excuse to text her. Then, I started the documentary again.

So I could not watch it for the third time as I tried to decipher what that winky face emoji meant, instead.

• • •

Mallory

"And just like that, the title of Best Scooter Whiskey Tour Guide has officially been stolen," I said, peeling my jacket off and laying it over the back of the chair in Logan's office before I plopped down into it. "Boom."

I was still making the bomb explosion gesture of awesomeness with my hands when Logan closed his office door and rounded his desk, shrugging his own coat off. "I have to admit, that was a pretty great tour."

"*Great*?" I asked, incredulous. "That was *fan-fucking-tastic*. I wouldn't be surprised if Mac doesn't burst through that door soon and tell us we got twenty-five new Yelp reviews — all five stars."

"I'm sure that group of young bucks from the University of Michigan would give you ten stars."

I snorted. "Still wouldn't give them a chance in hell — although the tall one did sneak me his number when he gave me his tip at the end."

"I'm sure that's not the *only* tip he'd like to give you."

Logan waggled his brows as my jaw flopped open, and I reached across the desk, smacking his arm.

"Pig!" I laughed, leaning back in my chair and folding my hands behind my head like a boss. "But see, they loved me because I have tits. The rest of the group loved me because I was charming, and witty, and I had stories galore." I quirked a brow. "Admit it — that wasn't bad for a rookie."

Logan watched me with the left side of his lips quirked, that dimple making a brief appearance before it was gone again. "You killed it. Although, I was impressed as soon as you introduced yourself. I knew it was going to be a good tour."

"Really? How?"

"Because you actually wore a shirt, and you didn't have any gum."

I stuck my tongue out at him, which earned me a chuckle.

"What *is* it with you and that gum, anyway?" Logan asked, cringing. "I swear, I was two seconds away from holding my hand out like a mom and demanding you spit it into my palm the first day you came into this office."

I laughed. "Well, let's just say I traded in one bad habit for another." I held up both hands like a scale. "Quit smoking, start chewing gum like a six-teen-year-old asshole."

"At least you *admit* the asshole part."

"Say what you want, Becker. Nothing can bring me down." I fished inside the pocket of my jacket hanging on the chair, pulling out a wad of cash. "*Espe-cially* not after getting this much in tips."

"Just wait until you get assigned to a tour of rich businessmen from some tech company in California or some brokerage in New York. The other female tour guides get five-hundred bucks *easy* on those ones."

I blanched. "Maybe I should forget my shirt for that one."

We broke out in a fit of laughter, but the noise died quickly when Logan's office door flew open, the handle hitting the wall so hard it rattled the room and surely left a dent. I jumped — out of my chair, nearly out of my *skin* — as Mac steamrolled his way into the office, face red and blotchy, breathing like a dragon again.

Uh-oh...

"Please, tell me what is so goddamn funny, because I could use a laugh after the shit storm you two just dropped on my desk."

Logan and I were both shocked silent, and we exchanged a glance before Logan cleared his throat. "Sir?"

"Sir?" Mac mocked him, slamming his phone down on the desk in front of Logan. "Thirty years. Thirty years we've been giving tours, and not once has a video been leaked. Not *once* has our most precious process been exploited to the public. Until today."

Logan's face was sheet white as he watched whatever was on that phone screen, and he swallowed a lump, not even looking at me before he slid the phone across the desk so I could see.

It was a video — one taken in the warehouse where the boys were raising barrels. What was worse, you could hear me in the background, explaining the entire process as whoever it was that snapped the video got a close up of the machinery we used, of the way Noah was arranging the staves, of *everything*.

"Mac, I—"

"It's my fault," Logan said before I could get another word out. He stood, meeting Mac's eyes. "I wasn't paying attention, I didn't realize the phone was out."

"Nor did you explain to *anyone* in that tour that there was no photography allowed in that part of the tour — as this little shit has repeatedly told me since he tagged us in the video and I've been private messaging him trying to get it taken down." Mac turned his glare on me next. "I knew it was a bad idea when your father told me you were going to work here. If you don't want any part of this company, fine — but don't try to take it down in a fire while you're here."

I narrowed my eyes, standing so I could look my uncle in the eyes, too. "I didn't do this on purpose," I defended. "And, besides — it's on our fucking *website* that we make our own barrels. And anyone who takes the tour can easily write up what we tell them about the process. It's not like it's a secret, or like we gave away any information that they couldn't find on Google."

"The reason we don't allow photos or videos is because they may know that we make our own barrels, but they don't know *how*. They don't know the products we use, the methods, the charring. This barrel process and our natural spring are the only things setting our whiskey apart from the competition — and you just gave one piece of that secret recipe away."

I had to clench my jaw to keep my mouth shut — mostly because Logan was giving me a warning look from behind Mac.

"It won't happen again, sir," Logan said, drawing Mac's attention back to him. "I'll make sure of it."

"Your damn straight it won't happen again, because until further notice, you're both suspended from giving tours."

"What?!" we both exclaimed, Logan taking a step toward Mac with the word.

Mac put his hand up, both as a note to Logan to stop where he stood and to signal that he was done with the conversation.

"I don't want to hear another word," he said, still fuming as he eyed us both down. "Now, I'm going to go do as much damage control as I can do and try to get this little fucker's video down before someone who actually matters sees it. In the meantime, you two are excused." He turned toward the office door, pausing at the frame. "And tomorrow, I'll have a new assignment for you."

"*Assignment?*" I asked.

"We're cleaning out the big storage closet, archiving what we need to keep and trashing the rest so we can make room for this year's files once the New Year passes." He gave us both a condescending grin. "I'm sure a little time in that dusty closet will be punishment enough for the two of you while I clean up your mess."

He turned and left at that, leaving Logan and me alone again, and I closed my eyes on a sigh.

Fuck.

It was *my* fault that video had been taken. Mac was right — I'd forgotten to tell them no photos or videos were allowed in that room, and I hadn't *seen* anyone filming — but they had. And now, I'd gotten Logan in trouble.

Again.

Here he was trying to get promoted, and was doing a fine job of getting himself there before I showed up and ruined it all. I'd landed him at the top of Mac's shit list.

And worse, I'd gotten him suspended from giving tours.

I turned, opening my eyes but keeping my gaze on my shoes. "Logan, I am so—"

But before I could get the words out, Logan zipped past me, shoving one arm in the sleeve of his coat before the other.

"Where are you going?"

"You heard Mac," he said, not looking at me. "We're excused for the day."

"So, where are you going?"

"Buck's."

He was already out the door, but I chased after him, offering awkward smiles to the other tour guides who watched us like hawks on our way out. When we were in the hallway, I grabbed his sleeve, forcing him to stop.

"Logan, I'm sorry. I'm so sorry. I'll talk to him, I'll—"

"It's *fine*, Mallory," he bit out, his gaze hard. "Please, just leave it alone. Mac isn't going to change his mind."

I swallowed, nodding as I released his sleeve.

"I really am sorry," I whispered.

Logan nodded, but didn't say a word before he turned, making his way toward the door at the end of the hall that led to the employee parking lot. I watched him go, feet glued to the floor, knowing that a glass of whiskey and a game of pool wouldn't fix what I'd done this time.

When the metal door slammed behind him, I let out a long sigh.

So much for starting over.

Chapter Eight

Logan

The hot coffee in my left hand did little to soothe the pounding of my head as I walked through the distillery halls the next morning. I sipped it anyway, hoping it could somehow erase the absurd amount of whiskey I'd consumed the night before. Going to Buck's to drown out what had happened with Mac seemed logical when I'd decided to do it, but hindsight reminded me that a Thursday night was *not* a Friday night, and reporting for work the day after drinking wasn't as easy as it had been when I was twenty-two.

The hot coffee in my *right* hand was for Mallory, but just like the one in my left, it did little to soothe my anxiety as I made my way toward the office. I knew she'd be there — even though I was early and she wasn't expected to be in for another hour. I knew, because I saw it on her face when I'd stormed out the day before.

She was sorry, and she felt bad for what had happened.

Which in turn made *me* feel like a bag of shit, because it wasn't her fault. What happened could have happened to any new tour guide, and in reality, it was more a reflection of *me* than it was of her. I'd been giving tours for years. I was the Lead Tour Guide. If anyone should have realized we didn't tell that group that there were no photos allowed, it should have been me.

And I didn't.

Because I was distracted.

I sighed, shaking my head at my own stupidity as I pushed through the door that led to the guide lobby. No one was in yet, not even Mac, so the lobby was empty.

But there was a blonde mess of hair in my office.

Her back was to me as she waited in the same chair she'd been in yesterday when Mac rushed into the office, her attention fixed on the swinging Newton's Cradle on my desk. I wondered if she'd left at all, if she'd slept, if she'd let go of what happened or if she'd simmered on it all night like I did.

When I rounded my desk and saw the bags under her eyes, I got my answer.

Mallory looked up at me like a little girl who got caught eating a cookie before dinner. She sat on her hands, her brows furrowed, eyes watching mine as I took a seat in my chair across from her. I could tell she wanted to speak, she wanted to apologize again, but I spoke before she had the chance.

"Mallory, I'm sorry for how I acted yesterday."

"No," she said, immediately shaking her head. "It was my fault. And you had every right to be pissed — to *still* be pissed. I am so sorry I fucked up... *again*."

I smirked. "You didn't fuck up. It could have happened to any new guide, and truthfully, it was on *me* to point that out if you missed it. I knew better — you didn't."

"But I *did*," she argued, shaking her head. "I asked you to start over last week, and then the first chance I get to show you that I'm serious now, that I care, I go and make the worst mistake I possibly could have."

I chuckled at that. "Mallory, it was a video of some stupid barrels being made — not a terrorist attack."

She smiled as much as she could, but it fell quickly, her eyes on my desk.

"It's okay — really. Mac made a bigger deal out of it than necessary. The video is down, and nothing proprietary was leaked. If it was really *that* top secret, they wouldn't let us take tours through there at all. Right?"

She tilted her head a bit at that. "I guess that's a good point."

I nodded, sliding the coffee I'd brought for her across the desk. "Here. A peace offering. So we can stop arguing about who was wrong and whose fault it is and focus on today's tasks. Deal?"

Mallory sighed, like she wanted to keep arguing and apologizing rather than accept my offer. It was kind of adorable, seeing the woman who'd given me so much hell look so upset that she'd let me down. And truthfully — *she* hadn't. It'd been my own damn self that had let me down.

Regardless of whose fault it was, the whole thing was in our past — and that's where I wanted to keep it. The sooner we got the storage closet cleaned out, the sooner we could both get back to tours.

I edged the coffee a little closer, waggling my brows. "It's mochaaa," I sang.

After a long pause, she reached forward for the cup with a long sigh, wrapping her hands around it. She nodded once, smiling a little more genuinely now, her shoulders visibly relaxing.

"Okay," she finally said. "Deal."

• • •

"Where do we even start?" Mallory asked, squinting through the dusty fluorescent light of the oversized storage closet. She hung her hands on her hips, surveying the mountainous stacks of file boxes and plastic storage containers that lined every single wall and filled three rows in the middle.

I followed her gaze with my own sigh. "I guess we pick a corner and go from there."

"And we're supposed to decide what's worth keeping and archiving, and what we can pitch?" She wrinkled her nose. "I feel like this is a job for a secretary who's been here for a long time and knows more about this stuff."

I tapped the printed list on top of my clipboard. "Lucy gave us a guide to go by, with a list of what to keep and what to pitch," I said, referencing the closest thing to a secretary the distillery had. Lucy sat in the front lobby, greeting guests and getting them ready for their tours, as well as handling all the admin tasks for our officers in her down time. "She said if we had any questions to call her or stop by the front desk."

Mallory shook her head, still not convinced, before pulling the highest box she could reach from the corner stack. "This sucks."

I chuckled. "It does, but hey," I offered, pulling my Bluetooth speaker from my backpack and propping it on one of the middle rows of boxes. "At least we have music."

I hit play on one of my go-to playlists on my phone, the familiar sound of "Fever" by The Black Keys filling the closet. Mallory paused where she was opening the first box, brows popping up into her hairline as she assessed me.

"*You* listen to The Black Keys?" she asked.

I shrugged. "Why is that hard to believe?"

"I don't know, I just took you for more of a country boy... you know, George Strait and the like."

"George Strait is the fucking man," I said, grabbing a box of my own off the stack she'd started on. "But so is Dan Auerbach."

She smirked, amusement dancing in her eyes as she assessed me. She took a step toward me, then another, and I hadn't noticed how small that closet felt until her chest was nearly touching mine.

"I couldn't agree more," she said, reaching behind me and turning up the volume on the speaker.

She backed away then, mouthing the words and moving her hips to the beat. My gaze fell to those hips, watching them sway like a hypnotizing pendulum. With her arms up over her head, a sliver of her toned stomach peeked out from under the Scooter Whiskey polo she wore, and I couldn't tear my eyes away from that stripe of bronze skin.

Not until her arms dropped, the sliver disappearing, and when I looked up, she was watching me with an even more amused smile.

"Let's get started, shall we?"

I swallowed, murmuring something close to a *yeah* before I turned and opened the box I'd pulled down from the stack. Mallory chuckled from behind me, but I didn't dare look back — not with my cheeks as hot as they were. I just bobbed my head along to the music, pulling the first file from the box.

And then we got to work.

As the morning stretched between us, it became overtly clear to me just how different Mallory and I were. Where she was huffing with each new box she opened, and sighing with each file she slapped down on the archive pile, and groaning when she came across something she couldn't decipher easily whether to keep or toss — I was in my own version of organizational heaven. The music helped me zone out, and I hummed or sang along to each new song as I filtered through the boxes, making neat piles, labeling anything that didn't already have an identifier, organizing by color and size so I could figure out the exact best way to re-pack it all in the end.

It was definitely a punishment for her, but as much as I wanted to be outside giving a tour, our task was something close to therapy for me.

I was still in the zone, flipping through some photographs from the Scooter Whiskey Single Barrel Soirée of 2004 when Mallory let out a larger sigh than usual, turning the music down a little and flopping down on the floor. She leaned her back against a stack of boxes, looking up at me with a pout.

"Can we take a break?"

I chuckled. "You can. I'm in a rhythm."

I wrote on a lime green label with Sharpie, sticking it to the folder of photos and placing it on top of the other files of photos I'd found that morning. I glanced at Mallory before I grabbed the next file in the box, and she smiled.

"God, you *love* this, don't you?" She shook her head. "I'm over here watching the minutes tick by like years and you're geeking out over putting everything in its place."

I smiled, peeking down at her before I flipped the new file open in my hands. "I can't help it. I've always been this way," I said. "There's just something so satisfying about putting things in order, giving them a place."

"You'd freak out if you saw the shop right now," she said, crossing one leg over the other. "There's not a corner of that previously empty space that's not covered with shit right now. I'm trying to set everything up, separate the room like I told you I envisioned. And Chris tried to help, but…"

"Chris has a different vision, I'd wager?"

She made a noise. "That's one way to put it. I mean, you know Chris — he'd have that place covered in glitter if I let him have his way."

I chuckled, because I *did* know Chris — at least, I knew him back when we were younger. He was the first person I'd ever known to come out, and the only one in our high school at the time. I didn't hang out with him, and didn't know him personally, but I remembered talking to Dad about it the day Chris told everyone he was gay.

I was confused, mostly because all the other guys in our school were being dicks to him suddenly — although he was the same guy he'd been the day before, when everyone adored him. Chris was the captain of the JV soccer team. He was on student council. He was hilarious, and was always surrounded by a huge group of friends who loved to watch him, to let him entertain them.

And it all changed overnight.

I could still remember Dad's furrowed brows as he listened to me, the calmness in his voice as he explained to me that people didn't understand people who weren't like them, and so they lashed out, afraid of the unknown. He told me not to be like them, not to run from what I don't understand, but to embrace it, instead.

And the last, most important thing, he told me was that I needed to be ready to stand up to those guys at school should they pull any shit with Chris.

Luckily, Chris proved that he could hold his own over the years, but he had a silent ally who watched his back from a far — just in case.

"It's my own fault," Mallory continued on a sigh. "I shouldn't have ordered everything at once. I don't even know where to start."

"Maybe I could help you," I offered — a little too quickly. My eyes darted to hers before I turned my attention back to the file in my hands, aiming for nonchalant as I shrugged. "I mean, if you want an extra hand. I could come by sometime this weekend, help you sort through it all."

"You'd give up your weekend to sort through the pile of crap in my art studio?" she questioned. "Come on now, I can't take you away from your hot dates."

I scoffed. "The only hot date I have this weekend is with a Nat Geo documentary on Sunday night."

She hummed a soft laugh. "That so? I've been wondering what you do outside of this place," she said, motioning to the closet around us. Her eyes skated over the mountain of boxes we had yet to get to before they found mine. "What's the documentary about?"

I scratched the back of my neck, murmuring a reply into my chest before tossing the file in my hand in the trash box and picking up the next.

"What was that?"

I sighed. "It's called *Creatures of Light Underwater*," I said, loud enough that she could actually hear this time. "And I know what you're thinking, but it actually looks really cool. It's all this new footage put together by deep sea scientists who are finally able to get deep enough to capture some of the wildest displays of light from species that live in pitch black water. No external light reaches that far down, yet they *create* light — to mate, to capture their prey, whatever."

Mallory bit back a smirk, shrugging and putting her hands up. "Hey, I didn't say a word."

"You were thinking of some, I'm sure."

"No, seriously. Zero judgment. If anything, I'm excited to see *you* so excited about something." She tilted her head. "So, you get off on biology, huh?"

I shrugged. "I guess. I just love learning, in general. That's why I like to read — to learn something new that I didn't know before. And I love watching documentaries, mostly because there's no acting or anything fake about it. There are so many fascinating stories that are *true*, that have real footage. It's incredible." I laughed through my nose. "Plus, I've lived in the same town my entire life and never traveled out of the state. It's nice to go places — to learn about other people, other cultures, other ways of life."

Mallory watched me for a long time without saying anything — so long that I peered down at her, and another shade of embarrassment tinged my cheeks when I found curiosity dancing in those blue eyes of hers.

"What?"

She shook her head. "Nothing. You just surprise me, that's all."

"Because I'm a nerd who listens to rock music?"

"No," she said easily. "Because you're smarter than you let on. And you're cool."

I snorted, deciding to make a joke rather than admit what her words did to my stomach. "If me geeking out over glowing fish is cool, don't get me started about my love for space."

Mallory laughed, tucking her feet closer and balancing her chin on her knees as she hummed along to the new song that had just come on. I eyed her from my peripheral, still flipping through the old training documents in the box I was working on, even though my attention was on her. I traced the black lines shaping her eyes, the long wisps of her lashes, the platinum strands of hair that had fallen from her ponytail and lined the edges of her jaw. I had the sudden urge to see her without makeup, to study the curves of her cheeks without them being covered with blush, or to look into her eyes without the tips of them being painted black, or to see the color of her nude lips, to feel them without smudging a line of lipstick...

To taste them.

That last thought zapped me out of my trance, and I cleared my throat, moving on to the next box in the stack. It was the one that had been buried on the bottom in the very back corner of the room, and it was extra dusty as I plopped it on the table in front of me.

I waved away the cloud, squinting. "Did it hurt?"

"When I fell from heaven?" Mallory snickered. "Come on, Logan. You've got better lines than that."

I chuckled. "No, I meant *that*," I said, motioning to the ring hanging from her nose. I pinched the septum of mine to illustrate. "I feel like that had to be painful."

Mallory reached up, fingering the diamonds that lined the bottom of the ring and shaped her too-perfect nose. It was ridiculous, really, that I noticed her fucking nose — but I did. It was perfectly sized for her face, the tip of it rounded like a little button, and that ring she wore only called my attention to it more.

"A little," she admitted. "But then again, I was eighteen and on a mission to piss off my parents. It could have felt like childbirth and I still wouldn't have backed down."

I cocked a brow. "You got that pierced to prove a point to your parents?"

"No, I did it because I liked it and I wanted to," she said, but the corner of her mouth lifted. "Driving my father insane was just a perk."

"I'm sure he loved the tattoos, too."

"Oh, the one on my lower back is his *favorite*."

I laughed, peeling the top off the dusty box. "Why were you so hell bent on pissing them off?"

A long sigh left her lips. "That's a very long story, and one that would require libations. Maybe—" Her words died mid-sentence. "Logan? What's wrong?"

I wanted to say *nothing*.

I wanted to shake my head, laugh it off, tell her to continue with her story.

I wanted to put the lid back on the box in front of me and pretend I'd never opened it and seen what was inside.

But I couldn't.

All I could do was stand there, gaping at the charred remnants of the most horrible day in all my life.

The box had been unlabeled — and now that I saw what was inside it, I knew why. It was a box not meant to be found, one not meant to be dug through. Black soot lined the edges of it, and the items that filled it looked like someone had cleaned out their desk after being fired, ready to make the walk of shame through the halls to their car with everything that had decorated their office loaded into a box.

The photo frame that sat on top was busted — the glass broken, the silver frame mostly black now, and the photo seared and water damaged. Only one little inch of it remained clear enough to make out.

It was my oldest brother's face — his smile, one sparked by the joke Dad had told us just before the photo was snapped.

I swallowed, gripping the edges of the folding table the box was on to keep myself from stumbling backward or passing out. All the blood drained from my face, from my neck, from every vein in my body.

"It's my Dad's stuff."

The words were barely out of my mouth before Mallory scrambled up from where she was sitting on the floor, peering into the box with me. "What?!"

I nodded numbly. "That... that's Jordan," I said, swallowing the lump in my throat as I pointed to what was left of the photo. "He had this picture on his desk. It was from our fishing trip the summer before he died."

"Jesus…" she murmured, reaching inside the box to retrieve the frame. She held it as delicately as she could, but already, her fingers were covered in black. She pulled the frame close to her eyes, studying it, and I watched her eyes trace the photo before they found mine again. "Logan, wasn't there an investigation done that day?"

I nodded, every movement slow and distant, like I was submerged under icy water just seconds from passing out.

"Wouldn't this have been evidence?" she asked, pulling the next charred item out of the box. Bits of ashes fell off the once-gold paperweight, now mostly black. It was one my mom gave him for Christmas, engraved with his favorite Colin Powell quote.

There are no secrets to success. It is the result of preparation, hard work, and learning from failure.

I couldn't speak. I just stared at the weight in her hands as Mallory stared at me.

"Logan?"

I blinked. "I don't know. Maybe they didn't think it was relevant."

"Maybe," she agreed, thumbing the small part of the quote that peeked through the grime. "But, if it wasn't relevant to the fire department or the police… then why did someone keep it?"

We shared a look then, and my heart kicked back to life in my chest, thundering hard in my ears as my hands dug into the box. One by one, I pulled out each item in that box — what was *left* of each item, anyway — until I got to the very bottom and retrieved a thick, heavy, dated and familiar rectangle that I never thought I'd see again.

Mallory gasped. "Is that…"

"His laptop," I finished for her, swallowing as I carefully sat it on the table. "Yes."

For a while, we both just stared at it, but then Mallory rounded the table to stand on the same side as me. She reached forward, carefully flipping the monitor of the laptop up to reveal the damage inside.

The screen was shattered and covered with a thick, black gunk, and what was left of the keyboard was melted and warped, revealing the plates and wires that made everything work underneath.

Mallory peered inside the box again. "Is there a power cord? Do you think it would turn on?"

"Look at it," I told her, waving a hand over the damage.

She sighed, nodding.

We both stared for a while again — me because I couldn't believe the ghosts we had found, Mallory likely because she didn't know what to do or say. But after a moment, her hand dipped into her pocket, and she pulled out her phone, typing something into a search browser.

"We may be able to recover the hard drive," she said, showing me an article she'd found. "And if we can get that, then maybe..."

"We can get answers."

The words sounded like they'd come from someone else's mouth, in someone else's voice. They shook and croaked out of my throat, and I swallowed, trying not to let the hope I felt building in my chest get enough air to surface. The longer I stared at that burnt hunk of computer, the heavier I breathed, and the more my pulse raced.

Little black dots invaded my vision, encroaching from every angle until I could only see through a lens the size of a pin hole.

I felt hands on my chest, on my neck, on my face, pulling me. Mallory's voice was somewhere in the distance, pleading with me to look at her, to breathe.

"Logan," she repeated, this time her voice clearing the fog in my head. "Look. At. Me."

I blinked, over and over, trying to find her through the darkness. It was her cerulean blue eyes I saw first, just an inch from mine. I felt her forehead against mine, her cool fingers framing my jaw, and the next thing I knew, my hands were reaching for her, wrapping around her waist, pulling her closer.

"Breathe," she said, and I sucked in the first breath in minutes, my lungs burning with the inhale before I let the air out again, slow and long through my mouth. "That's it."

I repeated the process, keeping my eyes open and locked on hers, but the more my body approached awareness, the more it buzzed to life at our proximity.

My cheeks heated under her fingers, breaths shallowing out again as I swallowed past the sticky knot in my throat. My gaze fell to her lips — dusty rose, plump and full, and now, parted just a centimeter, letting sweet breath through that met mine between us.

My eyes snapped to hers, but her gaze was on my lips now.

She let out a shaky breath.

Her tongue glided over her bottom lip, wetting it.

She leaned into me — just a fraction of an inch, the movement so subtle I couldn't be sure it happened at all.

All it took was the tilt of my chin, and our lips brushed, the slick heat of hers meeting the shaky coolness of mine. Mallory sucked in a breath at the contact, her fingers curling where they held my face.

"Logan..."

It was a warning, a whisper of desperation for me to stop — or maybe to *never* stop. I couldn't be sure, but I pulled away, wrapping my hands around her wrist as I pinched my eyes shut and took a real breath now that we had some distance between us.

"I'm sorry," I rasped out, shaking my head. "I... I think I was having a panic attack."

"It's okay," she assured me. "It's fine."

I released my grip on her wrists, breathing deep again before I let my eyes flutter open. My hands found balance on the flat of the table, and I stared at the computer, shaking my head.

"What do we do?" I asked — and I wasn't sure if I was asking Mallory, or my deceased father.

But it was her who answered, and her voice was steady and sure.

"We find a way to get that laptop home with you."

My eyes met hers, and the determination I found there lit a fire in my chest.

"Tonight."

Chapter Nine

Mallory

Later that Friday night, Chris sipped from his wine, commenting on the bogus drama happening on the reality TV show he was watching while I read the same sentence in *All the Light We Cannot See* ten times in a row.

I was actually enjoying the book — which was a new feeling, since I hadn't read for pleasure in as long as I could remember. College textbooks had turned me off to reading, especially since I preferred to make art in my spare time rather than read it. But this book was intoxicating, drawing me into another country, another time, another perspective. I loved reading it at night before I went to sleep, and since Chris knew how much I hated reality TV, he wasn't offended that I had the hardback splayed open in my lap while we hung out.

The problem was I couldn't read tonight any more than I could stomach watching two housewives fight over who had the best birthday party for their kids. As much as I wanted to escape into another world, I couldn't stop thinking about what was happening in my own.

Logan Becker had nearly kissed me.

Or was it *me* who had nearly kissed him?

It didn't matter, I'd decided, because either way — our lips had touched.

I shivered again at the memory, eyes glossing over that same damn sentence with my thoughts somewhere else entirely. I could still feel the coolness of his lips against mine, the warmth of his breath, the strong grip of his hands around my waist. I could see his eyes, honey gold and dilated as they searched mine before they fell to my lips. My fingers had curled where they held his face when that first bit of contact was made, and just a dip of his chin or a tip of my own would have sealed the deal, would have closed the final distance between us.

But he'd pulled away.

My stomach dropped, just like it did every time I replayed what happened in that storage closet. Logan pulling away felt like the most painful mix of relief and rejection — and I couldn't figure out how to decipher which feeling was more prominent.

I sighed, readjusting the book in my lap and trying again to focus on what

I was reading. It didn't take longer than sixty seconds for my thoughts to float back to Logan — this time, to the box of his father's belongings that we'd found.

We'd stashed that box away where we'd originally found it, stacking the boxes of items the distillery would keep and archive around it to hide its presence. Everything stayed in the box — except for the laptop, which I hid in my messenger bag as Logan and I walked to his truck after work. We checked to make sure no one was looking before I pulled it out, and Logan quickly placed it inside his truck and covered it with an old ratty towel.

"This is stealing," he reminded me, his eyes darting around the employee parking lot. "If someone catches us…"

"They won't," I was quick to assure him.

He still looked a little worried, a little numb, a little like he was going to throw up or pass out or both when he nodded, climbing into his truck. I'd stood there like a statue when he drove away, my fingers tracing the flesh of my bottom lip as I watched him go.

I could still taste him.

I let out another huff of frustration just as my phone lit up on the coffee table. I slapped the book closed, feet hitting the floor and heart hitting the ceiling when I saw Logan's name in a text notification.

Chris eyed me, one brow climbing. "I've never seen you move so fast for a text in your life," he commented. "Who is it?"

"No one," I murmured, but my eyes were glued to my phone now, reading and re-reading the text Logan had sent.

> **Logan:** *I got the hard drive out. It doesn't look damaged, but after some research, I think I'll need a USB hard drive enclosure to plug it in to my own computer and see if any of the files survived.*

My fingers flew over the keys, and Chris hummed, sipping his wine with a knowing grin. "Mm-hmm. *No one* my ass."

> **Me:** *Okay. This is a good thing, yes?*

> **Logan:** *I guess we'll see.*

> **Logan:** *Thank you, Mallory. For helping me get the laptop out. For everything.*

My stomach lurched.

> **Me:** *Of course.*

I stared at the screen, waiting, hoping — for what, I had no idea. But after a moment, the little bubbles that told me he was typing something popped up. I held my breath as I watched them, but then they disappeared again. I was just about to start typing something else when they reappeared, and just as quickly, they were gone.

He didn't know what to say any more than I did.

I wondered if he wanted to ask about the almost-kiss, if it was replaying in his mind as much as it was my own. Did he *want* to kiss me? Or did he want to make sure I didn't read too much into something that was nothing?

Maybe he wanted to clear the air, to let me know that he was having an anxiety attack and didn't actually want to hold me, or brush his lips against mine, or suck in the breath that I'd just let out.

Maybe he wanted a redo, and this time, he wanted to pull me into him instead of push me away.

Something close to a growl came from my throat when the bubbles disappeared again, and Chris paused the TV, turning where he sat on the opposite end of the couch until he faced me completely.

"Okay, enough with the animal noises. I can't focus with all the barking and growling you've been doing for the past hour." He snapped his fingers twice as he took a long sip of his red wine. "Spill."

"There's nothing to spill."

Chris flattened his lips, and then before I could react, he snatched my phone from me and read the screen as I wailed on him to give it back to me.

"Logan Becker," he mused with a smirk, handing my phone back.

I huffed, pulling it into my chest like I could protect what had already been seen. "It's just work stuff."

"Right. And I only cross dress during Pride Week." He rolled his eyes. "What happened? Did you get him in trouble again? Or is his grumpiness rubbing off on you?"

"I'm not grumpy," I defended. "And neither is he."

Chris cocked a brow. "That man has been a broody, keep-to-himself piece of eye-candy since we were teenagers. Who else do you know who sits at Buck's alone with a scowl and a glass of whiskey."

I opened my mouth to retort, but Chris held up his finger.

"*Besides* his brothers, because that will only prove my point further."

I shut my mouth again.

Chris chuckled. "Come on. Tell me what's going on so I can stop bugging you and get back to my show."

I covered my face with my hands, blowing a hot breath through the fingers. "I don't know," I groaned out. Then, I peeked through my fingers at Chris. "There may or may not have been lip contact."

"*Lip contact*? As in, *kissing?!*"

"No." I bit my lip. "Well... maybe kind of?"

Chris filled his glass of wine before topping off mine, and then he kicked back, making himself comfortable on the couch. "Tell me *everything*."

So, I did. I told him how Logan and I had started getting along, how I'd brought him into my studio that night after our walk, how we'd found a rhythm at work. I told him about my first *real* tour, how it had felt so good before we realized we'd forgotten the no photos allowed speech. I told him about Mac, about our punishment, about Logan's surprising taste in music and how his nerdiness somehow made me like him more. I told him about the box we found, the laptop, the hard drive.

And finally, the almost-kiss.

Chris was giddy the entire time, smiling like a loon and completely unable to keep still the longer I talked. By the time I finished, I thought he was going to squeal or giggle or jump up and down.

"This is *bad*, Chris," I pointed out. "We almost kissed. Or... at least... I *think* we almost kissed."

"Oh, you definitely almost kissed," Chris agreed. "Honestly, I'd say lip contact qualifies, but since there was lack of embrace or tongue, we can file it as an almost."

I sighed.

"Why are you acting like he kicked your cat?"

Dalí croaked out a meow from where he was curled up under the coffee table.

"Lip-locking is *fun*, Mallory — especially with a Becker boy." Chris waggled his brows.

"Did you hear what you just said? He's a *Becker*. His entire family hates *my* entire family — and honestly, if you ask me, it's for good reason. Plus, we work together. Plus, my father would *murder* me."

Chris scoffed. "And? Like pissing off your dad isn't your favorite pastime."

"It's different this time. He has me by the balls with this building being in his name," I said, gesturing to the studio apartment we were sitting in above the shop.

"Fine," Chris conceded. "But, does he even need to know? I mean, it's not like it has to be anything serious. It sounds like you like him, and from what you've told me, he likes you, too. Why not have a little fun?" He tipped his glass toward me before taking a sip. "From what I know of the guy, he could use it." Chris grimaced. "Who watches *space documentaries* for joy?"

I chuckled, flying through the list of reasons why entertaining any kind of feelings for Logan Becker — whether *just for fun* or otherwise — was a terrible idea. Still, just a centimeter of his skin on mine had sent me into this spiral, and now that I'd had a taste, I couldn't stop wondering what it would be like to dip the whole spoon in and take a full bite.

My phone vibrated, and Chris eyed me with a smirk. Before I could even think to reach for the phone, it was in his hands, unlocked with Logan's newest text pulled up — since I shared everything with my best friend.

Mistake.

"Still need help with the shop tomorrow?" Chris read, mimicking a deep voice that I presumed was supposed to be Logan's. He quirked a brow at me. "Help with what?"

"He likes to organize and clean and put things in their place," I explained with a shrug. "I told him he could help me put the shop together this weekend, if he wanted to."

Chris smiled triumphantly, tossing me the phone before kicking back and pushing play on the remote. "Sounds like *fun* to me."

I sighed, looking at the text with every quiet voice inside me saying I should decline. Logan Becker and I should have had a relationship that existed only within the walls of the Scooter Whiskey Distillery. He as the Lead Tour Guide, me as the guide in training. He'd show me the ropes, and I'd try not to get him into any more trouble.

Because he was a Becker, and I was a Scooter.

That was where all the lines should be drawn.

But the louder voices inside me wanted more of the Logan I got that night we walked Main Street, wanted to know what other music lived on his playlist, wanted to crack his shell, loosen him up, add a little color to his life.

Maybe it really couldn't hurt, I thought. *Maybe we could be friends, hang out, have a little fun…*

It was a stupid idea. Obtuse, really.

But it didn't stop me from sending the next text.

Me: *Tomorrow at noon. Wear something you can get dirty in.*

• • •

I was obsessed with the little wrinkle between Logan's eyebrows.

I stared at it all afternoon as he worked in my shop, opening up boxes and building furniture, hanging up signs and unpacking paint, organizing easels and brushes and sponges and cups. I loved how concentrated he was, how the same fire that fueled me when I envisioned the shop seemed to live inside him. It was like it was *his*, like he had something to fight for with me — something to lose.

We'd worked tirelessly all afternoon, and made a substantial dent in what was previously complete chaos. The studio was actually beginning to *look* like a studio, like a business, like what I'd always dreamed it could be. I could finally see the little sections I'd imagined, the division of the wide space, the different themes of each that helped them stand out while still bringing a cohesive feel to the shop.

My chest was light, wings fluttering against my rib cage.

It's happening. It's really happening.

The 1975 played on Logan's speaker — which he'd brought with him at my insistence. I'd offered a suggestion from time to time, but for the most part, it'd been his music, his favorite bands and artists, and I loved getting a sneak peek inside his soul. He listened to everything from yacht rock and country to

290

folk and classical — and he knew the words to every single song that came on. My favorite songs were the ones he couldn't help but belt out rather than just quietly singing along.

Right now, he was bobbing his head along to "Sincerity is Scary," one hand holding a slice of the pizza I ordered us for dinner and the other making more notes as he looked around the room at what we'd done and what was still left to do. I sipped on the sweet tea I'd made, watching him.

I'd told him to wear something he could get dirty in, so I guess I had myself to blame for the traveler sweat pants hanging off his hips, leaving practically nothing to the imagination when it came to how round and firm his ass was — as well as what he was packing in the front. And if those pants weren't already a distraction, the old, ripped, slightly stained Stratford High t-shirt he wore with the sleeves ripped off in such a haphazard way that the muscles that lined his ribs were visible, would have done the trick. When he'd first taken his jacket off, I'd had to turn away, clearing my throat and commenting on something about the mess of boxes to keep from staring.

Now, after a long day of working, his hair was disheveled, curling out from under the edge of his ball cap.

And that little wrinkle was present, his brows furrowed in concentration.

I bit my lip, watching him balance that slice of pizza in one hand as he made notes with the other. I swear, I *tried* talking myself out of what my fingers ached to do most, but instinct won out.

I slipped off the little bar stool I was on — one that would be used in the painting corner of the studio — and crept to the back office. My camera was on the desk there, and I strapped it around my neck, fussing with the lens and settings before I made my way back into the shop.

I stood off to his left, the setting sun casting his strong profile in an orange glow through the large shop windows. Shadows stretched out behind him, and I lifted the camera, looking through the viewfinder at my subject just as he furrowed his brows even more, jotting something down on the notepad.

Click.

The sound was soft and quiet, but still audible over the music, and Logan's head popped up, searching for the source. When he saw me still looking at him through the camera lens, he grinned.

"Did you just take a picture of me?"

I shrugged, lowering the camera. "Just testing some of the settings," I lied. "It's the golden hour, great time for shooting. I wanted to see how the light came through the windows."

He nodded, the corner of his mouth still quirked as he watched me from across the studio. "You're really into photography, huh?"

"It's one of my favorite mediums," I said, making my way back to the bar stool across from him. I pressed the button on the back of the camera that would show me the images I'd taken, and when I saw the one I'd just snapped of Logan, my heart squeezed. "Although, I still haven't managed how to capture the beauty of something you see with your eyes through the lens. Seems like, for some things, it's impossible to accomplish."

Logan was completely oblivious to the compliment, and he started in on his notes again. "I bet you do better than you think. Why don't you have any of your art down here yet? Your paintings, photographs..." He glanced at me before pulling his attention back to the pad. "I'm sure you have thousands."

"Most of them are upstairs," I said. "And I do have thousands, but probably only a dozen that are good enough to display."

Logan stopped writing, meeting my gaze. "I doubt that. I'd love to see what you've created."

His eyes were intense where they watched me, the air thick and heavy in the shop. He swallowed, taking to his notes again as I fiddled with the settings on the camera to keep myself busy.

"You'll have to show me some of your shots sometime," he said after a moment.

I nodded, watching his face level out as he got back to work, wondering why my lungs were being so weird with breath all of a sudden. It was like I was under water, or like I'd completely forgotten the simple, natural body functions of *inhale, exhale.*

It wasn't just me who was feeling it. I could tell Logan was off, too — and I was determined to change that.

Pulling the strap from around my neck, I set my camera down, circling the table we sat at and placing my hand over the notepad he was writing in.

He quirked a brow up at me. "Hard to write with your hand in the way."

"So take a break," I told him. "We've been working all day, and if I'm being honest, the stress rolling off you has been stressing *me* out."

I plucked the pen from his hands, shoving it and the notebook too far away from him for him to reach for them. He looked at them longingly for a moment before he let out a deep sigh.

"I'm sorry," he said, scrubbing his hands over his face. "Honestly, you giving me so much to do today has been a blessing for me. I can't stop thinking about the box we found, about my dad..." He swallowed, the thick Adam's apple in his throat bobbing. "Working on stuff like this helps me get out of my head for a while."

I frowned, crossing my arms to keep myself from reaching for him. I knew that feeling all too well, the need to escape, to move my hands in an effort to stop thinking — even if just for a while.

"I just... I can't figure out why that stuff was in there," he continued. "You know? Why was *that* stuff saved, tucked away? How did it survive as well as it did? Why didn't the fire department take it, or the police? Why wasn't it given to my mom, to my family, if it wasn't needed for evidence?"

I blew out a sigh of my own. "I don't know, none of it makes sense to me either."

Logan's frown deepened, his eyes falling to where he folded his hands in his lap.

I nudged his shoulder with my elbow. "Hey, you got the hard drive out, right? And you got the necessary equipment to see the files that are on it. That has to be comforting, at least."

"Yes," he agreed, lifting his gaze to mine. "But the hard drive is password protected. I can't access anything until I crack that code."

"And you will," I assured him. "But, until then, there's no sense in stressing yourself out over answers you can't find — no matter how many times you ask the questions."

His brows folded together again, and I chuckled, uncrossing my arms and taking a tentative step toward him. Before I could think better of it, I reached out, smoothing my thumb over the wrinkle I'd been marveling at all day.

"Have you ever painted before?" I asked, eyes on the skin that was smooth now that I'd run my thumb over it.

Logan's breath was shallow, his eyes locked on my face as I stared at where that wrinkle had been. "Not since elementary school."

I laughed, letting my hand drop from where I touched his face. "I think it's time we changed that." I held out that hand for his. "Come on, let's have some fun."

He grimaced. "I don't think I can. Not right now."

"Well," I insisted, wiggling my fingers and nodding toward his hand. "We're at least going to try."

Reluctantly, Logan took my hand, and I tried not to feel the warmth of his hand in mine as more than a friendly gesture as I guided him over to the corner of the room we'd started setting up for the painting workshops. A circle of easels faced the middle of that section, each station loaded with paint and brushes and palettes. I instructed him to sit, and then I moved to the corner, pulling out two large, blank canvases.

I placed one in the easel in front of him, the other in the one next to him where I would sit. As I poured paint for us and got rinse cups ready, Logan was quiet, not even singing along to the music anymore. He was staring at the blank canvas like it was a threat rather than a release.

"You'll like this," I promised him when I took the seat to his left. "Just try to relax and let go."

Logan nodded, another sigh leaving his lips as he picked up the first brush. "I don't really know what to do."

"That's the whole point," I said. "You don't have to know anything. You just... feel. Do. Whatever you want."

I turned my attention to my own canvas, hoping it would help release some of the pressure Logan felt to produce something. I let the music fill in the space between us, and after a few minutes of me working on my piece, Logan finally dipped his brush in the salamander orange paint and began.

We worked in a comfortable silence for a while, and the more time stretched on, the more Logan seemed to relax. He started singing again, and I just hummed along beside him until he surprised me when he belted out every word to "Man of Constant Sorrow."

"He's a bluegrass fan, too," I mused, keeping my eyes on my canvas. "Is there any kind of music you *don't* listen to?"

"Death core," he said easily. "And really, *all* metal music. Although, not because I didn't try to love it."

"I'm trying to picture you head banging and screaming with the rock on sign." I held my index and pinky finger up to illustrate, sticking out my tongue like Gene Simmons.

Logan chuckled. "I even went to a show in Nashville once, wondering if I'd appreciate it more live. And I did, but... not enough to listen to it on my own." He pointed the tip of his brush at me. "Did you know there are literally *hundreds* of sub-genres of metal music? It all depends on the vocal style, instruments used, what era or region or bands they draw inspiration from. I mean, there's literally a genre called Celtic Metal that's inspired by Celtic mythology."

It was the most enthusiastic I'd seen him all day, the excited grin on his face too contagious for me to fight.

"You're like a walking encyclopedia," I commented. "Like, you know a little something about *everything* it seems."

He shrugged, turning his attention back to his canvas. "It's all useless, except for maybe a trivia night. But like I said, I love to learn, so I usually find myself deep in the rabbit hole of the Internet reading about some subject I didn't even know existed before I stumbled upon it."

"You make me feel lazy, I never do anything productive like that — not now that I'm out of school. If anything, I avoid anything that looks suspiciously educational."

Logan gestured to the shop around us, to the canvas in front of me. "Are you kidding? Look at what you can create, at the art you can bring to life. And you're sharing that with your hometown, giving kids here the options that you never had to explore their creativity." He lowered his brush, pausing to look me in the eyes. "That's incredible, Mallory."

I wanted to hold his gaze forever, to lose myself in the specks of brown that dotted the gold irises of the man next to me. But I couldn't bare it, couldn't look at him any longer without wanting to shrink away from the parts of me he saw that no one else did.

I cleared my throat. "You know, it means a lot to me that you see it that way," I said, dipping my brush in the rinse water. "The studio, I mean. For a while, it's felt like this pipe dream, and even now that I'm making it a reality..."

I shrugged. "I don't know. It just seems like I'm the only one who takes it seriously, who sees what it can be." I looked at him again then. "Except for you."

Logan smiled, his eyes searching mine for the briefest moment before he turned back to his work. I did the same, and for a while it was just brushes over canvas, a soft rock ballad in the background.

"Mallory," he said after a moment, still painting. "The night we walked Main Street, you sort of mentioned that you had a deal with your dad. A deal regarding the studio." He didn't look at me, not even when my hand froze where I was painting a snowman in the yard of the Christmassy cabin scene on my canvas. "What does that mean?"

I blinked. "It's complicated, but long story short — he bought the studio in exchange for me finally working at the distillery. For at least five years, I have to be there Monday through Friday, and I'm free to use my evenings and weekends here."

My voice was low, tone short, my brush strokes on the canvas a little more violent.

Logan nodded. "I guess he's always been a little desperate for you to be a part of the family legacy, huh?"

I scoffed. "That's putting it lightly."

"What happened?" Logan asked, and this time, he stopped what he was painting to look at me. "The summer before high school, you said something happened that changed everything with your family."

I shook my head, the blood draining from my face as I recalled the memory. I thought about avoiding it, telling a lie, saying it was nothing and I was just a dramatic teen. But even now, even twelve years later, I still felt the same way about what happened as I did that hot summer night.

And for some reason, for the first time since I'd told my best friend Chris, I *wanted* to share it with someone.

"Something not a lot of people know about me is I have a very sharp sense of what's right and what's wrong," I said, continuing work on my canvas. "I've always had this moral compass, and a desire to be just, and to seek justice for others. I even thought about being a lawyer once," I confessed on a sarcastic laugh. "Until I realized how corrupt our judicial system is."

Logan was quiet, just listening, watching me.

"Anyway, one night that summer before high school, Dad had a big party at the house. It was catered, giant tents everywhere in our yard, a band and — of course — a casino. I'm sure you've heard of how he likes to offer the residents of Stratford a place to gamble since they have to drive out of state otherwise."

He gave me a face at that, because we both were well aware that my father's "underground" casino was nowhere near a secret — at least, not in this town. He was protected by the local police, and no one had ever reported him to any higher authorities — mostly because nearly everyone in town had participated at one point or another.

Logan and his family had an even more in-depth knowledge of it all, thanks to his older brother, Noah. Noah had started dating the mayor's daughter, Ruby Grace, and the mayor was now famous for his debt owed to my father from nights at the casino — a debt made public at what was supposed to be Ruby Grace's wedding to another man. It was the biggest scandal Stratford had seen in some time, and even now, six months later, it was whispered about.

"The casino part of the night was in our basement, and I went down there a little after midnight to get a soda. I also wanted to sketch, since I couldn't sleep with all the noise, and my favorite set of drawing pencils were down there with the rest of my art supplies — which I'd *begged* Mom to let me keep in my room, but she'd refused, saying the mess of paint brushes and pencils were eye sores."

I swallowed, still keeping my eyes on my canvas as I told the story.

"When I went down there, there was a group of guys playing blackjack. One of them was Randy Kelly."

"As in, *Chief* Kelly?"

I nodded. "Yep, the very one. He had just been appointed police chief, like two days before that. He was definitely celebrating that night, too, because he was so drunk he could barely keep upright in his chair." I pursed my lips, dunking my brush in the paint harder than necessary. "Not that it stopped him from groping me in front of everyone in that room and insinuating that when I was old enough for it to be legal, I should find my way to his bed."

"What the fuck?" Logan snapped. "You're joking, right?"

"Nope," I said, the word leaving my lips with a pop. I finally looked at Logan then, and even though it was cliché and made me want to roll my eyes at myself, I loved that his hands were curled into fists at his side, that his eyes looked murderous as it all sank in. "He even pulled me into his lap, refusing to let go of me until I punched him in the groin and high-tailed it out of there."

Logan's mouth fell open, his eyes flicking back and forth between mine in a look of horror. "What did you do?"

"I told my dad," I said. "Obviously. Because that's what any fourteen-year-old girl would do. I told my dad." I swallowed. "And I thought he would fly in like the superhero I thought he was, kick Randy's ass, save the day." My lip twitched, something between a smile and the beginning of a sob finding me. "But he didn't. He said it was nothing, that Randy was drunk, that he was sure Randy didn't mean any harm, that I was being *dramatic,*" I spat the word. "And that I should let it go."

"How could he say any of that?" Logan asked, that wrinkle between his brows again. "You're his *daughter*. That man practically molested you."

"Yeah, well, pissing off the police chief wouldn't bode well with my father's underground casino staying in operation, would it?"

Logan shook his head. "And your mom?"

I scoffed. "She's soft, weak, and does whatever Dad tells her to. She had nothing for me other than a hug and an offer to run me a hot bath."

"Jesus…"

I nodded, but as soon as the last words were said, I drew in a deep breath, picking up my brush like nothing had happened. "Anyway, I decided then that I didn't want anything to do with my family or their *legacy*. And that I was going to be my own person, and I didn't give two shits what they had to say about it."

Logan was quiet for so long that I paused where I was painting to make sure he was still breathing. He was, and in fact, it was about all he was doing — just looking at me, and breathing.

"What?"

"It's just that I've been trying to keep my father's legacy alive, to be everything he'd ever wanted me to be and more. I would give anything to have another moment with him, and meanwhile, you've been trying to escape *your* father for over a decade." He swallowed. "I can't imagine being in your shoes when that happened, or what you must have gone through ever since. You're really strong, Mallory. Really fucking strong."

My heart squeezed painfully in my chest, but I played off the emotion with a scoff. "Yeah, so strong that I had to come crawling back home to Daddy and take his money to make my dream come true."

"Hey," Logan said, reaching over to place his hand on my forearm. He squeezed until I looked at him, and I hated the sincerity I found there.

That The 1975 song was right — sincerity *was* scary.

"That's not what you did, okay? You're making your dream a reality, and doing whatever it takes to get there — that's a strong entrepreneur. That's a warrior."

The way Logan watched me in that moment, I knew he meant every word he said — and he wanted me to believe them as much as he did.

Suddenly, the air around us was too thick, too dense with emotions that I didn't want to feel. I blew a breath out loudly through my lips, pulling my hand from where it had been paused in front of my canvas. "Alright," I said, shaking my head. "That's enough of that. I brought you over here to paint to *relieve* stress, not make more of it."

"I'm not stressed."

"Well, you're not having fun, either," I argued. Then, my eyes flicked to the brush in my hand, to the paint on the palette between us, and I grinned. "But I think I know how to change that."

Logan quirked a brow, watching as I dipped the brush in the mahogany paint on my palette. I lifted the brush, made it look like I was going back to painting, and waited until Logan had turned back toward his own canvas.

Then, I flicked my brush and sent paint splattering all over him.

Specks of the orangish-brown color hit his biceps, the muscles of his rib cage peeking through his shirt, his neck, his eyebrow, the corner of his mouth — now popped open in surprise. He turned his head slowly, blinking several times before he wiped his thumb over the corner of his mouth where the paint had splattered. Logan looked at his thumb, at my challenging smile, and then he dipped his own brush.

"Oh, you're going to pay for that."

I squealed, jumping up from my bar stool and running away before he could even dip his brush. I took my palette with me, reloading my weapon before I turned back around. But Logan was there, and as soon as I was facing him, I saw paint flying my way in slow motion.

I closed my eyes just in time to feel the cool liquid splatter all over my face.

Logan laughed as I blinked my eyes open again, charging after him with my brush. He ran behind his canvas, and when I flung another attack, it landed all over the painting he'd been working on.

"Hey!" he said, peeking over the top at the new addition to his work. "You ruined it!"

"I made it better."

"Oh, yeah?" Logan swiped his brush over my painting, making a haphazard smiley face right over my snow man. "There. I returned the favor."

I laughed, walking over to marvel at the new addition. "Huh. You kind of did."

Logan peered over to look at the painting with me, like he wondered if it actually *did* look better with that smiley face, and it was just the distraction I needed to reach out and run my brush in a line from his ear to his collarbone.

I ran out of his reach before he could react, but he was on my heels quick, chasing me until I was hiding behind one of the chairs in the new pottery section. He hid behind his own barricade, and when I stood and slung another brush full of paint at him, it went everywhere — on the chair he hid behind, the new firing oven, the anvils and bevel cutters and other tools we'd arranged neatly in bins on the shelf.

Logan's mouth popped open as he stood. "Wait, stop," he said, putting his hands up before I could fire off another round. "You're messing everything up."

I laughed, ditching the brush all together and dipping my hands in the palette. A rainbow of colors stained my fingers and palms as I ran over to him and planted them right in the middle of his chest.

"Who cares! It's paint," I reminded him. "It'll come off."

"This is one of my favorite workout shirts!"

I shrugged. "Shouldn't have worn it to an art shop."

Logan narrowed his eyes, but then he dropped his own brush, hands on a path for the paint on his palette.

I took off screaming, looking for my next shield. Logan rounded the stack of boxes we had yet to unpack before I could hide behind them, catching me in his wet, paint-covered hands just as I slid around them. He wiped them down my arms, leaving multicolored streaks from my shoulders to my wrists.

"This shirt looks better with sleeves," he said with a grin.

I wiggled out of his grasp, panting and laughing as I sprinted across the shop to get more ammo. But I hit a wet spot, my shoe sliding over the gob of paint left by one of our attacks, and before I knew how to stop it, I was windmilling, the world tilting.

"Oh, shit!"

I tried to steady myself, but it was useless, and I wrapped my hands around my head to try to protect it from the fall.

But it never came.

Logan slid in like a baseball runner stealing home, catching me in his lap as I tumbled to the floor. It was a loud and awkward contact — me hitting him, him hitting the hard tile, both of us a mess of limbs and paint as we tried to figure out what had just happened.

"Are you okay?" Logan asked, hands framing my arms first, then my face, his eyes searching me for bruises or bleeding. He still had paint all over those hands, but I couldn't find it in me to care that he was getting it in my hair and all over my cheeks.

"I'm okay," I said on a laugh, giggling more when the worry didn't erase from his face as he continued his search.

I reached forward, running my own paint-covered thumb over that line between his brows again. It was like that touch pulled Logan into another room, another time, another world where it was just me and him and the warmth of my thumb on his forehead.

The music faded, the only sound now the steady thumping of his heart and mine.

Logan's next breath was a shallow rasp, a hard swallow rocking his Adam's apple as I continued dragging my thumb down, over the bridge of his nose, the tip, slipping down to catch his bottom lip before I dragged it off his chin. I watched my thumb making its descent, and when it fell from his face, my hand rested on his chest, fingers twisting in the fabric of his t-shirt.

I flicked my eyes back to his, but his were locked on my mouth now.

I smirked. "You want to kiss me, don't you, Logan Becker?" I whispered.

His eyes fluttered a bit, but otherwise, there was no response. There was no effort to deny or confirm, just his golden eyes locked on my lips, his hands still framing my face, my fist in his shirt, tugging him closer.

"Do it," I whispered, fingers curling more into his cotton t-shirt. I tilted my chin up, seeking him, heart pounding in my ears so loud I couldn't be sure I'd actually said the words.

A pained sound rumbled somewhere deep within Logan — his chest, maybe, or his soul. Those strong hands slipped farther into my hair, cradling my neck, pulling me closer, his eyes still locked on my lips.

But he stopped himself.

With less than an inch between us, Logan stopped, his lips parting, a shaky breath slipping from the new space. His fingers curled in my hair, and I closed my eyes, pulling his shirt once more until the man wearing it followed.

"I said *kiss me*," I urged, the words whispered against his mouth, our lips brushing now, eliciting that same electric charge I'd felt in the storage closet.

Logan took one last trembling breath.

And then he answered my plea.

Chapter Ten

Logan

I'd fantasized about it for years, what it would be like if I ever got the chance to kiss Mallory Scooter. In each and every scenario, I was timid and nervous, overwhelmed with a mix of fear and excitement. The possibility that I could ever actually taste her seemed so preposterous to me that all my dreams consisted mostly of disbelief.

So, when my lips crashed down on hers, capturing her next breath and a moan inside my mouth, I waited for those thoughts to hit.

Oh, my God.

This can't be happening.

Holy shit, it's happening.

I'm kissing Mallory Scooter.

I can't believe *I'm kissing Mallory Scooter.*

But none of those thoughts came.

Not when our lips met. Not when her hands slid up my chest, wrapping around my neck. Not when I tightened my grip in her hair, pulling her in, kissing her with such force I was sure I'd bruise both our lips.

There was no disbelief, no uncertainty, no nerves or timidness to be found.

I kept my lips pressed to hers as I waited for the *other* voices I expected to hear, the ones that would whisper *no, stop, you can't, you shouldn't.*

But again, they never came.

All I felt was a profound sense of *right*, and the most powerful wave of possession I'd ever experienced in my life.

Yes.

Finally.

Take.

Mine.

Those were the thoughts on repeat in my mind as I left one hand in her hair, the other sliding down to grab her by the hip and move her fully into my lap. Her legs straddled me, the warmth of her thighs surrounding my hips, the heat of her center calling to the growing bulge between my legs.

She gasped for air when I finally broke the kiss, only long enough for each of us to take a breath before my lips captured hers again, hard and urgent. My tongue broke the barrier of her lips this time, seeking hers, the taste of paint and sweet tea mixing on my taste buds.

Mallory didn't seem to have a single voice in her head warning her to stop, either. Her hands were in my hair, knocking the ball cap I'd been wearing to the ground as she tangled her fingertips in the strands and tugged, owning me in the same way I was owning her. She bucked her hips, rubbing the seam of her leggings over my erection, a lustful moan rolling through her at the contact.

My hands found her hips then, squeezing, locking her in place to keep myself from coming before anything even started. My body was reacting to hers in a way it'd never reacted to any other woman's in my life. It was like two magnets being held away from each other for years, finally being released and clashing together in the middle, touching for the first time, feeling what it's like to be whole.

I broke the kiss, biting and sucking my way over her jaw, her neck, up to capture her earlobe between my teeth. I sucked it gently, breathing a hot, wanting breath there that made her shiver, her thighs clenching around me.

"Take me upstairs," she breathed, and the words were barely out of her mouth before I was kissing her again, lifting us both up from the floor with her still wrapped around my waist.

I stumbled a bit, sneakers sliding over the mess of paint we'd stained the floor with as I blindly made my way to the staircase in the back that led up to her studio apartment. One hand gripped the rail to keep us from falling while the other held her against me, her arms tight around my neck, our mouths bruising each other in an effort to get closer, to taste more, to feel *everything*.

We crashed through her door at the top of the stairs, the handle swinging back and hitting the wall so hard I was certain it'd left a hole. Dalí jumped from where he'd been on her couch with a hiss, tail poofed as his nails skittered across the hardwood floor. He bolted between my legs and down the stairs into the shop, and I reached back for the door, slinging it shut before I dropped Mallory's feet to the floor.

As soon as she was standing, I twisted us until we'd traded spots, whipping her around to face the door and pressing her hard into it.

"This is bad," I warned, running my tongue up the back of her neck until my lips were next to her ear. "You know it. I know it."

Mallory whimpered, rolling her ass against my erection, her hands planted on the door, lips kissing the wood when she gave her reply.

"So stop, then."

Her words said one thing, but her body elicited another plea, chills racing from where my breath met her neck all the way to where her fingers intertwined with mine on the door frame. I lifted those hands above her head, leaning my body into hers more, not sure if I wanted to get closer or somehow put so much pressure on her that she'd push back, push me away, tell me to stop — and mean it.

"Stop what?" I whispered, leaving her hands above her head as I trailed mine down her arms, her rib cage, her waist. I slipped one arm between her and the door, holding her to me, as the other hand rounded over her ass, fingertips slipping between her thighs.

She gasped, arching her back, head falling back as she leaned into the touch.

"Touching you?" I asked, sucking the skin on her neck. "Kissing you?"

"No," she breathed, rolling her hips again, ass up, begging for me to slide my hand between her thighs just a little more. "Stop *thinking*."

Her request might as well have been a spell for how quickly it knocked every negative thought out of my mind in that moment. All the stress I'd felt the last twenty-four hours, all the worry, all the pain — *gone* with those two words and the roll of her body against mine.

It was only her now, my seductive little witch casting her charm, pulling me in.

And I dived willingly into her incantation.

My hand slipped farther between her thighs, the side of my thumb brushing her seam as she arched into the touch. Her hands flew down from where they were held above her head, reaching behind her, seeking me, but I clamped my hands around her wrists, forcing them up the door again.

"Keep these here," I demanded, my whisper a soft-spoken command that she whimpered in response to as if I'd whipped her, instead.

I kissed the back of her neck, her jaw, capturing the side of her lips as my hands trailed down again. One slid between her and the door again, holding her to me, but this time, the other dived under the hem of her leggings, fingertips dipping between the sweet swells of her perfect ass.

And my suspicion that she wasn't wearing panties under them was confirmed.

Her head fell back, lips no longer able to kiss me as they parted. Her neck was elongated, eyes closed, a desperate, shaky breath finding her as my fingers made their descent. I felt her asshole tighten when the pads of my fingers brushed it, and though I never would have even *approached* that topic the first time with any other woman, I realized quickly that Mallory Scooter was *far* from any other woman I'd ever known.

I paused my downward climb, circling the tip of my index finger over that sensitive opening, feeling it pucker beneath the touch.

Her entire body froze, but just when I thought she'd pull away, or open her eyes, warning me not to even think about it... she arched, instead. Her lips parted even more, the paint from my own staining those rose-colored swells, and I sucked her bottom lip between my teeth, releasing it with a hard pop as I applied just the slightest bit of pressure with my finger.

"You want it here, don't you?" I asked, voice rasping against the chills on her neck as I pressed a little more. It wasn't enough to penetrate, just enough to make her writhe between me and the door.

Mallory didn't answer, but she didn't have to. The way her ass poked up higher, her back arching so deep I wondered if she'd break told me more than her words could what she wanted.

I shook my head, kissing her neck as I pulled back on the pressure a bit. "I'll give it to you. But not tonight. Tonight," I said, slipping my fingers down farther until they slid between her drenched lips. "I'm taking *this*."

I dipped two fingers inside her at once, hips thrusting into the back of my hand to assist as she cried out, head falling back on my chest, eyes shooting open to watch me as I withdrew my fingers and repeated the motion, over and over, stretching her wider each time, reaching new depths.

Her eyes were an icy tundra, so blue they were somehow almost white as she watched me. Her eyes searched mine, lips parted, eyelids fluttering just slightly each time I pressed my fingers inside her again.

I let her watch me while I fucked her with my fingers, our breaths coming in short pants, mixing in the air between us. When it was too much not to kiss her any longer, I crushed my mouth to hers, keeping my fingers deep inside her and curling the tips on a search for that magic spot that would make her come undone.

Mallory's legs shook so violently I thought she'd fall if it weren't for me pinning her to the door. So, I gripped her tighter around the waist, taking her weight, my fingers continuing their assault as I sipped every breath of air she was finished with.

"Logan," she half-whispered, half cried into my mouth.

I waited for more, for her to tell me to stop, to keep going, to fuck her, to get on my knees and suck her clit. But all she said was my name, a longing, sigh of syllables, and then her legs seized, along with every other muscle in her body.

She came with a moan in my mouth, and I gobbled up that noise like my first meal in years, curling my fingers the same way I had been to keep her orgasm going as long as I could. Wetness sprayed from where I fucked her, soaking through her leggings and my sweat pants, too.

"Oh my *God*," she cried, finally pulling back from my kiss to ride out the rest of her climax. She screamed and moaned, back arching, legs shaking again as she surrendered to the feeling.

When she was done, she fell limp, and I really did carry her full weight as I slowly, carefully, withdrew my fingers.

Mallory panted, letting her hands fall from where I'd told her to keep them above her head. She turned in my grasp, pulling at my shirt, my hair, my pants, like she needed me closer — and I obliged in every way possible, holding her to the door, my lips trailing over her slick neck.

"Holy fuck," she breathed, pressing a hand to her forehead. I pulled back, locking eyes with her as she shook her head. "I've never... I didn't know I..."

I chuckled, kissing her nose. "That was fucking hot."

Mallory laughed, but as soon as the sound found her, it was gone again, her eyes heated, tongue rolling over her bottom lip. She fisted her hands in my shirt, pulling me to her for a long, hard kiss before she tugged on the fabric.

I leaned back, letting her pull the shirt over my head before I was kissing her again. She pushed us away from the door, her legs shaking as she backed me up to the couch. My legs hit the edge of it, but before I could sit, Mallory yanked at the hem of my sweatpants.

"Take these off."

I smirked, eyeing her as she stepped away from me, stripping her own shirt over her head and flinging it somewhere across the room. "Yes, ma'am."

We watched each other like animals about to fight rather than fuck as we stripped — me pulling my sweatpants and boxer briefs down my legs, her peeling her damp leggings to her ankles, kicking them the rest of the way off. Only a simple, black sports bra hid her breasts, and with one quick tug and maneuver of arms, it was over her head and on the floor, too.

I let my eyes devour her like she really was my prey, gaze sliding over the mountains and valleys of her goddess-like body. Her breasts were modest but round and plump, the peaks puckered and begging for my tongue. Her stomach was flat and toned, a dipped line running from the bottom of her rib cage down to just above her belly button — another trail begging to be licked. Tattoos that merely peeked out from the edges of her clothing before were now on full display — a phoenix starting at her hip and wrapping up her rib cage, a half-sleeve of flowers stretching from her elbow to her shoulder, a line of script highlighting the curve of her hip. Those lips I'd stared at for years were swollen, parted, her own eyes feasting on what she saw between my legs before they flicked up to mine.

She didn't say a word, just pressed one hand hard into my chest and shoved. I fell back, bare ass hitting the couch cushions, and as soon as I was sitting, she was on top of me, her mouth hard on mine.

And *that's* when it all hit me.

Maybe it was her being on top, me submitting, her taking control. Maybe it was her slim waist between my hands, her lips on mine before they kissed a trail over my jaw, down my neck, and back up again. Maybe it was her paint-matted hair falling in a curtain over my face, or the slick heat of her sliding over my shaft, eliciting a guttural groan from me that sounded like something off National Geographic.

Whatever it was, it finally hit me.

I was kissing Mallory Scooter.

I was touching her. She was touching *me*. It was bad. It was wrong. I needed to stop, to push her away, to rewind time and go back to when I would never even entertain that she could want me like this.

But it was too late.

My next breath was a shaky one, and now it was *my* hands that trembled as I held her, as she rocked her hips, coating me in her climax. She moaned when the tip of my cock brushed her sensitive clit, her eyes fluttering closed before they shot open again. In seconds, she was off me, digging in a drawer somewhere near where her bed was set up in the corner opposite the living room.

There were no walls in her studio apartment, just one giant, open space. Still, that distance between us was too far, and I found myself crossing it to meet her again, sliding my erection between the gap of her thighs just to feel her warmth again.

She sighed, falling back into me, and I flexed my hips again, fucking her thighs and somehow knowing just from that that fucking her pussy would be the end of me.

Mallory spun in my arms, holding up a shiny gold packet. "Condom," she rasped, and then she pushed me back again — this time, into her bed.

I fell into the sheets, her bed unmade from when she'd climbed out of it that morning. I smelled her all around me — in the sheets, on the pillows, in her hair that fell over me as she straddled my lap again. This time, she rolled that condom down over my shaft, and then she placed her hands on my shoulders, her eyes wide and locked on mine as she lowered down onto my tip.

I hissed, inhaling a breath so hot it felt like smoke in my lungs.

Mallory dropped a little lower, the tip of me stretching her open again, and with each centimeter that she dropped, I swore the fire spread. I felt it in my lungs, my veins, every muscle and joint and organ burning alive with one all-encompassing thought.

Mine.

I was fucked.

I knew it when she took me in completely, when she paused there with me inside her, our eyes locked, her lips parted and my bleeding heart in her fucking hands. She'd taken a part of me, and given me a part of *her*, and now — without the other — neither of us would be the same again.

Mallory's breaths worked in time with her movements — an inhale each time she lifted, a shaky exhale each time she lowered — over and over, again and again, her hands braced on my shoulders, her eyes locked on mine. My grip was so tight on her hips I knew I'd leave a mark, but I couldn't move them, couldn't release for fear she'd disappear like a fantasy I'd had so many times.

Her pace was so slow, so torturous. I felt every centimeter of her walls pulsing around me, and the climax was right there, waiting to release, but never quite reached.

I rolled us, maneuvering until I was on top, and I pushed up onto my knees with my hands braced on her thighs. With each pump of my hips, I pulled her toward me, reaching a new depth that made her eyes roll shut. Her fists twisted in the sheets, yanking until one corner popped off the mattress.

She moaned and writhed under my pulses, her beautiful breasts bouncing with each new thrust. I fell down over her so I could suck each mound into my mouth, tongue circling her nipples, hands kneading the flesh. She was everywhere — her nails on my back, her ankles locked behind my ass, her breasts in my mouth, my hands, her pussy tightening around my cock.

I sucked in a breath when she pulled my mouth to hers again, kissing me hard, and I pumped once, twice, a third time before I pressed so deep into her I saw stars.

She cried out, her moans living and dying in my mouth as I found my release inside her. Everything was still except for where I pulsed between her legs, and for that moment in time, I'd found the kind of ecstasy I thought only drugs could produce.

Maybe I blacked out.

Maybe I traveled through time, to another universe, another dimension.

I couldn't be sure, but when I came to, I was on my back, panting, my fingers tangled in Mallory's hair. Her leg was draped over my stomach, her arm over my chest, both of us riddled with such a fierce exhaustion that we couldn't open our eyes.

For a while, it was just us breathing, fingers gently moving — mine in her hair, hers trailing a path from my pecs to my abdomen and back again. When our breathing smoothed out, I could hear the distant sound of the music still playing on the speaker downstairs, and the soft whiz of a car driving by on Main Street.

Mallory lifted her head, balancing her chin on my chest as her eyes searched mine. She quirked one brow. "I think you ruined my pants."

I barked out a laugh, and I wasn't sure if it was because of what she'd said or because I'd just realized that it was real. What had only happened in my dreams before tonight had just happened in reality.

I had a naked Mallory Scooter sprawled across me, and it was so much sweeter than anything I'd ever dreamed.

"Well, paybacks are a bitch," I said, nodding toward my paint-stained shirt on the floor. "Told you that was one of my favorite shirts."

Mallory smiled, her eyes heavy and sated. She climbed up my chest, pressing her lips to mine, and when she pulled away, she watched me with questions and concerns dancing in those blue irises of hers.

But she didn't speak any of them out loud.

Instead, she rested her head again, wrapping herself around me even tighter as I pressed a kiss to her forehead.

And in the arms of denial, we both fell fast asleep.

. . .

I didn't know what time it was when I finally woke the next morning, only that the weight of Mallory's head was still resting on my chest.

It was warm, even with the comforter kicked down to my feet and the sheets covering only half of my naked torso. My body ached as I stretched my toes, flexing my calves, feeling the muscles in my quads protest at the movement after last night.

Sometime in the middle of the night, I'd woken up to Mallory's ass pressed against my groin. I didn't remember what time, or how long we'd been out. If anything, it felt almost like a drunken dream, like something I'd imagined — spooning her, kissing her neck, feeling her nipples harden under my touch, her back arch as I pressed my erection between the gap of her thighs.

Neither one of us had rested again until we were both spent, and then we'd curled back up easily, like we'd been together for years, like me being in her bed was the most natural thing in the world.

I ran my fingers through Mallory's hair, ready to gently wake her, but when the silky strands ended abruptly, I peeked one eye open.

Dalí flicked his tail from where he was curled up on my chest, croaking out something between a meow and a yawn as he watched me with lazy yellow eyes.

"Well, hello there," I murmured, scratching behind his ear.

I looked around the rest of the studio apartment for some sign of Mallory, but found nothing. It was just a series of messes everywhere I gazed — the wad of paint-stained sheets on the bed, our clothes littering the floor. I couldn't help but let my eyes wander over her own mess that had existed before I'd even been there, too — the dishes in the sink, the half-empty glasses and mugs on the coffee table, the wires from her curling irons and straighteners falling over the cabinet of the bathroom sink, the dozens of paintings and sketches and framed photographs leaning against the base of nearly every wall.

I smiled, feeling completely surrounded by her.

And in the next instant, my stomach dropped so violently I nearly puked.

I shot up in bed, causing Dalí to scamper off much the way he did the night before. He hid under the couch as I had my heart attack, and I pressed a hand to my chest, feeling the hard pumping of the frantic organ beneath.

Holy fuck.

I slept with Mallory Scooter.

I ran a hand back through my disheveled hair, cursing under my breath when I couldn't get my fingers through the matted paint. All the thoughts swirling around in my head now felt just as sticky and complicated.

Thoughts that were *nowhere* to be found last night.

I couldn't grasp onto one worry before another bounced in, like a set of ping pong balls let loose inside a rotating box. I thought about my mom, my brothers, about the fact that Mallory had been off-limits to me my entire life due to the last name she bore. My job was the next thought in my mind — the title I had, the one I wanted, the years of effort I'd put in to be the best at what I did.

I thought about the laptop, the hard drive, the password I wasn't sure I'd ever be able to decode to see if there was anything my father left behind. I'd been so fixated on that yesterday, and maybe that's why I'd had the lapse in judgment.

I wasn't in the right frame of mind.

But perhaps the biggest worry of all was that the number-one thought in my head *wasn't* that it was wrong, that I had fucked everything up by giving in, that I'd finally had Mallory Scooter in the way I'd always desired.

It was that I still wanted her, even *more* so now, and she was nowhere to be found.

Anxiety was still rippling through me as I let out a sigh, trying to calm my breathing and looking around the room as if it would have some sort of answer for me. When I looked past the pillow Mallory had slept on last night, I saw a sketch pad near her phone charger. It was propped open to a page somewhere in the middle, with chicken-scratch scrawling across it.

I reached over, pulling the pad into my lap, and when I saw the doodle next to the words, I smirked.

It was us — her mid-slingshot with her paint brush, sending paint flying across the page at me. And I had a brush in my hand, though my arms were crossed, shielding my face. We were both laughing, our features large and cartoonish.

And my awe for Mallory grew even more at the fact that she could bring that image to life, that she could bring *any* memory back with just a pencil, a sheet of paper, and those magic hands of hers.

Had to leave early for church — you know, princess of Stratford, and all. ;)
Help yourself to some coffee. - M

I was still smiling, but my stomach dipped and flattened at her words. Other than the half-hearted joke and a winking face scrawled after it, there was no indication of how she was feeling, of what she was thinking about what had transpired between us the night before.

Then again, I couldn't exactly blame her — since I had no fucking idea what to think about it all, either.

Another sigh left my chest as I crawled out of bed, tugging on my sweat pants before I tore out the note and the doodle, folding it into a square and tucking it in my pocket. I pulled on my t-shirt next, and then I padded my way over to the still-hot coffee pot, pouring what was left into a mug I'd plucked from the clean dish rack.

I sipped carefully on the hot liquid, leaning against her kitchen cabinet and looking around at the mess again. I couldn't de-tangle any of my thoughts, so I decided to put them to rest for now. I needed to talk to her — that much was fairly clear — and I couldn't talk to her right now. Until I could, I needed to calm down, to not let anxiety convince me I needed to break through the doors of that church and demand answers in front of God and the whole town.

I *did* need to get through those church doors, though — not to interrogate Mallory Scooter, but to show face and make Momma happy. I'd already missed the first service, but I could make it to the second one, and knowing Momma, she'd wait to make sure I showed up since I hadn't made it for the early one.

And though I was able to put *most* of my worries to bed, at least for the moment, I wasn't able to leave that apartment in the disarray it was in.

So, I finished my coffee, coaxing Dalí out from under the couch and loving on him while I made a plan. Then, I did the best thing I could do for my anxiety.

I cleaned.

And left a note of my own before slipping out the back door.

Chapter Eleven

Mallory

It felt like someone else sitting at the country club brunch with my parents. It must have been someone else's hand reaching for that mimosa, someone else's mouth moving, answering my parents' questions. It absolutely had to be someone else's legs crossing in the sun dress under the table.

Because in my mind, I was still in bed with Logan Becker.

I was across town, at the opposite end of Main Street, stretched out under the sheets in the morning sun with my bare chest pressed against his ribs. My arms were wrapped around him, his around me, my head on his chest, his breath on my ear.

Or maybe I was still stuck in a memory of last night. I could still feel his hands running gently over my spine, could hear the tender way he moaned my name in the middle of the night, could feel his lips pressing to the back of my neck before his hands slipped between my legs...

I bit my lip against a blush and a smile, sipping the delicious mixture of champagne and orange juice from the flute in my hand.

"I'll take that as a yes?" Mom asked.

I blinked, blotting my lips with the linen napkin in my lap. "Hmm?"

She chuckled. "You're so cheery today, but I swear, you're a million miles away," she commented. "I asked if you'd started unpacking at the shop yet, if things were coming together?"

A flash of last night hit me — paint and lips, music and eyes, a sigh and a kiss and a...

"Yes," I said, unable to hide my smile this time. My cheeks flushed as I traced the tip of my finger around the lip of the flute glass. "Things are coming together quite nicely."

My parents likely thought I was high, for how much I'd smiled at church that morning and now at brunch with them and my brother, Malcolm. I hated spending time with them — they knew it, I knew it — but every Sunday, our family was forced together.

At least, that's the way it was when I was in town.

I'd been able to escape the Stratford way of life when I was in college, but now that I was back — and, even though not living with them, *technically* living under a roof that they owned — I had to play by their rules again.

Dad beamed proudly, glancing at me over his menu. "That's my girl. I can't wait for the grand opening. We're going to throw the biggest party this town has seen." He cleared his throat, looking back at his menu — even though we all knew he'd order the same thing he always did and order it for Mom, too. "As long as it's in proper order, of course."

That was his nice way of saying that if he was going to show face and endorse my little *project*, it would have to be something bright and shiny and perfect. God forbid anyone with the Scooter blood in their veins make even the slightest mistake. He was still trying to fight off the rumors circling around town after the mayor of Stratford was called out for owing him a hefty debt from his nights in our underground casino.

Daddy didn't like stains on the family name, and he'd do anything to avoid them.

My brother, Malcolm, seemed bored at the table that morning. He was the spitting image of my father, only about a foot shorter and fifty pounds lighter. He was drinking champagne *without* the orange juice chaser, and constantly looking at his watch — no doubt counting down the minutes until he and Dad would go golfing.

When the waiter came, Dad ordered two eggs over easy, three slices of bacon, cheesy grits and one single pancake — for both him and Mom, of course. She hadn't ordered a meal for herself in the time I'd been alive, and I wondered if she even knew what food she liked anymore or if she just ate whatever her husband decided was fit for her.

Mom was the perfect southern belle that morning, her short hair freshly dyed brunette again — like no one in this town knew she was old enough to have grays — an Easter-egg-yellow sundress covering her shoulders and knees, and a classic string of pearls around her neck. She smiled and nodded and spoke when spoken to, chiming in when it was classy and helpful but keeping her mouth shut otherwise. She'd had years of training, and I knew part of it was that she grew up in a different time than I did.

Still, I wondered what went on in her head, what she would say if somehow I could rip that filter she wore to shreds. I had been around my mother for more than eighteen years of my life, and I still had no idea who she really was.

"So, things are all set up, then?" Dad asked when the waiter was gone.

"Pretty close. The different areas of the shop are in order for the most part. I need to work on the schedule, on what classes I want to offer consistently and brainstorm the first few special workshops. I'm waiting on some additional supplies and a few furniture items, too, and I'd like to get some art and décor on the walls before I consider announcing the opening. But, I think we're getting close."

My heart squeezed, because I couldn't believe I'd turned it around in such short notice, that everything I'd imagined coming to life was within my grasp.

It wouldn't have been possible without a certain man whom I couldn't stop thinking about.

My brother seemed to have read my mind, because he harrumphed a laugh, chugging what was left in his champagne flute before refilling it to the top. "I heard you had some help yesterday."

I narrowed my eyes at him, but he just smirked. I loved my brother — truly, I did — but he was a kiss up, and always liked to be on Dad's good side. Not that it was hard for him to be the favorite child, since he stayed out of trouble for the most part and did any and everything Dad asked of him.

I, on the other hand, would do the exact opposite of what my father expected on principle alone.

He'd told me one time in high school when we were in a fight that *I* was the favorite child, that I was all our parents ever talked about. I realized then that maybe part of him resented me for it. But what he didn't understand was that they talked about me because they wanted to *change* me, to stop my embarrassment on the family.

He was their pride and joy, and I was not after that title.

"Oh?" Mom asked, polite as ever. "Was it one of your girlfriends?"

I snorted, because my entire family knew there wasn't a single girl in Stratford whom I got along with.

Dad gave a disapproving grunt of his own. "Let me guess, it was that gay friend of yours, right? What's his name?" He waved his hand with a wrinkled nose. "*Christoph* or something?"

"Chris," I corrected, rolling my eyes. "His name doesn't morph into something more flamboyant just because he'd rather love a man than a woman. Also, there's no need to refer to him as my gay friend. He's my friend. No adjectives needed."

Dad waved me off again. "I'm sure he was helpful in the décor department."

I ground my teeth, but as much as his comments about my best friend perturbed me, I preferred that frustration to what I experienced when my brother spoke again.

"Nope. I heard Logan *Becker* was there. All. Day. Long."

My parents both snapped their eyes to me then, Dad's brows furrowing and Mom's mouth popping open in a shocked *O* as they waited for an explanation.

"Calm down," I said, holding up both hands like I'd just been accused of doing meth. I ignored the way my heart pounded hard inside my chest, hoping they couldn't see right through the lie I was about to tell. "He's good at organizing things, which I learned from our *punishment* this week." I gave Dad a pointed look. "Thanks for that, by the way. I'm sure you and Uncle Mac loved thinking that one up."

"I have no idea what you're talking about," Dad lied. I *knew* it was a lie, but I didn't press him on it. "And don't turn this on me. Why was Logan Becker at your shop?"

"Unpacking boxes, building furniture, hanging art, setting up and organizing supplies in a way that would make sense for classes. He was *helping*," I emphasized. "Which is more than any of you three have done, and you're my family. So, back off."

Mom seemed to relax a bit, reaching for her mimosa for a sip, but Dad narrowed his eyes in suspicion.

"I don't think it's a good idea for you to be hanging out with him outside of what's necessary during your training at the distillery."

"Yeah, well, you also didn't think it was a good idea for me to pierce my nose, but, here we are."

"Do not get smart with me, young lady," he barked, and Malcolm snickered, which earned him a swift kick to the shin under the table.

"Relax," I said as my brother rubbed his leg. "I'm not hooking up with Logan Becker, Dad."

Mom gasped. "Mallory Loraine!"

"What?" I shrugged. "That's what he's thinking. That's why he's all freaked out."

"That's enough, Mallory," Dad warned under his breath, and it was just as our appetizer of cinnamon bread was brought to the table. He smiled at the waiter, thanking him, and glared at me one last time before he unraveled his napkin. "I just want to remind you to keep your distance and remember the deal we have in place. I wouldn't want you to lose everything you've worked so hard for over something stupid." His eyes hardened, but then he pulled his gaze away, smiling at Mom and reaching over to squeeze her hand. "Now, I think we've had enough of this talk at the table. Malcolm, tell us how things are going in the marketing department."

That launched the conversation back into Scooter Whiskey territory — the most comfortable subject for my father — and launched *me* back into my own thoughts. I let myself tune out, hearing my father's warning as I envisioned Logan's smile, his honey gold eyes, his ridiculous arms that I'd felt up close and personal last night.

My chest tightened, because I never considered all the things that would come *after* a night like last night. And now that I was sitting at the table with three reminders of why I never should have even *thought* of kissing Logan, let alone going through with it, I realized how careless I'd been.

Normally, I wouldn't have cared. Normally, I would have freaking *married* Logan Becker, if it meant giving my father an ulcer and distancing myself more from the family name.

But normally, I didn't have an art studio on the line, and not a prayer of making it happen without my father's help.

My thoughts were a hurricane as I sat mute through the rest of brunch, and by the time I got home, all I wanted to do was take a hot shower and sleep the afternoon away. I walked straight upstairs, slung my keys and purse on the coffee table, and started stripping.

But I stopped right in the middle of the room.

Nothing in my apartment was how I'd left it. The dirty dishes were washed and laid in the rack to dry, my bathroom counter was wiped down, my hair product all put away on the shelf, flat irons and curling irons tucked away into a basket on the counter that I forgot I even owned. The bed was made, the tables cleared, and if I didn't know better, I'd say the floors were swept and mopped, too.

And every single wall was decorated with my paintings, sketches, photographs, and awards.

They were everywhere — the sunset photo I'd captured on the white, sandy beach in Alabama, the self-portrait sketch I'd been assigned to do my second year in school, the shockingly bright and vivid painting I'd done of a trio of jazz musicians on the street in New Orleans. Even my diploma — which, before, had been curled up and tossed into a box of other worthless things — was flattened and framed, the wrinkles of my treatment of it barely visible.

I covered my smile, shaking my head as I looked around the room. "Oh, Logan Becker," I whispered to myself. "What kind of strange creature are you?"

In the middle of the bed was a note, scrawled on the same sketch paper I'd left him one on that morning. When I picked it up, I laughed again at the stick-figure drawing — a girl and a boy in a very promiscuous position, her bent at the waist, him behind her, both of them smiling.

> *Thanks for the coffee, and for a great night. Made the bed, but fair warning — there's still paint on the sheets. I thought about washing them, but decided I wanted you to go to bed with a reminder of me. Try not to get too turned on without me here. See you at work.*
> *— L*

My cheeks shaded, and I pressed my hand to the heat there, shaking my head at the note.

I was in a special kind of trouble now.

• • •

Logan

Later that Sunday evening, all my brothers and I were gathered around the fire pit in Mom's backyard, kicked back, each with a drink in our hand. The night was quiet, save for the sounds of us sipping and the soft music coming from inside the house. Mom was in there making dinner, singing and bopping along to her favorite Fleetwood Mac album. Something about the quietness made me miss the summer, when the katydids chirped loud throughout the night, and the fireflies flickered on and off in the yard.

I'd tried my best to get my mind off Mallory, but had mostly failed. Church had been a small distraction, and I'd gotten in a good workout afterward, using my own bodyweight as torture until my muscles were aching and sweat was rolling off every inch of me. But now that I was quiet again, my hand wrapped around a glass of whiskey and my eyes watching the fire dance, all thoughts bounced back to her.

I hadn't heard from her.

I expected a text when she got home and seen that I'd cleaned up her place, but nothing came. Neither of us had initiated talking about last night, and the longer the silence stretched between us, the more my stomach turned.

I wondered if she regretted it.

I wondered if she was across town right now, cursing herself and thinking through excuses to blow off work tomorrow to avoid seeing me.

I wondered if I'd ever be the same again, now that I'd had her.

I knew the answer to that last musing, though I chose not to admit it. Instead, I lifted my glass, taking a sip of the amber liquid inside it and glancing at my older brother across the fire.

Noah could barely sit still, and every two seconds, he was pulling his phone from his pocket to spout off a text before tucking it back in. Tomorrow morning, he was getting on a plane to Salt Lake City to go see his girlfriend, Ruby Grace, for the first time in a month.

Jordan sat next to him, possibly more drunk than I'd seen him my entire life — and that was to say, he had a slight buzz. His eyes were glossy, lids heavy, and a permanent smile was fixed on his face — which, again, was rare, considering he smiled about as much as I left my bed unmade in the morning. The high school football team had finished out their season with an epic win at the state championship game Friday night, making it the second time he'd lead them to that victory as head coach. The trophy was inside, set up as a centerpiece on the dinner table for us to celebrate around tonight.

And Mikey, who was sitting on the other side of me, was the complete opposite of his oldest brother. I couldn't remember the last time I'd seen him smile, and watching him now — his eyes on the fire, his hands empty, no longer strumming on a guitar like they normally would have been around a fire before dinner, I wondered if this was one of those moments in his life where everything changed — namely, who he was.

I'd had a few of those pivotal moments in my life, and I knew there were some things you bounced back from, and other things that permanently shifted you. I guess if the love of my young life left me to go to Nashville when I'd always thought we'd chase her dreams together, I'd be fucked up, too.

Noah let out a frustrated sigh, kicking back in his chair with so much force he knocked a bit of whiskey out of the glass balancing on the arm of it. He wrapped his hand around it to steady it again, but his foot immediately started bouncing, taking his whole leg with it.

I smirked. "Nervous, bro?"

"I can't fucking sit still," he said, stating the obvious. "I should be excited to get on that plane in the morning, but instead, I feel so nervous I might actually vomit."

"Why in the world are you nervous?" I asked. "I was joking. I thought you were just so excited you couldn't wait for that six a.m. wake-up call."

"I haven't seen her in a month," he pointed out, wiping the sweat off the outside of his glass with his thumb. "What if she hasn't missed me. What if she's having the time of her life out there and not thinking about me at all. What if I get there and I'm only in her way and she can't wait for me to leave. What if she met someone who—"

"I'm going to stop you right there," Jordan said on a laugh. He held out his hands. "Ruby Grace loves you, Noah. She's probably so excited *she* can't sit still on the other side of the country. It's okay to be nervous," he added with a shrug. "It's been a while, and you guys went from living in the same town to being long distance overnight. It's going to be different. But the love you have?" He shook his head. "That's the same. If anything, it's stronger."

"But—"

"She walked out on her fucking wedding for you," Mikey said, cutting off Noah's rebuttal.

We all grew silent, turning to face our youngest brother who had said more to us in that sentence than he had in weeks.

"If that doesn't tell you that woman loves you, then I don't know what will." He tossed a rock he'd been turning over in his hands somewhere behind him, standing. "I'm going for a walk. Tell Mama I'll be back in time for dinner."

He didn't say another word, and none of us tried to stop him. He disappeared down the driveway, only the moonlight guiding him past that.

Jordan's mouth turned to the side as he watched him go. "We've got to do something to help him."

"It's only been a couple months," Noah said. "I'm sure he's just grieving."

"Maybe," I chimed in. "But, we may also have to come to terms with the fact that the young, carefree Mikey we knew before is gone now. I mean, didn't we all hit a point in our lives where all that perpetual joy left? When we realized the world could be a really fucking cruel place?"

My brothers were silent then, each of them remembering a time in their life when it happened, just as I was remembering mine. I was almost positive it was the same moment for all three of us — that unforgettable summer day when we lost the man who'd raised us.

Noah turned the subject to Jordan, asking him to recount the game Friday night. Mom had gone out of town with him to watch the game, but Mikey had asked to stay behind, so Noah offered to stay back with him. And I'd been at home trying to figure out dad's laptop — which I still hadn't told my brothers about.

My stomach turned, because for some reason, I didn't feel like I could open up to my brothers about anything going on with me — not the punishment I'd received at work, not the laptop I'd found, and *definitely* not the fact that I'd slept with Mallory Scooter and liked it.

I'd been able to go to my brothers with everything in my life up until that point, but something in my gut told me I couldn't go to them and get the answer I wanted to hear. What I *wanted* was for them to nod in understanding, to smile when I admitted I'd had a crush on her forever, and to high five me when I told them I'd had the best sex of my life last night. I wanted them to say they loved me and didn't give a fuck if I was dating a Scooter.

But the reality was that not a single one of them would say anything close to that.

And I couldn't blame them.

There was a tie between our families — Mallory's and mine — and though no one said it out loud, every single one of us thought that line was drawn in blood. In my *father's* blood, to be exact.

Something shady happened at that distillery the day my father died.

But maybe, if I cracked the hard drive open, I could find the answers we'd been looking for for years — and free Mallory of the stigma my family had for her in the process.

Still, I needed someone to talk to, and since Mallory wasn't texting me and my brothers all had their own shit going on, I turned to the other best friend in my life.

"I'm going to go see if Mom needs any help," I said, draining the last of the whiskey in my glass. "You guys need anything?"

They shook their heads, jumping right back into their conversation once I was standing. I made my way across the backyard and up the steps of the back porch, swinging inside just as Mom did a little twirl to the chorus of "Rhiannon."

She didn't hear me come in at first — not that I was surprised, with the level the music was blasting — and she bopped across the kitchen, swaying her hips and singing along on her way from checking whatever was baking in the oven to revisiting the cutting board where a parade of vegetables were in the middle of being diced.

I would have given anything in that moment to see my Dad sneak in behind her, twirling her out before pulling her back into him and kissing her nose the way he'd always do. I'd have given anything to hear her laugh, see the crinkle of her nose as she shoved him off playfully, only to watch him go back to the room where my brothers and I were, all the love in the world in those eyes of hers.

I swallowed past the knot in my throat, and I took his place as best I could. I stepped into the kitchen, slipping one of Dad's old aprons over my head and tying it behind my waist as I sang along with Mom. She smiled when she saw me, handing me the knife so I could take over where she was dicing and she moved to the bowl she was mixing the batter for dessert in.

"This is the best album in the world," she said, still bopping along to the song. She pointed a whisk at me. "And if anyone says otherwise, you tell them they'll have to fight your mama."

I chuckled, but didn't argue. The *Rumors* album was definitely one of the best albums in my mind, too.

For the rest of the song, we worked side by side just singing and swaying to the music. When it faded out, Mom crossed to the stereo in the living room and turned it down enough for us to talk over it. She gave me a knowing smile when she was back beside me in the kitchen, but then her eyes fell back to the task at hand.

"So," she said. "What's going on, Logan Daniel?"

I shrugged. "Nothing. Can't a son help his mom in the kitchen?"

Mama chuckled. "Yes, he certainly can. But, a mom can also know when her son has something on his mind." She lifted a brow in my direction, but kept right on working, scraping the batter she'd mixed into a small pan. I realized then that she was making her famous double chocolate brownies, and when she handed me the whisk to lick the excess batter off like I'd used to as a kid, my chest ached for those simpler days.

I took the whisk, running my tongue over the bottom where the batter was about to drip. "You're too smart for your own good, woman."

"You sound like your father." She chuckled, squeezing some caramel over the top of the batter that she'd weave in with a toothpick. "Now, talk to your Mama."

I licked one whole side of the whisk, hoping the time it'd take me to eat it and lick the excess chocolate from my lips would give me the chance to find the right words.

"There's a girl," I settled on, and as soon as the words were out of my mouth, there was a smile curling on Mom's.

"Ah," she said, eyes on the toothpick she was dragging over the brownie batter, creating swirls of chocolate and caramel. "As there always is."

"She's..." I paused, licking the whisk again as I tried to figure out the right way to put it. "She's unlike any woman I've ever known, Mom. She has a mind of her own and thinks for herself, instead of falling into the town gossip or doing what everyone else does. And she's creative, and talented, and smart..."

I smiled. "And funny. She's quick on her feet, and she doesn't take shit from anyone — least of all me. I don't know, I guess hanging out with her has just been... refreshing, if that makes sense."

"It does," Mom said, nodding with that same smile on her face. "You know, you're a lot like your father, in the sense that you never were entertained by the ordinary. You always craved the *extra*ordinary, even as a boy. You didn't want the same toys or video games that your brothers wanted. You wanted books, and Legos, and puzzles that challenged you." She chuckled. "If you ever fell for a run-of-the-mill girl, I'd probably croak from surprise."

"Mom," I said, frowning. "Don't even joke about that."

She waved me off. "Oh, stop it. You know what I meant." She checked the casserole in the oven, but apparently decided it wasn't done yet. She closed the door again, leaning her hip against it and folding her arms. "Are you and this girl dating, or are you just... what do the kids call it now? *Hooking up?*"

Mom made air quotes around that last part, and I barked out a laugh, shaking my head.

"We're not hooking up," I lied, because for all intents and purposes, that was probably the best way to describe what had happened between us last night. Still, it felt like more... even if we didn't have a title, or even a conversation about what had happened yet. "But, we're not dating either."

"So what are you?"

I sighed. "I guess that's part of the problem, isn't it?" I cleaned what was left of the batter on the whisk, dropping it into the sink before I turned to face Mom again, my hands braced behind me on the counter. "I think right now, we're friends."

"But you want to be more."

My stomach soured, because it was the first time I'd admitted it — to myself or otherwise.

I nodded.

Mom smiled, looking thoughtful for a long moment before she spoke. "Well, I think it's time you had a conversation with this girl. You know, your father and I always said that the reason our relationship worked as well as it did was because we were best friends first, and lovers second. We could come to each other with anything — even when it was uncomfortable to talk about. The other one was always there to listen, to understand — no matter what." Mom shrugged. "Maybe being honest with this girl about how you're feeling will be a test of sorts, to see if you have communication established, if you can go to her and make her feel comfortable to do the same with you."

I nodded, eyes on the old laminate floor between Mom and me. "Dad would have given that same advice," I mused. "He was always telling us not to shy away from our emotions, that it never made us less of a man to feel."

Mom's eyes glossed over a bit at that, but she smiled past them, shaking her head. "He was the best man," she whispered. "The best father."

I nodded, that thick knot back in my throat as silence settled over the kitchen.

"So," Mom said, swiping at a tear that had slipped free and fallen down her cheek. She forced a smile. "Do I know this girl?"

I frowned. "You do, actually... and that's partly why I haven't talked to her about how I'm feeling."

"What?" Mom shook her head, face screwing up in confusion. "Why on Earth would the fact that I know her be part of the problem?"

I didn't respond, just watched her with brows folded together, hands gripping the counter behind me. She shook her head again, waiting for me to answer, but then like a cloud passing over the sun, recognition slid over her face, slowly erasing the confusion as her mouth fell open.

Time stretched in that moment, a few seconds feeling like hours as Mom blinked, closed her mouth again, and turned her back on me.

She picked up the knife I'd abandoned for the whisk, chopping the tomatoes on the cutting board with more force than necessary as she shook her head. "No."

"Mom, hear me out."

"No!" She spun, facing me again with red cheeks and wide eyes. The knife was shaking in her hands. "Now, I'm sure Mallory Scooter is a nice girl, Logan, but it's so much bigger than that. Her family is trouble, son. You don't understand what they're capable of."

"Mom, come on..."

"I don't want to hear another word about this," she said, turning back to the cutting board with her mind made up.

She chopped away while I stood there with my hands open toward her, my jaw slack in disbelief. Mom had always been the most level-headed of the family, even when Dad was around. When he got up in arms about something, she was the one to cool him down. But now, she could barely cut a vegetable, she was so angry.

All because of me, and the feeling I'd given into after fighting it for half my life for this exact reason.

"Mom," I tried again, but she cut me off.

"Set the table and call your brothers inside." She dumped the tomatoes she'd cut into a large salad bowl, turning for a cucumber next.

She wouldn't look at me.

I swallowed, nodding numbly even though she wasn't looking at me to see my silent agreement. I set the table as she asked, called my brothers in, and crawled inside my thoughts for the rest of the night.

Dinner was lively, all of us celebrating Jordan's win at state, but the smile on my face was hollow. The questions I asked felt like they came from someone else's mouth, the jokes I made were distant and foggy, like I was playing host to a foreign entity running my body for me that night.

On the inside, I was the loneliest I'd been in my entire life.

If I couldn't even go to *Mom* about Mallory, I knew for sure I couldn't go to my brothers. And if I couldn't go to any of them, that meant I was facing what would happen next with Mallory on my own.

That cold sense of loneliness settled in like a thick fog, and by the time I was crawling back into my truck to head home for the night, I might as well have been in a one-man submarine in the middle of the Atlantic.

I stared at the Chevy emblem on my steering wheel until it blurred — hands on the wheel, mind somewhere far away that I'd never been before. When I finally blinked my way out of the daze and turned the key, bringing the engine to life, my phone lit up in the passenger seat.

And Mallory's name filled the screen.

You would have thought I was a shortstop diving for a ground ball for how fast my hand shot out, scooping the device into my grasp, fingers typing out my password until her text message popped up.

Mallory: *You bastard.*

The excitement I'd felt just moments before evaporated in a whoosh, taking my next breath with it. I watched the bouncing dots on the screen that told me she was typing more, and I ran through all the possible messages that might come next.

You didn't call.

Why did you clean my house, you weirdo?

The sex was awful, don't ever talk to me again.

But instead, an entire paragraph of text mixed with emojis came through.

Mallory: *I told you I'm not good with emotions, and you recommend this book??? Are you an emotional serial killer? Frederick just got beat up, and Werner went home with him, but now they're saying he's been lying and that he's 18 when he's actually 16 and all because they want him in Berlin to build technology for the Nazis. And then poor Marie-Laure is growing up and losing her innocence because she knows her dad isn't coming back and Etienne won't let Madame Blanchard run her rebellion out of his house anymore and… and…*

There was a pause, and then a single crying face emoji came through.

I chuckled, relief washing over me at the same time that a powerful ache rolled through my chest again. I remembered those feelings when I'd read *All the Light We Cannot See*, and the way the story unfolded, the incredible writing, the powerful emotions — they were all part of the reason it was my favorite book.

She was reading my favorite book.

And somehow, that string of emotions she was feeling while reading it was better than anything else she could have said in that moment.

Me: *You're reading.*

Mallory: *I'm reading.*

Mallory: *And can barely breathe let alone put this book down, all thanks to you. Asshole.*

I smiled, chest tightening as my fingers hovered over the keyboard, wondering what to say next. I didn't know if I should bring up last night, if I should take the opportunity to ask what she was thinking. But before I could decide, another text came through.

Mallory: *And maybe it was ME looking for an excuse to text YOU this time...*

My heart leapt like a fucking leprechaun, and I couldn't bite back the smile that bloomed on my face if I tried.

Me: *I'm glad you found one.*

I waited for another text to come through, but when it didn't, I slipped my phone into the cupholder in my console, deciding to save the words I really wanted to say for when I'd see her tomorrow. Then, I put my old truck in drive, and I drove home with a twist in my stomach — the same one that had been there all night, only now, it wasn't from anxiety, but from an unbearable excitement.

I couldn't wait to see her in the morning.

Chapter Twelve

Mallory

I was way too giddy to be going into work.

After the conversation I'd had with my dad, I should have been dreading walking through those distillery doors. I should have had a stomach full of knots because I'd have to tell Logan Becker that what happened Saturday night could never, *ever*, happen again, that we had to draw a line between us and stay firmly on opposite sides, that I had a lot to lose and so did he, and we should just stay away from each other.

But I realized as I bounced down the hall to the tour guide lobby that *should have* didn't matter much to me — and it'd been that way my whole life. I didn't heed the warnings I was given, and I didn't do what I was told.

I had two coffees in my hand when I slipped into Logan's office, and just like I knew he would be, he was already there, highlighting something on his clipboard when I set the coffee down in front of him.

"Happy Monday," I said, plopping down in the seat across from him.

Logan kicked back in his chair, and for the first time since he was inside me on Saturday night, our eyes met. "Mornin'."

I drank him in like *he* was the piping hot cup of coffee then, my neck heating as his eyes trailed slowly over me, too. My fingers ached to run through his hair, to pull on it until it was as disheveled as it had been that night in my bed. I let my eyes stop at every memorable spot as they grazed his body — that wide chest I'd laid my head on half the night, the abs I now knew he hid under that polo, those strong hands that had pinned me against my front door.

I squeezed my thighs together, meeting his eyes at the same time his snapped up from my lips.

"So... Saturday happened."

He chuckled, crossing one ankle over the opposite knee and folding his hands behind his head. "Indeed, it did." He frowned then, and I watched the Adam's apple in his throat bob. "I told my mom."

My eyes shot open wide. "You told your mom that we fucked?"

"No, no, no," he said, eyes doubling as he held his hands out toward me. "I would never... no. I just, she *may* have noticed that I was distracted at dinner last night, and I *may* have told her that... well, that *you* were the distraction."

Even though I could tell by his features that the conversation with his mom hadn't gone well, I couldn't help but smirk at the fact that he'd told her about me, at all. It was a silly, foolish feeling, like the kind I'd had as a teenager when bad boy Ronny Carmichael passed me a note between classes.

I'd been on his mind.

And he'd told his mom about me.

Why did that make me want to swoon like a fucking Disney character?

"I'm guessing she wasn't too thrilled that her son was being seduced by Mallory Scooter, huh?"

Logan cocked a brow. "I think we could argue who did the seducing that night."

"We could, but I'd win.

He let out one bark of a laugh at that, shaking his head. But the smile slipped off his face like a mud slide on the side of the mountain, his mouth pulling to one side. "You could say she wasn't exactly receptive..." He ran a hand back through his hair, and again, my fingers ached in jealousy. "Not that I should have been surprised, I guess."

"My father was the same."

It was his turn to blanch. "You told your *dad*?"

I laughed, folding my arms over my chest. "Relax. I didn't tell him you had my wrists pinned above my head and your hands under my yoga pants."

He smirked at that, the dimple flashing an appearance on his left cheek before it disappeared again.

"But," I continued. "My loud mouth brother dropped the bomb that you'd been at the studio helping me, and my dad drew his own conclusions." I lowered my voice and frowned, mimicking my father's voice. "*I don't think it's a good idea for you to be hanging out with him outside of what's necessary during your training at the distillery.*"

I waggled my finger with every word, and Logan chuckled, shaking his head.

"It's silly, isn't it?" he asked. "To let some old family feud define what we can and can't do."

"It is," I agreed, and though it sounded like we'd both just admitted that we didn't give a fuck about what our parents thought, we both knew it wasn't true. Logan loved his mother and his brothers more than anyone in the world, and I knew it killed him to disappoint them in any way, to let them down. As for me, I had an art studio on the line — one my father would rip away in the blink of an eye if he ever found out what happened between me and Logan.

"So... I guess we should just be..." Logan swallowed. "Friends?"

The way he asked it, the way his eyebrows bent together, his lips flattening — I knew it was a hollow offer.

I nodded. "Sure. Of course." A smile that felt like a wave of nausea found my lips. "Friends."

Logan watched me, and I watched him, both of us waiting for something more. It seemed like there were a million unborn words between us, floating in the air, waiting for us to reach out and grab them and bring them to life. When a long moment of silence had passed, Logan bit the inside of his cheek, picking up his highlighter he'd abandoned on the desk when I'd walked in like he was ready to get back to work.

"But," I said, and his eyes snapped to mine, the highlighter frozen over the page. "I mean... there's another option, isn't there?"

Logan dropped the highlighter, leaning back again. "There is?"

"I'm just saying," I said, voice shakier than I wanted it to be in that moment. I took a sip of my coffee, shrugging. "What if we kept things low key... casual... just between us?" My eyes found his again. "It is what it is, and it's not what it's not. Right? No need for anyone to know."

"Low key," Logan repeated, like he was tasting the words, checking them for poison with his tongue. "So, friends... with benefits."

I snorted. "If you want to be twenty-one about it, sure."

Logan nodded, over and over, just a slight movement of his chin up and down as he considered it. I watched him as he stood, and I expected him to start pacing the office, but instead, he crossed it, closing his door and turning to face me.

His eyes swept over me, sparking a fire low in my stomach.

He wet his lips.

He took a step.

And then I was out of my chair, meeting him in the middle, the two of us crashing together like magnets.

His hands weaved into my hair when he captured my mouth with his own, both of us sighing on an inhale, moaning on the exhale, leaning into each other like we could somehow melt together completely. All the electricity I'd felt that night came back like a tidal wave, and I surrendered to the waves, letting them drown me. I wanted him to fill my lungs, to conquer every breath, to imprison me.

It was a kiss that told me we were both lying. We both wanted more.

But if it was a choice between this, or nothing at all?

There wasn't a decision to make — not where I was concerned. It had already been made *for* us, without either of us having a say, without either of us having an ounce of control to throw this story in another direction.

We were inevitable, me and him.

And maybe we knew it from the start.

Logan backed me up to the desk, and when my ass hit it, I hiked both legs up, wrapping them around his waist and squeezing. He hissed, sucking my bottom lip between his teeth and releasing it with a pop, his hips rolling against mine. I broke the kiss to let out a gasp, and his mouth was on my neck in an instant, sucking and biting, my eyes rolling back at the contact.

He paused with his lips by my ear, breathing heavy. "I think this could work for me," he whispered, running his tongue over my ear lobe. "This... *friends* agreement." His hands squeezed where they held my hips, and the familiar pressure sent flashes of Saturday night barreling through my memory. I gasped, mouth still hanging open when he kissed my neck over to the opposite ear to whisper again. "What do you think?"

Against the voice inside me warning me not to, I ran my fingers through his hair, gripping those dark strands and pulling his lips back to mine.

That kiss was an answer.

That kiss was a lie.

And distantly, I realized that kiss might be the biggest mistake of my life.

• • •

Logan

For the first time in my life, I had a new routine, and it went like this:

Wake up early, so I could get in the workout I *usually* did in the evenings before I walked out the door for work. Then, I'd practically skip through those distillery doors, and wait as patiently as I could for Mallory to slip into my office and into my arms. It was easy to sneak time together under the guise of our "training" — especially when we finished up the storage closet and got back to tours. We ate lunch together, took break together, walked out together after work... and kept all the touching for behind closed doors.

After work, I went straight to the shop with Mallory. She sprung it on me that she wanted to have the grand opening on Friday — less than a week after we'd unpacked that first set of boxes. And though I thought she was crazy and that she needed at least another two months to be fully ready, I didn't argue — mostly because it gave me an excuse to spend every waking hour after work with her.

We'd paint, and build, and catalog and arrange. We'd test out equipment, and do calculations on the prices each class would have to cost to make a profit, and make plans for how to allocate supplies to each class so that we didn't overspend what we were making. We got the necessary permits and insurance — expedited, of course, thanks to her last name — and with every evening we spent together, working until after midnight, that dream of hers slowly came together.

And somehow, it felt like mine, too.

Mallory asked my opinion on everything, and I had a hand in every single corner of that space. It almost felt like building a home together, and I blamed that for the insane way I was feeling. It had to be that we were spending every day at work together, every night together, only separating long enough for me to shower and crash at my place just to wake up and do it all again. I brought food and toys for her cat and she cooked us dinner. I rubbed her shoulders after a long day and she straddled me at the end of a very long night.

I hadn't thought about the hard drive, or the password that protected it, or anything remotely negative since we'd made our agreement.

Because it was *easy*, playing house with Mallory — hell, playing *life* with Mallory.

And I found myself in extreme danger of falling faster than an anvil in an old *Looney Tunes* episode.

I was watching her read next to me on her couch Wednesday night when I realized it. It'd been another long night, and she was wearing only the t-shirt she'd ripped off me when the work was done. I was sated from her touch, smiling at the way she tucked her feet under her on the cushion, the way her wide eyes scanned each page, the way she nervously chewed her thumbnail as she read. Her platinum hair was grown out a bit, the darker, brunette shade showing at the roots, and she had all of it pulled back in the tiniest little ponytail, with loose strands falling all around her face and down the back of her neck.

In that moment — that quiet, seemingly average moment — she was the most beautiful woman I'd ever seen.

I'd never fallen for a woman, or for a girl — not in all the years I'd "dated." Women had mostly been a pastime for me, as ashamed as I was to admit it. I warmed a bed from time to time, let them give me a fun distraction from my routine, provide me company to combat the loneliness.

But, falling in love? I'd never been even *close* to that. If anything, dating those other girls was like walking in the plains of Oklahoma. There wasn't a cliff in sight, not an edge nearby to accidentally trip over and tumble down into an unknown territory of emotions. It'd been safe, level ground, and I'd walked it easily — and left it just the same.

With Mallory, it was a tight wire.

I knew I was balancing on that thinly stretched, wobbling wire the moment I met her. Even when she frustrated me, even when I wanted to throttle her more than I wanted to kiss her — I still somehow sensed it. I'd been walking that wire since she walked into my office that Monday after Thanksgiving, and now, I was balancing on one foot, with a stack of plates on my head and a glorious fall calling my name from below.

But I couldn't surrender to it — *that* was the kicker. Where we were now, this little hidden secret that we lived in — that was our world. That was where we could exist, and we'd drawn that line so we knew where we *couldn't* exist. Her father would rip this shop out from under her faster than she could say *wait* if he ever found out she'd slept with a Becker. And my own *mother* nearly had a heart attack when I'd told her I was interested in Mallory. She'd disown me if I told her I was falling for her, and if *she* couldn't even understand, there wasn't a prayer that my brothers would.

Everyone in my family had a sick feeling in their gut that Patrick Scooter was hiding something when it came to my father's death.

And here I was, pretending there was absolutely nothing wrong with the fact that I was falling for his daughter.

Still, there was a part of me — the larger part of me — that wondered what she'd say if I told her what I was feeling. If I told her *everything* I was feeling. Would she run, tell me I'm crazy, cut off what we have now because it's apparent that I can't handle it? Would she shake her head and tell me she wished I could be casual and low key like she suggested, that now I'd ruined everything?

Or would she fall into me, too?

I closed my book, setting it on her coffee table before I reached over and grabbed the one from her hands, too.

"Hey," she pouted, reaching for it even after I'd set it down next to mine. "Come on, Becker. You get me into reading and then you take my book away just when things are getting crazy? What sick kind of cruel are you?"

I didn't laugh, didn't make a joke back. I just pulled her into my lap, framing her face with my hands, and slowly, I pulled her lips to mine.

There was no roll of my hips — or hers. There was no quick rush of air on an inhale, or slick coat of desire pooling deep in my gut. With that kiss, I whispered things I couldn't say out loud against her lips, nipping at each one, my tongue seeking hers, hands sliding back until I cradled her neck, holding her to me.

She melted into the touch, but pulled away with a giggle, shaking her head and kissing my nose as she settled on my lap. "Nice distraction, but I'm still mad at you for taking me away from Marie-Laure and her fight against the Nazis."

"Come to my place tomorrow night."

I was stone-cold serious, and when she saw my expression, hers leveled out, too. "It's the night before the grand opening."

"I know, and we've done everything that needs to be done. You need a break before the madness takes over. Let me cook for you."

She smirked. "Macaroni and cheese, I'd imagine?"

"Let me cook a *real* meal for you," I said, still serious. My eyes searched hers, and I swallowed past the sinking in my gut that told me I was coming on too strong, that I was freaking her out.

I'd never felt this way in my entire life, and I refused to keep silent about it.

"I've never been to your place," she said — and I wasn't sure if it was an argument, or just a statement.

"Let's change that."

She bit her lip, considering, but then a smile bloomed over those rosy lips of hers, and she kissed my nose. "Okay, Chef Logan. But I expect a four-course dinner."

"And you'll get it," I said, kissing the corners of her lips before I pulled her mouth to mine again. My hands slipped over her arms, down her back, gripping her hips briefly before I smacked her ass. "Dessert, too."

She giggled, swatting at me with absolutely zero intention of actually getting me away from her before she wrapped her arms around my neck. The kiss deepened, all jokes gone, and I ignored the clock on the wall that told me it was late and I needed to go.

Maybe if I didn't point it out, if I didn't say a word, I could just stay there.

Stay the night.

Stay forever.

And maybe, if I played my cards right, I could get her to stay, too.

Chapter Thirteen

Logan

My place was the cleanest it had ever been — and that was saying something.

I'd rushed home from work to scrub down every corner, dusting and sweeping and mopping and tidying until it was time to run to the grocery store. And even now, with dinner cooking in the oven and my hands busy chopping veggies for the appetizer, I was looking around the space, making mental notes of things I wanted to tidy up or rearrange before Mallory got there.

It was the first time I'd ever invited a woman into my home.

It sounded crazy, because I'd *slept* with enough women that it should have been hard to believe that statement. But, regardless of what the town liked to think or gossip about, it was always me going to *their* place, not bringing them to mine. To me, there was something personal about the space I lived in — the photos on the walls, the books on the shelves, the magnets on the fridge. There were little pieces of me everywhere, and I had never wanted to share those pieces with anyone before.

Until now.

My stomach was a wreck the entire evening, and I wondered if I'd even be able to eat the dinner I was cooking. I'd gone all out, remembering from a brief conversation we'd had while cleaning out the storage closet that Mallory loved Greek food but rarely had it, since there wasn't a Greek restaurant within fifty miles of Stratford and her family was a steak and potatoes kind of family. So, I'd made homemade tzatziki, with fresh vegetables and hot pita bread brushed with seasoning to dip. I'd also made a classic Greek salad, and a creamy, feta-smothered chicken bake with artichoke hearts and olives and tomatoes and Mediterranean seasoning. And, even though it'd been a giant pain in my ass, I had baklava made and waiting to go in the oven as soon as I pulled dinner out — complete with the honey sauce in the fridge that I'd pour over top of it when it was done.

The meal and the way my house looked were the only things I could control that night. Maybe that's why I had obsessed, teaching myself more than

I really even needed to know about the Greek culture and their diet before choosing a perfectly balanced menu. And maybe that was why I'd cleaned every corner of my already-spotless house, as if even one photo frame being out of place would be the difference between Mallory feeling the same way I was or thinking I was a crazy person.

I sighed, shaking my head at myself as I arranged the freshly cut cucumber slices around the bowl of tzatziki. "Pull it together, man."

There was a knock at my door, and my heart thundered to life, kicking so violently in my chest I had to grip the edge of the counter to keep from toppling over. I ran my hands under the faucet, drying them on the towel hanging from my oven before I made my way to the door, checking each spot in my house one last time on the way over. I touched a few things — not really moving them, but feeling like I was doing *something* — and then I stood in front of the door, blew out a long breath, put on my best, easy-going, nothing-is-wrong-and-everything-is-casual smile, and turned the handle.

When the wooden door was open and only the screen door stood between us, I stood there like an idiot, not moving to open it and invite Mallory inside because I'd been stunned stupid by how incredible she looked.

Her hair was down and riddled with beach-like waves, the edges still framing her chin in the most perfect way. Her eyes were lined, a dark wing giving them an exotic look, the golden eye shadow making her ocean-blue eyes pop against her olive skin. She wore a jean skirt with dark leggings underneath, the thighs of them shredded to show little slivers of her skin between each black piece of fabric. That skirt was paired with an oversized white sweater that hung off her shoulder, and for some reason, that sweater made her look so adorable, so small and sweet and delectable that I considered forgoing dinner altogether and pulling her inside for the full, in-depth tour of my bedroom.

Those lips I loved to taste were painted my favorite shade of dusty rose, and they curled into a soft smile as she watched me gawk at her. "You going to invite me in, or should I grab a blanket from my car and throw a picnic out here on the porch?"

I shook my head, pushing the screen door open and clearing my throat.

I still couldn't speak just yet, and Mallory chuckled, slipping between me and the door and standing in my foyer as I shut the door behind us. I took her scarf and purse, hung them on my coat rack, and then stood there like an idiot again with my hands in my pockets, eyes trailing over her again.

"You look beautiful," I managed to murmur, and Mallory grinned wider, stepping into me.

"You look pretty handsome, yourself," she teased, tugging on the apron fastened around my waist. "Can I see you in *only* this later?"

That earned her a laugh, and like the first breath after being submerged under water, I relaxed, every muscle easing as I pulled her into me for a hug. "Only if you're a good girl."

She pulled back on a pout. "But, I thought you liked it best when I'm bad?"

Her hands slipped down, down, into the back pockets of my jeans, where she squeezed and pulled me closer. Her teeth grazed her bottom lip, eyes dancing over my neck, my jaw, my mouth.

A zip of electricity shot fast and hot down my spine, and I groaned, kissing her mouth hard and quick before I smacked her ass and ushered her toward the kitchen. "Stop distracting the cook."

She giggled again, but let me guide her deeper inside, and I ran back to check on dinner in the oven as she looked around.

"There's fresh tzatziki here," I said, motioning to the plate I'd set up on the kitchen island as I pulled the oven door open. The cheese was melting nicely, the chicken sizzling, the aroma making my stomach growl. "Fresh pita, cucumbers, carrots, tomatoes and such." I stood again, turning to face her, and she was watching me like I was some mystical creature she'd never seen before. "What?"

"You made me Greek food."

I grabbed the back of my neck. "You said it's your favorite."

"Once," she reminded me. "Like... in a passing comment. I can't believe you remembered that."

"I listen to you," I said on a shrug. "And I have a pretty good memory."

"Explains how you can recite some sort of knowledge about practically every event that's ever happened in history." She laughed, reaching for the bottle of wine I'd set out next to the appetizer and pouring us each a glass. She dipped a hot piece of pita in the dip next, shoving it in her mouth and letting her eyes roll back on a groan. "*Homgahgawd*, dis ish amazing."

I grinned, picking up my glass and cheersing it to hers. "Thank you for coming over."

She swallowed, sipping her wine to wash down the pita before doing a little twirl and giving herself a tour through the living room. "Thank *you* for reminding my taste buds why pita bread is the best thing to ever exist."

I watched her from behind the kitchen island as she swept through my home, running her fingertips over the top of my couch, the book-lined shelves, the photo frames that held memories made with my family. She paused in front of one of me and my mom, taken at my high school graduation. She was wearing my graduation cap, one arm around my waist and the other squishing my cheeks together while I pretended to be annoyed, rolling my eyes. The grin I wore gave me away, though — and it was one of my favorite pictures of us together.

Mallory smiled, tracing the glass over my face before she moved on, lifting her wine to her lips and letting her eyes wander the books on my shelf. "You have even more here than you do in your office," she mused.

"I've read all of them except the ones on the top shelf," I said, walking over to join her. "That's my *to-be-read* shelf."

Mallory lifted a brow, trailing her fingers over the spines of the books on the second shelf. "You've read *all* of these other ones?"

"I told you I'm a nerd."

She laughed. "I think reading is sexy." She folded one arm over her middle, balancing the elbow of the one holding her wine glass over it as she looked around more. Her diamond eyes danced in the low light of my living room, and she shook her head, still smiling. "Your place is so... *neat*. Not that I should be surprised, I guess." She looked at me then, poking me in the chest with one of the fingers wrapped around her glass. "You need a little color in here. And maybe a little mess, too."

"You volunteering to be that mess?" I asked, reaching out to hook my finger in the belt loop on her skirt. I tugged her into me, sweeping her hair behind one ear.

"I'd be honored," she whispered, and then her lips were on mine.

I pulled her into me as much as I could with one hand, each of us balancing our wine glasses while we drank each other in. The kiss was soft and sweet, and far too short when the oven timer went off.

"Mmm," I said, kissing her nose when I pulled back before I released her. "You better get over there and eat more of that tzatziki. Main course has got about ten more minutes after I add this last bit of cheese."

"Feta?"

"You know it."

She pressed a hand to her chest, closing her eyes. "My hero."

I finished up dinner with Mallory sitting at one of the bar stools at my kitchen island, sipping on her wine and snacking on the dippers and tzatziki as we talked. She asked me about every single picture in sight, begging for stories when I offered short explanations, and I asked her about her childhood and family, too. It was crazy to me that we grew up in the same town, with nearly the same tie to the same whiskey distillery, and yet, we'd had drastically different upbringings. Where my home was filled with laughter and love, with memories being made, hers was filled with business and agenda, with parties and reputation. She had so much expected of her at such a young age, whereas I was free to be a kid.

We ate the salad and main course at my small dining room table — the table that had only served me before that night. Mallory marveled at my skills in the kitchen with every bite she took, making unnecessary moans and asking for seconds, and I watched her laugh and sip her wine with my heart pounding in my rib cage, with words I was still too afraid to say dancing in my head.

The baklava came out of the oven right as I was putting our dishes from dinner in the sink, and Mallory poured the last of the bottle of wine in each of our glasses as I poured the honey over the fresh pastry. I knew it was best to leave that honey to set for hours before eating, so that it soaked down into the flaky dough, but I served it hot, anyway, and Mallory devoured every single bite. She even ran her finger over the plate to get the last bit of crumbs and honey.

"You're a god," she said on a final moan, dabbing her lips with her napkin and kicking back in her chair like a king would after a feast. "Seriously. You should open a Greek restaurant so I can have this type of food more often."

I chuckled, taking a long sip of my wine before I swirled what was left of it around the glass, watching the red liquid splash up the sides.

I could cook for you, I wanted to offer. *Every night. If we were together.*

"You've been so quiet tonight," Mallory observed, kicking those thoughts out of my head before they could materialize.

I peered up at her, offering a smile and a half-hearted shrug. "Just listening to you, enjoying the evening."

"Mm-hmm," she said, lips pursed. "You've got something on your mind. Spill, Chef."

I spun my glass again, eyes on the wine, before I abandoned the glass altogether and gathered my napkin off my lap, depositing it on the table. I stood, heart in my throat and voice a little shaky as I extended my hand for hers. "Dance with me."

One eyebrow arched high into her hair line. "Uh... I don't... I *can't* dance."

I beckoned her with my hand, smirking. "I'll lead. Come on."

Mallory looked at my hand like it was a spider that I'd swore wouldn't bite her, her face screwing up in a mixture of uneasiness and fear. But, to her credit, she took one last sip of her wine, and then she slipped her small hand into mine and stood.

I led her a few feet away from the table, in the space between my small dining area and the kitchen, and then I pulled her into me — one hand at her waist, the other still holding her hand — and to the soft, melodic voice of Leon Bridges, we began to sway.

She was nervous, at first, looking down at her feet and cringing, apologizing when she misstepped. But I guided her with my hand at the small of her back, encouraging her to keep her eyes on mine, and by the first chorus, we'd found a rhythm.

"My mom and dad used to dance after dinner," I said, spinning her out gently before I spun her back into my arms. "Every single night. My brothers and I would clear the table, do the dishes, and Dad would pull Mom into the living room, turn up the music, and dance with her."

Mallory's eyes sparkled, a smile tugging at the right side of her mouth. "That's so romantic."

"Dad always was," I said, laughing a little. "He always taught us to be vulnerable, to be emotional, to share what we were feeling even if we felt ashamed or embarrassed. And he taught us how to respect a woman, how to care for her, make her feel good." I swallowed, searching her eyes. "Make her feel loved."

Mallory swallowed then, too, and she pulled her eyes from mine, resting her head against my chest, instead. "My family was the exact opposite," she said, voice low. "We didn't talk about anything, least of all how we were feeling. I have no idea who my parents are, outside of the entertainer and business owner façade they present to everyone in town. And my brother?" She shook her head against my chest. "I don't know a single thing about him, other than that he likes to golf. And I don't even know if he really *likes* it, or if he just does it to do business with Dad."

"And they know nothing about you, either, do they?"

A soft laugh left her lips. "Not a thing."

I sighed, swaying to the music, holding her close. "That's a shame. Because if they knew you the way I do, if they could see what I see, they'd be the proudest family in this whole town."

She smirked, lifting her head from my chest and reaching up to thread her arms around my neck. We slowed to a two-step sway, back and forth. "Oh, yeah? And what is it that you see, exactly?"

It was my shot.

And I was taking it.

"I see a woman who isn't afraid of anything," I said, searching her eyes with my own. "I see an artist with heart and passion, and talent that she's so modest about that it somehow makes it even more impressive. I see a business owner with hustle and drive, with a dream that has no other option *but* to come true with her in the driver seat."

I swallowed, watching her eyes widen, her lips soften until they parted slightly.

"I see an intelligent woman, who had to grow up faster than she should have, but who handled it with grace. I see strength, and thoughtfulness, and care. I see someone who doesn't stand for being walked on, who refuses to follow the stream just because someone tells her it's what she's expected to do. I see a voyageur, someone who makes her *own* path, her own journey, and who gives off a light that draws everyone around her in like moths to a flame."

"Logan..."

"And I see someone who fights for justice, and who learns before she judges." I stopped swaying, sliding my hands up her back, over her arms, eliciting a wave of chills in my wake before my hands framed her face. I swept her hair back, looking into those almost-violet pools of her eyes as I spoke my next words. "I see the first woman to steal my heart, and the only woman I ever want to keep it."

Mallory's bottoms lip quivered, eyes glossing as they flicked between mine. For a long moment, we watched each other, those last words hanging between us, the air so thick I felt it pressing in on every side of me. Then, she took a breath, stepped back, away, my hands dropping from where they held her as she pressed a hand to her head.

"Gosh, I'm sorry," she said, swallowing and offering half a smile as she shook her head. "I'm feeling a little dizzy, I think. I should probably go lie down and get some rest." She was already walking toward the door, swiping her scarf off the coat rack and wrapping it around her neck. "We both have to work tomorrow, and the grand opening, it's going to be a long day." She laughed. "Need to be sharp, you know?"

"Mallory..." I tried, reaching for her and pulling her into me again. "I..."

She watched me, waiting, but I found I didn't have anything else to say. I didn't want to apologize, though by the way she was reacting, I felt like maybe I should have.

But I wasn't sorry. I'd said what I'd meant, and I'd said it because I wanted her to know.

What she did with it now was up to her.

I swallowed. "I can drive you home," I finished. "If you're feeling dizzy."

She shook her head. "No, no, I'm okay. It's not too far." Her eyes glanced at the table, where our dessert plates and half-empty glasses of wine still sat. "Thank you," she said, looking up at me again. The gloss in her eyes was gone, but her voice trembled slightly. "For the dinner, and the wine." She smiled. "And the dance."

I nodded, swallowing, unsure of if I was allowed to kiss her, to pull her into me even more than I already had.

"With the grand opening tomorrow, will you..." She reached for the back of her neck. "I mean, I know everyone will be there, and with our families... I just... I understand, if you can't come. If you don't want to."

I shook my head, sliding my hands back into her hair and bending to look straight into her eyes. "Mallory, I wouldn't miss it for anything."

She nodded, but her eyes slipped to my chest. She couldn't hold eye contact, and she avoided it even more when she pulled away, grabbed her purse, and opened the front door.

Mallory zipped out, leaving me inside with the warmth of our embrace battling against the cool wind whipping in now. But she paused on my porch, turning to face me.

"Goodnight, Logan," she spoke softly.

"Goodnight, Mallory."

Her eyes flicked between mine one last time, then she was gone.

And I was there, on the wrong side of the line she'd drawn between us, wondering if I'd ruined everything, wondering if she'd call it all off tomorrow, wondering if I'd have to live without her — all because I couldn't live within the terms she'd set for us.

Knowing I wouldn't be able to move on — not now that I'd known what it was like to have her.

With nothing left to do, and the ball firmly in her court, I swallowed, closed the door, and started cleaning.

Chapter Fourteen

Mallory

Twenty minutes before the grand opening of my very own, very first art studio, I stood upstairs in my loft apartment, staring at myself in the mirror, and hating everything I saw.

I hated that my hair was pinned up instead of straightened and framing my face. I hated that it was blonde instead of the bright violet I'd loved so much. I hated that I was wearing a white dress that was cut under my knees in the front but fell down to the floor in the back, like a goddamn bride, instead of my raggedy old jeans and a t-shirt and Chucks. I hated that I was a picture-perfect vision of what my parents wanted me to be that night, instead of who I really was.

"It's just for tonight," Chris reminded me gently from where he stood behind me. He fixed the strap of my dress, touching up a piece of my hair that had fallen before he handed me a tube of nude lipstick.

Nude, instead of the red or rose or burgundy I preferred.

"I look ridiculous."

"You actually look quite beautiful," he argued, but it was hard for me to believe him, considering he was wearing a fitted, fuchsia tuxedo. He did somehow manage to pull it off, though, and he looked — as he would have called it — *gay boy chic.* "And I know you hate hearing that, since this is the last thing you'd ever pick for yourself to wear. But, you do. And, regardless of what you're wearing, this is a night of celebration." He framed my arms, turning me to face him instead of the mirror. Then, he unscrewed the liquid lipstick tube, tapping my bottom lip until I parted my lips enough to let him paint them. "Tonight is the opening of *your* business, Mallory. Your art studio. And no one can take that away from you."

I mumbled, not really able to speak with him doing my lipstick, and he rolled his eyes.

"Yes, okay, except for your father. BUT, he won't. Because you're holding up your part of the deal. So, just relax, and try to find a way to not hate the world long enough that you can enjoy this?" He gave me a pointed look, and a smile, but my stomach was sinking as he turned away.

My father *wouldn't* take it away, what I'd worked for, as long as I held up my end of the deal.

But he would, if he knew about me and Logan.

I realized, very distantly, that the bigger reason why I was feeling agitated and shaky was because of last night more so than tonight. It was because I'd fled from the first man to ever confess he saw me for who I was, to confess he *liked* what he saw, to confess that he was into me — and more than just casually, like we'd agreed upon.

I'd ran out of there so fast you would have thought someone told me the studio was on fire.

But how could I *not* run? How could I not feel every nerve in my body warning of danger with Logan Becker that close to me, telling me in not so many words that he wanted more? It was impossible. His family would disown him, which would absolutely crush him. Everyone in that town knew how tightly bound that family was, and I couldn't stand to be the one to ruin that.

My family wouldn't just disown me, they'd make my life a living hell in this town until I had no choice but to leave it. And my studio? It would be gone before it even had the chance to get started. Everything I'd worked for, everything I'd sacrificed up until this point — my dignity, my pride, my weekdays, my fucking sanity — it would all be for nothing.

My father would rip it all away in a heartbeat.

I thought when I saw Logan at work today, we would be back to normal. I thought it'd be jokes and laughs and sneaking makeout sessions in his office.

But it was more like prison.

I'd barely seen him, and when I had, it'd been awkward, forced conversation — with both of us avoiding what he'd said last night while holding me in his arms.

I closed my eyes, pinching the bridge of my nose as a headache started, and Chris hurried over to me, framing my arms again. "Hey, are you okay?"

I let my hand fall to my thigh with a slap, sighing. "I'm nervous."

Chris narrowed his eyes. He didn't believe me, and if anything, now he *knew* there was something more on my mind than just the fact that I was in a dress and heels.

To his credit — *bless him* — he didn't push.

"It's normal to be nervous," he said, and his eyes searched mine, his hands rubbing my arms encouragingly. "But, ready or not, in about fifteen minutes, those doors are opening." He paused, mumbling the next words with a flick of his imaginary hair. "Of course, *not* with a blast of glitter, like there would have been had *I* been the one to throw this shindig, but still."

I tried to smile.

"Your family is downstairs waiting," he continued with a sympathetic smile. "I think it's time we join them."

I nodded, numbly, in lieu of an answer, and let my best friend guide me downstairs to where my father, mother, brother, uncle, aunt, and cousins waited.

It was all a blur from there.

The studio that Logan and I had brought to life shone like a new penny under the string lights Mom had installed. They hung from the rafters above, giving the shop a hip, industrial look. There was a jazz band playing softly in the corner of the room, right next to where the bar was. Servers waited at the ready, silver platters loaded with hors d'oeuvres in their hands. Each section of the studio was pristine — tidied, cleaned, decorated, and ready to be shown off. Tables near the front entrance held class and event schedules for the next few months, along with a pamphlet about me, my education, the shop and how it came to be.

If it were up to me, I would have just opened the doors. I would have just hosted the first class tonight, and maybe gotten drunk on a six pack by myself later tonight when it was all over with.

Still, I tried to find it in me to be thankful, to recognize that this was how my parents showed their love. They didn't know much when it came to parenting, but they *did* know how to throw a party.

Mom already had a glass of champagne in her hand when she scurried over to me, eyes watering as she took in my appearance. She went on and on about how beautiful I looked (though how I would have looked better had I taken the nose ring out), how stunning the shop was, how proud she was of me. Dad chimed in with his own prideful speech, saying he knew I had it in me. They both kissed my cheek, and my brother gave me a stiff hug, and my uncles and aunts and all the cousins bearing the Scooter surname shook my hand and congratulated me.

And all the while, I stood there, numbly smiling, responding to their questions in a way that felt like it was someone else speaking entirely. Someone handed me a glass of champagne — Chris, I presumed — and my father gave a speech. Some people laughed during that speech. Some people cheered. Mom dabbed at the tears leaking from her eyes.

Then, glasses clinked, bubbly was sipped, and the doors opened.

The first thing I felt was a suffocating kind of overwhelmed. My parents' friends were all the first to pile in, each of them pulling me into a hug or shaking my hand and marveling at how pretty I looked and how nice the studio was before they wandered off to find champagne and talk business with my dad. It felt like *everyone* was there — the mayor and his wife, all of Mom's stuck-up debutante friends, all the officers and board members from the distillery, the police chief and his wife, though he was smart enough to stay away from me. It made my stomach churn that he was there at all, but I knew my father, and if there was a chance to invite his high-roller friends and remind them how powerful he was, he'd take it.

Chris stood by my side with each person I greeted, smiling and taking over the conversation when I could no longer hold it. Of course, not many people stood to talk to him for very long. He was one of only a handful of openly gay people in our town, and let's just say that the first wave of people in attendance were very *old-fashioned* folks.

I thought I was living in my own personal hell, in a nightmare I wouldn't be able to escape for hours. I couldn't believe the grand opening of a studio I'd dreamed of for so long had turned into a social function for my fucking parents.

But then, slowly, people who had no ties to my family other than the fact that they lived in Stratford began to arrive. Families wandered in, with kids bright eyed and excited to play with the paint and the ceramic knick-knacks I'd laid out for anyone to bring to life with color and heat. I found myself flitting around the room, talking to young high school students who were interested in art but unsure of where to start, chatting with parents about after-school opportunities and summer programs, visiting with the secretary of the nursing home in town about field-trip opportunities for senior citizens. I was showing children how to paint, showing adults how to mold a pottery vase with their hands, showing a group of young adults pretending they were too cool to be there a brochure on a midnight photography tour where they could learn how to shoot the stars in the sky with long exposure.

So, the *second* thing I felt was that same pride my parents had. I felt joy, and accomplishment, and like I might actually be able to make a difference, to make art possible — even if it was just in the small town of Stratford, Tennessee. I watched so many eyes light up when I showed them something new, when they made the first stroke of color with their brush, when they lit up with the possibility that they could create something beautiful.

An hour ticked by, and then another, with people coming and going, and me floating around the room to do my best to talk to every single person who stopped in.

The third thing I felt was longing for the one person who had yet to show.

Logan assured me last night when I was mid-flee from his place that he would be here. He said he wouldn't miss it. Still, I didn't know why I was surprised that he hadn't come — especially after how I'd acted, how things had been at work. Why would he come? Why would he show up for *me* when I had run out on him?

I tried to ignore that hollowness in my stomach, filling it with champagne and what hors d'oeuvres I could keep down, and keeping busy with my guests. I convinced myself it was okay that he wasn't there, that I understood, that I didn't blame him and I didn't have a right to be a precious little baby about it.

But when Chris pulled me away from a family I was working on painting rocks with — rocks that I hoped would be little surprise Easter eggs throughout our town — and told me a special guest had just arrived, the way my heart stopped called me out on my bullshit lies.

Chris grinned at my dumbfounded expression, nodding to the door behind me before he sipped his champagne and twirled away to make himself busy. I closed my eyes, took a breath, and slowly — *very* slowly — turned around.

Logan was just inside the door, searching the room, with that damn wrinkle between his brows on full display. He shifted uncomfortably, holding a bouquet of flowers in one hand and a small white box in the other. His chestnut hair, which was normally ruffled and hidden under a baseball cap, was parted to one side, gelled, every strand in its place. He'd shaved, giving his scruff a clean line that somehow made his jaw and neck even sexier than before. He wore a light-blue button up, cuffed at the elbows, the top two buttons left unfastened. It was covered by a russet vest, one that showed off his broad shoulders and chest, accenting the narrow waist that drew my eyes down to his dark jeans. I smiled when I noted the rugged leather boots under those jeans — boots that matched his vest. He was so devastatingly handsome, my throat tightened, a knot forming that I couldn't swallow past.

His eyes were a fierce honey gold, even from across the room under the hanging string lights, and when they stopped on me, and a smirk crept up on the left side of his face, that damn dimple popping under his cheek — I knew he'd found what he'd been searching for.

My heart slowed as he walked toward me, as did the blood in my veins, and the breath filling my lungs. The people around me seemed to morph and fade until it was quiet altogether, until only the soft jazz music the band was playing and his footsteps walking toward me existed. He stopped with just a foot between us, and his eyes crawled over me, searing every inch, before he found my gaze once more.

"Hi."

I let out a long laugh of a breath. "Hi."

"You look…"

"Like a bride from the nineties?"

"Took the words right out of my mouth." Logan shook his head, brows folding together as he tugged on a piece of lace dangling from one of my wrists. "I mean, don't get me wrong. You're beautiful no matter what you wear. But… you just… you don't look like *you*."

"What does *me* look like?"

His eyes danced back up to mine, an uneasy smile finding his lips. "Effortlessly gorgeous in a pair of jeans, a t-shirt, and off-white sneakers. Hair down." His eyes fell to my lips. "Lips painted my new favorite color of dusty rose." When his eyes met mine again, I found I could barely breathe, and when he leaned in a little closer, I couldn't breathe at all. "Although, I prefer you in just my t-shirt and a messy ponytail."

Every inch of my skin heated when his breath touched my lips, but just as soon as the contact was made, he pulled back, handing me the bouquet of flowers.

He looked sheepishly at the pile of other flowers on the table next to the bar behind me. "I feel super original now."

I laughed, tucking the bouquet into my arms. "Most of those are for my mom, I assure you." I glanced around the room. "If you haven't been able to tell yet, this is more a party for *them* than for me."

"Explains your dress."

I smiled.

"I'm sorry I didn't come earlier," he said, grabbing the back of his neck with his now-free hand. "I was thinking maybe if I waited a while, it'd give your parents a chance to get busy with other things and not even notice when I arrived."

My eyes fell behind him, where my father was talking to the mayor, but looking directly past him at where we stood.

"I think you could have dressed up in a cat mascot costume, complete with the head piece, and my dad's radar would still go off when you walked in the room."

"He's looking at us, huh?"

"*Oh,* yeah," I said, but I brought my eyes back to him with an assuring smile. "But whatever, let him look. I'm glad you're here." I swallowed then, as the truth of that statement really sank in. "Really, I am."

Logan nodded, and a silence fell between us — with him looking at me, me looking at him. There were so many words left unsaid between us last night, so many things I knew I needed to tell him. I needed to put us back in the casual zone — *fast* — or perhaps, push us all the way back into the friend zone we'd existed in before.

But I couldn't.

The longer he stood there, the more I wanted to fall into him, to pull him into me and kiss him right there in front of God and my family and everyone else.

It was insane. I was absolutely certifiable to even consider it.

And yet, it was all I wanted.

"Speaking of the cat," he said. "Where is Dalí? It's not *Dalí and Mal's Art Studio* if Dalí isn't here, is it?"

"He's upstairs. God knows he'd probably shit himself and hide in the corner shaking being around all these people."

"Or he'd just walk under their feet and eat the crumbs they drop, flicking his tail in a bored fashion as he frolicked from person to person."

"And he'd whisper *peasants* under his breath."

"Of course, because it's his kingdom, after all."

I chuckled. The name of the studio had been the one thing I hadn't been able to figure out, and when we started filing the necessary paperwork to open the doors, we had to pick one. It'd been Logan who had suggested Dalí and Mal's, and when he'd said it, I could have kissed him for how perfect it was.

Okay, I maybe *did* kiss him.

My parents hated it, of course. Even Chris wrinkled his nose at the name when I'd told him. But it was perfect, for more reasons than just the fact that we had a shop cat. Salvador Dalí was one of the most unconventional artists of his time, and one of my biggest inspirations. Honoring his name with the name of my studio was perfect.

And, of course, Logan knew that.

Because Logan knew *me*.

"I... uh..." Logan held up the square, one-inch thick box in his hand, bringing me back to the moment with him. "I got you something else."

"Anal beads?"

Logan barked out a laugh, shaking off the tension that had been hanging over us like a cloud. "Not exactly, although now I kind of wish I had."

"Next time," I teased, and then I took the box from him, giving it a little shake like a kid at Christmas before I carefully pulled off the top. Inside was a simple gold frame around an all-glass, thin shadow box. There was a white rectangle in the center, and above it, written in black script, were the words *Dalí and Mal's First Dollar.*

I frowned, tracing the words with my fingertips before I looked up at Logan, confused.

"It's... you know, it's for your first sale," he said, shrugging and reaching for the back of his neck again. He pointed to the rectangle inside the frame. "You put your first dollar there, and then you can hang it up behind the register. I mean, I know it's a Square register now, and everything is digital, and your first class will probably be paid for with card. But, you could take a dollar out of the register, anyway. And pretend. You know? Just, as a symbol."

I smiled.

"It's a thing, a lot of old businesses used to do it. I think new ones still do. I don't know." He let his hand drop, reaching for the frame. "It's stupid. I'm sorry."

I yanked the frame out of his reach. "No! I love it."

"Are you sure?"

I chuckled, touching his arm. "Logan, I love it. It's thoughtful. It... it means you believe this place will be around for a while, that it will have history."

"It will," he said immediately, effortlessly, as if he'd never believed anything to be more true in his life. "It will, Mallory. Because it's you."

His hand covered the one I'd placed on his arm, squeezing it, holding it for a moment before he let it go and cleared his throat, taking a sizable step back from me.

"I'm going to go make myself scarce," he said. "Talk to the other tour guides who are here from the distillery, keep busy, stay out of the way. You know, just so I don't give your father an aneurysm, or anyone else in this town ammo for Sunday morning church gossip."

I laughed, looking around the room at the eyes that were on us. "Might be too late for that, but yes, good idea."

"I'll see you around."

"Wait," I said before he could turn away. "Can you stay after?" I swallowed. "There's something I want to show you."

He cocked a brow. "I'd love to stay after, but I think your dad might actually murder me if I'm here when everyone else is gone tonight."

"Sneak upstairs in an hour. If anyone asks, I told you to check on Dalí. And just wait there until I call you down."

Logan shook his head. "Sneaking around like teenagers. Why do I like it?"

"Because you're a troublemaker." I shoved him playfully. "Now go, be invisible."

We both laughed like it was a joke, and it might as well have been. I wasn't the only one who watched Logan for the next hour as he talked with families and couples and kids, showing them the different stations of the studio just like I would have if it were *me* talking to them. He handed out brochures, event schedules, showed pieces of my art on the walls and spoke of my education like he'd been the one to give it to me.

Logan treated that grand opening like it was his own.

And I wasn't the only one who noticed.

Mom's friends were tittering around the cocktail tables, eyeing Logan with suspicious glares. Dad hardly ever took his eyes off him, and even the other tour guides from Scooter were leaning in close, whispering conspiracies as they watched him.

I managed to call a toast near the end of the night, holding my champagne high as I thanked everyone for a memorable evening. It was the only way I could get the attention off Logan, and I watched out of the peripheral of my eyes as he slipped away and up the stairs while I talked. When the glasses were clinked and a hearty *hear, hear!* rang out, one by one, people began to leave, the band died down and started to pack up, and though everyone seemed to be looking around for Logan again, he was nowhere to be found.

"Proud of you, young lady," my dad said at the end of the night, when everyone was gone other than me, him, and Mom. Malcolm had ditched after an hour, and even Chris had finally left, at my insistence that I could clean up on my own. Dad pulled me into a stiff hug, one that felt foreign and awkward. "It was a great night."

"It was," I said. I gave Mom a hug, too, and kissed her cheek. "Thank you both for coming, and for doing all this," I said, gesturing to the lights, the tables of leftover food, the corner where the band had been. "I never would have made it so special."

"We're just so happy you've found your place in this town," Mom said, eyes welling again.

Dad looked around me, as if he was sure Logan was hiding in a corner somewhere. "That Becker boy was sure here a long time."

I shrugged, pretending like I didn't notice. "Was he? I was so busy making the rounds, I guess I didn't realize."

Dad narrowed his eyes at me, and I knew without him saying so that he didn't believe me for a second. Thankfully, he didn't press, just patted my arm. "Well, we're going to head home. Don't forget, Monday is Christmas Eve, and we have the annual Christmas Party at the distillery with all the employees and their families. I'd like you to be presentable," he said, waving a hand over my dress. "Wear something nice like this again."

"This is literally the only dress I own, Dad. Other than the one I wore to brunch on Sunday."

"It doesn't have to be a dress," he said. "Just… I want you to make a good impression. Okay? Can you please do that for me?"

I sighed — and I'll admit, it was a bit of a dramatic sigh, even for me. "Yes, yes, got it. I won't show up in jeans."

"Thank you." He leaned in, kissing my forehead before he placed his hand on the small of Mom's back and led her toward the door. They gave me one last wave after their coats were on, and then they were gone, and the door was locked, the lights were out, and the studio was finally empty again.

Well.

Almost empty.

Chapter Fifteen

Logan

Dalí was curled up in his favorite place — directly in the middle of my chest — when Mallory called for me to come downstairs.

I lifted a brow, scratching behind his ear as he closed his eyes and purred, leaning into the touch. "You're going to hate this, but I gotta go."

The cat creaked one eye open, as if he was telling me our relationship was *over* if I left that spot.

I chuckled. "I know, I know. But, there's a pretty lady calling me downstairs, and I can't make her wait."

"Are you talking to my cat?"

Mallory leaned against the frame of her front door, smirking at where I lay on her couch with Dalí. As if he sensed there was no use in trying to keep me in my spot, Dalí stretched on my chest, his claws kneading my skin, then he hopped down and trotted over to his food bowl.

"He's been the best conversation of the night," I said, sitting up.

Mallory shook her head. "Let me get out of this fucking dress, and then I want to show you something."

She disappeared into the bathroom with a handful of clothes, and moments later, emerged as the Mallory I found impossible not to fall for. Her hair was up in a messy ponytail, the tendrils that fell around her neck and face curled a bit from how it had been pinned back before. She wore an oversized Nirvana t-shirt and sleep shorts that were practically invisible beneath it, and I watched her legs with desire building like a storm inside me.

"Ready?" she asked, dropping the dress into her laundry basket before smiling up at me. Her face was makeup-free now, blue eyes tired, but shining, and I thought back to a passing thought I'd had, how I'd wished to see her without her eyes lined, her lips painted, her lashes slicked with mascara.

She was somehow even more beautiful, and I wasn't even slightly surprised.

I think I'd always known.

I swallowed, heart sinking and reminding me how quickly she'd left the night before. So, rather than tell her how devastatingly gorgeous she was, I just tucked my hands in my pockets and smiled. "Lead the way."

I followed Mallory downstairs, the shop quiet now that the band and guests had cleared out. The place was a mess, though, and I grabbed the trash can near the bar, tossing empty plates and napkins into it as I passed by the various cocktail tables.

"What are you going to do with all these champagne glasses?" I asked, piling them up on one of the empty tables.

Mallory shook her head, stealing the trashcan from me and putting it back by the bar. "I'll do a special event where basic bitches can paint a set to take home for when they host brunch," she answered, then she turned, pointing her finger straight at me. "Now, stop cleaning and follow me."

She looked so adorable, her little ponytail swinging, feet shuffling in her slippers as she led me over to the photography section of the shop. It was just a small corner, right next to the office she'd converted to a dark room, with shelves of lenses and tripods and photography books. There was something hanging on the wall above the shelf, but it was covered with a gray sheet, and she stood in front of it, waiting.

"I was going to uncover this tonight, but when you see what it is, you'll understand why I wanted to wait," she said when I took my place next to her. She stared at the sheet like it was a bed hiding a monster, like if she pulled it down, there was a chance she'd be screaming and running for her life.

I cocked a brow. "It's a beautiful sheet... thanks for showing me?"

She poked my rib, which earned her a yelp and a laugh. "Don't be a smart ass."

"Well, what exactly am I supposed to be looking at?" I rubbed the spot where she'd poked me.

"It's what's *under* the sheet."

"And are you going to show me?"

She pulled her mouth to the side. "I was... but now I'm nervous."

I laughed. "Why?"

Mallory turned, watching me with worried eyes before she shook her head, and let out a long, meditative breath. "Just... don't laugh, okay?"

I frowned, confused, but when she stepped forward, took another deep inhale, and tugged the sheet free from the wall — I understood.

And laughing was the last thing on my mind.

It was, perhaps, the most stunning photograph I'd ever laid eyes on. The colors were so rich, it was hard to believe they were real, that it was a moment captured in real life instead of one painted, one imagined. It was pensive, while somehow still being romantic — the decadent hues of orange and yellow bursting across the large photograph, playing with the deeper, darker shadows present there, too. It almost looked black and white, except for where those sun beams stretched, creating an illusion that made you look twice, three times, forever.

And it was me.

I sat on bar stool, back bent, brows furrowed and eyes focused on the notes I was making in a legal pad. It was the pad I'd jotted down all my thoughts for the shop in, from what furniture I still needed to build to how to lay out each section in order to bring Mallory's vision to life. I balanced a slice of pizza in the opposite hand, one bite taken from the tip, and I had one foot on the floor, the other on the second rung of the bar stool, knee propped up. My hair was wild and unruly, peeking out from under the edge of my old baseball cap, and the muscles that lined my rib cage were visible through the rips in my old Stratford High t-shirt that I'd cut into a muscle tee when I was eighteen.

It was just me. It was just a man eating pizza and writing down his thoughts.

And she'd somehow turned it to art.

The shadow from the window pane stretched over the left half of my face and body, up the wall behind me, cutting the image into four invisible window panes. Those shadows contrasted the soft glow from the sun setting over Main Street, casting me in its warmth. And the way she'd focused in on my face, somehow bringing the viewer's eye straight to where I was frowning in concentration, it brought a troubling feeling that sat deep within me, like the man I was looking at was going through more than anyone could know — that even though he was just eating pizza and jotting down a few notes, he was in turmoil.

And yet, he was at peace, too.

I stepped closer, eyes scanning the photo over and over, taking in every corner, catching more beauty with every round I made. I didn't realize how long it'd been, how long I'd remained silent, until Mallory stepped up, trying to throw the sheet over the photo again.

"It's stupid," she said, tucking the edge of the sheet behind the top corner of the frame.

My hand jutted out, catching her wrist, the sheet falling to the floor in a puddle at our feet. I was still staring at the photo, unable to take my eyes away until I pulled Mallory into me. I tilted my chin down then, looking into the eyes of an artist. "It's incredible."

"Really?" she whispered.

I shook my head, swallowing, not knowing what the right thing was to say in that moment. Instead, I tucked a strand of hair behind her ear, and then bent ever so slowly to kiss her cheek. She sighed at the contact, hands reaching for the edge of my vest, and she pulled me in, not letting me back away.

"It's the most amazing thing I've ever seen," I said, searching her eyes. "I don't have the right words to tell you what it means to me. Thank you."

She closed her eyes, leaning her forehead against mine with a relieved sigh. "I wished I could have revealed it tonight, shown it to everyone, you know? I wish..." She swallowed, hands tightening into fists around the fabric of my vest. "I wish so many things."

"What do you wish for most?"

"You."

She answered quickly and effortlessly, sending my heart into a spiraling rhythm. My hands trailed up her arms, sliding to hold her neck gently, her forehead still pressed to mine.

"You can have me, Mallory," I whispered. "If you want me, I'm yours."

"I'm scared," she confessed, her voice trembling with the admission.

I pulled her closer, our noses touching now, lips centimeters apart. "I'm fucking terrified."

She laughed, the sound barely a whisper, but thick with emotion. Then, she pulled back, her blue eyes flicking between mine. "I'm sorry I ran last night."

I nodded, brushing her jaw with the pad of my thumbs. "It's okay."

"Are we absolutely insane, or just somewhat certifiable?"

"Oh, we're a special kind of crazy, that's for sure."

"Good," she said, pushing up onto her toes. "I never liked being sane, anyway."

Mallory pulled my lips to hers, and the way she kissed me was so desperate, so thick with need, I was sure I was her lifeline. The oxygen she needed existed in my lungs, the shelter and protection she craved was provided by my hands, the care and understanding she'd been searching for, she found in my embrace.

And I found all I'd ever wanted in her.

She was the spontaneous to my well planned, the art to my logic, the unexpected welcome to my day-to-day routine I didn't even realize was suffocating me.

In that moment, I took my first breath on a new life with her.

We stayed connected at every point as we floundered up the stairs — hands in hair, lips locked, legs and limbs tangling and claiming until her back hit the comforter of her bed. The only light was the soft glow from the lamp in her living area, and that warm light spread over her like the glow of the sun as I stared down at her. My fingers began working open the buttons on my vest first, then my shirt, all the while with my eyes devouring that diamond of a woman I managed to find in the rough of Stratford, Tennessee.

She leaned up quickly when I moved for the button on my pants, clamping her hand over mine. I stopped, and she peered up at me, scooting until she sat at the edge of the bed. "Let me."

My breath was heavy in my lungs, chest rising and falling as I watched her hands carefully, slowly, shakily unfasten the button on my jeans. She tugged the zipper down equally as slow, pulling the denim off my hips, down my thighs, letting them pool at my ankles. Her lips parted when she saw my erection under the black briefs I wore, and she ran her hand over the bulge, making my next breath nearly impossible to take.

It was too much already, seeing her below me like that — her blue eyes on my shaft, and then looking up at me, her lips parted, hot breath touching the sensitive skin of my abdomen. She pulled at the band on my briefs, glancing up at me through her lashes before her tongue slicked out and over the tip of me. I hissed, hands fisting at my side, and she gave me a wicked grin before pushing my briefs the rest of the way down, and wrapping her warm hand around my shaft.

It was ridiculous, the jolt of energy that pulsed through me at her touch. She pumped, and I flexed, and she grinned, and my eyes fluttered like I was being touched by Aphrodite herself. When she lowered her mouth again, this time swirling her tongue around the tip once, twice, a little lower, a little lower still, before taking me in completely — I lost it.

My hips flexed forward, sinking deep inside her mouth as my hands found a home in her hair. I gripped and pulled, earning me a satisfied moan from her that vibrated around my cock. I grunted my own approval, and she started to work — bobbing and sucking, alternating sinful, teasing licks with taking me so deep she gagged.

Mallory released me long enough to flip herself on the bed until she was lying on her back, head hanging off the edge, and then her hands reached around me, grabbing my ass and pulling me back to her. She took me in her mouth again, and this time, the new angle of her throat allowed deeper penetration, and the hottest fucking view I'd ever had in my life.

She was spread out on the bed, t-shirt hiked up so much from her flipping over that the bottom of her breasts peeked out from the hem. They bounced with every gentle thrust of my cock inside her mouth, and I reached forward, tracing the bottom of them before I squeezed. She moaned, making my eyes roll back, and I continued my trail down her toned stomach, dipping one hand beneath the band of her sleep shorts. My fingers skated between her lips, and I groaned, circling her clit and slipping one finger inside her easily.

"Jesus fucking *Christ*, Mallory," I said, and she hummed, her lips vibrating over my shaft. She was soaking, and I knew I didn't have to say it for her to know. She rolled her hips against my hand, rubbing her wet clit against my palm, taking my finger deeper — and my cock deeper in her mouth in the process.

When I looked down and saw the bulge in her throat — that bulge being *me* — I pulled out on another curse, stopping myself from coming and flipping her over on the bed before she could wipe the corners of her mouth and ask my why.

"My turn," I whispered at the hollow space under her ear. I licked her lobe, sliding my hands under her shirt and peeling it over her head before I made quick work of her sleep shorts. I bent her over the edge of the bed she'd just had her head hanging off, and then I lowered myself to my knees.

Her pussy was swollen and dripping, her round ass poking out, back arched. I ran my hands over her spine, down the crease where her cheeks met, and then I spread them wide, and buried my face in that sweet deliverance.

"Oh, God!" she cried out, her legs already trembling. She held onto the sheets like they were what was responsible for the torturing pleasure, ripping at them until one corner popped off the mattress, and then the other.

I ran my tongue around her clit, between her lips, diving inside her pussy before I repeated the cycle. She spread her legs wider to give me more access, moaning, writhing, her thighs quivering on either side of my face. And if I thought she was close then, when I ran my tongue all the way up, running it in a circle around her perfect little asshole, she shook so violently I had to use my hands to hold her up.

"Oh fuck, *fuck*, Logan," she panted. "Yes."

"Yes?" I asked, sucking her clit between my teeth once more before I ran the flat of my tongue up and over, hitting that sweet ass again.

She arched. "*Please.*"

With that plea still hanging on her lips, I lowered my lips back to her clit, keeping all my focus there while I pressed my index finger against her puckered asshole. She rolled her hips, gasping, moaning, and when I slipped that digit inside her, feeling her pulse so tightly around me I thought she might break my finger, she let out the most guttural, animalistic groan I'd ever heard in my life.

She came fucking my finger, fucking my mouth, her hips rolling and thrusting, ass bouncing. Every part of her wanted more, and I gave and gave until I was out of breath and she was limp and gasping for air.

It was the sweetest addiction, making that woman come. And I decided then and there that I wanted that pleasure for the rest of my damn life.

She seemed a little dazed as I withdrew, standing and helping her roll over and slide up the bed until her head was on the pillows. I carefully lay down on top of her, elbows propped on either side of her head, body nestling into the space between her legs.

"Who even *are* you," she breathed on a laugh, pressing a hand to her forehead before she let it flop back into the pillows.

"I think I can help you remember my name," I said, kissing her neck and rolling my hips against her. My hard shaft slipped between her legs, into the wet space, making both of us groan in sync.

Her lips were on mine in the next second, and she kissed me hard and possessive, claiming me, urging me into her with her heels digging into my ass. But I kept just enough space there, sliding against her wet folds without actually entering her, just to drive us both crazy a while longer.

I pulled back, balancing on my elbows again, watching her eyes flutter, her lips part each time I rolled. But when her eyes opened again and found mine, that hunger faded, and vulnerability seeped in, slow and sweet, her eyes flicking between mine as both of our movements slowed to a stop.

"What is it?" I asked.

She shook her head, and instead of answering me, she slid her hands into my hair, pulling me down until our foreheads met. She closed her eyes, and I closed mine, and for a moment, we were just there, breathing, existing. Her chest rose to meet mine on every inhale, and with every exhale of mine, I tried to answer whatever questions she had that she couldn't even ask. I hoped she felt my sincerity, my assurance that whatever fear she had, I was there to fight it with her.

"Condom," she murmured.

I nodded, rolling off her long enough to dig in the drawer beside her bed. The moment that latex was covering me, she rolled until I was sitting, back against her headboard, ass on her pillows, and she straddled me, sinking down on me without so much as a second to let me brace for contact.

And I needed to brace. I *needed* to prepare for that overwhelming sense of ownership I felt when she took me inside her. I wasn't ready, and I had no choice but to give, to submit, to surrender everything. She was tight and hot around me, her legs pinning each side, arms surrounding my neck, forehead to mine. She kissed me softly, tenderly, sucking and biting at my lower lip with each lift of her hips. Every time she lowered back down, I groaned, louder and louder, my hands holding her hips to try to get her to slow down.

"I'm not going to last with you going like that."

"I don't want you to last," she breathed, biting my lip so hard I knew she'd drawn blood. "I want you to *come*."

The words were barely out of her mouth before I succumbed to her request. Hot lightning pulsed through me, and everything went blank. The only thing I felt, the only thing I could *ever* feel again was the point where we met, the emptying of me inside her, the sweet tightness of her throbbing out her second orgasm around my shaft. I pulled her close, wrapped my arms around her, flexed my hips into her harder, once, twice, again and again until every drop was spilled. Our bodies were slick and hot when we finally ebbed, our breathing shallow, lips numb where they met.

Mallory fell limp in my arms, burying her face in my neck. I held her for a moment, one hand at the small of her back, the other running back through her hair — which had come loose from her ponytail at some point. I rubbed her scalp before running my fingers through the roots to the ends, and repeated it again and again as she hummed a sated approval.

"That feels nice," she whispered.

I rolled us over until we were on our sides, disposing of the condom in the trashcan and shutting off the lamp before I climbed in behind her again. I pulled her into me, spooning her, wishing I could crawl inside her mind and know everything she was thinking in that moment.

For a long while, we were quiet. I watched my fingers running patterns over her skin, content to sit in that secret silence with her for as long as she'd let me. Her breath evened out, her eyes closing, and she snuggled closer to me. Before she could fall asleep, I wrapped my arms fully around her, tucking her into my chest, and whispered into her ear.

"Mallory?"

"Yes?"

"Do you think there's a universe that exists where you could be mine?"

Her eyelids fluttered open, and she turned in my arms. Even in the dark, those blue eyes of hers shone, and she locked them on mine, one hand crawling up to frame my face, sliding back into my hair, pulling me closer, her lips brushing mine when she gave her answer.

"Let's make one."

Chapter Sixteen

Mallory

That weekend was the best weekend of my life.

I woke the next morning with Logan's arms around me, his legs weaved through mine, my back to his chest. We'd kicked the covers off, but the warmth from his body alone was enough to sustain me. I'd rolled in his arms, watching him sleep and thinking over the promise we'd made the night before.

To make a universe — one where we could be together.

It didn't exist. That much, we both knew for sure. There wasn't a day anywhere in the future where his family or my family would be okay with us being together. But sometime in the last month, we'd decided it didn't matter anymore.

Logan had kissed my nose when he woke up, smiling and running his fingers through my hair as he watched me. I could tell he was just as worried as I was, that he was wondering if what we'd said in the dark still held true in the light. He'd told me to stay in bed, brought me coffee and made us breakfast, and then we'd sat there in the sheets we'd made love in, and we'd talked.

He'd asked me if I wanted to be with him, and I'd said yes. I asked him if he was ready for the consequences of being with me, and he'd said yes. And that was all it took. Neither of us were in a rush, we knew we had time before we needed to tell anyone. For a while, we wanted to keep it between us — mostly because we were selfish, but a little because I needed to find a way to talk to my dad before we told him.

Logan was sure his family would come around, that they would support him eventually — even if it took a while. And from what he'd told me about them, I believed it. They may never fully approve, but his brothers would stand behind their brother, his mom would stand behind her son. There was love there, and understanding, and communication.

All three of those things were missing in my family.

I couldn't imagine a day or scenario where I told my father I was falling in love with Logan Becker and he said, *"That's just swell!"* I needed to think, to figure out a way to prove to him that Logan wasn't whatever it was my father thought he was. I needed to show him that I didn't do this just to piss him and Mom off, but because I cared about Logan — more than I'd cared about anyone before.

If Dad found out before I had a plan, everything would crumble. He'd take my shop, kick me out of the apartment above it that I called home, and if I knew him well enough, he'd find a way to take it out on Logan, too.

That was what scared me most.

So, with a promise to each other that we were together, but that we both needed time before we told anyone, we ate breakfast in bed, and then Logan laid me down in those sheets and made love to me slowly, sweetly, with his eyes watching mine, his arms trembling on either side of my head where they held him above me.

And the best weekend of my life continued.

It was absolute bliss, playing house with Logan. It was the first weekend of the shop being open, so all day long on Saturday, I was downstairs, hosting classes and talking to potential customers who would stop in on their walk down Main Street to find out more about what we offered. Logan was there, too, for a while — helping restock supplies, ringing people up at the Square register, cleaning up after one class so that I could get ready for the other. But when Mrs. Brownstein came in with her children, casting us questioning looks, we knew it was a little too dangerous. Nearly everyone in town knew our family history, and we didn't need word getting back to either of our families before we were ready.

So, Logan went home for the day, working on cracking the password to his father's hard drive and — God bless — working on that perfect body of his, too. Then we met up for a late dinner at my place, and he told me about the Elon Musk book he was reading while I told him about the hidden art talent in Stratford. We spent Saturday night tangled up in each other, talking and laughing and never even bothering to get dressed, because we knew it wouldn't be long before we'd peel those clothes off once again.

And Sunday, we did it all over again.

Logan didn't leave my place until bright and early Monday morning, giving himself the day to shower and shop and get ready for our Christmas party at work. It was Christmas Eve, and the entire distillery was off for the next two days, but the Scooter Whiskey Christmas party wasn't exactly optional for the employees. It was always a grand affair, with Mom going all out with catering and a band just like she loved to do, and Dad giving himself an excuse to talk into a microphone, just like *he* loved to do. They'd both made it very clear that I was expected to be there, and Logan and his entire family would be there, too.

Even though the last thing I wanted to do was put on another dress I didn't feel comfortable in and play into the politics of Stratford, I knew it would be bearable with Logan there. I looked forward to stolen kisses in dark hallways, to watching him from across the room without anyone knowing I'd had him in my bed all weekend, and most of all, to coming home tonight and knowing he'd be coming home with me.

I floated on a high all day long, even when Chris dragged me an hour out of town to the packed mall crawling with last-minute Christmas gift shoppers to find me a dress to wear to the party. I didn't even complain when he had me trying on heels to match, or when he insisted on paying to get my hair and makeup done by one of the girls at the salon there. We stopped by his place long enough for him to put on a well-tailored, navy blue suit and a red tie that matched my dress, and then we were off, headed to the distillery.

"Logan is going to have to sit on his hands to keep from touching you all night in that dress," Chris said as we made our way across the parking lot. A hundred other cars were parking, too, and the clouds swirled with a threat of snow above us.

"I'll have to tell him to thank you."

"Oh, trust me, you wouldn't be okay with how I'd let Logan Becker *thank* me."

I poked him in the rib, and he laughed, holding his arm out for me to loop mine through.

"Come on. Let's see if your mom made any of that boozy eggnog we used to steal when we were teenagers."

The wind whipped cold against our faces as we huddled together and made our way inside the distillery. The party was being held in the only event space the distillery had, which was usually reserved for schmoozing possible partners or big clients. I gasped when we pushed through the doors, gawking and doing a full three-sixty turn as one of the pew boys from church took my coat.

"Whoa," Chris murmured, looking around with me. "Your mom really went all out."

And she had. It was a winter wonderland inside that old warehouse. Blue up-lights cast the walls and ceiling in a beautiful cerulean blue, and fake snow fell from the ceiling in the form of little foam bubbles. As soon as the flakes hit the ground, they disappeared, but there was scene after scene of wintery fun lining the room — a snow man, a little forest of trees, a small log cabin with the chimney churning out light smoke, an actual fire pit that had people sitting around it making s'mores. The dance floor was already covered with distillery employees and their families doing line dances to the country music the band was playing, and there were carolers making their way around the room, singing Christmas songs softly — just loud enough to be heard by those in very near proximity.

We made our way deeper inside with our mouths still gaping, and some-one handed us what appeared to be champagne, but it was tinged a light pink. When we tasted it, Chris's eyes widened.

"Peppermint," he said in awe.

I shook my head, a small laugh escaping my lips. It was an incredible party, and I had to give it to my parents. If they knew how to do one thing well — it was this.

Chris and I claimed our seats at one of the round tables in the back corner, me dropping off my clutch and him hanging his suit jacket on the back of the chair. Then, he led me to the dance floor, peppermint champagne still in our hands, and we danced.

I was never a big country music fan, but I couldn't fight back a smile as I did the old line dances I'd used to love in high school with the rest of the employees at the distillery. In a way, it felt like a big barn party, like just another night at The Black Hole, and I smiled despite the fact that I was in a dress and heels.

When I did a turn during *"Boot Scootin' Boogie"* and saw Logan watching me from across the dance floor, I smiled for a completely different reason.

I stuttered, but he moved easily into the next move, giving me a wink and a crooked smile that had his dimple popping out on his left cheek. I smiled back, finding my place in the dance again, but unable to take my eyes off him. His own eyes swept over me, and he shook his head, mouthing a *"wow"* that made me blush.

Blush.

Who even was I?

We were still staring at each other when Logan's older brother, Jordan, narrowed his eyes — first at Logan, and then at me. I swallowed under the intensity of his glare, offering a small, noncommittal wave. Jordan lowered his brows more, turning his gaze to Logan, who finally tore his eyes off me and continued dancing, acting like nothing had happened at all.

My stomach sank, remembering the universe we still lived in, regardless of the one we'd promised to make together. But I didn't have time to stew on it before Dad was on the microphone, telling us to make our way to our tables for dinner to be served.

I wasn't able to steal away time with Logan like I'd hoped — not during dinner, and not after, when the white elephant gift exchange was happening between the employee children on the dance floor. When the band picked back up again and people started making their way to the floor, I caught his attention from where he sat at a table with his mother, Jordan, and Mikey, and I nodded toward the hall where the bathrooms were.

Logan nodded, and my stomach was a mess of nerves as I made my way across the room, like I was about to steal a car instead of talk to my boyfriend.

My boyfriend.

An audible sigh left my chest at that, and I shook my head, giggling to myself and looking back over my shoulder to see if Logan was following. I stopped short, frowning when I saw he'd been pulled aside by the other tour guides. They shoved him toward the dance floor, relentless, and he laughed and laughed, but his eyes were sad when they met mine.

"*Sorry,*" he mouthed.

I smiled, waving him off and letting him know it was okay.

Maybe I wouldn't get time alone with him at the party, but I'd have him all to myself when it was all over.

That was enough for me.

Chris and I made another drive by at the peppermint champagne table before we were back on the dance floor, too — on the opposite side of where Logan was. We exchanged glances now and then, shared a smile or two, and all the while, I counted down the minutes until the party would be over and I would be in his arms again.

"If I could have everyone's attention, please," my father said when the next song died out. Everyone on the dance floor turned to face the makeshift stage, where he stood behind a podium with a microphone, smiling and beaming out at his employees. Mom stood beside him, both of them dressed in pearly white — Dad in a tux, Mom in a gown — looking like the Groom and Bride or like the King and Queen, themselves.

I would have rolled my eyes if I wasn't in such a good mood.

As it was, Chris and I gathered in the middle of the dance floor with everyone else, holding our glasses out when a server came around to refill champagne glasses. That meant a toast was coming, and if I knew my father, he'd be toasting to how successful the distillery was this year.

AKA — how successful *he* was this year.

"Mrs. Scooter and I would like to sincerely thank each and every one of you for attending tonight," he said, putting an arm around Mom as they swept their eyes over the crowd. "This is the twenty-seventh year that we've had the Christmas Eve party — a tradition that my grandparents started that I'm happy to keep alive today."

There was a light applause, and my mom squeezed Dad's arm. I swore I saw him getting choked up, which was laughable — considering him and grandpa were fighting about almost everything up to the very day he passed away.

Dad went on to talk about how well the distillery had done, talking about new partnerships and advances. The entire room was abuzz when he revealed that my brother, Malcolm, had secured us a sixty-second advertisement during the upcoming Super Bowl. Dad said there would be filming happening at the distillery, because they wanted to show the faces that made America's favorite whiskey come to life.

I zoned out a bit after that, sipping my champagne that I was supposed to be saving for the toast while my eyes scanned the room for Logan. I found him over to my left, closer to the stage than I was, surrounded by his mother and two brothers. Noah wasn't there this year, since he was visiting the mayor's daughter in Utah. It looked a little strange, seeing the family without one of the brothers — like a puzzle with one piece missing right in the center.

Logan must have sensed me watching him, because he took a sip of his whiskey, casually glancing around until he found me, too. He smiled, tilting his glass toward me, and I tilted mine.

With just our eyes, we had an entire conversation in that moment.

You look beautiful, he said.

I can't wait to get you home, I said.

Soon, he said.

Soon, I echoed.

Then, my father asked my uncle to join him on stage, and the applause pulled both of our gazes back to the front.

It was always my father who had the charm to bedazzle a crowd. Uncle Mac, on the other hand, always looked like he was perturbed, like he was biding his time until he could be alone again. He gave an awkward smile at the applause, standing next to my father with rosy cheeks and a glass of whiskey in his hand.

"As you all know, my little brother has been instrumental in this distillery's success since our father passed away. It was his idea to implement a tour department — an initiative that continues to pull visitors in from across the country and the *world* every single day."

There was another roll of applause, and Chris nudged me. "That initiative has also brought a plethora of gay tourists into Buck's," he said, wagging his brows and taking a sip of his champagne. "*Thank you, Mac.*"

I chuckled, nudging him back as my father went on about all of my uncle's accomplishments. I was tempted to zone out again, to see if I could eye-fuck Logan from across the room a while longer, when I heard my name called.

Applause started again, but I stood there frozen, confused, wondering what I had missed. Chris cleared his throat, nudging me forward before he began clapping around his champagne glass, too.

I smiled, cheeks heating as I made my way to the stage. One of the pew boys helped me up the stairs, and then I was standing next to my mother, facing practically the entire town of Stratford. I found Logan, and his comforting smile anchored me, steadying me as my father beamed at me from the podium.

"We've been trying for a long time to get our daughter, Mallory, to take her role at the distillery. But, as many of you know, she is a colorful bird who likes to fly her own course."

There were a few chuckles, and I forced a smile, despite the fact that I wanted to roll my eyes at the backhanded compliment.

"When Mallory told us she was coming back home to Stratford after she wrapped up her masters degree, we were thrilled. Not only because — as many of you know — she was opening her very own art studio, but because it meant we'd have our family together again, too." He paused, beaming at me like we were best friends. "And we are so proud of her, of all she's accomplished." He turned to the crowd then. "What do you guys think? Do we love the new addition of *Dalí and Mal's* to Stratford?"

The applause roared then, and Logan let out a whistle between his teeth that had me *actually* smiling and blushing. I covered the smile with one hand, and Logan grinned up at me, tossing me a wink that I held for my own.

"What you might not have known was that while she was building that studio up during her evenings and weekends, she was *here,* working as a tour guide during the week days. And from what her uncle has told me, she has excelled at that — after a few minor setbacks, of course."

Those who knew of those *setbacks* chuckled throughout the room, and I found myself forcing a smile again, wondering when all this hoopla would be over.

"We've had more compliments for Mallory's tours just in the past month than we've had for any other tour in the past *year*," Dad said, and that had my eyebrows shooting into my hairline — one, because it was news to me, and two, because I found it hard to believe — especially given how many compliments came in for Logan each and every day.

And that's when my stomach sank to the stage floor.

Because I knew, right then, that my father was up to something.

And I knew it was something I wouldn't like.

"She's put personal touches on her tours, telling our visitors about fond memories she had with her grandfather, about growing up around the distillery, about the history only our family knows. She's even volunteered to help out with tasks *outside* of her normal duties — like cleaning out an entire storage closet to make way for new equipment that will help our brand excel."

I frowned, opening my mouth to mention that I did *not* do that alone — or by choice — but my father kept talking.

"That's why, it is my absolute pleasure to announce to all of you tonight that my brother, Mac, is retiring after the new year. And it is my *distinct* pleasure to also announce that we are filling his position with another deserving member of our family — a member we weren't sure would ever come home, one we are so happy to have back in Stratford, and one who has already made us proud in her short time working at Scooter. We know she will have a long and successful career ahead, and we can't wait to see where she takes this instrumental part of our company. Please help me congratulate Mallory Scooter — our new Manager of Tour Guide Operations."

Dad started the applause, Mom teared up, Mac looked bored — and I tried my best but failed epically to hide my expression of horror.

No.

No, no, no!

Mom wrapped me in a hug, and Dad made some comment about me being stunned, a laugh rolling off his lips. All the while, I searched for Logan

— and it wasn't hard to find him, because the entire distillery was watching him, too.

They were watching the entire Becker family.

Logan stood like a statue, just as stunned as me, his eyes on my father while Jordan held a firm hand on his shoulder. Their mother, though small beside them, was standing tall, head held high, a determined-level expression on her face. Their youngest brother, Michael, stood just as tall and silent on the other side of her, shaking his head, his brows furrowed over angry eyes.

I willed Logan to look at me as my father reached to pull me into a hug next. The room was a mixture of awkward applause and animated chatter. Suspicious eyes glared up at me, and I didn't have to read lips to know the things they were saying about me weren't flattering. I didn't blame them. I hated myself in that moment, too.

This job shouldn't be mine. It was never *meant* to be mine.

It belonged to Logan, and I wasn't the only one who knew that.

The man I'd had in my bed all weekend looked like a stranger under that pale blue light. And when his eyes found mine, he looked at me like *I* was a stranger, too — like everything between us was a lie.

I pleaded with him as much as I silently could to wait, to not draw conclusions, to let me think, to let me *fix* this. But he pursed his lips, shook his head, and then he was shaking his brother off him and tearing through the crowd.

I pulled out of my father's grasp, running down the steps and chasing after him. I didn't give a fuck what anyone said about me, about *us*, because at this point — they were talking, anyway.

The only thing I cared about was getting to Logan and making him see that I had nothing to do with this.

It was snowing lightly when I shoved through the doors that led to the parking lot, and my breaths racked through my chest painfully as I searched for Logan. I found him storming across the wet concrete toward his truck, and I ran, feet screaming in my heels the entire time.

"Logan!" I called, but he didn't so much as stutter or pause. "Logan, wait!"

He spun then, and I nearly crashed into him, skidding to a stop with just a foot between us.

I held up my hands, trying to catch my breath. "Logan, I am so sorry. I had—"

"You had *what*, Mallory?" he fired back, standing tall. "You had no idea that was coming? You had nothing to do with it? You had no intention of hurting me?"

I gaped at him, because of course that was exactly what I was going to say. But when those words rolled from his lips, shame shaded my cheeks, because he knew as well as I did that somewhere, in the back of my mind, I suspected this might happen.

He suspected it, too.

And I did nothing to stop it.

"Do you know how long I've fought for that job, Mallory? How many hours I've put in, how many years of my life I've dedicated to this company, just *trying* to keep my own family's legacy alive, *trying* to fight for my father — who has no voice to fight for himself anymore?"

"Of course, I do," I said, reaching for him, but he pulled away like I was poison. I swallowed, letting my hands fall limp at my sides. "Logan, of course I know that. I know *so much* about you, and I want to know everything. I'm falling in lo—"

"Don't," he warned, his voice a thunderous growl. "Don't you *dare* say that to me — not right now. Not when you just ripped my fucking heart out on that stage in front of everyone in this goddamn town."

My throat closed in, emotion strangling me from the inside.

"I *trusted* you," he breathed. "I let you in like I've never let another woman in before. I told you things about myself that not even my *family* knows. And you know what?" He laughed, fist hitting his chest hard. "It's *me* I'm pissed at the most. It's me who was the fucking idiot, trusting a Scooter, giving myself to a woman who has showed this whole town time and time again that the only thing she cares about is herself."

I gasped. "Logan... you don't mean that."

"You're going to tell me you had *no* idea that this was coming?" he asked, stepping into my space. I took a step back. "You're going to look me in the eyes and say your father never hinted at this, that you never thought to talk to him about it, or to talk to *me* about it — especially after everything that's happened between us?"

I swallowed, body trembling as more snow fell down around us. Little flakes caught on his lashes, in his hair, and he looked so devastatingly beautiful in that moment that I had to cross my arms to keep from reaching out for him.

I wanted to pull him into me, comfort him, tell him I would never hurt him...

But he was right.

There *was* a part of me that suspected my father had this in his plan. I wondered why the timing was the way it was, why he wanted me in the tour department out of all the departments there were at the distillery. I was an *art* major — I should have been in marketing with my brother.

The truth was — I knew.

Deep down, I knew.

And I'd been too chicken shit to do anything about it.

"I can fix it," I breathed, sniffing against the cold. "Please, just give me a chance to fix it."

"You *can't*," he said, stepping into me again. This time, I didn't move away. I looked him right in the eyes as he gave me the lashing I deserved.

"Your dad just announced that you're the new manager in front of everyone. You can't convince him to go back on that, and you can't do *anything* without him taking the studio away from you. Admit it, he played you, and a part of you knew it would end up like this." Logan shook his head. "It's actually kind of perfect, isn't it? Playing with me the way you have been the past month. Was it one last dig at your father? One last way to piss him off before he locked you into a life you never wanted?"

I choked on a sob that had no tears to back it, a result of years of me training myself not to feel. I would have given anything to cry in that moment, to throw myself into Logan's arms and beg for his forgiveness.

But I didn't deserve it.

"I was just another way to rebel, wasn't I? When everything else was out of your control, when you knew you had to play by his rules, I was the only way you could get your hits in, huh?"

I shook my head, bottom lip quivering, but I had no words to fight back. I had nothing but my bleeding heart in my hands — a heart I knew Logan wouldn't take. Not now. Not ever again.

I didn't deserve Logan Becker, because I was exactly the piece of shit he was describing me to be.

And the best thing I could do for him was let him go.

Logan sighed, pinching the bridge of his nose before he let his hand fall to his side. His eyes searched mine, and they welled with tears the longer he stared. He opened his mouth, closed it again, and then his head fell as he shook it. When he looked at me again, it was with a single tear slipping down his cheek.

"I was so blinded by you that I couldn't see," he whispered, his voice shaking. "All I wanted was to love you. Nothing else mattered. And now..." he swallowed. "Now, I've lost everything. Including you — and I never even had you at all, did I?"

My face twisted, again, all the signs of crying without the actual tears making themselves known. My heart ached so violently inside my chest I thought it would revolt and tear itself out of my body just to escape the pain.

He was *everything* to me.

But how could he ever believe me if I told him that, after everything that had happened?

When I didn't answer, Logan shook his head, putting his hands up as if it was his final surrender. Then, he turned, storming the rest of the way to his truck. He climbed inside, slammed the door, roared the engine to life, and peeled out of the parking lot, leaving me damp and cold in the falling snow.

And it was right where I deserved to be.

Chapter Seventeen

Mallory

On my phone, there were a dozen missed calls and texts.

There were texts from my mother, asking where I was, and from my father, warning me to not upset my mother on Christmas Day. There were missed calls from my brother, from my grandparents on my mother's side, and from Chris — who had left a few threatening voicemails that he'd beat down my door if I didn't answer him soon. There were texts from acquaintances and "friends," wishing me a Merry Christmas and a happy new year.

But there wasn't a single word from Logan.

I didn't know why I hoped for it, why my heart leapt into my throat every time my phone buzzed, or why I ever expected to see his name on the screen when I unlocked it. Last night hadn't been a small fight. It hadn't been a little misunderstanding that would feel silly and insignificant in the morning light. It had been the final blow in a fight neither of us even realized we were in. It was a total knock out.

And now, here I was, beaten and bruised on the cold floor of what I hoped my life would be, wishing I could go back in time and do everything differently.

If I had Doc's DeLorean, I'd set the dial to send me back a little over a month ago. I'd go back and tell my father to take his deal and shove it right up his ass, because I would have listened to that little voice inside me that *knew* he wasn't exposing all his cards. I'd known who my father was my entire adult life, and I'd been naïve to ignore what I knew about him just so I could selfishly pretend there was no reason not to take the deal he offered me, to get my dream if all I had to do was sacrifice a little time at the distillery.

If I hadn't realized it from the beginning, I *definitely* should have figured it out once I got on the inside.

Once I saw how everyone in that department looked up to Logan, once I saw how, effortlessly, he was the best on that entire team, and once I put two and two together that my uncle was retiring, and that I'd been sent to that department *despite* the fact that I was the least qualified in our family to give tours...

I should have known.

I should have stood up, found my voice, fought for justice like I always did.

I should have stopped it.

But I didn't.

Part of me ignored it because I didn't want to have my dream ripped from me when I'd only just had the chance to hold it in my hands. Part of me ignored it because I was scared, because I had nowhere to go, because failing didn't feel like an option for me — and I would avoid it at all costs.

And perhaps the largest part of me ignored it because the more time I spent with Logan, the more I fell for him — and I thought if I ignored everything else that wasn't him, I could live in a blissful little bubble where nothing could touch us.

I didn't think of him, of his dreams, of his happiness — when it seemed all he'd done the past month was put *my* dreams and happiness first.

My chest ached as memories of us working in the shop filtered through my mind. I longed for those long afternoons, laughing and listening to music and learning more about him. I yearned for a different last name, for a different family, for a different circumstance where I could have met Logan Becker and fallen for him and let him fall for *me* without any of this shit being an issue.

But that wasn't the world I lived in.

My phone buzzed on the coffee table again, but this time I didn't even move to check the screen. I knew it wasn't Logan, and I knew that whoever it *was*, I didn't want to talk to. I didn't want to talk to *anyone*. It didn't matter that it was Christmas Day — I was perfectly content being miserable.

And alone.

It was what I deserved to be.

I hadn't eaten since the night before, the thought of food so revolting I couldn't stomach so much as a piece of toast, so my legs were a little wobbly as I wrapped my thick robe around me and padded downstairs to the shop. Snow had covered the town last night, leaving us with a beautiful white Christmas that every little kid and mother, alike, had prayed for. Under different circumstances, I might have run out to play in it. I might have been having a snowball fight with Logan, or laughing as I got soaked making snow angels.

As it was, Main Street was empty, everyone home with their families celebrating the birth of Christ, and I found the vacancy comforting. It left me alone with my thoughts, alone with my misery, alone with my broken heart — and my ability to use it to create something.

It was the only thing I wanted to do, other than sit around and feel sorry for myself. I wanted to bring something to life — and before I could make a choice of how, my body made it for me. My feet carried me numbly over to one of the stools in front of a blank sketch pad, and I sat with my back to the store windows, letting the late afternoon light cast its light over the cream paper.

It was cold in the studio, but I didn't turn the heat on. If anything, I wanted to feel that cold down to my bones. I sat there, shivering, pulling the sketch pad into my lap and propping my feet on the footrest of the stool. For a while, I just stared at that blank sheet, vision blurring, heart slowing to an almost nonexistent beat within my chest.

Then, I drew.

Time slipped away easily, just like it always did when I lost myself in art. The afternoon light turned to evening light, a bright glow from the setting sun reflecting off the snow and casting the studio in a halo so beautiful it might as well have been sent from the heavens. I found comfort in the familiar scratching sounds of the pencil against the paper, in the way nothing slowly turned to something. Gray dust covered my hand, and my back and shoulders ached from poor posture, but still, I drew.

And blended.

And created contrast and depth and everything that was so challenging with sketching — that challenge usually the medicine that healed all my ailments.

But when the pencil fell limp in my fingers and I stared down at the face that stared back at me — the one that had haunted my dreams all night, too — I didn't feel any relief.

I only felt the deep, all-encompassing, impossible-to-ignore urge to make everything wrong right again.

I'd brought Logan to life on that paper — the crinkle of his eyes when he smiled, that dimple on his cheeks, one hand seeming to hold the face of the person looking at the drawing while the other rested under the pillow he laid his head on. My sheets pooled around his waist, allowing me to bring the lean lines of his toned stomach to life. His hair was a mess, just the way I liked it, and he was looking at me like I was the only thing that mattered in this entire world.

Like the way I looked at him.

I sighed, dropping the pencil to the pad and scrubbing my hands over my face. I didn't even care that I was surely marking my face with pencil dust. I wanted to rub away the exhaustion, the headache, the stress.

When I lowered my hands again, I found myself staring at the photograph of him eating pizza and taking notes that first day we'd worked on the shop. My heart crawled into my throat, and I tried and failed to swallow past it as I looked at him.

I could only remember one life-altering moment in my life.

That night my father chose his reputation over me, the night he made it clear that my safety and wellness came second to the connections he needed to run business — I made a choice. I chose to never lean on my family again, to never abide by the rules they set for me, to forge my own path and forsake what anyone in this town ever had to say about it. I chose what was right over what was wrong, what was hard over what was easy, and what was just over what was *unjust*.

Now, I found myself sitting in that same, hollow, yet somehow exciting kind of moment.

I was on the precipice of making a decision that would alter everything. I would no longer be able to wake up in the life I'd known, in the comfort I'd made a home in, in the certainty I'd found peace in. Because once I made the choice that I was teetering on making, everything would change, and though it was the harder path to walk — it was the right one.

I stood, setting my sketch to the side and walking over to stand in front of the photo of Logan. My heart clambered in my chest, and I placed a hand over the spot where it ached, soothing it as best I could.

He was worth it.

He was worth everything.

And no matter what it cost me, I *would* do right by him.

That was a promise.

• • •

Logan

I told you so.

It was the unspoken theme of that Christmas Day.

I felt those words floating in the air, could practically hear them coming from my mother, from my brothers, from my*self* — though no one spoke them out loud.

For all intents and purposes, it was a Christmas like any other. We all gathered at Mom's last night after the party at the distillery, and Mom made cookies that we decorated just like we did every Christmas Eve since we were kids. Her favorite Frank Sinatra Christmas album played on the speakers, we all wore matching flannel pajama bottoms, and though we were quieter than usual, and I was a fucking wreck inside, we all kept it together on the outside.

No one spoke about the promotion.

No one asked me about Mallory.

No one gave away that we were all hurting, that we were all upset, and that once again — our family had been disrespected by the Scooters.

Instead, my brothers and I put on our happy faces for Mom, and she put on her happy face for us, and we made cookies and watched old Christmas cartoons and then we made a big pallet in the middle of the living room floor. The three brothers slept there while Mom slept on the couch, and though it felt wrong to not have Noah there, it was still home.

It was still Christmas.

I wished it was a rainy, cold day in the middle of November that I felt this kind of pain. I wished I could be alone, in my bed, in my own home. It felt like a betrayal to my soul to open gifts that morning, to eat a lavish Christmas dinner, to pretend I gave a shit about anything other than running to the person who had caused me more pain than I'd felt since my father passed away, and somehow finding a way to make it right with her.

And perhaps more than anything else, I wished I could open up to my family about what I was feeling. I wished I could lean on my brothers, on my mom, on the ones who had always been there for me. But I already knew what they would say.

They'd say *I told you so.*

And I couldn't stand to hear it — not now, maybe not ever.

I'd been so sure that they were wrong about Mallory, that the acts of her father didn't speak for her. I was so sure she was different — not just from the other Scooters, but from every other person in this town, period. I'd seen this deeper side to her, this diamond she kept hidden from everyone else — at least, that's what I'd convinced myself.

And even now, even in the middle of the pain caused by her hand, by her father's hand — I still believed it.

I'd lashed out at her the night before, and shame heated my neck again at the memory of it. I was hurt, and unable to control my anger, and I'd taken everything out on her when I knew she hadn't meant to hurt me.

But she *had* hurt me.

And I didn't know if the intention *not* to even mattered anymore.

She had her hands tied. That, I could understand. She was out of college, without a job and without a home, and her father gave her the opportunity to have an art studio of her own, a home above it, a place and a purpose. Could I have said no, had that same opportunity been presented to me — even if the strings attached to it were sticky and dirty and suffocating?

I sighed, readjusting the pillow behind my back on the couch. Jordan, Mikey, and I were taking turns playing Madden while Mom cleaned up in the kitchen. Pie would be served soon, and then I could make an excuse to leave and finally be alone.

"You sound like a bull with all that huffing and puffing you've been doing," Jordan said, keeping his eyes on the screen where he was currently making an offensive running play against Mikey. Mikey's defensive end took the running back down easily, and the screens popped up for each of them to select their next formation and play.

"My back is aching," I lied. "Just trying to get comfortable."

"You know you can cut the bullshit anytime, right?" He hiked the ball. "I think we're all tired of pretending like last night didn't happen."

"I'm not pretending anything. I just don't feel like talking about it."

"Why? Because you're too big and bad for feelings?" His tongue jutted out as he pressed the buttons that sent the ball flying out of the quarterback's hands and down the field to a wide receiver. It was caught, and he ran it all the way to the ten-yard line.

"Bullshit," Mikey mumbled. "You're not getting into that end zone, brother."

"We'll see," Jordan replied with a smirk as they picked their next plays.

"No," I said, answering his assessment. "Because I already know what you guys will say, and I don't want to hear it."

"Oh, you hear that, Mikey? Logan's a mindreader now. Knows what we'll say before we do."

"Should sign him up for the circus," Mikey chimed.

I rolled my eyes. "Come on, like you're both not waiting for the chance to say you told me so, that Mallory is a Scooter and I should have known better? That I should have kept my distance?"

Jordan paused the game, and he and Mikey both turned, confusion on their faces. "What are you talking about?"

The color drained from my face. I realized then that the only person I'd told about my interest in Mallory — past the fact that she worked with me, anyway — was Mom.

I shook my head. "Nothing."

"I was thinking about the fact that the promotion rightfully owed to you was given to a Scooter, yes, but it doesn't reflect on you," Jordan said, one eyebrow lifted. "This was on them. There was nothing you could have done to prevent it."

"He's talking about the fact that he's in love with Mallory and feels like a sucker now that he realizes she was taking his job all along."

Jordan's attention snapped to my youngest brother, and I gritted my teeth, hands fisting at my sides.

"I'm not in love with her." Again, a lie.

"Wait," Jordan said, pointing at Mikey when he looked back at me. "What does he know that I don't?" He narrowed his eyes, pointing his finger at me this time. "Have you been hooking up with Mallory Scooter?"

I sniffed, crossing my arms over my chest without an answer.

Jordan let out a bark of a laugh, eyes wide. "Wow."

"She's not what you think she is," I defended.

"Clearly."

"She's not. She hates her father almost as much as we do. She knows the shitty things he's done, and she's spent her whole life trying to get away from that legacy."

"Well, obviously, she's doing a fine job of that."

"She didn't know he was going to do this," I growled.

"Then why are you so upset?" Jordan threw back. "If Mallory is so innocent, and you're so in love, then why are you moping around like someone rearranged the books on your bookshelf?"

"Because everything I was afraid of losing I lost in a matter of minutes!" I stood, glaring down at my brothers on the floor. "Because that job was the only chance I had of doing my part to keep the Becker name alive in that distillery. Because they're trying to wash Dad out of their history altogether, and it's working. Because I can't do anything about it. And yes, because for the first time in my fucking life, I thought maybe I could have what Mom and Dad did, that I could be with a woman who understood me, who challenged me, who made my life better instead of just making me roll my eyes at all the fucking town gossip that most girls in Stratford are obsessed with. She was different, and for the first time since Dad died, I was actually fucking happy." I didn't even bother hiding the tears that flooded my eyes, because with my brothers, I was never afraid to cry. "All I do, all I've ever done is try to keep the peace. I need steadiness — routine and dependability. And right now, I don't have any of that. Right now, I'm on a piece of fucking driftwood in the middle of the ocean without a paddle or a prayer in hell of finding land again." I swallowed, holding my chin high, though every part of me was trembling. "*That's* why I'm upset. Are you fucking happy now?"

Neither of my brothers could look at me then, and I took their eyes being glued to the carpet as an answer. Mom had peeked out of the kitchen, and the look in her eyes when I turned around was so heartbreaking, I couldn't hold it together any longer. I swiped my laptop off the kitchen table and barreled outside, not bothering to grab a jacket. I needed space, and fresh air, and to not have anyone's pitiful stare on me for a while.

Of course, I should have known better with my family. It didn't take long before Jordan and Mikey walked outside and sat on the porch with me. Jordan handed me my jacket, and I tugged it on without looking at him, keeping my attention on the laptop. They let me stew for a little while longer, but then my little brother got up from the rocking chair he sat in, flipped my laptop lid shut, and forced me to look at him.

"We're sorry," he said, leveling his hazel eyes with my own. We both favored Mom, and sometimes, when I looked at him, I saw a younger version of me. "I'm saying that on behalf of all of us. But you should know that we love you, and we would never judge you. Not even if you robbed a bank and tried to get away in a go-kart."

I sighed, smile tugging at the corner of my lips. "I know. I'm sorry, too. I just... I don't know how to handle all of this. I hate feeling anything negative, and right now, I'm drowning in *everything* negative."

"I know the feeling," he said, and Jordan and I exchanged glances.

Our little brother had been battling a broken heart for months, and here he was, ready to go to war for *mine*.

That was the Becker way.

Mikey pulled his rocking chair over so he could face me, and Jordan leaned against the porch railing, quiet for now.

"I didn't realize it until Noah got with Ruby Grace, until Bailey broke up with me, maybe not even until just now, when you said what you did inside, but..." Mikey shrugged. "I think we're all looking for what Mom and Dad had. And if I'm being honest, I think we're wasting our time."

Jordan shifted his weight, but kept quiet, watching our little brother as he continued.

"I don't know what happened between you and Mallory, but I can tell you now, if it's over?" He shook his head. "Just let it be over. Find a way to let her go. I know it feels impossible. Trust me — I'm *still* holding on to a girl who tossed me aside so easily, I got whiplash. But, the more time that passes, the more I see that... well... maybe the kind of love Mom and Dad had really is so rare that not everyone can find it. Noah did, and I love that for him. But, I don't know... maybe it's not in the cards for all of us."

My throat tightened, the grip so tight I couldn't swallow past it.

"That's probably not what you want to hear," he said. "But, it's what I believe to be true. And you know, there's more to life than love. We can find joy in other things, you know? Our careers, our family, our hobbies. Travel. Maybe live in a new city, a new place that doesn't have the same weight as this town always has for us."

He swallowed at that, and I narrowed my eyes, because if there was one thing our family always agreed on — it was that our place was in Stratford. We had a legacy here, and we would fight to keep it. But the way Mikey was talking, it was like he wanted to be free of it all. In a way, I guessed I couldn't blame him.

"You forget that I lost my career," I pointed out.

"No, you didn't," Jordan said from where he stood. "You lost a promotion, but that's all. And who knows, maybe Mallory will crash and burn and they'll have no choice but to give the job to you."

"Or to a rookie, since they seem hell bent on keeping Beckers out of leadership," I argued.

"Maybe," Jordan conceded with a shrug. "But, that's the fight we all knew we'd be in, right? When Dad died, when that company covered it up and made it seem like an accident, even though we know there's something more to it... we all agreed to keep Dad's memory alive in this town, in our own ways. You and Noah and Mikey knew going into jobs at the distillery that it wouldn't be easy, but you're still there. And you're going to tell me that because of one setback, you're ready to quit? To leave it all behind?"

I blinked, shaking my head as my gaze fell to the chipping wood planks of the porch. "I don't want to quit."

"Then don't."

I nodded, letting their words settle over me. They were both right, of course — another annoying trait of the Becker family. When one of us lost our cool, we found it hard to see clearly, but the rest of the crew was always right there to help light the way back to rationality.

When we fell, we fell hard. When we loved, we loved with all we had. When we fought, we fought until we dropped. And when one of us was knocked down, the whole team stopped everything to get them back on their feet.

That was the Becker way.

I sighed, deciding in that moment that there was nothing more to say. Jordan was right, there was no way I was going to walk away from the distillery. If anything, I reckoned that was what Patrick wanted me to do — and I'd be damned if I'd give him what he wanted. I was there to stay — even if it would suffocate me to see Mallory in that job every day.

And as for what I felt for her, maybe Mikey was right about that. Maybe what I thought we had, what I desired from her, from us... maybe it didn't actually exist. She had ties to her family, and I had ties to mine, and for that reason alone, it didn't make sense that we would ever be together. I'd lived in the apartment above that shop with her in a secret hideaway, a place where we could pretend we were someone different, that what we had could last.

Now, we were back in the real world.

And it just was what it was.

I stared at the laptop in my hands, and my chest ached for a completely different reason. "There's something else I need to tell you guys," I said, looking up at both of them.

Their frowns mirrored each other as I opened my laptop again, and I swallowed, turning the screen toward them.

Jordan squinted at it. "Username: Becker dot John at Scooter Whiskey dot com," he said, shaking his head. "I don't get it. Are you trying to break into Dad's old email?"

"I'm trying to break into his old laptop."

Mikey leaned in closer. "But his laptop is gone," he said. "They never recovered it from the fire."

"They did," I corrected. "They just never told us."

My brothers watched me for a long moment before Mikey pulled the laptop into his hands, and Jordan watched over his shoulder while I told them the whole story. I told them about the storage closet, the laptop, how I'd extracted the hard drive, but it was password protected. I told them that I didn't want to tell them at first, because I thought it was hopeless. But, I'd tried everything that I knew, and now, I needed their help trying to figure out the password.

"If we can get into it, maybe we can find something," I said. "I don't know what I'm looking for exactly, but maybe..."

"Maybe there are answers," Jordan finished, his eyes scanning the screen.

"Ky knows a little about hacking," Mikey chimed in. "She's big into gaming and computers, and one time she hacked into the school system and changed everyone's grade to an A in Mr. Zee's anatomy class because he was such a stickler and never taught us what was actually on our tests."

"Oh shit, I remember that. Your sophomore year, right?" I asked

He nodded. "Maybe she can help."

"Here," I said, reaching for the laptop. I safely ejected the external hard drive that now housed the one that had been inside Dad's computer and handed it to Mikey. "Take it. You guys can work on it for a while. I've been obsessing over it, anyway. Need a break."

"Okay. We need to tell Noah, too."

"I will," I said. "As soon as he's back. He's happy right now, I want to let him have that."

For a long pause, my brothers and I were quiet. I felt marginally better, though my chest was still tight. I figured it would be that way for a while, until time could do its work and heal me, my heart, my soul. It'd been that way when Dad passed away, too, and I'd survived.

If I could make it through that, I could make it through anything.

When we all stood to make our way back inside, Jordan nudged Mikey with a smirk. "So... you and Ky are hanging out again, huh?"

Mikey frowned with a noncommittal shrug. "So? We've been friends forever. Why is it weird that we're hanging out?"

"No reason," Jordan said, but he and I exchanged a knowing look. That girl had been in love with our brother since they were toddlers, and I had a feeling Mikey was going to discover that real soon.

I just hoped he could give her a chance, open his heart to that possibility after Bailey.

And I hoped that maybe, one day, I could do the same with mine.

Chapter Eighteen

Mallory

I shouldn't have been as angry as I was that Christmas decorations still lined Main Street when I woke up the next morning. Of course, no one was going to take them down over night. In fact, I knew they'd still be up for another week or so, spreading joy through the new year.

Damn them.

It was just that it didn't match my mood as I flew down the road in my old Camry, the one I had insisted on buying with my own money that I saved up before I went to college. It was a piece of shit. It needed a new air conditioner and a new radiator and a new everything.

But it was mine.

I wondered briefly why I never saw my situation now the way I saw buying this car when I was seventeen, but I tried not to dwell on it. What was done, was done.

I only had my actions and choices *now*.

It was a little harder to breathe when I pulled through the gate at the end of my parents' long driveway. I didn't grow up in a house, I grew up in a giant, southern-as-can-be Tennessee estate. It sat on one-hundred-and-fifty-two acres on the north side of town, which was entirely too much land for a family of four. Of course, my father needed land to entertain — to shoot skeet, have a driving range and putter course for business talk, and, for some reason, horses. I never did figure that one out, since he wasn't a rider, and neither was Mom, nor were Malcolm or myself.

And where Dad wanted the land, Mom wanted the large house. She wanted enough room to have servants' quarters, where those who worked for her could live and be readily available. She needed multiple kitchens, dozens of rooms to house guests who were too inebriated to leave, and, as she would tell anyone who would listen, *"Plenty of room for future grandchildren to have adventures and get lost."*

It was always too much for me. I'd felt suffocated in that massive home, and when I parked in the driveway next to the elaborate fountain, I found myself struggling for air once again.

I pushed through the front door without knocking, handing my coat and scarf to Larry — one of our butlers — before I made my way into the dining room. Mom lit up when she saw me, clapping her hands together, whereas Dad just barely glanced at me over his newspaper. Malcolm was there, too, but he was on his phone, and I was pretty sure he didn't even realize I'd walked in.

"How nice of you to finally join us," Dad murmured. "Sit. I'll have Amada bring your breakfast."

"I'm not hungry. Can we talk in your office?"

Dad waved a hand over his half-demolished plate, not taking his eyes off the newspaper. "I'm eating."

"Looks like you're done to me."

"Mallory," Mom scolded, in the sweetest, most unassuming voice. It annoyed me more than if she would have yelled at me. "You missed Christmas Day and now you won't even eat breakfast with your family? What has gotten into you?"

"Sorry I missed yesterday, I wasn't feeling well," I said, then I turned back to Dad. "Your office? Or do you want to do this here?"

Dad gave an exaggerated sigh, taking his sweet time folding up the newspaper he was reading before he grabbed his coffee, kissed Mom on the forehead, and assured her and Malcolm that he would be back.

Again, Malcolm didn't seem to notice any of it.

Dad followed me down the hall to the west wing of the house where his office was. As much as I hated the business done within those walls, I absolutely loved the office. Three of the four walls were covered with books — which was laughable, considering the only books my father had ever read were end-of-the-year reports on the distillery — and the last wall was a floor-to-ceiling window that overlooked the rolling hills of our property, the Smokies peeking out over the horizon far in the distance.

He closed the door once we were inside, taking a seat behind his desk.

I remained standing.

"What is it that you're being so dramatic about?"

"Stop acting like you don't know," I said. "What the hell was all that about at the Christmas party? I've worked at the distillery for a *month*, Dad. I'm still in training. I'm not fit to take that job from Uncle Mac any more than you're fit to be a good father."

"Watch your tone, young lady."

"That position was *Logan's*," I said, pressing my index finger on the top of his desk like I was pointing at indisputable proof. "And you know it."

Dad rolled his eyes. "Cut the theatrics. This was a business move. We can't have a Becker running an entire department, let alone the most important *local* one, lucratively speaking."

"*Why*?" I asked, tossing my hands up in exhaustion before they fell back to my thighs with a *whack*. "What is your vendetta against that family? They lost their father in the one and only fire our distillery has ever had. We owe them. Besides, Papa *loved* their grandfather. They were partners."

"They were *not* partners," Dad said, nose flaring and face reddening. "That was never officially written on any paperwork."

"It didn't *have* to be written. They knew it because they were friends — you *all* were. I remember Papa telling fond stories of Logan's dad, John. How much he saw him as a son. And I also remember seeing pictures of you and their mom, Laurelei, when you were high schoolers. You two seemed like friends then. What happened?"

Dad slammed his fist on the desk, his face so red I thought he'd burst a blood vessel if he didn't calm down. "That's *enough*. What decisions I make for my business are just that — *my* business. I don't owe my daughter an explanation."

"You do when it concerns me!" I argued. "When it's my life, my job, my friends—"

"Logan Becker is *not* your friend."

"You're right. He's more." I stood tall, swallowing down whatever hesitance I'd had before that moment. "I love him, Dad. And I don't care if that's not *permitted* in your mind. And I also don't care what you had in plan for me at that distillery, because I'm done. I'm quitting. And you're going to give that position to Logan."

Dad watched me for a long, slow moment, blinking several times before he let out a bark of a laugh. Then, he gave in to a whole fit of laughter, swiping at tears coming from his eyes before he spoke again. "Oh, child. Your spunk is so adorable."

"You will give that position to Logan," I said again, not backing down. "Because he deserves it. Because he's the right one for the job. Because it's the right thing to do."

"I will not."

"You *will*," I said again, folding my arms. "Or I will go see your favorite journalist at the *Stratford Gazette* and tell her everything about that night when I was fourteen, when our police chief sexually harassed me and my father did nothing about it."

All the color drained from my father's face.

Miranda Hollis loved to publish scathing articles about my father and the distillery. It seemed her mission was to get Scooter Whiskey out of Stratford, to disconnect the town from what she thought was a *garbage business*. Since her father was involved in politics, Dad had never been able to silence her.

Much to his dismay.

And he knew as well as I did that if she got this story, there would be a shit storm for him, for our family, for the police chief and the entire town.

He placed his palms flat on the desk, stood very, *very* slowly, and waited until he was towering over me to look me dead in the eye. "You will do no such thing, young lady. Now, I don't know what the hell has gotten into you, but if you remember right, it's *me* who pays the bills on that little studio you love so much. It's *me* who bought that apartment above it where you sleep every night. And it's *me* who can take all of that away," he said, snapping to illustrate the point. "Just like that."

"Fine," I said, shrugging. "Do it. Take the studio, take the apartment. I have my car, and my dignity, and that's fine by me."

Dad laughed, shaking his head like I was delusional. "You've lost your mind, little girl. You'll be excommunicated from this family, from our money, from *everything* — and that shop is gone. That's not a threat. That's a promise."

I shrugged, though my heart squeezed painfully in my chest. I knew this was how he would react, and I knew when I walked out of my studio this morning that the dream I'd built inside it would be gone.

It was a sacrifice worth making, because this was the right thing to do.

"That's fine, if that's your choice," I said calmly. "But this is mine."

Dad shook his head, face screwed up in confusion like I was certifiably insane. And maybe I was. All I knew was I could never live with myself, playing a part in his game just to have a studio that I could maybe have on my own someday. It would take longer. I'd need a loan, and a business plan, maybe some investors. It wouldn't be easy.

But nothing in my life had been.

I knew one thing for sure — I never wanted to be in debt to my father, and I never wanted to be a part of any plan that hurt the man I loved.

"I know you don't want another scandal rocking this family, and I *definitely* know that with everything in the news right now, with the way companies and celebrities are getting shut down by women coming forward with their stories, this is the kind of scandal you never want to leak. So, if you want me to keep my mouth shut, I will. But you have to do this for me."

Dad's jaw clenched, face red. I gave him one last pointed look before I turned and crossed the office, opening the door that led to the hallway.

"Make it right, Dad," I said. "You have until New Year's."

Then, I slammed the door on the devil, and vowed to never make a deal with him again.

• • •

Logan

A week off from work was too long when you were miserable.

Having Christmas off was a blessing. The distillery was the absolute last place I wanted to be after the party on Christmas Eve, and spending time with my family was exactly what I needed. But that night, when I'd gone home, I'd realized it was going to be a long, lonely week.

I was so used to filling all my time with Mallory, I didn't know what to do with myself. My usual routine felt stale and suffocating now, like I was wasting time instead of making the most of it. I longed to reach out to her, to talk to her, to hold her — even with the sting of the burn she'd left fresh on my skin.

My brothers said leave her be, let her go.

My heart said go to her, hold on.

I sat in that tornado of thoughts all week, trying anything I could to keep my mind off things and failing. Working out didn't help. Reading didn't help. Cleaning didn't help. Not even an all-day marathon of murder documentaries on Friday helped. The closest I'd come to feeling okay was Saturday night at The Black Hole with my brothers. Noah was back in town, and we'd taken him out to get his mind off leaving Ruby Grace. It'd been a night of Becker debauchery, and then we'd ordered pizza at one in the morning and sat up all night trying to crack the password on Dad's hard drive.

It felt like old times, like when we were kids staying up too late during winter break, dreading the time when we'd go back to school.

And that's what it felt like, dragging myself back through the distillery doors on Monday morning — New Year's Eve. As much as I couldn't wait to get back to work, to have something to keep my mind off everything, it was a catch twenty-two.

Because everything I wanted to forget about was inside those walls.

The sympathetic looks started in the lobby, with Lucy, and they followed me all the way back to my office. A few people stopped me on the way, shaking my hand and holding my shoulder in sincerity when they said they were sorry, that it was all bullshit, that they were on my side.

Like it mattered.

My stomach churned, even after I was in the solace of my office, because I knew at any moment, Mallory would be there, too. I didn't know if she'd walk in and go straight into Mac's office, start working on transitioning, or if she'd be doing tours with me — business as usual. I didn't know if she'd try to apologize again, if I'd be able to listen.

If I'd be able to stay away.

Again, I found myself at war with what my brothers had said at Mom's. They urged me to stay, to not give up on the career I'd built, the reputation I had, the legacy our father started that we were keeping alive.

But now that I was in my office, in a place that used to bring me hope, and fuel, and drive — I only found hopelessness.

I sighed, staring at my desk for far too long before I actually sat down at it. I pulled up my emails, whipped out my highlighters and schedule and clipboard, and tried to get into the groove just like I would have any other

Monday morning. And twenty minutes in, I found myself slipping away, into work, out of my mind.

Until there was a knock at my door.

My stomach dropped, heart leaping into my throat as I stared at the door. I didn't know who was on the other side of it, only that if it was the person I thought it was, I wasn't ready.

But I had no choice.

"Come in," I croaked out, keeping my eyes on my schedule and pretending it needed my full attention. I started highlighting things that didn't need to be highlighted, just so I wouldn't have to look up.

"A word, Becker?"

My head popped up at the sound of Mac's voice, and now he was playing the same game I had been, looking at his clipboard like he was on a tight schedule and I was just a stop along the way.

"Yes, sir. Of course. Do you want me in your office?"

"No, this is fine," he said, closing the door behind him. He set his clipboard on my desk, taking the seat opposite me. For a long while, he just looked at me — as if he were truly seeing me for the first time since I'd worked there. Then, he sighed, pinching the bridge of his nose. "I want to apologize for what happened at the Christmas party. None of us were expecting that, least of all me, but when my brother makes up his mind... well..." He shrugged, folding his hands in his lap. "I guess I don't need to tell you that there's no arguing with him."

I didn't answer. I had nothing to say.

"Anyway, I came in here today to tell you that we spoke this weekend," he said, shifting uncomfortably. Mac was one of those men who was easy to read. He always had been. I knew when he was lying, because he could never look you in the eye when he did, and he fidgeted uncontrollably. "I argued that Mallory wasn't ready for a leadership position, and after much convincing, he agreed. So, we're offering the management role to you."

My jaw dropped. "You're... what?"

"I don't know why you're surprised," he said, cocking a brow. "I think everyone in this town knows the position is rightfully yours."

I swallowed. "But, they announced at the party that the position was Mallory's."

"Are you deaf, son? Did you not just hear me?"

"I did," I assured him, shaking my head — because it didn't make sense. Patrick Scooter didn't go back on his decisions, especially once he'd announced them to the entire town. "I'm sorry, sir. I guess I'm just a little confused."

"Yes, well, that makes two of us," he murmured, standing. Apparently, the conversation was done. "Anyway, we've got about a month before I'm trading in this name tag for a life of golfing and fishing. So, we have work to do.

Have Joseph take your tours today. I want you to figure out a transition plan, and then set up time for us to train."

"Yes, sir."

He nodded, but before he could make his way out the door, I called after him.

"Mac?"

"Hmm?"

I swallowed. "What does this mean for Mallory? I mean… is she… is she taking my spot, or?"

Mac shrugged. "Apparently, she's not working here at all anymore. Once she found out we were giving you the position, Patrick said she quit. And is selling her studio, too, I guess. Said she's done with this town, that she's leaving and never coming back." He shook his head. "I'll never understand that niece of mine. Go through all that trouble to buy and build a studio, have a grand opening, just to shut it down a week later?" He scoffed. "This is why women shouldn't run businesses. Too emotional, you know?"

I kept my mouth shut, offering him an awkward smile and a nod before he let himself out of my office. When I was alone again, I blew out a breath, mind racing as I tried to piece it all together.

Patrick Scooter would never go back on a decision he'd made. Never. Not without there being a *very* good reason.

And Mallory wouldn't give up her studio — not after all she'd done to bring that dream to life.

Something was off. Something was wrong.

I put an *out of office* email up before I stood, swiping my jacket off the back of my chair and practically running back out to my truck. Mac wouldn't miss me for a day, not if this really was the new direction we were going. Hell, I could make a transition and training plan in an hour.

And I needed to find out what the hell was going on.

I needed to find *her*.

If what Mac said was true, and the studio was being sold, I didn't have a clue where to find her. That was her place — her home, her getaway, her sanctuary. I didn't know where to even start, aside from hunting down her best friend, Chris. Maybe he'd tell me where she was.

Then again, maybe he'd spit in my face. After the way I'd talked to Mallory, I deserved it.

My stomach twisted into a tight knot as I threw my truck in drive and peeled out of the parking lot, wondering what had happened, what Mallory's father had done.

Suddenly, the only thing that mattered was making sure she was safe.

And finding her before she left Stratford — and *me* — forever.

Chapter Nineteen

Mallory

Crying was disgusting.

I remembered now why I had avoided it at all costs during my adult life. I was snotting all over myself, my eyes were red and puffy, lashes wet and clouding my vision as I added in the final details to the painting I'd been working on all day. I kept wiping my nose on the back of my wrist because I was too engrossed in what I was creating to get up and get a tissue, and besides, what did it matter? I was alone in the half-empty studio that would soon be completely bare again, just like I'd found it, and then auctioned off to the highest bidder.

I knew I looked like a complete wreck in my baggy black sweatpants and oversized Nine Inch Nails t-shirt, my hair piled on top of my head, and now, an ugly cry face, too. At least I hadn't bothered to put on makeup, so there was no scary mascara streaking down my face.

Again, not that it mattered, since I was very, *very* alone.

It was, perhaps, the loneliest I'd felt in my entire life, sitting in that studio with my hands creating art in an attempt to remind myself there was something worth breathing for. And as another wave of tears hit me, my face twisting with the gut-wrenching arrival of them, I tried to pinpoint what had set them into motion — but I couldn't.

It had all hit me at once.

I'd been holed up in my room upstairs all morning, *not* packing — though I should have been, and reading the end of *All the Light We Cannot See*, instead. Maybe it was because I wanted to escape my new reality. Or maybe it was because I wanted to feel some sort of tie to Logan again — no matter how small.

Regardless, when I finished, I closed the book, stared at the wall, blinked several times, and then, I sobbed.

I cried for Maurie-Laure, for Verner, for the horrors and tragedies of war and for the beautiful victories of life lived after. I cried for the man who had given me that book, who I wished I could call and talk to about it, who I wished

I could laugh and play with like I had just weeks before. I cried for my art studio, for the dream I'd barely seen brought to life before I'd forfeited it. And I cried for my family — or rather, my lack thereof — for the little girl who had her innocence stolen and for the woman who realized maybe no family was better than the family she had.

Not that I had a choice. My father had made that for me.

Just like he threatened, I was excommunicated from the family. He didn't even let me talk to my mom or my brother again, and explained to me that they were already told what I'd done, and that they had no interest in speaking with me, anyway. I figured it was true for my brother, who believed whatever Dad said, but I couldn't stomach that Mom felt the same. And I knew even if she didn't, she was too scared of my father to come find me, to try to make it right.

And so, I was alone.

I had roughly a week left to get out of the studio before Dad would have me formally evicted. Chris had offered his couch for as long as I needed, but past that, I didn't have a plan.

I didn't have anything.

Something inside me surged, like a warm, bright burst of morning light, because that wasn't true. I *did* have something — my pride. My dignity. My moral compass, pointing due north.

I had done what was right, even knowing it wouldn't be easy, and that was enough to ease the pain.

It was another cold night, and since Dad had already cut off the electricity, I was painting by the light of several candles, wrapped up in a blanket on one of the few bar stools left. My arm and hand were freezing, but I was almost done with the painting I'd started that afternoon, as soon as I'd finished the book.

It was the most powerful scene I'd ever read — the version that I saw in my head, anyway. It was my Maurie-Laure and Verner, sitting on the curb in Saint Malo. It was a young, innocent boy trapped in a war as a villain he never intended to play, and a young, innocent blind girl who fell in love with a world she could not see — even when it was at its ugliest.

That scene was one I would never forget. Just like the book. Just like the boy who *gave* me the book.

And I wanted to immortalize all of it with that painting.

Fireworks were already spouting off here and there outside, even though we were far from midnight and the hour that would welcome in a new year. The sounds were dull and distant, so when a knock sounded at the shop front door, I nearly jumped out of my skin.

When I turned and found Logan on the other side of the glass, I was paralyzed altogether.

Small bursts of fireworks were going off somewhere in the distance behind and above him, casting him in soft pink and purple and blue glows as he stood there, hands in the pockets of his Carhartt jacket, hair a mess under his navy blue ball cap. My feet carried me numbly to him, and it felt like someone else's hand unlocking the door, someone else stepping back to allow him inside. When the candlelight reached his face, I saw how dark his eyes were, how his beard was longer than usual and scraggly like I'd never seen it.

He didn't say anything at first. He just looked at me, at the blanket around my shoulders, the tears marking my face, the bird's nest of hair on top of my head. Then, he looked behind me — at the painting, at the book on the stand next to it — and then back at me.

My bottom lip quivered, and I sniffed, trying and failing to fight back another wave of tears. "I told you I'm not good with emotions."

Logan smirked, opening his arms, and I padded forward until I was in them. He wrapped me up in a tight hug, and I cried harder when I felt that embrace, when my head rested against his chest, his chin on top of my head, his distinct scent of whiskey and wood and old books surrounding me in comfortable familiarity.

He sighed, as if that embrace was all he'd been wanting, too. And for the longest time, he just held me there, arms wrapped tight, hearts beating in sync, me crying on his shoulder.

"I take it you finished," he said, voice rumbling through where my ear rested on his chest.

I nodded. "I told you not to make me cry, Logan."

"Well, you made me cry first, so I think we're even."

My heart ached at that, and I pulled back, looking up at him through my wet lashes. "You're right. I guess I deserved it, huh?"

He chuckled, sweeping the mess of hair that had fallen loose from my ponytail away from my face. His eyes catalogued every part of me, but he didn't look at me like I was the hot mess express in pajamas.

He looked at me like I was a priceless, one-of-a-kind, first edition of his favorite novel.

"I thought you were gone," he croaked, voice low. "I came by earlier this morning, and the shop was so empty, and you didn't answer... I've been looking all over town for you."

"You have?"

He nodded, that favorite wrinkle of mine making its appearance between his eyebrows. "Mac came to my office first thing this morning and told me he talked to your dad, that he convinced him they made a mistake by giving you the management position. He said it was mine, and that you had quit, that you were selling the studio and leaving town and..." He swallowed, shaking his head. "I just knew something was wrong, something was off. I had to find you."

I laughed, wiping my nose with the back of my wrist with a shrug. "Welp. Here I am."

A hint of a smile touched his lips, but it disappeared quickly, his eyes searching mine. "What happened?"

"I don't even know where to start," I said, blowing out a breath. My hands gathered at the center of his chest, and I looked at them instead of at his golden eyes. "I was sick all that night, after what happened. I wanted to run to you, to beg for you to believe me when I said I had nothing to do with what happened. But after our fight..." I shrugged. "You were right. I may not have played an active role in it, but somewhere, in the back of my mind, I knew what my father was capable of. I knew making any kind of deal with him was dangerous."

"I'm sorry for the way I spoke to you."

"You shouldn't be," I said, shaking my head. "I deserved it. And that next day, after wallowing in self-pity, of course, I came down here and I drew a sketch of you in my bed. And I looked at that picture of you on my wall. And I felt you in every inch of this room, of the room upstairs, of my *life*," I confessed. "And I knew I had to make it right somehow."

Another tear slipped down my cheek, but it didn't make it far before Logan was thumbing it away, and somehow, that made my chest squeeze even tighter.

"I told my dad he needed to make it right, that he knew as well as this entire town did that that position was yours — not mine. I told him if he *didn't* make it right, I would go to the *Gazette* with what happened that night when I was fourteen."

Logan inhaled. "Mallory..."

"I know," I said, glancing at him before my eyes fell to my hands on his chest again. "I know. Trust me, I didn't want to. I don't want to *ever* talk about that night with anyone ever again. But, I was willing to do it, if I had to. And I knew my father well enough that it wouldn't come to that. He doesn't want another mark on our name — not now, especially after everything that happened with Mayor Barnett this summer." I sniffed. "Anyway, the next day, he told me I had two weeks to get out of my apartment, that he was sending movers to take all the furniture and art supplies to auction, and that I was never to talk to anyone in my family ever again."

Logan shook his head, framing my face with his hands and forcing me to look at him. "Why would you do that?" he asked urgently, searching my gaze. "It's just a job, Mallory. I could have done something else. I could have—"

"It's not just a job, and you know it," I argued. "It's your family's legacy. It's the position you've worked your entire adult life for — and the one you damn well deserve, too."

"But, your family," he whispered, then he looked around. "Your dream."

"My family was never family to begin with. Family sticks together, no matter what. They love each other and understand each other and they would never, *ever*, do what my father did to me — not when I was fourteen, not now."

I shivered. "And my dream is to bring art to kids. But, I don't need my father to make that happen. Maybe I'll go into education, or maybe I'll open up a shop of my own. Whatever I decide to do, I know one thing for sure — I don't need my father to do it. I don't want any part of his legacy, not with the way he's living it. I'm ashamed I even came back and agreed to that deal with the devil in the first place."

"You didn't do anything wrong," Logan assured me.

"No, I did. I did. And that's okay, I admit it, and I did what I had to do to make it right. When I came back, I was lost. I was fresh out of college and jobless with no money or career possibilities ahead of me. I fell right back into the trap I fought my whole life to escape. It was a moment of weakness, a moment of being on my knees. But, I'm standing again now."

The left side of Logan's mouth quirked up, and he nodded. "You are."

"On top of all that," I continued. "I realized something very important that day after I watched you walk away from me."

"What's that?"

"That if it means I can't have you, if it means hurting you, then it's not right. I don't care what *it* is." My hands began to tremble as I slid them up the rough fabric of his jacket, my eyes flicking to his mouth and back to those honey eyes. The blanket I'd been tucked under fell to the floor at our feet. "And I'm going to say something so crazy, you're going to want to commit me. Because I know it's too soon. I know that to most people, it would seem impossible. But..." I swallowed, shaking so bad I had to fist my hands in his jacket to keep from tumbling over. "I think I love you, Logan Becker. You poor sonofabitch."

Logan laughed, his eyes sparkling in the candlelight as he pulled me into him more, as if his warmth could stop the trembling that came with that admission.

"I can one up your crazy," he said.

"Oh, yeah?"

"Yeah. Move in with me."

My next breath didn't come, though my jaw dropped low enough to let in a giant gulp of air, had my lungs allowed it.

Logan smirked, chucking my chin with his knuckles until my mouth closed. "Move in with me, Mallory. We can figure everything else out together. Wanna know how I know?"

"How?" I barely whispered, still riddled with shock.

"Because I love you, too," he said, leaning down until his forehead met mine. "And I don't just think it. I know it."

"You're *insane*."

"As long as we can be crazy together."

Before I could laugh, his lips were on mine, hands sliding back to hold my neck and pull me into him. Two more tears slipped free when that man kissed me, and I leaned into it — into the pain, into the love, into the crazy. I leaned into the uncertain future that kiss promised me, into the man I trusted to get me through anything, and into the choices we'd both made that led to that moment.

He was my Romeo, and I his Juliet, and our families be damned — we were going to make it.

And this story *wouldn't* end in tragedy.

It was the wildest, most whirlwind of a month I'd ever experienced in my life — that month I spent falling for Logan Becker. When he took my hand and led me outside to watch the fireworks, bringing the blanket with him, I curled up inside that warmth with him with the most relieving sigh finding my lungs. I'd never felt so right, so sure, so... *at home*.

He leaned against the storefront of the shop — the one that we'd built up together, the one now empty once again — and I rested my back against his chest, eyes cast toward the sky. We watched those bursts of light fire off in the sky, talking about the week we'd spent apart and what each of us had been through. Logan promised me his family would come around, that he would find a way for that to happen, that somehow, we'd make it work. And though it scared the absolute shit out of me, I believed him.

For hours, we sat there in the cold, talking and holding each other and watching the town of Stratford say goodbye to another year passed.

When the clock struck midnight, Logan pulled me to stand, wrapped me in his arms, and kissed me into the new year, into a new future, into that new universe we promised to make — one where it was me and him against the world.

Then, he dragged me inside, up the stairs, and we made some fireworks of our own.

Epilogue

Logan

"Oh, come on, Mom! It's his graduation," Noah pleaded, holding the shot glass filled to the brim with Scooter Whiskey. "Just one shot."

"Absolutely not," she said, pointing a finger at Noah in warning. "I said no, and I mean it. I'm not naïve enough to think you boys didn't drink before you were twenty-one," she said, waving that finger across all of us older boys. "But, I've managed to keep this one away from the stuff so far, and I intend to keep it that way." She said the last part pointing at Mikey.

"I don't know what you're talking about," Jordan defended. "I was an innocent, law-abiding child."

Mom rolled her eyes, taking the shot glass from Noah and slamming it back herself. A wave of whistles and cheers rang out when she slammed the empty glass back down on the table, cringing and shaking her head against the burn.

"Atta girl, Laurelei!" Betty yelled, throwing her hand into the air for a high five.

Mom slapped it, smiling victoriously. "Now that that's settled, who's ready for cake?"

A unanimous show of hands went up, and she laughed, waving us off as the chatter kicked back in and she escaped to the kitchen to retrieve the massive graduation cake she'd ordered for Mikey.

My younger brother sat on the opposite side of the table from me, an easy grin on his face — and the closest thing I'd seen to his full smile since the fall. He'd changed since he and Bailey broke up. He'd grown quieter, more serious, and he preferred to be alone more now than he ever had before. Still, he seemed relaxed that day, and happy — and he was surrounded by everyone who loved him most to celebrate his accomplishment.

His best friend, Kylie, sat to his right, laughing at a story Betty was telling. Betty was a relatively new friend of the family, one Ruby Grace had brought with her when she and Noah started dating. Ruby Grace had worked down at the nursing home where Betty lived, and through that connection, she'd become one of Mom's best friends — and like a grandmother to all of us.

Ruby Grace was there, too, sitting next to Noah, who had his arm around her and a soft smile on his face as he watched her listen to Betty's story, too.

Jordan was on the other side of Mikey, currently holding his shoulder firmly as he bent low and whispered something meant for just the two of them. I was sure it was something similar to the advice he'd given me on my high school graduation day — advice that I still carried with me every day.

Fight for what's right, stand up for those who can't stand for themselves, give yourself permission to love and to lose and to be loved and lost in return, and above all else, family first — always.

And, perhaps my favorite addition to that family table at Mom's was the woman sitting next to me.

Mallory sipped on her gin and tonic, smiling at Betty while her fingers drew circles on my knee under the table. Her hair was a neon mix of orange and pink, bright colors that set her blue eyes aflame against her pale skin, and she had a fresh tattoo healing behind her ear. It was a small lotus flower, a symbol she'd told me reminded her that, like the lotus flower born from the mud, we must embrace the darkest parts of ourselves to become our most beautiful selves.

I reached down and covered her hand with my own, giving it a squeeze. She smiled, tossing me a wink before she turned her attention back to Betty, chiming in with her own story next. And I was content to sit back and listen, to watch her fit in with my family just like I knew she always would. It seemed she'd grown on everyone — even Jordan, who was perhaps the most hesitant. Once she moved in with me, they had no choice but to accept her as part of me.

That's what family did.

And it seemed like everyone was beginning to love her.

Well, everyone except for Mom.

She'd been quiet when I'd told my family that Mallory and I had made up, that we were in love, that she was moving in with me. She'd been quiet the first time I brought Mallory to dinner, too — but polite, of course. And though she hadn't warmed up much over the past five months, she hadn't disowned me, either.

I guessed that counted for something.

As for Mallory's family, they'd kept their word of disowning her. She hadn't spoken to any of them since that day she'd told her father off in his office, and though she tried to hide it, I knew it hurt her sometimes.

But *I* was her family, now. *We* were her family.

And unlike what she'd been used to before — we'd be a real one to her.

"Mallory, can you help me in the kitchen?" Mom called, and the table went silent for a moment.

Betty was quick to kick the conversation back in gear as Mallory stood, squeezing my shoulder. "Of course." She disappeared into the kitchen, and I worried my cheek wondering what Mom was saying to her.

"It's getting pretty serious with you two, isn't it?" Jordan asked, nodding toward the kitchen.

I couldn't hear what they were saying, but I kept my eyes on the women inside those walls, anyway. "Serious as the last two minutes of a tied Super Bowl."

Jordan chuckled, lifting his glass of whiskey. "Better hope Mom doesn't eat her alive, then."

I cheersed my glass to his, taking a long sip and letting it burn on the way down. Watching Mallory in the kitchen with Mom, I couldn't help but feel a surge of pride at the woman she was, the woman I loved, the woman who would someday be a part of our family. I knew it without a single doubt in my mind, especially after all we'd been through.

If the first month of our life hadn't been enough of a ride, the last five months would have sealed the deal. Between learning how to live together — her perpetually a mess, me perpetually a neat freak — and adjusting to a new way of life with each of our new careers, it had been a whirlwind. Mallory was spending every hour of her day creating, whether it was painting or sketching or crafting or photography. Anything she could make and sell at the craft fairs around the state, she made. It was all part of her plan to save up to buy a shop of her own one day, and I helped her in whatever way I could — even when she asked me to pose nude for an exotic series of black and white sketches she sold for fifteen grand at a romance novel festival.

As for me, I was working longer hours at the distillery, turning the tour guide department into what I'd always envisioned it could be. We had more tours being booked than ever before — more than we had people to *give* tours — which meant I had my hands full trying to figure out how to accommodate the new demand.

And while I loved chasing my dreams with her, my favorite moments with Mallory were the quiet ones, when we were on the couch, Dalí curled up in a ball between us, a book in our laps, soft music playing in the background. I loved reaching over to close her book, to kiss her, to pull her into our bedroom where we made love.

I loved sharing my life with her.

And I knew without hesitation that I wanted to do it forever.

Mom carried the cake in, setting it down in the middle of the table with slices already pre-cut. She distributed small paper plates and my heathen brothers dug in immediately as Mallory took her seat next to me again.

"Everything okay?" I asked.

She smiled, unfolding her napkin and putting it in her lap again. "Everything's fine. She was just threatening to hang me by my neon ponytail if I ever hurt her baby boy."

I blanched. "She didn't."

"Oh, she did," Mallory assured me on a laugh, patting my knee. "But, I don't blame her. And it was a good talk, one I'm glad we had. I have to prove to her that I'm not like the rest of my family, and I don't think that's an unfair request. It's also not a challenge I'm not willing to take on." She leaned in, pressing a quick kiss to my lips. "Especially for you."

I smirked, squeezing her hand where it grabbed mine under the table just as Mom called our attention.

"Now, before you go digging in," she said, swatting my hand where I was about to put the first bit of cake in my mouth.

"Hey!"

"I'd like to take a moment to say something," she said. She clasped her hands gently in front of her, and with the evening light pouring into the house, the silver of her hair shone a brassy gold. "Michael, this is one of the most important days of your life. It is a day you will never forget, a closing of one door and opening of the next. And no matter where this life takes you, I want you to always know that you have a home to come back to, and a family that loves you, very, very much."

"Hear, hear," Jordan said, lifting his glass. The rest of us lifted ours in unison.

"To Michael," Mom said, tears in her eyes now. "Our baby boy, a baby no longer."

We all cheered and whistled, taking a drink before digging into our cake. Mikey stood and wrapped Mom in a big hug, and as soon as they had both sat down, Noah stood. He seemed nervous, and when I realized he hadn't touched his cake, I narrowed my eyes, looking between him and the offending slice.

"Uh, while we're all gathered here," he said, clearing his throat. "I wanted to let you all know we have another cause for celebration."

The whole table went quiet, and we all knew before he even said his next words.

He reached for Ruby Grace's hand, and when she stood with him, it was the first time we'd all taken our heads out of the sand and noticed the rock on her finger.

"Yesterday, I asked Ruby Grace to marry me," he said, beaming at the red-haired beauty beside him. "And she said yes."

Betty was the first to jump up, wrapping Ruby Grace in a fierce hug as she went on and on about Richard Gere, for some odd reason. Mom was *really* crying now as she stood to hug Noah, and we all took turns embracing each of them and offering our congratulations.

"What an exciting day," Mom said when we were sitting again, dabbing at her eyes with her napkin. She laughed when Jordan offered his, too. "I'm just a mess."

"You had to know this was what you were getting yourself into with four boys," Kylie said.

Mom chuckled. "Yes, I suppose I did."

Kylie was a tiny little thing — maybe five-foot-two wearing heels. She had long, dark, chestnut hair and the classic girl-next-door face. She'd always kind of felt like one of the guys when we were younger. I remembered her playing man hunt with all of us out in the backyard, and had a distinct memory of her knocking one of Mikey's teeth out when he said something she apparently didn't like. Now, though, she and Mikey both looked like they were caught in some strange in-between — not yet a man and woman, but far from a boy and a girl.

It made my chest hurt a little to see them growing up like that.

She'd been around more that spring, trying to help Mikey break into our dad's hard drive. It apparently was more encrypted than we knew, though, and she said she could do it, but it would take time.

Michael took a sip of his water when we were all settled again, clearing his throat with his eyes on his glass. "While we're making announcements, I guess now is as good a time as any to tell you guys…"

"Tell us what, sweetie?" Mom asked.

Mikey looked around the table, and then he sniffed, eyes back on his glass. "I'm going to spend the next few months here in Stratford, enjoy one last summer in my hometown. But, after that, I'm moving."

Everyone stopped what they were doing — forks suspended in mid-bite, hands paused around glasses, all eyes on my baby brother.

"To New York."

There was a very, *very* small stretch of silence — and then all hell broke loose.

Mom started crying — this time, they weren't happy tears. Jordan immediately launched into not making hasty decisions while Noah argued that he couldn't leave the distillery. I opened my mouth to chime in, but Mallory squeezed my knee in warning under the table, and when I looked at her, she just shook her head.

"You guys can yell and holler all you want, but my mind's made up," he said over the chaos, standing and tossing his napkin down on the table. "I'm eighteen now and this isn't a choice that any of you get to make for me. So, you can either support me, or not, but either way, I'm going."

With that, he stormed across the house and out the front door, footsteps thumping down the porch steps.

Kylie grimaced, folding her own napkin and setting it on the table beside him before she stood. "I'll go talk to him."

When they were both gone, Mom's whimpers were the only sound at the table. Jordan reached over to hug her, and Betty smiled, turning the attention back to the good news of Noah and Ruby Grace's engagement.

"So, tell us how he proposed," she urged.

And, at least for the moment, Mikey's news was put aside.

I was still reeling from it all when Mallory and I pulled into our driveway later that evening, and I felt like a zombie opening the car door for her, carrying the leftovers Mom sent with us inside, and plopping down on the couch. Mallory sat next to me, running her fingers through my hair and watching me with worried eyes.

"You okay?"

I nodded, though I wasn't entirely sure. "I just... I can't believe he wants to move. To *New York*, of all places." I shook my head. "This has always been our home. I guess I never considered the possibility that one of us could leave it."

"Maybe he'll change his mind," she soothed.

"Maybe. But if he doesn't, I'll support him. That's what he would do for me in the reverse. I should put it on my work calendar now that I'll be out a couple weeks at the end of summer, just in case he needs help moving."

Mallory smiled, moving until she was lying on my chest. "You're a good brother."

We laid there like that for a while, both of us quiet, until a soft chuckle left her lips.

"What about your other brother? Getting married?"

I smiled. "That wasn't as much of a surprise. I knew when he first got caught up with that girl that he'd marry her one day."

"Oh, yeah?" Mallory asked, scooting up to look at me. "How'd you know?"

"He looked at her the way I look at you," I explained easily, moving her hair away from her face. "Like forever was sitting right there in her eyes."

Mallory made a gagging notion with her finger, rolling her forever eyes.

I laughed. "What? You don't like the sweet romance?"

"Not when it's cheesier than a pizza from Mario's."

"You'll let me cover you in all the romantic cheese I want to," I said, wrapping her in my arms while she squealed and played like she wanted to get away.

We both knew she didn't.

"And you'll like it, too," I said, kissing her.

She chuckled. "Fine. But when you and I decide to tie the knot, promise me one thing?"

"Anything."

Mallory grinned. "Let me shove cake in your face."

I blanched. "But then I'll have icing all over my face."

"Mm-hmm," she agreed, still grinning as she kissed my nose. "And probably all over your tux, too."

I wrinkled my nose. "Sounds messy."

"Well, you did agree to let me be the mess in your life," she reminded me.

And when she leaned in to press her lips to mine again, I held her there, deepening the kiss with a promise that I'd do anything she ever asked.

Because what a beautiful mess she was.

Manhattan

Here's to the raw pain of being the friend,

the just friend,

the one who's everything, and yet somehow,

not quite anything at all.

And to those who hold onto the possibility that maybe,

just maybe,

there could be something more.

This one's for you.

Prologue

Kylie

My high school graduation was a day of fireworks.

Everything felt like a dream, the way it always does when you stare up into the night sky on the Fourth of July and watch those glowing sparks fill the air.

I got dressed in my white, tea-length dress and put my burgundy gown on over it, finishing the look with the matching graduation cap, the tassel on the right, waiting to be flipped over once I walked across that stage.

Boom.

I stood in the living room of the tiny apartment I shared with my father, trying not to cry as his eyes filled with tears and he placed my honors cords around my shoulders, adjusting the golden fringes so they sat just right.

Pop.

I smiled with my chest swelling like a balloon as my father hugged me, held me in his arms, and whispered, *"She'd be proud of you"* in my ear.

Fizz.

Every moment, every second that filled every hour that filled that day was a series of bursts. Booms and pops and fizzes, bright lights and smoke, a dream that someone else was living and I was merely watching.

The only moment of clarity came when I drove over to my best friend's house for pictures before the ceremony.

Michael Becker waited for me on the porch, something close to a smile on his lips when he saw me climb out of my truck, Dad pulling in right behind me. Our families hugged and exchanged choked-up *"Can you believe it"* as Mikey and I laughed and shook our heads.

He teased me about the fact that I was wearing a dress.

I teased him about the patchy scruff on his chin.

But in that moment, when he took my hand and said, *"Let's go walk that stage,"* I felt the fireworks more than ever.

Boom.

Pop.

Fizz.

My eyes found his when he walked across the stage in our high school gym, "Pomp and Circumstance" playing in the background just like we knew it always would. And when it was my turn, he cheered the loudest — which was saying something, considering how loudly my dad whooped and hollered.

Then, to the tune of hundreds of families applauding and our fellow graduates cheering like we'd won the lottery, we tossed our caps into the air.

My eyes were on Mikey.

Boom.

Pop.

Fizz.

Fireworks. Endless sparks and an undoubtable feeling that the best was yet to come, that we were on the precipice of something new, something unforgettable.

A new adventure.

And when we all gathered for dinner at Mikey's after, the feeling of family surrounded me. My best friend was on my right, his family that had always been mine, too, sat all around us, and there was so much to celebrate.

First, his mom delivered our cake, and made a cheers to her youngest son on his accomplishment.

Then, Mikey's older brother, Noah, announced his engagement to Ruby Grace Barnett.

The smoke from that firework hadn't even settled before Mikey cleared his throat, and announced that he had something to say, too. I thought maybe a toast, or a thank you, or perhaps a gift for his mother.

But instead, he opened his mouth and dropped the biggest bomb of them all.

"I'm moving to New York."

The chaos that ensued was lost on me, mostly because I was sitting next to him, shell shocked, wondering if I'd heard the words correctly. I was so sure I hadn't.

It couldn't be my best friend who just said he was leaving our hometown, the one he grew up in, the one his father died in, the one he loved. It couldn't be Michael Becker, the boy I'd shared everything with for years, saying he was spending one last summer in Stratford before he packed up and made his way to the big city.

It couldn't be Mikey, the boy I'd loved in secret for years, saying that my time to tell him that was running out.

But it was.

And I knew exactly why.

Bailey Baker.

The first girl Mikey dated. The first girl Mikey fell in love with. And the girl who left him completely behind in October, when she dropped out of school to chase her dreams in Nashville — *without him*, even though their plans were always to go together.

It was *her* he wanted to flee from, her he was trying to escape. I knew maybe more than anyone at that table that his motivation to leave our town and live in the city that never sleeps was born and bred in that girl we all wished we could help him forget.

And that's when it hit me.

The fuse I'd thought was endless shortened in a breath, the bright flash of a mortar blinding me with one searing truth.

This was it. My last chance to tell my best friend that I wanted more, that I always had, that he couldn't leave me — not when I'd just gotten him back.

So, right then and there, as his brothers drilled him with questions and his mother sobbed as he flew out the front door, telling all of them that his mind was made up, I made a plan.

One summer.

One list of adventures to remind him that our small town has more to offer than memories of the girl who left him behind.

One last chance to tell him I'm in love with him.

And in that moment, I was just dumb enough to think that maybe he could love me, too.

Boom.

Pop.

Fizz.

Chapter One

Michael

I woke up the day after my high school graduation feeling completely under-whelmed.

This day I had looked forward to for so long had come and gone like any other Saturday, and though I was skeptical that I'd feel any different, part of me hoped I would. Part of me wished to feel something — *anything* — other than the hollow emptiness I'd been drowning in since October.

But, here I was, eighteen years old and no longer bound to the fluorescent lights and locker-lined halls of Stratford High, and all I could think as I stared up at the popcorn ceiling in my bedroom was how absolutely disappointing it all was.

I sighed, kicking off my navy blue, flannel comforter and padding bare-foot down the hall to the bathroom I'd once shared with my three older broth-ers. Now, it was all mine, save for the few times a year that one or two of them stayed the night.

I was on autopilot, going through the same routine I had every morning, feeling the same numbness that I'd lived in since the light of my life walked away from me like I was nothing to her. That rainy day in October had splin-tered my life into two: Before Bailey Left and After Bailey Left.

B.B.L. was the best part of my life. It was filled with music, and laughter, and romance. I was needed and wanted, I had a purpose, I had someone to take care of, someone to take care of *me*. I had a partner, a plan, a life just waiting for us to live it — together.

A.B.L. had, so far, been the most miserable part of my life — and that was saying something, considering my father passed away when I was a kid. But I'd been young then, and I'd continued on, finding solace in my family and childhood best friend. As crazy as it sounded, even *that* loss didn't compare to the all-encompassing one I felt when Bailey broke up with me, telling me she was going to Nashville to pursue her music dreams *without* me, instead of *with* me, like we'd always planned.

It was supposed to be me and her — always.

It was supposed to be high school graduation, then us moving to Nashville together.

It was supposed to be her working with her label, playing at the bars on the Nashville strip, traveling the country to visit radio stations and play sold-out shows at local country bars before she hit it big and burned up the Country Top 100 charts.

And it was supposed to be me, right there beside her, supporting her and building that life we always envisioned we'd have together.

Instead, she'd dropped me like I was a weight holding her back instead of a hand pushing her up and forward and *on*. She asked for time, for space, for the chance to focus on her music — as if I'd ever asked her to give any of that up for me.

Bailey was my high school sweetheart, but I'd never classified her as that. I'd always seen her as my *everything*. She wasn't just high school. She was college, and first job, and marriage, and first house, and four kids of our own. The simple fact that we started dating my sophomore year didn't make me see her as a stage in my life — one that existed only in high school. No, that fact didn't mean anything to me, really, because I always felt like we'd have found each other one way or another, at some other point in our life, had we not grown up in the same town.

But obviously, my romantic view of what we had was warped — because I didn't ever think she'd leave me, and here we were.

When she left, I realized that she didn't just take part of me with her — she took *all* of me. I didn't have an identity outside of who I was when I was with her, and once she was gone, it was as if I'd disappeared into thin air. I was still here, breathing, existing, but past that?

Nothing.

Seven months after our breakup, and I still ran through all those thoughts every single morning as I brushed my teeth, combed my mess of hair, shaped up what little stubble I could grow on my face and neck, and said a silent prayer before facing whatever I had ahead of me that day.

But, in *one* way, today was different.

I might have still been miserable, and lonely, and lost. I might have still felt like the same kid I was the day before I graduated now that I was here on the other side. But, the Michael Becker *before* high school graduation was just another country boy living in Stratford, Tennessee.

The Michael Becker *today* was on his way to The Big Apple.

A flitter of something close to excitement whirled through me at the thought as I made my way down the hall and into the kitchen. I'd been sitting on the decision for months now, knowing I didn't have anything here in Stratford for me anymore, and knowing that in every book and movie and song, New York City was where you went to find yourself.

Still, it didn't go over well with my family — not my three older brothers, who were adamant about all of us staying here in this town together and keeping our late father's legacy alive. And not my mother, who would have an empty nest, once I left this house she and my father had bought together just after their marriage.

The house we'd made a home.

The house we'd stayed in after my father died.

The house each brother left, one by one, until it was just me and Mom and the memories within these old walls.

The wood floor of the kitchen creaked under my foot as I dipped inside the fridge, pulling out the jug of milk and drinking straight from it. Mom was on the porch just like she was every Sunday morning, rocking in her favorite chair and drinking her coffee with her eyes washing over the front yard.

I took a moment to watch her from inside, noting the gray of her hair that had appeared in the last couple of years, the laugh lines that were more pronounced on her cheeks. Her eyes were the same goldish-green as mine, and even from this angle, I could see the sun reflecting in those forest-like pools.

Every time I saw her out there, I had a flashback of the same vision, but with my father there beside her — one hand holding the newspaper, the other on her knee, both of them rocking side by side.

I shook the thought away, pushing through the screen door with a little more hesitance than I was used to. Mom's eyes were still a bit swollen from all the crying she did last night — and those tears were my fault. I'd told her and the rest of my family at my graduation dinner that I was leaving for New York at the end of the summer.

To say they hadn't taken it well would be a gross understatement.

"Mornin', Mama," I said, leaning a hip against the porch railing.

She blinked, as if she hadn't even noticed that I'd joined her, and then she gave me the best smile she could manage — one tinged with sadness and worry. "Ah, good morning, my high school graduate. Feeling like an adult yet?"

I attempted a smirk but wasn't sure if my mouth actually moved from its perpetual state of flatness. "Totally. Going to invest in some stocks today and go to bed at eight-thirty. Growing some facial hair, too," I said, rubbing my chin where the most impressive amount of scruff I'd had so far in my life was coming in. "See?"

Mom chuckled, cupping her mug of coffee and rocking gently. "I'm so proud of you, Michael Andrew." She paused, brows folding. "But, I'm so worried about you, too."

"Mom..." I warned, letting my eyes roll up to the porch awning. "Please, I don't want to rehash what we already talked to death last night."

When I looked back at my mother, her bottom lip was trembling slightly, and as much as I didn't want to cause her any pain, I also didn't want to argue with her over why me moving to New York was my decision and no one else's.

I pushed away from the railing, opening my arms wide. "Come here."

Mom sniffed, setting her coffee cup down and standing to give me a hug. I wrapped my arms completely around her, and she sighed, resting her head on my chest.

"I just… I don't know what I'm going to do without you here."

"I'll visit," I promised. "And *you* can visit *me,* too. See the big city, the lights, Times Square. Doesn't that sound fun?"

"Sounds scary," she murmured against my shirt.

I kissed her hair, resting my chin on the crown of her head. "It's all going to be alright, Mama. I promise. Just trust me, okay? Trust that you and Dad raised me well, and that I wouldn't make any decisions without thinking them through from every angle first."

She nodded, wiping a tear away when she pulled back from my grasp. She forced a shaky smile again, her eyes still glossy. "You too adult to join your mother at church?"

I shook my head. "Never. Leave here in twenty?"

"And not a minute later."

I still felt the weight of my mother's grief on my shoulders as I went back to my room to change, pulling on a simple button-up and khakis before grabbing the Bible that used to be my father's out of my bedside table drawer. I tucked it under my arm, grabbing my phone off the charger just as the screen lit up with a new text message.

Ky: Hey, can we meet up after church? It's important.

I smiled at the text from my best friend — mostly because it was just like her to be dramatic before nine AM.

Me: If this is because you forgot to sleep with your retainer in again, I'll only say it one more time — your teeth will not go back to being crooked over one night.

Ky: Ha, ha. First of all, it's possible for teeth to move substantially within a forty-eight-hour period. Secondly, stop being a jerk and meet me at Blondie's after church.

Ky: I'll even buy you a pistachio brittle cone.

Me: Twist my arm, why don't ya? I'll be there.

Kylie and I had been thick as thieves since we were kids — well, aside from the two years I'd dated Bailey. She hadn't exactly been okay with me having a female best friend — even when I *assured* her that I didn't even see Kylie as a girl — so, we'd taken a step back, going from hanging out nearly every day to just texting now and then and seeing each other at school.

But when Bailey left, and I had no one, Kylie was right there for me. And it was like no time had passed at all.

If I was being honest, I wasn't sure I'd still be alive if it weren't for that girl.

Ky: For the record, that's still a disgusting ice cream flavor, and you're still weird for liking it.

Me: If I wasn't weird, you wouldn't be my friend.

Ky: Touché. See you soon.

I checked my appearance in the mirror one last time, smoothing a hand over my shaggy, walnut hair, and then I drove Mama to church just like I did every Sunday morning.

And the feeling of nothing changing after high school graduation continued.

Chapter Two

Kylie

I fell in love with Michael Becker at the ripe old age of eight years old.

Of course, no one knew that fact except for me, because Mikey and I had always been in the proverbial land known as "The Friend Zone." But, it was true. I fell for that kid like a penny off the Empire State Building — fast and silently and unbeknownst to anyone other than the poor concrete that I hit and dented when I crashed to the ground.

And me.

I would never forget the way I fell for him, not in all the years I lived. And no matter how I tried to *unfall* for him, it was useless. Something about that boy had me wound up tight — breath shallow, heart beating a little too fast, eyes wide and child-like. Maybe that was why I hadn't batted an eye at us becoming friends, at him eventually telling me I was his best friend, at stepping up and taking that role with pride — like *first best friend* was somehow a sure stepping stone to *first true love.*

It had been the longest summer of my life, the summer after second grade, because I'd watched my mother wither away like a flower starved of water in just six short weeks. The day after school, she was completely fine. We went camping — her, my father, and me — just like we did every year when school let out. It was a celebration of summer, a weekend full of s'mores and swimming and Dad attempting to teach me how to fish.

But the day we got back home, Mom got sick.

And she never got better.

The doctors couldn't figure out what was wrong, and the specialists they referred us to were just as lost. Mom suffered from chronic headaches so bad she couldn't leave the dark bedroom — a room that I remembered smelling like dirty laundry and dust. She couldn't keep anything down, and even when we moved her to the hospital so they could administer fluids, her body rejected them.

A mysterious disease, they said.

Perhaps a tick or mosquito gave it to her, they guessed.

Nothing we can do, they admitted with sad eyes.

Six weeks. That was all it took for me to lose the mother who was supposed to be there for me always, and for how it took my father down, he might as well have died along with her.

So, when I went back to school on that first day of third grade, I didn't know who I was or what to feel or who to turn to or what to do. The first day of school had always been fun for me — new clothes, new supplies, new backpack, new classroom, new teacher, new friends. I loved to learn, loved to discover, loved to read, even loved homework and tests and all the things that most kids hated.

But I couldn't love anything — not after that summer.

At least, that's what I thought — until Michael Becker sat next to me on the playground.

He had the same miserable look about him, his eyes on his shoes, arms wrapped around his knees. He'd sat down on the other side of the tree trunk where I was hiding, watching the other kids play, wishing I wanted to play, too.

"Hi," I said tentatively.

"Hi," he barely murmured back.

Silence.

"Are you okay?" I asked.

He shook his head.

I nodded, drawing a circle in the dirt with my finger. "Me either."

"My dad died," he said, simply and without emotion, like he was telling me what his favorite color was.

Something in me changed then — right in that moment — because I looked at Michael Becker over my shoulder, and for the first time, I really saw him.

We'd been in the same class in first grade, but I hadn't seen him then. We'd played on the playground a few times in second grade, but again, I hadn't seen him then, either.

It was only then, on the playground the first day of third grade, that I truly saw the boy with the dead eyes and the perpetual frown.

"My momma died, too."

He looked up at me, his shaggy brown hair blowing in the wind, and then he scooted over — once, twice — and reached out his hand for mine.

And that was it.

That one, seemingly insignificant exchange between two eight-year-olds was what did me in. Michael Becker grabbed my hand, and we somehow found a friendship in the hollow darkness of the pain we both shared.

The rest was history.

I didn't mind being friend zoned — mostly because, when I was younger, I didn't know that was what was happening. All I knew was that Michael and

I were spending every recess together, and every afternoon after school, and every weekend. All I knew was that his three rambunctious older brothers and angel of a mother felt like they were mine, and my father loved Mikey like he was his own, and we knew more about each other than anyone else.

It wasn't until the end of middle school that I realized I was ready for more, that I wanted to cross over that friend line into something that might involve more hand-holding, and maybe some kissing, and *definitely* a different title.

I wanted to go from *best friend* to *girlfriend*, and the way I saw it, there was no way it wouldn't happen.

Mikey loved me, even if he didn't realize it. He so effortlessly knew what I needed and when I needed it, we hung out every single day, he told me things he didn't tell anyone else. All I needed was for him to open his dumb boy eyes and see that I was, in fact, a *girl* — with boobs and everything.

Okay, so *maybe* my boobs didn't come in until junior year, but still.

I was ready. And I was patient. I had faith that the day would come when he'd look at me and see me in a different light.

But all of that went to hell at our sophomore homecoming — because Bailey freaking Baker asked Mikey to dance, and from that moment on, my best friend was a stupid, pathetic, love-sick teenage boy.

And not over me.

I watched the boy I'd loved my whole life fall in love with someone else, and I'd somehow smiled through it all.

I'd been there to offer advice when he wasn't sure how to ask her on a date, to help him dress for said first date, and to listen to him gush and freak out *after* said first date. I was there the day he asked her to be his girlfriend, the day they had their first make-out session, and the day they got into their first fight.

Which just so happened to be because of me.

Bailey didn't like him hanging out with me all the time, and she *definitely* didn't like the fact that I was a girl — although, that was still a fact that Michael was completely oblivious to.

And so, I'd smiled and assured him it was okay, that I understood, that *of course* we could cut back on hanging out after school and on the weekends. We always had school, right? We always had each other, right?

Wrong.

Day by day, week by week, month by month, we talked less and less, and my best friend became a stranger.

And still, I loved him.

Maybe that was why I was double-checking the list I'd stayed up making all night, reading over each bullet point, fine-tooth combing through it like it was a college application and not a silly last-ditch effort to keep Michael Becker from moving across the country.

When Bailey broke up with him and left Stratford for Nashville, it was me who was here to pick up the pieces. For the first time in two years, that piece of me that had been missing was back — even if he was a battered, bruised, and broody version of the boy I knew before.

Now, he wanted to leave.

And the simple fact of it was that I *refused* to accept that.

I wasn't ready to lose my best friend — not when I'd just got him back.

"In case you missed the news, school is out. You did it. You graduated. You don't have to study anymore," Dad said on a chuckle, taking the seat across from me at our small dining room table.

It was a piece of junk we bought when we moved into the tiny, two-bedroom apartment in the complex at the edge of town after Mom died. I sat at it every morning wishing we'd stayed in our old house so I could sit where Mom used to at our *old* dining room table — the one built by her dad, with a big leaf we'd put in the middle for holidays.

I made a face at his joke, which made him laugh again, and then my attention was right back on the notebook in my hands. "Got to keep sharp during this gap year, Pops."

"Maybe, but you know, a gap year is made for you to have fun — discover yourself, travel, forget about school for a while."

I cocked a brow. "Do you even know me? All I *do* is school."

He tipped his coffee mug at me. "Fair enough. You know, I think I still have your mom's journal from her gap year. I could dig it out for you," he offered. "Maybe it'd give you some ideas."

Something in my stomach twisted at the mention of Mom, the way it always had since she'd passed on. It felt a little like a hug from her and a little like a knife between the ribs all at once. "Really?"

Dad nodded. "She *is* the reason you're taking the gap year, after all," he said on a shrug. "Maybe you could see some of the same places she did."

I smiled, reaching over to squeeze Dad's hand with mine. "I'd love that."

When I pulled my attention back to the list in my hands, my stomach was fluttering for a completely different reason. Even though I'd known it was coming, high school graduation had somehow snuck up on me, and now, here I was, without a single plan on what was to come next.

It made absolutely zero sense, seeing as how I *loved* school and knew without a doubt that I wanted to go to college. But I hadn't submitted even a single application.

My memories with my mother were foggy, faded, similar to the dream that graduation had felt like yesterday. But one thing I remembered, when I sat in her lap one evening when we were camping, the fire crackling in front of us and the katydids chirping loudly in the trees, was how fondly she talked about her gap year.

I was only seven, and yet I could still remember her animated eyes as she told me about the road trip she'd taken, the places she had seen, the weird hotels she'd stayed in and the many car breakdowns she'd had along the way. She told me that was the year she'd found herself, the year she'd known she wanted to dance not just as a hobby, but as a career, and — eventually — she wanted to *teach* others to dance, too.

When she'd passed, I'd made a vow to do my own gap year in her honor, to take the year off after high school to find myself.

Now that it was here, it felt more scary than it did exhilarating, and I packed that fear away, focusing instead on the more pressing task at hand.

Dad frowned, peering at my notebook as he reached out a finger, trying to drag it toward him. "What are you working on, anyway?"

I snatched it out of his grasp before he could sneak a peek. "A list of places to travel, of course."

"You've always been the worst liar, Smiley."

I smiled at the nickname, one Mom had given me when I was younger on account of me having a smile the size of my face — even if it was full of crooked teeth at that time.

"My Smiley Kylie," she'd always cooed.

"It's nothing really, just something for Mikey."

"Ah," Dad said, sipping his coffee before he opened the Civil War book he was reading he was no longer interested. "You still upset about his big news from last night?"

Dad asked the question like it wasn't a big deal, like it was casual and he already knew I was fine, but we both knew otherwise.

"I'm fine," I lied. "I'm happy for him."

Neither of us said another word, but Dad reached for my hand, giving it a squeeze before he left me alone to work on my list while he read.

My father was the spitting image of Hugh Jackman — except a little older, a little grayer, and maybe a little pudgier around the middle. I used to joke with him when the *X-Men* movies came out that he was my real-life Wolverine — hairy knuckles and all.

But, the point was that my father was handsome — even in his old age. Every single woman over the age of forty had tried at one point or another to be his next wife after Mom had died, but he'd showed no interest. *Your mom was my one and only, and that's just that*, he'd say.

I got a mix of the two of them, my mom and dad — Dad's wide smile and chocolate brown eyes, Mom's heavy and straight-as-straw hair, Dad's narrow frame, Mom's petite height, and somehow, the perfect mix of their skin color, which meant I was white as snow in the winter, and dark as mud in the summer.

In theory, it sounded like a beautiful mixture of two perfect specimens, but I had somehow managed to be just completely average looking my entire life. In fact, I'd cried when I got my braces off because they were the only thing that brought a little spunk to my appearance. I was the classic, country, girl-next-door, slightly-nerdy and not at all girly wallflower of Stratford, Tennessee, who tutored the delinquents and made sandwiches for the homeless — because, as my father always loved to point out, helping others was in my blood, just like it had been in my mother's.

Sometimes, Dad would argue that I took care of *him* more than he took care of me.

But, I'd argue right back.

My father was a quiet man, but he was also a *hard-working* man, and — though it pained me to admit — he was also a *different* man than the one I'd had as a father before Mom passed away. She took a part of him when she went, and the piece of him left behind smiled a little less, laughed a little softer, worried a little more.

Dad worked fifty hours a week as a forklift operator at the Scooter Whiskey Distillery. He'd been in that job for as long as I could remember, with no intention of moving up or out. Work was just that to him — a job, a way to make ends meet. For him, it was the life *outside* of work that made a man. And outside of work, my father liked to study, investigate, and relive the Civil War. Three times a year, he would get all dressed up in his Union soldier attire to reenact some of the bloodiest wars in Tennessee, and it was during those times that I wondered if my father had lived a past life, one where he really *was* a soldier on those fields, because he came to life more with that uniform on than he ever did in a Scooter Whiskey t-shirt.

I stared for a long moment at the hand he'd squeezed before I pulled my attention back to the notebook I'd been scribbling in all night. I knew I only had one shot to convince Mikey to listen to me, because as much as any other Becker boy, he was stubborn as all get out.

From the way he spoke last night, he'd already made up his mind.

It was New York City or bust.

But when we were eight years old, that boy wrapped his pinky around mine and he made a promise to me that he would always listen to me, no matter what.

I could only hope he'd follow through on that promise all these years later.

Chapter Three

Michael

The outrageous line at Blondies was the first sign that summer had finally arrived.

Blondies was the one and only ice cream shop in town, and during the off-season, a small line would form in front of the window — mostly after school or right after the public pool shut down. But in the summer, that line curled its way around the entire building and into the parking lot.

I smirked at my best friend — who was still at the window, even though we'd already been given our cones and cashed out — while licking swirls around the top of my pistachio brittle masterpiece. I watched Kylie's exchange with the mom of three who had been in line behind us, both of them animated and smiling before the mom wrapped Kylie up in a big hug. Then, she was on her way over to the table I'd snagged us, blush shading her cheeks.

"Tell me you didn't just pay for that woman's ice cream," I said when Kylie took her seat across from me.

She avoided my eyes guiltily, licking the top of her strawberry cone littered with sprinkles.

"Ky..."

"What?" she asked, gesturing toward the mom still in line like there was no other option. "You heard her when we were talking in line. She's new to town, a single mom of three. *Three*, Mikey. Can you even imagine?" Kylie shrugged. "It was the least I could do. A little pay-it-forward action."

I shook my head, taking another bite off my cone in lieu of responding to her reasoning. That was just who Kylie was. She'd bend over backward and lay her body as a bridge over muddy water if it meant saving a family of ducks or helping a fellow human.

Kylie still somehow looked like the girl I'd met in third grade, and sitting across from her now, at our favorite place in town, I felt an uncomfortable ache in my chest for a past life, a past version of myself — one who hadn't experienced heartbreak or lost himself completely. It seemed like simpler times when it was just me and Ky hanging out after school, playing video games or hiding out in the treehouse my father had built.

Again, all of that was B.B.L.

When Kylie came up and sat with me at lunch a couple weeks after Bailey was gone, I didn't even know what to say. Sure, we'd still texted every now and then, but for the most part, I'd lost touch with my best friend over the two years I'd dated Bailey. And still, when she saw me hurting, Kylie was the first one there and ready to help.

It was in her DNA, and I was thankful for it.

I was still a miserable, lost soul all these months later, but at least I had someone there for me. And when we were together, the pain was a little more subdued.

"So," I said, licking around the melting edges of my ice cream. "Now that you've got me buttered up with my favorite ice cream, are you going to tell me what you want?"

Kylie frowned, a strand of her long, thick hair falling in front of her face before she swiped it back behind her ear. We used to joke that her hair was thick and long enough to strangle someone, should we ever be attacked. In all the time I'd known her, she'd worn it at the same length, just past her shoulder blades, and in the same style, straight and parted down the middle. It was, perhaps, what I loved most about Ky.

She never changed.

She was the one thing in my life that always remained a constant.

"I never said I wanted anything," she pointed out defensively. "I said I have something to talk to you about, and that it's important."

"Right," I agreed. "But, if something was wrong, you wouldn't have even asked me to meet you. I would have had to figure it out by you retreating into yourself for days and saying everything was fine. Then, I would have had to tickle it out of you or sit in bed with you until you got so annoyed with my presence that you told me what was wrong."

She frowned more, because she knew I was right.

"And," I continued, "if it was something exciting, you would have barged through my front door or climbed through my window if it was late and told me on the spot, like you did when you found out you got the volunteer position at the nursing home. When do you start, by the way?"

Kylie was all but pouting now. "Next week," she admitted on a sigh. "It's ridiculous how well you know me."

"Now you know how I feel when you call me on my bullshit."

"To be fair, you *require* that kind of tough love. It's, like, written in your How-to-Friend-Michael-Becker manual."

I just lifted a brow and shrugged noncommittally. I didn't have to answer for her to know I already knew that. Mom said I got that from Dad — the stubbornness, the tendency to shut down and reject anything that made me rethink my actions. I wasn't sure if that was true, since my memories of my father were distant and hazy, but I *did* know that Kylie calling me on my shit was all that had saved me from making an ass of myself many, many times in her presence.

When I didn't say anything more, Kylie sighed, holding her cone carefully in one hand while she dipped the other into her backpack and retrieved one of her worn notebooks. That girl was always writing stuff down — namely math equations or coding challenges, or half-brained notes about inventions she could make that would somehow save the world.

"Okay, before I say anything else, I need to remind you of something," she said, pressing her hand over the top of the notebook protectively, like it held all the secrets of the universe in it.

I waved a hand for her to go on.

"When we were eight, you pinky promised me that you would *always* listen to me — no matter what."

I nodded. "I remember."

"I need you to keep that promise."

I pressed a hand to my chest in mock offense. "I can't believe you'd insinuate that I'd ever break the sacred vow of a pinky promise."

Kylie rolled her eyes, but when they found me again, they were so serious I started to worry. "I mean it. Please, Mikey."

I reached over with the hand not sticky with ice cream and squeezed hers with it. "I'm listening."

Her eyes stared at that point of contact for a long while, and when her breathing picked up, the worry I'd felt building in my chest doubled. Maybe I had been wrong about her shutting down when something was wrong. Immediately, I thought of her dad.

And then, I thought of mine.

My father died in a mysterious fire at the Scooter Whiskey Distillery — the *only* fire to ever happen in the history of the distillery. I'd been so young, I didn't remember much — except for the hopeless, empty feeling I'd had once I realized that my father was never coming home again.

Over the years, as I grew up, I learned from little comments here and there that my older brothers and my mom didn't believe the story we were fed by both the fire department and the owner of the distillery. They said it was started by a cigarette, but we all knew my father never smoked.

There was foul play — at least, that's what my family had always suspected. But, we never had proof... that we knew of. But when my older brother, Logan, found a box of our father's things — all half charred from the fire — we found a few more clues as to what happened that day.

The biggest one was the damaged laptop that hid a still-working hard drive.

Logan had kept quiet about it for a long while, trying to break into it on his own, but when he'd finally told me and our other brothers about it, I'd offered to take over.

Well, technically, I'd volunteered *Kylie* to take over.

She'd been into coding and HTML since we were kids. Provided, it had mostly been for fun — like the year she coded one of the Christmas trees outside the lighthouse to dance and sparkle with whatever colors she wanted it to. Still, I knew if anyone could break into that hard drive, it was her.

So, suddenly, my heart was in my throat, and I pulled my hand away from hers with the next breath leaving my chest completely.

Was this it? Had she broken in? What did she find?

Kylie abandoned what was left of her ice cream cone, tossing it in the nearby waste bin before she blew out a long breath, closed her eyes, and spoke.

"I know you've already made up your mind about New York, but I want you to reconsider."

The tightness in my chest evaporated instantly with her words, the anticipation that she'd found something on the hard drive gone — along with my appetite.

I sighed, taking one last bite of my waffle cone before I tossed the rest of it in the same trash can she'd just threw hers.

"Hear me out," she said, opening her notebook.

"Why is it so hard for everyone to just accept that this is *my* decision, and to be happy for me?" I asked, anger heating my neck. I expected this from my mom, and even from my brothers, but from Kylie?

She was the one person I thought understood.

"I do accept that it's your decision," she clarified. "I just... I want the chance to show you the other option."

"As in, staying in Stratford," I deadpanned.

She swallowed, her big doe eyes doubling in size. "Yes."

"I already know that option. I've been *living* in that option since I was born."

"But you've forgotten everything that's good about this town."

I scoffed. "Oh, right, because there's *so* much to count in that category."

Kylie smacked her hand down on the picnic table, cheeks red again — but this time, not from a blush. "There *is*, Mikey, and you thought so, too, before a stupid girl soured everything for you and made you want to leave it all behind."

Her words were so loud that the people sitting at the table next to us glanced our way — a table full of freshly graduated seniors from our class. They watched us with a mixture of pity and wariness before they turned their attention back to their own conversation, and the anger I'd felt before bloomed like an angry ivy up my neck.

"Thanks for the reminder."

"I'm sorry," Kylie said quickly, smoothing her hand over the page she'd opened to in her notebook. "But, you promised you'd listen. So, just... listen. Okay?"

If it were anyone but Kylie, I would have gotten up and walked away. But, as it was, I *had* made her a promise all those years ago, and I wasn't backing out on it now.

I crossed my arms, waiting.

"Here's what I'm proposing," she said, blowing out a tentative breath with her hand smoothing over the page of her notebook. "You said you're moving at the end of the summer, right?"

I nodded.

"Well, I want the next two months to show you everything you used to love about this town, and remind you that there's more here for you than just the memories of Bailey."

Something akin to a sharp, hot knife hit my chest at the mention of her name, like just those two syllables were a warning to my entire body that pain was about to be inflicted. I swallowed, and Kylie must have noticed the fault line in my demeanor, because her eyes softened where she watched me.

"I made a list," she said, scooting the notebook toward me.

"Of course you did."

That made her smirk, and the knot in my chest loosened as I glanced down at the page.

"*Mikey and Ky's List of Epic Stratford Adventures,*" I read aloud, cocking a brow when I looked at my best friend again. "That's an oxymoron, you know — *epic* and *Stratford.*"

"Ha, ha," she said, swiping the notebook back from me and petting it like it was her dog that I'd kicked. "You used to love this town, and believe it or not, even though Bailey is gone, it's still the same town it was when you were happy and in love."

"That's just the problem," I pointed out. "Nothing ever changes in this town. It's stale, boring, dried up. I need something new, something exciting, something..."

"That doesn't remind you of her."

I swallowed, looking down at my hands folded on the table top.

"It's not just that," I tried to explain, not really sure where to start. "When I was with her, I had everything figured out. I knew exactly who I was, where I was going, who I would be in the future. Now, that's all been erased." I looked at her. "I'm lost, Ky. I don't know who I am or where to go or what to do next. All I know is that being here feels like sitting in a burning room with the smoke suffocating me when all I have to do is stand, walk to the door, and open it to get out and find relief." My chest tightened. "New York City is the place where the lost ones go, and it's where I want to be."

Kylie's eyebrows drew together, and for a long moment, she just watched me — silent, understanding.

Just like she always had been.

"Look," she said after a long pause. "I'm not asking for anything crazy. You're going to be here for the next two months anyway, right? So, all I'm asking is that you hang out with me for a large portion of that time and give me this chance."

"You're wasting your time," I told her. "I can't wait until the end of the summer to start preparing for the move. I have to find an apartment, a job."

"I know," she said softly, and it was the first time I saw the real hurt behind her hopeful eyes. "And that's fine. I get it. Maybe none of this will change your mind. But, even if it doesn't, you have nothing to lose by agreeing. If anything, it can be like one last hurrah. A summer of fun with yours truly before you ditch this town and leave it in your dust."

I blew out a long breath through my nose, shaking my head, because I already knew nothing would change my mind, but I *didn't* know how to tell that to Kylie — who was looking at me with big puppy eyes right now.

"*Please*, Mikey," she said, leaning down to catch my gaze. "Let me remind you why you love Stratford, and show you that Bailey was just a *part* of your story here — not all of it."

The afternoon sun slipped past the umbrella covering us, catching the gold flakes in her otherwise brown eyes as she watched me. I knew those eyes as if they were my own, because they'd been a part of my life since I was eight years old.

And so had Kylie.

She'd been the only one to truly understand what I was going through that first year we became friends. We'd mourned our parents' death together, gone through puberty together, laughed and cried and celebrated and hurt together. And even though I didn't deserve it, she'd been right there for me when Bailey had left, and she hadn't asked for a single apology — even though I owed her several.

It didn't matter that my mind was already made up. It didn't matter that I knew she didn't have a chance of convincing me to stay. All that *did* matter was that she was my best friend, and she deserved the time she was asking for in my last months in town.

So, I propped my elbow up on the table, and extended my pinky toward her with as much of a smile as I could muster.

The worry on her face washed away immediately, eyes flicking back and forth between my gaze and my hand. "Really?"

I nodded.

A little squeal came out of that girl as her smile took over her entire face — just like it always did.

Then, she looped her pinky through mine, and the deal was done.

...

Kylie

Having dinner with the Becker family was like having dinner in a circus ring.

The level of noise always hovered somewhere right around *roaring tiger* and *carousel of screaming children*, thanks to four brothers who thought the only way to be heard was to speak even louder over the other. Tonight, all four of them were gathered around that long table that we'd sat at for more nights than I could remember, plus Noah's fiancé, Ruby Grace, Logan's girlfriend, Mallory Scooter, and perhaps my favorite new addition to the family, Betty Collins, a spunky senior citizen brought into the family by Ruby Grace and the time she spent volunteering down at the nursing home.

The same nursing home *I* would be volunteering at this summer — thanks to Ruby Grace pulling some strings.

Michael belched so loud beside me once he'd cleared his plate that my jaw dropped, and he just grinned at me before high-fiving his older brother, Logan.

Mama Becker shook her head. "Manners, Mikey."

"Maybe he's practicing for his move to The Big Apple," his brother, Noah, teased.

"Ohhh, yeah," Logan agreed. "He's got to work on his Jerk Face."

"And on his accent. Hey, Mikey — say '*Car*', but without the *r*," said Jordan, the oldest.

Michael rolled up his napkin and tossed it at them, making everyone laugh. It was sort of dizzying, sitting at a table with all of the Becker boys. Mikey and Logan favored their mother, sporting the same olive skin and hazel eyes, whereas Noah was the spitting image of their father — not that I'd ever seen anything more than just a photo of him. At least, not that I could remember. But those piercing blue eyes and that sideways grin that hung in several photos on the wall looked just like Noah.

Jordan was perhaps the only one who stood out a bit, being that he was adopted. His umber skin and dark, short hair were about the only things that were different, though. He somehow had that Becker smile, even if it was biologically impossible, and more than anything, I knew Becker blood ran deep in that man. He was a brother and a son above all else — and one hell of a football coach right after that.

"Don't start," Michael warned, but he wore as close to a smile as he'd had in months as his brother teased him. Part of me wondered if making the decision to move had lightened the load on his shoulders a bit, if he was feeling like he could relax a little more now that he'd told his family that he was leaving.

The other part of me wondered if I stood a chance in hell of changing his mind.

I'd gotten him to agree to let me try earlier that day outside of Blondies — even if he assured me it wouldn't work. Maybe it was silly and naïve to find hope in the pinky promise he'd made me, but I clung to it anyway.

I had one summer to convince him that he didn't need to leave this town to get over Bailey.

I just hoped I could actually do it.

"I agree," Mama Becker said, tidying her napkin on her lap before she played with the fork on her dessert plate. The leftover graduation cake from yesterday that she'd served us was gone, so she had nothing to play with, but her eyes stayed on that plate, anyway. "I don't want to talk about my baby boy moving across the country."

"Mama..." Michael said, frowning.

Lorelei shook her head, eyes glossing over as she forced a smile, and pointed it right at me. "Ky, tell us about all the amazing plans you have for your gap year."

A blush heated my cheeks, traveling quickly down my neck to my chest. I gave a tight-lipped smile, aiming for casual and funny as I tried to joke about it. "Well, I would — if I *had* a plan."

"Isn't a gap year supposed to be about traveling?" Betty asked from the end of the table. She whistled. "I tell ya, they should give *me* a gap year. I'd blow this popsicle stand and high-tail it to Italy. Get me some of that fancy ice cream. What's it called? Gaston?"

Ruby Grace chuckled, touching Betty's arm. "Gelato, Betty. Gaston is the name of the villain guy in *Beauty and the Beast*."

"Oh," Betty said, but then she waved her off. "Well, if there's a guy who looks like him over there, toss him into the mix, too. I can handle it."

The table roared with laughter, and Ruby Grace shook her head. "Gaston is French, not Italian."

"Then I guess I'll have to go to France, too."

I was hopeful that Betty's charm and the laughter would distract everyone long enough for a new subject to be raised, but of course all eyes turned back to me.

"I just can't believe you're not going straight to college," Logan said. He nudged Mallory, then. "This girl is in love with math and science the way most girls are in love with Justin Bieber."

I could have fried an egg on my cheeks when the table chuckled in unison.

"Oh, don't worry," Mikey said, clasping his hand on my shoulder like I was one of his brothers. I might as well have been. "She'll be saving the world soon enough."

Ruby Grace lit up at that. "Are you thinking of AmeriCorps?"

I shook my head, playing with the napkin in my lap so I had something to do other than internally cringe at the attention being on me. "No, although

I think it sounds amazing," I added, knowing that was close to her heart. "I'm more of the in-the-lab, nose-in-the-books kind of girl."

"She's going to be a part of the team that ends our water crisis," Mikey said confidently. "Or figures out how to power vehicles off garbage. Or finds a bio-degradable and affordable substitute for plastic."

Jordan sat back in his chair, assessing me like he was impressed. "You really think those things are possible?"

I shrugged, taking a sip of my water as I found the words. "I mean, in theory, yes — of course it's possible. Everything is. The way I see it, the world we live in, the universe, it's all one big math problem. The issue is that as a human race, we only know so much. There are too many variables to have all the answers we want, at least, at this time. But, each decade that passes, we discover more and more. Theories change, new science is born, math problems are solved. Think about our grandparents, or *their* grandparents… do you think they ever imagined we'd hold tiny computers in our hands that could answer any question we ever had? That could guide us across the country with a navigation system? Do you think they ever thought we'd have stem cells, that we'd be able to grow a lung, that we'd be able to manipulate DNA to possibly eliminate life-threatening diseases?"

My heart was racing, and the smile on my face was so big it hurt as I pulled my hands from my napkin and used them to animate my point.

"It's like being in algebra class. You have all the other variables, and you just have to figure out what x is." I shrugged. "Once we have the variables we need, it's a matter of solving an equation. And there's nothing I love more than a good challenge."

I sat back on a grin, but one passing glance at each person at that table, and my stomach dropped.

Logan and Noah wore identical faces of confusion, their mouths hanging open. Ruby Grace and Mallory were smirking like they were impressed, but still didn't quite see it the way I did. Jordan watched me like I was something out of a National Geographic film — like a snake eating a mouse, or worse. And then there was Mikey, who looked at me with a chest swelled with pride.

"My nerd is showing again, isn't it?" I asked on a cringe.

That broke the table into laughter, and I let out a long breath of relief.

"I think you're going to be famous one day with a brain like that, young lady," Betty said, matter-of-factly. "And I just hope I'm around to see it."

"So, science major?" Noah asked.

"Bioscience, yes," I answered. "I'm thinking microbiology, or science engineering."

"That's amazing," Mallory mused, leaning toward me over the table. "So, why a gap year? If you're so into this kind of stuff and you know what you want to do… why wait?"

A smile found my lips, and I looked down at my hands. "My mom took a gap year after she finished high school," I explained. "I've always wanted to do the same. You know, to honor her." I looked up at her, then, and her smile was soft and understanding. "I just have to figure out what to *do* with said gap year."

A soft chuckle from the table, and Lorelei reached over to pat my hand.

"It's okay to not have everything figured out," she said. "I think it's great that you're taking a year to decide what you want to do next." She side-eyed her youngest son. "I wish someone *else* would do the same."

"Mom," he warned.

Betty snapped her fingers. "Say, Kylie — if you're so good with techy stuff, does that mean you can help me set up my Face Space while you're volunteering at the nursing home?"

"Face*book*, you mean?" Ruby Grace chimed in.

"Whatever," she said, waving her off. That earned another fit of laughter, and then Mallory asked Ruby Grace if she and Noah had chosen a wedding date yet, and all attention was officially off me.

Thank God.

At our graduation dinner last night — right before Mikey told everyone he was leaving for New York — Noah told us he and Ruby Grace were getting married. Their love had been a whirlwind, a summer affair that was taboo — being that she had been engaged to someone else. But now, seeing them together at that table, I couldn't imagine either of them with anyone else.

They were meant to be.

Oddly, I could say the same for Logan and Mallory, even though I was probably the *only* one at that table who would say it. After all, Mallory was a Scooter — the daughter of the current owner and CEO of the whiskey distillery our town was built on, Patrick Scooter. And it was no secret in this family that the Beckers and the Scooters didn't get along.

At least, not anymore.

They say there was a time when the two families were practically one. In fact, it had been Michael's grandpa who had essentially built the Scooter Whiskey brand *with* Mallory's grandfather — the original founder. They had been best friends, business partners, but when Robert J. Scooter passed away, he didn't leave anything in his last will and testament that said the Becker family was owed any part of the distillery. Patrick, the oldest Scooter son, assumed full ownership and top responsibility.

And the feud began.

I didn't know much about it, being that I was young and wholeheartedly uninterested in the town gossip, but being best friends with Michael, I knew that they slowly smoked his father out of his role on the board, down to practically a paper pusher.

And then, there was the fire.

The fire that John Becker died in, leaving a wife and four boys behind. The fire that the town claimed was started by a cigarette, knowing full well that Mr. Becker never smoked.

The fire that changed these boys forever, and left a mystery that they were still trying to solve today.

Suddenly, I had the urge to go home and fuss with the hard drive they'd found in their father's old, half-burnt laptop. Logan had found it over the holidays, and Michael had convinced him to let us take a crack at it. He'd volunteered me for the cause mostly because I'd gone through a phase of being obsessed with coding, but it was all child's play, little video games and website designs that I'd toyed with for a small period of time. I *had* hacked into our school's system our sophomore year, just to see if I could do it. But that had been a joke, one somewhat-legit looking email to the principal and he'd clicked my link and typed in his username and password like the dummy I always knew he was.

This hard drive was different.

It was encrypted, backed up by the Scooter Whiskey Distillery firewall and too difficult for me to crack swiftly. I'd been trying to break into that thing for months now with no luck, and we'd recently started trying ten random passwords an hour — the max before it locked us out — instead of trying to break in. Sometimes we'd work for one hour, sometimes for a couple, sometimes we'd take an entire week break from it.

I wondered if I cracked it over the next two months, if Mikey would stay.

That urge to get home and try fired up even more at the thought.

Betty started cleaning up the dishes off the table, and when she stood, Jordan wiped his mouth with his napkin and placed it on the table before extending his hand for his mom's. "Well, I think it's about that time."

Lorelei smiled, slipping her hand into his, and Logan crossed to the stereo in the living room, turning on a song I'd heard dozens and dozens of times inside those walls.

"Wonderful Tonight" by Eric Clapton.

It was the song Lorelei and John had danced to at their wedding so many years ago, the song he used to dance with her to every night after dinner, and a song that the Becker brothers *still* danced with her to in his place.

Jordan was already swaying softly with his tiny mother in his arms, and Logan pulled Mallory onto the dance floor, too, giving her a spin that made her laugh nervously as she gripped onto him like she would fall if he stepped too far away. She clearly was not a dancer, and my heart swelled when Logan leaned into her and whispered, "I got you."

Noah and Ruby Grace were next, and they fell into a beautiful waltz, showing those dance skills that they both had. Betty leaned against the door frame of the kitchen with a smile, watching the three couples in the living room along with us.

"Why don't you two get out there?" she said, nodding at us.

I flushed so hard I thought lava would burst out of my eyeballs, and Betty narrowed her eyes at me like I'd just exposed all my deepest secrets to her.

Like that I was completely in love with the boy she just casually recommended I should dance with.

"Oh, no," I said, shaking my head with a nervous smile. "We don't... We aren't..."

"Pshhh." Betty waved her hands in the air before she shooed us toward the floor. "You don't have to be married to dance. Go on, now. Get."

My nervous laughter turned into something close to a goose call, but everything stopped altogether when Michael grabbed my hand, leaning in to whisper by my ear.

"We better dance before that old woman smacks us both upside the head."

"I heard that," she warned, shoving us forward now that we were standing. "I may be old, but you're damn straight I could still whoop your butt."

We both laughed, though my laugh was strangled with my hand in his like that. It wasn't like he hadn't ever grabbed my hand before. It wasn't like that electricity I felt pulsing through his palm to mine wasn't the same thing I'd felt since we were eight years old. But feeling him drag me toward the dance floor, falling into step next to his brothers and their loved ones, next to his mother, it was too much.

Because it felt natural.

Because it felt like I was already family, like I belonged... like *we* belonged, together.

Because I knew dancing with me didn't mean anything to Michael.

And because I hated that it meant *everything* to me.

Michael smirked a little as he pulled me into his arms, and I aimed for completely cool and calm as I threaded my own around his neck, stepping in time with him. It was just a simple two-step sway, but then he grabbed one of my hands, twirled me out to the center of the dance floor, and spun my hips fast so that I twirled twice more before landing back into his arms.

"Show off," Logan murmured as their mother laughed with delight.

I shook my head, breathless and a little wobbly after that stunt. "Good thing you were here to catch me, otherwise I'd be on the floor right now."

"I'm always here to catch you," he teased with a wink.

My chest ached.

"So," he said, tugging on a strand of my long hair. "What's first on that list of yours."

"That's for me to know and you to find out."

"Oh, keeping secrets now? I should have studied that notebook harder when I had the chance."

"This will make it even more fun," I pointed out. "It'll be like you're a secret agent, never knowing when the next mission is going to come or what it's going to be."

"Speaking of missions," he said, glancing at his mom before he lowered his voice even more. "Any luck on the..."

He didn't have to finish the sentence — the hope in his eyes told me all I needed to know about what he was asking.

I gently shook my head, hating that I didn't have better news. "Not yet. But, it's not hopeless."

Michael deflated, but forced a small smile and a nod.

That urge to get home and work on the hard drive struck again, this time as hot as lightning.

Mikey watched his mom dancing with his oldest brother, and a softness came over him that was rare nowadays. I couldn't help but stare at him as he stared at them, noting the strong set of his jaw, the slope of his nose, the flecks of gold in his eyes. He was stuck between a boy and a man, still that eight-year-old boy I fell in love with, and yet somehow, a man I didn't know at all, too.

He sighed the longer he watched them, and the next time he spoke, it was three words that turned my stomach and stole my breath.

"I miss her."

I didn't have to ask who *her* was. I knew it, he knew it, we *all* knew it.

I swallowed down the pain I couldn't let him see, leaning in to rest my head on his chest, instead. "I know," I offered softly, squeezing him a little tighter. "I'm here."

He nodded, squeezing me back, and I thought about my list, about the promise he'd made me, about the one last shot I had to shoot. I thought about all the years I'd kept silent, about the years I'd stepped back and let him love another, never telling him how I felt.

I wondered how much longer I could keep quiet.

I wondered what would happen if I ever spoke the words out loud.

And on the drive home, I prayed to God that I wouldn't completely shatter my heart in an attempt to keep that boy in my life.

Chapter Four

Michael

The Scooter Whiskey Distillery Gift Shop was my own personal hell.

It was my first job, one I acquired just after my sixteenth birthday, and one I *used to* enjoy. In fact, I'd loved it so much when I'd first started that I'd volunteered for other people's shifts, working as much as I possibly could as a minor.

I loved talking to the tourists passing through our little town, suggesting the best diners and restaurants in town, recommending a drive up the old, windy road to our north that would take them to a little hidden waterfall and view of the mountains. I loved hearing who was in our town, how they'd found out about it, and why they were here. Some of them had stumbled upon it by mistake. Others were more obsessed with whiskey than I'd ever care to understand. Either way, I was their last stop before they left our distillery, and it was always fun for me to tell them where to go next.

Bailey used to love it, too.

She'd visit me, lean over the counter and smile at me with that dazzling smile of hers, those moss green, almost transparent irises sparkling in the natural light that poured in from the gift shop windows as she told me about whatever song she was writing. And when a tourist interrupted to buy their gifts, she'd chime in with her own suggestions, and I'd watch as each and every guest fell just as much in love with her as I was.

It was impossible not to.

I was convinced that was why Nashville had been so receptive to her, why a label had been so quick to sign her and so urgent to get her started on her music career. There was just *something* about that girl — even when she wasn't singing. And when you put a guitar in her hands and gave her a stage to perform on?

Forget about it.

Might as well kiss your heart goodbye.

And as much as I hated to admit it, I knew deep down in my black heart that she was the reason I'd lost the love for this job — for this distillery, this town.

This life altogether.

Now, I didn't care to talk to the tourists. I didn't care to greet them with a smile or ask how their tour was or offer suggestions on which bottle of whiskey was worth it to pack in their suitcase to take home with them. I didn't have a long list of suggestions for them to round out their trip to Stratford, and if anyone ever did ask where they should eat, I gave the same answer every time — a short, clipped response that told them they were better off stopping for food in the next town over than to eat any of the garbage here.

I wasn't too stubborn to admit that Bailey had made me prickly.

But I *was* too stubborn to do anything about it.

In a way, I kind of liked the new way people responded to me. Everyone who knew me in this town watched me warily, from a distance, like I had a bomb under my coat that I could pull the cord on at any moment. The tourists seemed to pick up on it, too, which meant my long shifts that used to be filled with people-pleasing now mostly consisted of me surfing the Internet on my phone and occasionally breaking contact with the screen long enough to ring someone up.

It wasn't a career, but it was a job that paid me well enough to save for my first few months in New York. And that was all I needed.

Still, Mondays were the worst, it seemed, and I was grumpier than usual that I was still at the same job even though I'd graduated high school. It was yet another sign of proof that nothing had changed by me receiving that diploma.

"Twenty-two ninety-one," I told the girl I'd just rung up, who, by the looks of it, was just old enough to do the distillery tour and tasting. She couldn't be a day over twenty-one, and she smiled at me like she'd just bought a prized pig as she handed me her credit card — along with her driver's license.

I handed the latter back to her without looking at it.

"It's my birthday," she said as I ran her card. "First day getting carded and not having to show my fake."

She added that last part with a laugh, and I cocked a brow, glancing up at her just as she leaned a little over the counter.

Flashes of Bailey assaulted me — the way she'd leaned over that same counter in just the same way — and for a moment, it was her I saw instead of the blonde tourist.

But it was gone in a flash.

I scowled, ripping the receipt from the machine with more force than necessary and handing it to the girl along with her card. "Happy birthday," I murmured. "Do you want a bag?"

Her face crumpled, and she swallowed, shaking her head and grabbing the bottle of whiskey off the counter. She opened her mouth to say something more, but didn't follow through with it, and as soon as she was away from the counter, I took a seat on the bar stool again, pulling up the search for Manhattan apartments I'd been going through on my phone before she interrupted.

I'd only scrolled past three more shoe-box-sized, ridiculously priced apartments before there was another girl at the counter.

"Ouch," she said, clucking her tongue as she looked over her shoulder at the one who'd just left. "That girl is going to have a complex, thanks to you. Bet she never attempts to flirt with a stranger again."

I rolled my eyes at my best friend without even looking up from my phone. "She wasn't flirting. And I was nice enough. I told her 'happy birthday'."

"You *growled* 'happy birthday'," Kylie corrected. "And if you couldn't see that that girl was flirting with you, then you're even more helpless than I thought."

I shrugged. "Even if she was, I'm not interested."

"Yeah. Apparently you've got an internet girlfriend there," she said, snagging my phone out of my hands before I could react.

I didn't even reach for it back, just sighed and waited.

Kylie wrinkled her nose. "These apartments are awful."

"Well, that's what happens when you start at the bottom in the biggest city in the United States. Gotta struggle for a while."

Kylie swallowed, a shadow of something passing over her face before she tossed the phone back to me. "Do you have anything going on after work?"

"Actually, I was going to—"

"Great. We're going mudding."

My eyebrows shot up into my hairline at that. "We're... I'm sorry, what?"

"You heard me. You made me a pinky promise, and we start today."

"You hate mudding."

"But *you* used to love it," she said, pointing her finger right at my chest. "And I have a truck. Therefore, we're going."

I fought back a laugh at that, but failed to hide it long. "Kylie, you have a Tacoma. It's a two-wheel drive."

"Last I checked, two wheels drive it just fine."

I full on laughed at that. "You can't take it mudding. You'll get stuck."

"So... we get stuck," she said on an exasperated breath, throwing her hands up in the air. "You said you were down. You *pinky* promised, Mikey. So, stop being such a fuddy duddy and just meet me at my house after work."

My eyes rolled up to the ceiling, and I cursed myself for making that damn agreement without asking to see the notebook again. I didn't remember a single thing that was on her list, but if this was just the start, I was convinced I'd made the worst deal of my life.

"It'll be fun," she said, leaning over the counter the same way the blonde tourist had.

The same way Bailey had.

I swallowed, picking my phone back up to search through more apartments with a pair of green eyes haunting me just like they always did.

"Can't wait."

• • •

I knew the smile on my face was a smug one as I watched a wide-eyed Kylie take in the scene around us.

The mudding park just outside of Stratford was busy, even on a Monday night, because it was summer and the mud was fresh. Warm weather and longer days called to the country boys with big mud tires, to the men with tricked-out trucks just begging to get a little dirty.

Kylie's brown eyes took up half her face as she surveyed the truck — on tires twice the size of her — currently slinging mud from the puddle it'd just dived into. The mud was thick and clay-colored, spewing up from the back tires like a reverse waterfall as the crowd cheered and hollered and raised their beers to the driver. He was in a Chevy Silverado, jacked up on after-market tires that I knew he'd sunk no less than three-thousand dollars into, not including whatever it cost him to lift the truck on suspensions.

And he wasn't the only one.

We were surrounded by men and women of all ages who had more money in their truck than they probably did in their home. There were Broncos and F-150s, Tundras and Rams, Jeeps and Hummers — all lifted and tricked out and well equipped to take on the fresh Tennessee mud.

And then, there was my adorable, naïve, hopeful best friend and her little Tacoma.

Kylie swallowed as a group of girls in full camo gear walked by us, eyeing her truck with curious smiles before they made their way over to a hot pink Jeep that had a vinyl sticker across the front window reading *Swamp Girl.*

"Still think this is a good idea?" I asked, crossing my arms over my chest.

"Yes," she squeaked, faking confidence. She forgot too often how well I knew her. "So, we might not be able to put on a big show," she offered on a shrug. "We can still get some mud on the tires, you know, like Brad Paisley said."

I chuckled. "Maybe we should go hit one of the smaller trails," I offered, nodding toward the woods behind her. "Something not so muddy."

"That's not what you would do when you came out here when we were younger," she pointed out, shifting her weight to one hip. "You'd go right there in that big mud pit and you and your brother wouldn't leave until you were completely covered in muck."

"My brother also drives a Bronco," I reminded her.

"Ugh! You're impossible," she said on a huff, yanking the door handle on her truck. "Just get in."

I shook my head, already knowing what a disaster it was going to be but knowing there was no arguing with Kylie when she had her mind set on something.

She was right, I *did* used to love mudding with Jordan. It was my favorite way to bond with my oldest brother, who stuck to himself for the most part. When we climbed in his Bronco and came out here to the trails, we got away from everything. Sometimes we'd talk for hours, sometimes we'd laugh and jam to music as loud as his speakers could play it, and other times, when the mud was gone and it was just old bumpy roads, we'd ride in silence with the windows down, both of us lost in our own thoughts.

I hadn't been mudding since Bailey left, even though Jordan had invited me plenty of times, and I knew the biggest reason why. I didn't want to talk to him about her. I didn't want to jam out to music and laugh and pretend I was fine. And I damn sure didn't want to be alone with my own thoughts with anyone else around to witness the suffering.

I just wanted to be left alone.

Too bad my best friend had missed that cue.

I sighed, following her lead and climbing into the passenger seat of the truck. "Are you sure you don't want me to drive?" I asked, shutting the door behind me as she fired the truck to life. "It can be a little tricky maneuvering the pit and knowing when to give it gas and when to lay off."

"I watched several YouTube videos and I am fully prepared."

She said the words so seriously, so matter-of-factly, that the laugh that shot out of me was absolutely unavoidable.

Kylie's eyes narrowed, and she revved the engine, tiny fists curling around the wheel as she focused her eyes on the pit in front of us. The tiny roar of her engine had a few people looking at us, but most of the crowd was gathered around the Silverado who'd just emerged on the other side of the pit.

"Just be careful, okay? If you fall into the deepest part of the pit, give your engine some time to shed the water before you—"

My next words were cut off by a string of expletives as I grabbed what my brother always referred to as the *oh-shit handle* above the passenger side window and held on tight, the truck flying forward with Kylie gripping the wheel in determination. She could barely see over the dash, and it was still a mystery to me how her tiny legs were long enough for her to reach the pedals — but reach them she did. And with her foot on the gas, we propelled forward, the lanyards from her many volunteer gigs swinging wildly from where they hung around the rearview mirror.

There were some encouraging hoots and hollers as we rolled toward the pit, and when the front end dipped in, water and mud splashing up around us, the cheers rose, and that determined look on Kylie's face morphed into a giant, mega-watt smile.

"Oh my God! We're mudding!"

The truck slipped deeper, and a giggle escaped her lips when the back tires fell into the pit with a *thunk*.

I loved that look on her face, the same one she got when she tried something new, or helped someone in the community, or when she managed to beat me at a video game. Her eyes were wide and shining, smile splitting her entire face, long, brown hair falling over her face just enough for a few strands to get stuck on her lips.

But there was something different about that smile, somehow. Something... *new* that I couldn't quite place. Warmth spread through me at the sight of it, and my own lips curled into a grin. "You're mudding," I echoed.

"This is so fun!" she said, revving her engine so the tires whirred and spewed mud up behind us.

We were still going forward, but then the pit deepened, and the front of her truck sank a good foot more into the mud, causing little wisps of smoke to emerge from under the hood.

"Oh, shit," she said, and her foot came off the gas pedal before I could tell her not to stop.

"No!" I said, reaching over to grab the steering wheel and try to steer us toward the bank to get some traction. "Keep going! Gas, gas, gas!"

"I thought you said not to put on the gas when we sink!"

"I said if you were taking on water! We're going to get stuck, GIVE IT GAS!"

Kylie screamed, slamming her foot down on the gas with wide, panicked eyes, her hands framing mine on the wheel as she tried to help me steer us toward the ramped dirt that could get us out of the pit.

But it was too late.

The wheels spun and spun, the engine roaring violently under the hood, smoke billowing, but the truck didn't move more than an inch.

Cheers rang out around us, but when she cut the gas again, the cheers turned to laughter, and I watched, mortified, as everyone around us pointed and shook their heads at our failed attempt to clear the pit.

I frowned, shaking my head on a curse word as I released the wheel and threw my hands up. "I *told* you your truck wasn't a mudding truck!"

"It's okay," she said, swallowing and shaking her head before she forced a smile. "It's okay! So, we're stuck. No big deal, we'll just..."

She put on the gas again, which made the truck sink deeper before I yelled for her to stop. When she did, I let out a long, exasperated sigh, scrubbing my hands over my face before letting them fall to my lap.

"Everyone is laughing at us."

Kylie looked around then, as if she'd only just noticed. "So? Let them laugh. Who cares?"

"*I* care," I said. "We look like idiots."

Her little mouth clamped shut at that, and she shook her head. "You know, my old best friend wouldn't have cared. He wouldn't have given two shits if the people in this town were laughing at him or not. He would have been *nice* to me. And he damn sure would have had a little fun instead of being such a grump."

"Well, I'm not your *old best friend*, anymore."

"Clearly," she said, shoving her door open. "I'm sorry I even tried. Forget about the pinky promise. Clearly, this WHOAMYGOD—"

As soon as Kylie stepped out of the truck, she slipped on the step that led down to the ground, and in a whirling of arms and legs, I watched her fall, landing in the mud below the truck with a wet *smack*.

Another roar of laughter sounded as I climbed over the middle console, jumping down into the mud with her to help.

"Shit, Kylie. Are you alright?" I reached my hand down to help her stand, but instead, when she pulled, I lost my footing, and down in the mud I went, too.

The laughter around us doubled as mud sank into every crevice of my shorts where I *never* wanted mud to be.

"Oh my God, I'm so sorry!" Kylie said, covering her mouth with her muddy hands as her eyes widened. "I'm so sorry. Here, I'll just—"

She tried to stand, but slipped and fell again, this time face planting in the mud beside me. When she leaned back onto her knees, she looked like my mom did once a month when she put on her weird face mask thing.

And to make her even more adorable, her bottom lip quivered, face twisting as she tried not to cry.

"I'm so sorry," she said on a trembling voice. "I... I ruined it. I ruined my one shot."

She buried her face in her hands again, and for a long pause, I just watched her — shoulders hunched, mud covering every inch of her — matting her hair, speckling her arms and chest, completely covering the lower half of her body. I blew out a breath, leaned up slowly until my palms held me upright, and then, the strangest thing happened.

I laughed.

Truly laughed — not a snort, not a sarcastic chuckle.

A real, genuine laugh.

It was a little painful, that first laugh shaking the rust off my rib cage as it broke through the fortress of my depressed soul. It was as if my body had forgotten how to do it altogether, but the longer I laughed, the more the chains around my chest loosened.

Kylie glanced up at me through her fingertips, first with a curious cock of one eyebrow, and then with a timid smile.

The mud was still caked on her face, and the thought of my mom and her stupid face mask hit me again, and I laughed harder, covering my stomach at the strange pain. I couldn't talk, couldn't breathe — all I could do was laugh.

Kylie chuckled, and when I surrendered to the laugher and fell back into the mud, she laughed with me, though hers seemed to be mixed with a bit of crying, too.

I reached for her, and when she slipped her muddy hand in mine, I pulled her back down into the pit, which made us both fall victim to another round of laughter. The crowd around us cheered, and already I could see the man who'd just cleared the pit in the Silverado getting his chains out to help tow us out of where we were stuck.

"You're not mad at me?" Kylie asked when the laughter subsided, leaning up on one elbow to look down at me.

"No," I breathed out, chest light, head even more so after all the exertion. "You're a mess, and stubborn as hell, and entirely too hopeful for my grumpy ass," I said, but then my eyes found hers, and I smiled. "But I could never be mad at you."

She smirked, eyes wandering over me. "To be fair, you're a mess right now, too."

"And who's fault is that?"

I yanked her back down into the mud, rolling until I was covering her with the gunk that was slowly caking all over me. She laughed and squealed, trying to escape my hold. When I was firmly on top of her, her arms pinned under mine, we both stopped laughing, and a foreign, almost completely forgotten feeling flooded me just like the mud had flooded her engine.

Gratitude.

Because for the first time in months, I'd laughed.

And it was all thanks to my best friend who never gave up on me, no matter how many times I told her she should.

"Thank you, Ky," I said, searching her brown eyes under me. "Thank you for not listening to me. For bringing me here."

Something in her eyes softened, and she smiled, her cheeks shading pink under the brown smattering of mud. "You're welcome."

The longer I stared at her, the more I realized how much she'd grown up in the two years we'd spent apart. I'd seen her around school, of course, but I'd somehow missed how the roundness of her cheeks had slimmed, and the lashes that framed her eyes had lengthened, and that little girl face she'd always had had changed into something different, something that wasn't yet a woman, but was far from the girl I'd met so many years ago.

I was still studying what I'd missed when a shadow broke the sunlight hitting those flecks of gold in her eyes, and we both looked up to find a tall man in overalls staring down at us with a crooked grin.

"Whatd'ya say we get you guys pulled out of this muck, huh?"

Chapter Five

Kylie

"So," Betty said, removing her swim cap before she leaned against the edge of the nursing home swimming pool. "How long have you been in love with Mikey?"

Her question jolted me from the daze I'd been in all morning, and my eyes bulged, something between a choke and a laugh leaving my chest as I shook my head a little too violently. "What? I'm not... I don't..."

"Oh, cut the crap," she said with a bored roll of her eyes. "Anyone with more than a pea-sized brain can see you've got heart eyes for that boy. Except for maybe him, which I'd wager is part of your whole dilemma, isn't it?"

I just gaped at the sassy old woman, wondering how she had figured out my biggest secret after only hanging out with me at a handful of Becker family dinners before this week at the nursing home.

It was Thursday, just three days after the mudding incident with Mikey, and somehow it was still the only thing I could think about — even with my exciting first week volunteering at the nursing home. Ruby Grace had pulled some strings to get me the gig, even though the staff and current volunteers were plenty for the summer, and I was more thankful than she'd ever know. This was my element. I loved to be around other people, to help them in whatever way I could, to volunteer my free time for a higher purpose. With high school over now and all those previous volunteer jobs I'd had within the Interact program ripped from my grasp after graduation, I didn't know what I'd fill my summer with as I tried to figure out what to do with my gap year.

Other than my planned adventures with Mikey, of course.

Not that the first bullet on my list went over very well. Mudding had been a foolish idea, one that exploded quite literally in my face. My cheeks heated at the memory of getting my truck stuck, just like he said I would, and of falling into the mud the minute I stepped out of my truck.

It was the most mortifying experience of my life.

Still, Mikey had laughed for the first time in months.

And he had thanked me for taking him out there.

That had to count for something, right?

And there was that moment, when he had pinned me in the mud, when his eyes were dancing over my face as if he'd never seen me before...

Betty flicked some water on my face, waving her hands in front of my eyes. "Wake up, girl. You may not know this about me yet, but I'm a stubborn old woman, and if you think I'm dropping this subject before you tell me everything, you're as wrong as a chicken in a tuxedo."

I chuckled, finally closing my mouth before I lifted myself out of the pool, sitting on the edge with my feet in the water. I'd just taught my first class of water aerobics — a class that Noah had apparently made *very* popular here. I could see the disappointment in all the women's faces when they showed up for class and it was me instead of a shirtless, glistening Noah Becker.

And even though it had only been a few days for me at the nursing home, I could already tell Betty was a handful. She was on the verge of being diagnosed with dementia, but Ruby Grace had let me in on the secret that the woman was as sharp as a tack, and only had *selective* memory when it was convenient for her.

Everyone at the nursing home loved and respected her. Everyone in the Becker family absolutely adored her.

And now that we'd spent a few days together, I could see why.

"There's nothing to tell," I said, digging my heels deep into denial as I offered her a shrug. "We're friends, that's all."

"Uh-huh. And I'm Doris Day." She shook her head, running her hands through the wet, thin, white wisps of hair on her head. "I saw the way you blushed when I suggested that you two dance together at dinner on Sunday. And the way you watch him — *all* the time. If I'm being honest, honey, you're about as obvious as a pumpkin in a hay stack, though I'm sure you'd much rather be a needle."

I sighed, looking up to the white clouds floating above us like they'd somehow deliver me from the current moment. "You really aren't going to let this go, are you?" I asked.

"Nope," she answered with a pop. "Now, how long have you been in love with him?"

I cringed, biting my lip as I brought my gaze back to hers. "Since we were eight years old?"

It came out like a question, like a permission I was seeking, as if Betty Collins would somehow be able to grant me access to the boy who had been off-limits my whole life.

Sure, honey. Go right ahead! Tell him how you feel and he'll be yours. You're welcome.

Betty shook her head, clucking her tongue. "It's even worse than I thought. And he has no idea, does he?"

"Completely clueless," I said on another sigh.

She was quiet for a moment, her eyes reflecting the turquoise water of the pool as she thought. It was a perfect summer day — just a few white clouds in the sky, temperature in the mid-seventies, a cool breeze coming in from the north. It was the kind of day that made you feel like no matter what was going on in your life, it would all be okay, somehow.

"Well, I think there's only one solution to your problem, and it's an obvious one."

"I can't just tell him how I feel."

"Ah, so she does know," Betty said, pointing at me.

"It's not that simple," I said, dropping back down into the water. It hit just above my waist now, and I let my fingertips run along the top of the water as I paced, trying to explain. "He's still heartbroken over Bailey. He couldn't see me as a possible girlfriend *before* Bailey messed him up — how could he possibly see me like that now? When she's the only thing taking up space in his head, other than moving to New York?"

I was surprised by how easily the words came out of me, as if I'd been waiting my whole life for someone to figure out the secret that I'd been hiding so that I could *finally* talk it through. The sad truth was, Mikey had always been my person. So, when he ditched me for Bailey, I didn't have a girlfriend to spew all my feelings to. It wasn't for lack of trying — hell, I'd even joined three more clubs that I had absolutely zero interest in in the hopes that I'd find a new friend. But everyone in our school had already been cliqued off by then, and though I made some casual friends to talk to at school and during club meetings, none of them were eager to hang out with me outside of that.

Dad was my best friend outside of Mikey, and *clearly* I couldn't talk to him about my boy troubles.

Maybe it was because it was Betty, and if the Becker family trusted her, I knew I could, too. Maybe it was because I'd had it all bottled up for years, and for some reason, I felt like that moment when Mikey had hovered over me in the mud pit — like he saw a little something more than he had before — had somehow busted the top right off, my insides spewing and fizzing to get out. Or maybe it was just something about that perfect summer day, about the whisper of promise that floated in on the cool breeze.

Whatever it was, relief washed over me with each confession I made.

"Speaking of which," Betty said, calling me back to the moment. "What are you going to do when he makes the move to the big city?"

I shifted uncomfortably. "Well, as of now, I'm trying to stop him."

"How?"

"I made a list of things he used to love about this town, things that made Stratford home to him — his favorite things to do, favorite restaurants, favorite places. I want to show him that he still loves this town, and that Bailey isn't the only thing that he loved about it."

Betty nodded, a small smile on her thin lips. "Smart. I like it." She frowned again. "Let me ask you something. Have you ever dressed up around him? Did you guys go to homecoming together, or prom?"

I wrinkled my nose. "I don't *need* to dress up around him. That's the best part of our friendship. I can be in sweatpants and a t-shirt and he still treats me the same way as if I was all dolled up. And, no. I mean, we *did* get dressed up for freshman homecoming, but we both felt awkward and neither of us really wanted to go. So, we bailed out and opted for an all-night *Halloween* movie marathon, instead. And then..." I shrugged. "Well, then he had Bailey."

"Hmm..." she mused. "Well, I'm glad you feel comfortable around him, and you don't strike me as a girl who likes to paint on a full face of makeup and wear high heels."

I wrinkled my nose again. "Definitely not."

"But, have you ever thought that maybe he doesn't see you as a possible girlfriend... because he's never really seen you as a *girl*, at all?"

I opened my mouth to argue, but her words hit harder than I expected, and memories of countless nights spent together in close proximity in his bed or mine flashed through my mind. He was a teenage boy. Even if we *had* been friends before, why did he never get an unfortunate boner at our close proximity, or try to make a move on me with all those raging hormones?

My mouth snapped shut again, because Betty was right.

I might as well have been a teenage boy, too.

"Listen, you two haven't really hung out in the past two years while he dated that girl, right? Not until these past few months?"

I nodded.

"Well, boys and girls change a lot when they're your age, and I'd bet that you have some..." Her eyes dropped to my chest. "*Assets* now that he might not have noticed before."

I gaped, covering my bikini top with both arms. "Betty!"

"I'm just saying!" she said, throwing her arms up. "God, I know it's archaic. It goes against every feminist bone in my body and I *know* Julia Roberts would be ashamed of me if she could hear me saying this. But... the truth is, boys — especially boys his age — tend to think with only one part of their anatomy." She paused, one eyebrow arching. "And it ain't the brain, sweetheart."

I snorted.

"Maybe wearing makeup and a fancy dress and high heels is too much," she continued. "But you can still show him how *very* womanly you are in other ways."

I laughed, shaking my head. "You are a dirty old woman, you know that?"

"And proud of it, sweetheart." She winked. "Now, that list of yours with all of Mikey's favorite things in town... any of them involve swim suits?"

Her grin was wicked, and I was already shaking my head.

"Yes, but I don't like the way you're looking at me."

Betty chuckled, walking over to where I'd stopped pacing in the pool to frame my face with her wet hands. "It's now or never, little lady. Get that boy to see you in a new light. As a *woman*, not just the girl he's been best friends with for years." She smacked my cheeks softly, letting my face go with a knowing smile. "I promise, it only takes one time for them to see it. After that?" She shook her head. "They can't *unsee* it. Even if you do go back to sweatpants and t-shirts."

"Is this you speaking from experience?"

"Oh, heavens no," she said, waving me off. "I had one man and one man only, and he made it very clear how in love with me he was from the day we met. But," she said, pointing her finger at my nose. "I watched a *lot* of romantic comedies, and I promise, this is the trick."

Something between a whine and a laugh came from my lips, and I sighed, dropping down until every inch of me was under water. I blew bubbles from my mouth, sinking down to sit on the pool floor, and with only my heartbeat in my ears, I internally chastised myself for taking advice from a nearly senile woman whose advice was built from too-good-to-be-true romance movies.

Still...

At this point, what did I have to lose?

• • •

Michael

Logan was the first one in the water when we drove out to the lake on Saturday.

He barreled past the rest of us, setting up blankets and chairs on the grass, tearing off his shirt and throwing it at Mallory as he ran past her. She was still laughing when he grabbed the rope swing at the end of the dock and swung high into the air without a second thought, letting go of the rope when he was at the highest point of the swing and then plummeting down into the water with a giant splash.

Jordan and Noah rewarded him with whoops of encouragement when his head emerged from the water, and Mom laughed from where she was spreading out a giant picnic blanket beside me.

"Gosh," she said, shaking her head and pulling some grapes from the cooler we'd packed. "It's been so long since I've been out here... feels like another lifetime."

I nodded, knowing without asking that the other lifetime she was thinking of was when she and Dad would bring me and my brothers out here when we were younger.

I didn't have much recollection of all the lake trips we took, but I did remember one time — the summer before my dad passed away. I remembered the sunburn, the first fish I ever caught on my own, and that I'd been missing my front tooth.

It was hard, because I didn't know how much of that I *actually* remembered, and how much was only a memory because someone else had told me the story about it. I was so young, I couldn't actually close my eyes and remember catching that fish. But I could look at the photo of our family in front of our tents, of my missing front tooth, of the sunburn on my cheeks.

It was one of the most difficult parts of losing my father at such a young age.

I could barely remember him.

I never admitted it out loud — not to anyone but Kylie — mostly because it made me feel ashamed for some reason. But it was the truth, and if anyone understood it, it was Kylie. When I looked back on my younger life, I hardly remembered anything that happened with my dad past what someone told me or what a photo or video had captured, and it was the same for Ky.

I knew what Mom meant by it feeling like another lifetime.

For me, it felt like another person's life altogether.

"Well, we all know the stubborn girl you can thank for bringing you back," I finally said on a smirk.

Mom's smile brightened at that, and she cast a glance across the way where Kylie was setting up her own blanket. She was the reason we were all here today, and she'd organized it all before she even told me, which meant I couldn't say no. There *was* no saying no to my mom, and when the rest of my brothers were involved, I knew there was no use even trying.

Not that I would have tried to back out, not after the promise I'd made Kylie. For whatever reason, her showing me what I used to love about this dump of a town was important to her. And even though I knew she'd never change my mind about moving to New York, I *would* follow through on the promise I'd made to let her try.

"That girl has always been something special," Mom said, still eyeing Kylie.

Before I could respond, I was hoisted up over Noah's shoulder, and he took off after Jordan toward the water. There was no use fighting it, so I rally cried all the way until Noah threw me into the water, him and Jordan jumping off the dock right after.

Logan threw his fist in the air, immediately shoving Jordan back under water as soon as he surfaced. They were still wrestling as I reclined back, eyes cast toward the blue sky dotted with puffs of white clouds. The air was hot and humid, but the water was cool and crisp, and nothing said summer more than that combination.

"Look at that," Logan said, nodding toward the shore with a goofy grin. "When's the last time you saw Mom have a smile like that?"

My brothers and I all turned to look, and Mom was mid-laugh, sitting on the picnic blanket with Ruby Grace as they both lathered on sunscreen.

"I don't know why none of us ever thought of bringing her out here," Jordan said, voice low.

Noah shrugged, running a hand over his face to wipe off some of the water. "I guess I thought it would bring up memories of Dad."

"I'm sure it does," Logan chimed in. "But, maybe that's okay. It's not like she's ever going to forget him."

We all fell silent at that.

"Speaking of dopey smiles," Jordan said after a long pause. "I think this is the first time the four of us have been alone since your big news, Noah."

That dopey smile Jordan spoke of doubled, and Noah's cheeks flushed like he already had a sunburn coming on.

"Congrats, big bro," Logan said, clapping him on the back. "Let's hope this town is ready for a Becker wedding."

Noah laughed through his nose. "Let's hope they're ready for *two,* since I bet you won't be too far behind me." He cocked an eyebrow, looking up the bank at where Mallory was taking a seat next to Ruby Grace.

"Ugh, you guys are disgusting," I finally said, splashing them both. "Can we please talk about football or fighting or literally anything but this."

Jordan high-fived me, but Noah and Logan just laughed, both of them shaking their heads.

"Just you wait," Noah said. "It'll be *you* talking like this soon enough."

I rolled my eyes hard enough to cause an aneurysm. "Fat chance. I gave up on the whole love thing months ago."

"What about Kylie?" Jordan asked.

Something about the way he said her name, about the way all three of my brothers watched me once he'd said it, made the blood in my veins turn to ice.

"What *about* Kylie?" I echoed.

"You guys hang out almost every day," Logan pointed out.

Noah nodded. "And she clearly has feelings for you."

The laugh that bubbled out of me was loud and surprising — just as surprising as the words that had just come from my big brother's mouth. I shook my head. "She does *not* have feelings for me. Guys, it's *Kylie,*" I said, as if just reminding them of that simple fact would put all their idiotic questions to bed. "We've been friends since we were in elementary school. Yeah, we hang out every day, but we play video games and listen to music and try to crack the code on Dad's hard drive — not make out and feel each other up under the covers."

They all smirked at that.

"Seriously, we're not even remotely attracted to each other. She's my *friend,*" I reiterated. "The way our relationship is, she might as well be a boy."

Logan's eyebrows shot up into his hairline as he looked somewhere behind me, and a low whistle came from his lips. "I don't know, little bro. Not sure I know a single boy who looks like *that.*"

I turned, following his gaze up to the shore where Kylie was, and when I saw her, something inside me grabbed my next breath in a hard fist and squeezed.

She had her tank top in her hands, suspended above her head as if she was moving in slow motion as she stripped it off. Her long, dark hair tumbled free from the neck of the shirt once it was over her shoulders, falling down her back as she let the tank top drop to the ground. Her stomach was tight and toned, the tan she always attained easily every summer already starting to bronze her skin. But what made the fist around my lungs impossible to escape was the tiny, red scrap of fabric that covered her chest.

No, not her chest.

Her breasts.

Maybe it was because I'd been so wrapped up in Bailey for two years, or maybe it was because we hadn't been swimming together since before Bailey and I started dating, or maybe it was just because I was a blind fucking idiot. Regardless, one thing was sure — I had never seen Kylie like that.

Her breasts were small, but perfectly round and perky, and exactly the right size for how small she was. They stretched the fabric of the cherry red bikini she wore, the bottom of the round swells peeking out in a little hole that was cut in the top.

She had cleavage.

My best friend had fucking *cleavage.*

How had I never noticed that before?

She was oblivious to the stares she was getting from me and my brothers, and she flicked the top button on her jean shorts next, sliding the zipper down before she moved her hips in time with her hands, shimmying the denim off to reveal a little strap of fabric that matched the top. Tiny strings zig zagged on each hip, the V of the bikini bottom accenting her toned stomach, her lean legs, her narrow hips.

And when she turned, taking both her shirt and her shorts and shoving them in her bag, I saw more of my best friend's ass than I'd ever seen in my life.

That bikini was practically a thong, the center of the fabric bunched together at the small of her back. It hiked that red fabric up, and the bottom swells of her ass mimicked those of her breasts.

Gone was the Kylie who was all knees and shoulders and braces.

And the Kylie I saw now?

I didn't recognize her at all.

The hyena cackle of laughter that erupted behind me shook me from my thoughts, and I picked my jaw up from the ground as I turned to face my brothers again.

They all wore shit-eating grins, and Jordan looked at me with a mix of amusement and pity. "Yeah. The way you just watched her strip down to that bikini *definitely* screamed '*not even remotely attracted.*'"

That earned another fit of laughter from Noah and Logan, and I narrowed my eyes. "We're friends. That's it."

"Uh-huh," Noah said, floating on his back. "Say that again when the dude down the beach comes over and asks her for her number."

My eyes narrowed farther, this time in confusion as I glanced back over my shoulder. And sure as shit, there was a group of guys from our high school down the beach from us.

And one of them had his eyes locked on Kylie like he was a wolf and she was his next meal.

I recognized him — a jock from the grade below us named Parker. He and his group of friends were seniors now, and I could see it in the confident way he watched Kylie that he was just as full of himself as any new senior football star was. He had a reputation around Stratford High for being both a straight-A student and a playboy. He was one of those guys you wanted to hate, but couldn't really because he was funny and charming and talented as hell on the football field.

Still, everyone around that high school knew he had a specific taste for good girls, ones he could pull in easy and leave just as easy when he'd had his fill.

One thing *I* knew for sure — there was no fucking way I'd let him hurt Kylie.

It was absurd, that that was where my brain went. He hadn't even *talked* to her and a wave of possession had swept in on me like a surprise summer storm. In fact, that entire *moment* had hit me like a bolt of lightning, like a crack of thunder, loud and quaking as it rattled everything I thought I knew.

My jaw clenched, and I turned back to my brothers long enough to flip them all off before I started swimming toward shore. I could still hear their laughter when my feet hit the sand, but I didn't care.

I had a different focus now — and it was keeping that slime ball away from my best friend.

Chapter Six

Kylie

*W*orst. Idea. Ever.

Those words were on repeat in my mind as I tried to calm my breathing and my shaking hands enough to put sunscreen on my *very* exposed body. I couldn't believe I'd let Betty talk me into this, and while I'd bought into her theory when she'd first explained it all to me, I felt like an idiot now.

A very naked idiot.

I could feel eyes on me coming from every direction as I lathered up — perhaps the worst being the eyes from Mikey's mom. She'd never seen me dressed like this — hell, *no one* had — and I tried my best to stay calm and pretend like I was unaffected by the stares, but I wondered how many of them could see the tremble in my hands.

I wondered how many of them could see the scared little girl living inside of the seemingly confident young woman putting on sunscreen.

"You've got to fake it till you make it, sweetheart," Betty had told me when I'd brought the swim suit to the nursing home on Friday to show her. *"If you're covering yourself and fidgeting, you might as well be in a muumuu. That little red bikini isn't just a piece of clothing, it's an attitude — embrace it."*

I forced a breath as I rubbed the lotion over my cleavage, reminding myself how I felt when I first put the swim suit on. I'd looked in the mirror and nearly gasped, surprised as I assumed everyone else was now that I had a body like that hiding under my t-shirts all this time. The truth of the matter was that I'd always been so obsessed with school and books and video games and volunteering, that shopping had never been a hobby for me. I'd never cared to be fashionable, or to wear clothes that showed what only I saw when I got undressed to take a shower.

But when I'd looked in that mirror, when I'd seen the girl staring back at me with a body that felt as foreign as the swimsuit covering it... something had come alive inside me.

Maybe it was confidence.

Maybe it was self-love.

Maybe it was just nausea, and I was an idiot to mistake it for anything else.

Regardless, I let out another long exhale and tried to channel the girl who had put on this swimsuit in the dressing room and smiled. At this point, I was committed, and what did it matter if I didn't get the reaction out of Mikey that I wanted? *I* felt good — and that was what mattered.

"Need help with that?"

I'd been so caught up in trying to get my hands to stop from shaking that I hadn't noticed Mikey getting out of the water. But there he was — standing in front of me with water dripping down every valley and over every little hill of his body, accenting the lean, toned abs he'd had since our freshman year of high school. I could still remember the first time he took his shirt off after the summer of eighth grade, when I'd noticed that little boy body was changing into something else... something *more*.

Now, he was eighteen, and every part of his body screamed that fact in my face. His biceps were cut, the veins of his forearms winding like ropes all the way down to his wrists. His chin was no longer smooth, but peppered with a scruff I was desperate to touch. That shaggy hair of his that I'd always loved fell a little into his eyes now, dripping water down his face, his neck, his chest and abs, collecting in a little river that disappeared somewhere under his black swim trunks.

I gulped.

"Hmm?" I asked, tearing my eyes from his abdomen and trying desperately to remember what he'd asked me.

He smirked, reaching out a hand for the bottle of sunscreen in mine. "Figured it would be kind of hard to get your own back," he said calmly, easily, as if the fact that he was offering to lather lotion on me when I was the most naked I'd ever been in front of him was no big deal at all.

I realized, even when my shaking hands handed the bottle to him, that it probably *wasn't* any big deal to him. Our entire friendship, Mikey had seen me through lenses that masked the fact that I was a girl — and deep down, I knew a bathing suit wouldn't change that.

"So," he said when I turned and swept my hair together, gathering it in front of my left shoulder so he could apply the sunscreen. The lotion was chilled, but his hands were warm, and when they touched down on my upper back, my eyes fluttered closed on as soft of an exhale as I could manage. "Since when do you own swimsuits like this?"

My eyes flew open, nearly popping out of my head as my heart thundered to life in my chest. His warm hands weren't enough to soothe me now, and if anything, they felt like a warm breeze on a pile of embers, stoking them back to a roaring fire.

Maybe Betty was *right.*

I cleared my throat, shrugging and aiming for nonchalant when I answered. "I don't know, I wanted to try something new," I said. "I know it's not really my style, but…"

Mikey didn't say anything else, but his hands slid beneath the crisscrossed straps on the back of my swimsuit top, skating down my spine and over my ribs. A shiver ran over me, one I couldn't even try to hide.

I peeked at him over my shoulder. "Do I look stupid in it?"

His hands stilled where they were on my lower back, and his eyes floated up to meet mine. He swallowed, and something close to a smile touched his lips, but it fell before it could reach his eyes. "No, Kylie," he said, his voice low. "You don't look stupid."

Mikey watched me for a long moment, but then his eyes fell to where his hands were on my back, and he got back to work as I turned around to face the water again.

Every nerve of my body was aware as his hands ran over it, spreading the sunscreen over my hips and lower back. When his fingertips dipped down just below the band of my bottoms, my eyelids fluttered again and I was so close to moaning that I tore away from his grasp, offering him an awkward smile as I snatched the sunscreen bottle from his hands again.

"Thanks!" I said, still smiling like a loon. "I think I can get the rest."

Mikey smirked, throwing his hands up in a surrender before he rubbed what was left of the sunscreen on them over his shoulders. He plopped down on the blanket I'd set up next, leaning back on his hands and looking out at the water.

When every part of my skin was covered with sunscreen — including the *very* large portion of my ass that hung out in this little bikini — I took a seat next to him, sliding my sunglasses on and pulling my long hair up into a pony tail. Jordan was still in the water, floating on his back and looking up at the sky, while Logan toted Mallory around on the floaty she was reclined on. Noah, Ruby Grace, and Lorelei were all on the blankets just down the bank from us, talking and laughing about something as they ate lunch.

"This was a good idea," Mikey said after a long pause. "My brothers and I were just talking about how none of us ever thought to bring Mom out here. I guess we thought it might be hard for her, since we used to come here with Dad. But…" He smiled, nodding toward where Lorelei was. "Look at her. I haven't seen her laugh like that in so long."

My heart squeezed, and I tried and failed to stamp down the little parade of hope that sprang to life in my chest at his words. I wanted so badly to show him that Stratford was more than just the memories he'd made in it with Bailey, and for the first time, I thought that maybe I had a chance.

"It'd be even better if we could get you playing on your guitar," I said, leaning over on my left hand until my shoulder nudged his. Mikey's smile faltered, but I kept my gaze on him. "You ever going to tell me why you threw it in the fire at The Black Hole?"

The Black Hole was the most popular town hangout, a weekly bonfire that people of all ages would show up at to party. There were high schoolers way too underage to be there, college kids back on break or those who stuck around after high school and got jobs in town, and of course, the residents who had been in Stratford for decades, drinking the same beer or whiskey and talking about the same town gossip every week.

Sometime just after Thanksgiving, Mikey had gotten rip-roaring drunk and caused a scene, breaking his guitar and throwing it in the fire while everyone watched from a distance. For them, it was just one more thing to gossip about.

But for me, it was a sign that my best friend needed help more than I thought.

That had been when I started forcing myself back into his life — whether he wanted me there or not. Still, to this day, we never talked about that night at the bonfire, about what drove him to throw away the thing that brought him the most joy in life.

And if it was just *a* guitar, maybe I wouldn't have been so worried.

But it was the one his father gave him before he died, one he'd held onto even when he knew he needed a new one.

Now, it was ash.

Mikey let out a long breath, eyes still fixed on the water. "I was drunk," he said, then muttered under his breath, "obviously." He sighed again. "And you know I don't drink. But, for my brothers, that has always been their answer to everything. Bad day at work? Whiskey. Girl problems? Nothing a few beers can't fix. So, I thought that was my answer, that if I got wasted, everything that had happened between me and Bailey would melt away."

My chest ached, because I could understand the feeling. If I knew a bottle of wine would kill my desire for my best friend to fall in love with me, I'd have become a drunk at age fourteen.

"Well," he continued. "Turns out that when *I* get drunk, I don't forget about my problems — I text them."

I chuckled, and something close to a smirk found his lips before they leveled out again.

"It was sort of funny at first, and Bailey did answer. But, the longer we talked, and the more it felt like us — like *us* before she left — the angrier I got. I started writing her these long texts that ranged from furiously demanding more explanation for why she left, to desperately begging her to come back. And then, she told me not to text her anymore, that I needed to let her go. And even though I sent another mountain of texts, she stopped responding."

Everything inside me deflated. "Ouch."

"Yeah," he said on a nod. "Ouch."

"So you threw your guitar into the fire."

"I threw my guitar into the fire," he echoed. "Because in that moment, it wasn't the guitar my father gave me. It wasn't the musical instrument that brought me joy. It was a torture device, one that would always remind me of the nights I sat with Bailey, of when I'd strum on those strings and she'd bring a song to life with her angelic voice. We made music together, you know?" he asked, turning to look at me, and I hated the pain I saw in his eyes, because it was a pain I knew would never be erased. "And I guess you could say that was the day the music died."

I frowned, sitting up until I was fully facing him. "I'm really sorry, Michael," I said, eyes searching his. "For everything she put you through."

The little muscle that hinged his jaw tightened and released, and he tore his gaze from mine, standing before I had the chance to say another word.

"Come on," he said, reaching his hand down for mine with a forced smile. "Let's get you on that rope swing."

I blanched. "Uh..."

"*Now*, Ky," he said, grabbing my hand and yanking me up to stand. When I was on my feet, we stood toe to toe, our chests close, and his breath heated my lips as my own caught in my chest.

Up close, I could see the ring of a slightly darker olive green surrounding the hazel of his irises, and those eyes watched mine before they fell to my chest — and all the blood in my body rushed to my cheeks in the most furious blush of my life.

"Better hope your new wardrobe can hold up," he said on a smirk.

I still hadn't taken a breath when he grabbed my hand in his — just like he had a hundred times before — and tugged me toward the dock.

And, at least for the moment, Bailey was forgotten.

Though I knew it wouldn't last.

• • •

Michael

By the time the sun began its descent behind the Smoky Mountains in the distance, we were all sun-kissed and pleasantly worn out. Mom and Jordan were working on packing up the coolers while Logan and Mallory folded up the blankets. Ruby Grace and Noah were sitting at the edge of the dock, feet hanging down toward the water, Ruby Grace's head resting on Noah's shoulder.

Kylie watched them with bent brows, as if she was such an empath that she could feel every emotion between them. Tomorrow, Ruby Grace would head back to Utah for the last part of her year with AmeriCorps, and I knew now that they were engaged, it would be even harder to say goodbye.

"I'm proud of you for jumping off that rope swing," I said to her as we toweled off, trying to distract her from my brother's sadness. If there was one thing I knew about Kylie, it was that she felt the human condition like no other person ever could. It was part of what made her an amazing daughter to her father, who was a lost soul after the death of her mom, and it was part of what convinced me that she'd somehow save the world one day, too.

A soft smile touched her chapped lips. "I don't know if I can say the same, seeing as how I felt like I was all flailing arms and legs coming down into the water."

"Oh, you were," I teased, running my towel over my hair. "Looked like one of those wavy blow-up guys in front of Big Dog's Auto Sales, but at least you did it."

She smacked my chest, but my hand shot out and grabbed her wrist, tugging her into my arms before she had the chance to fight it. She dropped her towel and mine fell from off my shoulders as I prepared her for the classic noogie I'd tortured her with since we were kids.

"DON'T YOU DARE, MICHAEL BECKER!"

I just laughed harder, tickling her until I could get her in a firm hold. And I did. I had her — right there in my grasp, squealing and trying to worm her way out, my knuckle just above her head — when a third, unwelcome party joined us.

"Hey, Kylie," Parker said, sliding his hands into the pockets of his swim trunks when he was in front of us.

Kylie went completely still in my arms, her eyes wide, damp hair falling in front of her face. Then, she scrambled out of my hold, as if she was suddenly embarrassed by us touching.

Parker's eyes eagerly devoured her once she was standing on her own, like there wasn't an ounce of shame in him, but his charming smile when his eyes found hers again masked the wolf that I saw underneath it.

"Hi," she squeaked.

That made him smile wider, and only then did he give me a half glance. "Mikey," he said simply, nodding his head up a bit as if we were best buds.

"Parker," I replied flatly.

"I saw you going off the rope swing," he said, turning his attention back to Kylie. "That was pretty cool. We tried to get some of the girls here with us to do it, but they were all worried about getting their hair wet."

He laughed and rolled his eyes, and Kylie laughed a little, too which, for some reason, made my neck heat.

"Yeah, well, they probably actually know how to *do* their hair," she said, tugging on a handful of her own. "Not such a big deal to get it wet when it's just limp and straight like this."

Parker reached forward, tucking the hair she'd just pulled on behind her ear. "I like your hair," he said — simply, stupidly — but with the way Kylie's eyes doubled in size, you would have thought he was a god telling her he would make her immortal.

I cleared my throat. "We should probably help pack up the cars," I said, reaching for Kylie's hand. "Nice talking to you, Parker. Good luck with your senior year."

Parker smiled, but not at me — his attention was all on Kylie, and the fact that her hand was in mine didn't seem to faze him at all. "Thanks, man," he said, but then he took a step closer to Kylie. "I hope I see you around this summer."

She swallowed, trying and failing to smile back. "Yeah. Me, too."

Parker nodded, giving her one last dazzling smile before he turned and jogged his buff, shirtless, douchebag self back to his group of friends.

Kylie turned, looking at me with eyes the size of baseballs. "What the hell was *that*?" she asked me, laughing hysterically as I tugged her toward Mom and Jordan.

I smirked, trying to ignore the knot in my throat. "I think Parker Morris was flirting with you."

She snort-laughed, slamming her hand over her mouth as soon as the sound let loose. She shook her head. "That's absolutely absurd."

I shrugged in lieu of an answer, mostly because I was having a hard time understanding why my jaw was so tight, why the fingers not laced with hers were curled into my palms with a pressure that would surely leave a mark. My heart was beating too fast, the hair on my neck raised like my territory had just been threatened.

What the hell was wrong with me?

I blew out a breath, releasing her hand when we reached the rest of our crew, and I got to work loading up the cars without another word on the subject.

• • •

Kylie

Brett Eldridge crooned on the radio on our drive home, and I tapped my toes on Michael's dashboard, a permanent smile on my face as I watched dusk slowly turn to night in front of us. We had the windows of his old Camry rolled down, and the warm summer breeze danced through my hair. I was humming along to the song, thinking about how perfect the day had been, about how everything had gone right.

Mikey had fun.

I knew it without asking him. I'd watched him laugh and wrestle with his brothers, heard him scream like a banshee before flying off the rope swing, and felt the calmness of his heart like I hadn't in months as he spent the day with his family.

Maybe mudding hadn't been the best idea, but today was a win.

And I'd take it.

"We should go to Blondies," I shouted over the music.

Mikey seemed a little lost in his own thoughts, but he shook them away, offering me a smile. "Okay."

"You alright?"

He watched me for a long moment, like he was looking for something, but then his gaze found the road again and he nodded. "Yeah. Just a little tired."

I smiled mischievously, leaning forward to crank the radio up. "Nothing a little dance party can't fix!"

One eyebrow climbed on Mikey's face as we pulled up to the first stoplight in town, and I mouthed the words to "Don't Ya" while holding a fake microphone. My shoulders shimmied and shook, hips wiggling, and I even did a hair flip for some added drama.

He laughed at that, shaking his head when I leaned over the console toward him and stuck the invisible microphone in his face. He pushed my fist away, so I leaned out my car window and sang to the car next to us. It was an older couple, and they smiled and bopped their heads along, encouraging me.

"Get back in here, crazy girl," Mikey said, tugging on my tank top until I was firmly seated again.

"Only if you sing with me!"

I shoved my fist back in front of him again, and he stared at me, still not cooperating. But when the light turned green and I shrugged, about to lean out the window again, he grabbed my wrist in his hands and belted out the chorus into my invisible mic.

Laughter rolled through me, and I shimmied and sang along, passing the microphone between us like we were doing a karaoke duet on stage. When the song ended and we made the turn on Main Street toward Blondies, I held up my hand for a high-five, and Mikey slapped it as he fought against a smile.

"Nerd," he said, shaking his head.

"Don't act like that wasn't fun."

He didn't respond, and I wished I hadn't been so fixated on him that I missed what was being said on the radio. I wished I hadn't been tracing the bridge of his nose, the plumpness of his bottom lip — the one I used to tease him and say was his *broody boy pouty lip*. If only I hadn't been cataloging the way his hair dried when it was wind-blown, or the olive color of his sun-kissed skin, or the way dusk touched the green in his eyes, maybe then I would have heard the announcer on the radio say which song was next before it was too late to change it.

"*... New from Nashville, it's Bailey Baker with her brand new, debut song — 'Mama's Front Porch'.*"

All the blood drained from my face, the laughter gone immediately, and I watched as every muscle in Michael's body tightened at once — his fists around the steering wheel, his shoulders up to his ears, his jaw, his chest. He was as stiff as a board as the first few notes of the song played, and as soon as her voice blasted through the speakers, my hand jutted out and hit the power button, leaving us blanketed in silence, but for the other cars on the road.

He didn't relax even an inch.

His eyes stayed on the road, and when he drove past Blondies, I didn't even bother telling him. Because I knew.

That was it. The night was over.

"Hey..." I tried, reaching for him. But as soon as my hand touched his forearm, he shook me off, and I pulled away like I'd touched a hot stove.

"Don't."

I swallowed, because I didn't know a single thing I could say in that moment that would fix what just happened. No matter what I had to offer, nothing could erase the fact that the only girl he'd ever loved, the only girl to ever break his heart, now officially had a song on the radio.

And he'd have to hear her, no matter how badly it hurt.

He pulled up to the curb in front of my house, not even bothering to put the car in park. He just sat there, hands wrapped around the wheel, eyes losing focus somewhere in the distance as he waited for me to get out.

"I don't want to leave you like this."

"Like what?"

I swallowed. "I don't know..."

"I'm fine," he said curtly. "Like I said, I'm tired. I just want to go home and get some rest."

"I know, but—"

"God*damnit*, Kylie!" he screamed, beating his fists on the wheel before he gripped it again. He turned and pinned me with cold, hard eyes. "Please, for Christ's sake, just stop trying to fix me or save me or make me happy again or whatever it is you're trying to do and just leave me alone."

The stinging hit my nose first, and my bottom lip trembled before I rolled it between my teeth. "I'm your best friend," I reminded him. "Best friends don't leave each other to drown in their own misery."

He blew out a breath through his nose like a dragon, finally putting the car in park before he ran his hands over his face. When his palms hit his lap, he turned to me, marginally calmer this time.

"Kylie, please," he said, and my heart cracked just like his voice did as he fought back emotion. "I need to be alone right now. *Please.*"

Everything inside me told me to reach for him, but if I was his friend like I'd just pointed out, then I knew reaching for him wouldn't be for him.

It would be for me.

It didn't matter what I wanted right then. It didn't matter that I wanted him to let me in, to let me help, to let me hold him and comfort him and take his pain away.

Because he just told me what *he* needed, and I had no other choice but to give it to him.

I swallowed, nodding with my lip still pinned between my teeth as I gathered my bag and towel and draped them both over my shoulder. I turned, hand on the door handle, words I wanted to say lodged somewhere deep in my throat. But I ignored them, tugging on the handle and stepping out of his car, instead.

As soon as I shut the door again, he was gone.

Chapter Seven

Kylie

I'd never stared at my phone more in my life.

I had the screen memorized, every color in the sunset I had set as my background, every number and letter that lit up on it when it was locked — the time, the date, the provider and battery life. I even catalogued the three hair-line cracks I had in the screen protector, and the way they made a sort of wishbone shape.

But no matter how I willed it, Mikey wouldn't text or call me back.

It'd been four days since our day at the lake, and I hadn't heard a single word from him.

A heavy sigh left my lips as I locked my phone again, this time flipping it face down on the middle couch cushion and pulling my attention back to the TV screen. The History Channel was running a Civil War miniseries — one Dad had been counting down to — and so my evenings had been filled with the blood and gore and treacherous history of our nation's past.

Which, admittedly, was somehow less depressing than the current state of my own life.

Staying busy was the only thing keeping me afloat that week. I spent my days at the nursing home and my evenings making dinner for Dad. Then, we'd plop down in the living room and watch the show while I scribbled more ideas in my adventure notebook, wondering if I'd get the chance to try any of them or if my time had passed.

"Your sighs tonight have been powerful enough to steer a sailboat, Smiley," Dad said, eyeing me from his recliner — the same one he'd had my whole life — before his attention was on the screen again.

I sighed to drive the point home. "I'm sorry, just a little distracted."

"Anything you want to talk about?"

I shook my head, but a commercial came on the television, and Dad muted it, putting his full attention on me.

"Is this about your gap year?"

I picked at the fraying strings on the end of my hoodie, ones I'd chewed up throughout the years of wearing it. All of my hoodies were victims to my nervous chewing habit, and they all wore the scars.

"You know, you don't have to wait to go to college," he said when I didn't answer. "Your mom took that year off because she needed to, because she *wanted* to. You know what you want to do, and that you want to go to college," he reminded me. "And you could still get in for spring semester, if you started applying now."

"It's not that," I said on a long exhale. "I mean, I'm still not sure what to *do* with my gap year, but I know I want to take it. Not just for mom," I said, though that was a driving force. "But for me. I can't explain it, but I feel like it's what I'm supposed to do, like there's something I need to learn, or some place I need to go or see before I go to college." I frowned. "It's weird, like a gut feeling that makes no sense but that I trust implicitly."

Dad smiled at that. "You got that from your mother. She used to call it her sixth sense. She would get a gut feeling about something and there was no talking her out of it, no matter how crazy it seemed." He chuckled, looking at me like he saw her, instead. "That gut feeling saved us from one of the biggest pile ups on I-65 the year after you were born."

"Really?" My heart squeezed, a soft smile finding my lips at the thought of having something in common with Mom. Any time Dad told me that — *you look like her, you sound like her, she did that, too* — it warmed me from the inside out. I longed so badly to have her in me, to be a way she could live on.

He nodded. "Tell you what, I never questioned her gut feelings again." Dad watched me for a long pause. "Alright, if it's not the gap year, then what is it?"

I shifted. "Rhymes with *Nike.*"

"Ah," Dad said, as if now that I'd said it, he felt like he should have already known. He sat back in his chair with a thoughtful pause. "Sad that he's leaving?"

I nodded.

"Still trying to get him to stay?"

My mouth popped open at that, but Dad just smirked. "How did you know?"

"You're not as sneaky with that notebook as you'd like to think," he said, nodding to the offending object in my lap. "Had it open all dinner. Can't fault me for being a nosey old man when you leave stuff like that for the taking."

I chuckled. "Dad! That's invasion of privacy," I teased, but another sigh left me as my eyes fell to the notebook. "Not that it matters. The two *adventures* I've convinced him to take so far both blew up in my face."

"The lake day seemed great," he countered. "Lorelei called me to tell me how thankful she was to you for organizing it all."

"It *was* great," I said. "Until the car drive home, when the stupid radio played Bailey's song."

Dad blanched at that. "They're already playing her on the radio?" He shook his head. "She's only been in Nashville for… what… five months?"

"Eight," I corrected, because yes, I'd been counting. "But yeah, it seems pretty fast. Mikey said the label that signed her was obsessed with her, that they couldn't wait to get her album recorded." I shrugged. "I guess she's making waves over there."

Dad was quiet for a long moment as I picked at my hoodie strings. "Well," he finally said. "I'm sure that was hard for him, but I'm also sure he appreciated the lake day. And that he had fun."

"He hasn't texted me since then," I confessed, staring at my phone. "Hasn't returned my calls, either."

"Give him a little time, he'll come around."

"Tomorrow is June ninth," I said, peeking up at my Dad to see if he understood why that was important. His frown told me he did. "I can't leave him alone."

Dad nodded. "Well, if I know anything about Mikey, it's that he loves you."

My heart ached, for a reason I wasn't ready to tell Dad yet.

"And he will be happy to see you tomorrow, even if he doesn't realize it at first."

"I'm not even sure he'll let me through his front door."

"You're my daughter," Dad said. "And you won't take no for an answer. That's one of the most special things about your love and your friendship." He pointed the remote at me. "It's relentless."

I chuckled, glancing at my phone again as Dad unmuted the television. The miniseries stole his attention, and I thought about what he said, wondering if my *relentless friendship* would save me or drive the final nail into my coffin tomorrow.

I'd find out soon enough.

• • •

A mixture of determination and fear swirled within me like a stiff current as I wiped my sneakers on Mikey's door mat the next evening. The sun was still warming my back, even though it was just past seven, and that was one of my favorite things about summer time. The days were long, the evenings full of promise instead of darkness.

It'd been a long week, namely because Michael had ignored me for all of it. Giving him space when all I wanted was for him to talk to me had been tough, but what had made it worse was knowing this day was coming at the end of the week. I wished he would have broken the ice before now, but he hadn't, and regardless, I wasn't leaving.

The constant ache that had lived in my chest all week was one I was used to. I'd experienced it the first time I realized I was in love with Michael, that I wanted more, but didn't know how to tell him. It'd been twice as bad when he started dating Bailey. I couldn't even be sure I'd ever been rid of that ache in the two years they'd dated, only that I'd gotten used to it, welcomed it, gave it a home to live in.

But for the past eight months, it'd been me and Mikey again. It had been so close to normal, to the way things used to be... and somehow, maybe, with a promise of more.

Until Saturday night.

My ribcage was suffocating as I remembered the look in his eyes when Bailey's song came on the radio. An entire day of fun was wiped away in just seconds, with just one song from one girl who held the key to everything for him.

And as soon as he'd driven away that night, that ache I'd said goodbye to came right back, climbing into the bed of my chest and making a home again.

The days had blurred together, filled with long hours of volunteering at the nursing home and long evenings of watching TV with Dad. Our conversation from the night before floated back to me, and I held onto my father's words, to his promise that everything would be okay in time.

It was Thursday, and for five long days, I'd left Michael alone.

But tonight was different.

He didn't get to have space tonight.

The screen door squeaked shut behind me when I stepped into the living room, and the sight of Lorelei at the dining room table with her hands wrapped around a glass of white wine nearly broke me. She was in robin's egg blue pajamas and her rose-pink robe, hair tied up in a messy knot, eyes long and tired as they stared at the liquid in her glass. Her reaction to me coming inside the house was delayed, but bless her heart, she forced as much of a smile as she could through the tears — the ones dried on her face and the new ones forming in her hazel eyes.

"Well, aren't you a sight for sore eyes," she said on a sniff.

I offered her a sympathetic smile back, setting the basket I had in my arms down on the table. My hands were a little shaky as I pulled out the small bouquet of flowers I'd picked out for her first — daisies and carnations, two of her favorites — and immediately grabbed her favorite vase from under the kitchen sink, putting the oven on to pre-heat while I was in there.

Lorelei just watched me with wide eyes, not saying a word until I'd cut the stems and arranged the flowers the way I wanted them. I sat them down in front of her on the table, refilled her glass of wine with the bottle next to her, and went back to my basket.

"I brought some lasagna for dinner," I said, pulling the large, glass casserole dish out. "It'll just take an hour in the oven to heat up. I know you're probably not hungry, but I'll put it in now, just in case."

She still stared up at me with those glossy eyes as I returned to the kitchen, popping the dish in the oven and setting a timer. When I got back to the table, Lorelei squeezed her eyes shut, letting a river of tears run loose down her cheeks. She buried her face in her hands for just a split second before she was up out of her chair and in my arms.

"I know, I know," I said, hugging her tight and fighting against my own urge to cry. "It's okay."

For a long while I just hugged her, smoothing my hand over her back to bring as much comfort as I possibly could. When she finally pulled back, her eyes were freshly red and puffy, and she sniffed, wiping at her nose with the sleeve of her robe.

"You are an angel, Kylie Nelson. Do you know that?"

I smiled. "Not an angel. Just a friend."

Lorelei shook her head, sitting back down at the table carefully and reaching for her wine. She took a sip, took a breath, and then smiled at me as best she could again. "He's in his bedroom."

I frowned, nodding. "I'll come grab the lasagna in an hour, okay? Let me know if you need anything."

She reached out for my hand and squeezed it, then I grabbed my basket with shaking hands, striding toward the bear's den.

I didn't bother knocking on Mikey's door, just let myself inside. It was dark and depressing inside that little room — the navy blue curtains pulled shut to block the last of the sun's light from breaking through. The only light was that from the television, which flickered between dark and light with each action scene that passed over the screen. Clothes littered the floor, empty soda cans and snack wrappers littered his desk, and then there was him — sitting on the bed with a black hoodie on, the hood up and covering most of his face, Xbox controller in his hands.

He didn't take his eyes off the screen when I came in. They were long and worn just like his mom's, and little greasy tufts of his dark hair spilled from under the hoodie and over his forehead. He looked sort of menacing with the light of the TV hitting all the hard edges of his face — his long nose, his square jaw, the thick Adam's apple that protruded from his neck.

He looked like he was about to rob a bank.

He also looked like the saddest boy in the whole world.

"I don't want company," he said — again, not taking his eyes off the screen.

His fingers moved over the buttons on his controller with precision, and though his words stung, I ignored them, dropping my basket on his bed before I climbed up into it, too.

Mikey blew out a hard breath. "I mean it, Kylie. I don't want to hang out."

"Well, that's just too damn bad for you," I said, reaching over him for the extra controller on the edge of his desk. I hit the power button, snatching the large bag of Butterfinger minis I'd brought out of the basket and dropping it in his lap.

He sighed, finally pausing his game to look at me. "What do you want?"

"Nothing."

"I don't want to talk."

"Neither do I."

He huffed. "Why are you here, Kylie? I just want to be alone."

"Well, you can be alone tomorrow, if you still feel that way. Because tomorrow is June tenth. But today is June ninth, and I'm your best friend. And in case you forgot, best friends don't let best friends be alone on the anniversary of their parent's death."

Mikey swallowed, his nose flaring a bit before he turned back to the TV.

"You've ignored me all week, and I gave you space because I knew you didn't want to talk about what happened on the drive home from the lake. I gave you time. I left you alone. But you don't get space or time today, Mikey. You get your stubborn ass best friend in your bed playing video games with you. And it's fine if you don't want to talk, but you're not going to be alone. Not tonight."

My heart squeezed painfully in my chest when those last words came out, that familiar ache of loss making itself known inside me. I knew exactly how Mikey felt right now — how he wanted so desperately to skip this day, to not think about how long it'd been since his dad left the Earth, to not consider how much of his life has passed without his father being there to witness it all. It was the deepest, loneliest, most severe pain I'd ever known in my life.

And the only thing that ever made me feel better was knowing I wasn't alone.

It was knowing that every year on July twelfth, my best friend would be there with me in my misery, silently promising me that everything would be alright.

The muscle in Mikey's jaw flexed under the skin, nose flaring again, a long, hard swallow rocking his Adam's apple. For a long moment, he just stared at the TV, his breaths long and heavy, and though I'd never tell him, I saw how his eyes welled up with the threat of spilling over, but he held those tears back as if it was his only job in life.

After a long sixty seconds, he took a breath like it was his first, like he hadn't been breathing at all that entire time.

Then, he grabbed a Butterfinger from the bag, clicked a few buttons on his controller, and ended the game he'd been playing, changing it to two-player mode.

Chapter Eight

Michael

Kylie sat in my bed, silent as promised, and played video games with me for the next hour.

After that, she brought me a plate of lasagna and a glass of water, and even though the last thing I wanted to do was eat, she convinced me to take at least one bite. One bite lead to two, two to three, and before I knew it, I'd devoured it all.

Once she'd taken my plate to the kitchen, she came back and convinced me to take a shower.

"We can play more games when you're out," she'd said. "But you smell, and I know you don't want to go to bed like that."

So, here I was, standing in the shower, numb as I always was on June ninth.

The water was neither hot, nor was it exactly cold. It felt almost the same temperature as the room, like the air had liquified and was surrounding me in every way possible. I went through the motions — washing my hair, scrubbing my body — before I just stood there and let the water run down my back, thinking about the day.

Every year, my family and I knew this day would come.

We knew that January would turn to February, and then to March, and so on and so forth until June ninth popped up. Noah, Logan, and I knew that Patrick Scooter — Mallory's dad and the current owner of the distillery — would make an announcement on the loud speaker at work and ask for a moment of silence for our dead father. We knew he would pretend like he was sorry, pretend like he cared, pretend like it was all an unfortunate accident, even though something deep in our guts told us otherwise.

Jordan knew his football team would show up to summer training with something to commemorate the loss — sometimes a framed photo with their signatures, sometimes a football with Dad's name on it — to show them he wasn't alone. This year, they made a jersey with Dad's name on it, and they issued him the number ten.

Mom knew she'd get a slew of phone calls and drop-by visits, most of which she ignored, since she hardly left her bed and definitely *never* changed out of her pajamas on this day. And we also knew that this Sunday at church, the pastor would huddle us all together after service, and he'd whisper his sincere apologies and remind us that he was always there for us should we ever need him.

We knew all of that.

And still, it never made the day any less difficult to endure.

I scrubbed my hands over my face once I shut the faucet off, reaching for my towel hooked just outside the curtain. I was thankful my body knew what to do to get me dry and in clothes again, because if it was up to me, I wouldn't have been able to do it.

Every year on this day, I was numb.

But there was something worse this time.

Because today marked ten years.

Ten years without my father sitting at the dining room table, laughing and asking about our days as he held Mom's hand under the table. Ten trips around the sun without him taking me and my brothers out to our old tree-house to repair it or add to it, without trips to the lake, without trips anywhere with him. An entire decade without my dad's advice, without his jokes, without his hands holding Mama as they danced in the living room.

Somehow, for some reason, the ten-year mark made everything hurt even more than usual.

What made it even worse, I imagined, was that I'd been in my head about Bailey all week — ever since I heard her stupid song on the stupid radio. What pissed me off the most was that it *wasn't* a stupid song... it was a brilliant one.

One that she'd played for me the first time *we* finished writing it.

One that I'd *mostly* written.

One that the entire country would fall in love with now that it was on the radio, just like I did when she played it for me.

And it was proof of what I'd feared most.

She was making it happen. She was in Nashville writing songs and recording in the studio and playing on stage for hundreds of intoxicated tourists. She was moving on without me, and she was doing just fine.

And then, there was me.

Unfollowing her on social media had been such a huge step for me, and I'd thought in that way, it would at least be a few years before I had to see her or hear her. That song on the radio had proven me wrong.

So, there was Dad, and there was Bailey, and those two pains merged into one inside my heart over the past week.

But there was something warm there, too... something that perhaps had me more tied up than anything.

I couldn't stop thinking about Kylie.

I couldn't stop replaying that day at the lake — watching her laugh as we swung off the rope swing, seeing her palling around with my brothers, listening as she spoke with my mom like they were just as close of friends as we were. I could still feel the tenseness of my body when Parker came over to talk to her, and I could still hear the dizzying thoughts that assaulted me on the drive home that night — *before* Bailey's song played on the radio.

It was confusing, why I was so aware of her that day, why suddenly things that she'd always done stood out to me and gave me pause.

But I hadn't had time to process it, not with everything else taking up space inside me. So, with a sigh, I put it to rest for the night.

My room was clean when I pushed back through the door, scrubbing my hair dry with my towel. I scanned the now-clear floor, all my dirty clothes put in the laundry basket, and my now-clean desk, all the clutter and junk and garbage gone. My bed was made, and Kylie sat on top of the comforter, leaning against the wall with her laptop in her lap.

She clicked away on the keys, only looking up at me for a brief second before her eyes were on the screen again. "Feel better?"

"A little," I said, and it wasn't completely a lie. A shower might not have been able to bring my dad back, but it at least washed the stink off.

I hung my towel around my shoulders, watching Kylie and wondering what she was made of. Whatever it was, I knew it was stronger than the material that made me. And more thoughtful, too.

She'd come over even when she knew I'd be an asshole.

She'd fixed dinner for me and my mom.

She'd cleaned my room and forced me into the shower.

My stomach ached, because I knew not everyone in the world who felt like me had someone like her looking out for them.

And I also knew that I should appreciate it more.

I tossed my towel in the laundry basket, hopping up on the bed next to her and leaning back against the wall. She had my father's hard drive plugged into the side of her laptop, and the password screen up, as well as a list of randomized passwords she'd curated based on questions she'd asked me.

What's his middle name?

What town was he born in?

Did you have any pets? What were their names?

Hundreds and hundreds of passwords were on that list of hers — some with lines through them, some yet to be tried. I watched as she tried a few more, scratched lines through them, and then waited, because we'd learned that if we tried too many too quickly, we'd get locked out for a day.

"Kylie," I said as she typed up a few more possible passwords on the list.

"Mmm?"

"Thank you."

Her fingers paused over the keys, hovering, and her big brown eyes slowly lifted until they met my gaze. When she looked at me like that, I found myself flashing back to Saturday, to seeing her at the lake, as if I'd seen her for the first time in years.

So much about her had changed in the two years I'd been tied up in Bailey, and even when we reconnected, it was like I was blind to it all.

But I'd seen her on Saturday, and I saw her now — for *all* that she was. I saw how her cheeks had hollowed out, how her hair was longer now than it ever had been, how her body had changed, morphed, from bones and skin to curves and muscle. She wasn't a little girl anymore, and I wasn't a little boy, and through all the shit that had happened in my life, she was the one and only constant.

How long had I taken that for granted?

"You don't need to thank me," she said after a moment, her eyes still locked on mine. "You're my best friend. Where else would I be today?"

"I don't always act like it," I confessed. "Your best friend. Sometimes, I don't act like a friend at all. And I'm sorry for that."

She smirked then, punching my arm. "Don't go getting soft on me, Becker."

I bit back a smile of my own, lifting my fist with the middle knuckle protruding. Kylie's eyes doubled in size, all traces of a smile gone, and she shook her head, glaring at me in warning. "Don't even *think* about giving me a noogie, Michael Andrew."

I lunged for her, and she squealed, worming her way out of my grasp just before I could land my knuckle to her scalp and rub it in. Still, I was stronger than her, and I pinned her easily, her long hair splaying over my pillows like a curtain, laptop sliding off her lap and to the side.

"You're going to break it!" she warned, but I closed the screen and set it on my desk before pinning her again.

"There. It's safe." I grinned wider. "But you, my friend, are not."

She squealed as I tickled her, her familiar deep-belly laugh filling my ears and conjuring up the first real smile I'd had since we were at the lake that Saturday. And then, from the living room, a familiar melody found its way into my room, stopping us both in our tracks.

Eric Clapton's voice filled the house, a little louder than usual, the song my parents danced to at their wedding filling every empty space.

"Wonderful Tonight."

I still had Kylie half-pinned, and we exchanged a knowing, sad look before I released her, and we both sat on my bed for a moment, just listening to the song.

"I'll be right back," I said, and Kylie nodded without asking where I was going, because she already knew.

I found Mom sitting on her knees in front of the stereo in the living room, her hands still on the buttons that made the song play, eyes glossed over and distant, as if she wasn't looking at a stereo at all — but into a whole other life.

One where she wasn't alone.

I ignored the stinging in my nose as I held a hand down to her, and it shook her from her daydream. She smiled up at me, letting me take her hand, and once she was on her feet, I took her right hand in my left, secured my other hand at her waist, and we danced.

Mom didn't cry when this song was on — ever. She smiled, and danced, and leaned her head on my shoulder and swayed to the rhythm. My brothers and I had a theory that this song was a time machine for her, that when it played, she went back in time, back to Dad.

I leaned my cheek on the crown of her head, swaying in time with the music, maybe escaping to another time myself. I left my eyes closed until the end of the song, and when it was over, I kissed Mom's forehead, and she squeezed me tight.

"He would have been so proud of you," she whispered, and my throat tightened with emotion I refused to let through.

I nodded. "He's still with us," I assured her. "Always will be."

She returned my nod, burying her face in my chest with one last hug before she pulled back and gave me the best smile she could. "I think I'm going to make some hot tea and sit on the porch for a while before bed."

"That sounds nice. I'll go get Kylie and we'll join you."

Mom's smile doubled at that, and she pinched my cheek before turning and heading for the kitchen.

I took one step toward the hall, but when I made the full turn, I stopped before another step could be made. Kylie was there, shaded by the dark hallway but for the glow of her laptop screen that she held open in her arms. Her eyes were wide and fearful, like she'd seen a ghost, and her mouth hung open for the longest time as she watched me.

"What?" I asked, not daring to take another step. "What is it?"

She finally closed her mouth and swallowed, but the fear in her eyes didn't ebb.

"I got in."

• • •

Kylie

I'd chewed all the plastic off the end of the string on my hoodie the next evening, sitting on Michael's front porch with all of his brothers gathered around my laptop, gaping at the screen.

Logan hadn't stopped asking questions.

What was the password?

Answer: *WonderfulTonight1985!*

What did you find?

Answer: email archives, financial documents for the distillery, miscellaneous projects he'd been heading, minutes from the board meetings for the five years leading up to his death, and — most importantly — a daily journal log.

What's in the journal?

That one didn't have an answer yet.

Noah was texting furiously to Ruby Grace, all the while nodding and listening, cataloging everything we told them.

Jordan hadn't moved, except to lift his Old Fashioned to his lips from time to time. He'd take a sip, swallow it down, and keep his eyes locked on the laptop screen.

"It's weird," Mikey said, elbows propped on his knees as he tried to explain to his brothers what we'd discovered. "Most of the entries are boring, day-to-day stuff. We skimmed some of them, but I think there's something we missed. Because all of a sudden, the entries go from being written in English to..." he paused, glancing at me as if he thought he was crazy for what he was about to say. I nodded to assure him. "Latin."

"*Latin?*" Noah and Logan asked at the same time, the surprise and confusion evident in both of their voices.

Mikey nodded. "Yeah. At least, I'm pretty sure that's what it is. Hang on." He pulled up one of the later entries in the document, showing the gibberish to his brothers.

"Definitely Latin," Jordan said, the first words he'd spoken since we'd sat down on the porch.

"Wait... I think I remember something about that..." Logan said, rubbing the stubble on his jaw. "I remember Dad saying something about how he didn't know any foreign languages, how he'd read an article in the paper about how Latin can prepare you to learn other languages, since it's tied to so many of them."

"Oh, shit... I remember that now, too," Noah said.

I felt like a fly on the wall, a silent bystander, just there to answer questions when they were asked to me, but otherwise to sit back and listen. Truth be told, I was thankful — because I was still in shock.

There was a very, *very* small part of me that was hopeful in the beginning, when Mikey and I first started trying to crack into the hard drive. I thought maybe one of the softwares I'd heard of would do the trick, or that we could guess it. But, as time wore on, I started seeing it less as a possibility, and using it more as an excuse to be around Mikey.

Now that we'd actually gotten in, I had no idea what it would mean — for Michael, for his brothers, for his mom.

For our entire town.

Something stirred in my gut, low and rumbling, like a storm about to let hell loose.

Whatever the reason was for his father writing his journal in Latin, I knew those gibberish words held secrets that would change everything.

"Logan, what else did you guys find when you found Dad's old laptop?" Noah asked.

Logan pinched the bridge of his nose. "I can't really remember all of it. I know that picture of us at the lake was in the box, in a frame, partially burned, partially water-damaged." He paused, shaking his head. "That paperweight Mom got him for Christmas one year, with the Colin Powell quote. That's all I remember before my focus was on the laptop."

"It doesn't make sense," Noah said. "Why would *his* things be in Robert J. Scooter's office? I mean, I know Dad was cleaning it out, organizing it, whatever, but... he still had his *own* office. Why would the things from his office be burned if it was Robert's office that the fire happened in?"

That question made my stomach sink like an anvil, and judging by the white-as-snow looks on the rest of his brothers' faces, I knew I wasn't the only one.

"We have to figure out what that journal says," Logan whispered.

"We're on it," Mikey said. "We just have to use a translating tool. It'll take some time, but—"

"Let me do it."

All eyes turned to Jordan, who had drained the last of his drink before speaking those words.

He sniffed, looking each of his brothers in the eye as he leaned forward, balancing his elbows on his knees, hands folded between his legs. "It's summer. Besides football camp, I've got nothing going on."

"But that takes a lot of your focus and energy," Mikey pointed out. "I really don't mind—"

"You're leaving," Jordan reminded him — reminded *all* of us. "You need to be looking for apartments, and a job, and figuring out what you're taking with you and what you're leaving behind."

Those words sent another wave of nausea through me.

"Besides," Jordan said, leaning back in his rocking chair. "You've all been a part of this in some way or another. It's my turn. Let me take over. I studied Latin a little with Dad when he first started, and a little on my own after high school, before I started coaching."

"Wait... you studied Latin?" Logan asked.

Jordan shrugged. "Not a lot, just a little. Enough to know the basics. And like Mikey said, I can use a translation tool for the rest."

Everyone was quiet for a moment, but I knew from the look on Mikey's face that he was hesitant. I reached over, squeezing his forearm.

"I think this is a good plan," I said, more to him than to the group. "We've been caught up in this for months. Take a break, let Jordan look through what we found."

His mouth pulled to one side, and I knew it was because we'd worked so hard to get into the hard drive, he didn't want to hand it over to someone else now that we'd finally gotten in. But, when he looked at his oldest brother, at the one who everyone knew only spoke when he really had something to say, he softened.

"Yeah," he said finally, nodding. "Yeah, you're right. I'd get too tangled in this and wouldn't focus on what I need to right now, like apartments and stuff. I think you should take over."

Everyone nodded in agreement just as the screen door flew open.

"Dinner's almost ready," Lorelei announced. "Now, all of you get in here and get washed up."

We'd all jumped when she came out, Jordan reaching for the laptop and slamming it closed, tucking it under his arm.

Lorelei narrowed her eyes and folded her arms over her chest. "Why so jumpy? What were you doing?"

"Just looking at porn, Mom," Logan answered easily, standing first and squeezing her shoulder as he passed. "So you're right, better go get washed up."

Lorelei grimaced as we all laughed. "Logan Michael, that is not funny."

She chased after him, still chastising him as we all took a breath once she was off the porch.

"I think we all agree, best not to tell Mom about this until we have something more to tell, yeah?" Jordan asked.

Noah and Mikey nodded, and though I knew what I thought didn't matter, I nodded, too. That woman had been through enough. The last thing she needed was to be worrying about some Latin journal when none of us knew what it meant yet.

Jordan and Noah got up next, whispering quietly to each other as they made their way inside for dinner. I grabbed Mikey's arm once they were inside.

"Clear your schedule tonight," I said. "After dinner, we're going line dancing."

Mikey groaned, face twisting up like a child just told to take the trash out. "Not tonight, Kylie. It's been a long week, and Jordan's right — I really do need to get serious about my apartment and job hunt."

My stomach tightened, but I ignored it. "Exactly. It *has* been a long week, and what better reason to have a little fun? Besides, you made a pinky promise, remember?"

His face twisted even more at that.

I chuckled. "It'll be fun. I promise. And you can use the rest of your weekend to be boring and look for jobs, if that's really what you want to do."

He sighed, using his hands on the rocking chair armrests to lift himself as if it was the hardest task in the world. "Fine," he said, dragging the word out. "I'll go. But I'm not dancing."

I just smirked as I followed him inside, because we both knew that was a lie. And now that we'd made it past his father's death anniversary, and cracked into the hard drive, *and* he'd forgotten about Bailey's song on the radio — at least, temporarily — I could finally get back to my summer mission.

Mikey loved to line dance, no matter how moody and broody he wanted to play right now. And if I knew one thing about New York City, it was that line dancing wasn't going to be easy to find.

Tonight, I fully intended to remind him of that.

And when we bowed our heads before dinner, I said a silent prayer of my own that it would somehow be enough to make him stay.

Chapter Nine

Michael

The last time I went to Scootin' Boots, it was with Bailey.

It was the night before our first day of school as seniors, and she insisted that we go dancing. Of course, it wasn't like I could ever say no to her. All she had to do was smile at me and bat her lashes and *bam* — whatever she wanted, I'd move the Earth and moon to get it for her.

I remembered that night differently than how I used to. If she'd have stayed, I would have just looked back on it as another night of line dancing. But, after she left, I scoured our past few months together for clues that I'd missed, anything that might have been a warning sign of the imminent heartbreak ahead — and I always landed on that night. Because I remembered one slow song when I held her close, swaying gently, and she laid her head on my chest and let out a soft sigh before whispering, "*I wish we could always be like this.*"

In the moment, I thought she'd meant young, free, kids going into senior year who were crazy about each other without another care in the world.

But now, I knew she had already known the decision she would make, that she would leave, that I would be left behind.

I tried to shake that memory away as I opened the door to Scootin' Boots for Kylie, ushering her inside first. I paid our cover, that numb memory still hovering over me as they stamped our hands to show we were too young to drink, and then we were inside the sea of people — half of them dancing, half of them watching.

Scootin' Boots was a two-story bar, with a large dance floor in the middle of the bottom floor and a viewing deck up top. You could also dance in the slightly smaller dance floor on the second floor, though it was a different kind of dancing, since they only played hip hop and pop music upstairs. But the big floor, the one everything in that bar was centered around? It was for line dancing.

The memory of Bailey started to wane the closer we got to the floor, along with the heavy ache I'd felt in the pit of my stomach since we'd cracked into my dad's hard drive. I knew my older brother was handling it, but until now, I hadn't been able to let it go.

This was what music did for me.

It slinked its way into all the cracks of my broken soul and filled it with hope, with movement, with rhythm and passion.

Standing on the edge of that dance floor, I recognized for the first time that I missed it.

I missed music.

Even if it did hurt a little, now that Bailey had left her mark on the one thing I loved so much.

Kylie and I huddled off to the side of the floor, watching as a dozen lines of dancers moved in sync, kicking and stepping and spinning in time to a Luke Bryan song. Already, that familiar itch to get out there and join them was creeping up my spine, and the wide smile on Kylie's face served to push my memory of Bailey a little further out. She'd been there for me that week, even when I didn't deserve it. And now, I hoped I could pay her back with a night of fun.

"Look at how fast they're moving!" she said, pointing to the dancers.

But I only looked out on the floor for a split second before my eyes were on my best friend again.

Something had changed about her since we graduated.

I still wasn't sure what it was — at least, I hadn't put my finger on it yet. But there was *something* that had changed. She was still the same girl I held hands with on the playground when I was eight years old. She was still the same girl who played video games with me and knew my favorite candy bar. She was still the same girl who bent over backward to help everyone around her, just because that was what she did. It was what made her Kylie Nelson.

But, she looked differently, spoke differently, *existed* differently.

I didn't know if it was just me that was oblivious to it all before now, or if there really had been a change in her in the time I'd been with Bailey. Either way, she was the girl I knew before, and somehow, someone I didn't know at all.

That was the same dark hair I'd seen in pig tails and messy buns and pony tails and fresh out of the shower — but it was longer now, thicker.

That was the same sunshine yellow tank top I'd seen her wear a thousand times, one she'd had since she was fourteen — but it fit differently now, stretched in places where it used to gape before.

Those were the same legs I'd seen cut up on the playground, and folded criss-cross style on my bed when we had movie marathons all night, but I'd never seen them in the cut-off shorts she was wearing, the frayed edges of them somehow making those legs feel foreign and completely new.

Even the boots on her feet, I knew they were the ones her dad got her for Christmas our freshman year, and that she loved them so much she refused to get different ones, even though they were a touch too small and hurt her toes — but paired with those shorts...

Everything was the same.

Yet, *nothing* was the same.

Kylie glanced up at me with the smile of a kid at the circus, shaking me from my thoughts again.

"I could never do that," she said over the music.

"Sure you could. You will."

Kylie shook her head. "My feet don't move like that."

"Come on," I said, offering her my hand. "I'll show you how."

Her eyes bulged, but before she could argue, I was already tugging her toward the dance floor. It was the perfect timing, since the song had changed to an old favorite of mine — "Chattahoochee" by Alan Jackson. It was an easy line dance compared to some of the newer ones, and I pulled Kylie to the back corner of the dance floor so I could teach it to her.

"Okay," I said, lining us up side by side. "Just watch my feet and listen to my instruction. It's only a few moves and then it just repeats."

"You make it sound so simple, when I know for a *fact* that it's not."

I grinned, reaching over to squeeze her hand in mine. "You trust me, right?"

Something passed over her face, like a shadow in the night, and she swallowed hard, nodding in lieu of a verbal response.

"I've got you," I said, squeezing her hand again before I let it go. "I promise. Now, you ready?""

Her eyes were wide, lips parted just a bit, but she nodded tentatively again.

And then it was show time.

I called out the moves to her as we did them — the kicks and stomps, turns and steps, grapevines and shuffles. For the first few repetitions, she was a mess of legs and boots and flailing arms. She laughed and laughed, shaking her head and yelling at me over and over again, "I can't do this! It's too hard!"

But, just like I knew she would, Kylie started to grasp it after the second chorus. She fell into sync next to me, and even though she still had to watch me and listen to me call out the moves, her body was responding, memorizing, dancing with more ease. And by the last round, she did it without messing up even once.

The song ended, and Kylie jumped into my arms, screaming with excitement.

"Oh, my God!" she yelled. "I did it! I did it!"

I spun her around, laughing before I set her back on the ground. "I told you."

She stuck her tongue out. "Don't make this about you being right, asshole. This is about me — being the best damn line dancer in the history of ever."

A laugh shot out of me, but I didn't argue, just fell in line next to the other dancers as the next song began. "Ready for more?"

Kylie bit her bottom lip, excitement flashing in her eyes before she took her place next to me. All the fear, the hesitation, the nervousness I'd seen in her just four minutes before was completely erased, and now, my fearless best friend who could take on anything was all I saw on that dance floor. And I wasn't even a little surprised — because that was just who she was.

She could do anything, be anyone, accomplish whatever she set her mind to.

It was something I'd always admired about her.

It was something no one else in the world could do quite the same way she could.

And just like her nerves had evaporated, so did the heaviness I'd carried around on my shoulders all week. The more we danced, the less pain I felt reverberating through my chest. I'd forgotten how easy it was to lose myself in the music, to succumb to focusing on the next move, the next spin, the next song.

Before I knew it, we'd been on the dance floor for an hour, and Kylie finally tugged me off after the fast, spin-heavy dance to "T-R-O-U-B-L-E" by Travis Tritt.

"I need water," she screamed over the music as she pulled me off the floor, making a bee line for the bar.

We slid onto two empty bar stools, calling out our water orders to the bartender, and then Kylie reached just behind the bar for a wad of napkins, handing me half of them.

"I'm disgusting," she said on a laugh, peeling her long hair off her neck with one hand and wiping the sweat off her forehead with the other. I started to laugh, too, until she dipped her hand holding the napkins down her long neck, wiping them over her glistening chest, which, as the lake day had revealed to me, was not flat anymore like it had been when we were kids.

I swallowed, tearing my eyes away from her cleavage just in time to take our two waters from the bartender. I gave her a couple dollars for a tip, and as soon as the water was in Kylie's hands, she'd drained half of it.

"Ahhh," she said, letting the straw go and collapsing back on her bar stool. She fanned herself with the ball of napkins still in her hands, laughing again. "You know, I didn't realize I was going to get a cardio workout by asking you to come here."

"You've been here before though," I reminded her, sipping from my own cup. "It's not like you didn't know what you were in for."

"I've *been* here, yes," she agreed, pointing her straw at me. "But I've never *danced* here. That's the difference. I'm usually sitting at one of the tables in the back, or playing a solo game of pool like the loser I am."

Kylie laughed.

I didn't.

"Wait... you've *never* danced here before?" I asked, frowning as I tried to think back on the other times we'd been to Scootin' Boots. As soon as we were sixteen, we started coming for teen nights. I couldn't even recall all the times we'd been since. "That can't be right."

"Ohhhh, trust me. It's right. There was no way I was going to get out there by myself, and as shocking as this might sound, the teenage boys of Stratford weren't exactly clamoring to dance with me."

She rolled her eyes, chuckling, but I was still racking my brain, thinking about the dozens of times we'd been here and the fact that I couldn't recall a single time that I'd seen Kylie dance.

"It just doesn't make sense," I said, shaking my head. "I never pulled you out there?"

At that, the smile slipped off Kylie's face like a runny egg, and she shrugged, chewing on her straw a bit before she took another drink. "You had Bailey," she said, softly, almost so quietly I didn't hear her at all.

She opened her mouth to say more, but not another word came.

Not another word was needed.

A sickening wave rolled through me, one as foreign as it was familiar. We both knew I hadn't been the best friend when I was tied up in my relationship with Bailey, but still, neither of us had ever really discussed it.

She'd never really told me how it had felt, for me to abandon her the way I did.

And I'd never really apologized.

I set my water down, folding my hands between my knees and staring at my knuckles as I tried to find the words. "Kylie..." I started. "I know we never talked about it, but I'm really sorry for—"

"Well, I'll be damned."

Parker Morris interrupted my apology, sliding up next to Kylie's bar stool with an easy, care-free grin. He tucked his hands in the pockets of his Wranglers, hooking his thumbs on the leather of his belt. The buckle was huge, a gold and silver oval that boasted first place in goat roping at the youth rodeo, and though I normally would have found that impressive, I presently only found it annoying.

"First, you're jumping off rope swings. Now, you're breaking a sweat on the dance floor?" Parker shook his head. "You're just full of surprises."

He said all of that to Kylie, and the blush that shaded her cheeks made my stomach knot for a reason I couldn't understand. Parker smiled wider, and only then did he turn to me.

"Hey, Mikey. Been a long time since I've seen you out here."

"I thought Thursday was teen night," I said, admittedly a little more like a bull dog than I intended.

Parker blew a laugh through his nose, assessing me like he'd just realized

I was the one stepping into the ring with him at a fight. "It is. But we have fakes," he said, motioning to himself and a crew of seniors standing not too far behind him. All of them were watching us — some curiously, some like we were gum stuck to the bottom of their boot.

That was the thing about becoming a senior in a small town. There was a false sense of importance that came with it. I had felt it, too, like a prized pig owner at the state fair. Bailey and I had walked around town like we were top dogs, and that feeling had stuck around even after she left.

Until I graduated and realized being a senior in high school didn't mean shit, except that soon, you'd be on your own, and lost, and — if you were lucky — stuck in a major you didn't really care about at a college that's so expensive it'll put you in debt for life.

If you were unlucky, you'd just be depressed.

Like me.

"Anyway," Parker said, still wearing a smug smile as he turned his attention away from me and back to Kylie again. "I came over to ask if you'd like to dance with me."

Kylie blanched. "I... uh... I'm not really good at it."

"That's okay," he said. "I pulled some strings at the DJ booth. It'll be a slow song, and I'll lead."

Parker looked behind his group of friends, nodding to the DJ in the booth above the dance floor, and the guy nodded back, fading out the line dance that was on and replacing it with "Neon Moon" by Brooks and Dunn.

He turned back around, grinning again, his sole focus on my best friend.

"It's a cha cha," he explained. "Nothing too crazy." Parker offered his hand to her next, holding it out like he was motherfucking Prince Charming waiting to help her into a carriage. "What'dya say?"

Kylie bit her bottom lip, cheeks still flushed red as she eyed his hand, and then me.

Her eyes hit me like a freight train.

It was impossible, the things I felt when she looked at me the way she did. Because in my mind, for some twisted reason, she was asking me something in that moment.

To save her.

To stop her.

To steal her for myself.

I knew none of those things could be true. I knew we were just friends, that we'd *always* been just friends.

But just like I knew something had changed about her that summer, I knew she was asking something of me in that look.

Whatever it was, I was too slow to decode it, and she tore her eyes away, looking back at Parker.

Then, she smiled, and slipped her hand into his. "Okay."

Parker's grin doubled in size as she slipped off the bar stool, and he turned, her hand in his, tugging her toward the dance floor.

Kylie looked over her shoulder at me, again with a question I couldn't quite hear, but then Parker reached the dance floor, and she turned, falling into his embrace as he took her right hand in his left, and wrapped the other around her small waist, pulling her closer to him than necessary for this kind of dance.

He said something that made her laugh, and my neck burned with a fierce heat.

Their first steps were awkward, and she tried to bury her face in his chest, but he kept leaning down to look at her, to get her to look at him. And before long, they'd found a rhythm, dancing with the other couples on the floor as I watched from the bar.

I was only eighteen.

I was only eighteen, and yet, I could remember moments in my life that changed everything.

I could remember the first time I picked up a guitar, how it felt to pluck the strings and feel the vibrations through my hands, traveling up my arms, making a sound that I controlled.

I could remember how my father's death changed me — monumentally — in a way that was irreversible.

I could remember the way my body changed when I hit high school, and how my heart shifted when I met Bailey, and how my entire world came crashing down when she left.

Maybe that's why I recognized it earlier that night — that feeling that something was off, that something was weird, that something had changed.

But it wasn't until I saw Parker's hands slide down to the small of Kylie's back, until I saw them thread together and pull her closer, until I saw her laugh and blush in the arms of someone else, that it all clicked.

I didn't want her to dance with Parker Morris... or with anyone else, for that matter.

Because I wanted her to dance with me.

With *only* me.

I couldn't digest it, couldn't sit there and ruminate on *why* that was because the song was already halfway over and all I knew for sure was that I'd be damned if it ended with her still dancing with him.

My body moved without me telling it to, feet carrying me across the bar, across the floor, until I was standing right beside Parker and Kylie and my finger was tapping on his shoulder.

I cleared my throat when they both looked at me, as if their eyes had zapped me back into the moment, and only then did I realize what I was doing.

"May I cut in?"

He could have told me to fuck off. I knew that was a possibility, but not a probability, as no southern gentleman would act that way. And if I knew one thing about Parker, it was that his reputation was as important to him as the shiny buckle on his belt.

His jaw tightened, but to his credit, he managed a smile that seemed almost genuine as he released his hold on Kylie and stepped back, offering her hand to me.

"Of course," he said through his teeth. Then, he turned to Kylie, pressed a kiss to the top of her hand. "Save another one for me later?"

Her eyes were wide, stuck on the place where his lips still hovered over her skin. "O-okay," she managed on a squeak.

He smiled, eyeing me like he'd already won before he relinquished his dance partner and walked back to his group of friends.

I stamped down the irrational urge to throat-punch him, schooling my breath and focusing on the fact that Kylie was in *my* arms now. She glanced over her shoulder, watching Parker go, and then she looked back at me with one raised eyebrow.

"You're welcome," I said.

At that, her other eyebrow shot up. "I'm sorry?"

"For saving you from that creep," I finished, like the answer was obvious. "You're welcome."

Kylie snort-laughed, but already, she was more relaxed, her hands wrapped around my neck as I swayed us to the music. "I'm sorry, I wasn't aware I asked to be saved." She smirked, moving her head side to side like in a sort of dance of her own. "Seems to me like someone's *jealous*."

She sang the words on a tease, but everything in me tightened, like the wheels and axles that powered the machine of my body all locked up at once.

I swallowed, searching her gingerbread eyes and seeing so much more than I ever had before. "What if I am?"

She froze in my arms, her smile gone in a flash, the blush Parker had conjured up on her cheeks replaced with a sheet of pale white, like she'd just realized she was dancing with a ghost.

I stilled, too, and in the sea of a dozen dancers, we stood paralyzed in each other's arms, looking at each other for what felt like the first time.

Kylie's lips parted, and even if I'd wanted to, I couldn't have fought the way my gaze dropped to her mouth at the motion.

Her breaths were hard, her chest rising and falling to the beat of the music, but my own breath was steady as one hand glided around her waist, up the back of her arm, her neck, until my hand found the thick strands of hair that had fallen in her face. I swept them away, tucking them behind her ear, and all the while, my eyes never left her lips.

Her full, pink lips, shaped like a bow.

Lips I'd known nearly all my life.

Lips I'd never truly known at all.

Lips that I realized — suddenly and acutely — that I wanted to taste.

Kylie's breath stopped altogether when my hand slipped from where I'd tucked her hair behind her ear to frame her jaw, and my thumb snaked out, sliding over her bottom lip, her mouth parting more.

I was under a spell, a trance, living in another world, another universe.

But the song changed, and a familiar tune broke through the haze.

And everything came crashing down.

"Alright, y'all. If you're not already on the floor, grab someone special and pull them out here. This one's new from Nashville, from Stratford's own Bailey Baker, our small-town rising star. Let's get on the floor and show our girl some love!"

Cheers erupted from all around the bar, and somewhere in the fog of my mind, I realized more and more people were flooding the dance floor. But Kylie and I were still frozen in the middle of it all — only now, she was watching me with wide, terrified eyes.

"Mikey…" she tried, but I couldn't.

Couldn't listen.

Couldn't respond.

Couldn't stay.

I let her go like she was on fire, the crowd dizzying as I shoved through it, earning a few *"Hey's!"* and *"Watch it's!"* along the way. I didn't care about manners in that moment, or that Parker and his friends were laughing when I passed them, or that I'd left Kylie behind.

Bailey's voice surrounded me, drilling into my brain, into my memory, into my broken heart, cracking it just a bit more.

All I could focus on was getting out of that damn bar.

Getting out, and never coming back again.

• • •

Kylie

"Mikey!"

I called out his name, over and over, trying to keep him in sight while I pushed through the crowd. It was much more difficult for me, since I was about half as tall as everyone else in there, and by the time I broke through the crowd at the back bar, I'd lost him.

"Shit," I murmured, heart pounding in my chest as I scanned the place looking for him. Of course, I didn't know if my heart was a snare drum because Bailey's voice was ringing in my ears and driving Mikey crazy, or if it was because he'd just told me he was jealous of Parker Morris dancing with me.

And he'd looked at my lips.

He'd looked at my lips like he wanted to kiss them.

A shiver split through me, but I brushed it off, pushing through the men's bathroom door.

"Mikey!" I called out, shielding my eyes and wishing I could unhear the men peeing in the urinals. "I swear to God, Mikey, if you're in here, you better answer me."

"I don't know who Mikey is," a voice said. "But I'll be whoever you want me to be, cowgirl."

A few whistles rang out at that, and I shook my head, bolting out of the bathroom as fast as I'd gone in. Bailey's song was still on as I made my way toward the exit, and as much as I tried not to listen, the second verse of the song stuck me like a knife in the ribs.

It was you and me, that warm September night.
I wore your hoodie,
and you wore my hair tie.
It was right there, hanging on your wrist,
when you leaned in and gave me my first kiss
On Mama's front porch.

My stomach rolled, because I knew as much as our whole high school did that those lyrics were about Mikey. He'd worn her black and red scrunchy on his wrist the entire time they'd dated.

He still had it, hanging from his old guitar stand in his room.

The fresh air did little to relieve me when I finally pushed my way outside, but when I saw Mikey standing by my truck, I found the next breath a little easier.

When I was twelve, my dad had taken me hunting with him. It was his attempt to bond with his pre-teen daughter after years of essentially being a shell. It'd been me taking care of him after Mom died, not the other way around, and apparently hunting was his way of showing his thanks.

Still, it only took one time for me to discover that hunting was *not* for me. My tender little heart just couldn't take it. But, I remembered what it felt like. I remembered how quiet we had to be, how my heart had thumped loudly in my ears as we waited for deer, and how it had tripled its pace when we'd accidentally come too close to a mother black bear and her cub.

Dad had warned me we were in danger, but if we stayed quiet, and kept our distance, we'd be okay.

I could sense it, the fierce protectiveness of that mother bear, and the awareness that if I made one wrong move, I'd be her lunch.

That was how I felt walking toward Mikey, who was leaned up against my still-muddy truck, arms crossed, nose flaring, eyes on his boots. He looked so handsome, so *devastatingly* handsome, like a rare, leather-bound book on the top shelf, just out of reach.

I slowed my pace the closer I got, fearful of spooking him, of threatening him in any way that might make him lunge out and take my head off.

When I felt like I was close enough, I paused, picking at my nail polish and staring at my best friend, wondering what I should say.

"Mikey..."

"Let's just go."

"I'm so sorry," I said, voice just above a whisper. "I... I didn't think..."

At that, Mikey's head jerked up, his eyes landing on me and pinning me right there where I stood. His jaw was flexed, the muscles in his neck tight. "No," he said. "You didn't."

I opened my mouth to say something more, but nothing came.

"I told you to leave this alone," he said, pushing off the truck and taking a step toward me. My instinct was to flinch, to back away, but I stood my ground as best I could. "I *told* you we shouldn't fucking come here."

"I-I'm sorry," I said on a tremble. "Why are you mad at me? Obviously I didn't know they would—"

"Of *course* you didn't know!" He raised his voice, throwing his hands up in the air like it was the most obvious thing in the world. "Because in your world, everything is fine and fixable. In your world, nothing is ever wrong. You wouldn't think of something like this happening because you *never* think about anything other than rainbows and butterflies and, and..." He waved his hands around. "Glitter."

I narrowed my eyes, lips flattening as I took a step toward him this time. Heat creeped up my neck, and every nerve in my body screamed *fly!*

But my heart said *fight*.

"Oh, my *God*, Mikey. Do you hear yourself right now?" I shook my head, raising my own hands in the air before letting them fall and smack against my sides. "She is just a freaking *girl*. Okay? You dated her for two years. You had your heart broken when she left. Yes, we all get it, but for fuck's sake, it is not *this* big of a deal."

His head snapped back like I'd slapped him. "Oh, I'm sorry, I didn't realize you were the expert on dating, seeing as how you've never even *had* a boyfriend."

I ignored the sting of those words, taking another step toward him instead and putting on my best bitch face. "Oh, trust me — after I realized what a mess you and Bailey were, I figured out pretty quickly that a boyfriend was the *last* thing I wanted."

The muscle in his jaw ticked at that, and he rolled his eyes, turning away from me to round the truck. "Whatever. Let's just go."

"No."

He stopped, turning over his shoulder to eye me before he faced me fully again. "No?"

"I'm having a great time. I don't want to leave."

"And I can't go back in there."

"*Why not*?" I asked, exasperated, my hands framing the air like it was the question itself. "You're letting that girl drive you out of this town, out of the places you love most, away from the *people* who you love most. And I'm trying to show you why that's a mistake."

"I don't need you to *show me* anything," he said, but I didn't miss the crack in his voice, the way his eyelids fluttered a little as he fought against the emotion I knew he was feeling.

She'd broken him, that girl who'd run off to Nashville.

And I didn't know if he'd ever be the same again.

I softened, shoulders relaxing as I lowered my voice and made my way over to him.

"You're more than what that girl did to you, Mikey."

The lines in his forehead eased, his brows resting, something passing over his face at my words. And for a split second, I thought maybe, just *maybe*, I was getting through to him. I reached out for him — slowly, tentatively — touching his arm gently before I slid my hand down into his, and I squeezed.

He followed my hand with his eyes, swallowing when he found my gaze again, and as soon as his eyes had locked on mine, they fell a few inches.

To my lips.

That same rush that had stormed me on the dance floor came back full force, like it'd never left at all, but had only been temporarily muted.

"Ky?"

My next breath was short. "Yes?"

His eyes snapped to mine, and the whole world stopped spinning.

"I'm going to say this slowly, so you hear me clearly. Okay?"

I nodded, still not breathing.

A moment passed, and then Mikey leaned in and lowered his voice to a whisper.

"You. Do. Not. Understand."

I blinked, not sure I'd heard the words right, but there they were, hanging between us, and Mikey stared at me, unapologetically backing them up.

I scoffed, ripping my hand free from his. "Unbelievable."

He let me go, and something between a laugh and a growl broke through my calm façade.

I was done.

With playing nice, with playing the game, with trying to open my best friend's eyes when he was so damn set on keeping them shut.

With everything.

"*I* don't understand?" I finally said, repeating his words as I shook my head. I pointed, jabbing my finger into his chest before I backed away. "It's *you* who doesn't understand. It's you who's blind to the fact that you love this town, and the memories you've made in it, and that the people here love *you*, too. But you know what?" I laughed, looking back at the neon Scootin' Boots sign with my tongue in my cheek. "If you can't walk back into that bar with your head held high because you're better than her? If you want to let a *girl* be the reason you uproot your entire life and leave this town and the people in it behind?" I looked at him again, shrugging. "Fine. Go. In fact, let me know the official moving date," I added with a scoff, fishing my keys out of my pocket and turning on my heel. "I'll throw you a going away party."

The words were barely out of my mouth when his hand shot out, gripping my wrist and whipping me back around. My keys fell from the opposite hand, and I frowned, opening my mouth to lay into him again.

But I couldn't.

Because he kissed me.

My next breath was a gasp and it lodged in my throat when our lips met, hard and fast, angry and hot. He kissed me like a punishment, and I took it like a sadist, the shock gone as fast as it had come as I leaned into him. My hands snaked around his neck, fingers curling in his hair and pulling him closer, desperate for more.

He tasted familiar somehow, like my favorite candy or the toothpaste I'd used my entire life. When his arms wrapped fully around me, pulling me into him, crushing me with the need to be closer — I saw stars.

My breath was shallow and loud, my inexperienced mouth slow compared to his, and my entire body was hot and sensitive like an exposed wire. I couldn't wrap my head around what was happening, couldn't grasp the fact that we were kissing — not until he nipped at my bottom lip with a guttural groan that sent me slamming back into reality like a car into a brick wall.

I ripped away from him, and though I couldn't be completely sure, I thought I screamed something like *no* or *stop*. And then, with a hand that didn't feel like my own, I slapped him.

Everything went quiet.

There was no music thumping from inside the bar, no laughter from those who had filtered into the parking lot, no trucks roaring to life or cars passing on the road. It was just me, staring at my best friend holding his cheek where I'd slapped him and watching me with wild, confused eyes.

My breath came back all at once, and I gulped the fresh air down, swallowing it and shaking my head as tears welled in my eyes.

"I've been waiting my *whole life* for you to kiss me, Michael Becker," I said, voice trembling and hoarse. One lone tear slipped from my left eye, and I swiped it away before it could fall past my cheek bone. "How dare you do it when you're thinking about her."

Mikey deflated like a leaky balloon right in front of my eyes, his shoulders sagging, mouth falling slack as he ran his hands back through his hair and braced them on his head. "Kylie..."

I shook my head, covering my mouth with one hand as I bent down for my keys with the other. I kept my fingertips on my lips as I turned, climbing into my truck.

"Find another ride home," I said without looking at him again.

Then, I shut the door, revved the engine to life, and drove away from my best friend and my first kiss, determined to forget them both.

Chapter Ten

Michael

I*'ve been waiting my whole life for you to kiss me.*

Eleven words.

Eleven words that might as well have been a giant bucket of ice-cold water for how they woke me up on Friday night.

Eleven words that played on repeat, over and over, assaulting me from every angle as I sulked in my own misery all day Saturday.

Eleven words that changed everything.

I wish I could say I spent Saturday coming up with some grand plan to apologize to Kylie, that I had swallowed my pride and knocked on her door first thing that morning. But the truth was I'd submitted myself to a sort of torture, an awakening in the form of replaying every moment I'd ever had with my best friend through different-colored lenses.

Because I couldn't for the life of me believe that I'd missed it.

Since we were eight, we'd been practically inseparable. We'd had sleepovers and video game marathons and ice cream trips after school and lazy days watching movies and early mornings of her dragging me to some other volunteer thing that I never understood but did because I knew it made her happy.

We'd spent birthdays together, and Thanksgivings, and Christmases and Fourth of Julys and — perhaps most importantly — our parents' death anni-versaries.

I knew when she was hiding something that upset her, and she knew when I was really sad but disguising it as anger. I knew her favorite books and movies and candy bars, and she knew all my moves in Mortal Kombat.

I'd helped her pick food out of her braces, and she'd helped me think of what to do for my first date with Bailey. She'd cried when she heard me play my first original song on the guitar my father bought me — a song I wrote for him — and, though she never knew, I'd cried on her sixteenth birthday when her dad gave her her mother's favorite pair of diamond earrings as a gift.

She never took those earrings off, not since that day.

My mother saw her as a daughter, and I was the only person other than herself that her father could stand for longer than an hour at a time. In every single way possible, we were tied together, Kylie and I.

She'd always been there for me.

And I'd always been there for her.

How had it never occurred to me that maybe she wanted more than just a friendship?

How had I never known that she'd wanted me to kiss her?

And why did it take her finally turning her back on me for me to realize I wanted to kiss her, too?

It took an entire twenty-four hours of me lying in my bed, staring up at my ceiling and running through every memory I had with Kylie, trying and failing to dissect it for clues I'd missed before I realized one very important thing.

It didn't matter that I hadn't known before.

What *did* matter was that I knew now.

And what mattered *most* was what I did now that I knew.

I felt like a dog with my tail tucked between my legs when I parked at the nursing home on Sunday afternoon, and I wagered I probably looked like one as I made my way inside, a small box of Kylie's favorite caramel candies from the next town over in my right hand. I had approximately zero clue of what I would say when I saw her, or how I would explain my actions on Friday night.

All I knew was that I had to see her.

"Oh! My goodness," the woman at the front desk said when she saw me enter. She was petite, with short blonde hair and a gap between her two front teeth, and she felt familiar in some way I couldn't place. She pressed her hand to her chest, shaking her head as she looked me up and down. "Heavens, I'm sorry, it's just... you look so much like your older brother. For a second there I thought I was going to be able to tell the ladies that their favorite water aerobics teacher was back."

I chuckled, placing the box of caramels on the counter as I realized she was Ruby Grace's best friend. I remembered Noah talking about her when he and Ruby Grace were dancing around each other like they were *just friends.*

"Noah taught *water aerobics* here?"

"Indeed, he did," she said, with a far-off gaze that told me *she* might have enjoyed his instruction more than the women of the nursing home. "And trust me, he was *quite* a hit around here. I'm Annie, by the way. Ruby Grace's friend."

I reached over to shake her hand. "Mikey. I'm surprised Ruby Grace didn't drag my brother down here when she came back to visit."

Annie waved me off. "Oh, please. Like those lovebirds could leave the bedroom long enough for a trip to the nursing home."

I grimaced.

"Sorry," she said, making a motion as if she were zipping her lips shut. "I'm sure you don't want to think about your brother that way."

"It's not exactly at the top of my list of things I like to picture, no."

She chuckled. "What can I do for you?"

"Uh..." I cleared my throat. "I was actually hoping to speak with one of your volunteers... Kylie Nelson."

Recognition lit up Annie's eyes, a coy smile finding her lips. "Oh, you're a friend of Kylie's, huh?"

I grimaced again. "Well, before Friday night I was. Now, I think the term *friend* is debatable."

She eyed the candy on the counter before looking up at me again. "What'd you do?"

"What does every man do?"

"Something stupid, that's for sure." She sighed, nodding down the hall to my left. "Room one-oh-nine." She paused, smirking as I grabbed the box of candies off the counter. "Good luck, Becker."

I held up the box in a thank you, making my way down the hallway with a sinking feeling in my gut. When I reached the end of the hallway, the door on room one-oh-nine was covered with a red and white wreath, and it was ajar. I peeked in, smiling when I saw Betty rocking in her chair, and Kylie sitting on her bed, reading a gossip magazine out loud.

"Now just wait a second," Betty said, interrupting her. "You mean to tell me that *the* Dennis Quaid, as in hunky Nick Parker from *The Parent Trap* is now dating some Texas college student?"

Kylie pressed her lips together. "Apparently."

I stared at those lips, at the ones I'd kissed so haphazardly Friday night. That kiss had been hot and fast and I hadn't even truly realized it was happening until she'd shoved me away and slapped me.

Rightfully so.

Just looking at them brought the memory back in a rush, and I could feel them — soft as velvet, timid and giving under my own. Already, I wanted to taste them again.

I wanted the chance to kiss her proper.

Betty tsked, snapping my attention away from Kylie's lips. "But he had that beautiful wife! What was her name... Kim? And they had those gorgeous twins together..."

"Well," Kylie said, flipping the page. "What can I tell you, Betty? Guys suck."

I figured that was as good a cue as any, and with that tail tucked securely between my legs, I knocked on the door, opening it farther as I stepped inside. "You can say that again."

Kylie looked at me like she wasn't sure if she wanted to leap into my arms or run for her life.

Betty, on the other hand, glared at me — and there was no mistaking what she was thinking.

"Oh, lookie here," she said, still rocking in her chair. "If it isn't sweet Mikey Becker." She said *sweet* like an insult, and her smile was sarcastic and wide.

"Afternoon, Betty. Catching up on the latest celebrity gossip?"

"Oh, you know, just reading up on how many good men are left in the world," she bit back, tilting her head at me. "Seems that number is increasingly low nowadays."

I managed a smile, clearing my throat. "Yeah, well, I hate to admit it, but we men have a tendency of walking around with our heads up our butts half the time."

Betty scoffed. "You can say that again."

"Do you mind if I steal Kylie away for a minute?" I asked, turning my attention to her then. Her eyes were still wide, her pink lips parted as she watched me.

"Depends," Betty said. "You going to give her another reason to smack you?"

Heat creeped up my neck, and a blush covered Kylie's face, too, as she gave Betty a pointed look.

"That's not my plan," I answered. "But, to be fair, she has plenty of reasons if she really needs an excuse."

A small, noncommittal smile tugged at Kylie's lips, and Betty made a condescending noise before slowly pushing herself up from her rocking chair. I crossed the room to offer her my help, but she waved me off with another *harrumph.*

"I'm going to sit by the pool," she said, glancing back at Kylie when she was standing. "You holler if you need an old woman to put this young man in his place, you hear me?"

Kylie bit back a laugh. "Yes, ma'am."

Betty gave me one last glare before she walked past me and out into the hallway, closing the door behind her when she was gone.

The *click* of the door closing left me and Kylie in a muffled sort of quiet, with only the distant sounds of games and voices and a vacuum cleaner going somewhere down the hall. I looked at Kylie, and it was for what felt like the first time in my entire life.

Because I saw her.

I really, truly *saw* her.

Those brown eyes of hers — the ones she hated, the ones I'd always thought were perfect — were bloodshot and tired. She never wore makeup, so there was nothing to disguise the fact that she'd been crying, or that she seemed to have had as much sleep that weekend as I had — which was to say, none. The tan she was already building that summer was somehow faded, her skin ashen white, and she folded her legs up under her on the bed, wrapping her arms around herself as if to shield her heart from me.

I couldn't blame her.

With a deep inhale, I sat on the edge of the bed, giving her space, but facing her head on even if she wouldn't look at me. My fingers drummed on the box in my hands before I slid it across the quilted comforter to her.

"From Maribel's," I said, as if Kylie didn't already know that turquoise and gold-ribboned box so well. It was her favorite candy store, one that was a special treat, since it was forty-five minutes away.

She glanced at the box, but didn't move for it, wrapping her arms around herself tighter, instead.

"I'm sorry, Kylie," I said, because I knew that even though those two words weren't enough, they were the only place to start.

Her eyes found me then, and she didn't say anything, but she didn't look away, either.

"I don't have anything that excuses my behavior Friday night," I started. "Nothing that isn't just that — an excuse. My father taught me many things before he died, even as young as I was, and the biggest thing was to not make excuses."

Her eyes softened, and I took my chances, scooting a little closer to her on the bed.

"That song..." I said, swallowing as my nerves jolted just at the memory. "It triggered me. And I know it seems weak and stupid to you, but to me? In that moment?" I shook my head. "It was like trying to breathe under water, like trying to run in quick sand. I felt suffocated and confined, with everyone's eyes on me, knowing they knew she was my ex, that some of those lyrics were about me..." I sniffed. "And that she left me behind, and when she did, I broke."

Kylie lifted her head then, frowning in sympathy as she watched me.

"I'm embarrassed, Kylie," I finally admitted. "I'm embarrassed, and depressed, and ever since she left, I feel..." I swallowed. "Lost. In every sense of the word. I don't remember who I was before her. I *can't* be who I was with her. And who I am *after* her?" I shook my head, trying to make her understand. "I don't know who that guy is supposed to be. I don't know what he loves or hates or where he wants to go or what career he wants to make or what his future looks like, because for two years, all those things were tied up in her."

I reached over, and blessedly, Kylie let me take her hand in mine.

"But, I'm sorry I took out my embarrassment on you. I'm sorry I blamed you, like you could have known they would play that song, or that I'd react that way. And I'm sorry I said you don't understand, because if anyone knows how low I've been, it's you. And for some reason *I* will never understand, you've stuck by me — even when I was a depressing mess, and even when I was an asshole."

Kylie smirked. "You really were an asshole."

"I know," I said on a short laugh. "I know, and you didn't deserve it. And I am truly, truly sorry. I promise, I won't do that again. I will not take out what I'm feeling on the one person who's actually here for me, trying to help me out of the dark."

Her shoulders deflated on that, and for a long while, she just watched me — her eyes flicking between mine, looking for signs of a lie or something else I couldn't quite decipher. Then, she pulled her hand away from mine, balanced her elbow on her knee, and stuck out her pinky.

I smiled, looping mine through hers, and we hooked them, kissed our thumbs, and pressed the pads together to seal the deal.

"Thank you," she said, letting out a long breath like she'd been holding it since Friday night. "I've been... well, let's just say it's been a rough weekend."

"For me, too," I said.

She reached for the box of candies next, hastily unwrapping a caramel and popping it into her mouth. They were small and delectable, and she closed her eyes on a moan, sucking on it until it evaporated. "Besht cawamels evew."

I smirked, but I was already debating my next move, because I wasn't done talking — not yet.

I *could* have been. I could have stopped right there, right then, and left the apology where it was. The fight was squashed, we were friends, and everything could easily go back to normal.

Except I actually *couldn't* stop there.

Not now that the curtain had been lifted, and I'd seen what I'd never seen before.

"Ky."

"Yeah?" she said, swallowing the last of her caramel and reaching for another.

I licked my lips, holding her gaze. "There is *one* thing you were wrong about Friday night."

She scoffed, crossing her arms. "Oh, yeah? Please, do tell me how I was wrong and you were right. I know you love to do that."

Kylie chuckled, but not even so much as a smile found my lips, and when Kylie saw the seriousness in my eyes, her laugh faded.

I scooted closer, pulling both of her hands into mine — even the one holding on to the caramel for dear life. My thumbs rubbed her wrists as I held her, soothing my anxiety as much as I hoped I was soothing her with my next words.

"I wasn't thinking about Bailey when I kissed you."

She stilled, her lips parting, eyelids fluttering as she watched me.

"And if it's alright with you," I continued, still holding her tight. "I'd like to try that again."

A shallow breath slipped through her lips, the sweet scent of caramel touching my nose. I felt like I was hanging onto the edge of a cliff by one hand, reaching up to her with the other, hoping I hadn't read the entire situation wrong and that she'd tug me back up to solid ground with her and not let me tumble to the unforgiving waves below.

"*Now?*" she whispered.

I choked on a laugh, something between relief and a heart attack hitting my chest at the same time. Then, I shook my head, smoothing my thumbs over her hands again. "No," I said, still chuckling. "No, not now. But… soon." I swallowed. "If you want to."

"I want to."

The words flew out of her mouth quickly, and her eyes shot open just as fast, like she was wondering if she'd actually said them.

I smirked, nodding. "Good. Because I want to, too."

"Really?"

"Really."

She flushed the deepest shade of crimson I'd ever seen, and the way her wide, innocent eyes watched me, it made me want to go back on my word that I didn't want that next kiss to be right here, right now.

"What are you doing tonight?" I asked instead.

Kylie shrugged, blowing out a breath through her mouth like it was hard to breathe in that little bedroom. In many ways, it was. "I don't know," she said, looking around. "I'll be here until three, but after that, I was just going to go home and hang out with Dad." Kylie found my eyes again. "Why? What did you have in mind?"

And just like I had Friday night, I felt a shift in that little room, in my little world, in the entire atmosphere — one that told me things would never be the same.

"Come with me to pick out a new guitar?"

• • •

Kylie

The English language is weird.

We have a word for *almost* everything. *Calxophobia* is the word we use to describe someone who's afraid of chalk. *Serendipitous* is the word we use to describe something amazing that happened by chance. *Lackadaisical* is the word we use to describe something or someone lacking spirit or zest.

More than a million words in the English language, and yet, not a single one for what I was experiencing on Sunday night as I sat one chair over from Mikey, watching him tune his guitar in the light from the fire we'd built in his backyard.

Where was the word for "*day that turned one's entire life upside down?*" Where was the word for "*giddy as hell but also equally terrified and nauseous?*" Or, what about "*moment in one's life when one's best friend who one has been in love with forever says out loud that he wants to kiss you? Er… one?*"

No, I couldn't rely on the English language to help me summarize what was happening in the pit of my stomach, that mix of contentment and uneasiness that seemed so at war and yet so perfectly comfortable co-existing inside me. All I knew was that it was night and day different from how I'd felt Friday night when I'd crawled into bed and sobbed myself to sleep. And it was *definitely* different from the day of misery I'd succumbed to on Saturday, when I'd let myself throw the biggest pity party of my life.

Mikey had finally kissed me.

I'd waited so long for his lips to touch mine, for a moment when he'd look at me and see something more than just a girl he liked to hang out with. And when it had finally come, it had been at the height of the biggest fight we'd ever had.

About his ex-girlfriend.

The reminder soured my gut again, and I sipped on my Dr. Pepper, watching Mikey's furrowed brows as he toyed with the strings on his new guitar. How was it possible to feel so low and so unsure one day, and then so high and elated the next?

Earlier, at the nursing home, he told me he wasn't thinking of Bailey when he kissed me.

And he asked if he could kiss me again.

I still couldn't believe it, especially not after spending what felt like an everyday, normal afternoon with him. We'd met at Carl's Music Center — the only place to buy a decent guitar without driving at least an hour — and walked the aisles together while Mikey eyeballed his options. Carl had helped him, giving him a few options to play and hold and feel that were up the alley he was searching in.

He wanted a good acoustic, one like the one his dad had given him — the one he'd thrown in the bonfire at The Black Hole over the holidays. And in the end, he settled on a used Blueridge BR-160 that was in good condition and had a faded Eagles sticker on the body.

Everything had felt normal.

We'd horsed around in the guitar shop. I'd made him play a diddy on a small, pastel-pink guitar with *My Little Pony* stickers all over it while I recorded him on my phone, and we'd stopped to get ice cream at Blondies when the deal was done. Then, we'd come back to his place for Sunday dinner with his family, and now we were here — sitting around a small bonfire in his backyard like we had a hundred times before.

He didn't *feel* any different to me.

But in the back of my mind, I knew he wanted to kiss me.

And that was all it took to have my stomach in a knot the size of a Case Tractor.

"There she is," Mikey cooed, like he was talking to a two-year-old instead of a guitar as he plucked at the strings on the neck and strummed. For the first time since we sat down by the fire, it sounded right, the tuning done, and he looked up at me with a grin splitting his face. "I got a new guitar."

I smiled back. "Indeed, you did. How does it feel?"

He sighed, looking back down at his new baby as he played the first few notes of "Hotel California" softly. "It feels good, I guess. But a little weird."

"Because it's not Vanessa?"

He sighed again, deeper this time. "She's definitely not Vanessa."

Vanessa was the name for his old guitar — the one his dad had given him shortly before he passed away. His dad had always named *his* guitars, and so Mikey did the same, naming it after his biggest crush at the time — Vanessa Hudgens. He'd never admit it to anyone but me, but he'd been obsessed with her after *High School Musical. That* guitar had been entirely too large for him when he was eight years old, but it was the one he learned on, anyway. And he'd played that old thing well past its prime... up until the day he tossed it in the fire and watched it burn.

"What are you going to name this one?" I asked.

"Hmmm..." He stopped playing, smoothing his hand over the body, the neck, over the strings. "That's a good question."

"What about Emily?" I suggested. "After that hot model slash actress. Emily Ratzkowski."

He made a face. "Nah."

"*Nah?*" I mimicked, cocking a brow. "She's a smoke show. Okay, fine. What about Carrie? As in, Underwood?"

Mikey made another face.

I chuckled. "Alright. I give up. Who's your biggest crush right now?"

He looked at me curiously, with the smallest smirk on his lips.

"You named your first one after *High School Musical*'s bombshell who had the voice of an angel," I reminded him. "Vanessa Hudgens. Eight-year-old Mikey's biggest crush. So, who's your biggest crush now?"

He just kept looking at me with that dumb face, and then he nodded — just once — mind suddenly and definitively made up. "Nelly."

"*Nelly?*" I repeated, scrunching up my nose. "As in Furtado? Or the rapper with a Band-Aid on his cheek? Because depending on the answer, we might have more to talk about."

Mikey barked out a laugh. "Neither."

"Nelly who, then?"

"C'mere."

I frowned, looking at him like he was having a seizure or something.

"Come *where*?" I gestured to the small space between our chairs. "I'm already sitting next to you."

Mikey didn't say another word, just sat his guitar beside him, leaning the neck of it against his chair, and then, he patted his lap.

I stared at his basketball shorts for a long time — maybe a creepy amount of time — before I glanced back up at him again.

He chuckled. "Ky, come *here*."

I swallowed, setting my Dr. Pepper in the cup holder of my camping chair before I stood on legs as shaky as a newborn calf's. Then, I stood in front of him — stupidly — waiting to make sure I hadn't really, *really* misunderstood him.

His smile climbed, and he reached out, wrapping one hand around my waist as the other hit my thigh. And despite the heat coming from the fire and the already seventy-two-degree summer night around us, I was trembling as he pulled me into him, onto his lap, his arms wrapping around me easily as he adjusted me there.

"Nelly," he repeated when I was on his lap, the firelight dancing in his eyes as he looked up at me. "As in my own little nickname for Nelson."

"Nelson..." I whispered, not sure why my voice was suddenly gone. In fact, not sure that word had come from me at *all*, because with me in his lap, with one of his hands on my hip and the other resting on my thigh, and his big, olive eyes looking up at me like that — I wasn't sure of *anything*, really.

He nodded. "Nelson. As in, Kylie Nelson." Mikey shrugged. "If we're sticking to the biggest crush theme, then it fits perfectly."

My cheeks heated, and not a bit of it was from the fire.

"Can I ask you something?" he asked, brushing my long hair back behind my ear with his fingertips.

I shivered at the touch, nodding in lieu of a verbal response.

"Friday night... before you left..." He swallowed. "You said you've been waiting your whole life for me to kiss you. Is that true?"

My tongue was like sandpaper in my mouth, dry and impossible to swallow past as I nodded.

His brows tugged inward, his hand framing my face as he slid his fingertips into my hair, his thumb brushing the skin in front of my ear. "Can I ask you something else?"

"Mmm," I think I answered.

"If I kiss you again, right now, can we pretend that one on Friday never happened?" His fingers curled at the back of my neck. "Can we pretend this is the first time?"

I think I nodded. I think I whispered something close to *yes*, because Mikey pulled me into him — his hand at my waist tugging me closer, his hand in my hair pulling me down — and with his eyes searching mine before they fluttered shut, he pressed his lips to mine.

Heat spread like gooey liquid from that point of contact, from where his soft, warm, determined lips found mine, all the way to my toes. And even still, with the heat from the kiss and the heat from the fire, an inexplicable shiver rocked through me.

But it only made Mikey hold me tighter.

When the first kiss was broken, a soft sound from our lips breaking contact, he came back for more — and this time, the kiss was deeper, insistent, and sure. I inhaled a stiff breath, and he groaned, both hands framing my face then as he held me to him.

It was as if the whole world was tilting, like we were spinning out of orbit, like all the laws of gravity were being broken with that singular kiss.

I felt every part of him as if it were my own — his hands on my skin and in my hair, his lips parting, his tongue slipping inside my mouth to meet mine. I felt his rapid heartbeat reverberating through me, matching my own heart's rhythm, a new song coming to life inside us.

And when he pulled away, we pressed our foreheads together, both of us breathing like we'd just climbed a mountain.

I let out a shaky exhale. "Well..." I whispered, wetting my lips. "That was a much better first kiss."

Mikey smirked, nodding slightly with his forehead still to mine. "It was a solid silver medal."

I frowned, pulling back to look him in the eyes, but he just smiled wider.

"Meaning, I think we should go for gold."

He pulled me back into him, and for the next hour, neither of us came up for air.

Chapter Eleven

Michael

"He's going to *love* this one," I said to Katie — who, I'd just found out during our conversation, was visiting the distillery from Portland. She was on summer break from college and her boyfriend had just turned twenty-one back home. "It's the most popular one from our limited barrel release this spring. There aren't many bottles left, either, so you got here just in time."

I bagged up her whiskey and shot glasses, and the t-shirt that said *Scooter Gal* with our logo on it, handing it all to her with a smile.

"Thank you so much for your help," she said. "I'm going to stop by the front and tell them what a great job you all are doing here. The tour was fantastic, and you were just the cherry on top."

"Ah, stop it. Now you're just trying to make me blush," I teased.

She giggled and waved me off, making her way out of the store with her brother and parents as I tucked her signed receipt in the register drawer. As soon as she was gone, I checked to make sure no one else needed my help, then dug in my pocket for my phone.

Two texts from Kylie.

I smiled, typing out a reply to her comment on how we needed to see the new Marvel movie before social media spoiled it for both of us. As soon as the text was sent, there was a knock on the counter.

"Well, I'll be damned," Logan said, shaking his head. "You really *are* smiling. I guess not all the rumors that go around this place are false."

I rolled my eyes, tucking my phone back in my pocket. "I always smile."

Logan cocked a brow.

"At customers."

He lifted the other one.

"Okay, fine," I conceded. "So, I've been a little grumpy. Sue me."

Logan chuckled, looking around the shop to make sure no one was close enough to hear us before he leaned a little more over the counter. "I still can't believe you and Kylie got into the hard drive."

My smile slipped, chest tightening. It wasn't that I'd forgotten about the hard drive, but it hadn't exactly been at the top of my mind that week. No, that spot had been reserved for Kylie, and for my new favorite pasttime.

Which just happened to be kissing her.

"I know," I said, lowering my voice, too. "It's crazy. I think there was a part of me that never really thought we'd get in, you know?"

Logan nodded, adjusting the curve on the bill of his baseball cap. "Same here. I wonder what Jordan's found so far."

"He won't tell us unless it's important."

"True," Logan agreed. "Do you think..." His voice faded, and he looked around again, frowning. "Is it stupid to hope that maybe there are some answers on there?"

"No," I assured him. "But, it's not stupid to think we probably won't find anything at all, either." I shrugged. "I mean, from what Kylie and I looked at, it was just sort of a daily log of what he was working on, some brief summaries of conversations he'd had with the board. And it's not like he could write in it after he..." My throat tightened. "I just think if he would have known something before that day, if he would have felt something off... well... wouldn't he have told us? Or at the very least, told Mom?"

Logan nodded again, his brows furrowed. It wasn't the answer either of us wanted, and I knew it. It was easy to hold onto hope that there'd be something monumental on that hard drive, but the truth was, we'd gone ten years without answers to what happened to our dad that day.

My bet was that we'd go our whole lives just the same.

My phone buzzed in my pocket, and I fished it out, smiling at Kylie's suggestion that we play a game of Mortal Kombat before the movie, and loser has to dress up like a Marvel character.

Logan nodded at my phone with a grin when I tucked it away again. "Who ya texting?"

"Kylie," I answered easily, rearranging some shot glasses in front of the register that didn't need any adjusting at all.

"That's a pretty big smile for texting Kylie," he observed. "Something you wanna tell me, baby bro?"

"Nope."

He laughed, smacking the counter before pointing at me. "Oh, but I think there is. She's the reason you're all smiley and being nice to people again, isn't she?" He leaned closer. "You guys made out, didn't you?"

"I'm not all *smiley*," I argued, fidgeting with the shot glasses again. But no matter how I tried, I couldn't fight back the stupid grin that hit my face. "And who I'm making out with is none of your business."

His jaw dropped. "Holy shit," he whispered. "You really did kiss her?!"

I didn't answer. Hell, I didn't have to by the way Logan was already whooping and hollering.

"Well, hot damn!" he said, smacking the counter again. "About time you made that girl your girlfriend."

I smirked. "Hold your horses, hoss. We're not there yet."

At that, Logan's face went as still as stone. "What do you mean *you're not there yet*." He eyed me. "Please tell me you aren't just making out with Kylie without actually dating her."

"I'm just saying we haven't put a title on anything. It's new."

"Mikey," Logan said, like I just told him I stole twenty dollars out of Mom's purse.

"What?"

"This is *Kylie* we're talking about," he said. "She's tender."

"You saying I'm going to break her?"

"What I'm saying is you might want to make sure you're on the same page."

I rolled my eyes, but we put the conversation on pause while I rang up a family from Detroit. Once they were gone, Logan leaned over the counter again.

"Not everything in life requires a PowerPoint presentation, big bro," I said. "As much as I know you love them."

"Maybe so," he agreed. "But, I think *this* at least requires a conversation." He knocked on the counter once, standing upright. "I have to get back for the next tour, taking another one of Susie's since she's sick today."

"Manager of the year," I teased with a shit-eating grin.

Logan ignored me, but he didn't drop the other subject. "Just think about it, okay? If you really are leaving at the end of the summer... what does that mean for her?"

He left me on that, and when he was gone, I pulled out my phone with a sour twist in my gut.

I understood what my brother was saying, but what he didn't get was that it was early. *Really* early. We had only kissed for the first time that weekend, and now, here it was Wednesday. It hadn't even been a full week. Right now, we didn't need to have a full-blown conversation about where we go from here.

If anything, we were still trying to figure out how it felt to be in this new territory. After years and years of being friends, crossing the line into more was uncharted for both of us. We needed to go slow.

And *that* was something none of my brothers would understand, provided their track record.

I typed out a text to Kylie.

I want to see you.

The little bouncing dots showed up immediately, letting me know she was typing, and then a picture of her and Betty out by the pool making silly faces filled my screen. She wasn't wearing sunglasses, so she was squinting against the sun, and her long hair was wet and sticking to her cheeks.

She was the cutest thing ever.

Keeping that one forever. But I meant in real life. What's next on that list of adventures you have for us?

A few more customers checked out, and when they were gone, it was just me in the gift shop. I sat on the bar stool behind the counter, and when I saw the text lighting up my phone, I smiled.

Pick me up at eight and find out.

• • •

Kylie lived with her dad in a small, two-bedroom apartment on the edge of town.

I could still remember when they moved out of their old house, the one she'd grown up in, the one she'd made memories with her mom in. She'd been so heartbroken to leave it, but she'd tried so hard not to show it so that she didn't upset her dad.

It seemed she was always afraid to break him even more than her mother's death already had.

That's why it was no surprise to me when I pushed through the front door and found them there at the little folding table they called a dining table, Mr. Nelson wiping his mouth with a napkin while Kylie cleared the table.

"Evening, folks," I said in my best southern Tennessee accent. "Leave any for me?"

"Mikey, my boy!" Mr. Nelson exclaimed, opening his arms wide. He grinned at me with what I always called his Wolverine smile — the one that creased the edges of his tired eyes. "I didn't know you were stopping by."

"I told you we were hanging out tonight," Kylie argued, rolling her eyes as she stacked their plates together. She turned to me then, and a smile that hit me square in the chest bloomed on her beautiful face. "Hey."

I smiled back. "Hey, yourself."

"Are you really hungry? I can heat up a plate for you," she said, already hurrying to the small kitchen that was just a few steps away.

I let myself in, closing the door behind me and tucking the box I'd brought with me under one arm. "Nah, you know Mom wouldn't let me leave without stuffing me like a turkey first."

"Woman after my own heart," Kylie said, flipping on the faucet to rinse the dishes.

"I know *that* feeling well," Mr. Nelson chimed in, eyeing his daughter with a rueful smile as he rubbed his belly. "Been trying to lose ten pounds, but it's impossible living with this one."

"Trust me, Pops," she said over the running water. "Eating Easy Mac and hot dogs would not help you lose ten pounds. Maybe ten years off your life, but not ten pounds."

"I'd throw some tuna salad sandwiches in the mix from time to time," he argued. His daughter rolled her eyes again, which made him chuckle before he turned back to me and patted the now-empty seat next to him at the table. "Come sit, Mikey. Haven't seen you in a month of Sundays. How ya been?"

I took the seat next to him, setting the box I'd brought on the table. "Oh, you know me. Staying in trouble and out of grace."

"Only way to be as a young man," Mr. Nelson said. "I heard through the grapevine that you're moving to The Big Apple at the end of the summer?"

The sound of dishes clinking and sponge rubbing against plate ceased in the kitchen — just for a split second — almost short enough that I thought I imagined it, and then Kylie was back to scrubbing. I cleared my throat, swallowing against the sense that I was about to say something wrong. "That's the plan."

Mr. Nelson whistled. "I've never been, but Patricia spent a year there. She loved that city of lights. Said she didn't sleep the whole time she was there."

"Mom lived in New York?" Kylie asked from where she was rinsing the dishes now.

"She did."

Kylie frowned. "I didn't know that."

"She never talked about it," Mr. Nelson said. "I think she wanted everyone to think this had always been the plan — to be a dance teacher here in Stratford. And not that she wasn't amazing at that," he added, throwing his hands up. "Because she was. Best damn dance teacher this town ever had. But, when we were younger, before college and all that... well... she wanted to be a ballerina. And you know what? I think she could have been. She was a damn good dancer."

"What happened?" I asked.

"Oh, she fell in love with an old fuddy duddy who didn't want to leave the comfort of southern Tennessee." He winked at me, but something in his eyes tinged him with a true sadness. "A year apart was already too long for her, and she didn't want to do another year without me. So, she came back home, drove to and from Nashville three times a week to earn her degree and made a different career out of her passion."

"I didn't know any of that," Kylie said, and I glanced at her over my shoulder, chest tightening at the sorrow in her own eyes.

"Well, again, it wasn't something we talked about often," Mr. Nelson said, slapping his thighs and forcing a smile to change the subject. "Anyhoo, the city never was my thing, but I reckon you'll love it. You got a job lined up?"

"Not yet," I said, rubbing the back of my neck. "But I'm working on it. Figured at the very least, there oughta be a few gift shops there, don't ya think?"

He chuckled. "Yeah, I don't suppose you're wrong about that." He nodded toward the box in my hands then. "You bring dessert?"

"If I was a smarter man, I would have," I replied, pushing the box across the table toward him. "It's actually a gift. Something I picked up that I thought you might like."

"For me?" Mr. Nelson raised his eyebrows, looking at his daughter like he was impressed before he popped the lid on the box. Then, his smile covered his entire face and he clapped his hands together in joy. "Well, I'll be damned! Look at that!"

He pulled the hat from the box, smoothing his hands over the felt before he put it on his head and looked to Kylie for approval.

"Looks great, Dad," she said. "Now you've got the complete outfit."

"It's the right kind, right?" I asked, nervous. "I saw it in the pawn shop window, and thought it looked pretty legit, but wasn't sure."

"Oh, yeah," Mr. Nelson said, taking it off to inspect it closer. "This is a mighty fine Union kepi hat. Looks even better than the one I lost."

"Well, I'm glad that hat was all you lost in battle, sir."

Mr. Nelson chuckled, reaching out to take my hand in his and shake it firmly. "You're a good kid, Mikey. Thank you."

"Alright, dishes are all done. There's sherbet in the freezer. You can have *two* scoops," Kylie warned her father, pointing a finger at him before she tucked her hair behind her ear and slid her hands in her back pockets. "Don't think I won't know if you take more."

Mr. Nelson grumbled something under his breath, but Kylie just smiled and bent over to kiss his forehead.

Then, she turned to me.

She was in a soft, winter-green shirt that I'd seen her wear a hundred times, one she got for volunteering at the summer bake-off the church had the summer after eighth grade. Her jean shorts were dark and modest, cuffed mid-thigh, and her long hair was still a little damp, which told me she was freshly showered.

I'd seen her like that a million times before.

And yet, I couldn't help but see her differently every single time I looked at her now.

"I just need to grab my shoes and I'll be ready," she said, thumbing toward the hall behind her. "Be right back?"

"Okay," I said, grinning.

"Okay," she responded, and with a blush shading her cheek, she scampered down the hall.

When I looked back at Mr. Nelson, he had one eyebrow in his hairline and an amused, slightly scary smile on his face.

I swallowed.

"Something you wanna tell me, son?"

I cleared my throat, crossing my ankle over my knee. "No, sir."

"Mm-hmm," he said, still watching me. "Listen, I may be old, but I'm not blind, and I know when there's a change in my daughter. She came home and cried herself to sleep in that bedroom Friday night, and then came home happy as a clam Sunday evening. And while I may not know the details of what's going on, I'd wager it has something to do with you."

I gulped again, but kept my eyes on his.

"Now, it's none of my business what you two do as friends," he said. "But, the minute you become more, my need-to-know-basis requirements double. You understand?"

"I do, sir."

"Good," he said. "You're a good kid, and I know you care about Kylie. But I also know you're a boy, and since I was one myself, I know all too well how stupid a boy can be. So, before you do anything that might break that girl's heart in there," he said, nodding down the hall. "You best remember that's my one and only baby, and you'll have me to answer to."

I'd had a similar talking to from Bailey's father the first time I'd picked her up to go on a date, but for some reason, this time felt more intense. This was Kylie's dad, a man I'd considered a second father since I was eight years old. I'd stayed so many nights on his couch that I couldn't count them up if I tried to. We'd had holiday dinners together, spent summer nights watching movies as a family of sorts, and when Kylie had gone through something that had her shutting down from the world, he'd always turned to me for help.

One thing was clear: it didn't matter how much history we had. Mr. Nelson was making sure I understood my place, and his expectations for what would come next.

My brother's warning from earlier rang in my ears, but I ignored it, nodding instead and smiling at Kylie's dad. "I would never intentionally hurt her," I promised him. "And I'll fight off my natural stupidity as best I can."

He smirked at that, reaching over to pat my hand. "'Atta boy."

"Ready?" Kylie asked in the next breath, but when she saw my face, she narrowed her eyes at her father. "Dad, what did you just say to him?"

"Just talking about sports, Smiley," he answered, picking up his new hat and dusting a piece of lint off it. He shooed us away. "Have fun."

She narrowed her eyes farther, but I hopped up, putting my arm around her shoulders and guiding her out the door before she could ask anything else.

When we were in her truck, she paused, holding the key in the ignition without turning it. "What did he say to you?" she asked.

"Nothing that concerns you."

She pouted, which earned her a chuckle and a kiss on the cheek, and that seemed to flush any other questions she had out of her mind.

"Now," I said, slipping my hand over her knee. She looked down at the embrace with another blush, her hair falling in front of her face a bit before she looked up at me and cranked the engine to life. "Where we going?"

Chapter Twelve

Kylie

"I think I might throw up."

"You better not!" Mikey screamed up at me. "Remember, I'm below you here. I didn't sign up for the splash zone."

I laughed, gripping onto the rusty metal ladder even tighter. My next step was just as trembly as the one before it, and I forced a breath, blowing it out through pursed lips.

"I don't remember it being this scary when we were ten," Mikey called up.

"We were fearless. We didn't think we could die."

"Well, I seem to be acutely aware of that fact now."

I laughed again, stopping to get my balance before I took another step. "Stop making me laugh! I'm going to fall."

"You won't fall. I'd catch you."

"Sure. You'd catch me. Right before we both tumbled to our death."

"Hey, this was your idea, Indiana Jones. Now, climb. We're almost there."

Steadying myself, I took a few calming breaths before I started climbing again. The rest of the journey was silent, and when I reached the top, I peeled my backpack off and collapsed, feeling the cool grate of the metal on my damp back.

"Oh, thank God," Mikey said when he joined me, flopping down on the other side of the opening where the ladder met the base. "You know we'll have to die up here, right? Because there's no way I can climb back down."

A hearty laugh left my chest, and I sat up, still winded, breathing like it was Everest we'd just climbed and not the Stratford water tower on the south side of town. My eyes traced the bright red letters that spelled out our town's name, each one outlined in black, and our only claim to fame in small, italic print below it.

Home of the Tennessee State Champions Football Team — Go Cats!

Beneath that, in everything from Sharpie and pencil to spray paint and knife-carvings, were names and phrases and years that had been scrawled over time, people marking their place.

Jessie was here.

Color guard team 2005.

Mark and Lisa 4ever.

I smiled, reaching into my bag for a bottle of water. I tossed it to Mikey before digging one out for me, too.

He sat up, took a long swig, and then crawled over to sit next to me, both of us leaning back against the tower with our eyes on the town spread out below us.

"It looks kind of pretty at night," Mikey said, scanning the lights. He pointed to the American flag blowing in the breeze on the hill east of town, the one that welcomed visitors to our little map dot. The flag was lit up with a spotlight, and right behind it was a giant, illuminated cross.

"It does," I agreed. My gut twisted as I took another sip of water, eyes falling to my lap. "Sure you won't miss this view when you leave?"

"Nah," he said easily — so easily my heart broke a little more. "This is nothing compared to the Manhattan skyline."

"You're not scared of a city that big?" I asked. "Of all those people, all those buildings and cars and… and…" I waved my hand. "Just, all of *that*?"

Mikey leaned his head back against the tower, thinking. "Honestly? No, not even a little bit. I think that's what I'm most excited about. No one will know me, and I won't know anyone, either. And there's so much to do, so much to see, so many possibilities of how to fill your time. There are paths of life there that I don't even know *exist* yet, you know? It feels like… I don't know, like I can be whoever I want to be. Like a rebirth."

I nodded, with my eyes still on my hands, unable to look at him when he talked about leaving so easily.

"Hey," he said, thumbing my chin until I looked at him. "I'm not gone yet, okay?"

I nodded, attempting a smile. And even though I wanted to pout and give up on my stupid idea that our list of adventures would open up his eyes to how much he loved this town and make him stay, I couldn't give up hope. Not yet.

Especially not now that we were… whatever we were.

I chewed the inside of my cheek, the words on the tip of my tongue to ask him to define exactly *what* that was. Because if the end of the summer came and I *couldn't* make him stay, then what did it mean when he left?

I knew it was still new. I knew it was silly to already be anxious and wondering if we had a title or a definition. But now that we weren't just friends anymore, I didn't know where to put us.

And it felt a lot like I was in danger of something I couldn't quite put my finger on.

"What about you?" he asked, tapping my nose before he sat back again. "You've got this whole gap year to fill. What do you want to do with it?"

I groaned, leaning my head back against the tower with my eyes on the town again. "I wish I knew."

"You don't have any ideas?"

"I mean, I want to travel... but I don't know *where*. Or how far I could actually get with what little savings I have. And then there's... well, I just don't know if traveling is the best thing for me to do right now."

"Because of your dad."

My stomach turned. "Yeah."

Mikey leaned up, turning in place until he faced me. "You can't stay in that apartment with him forever, Ky. He's a grown man. He'll be okay. And he wants you to go live your life."

"*Will* he be okay, though?" I asked, looking at him then. "I mean, *really* okay? I've taken care of him for so long now, I'm not sure."

"Trust me," he assured. "Once you leave, he'll figure it out. It might take him a little while to get a rhythm going, but he will. And regardless, it's not your job to care for him."

"But I love him. I care about him. I want him to be okay."

"And he wants *you* to get out and live," Mikey said. Then, he wrapped his hand over my knee, holding it like it was the most natural thing in the world despite how it made a wave of chills race up my shorts. "If money wasn't an issue, and you knew your dad would be one-hundred percent okay in your absence, where would you go?"

I looked up at the sky, at the stars that broke through the dim light our town gave off. "I think I'd take a road trip," I said, smiling. "Rent a camper van, check out some state parks and national parks, hike, camp." I looked back at him with an embarrassed grin. "And probably stop at every animal shelter I could along the way."

He chuckled, his eyes wide and sparkling in the soft light from the tower. "That sounds amazing, Ky. You should do it."

I shrugged, looking at where his hand held my leg. I covered it with my own, feeling the smooth skin that stretched over his knuckles. "I dunno. We'll see." I swallowed. "Who knows, maybe New York will be on my list. Seems like it was a big place in my mom's life... maybe it'd be great for me to see, too." My eyes found his briefly. "Maybe I could visit."

Mikey flipped his hand over, and I traced his palm with my fingertips until he folded his fingers in with mine. "I'd like that," he said.

Then his other hand found my chin, and he tilted it up, tilted his own down, and gently, his lips found mine.

We both exhaled a shaky breath at the contact, and he squeezed my hand in his, pulling me closer. Just that little squeeze, that centimeter of movement had my heart doubling its pace, thumping so hard in my chest I knew Mikey had to be able to hear it.

I reached for him, fisting my hands in his t-shirt as I deepened the kiss. A tingling sensation trickled through me when our tongues touched, and when a soft groan came from his throat, I felt muscles in a place only I knew about tighten and pulse.

I broke the kiss, pressing my forehead to his as a long breath left my lips. "Does kissing always feel like that?"

"Like what?"

"Like…" I shook my head, wetting my lips. "Like if you kiss me any longer, I'm going to explode?"

He smirked, sitting back and brushing my hair from in front of my face. His eyes searched mine as he played with the strands. "Was I your first kiss?"

I blushed. "I mean, if you don't count Zachary Hoggins holding his lips on mine and counting to five behind the middle school when we were twelve, then yeah."

"Zachary Hoggins?" Mikey grimaced. "You can do better."

"Hey, he wanted to kiss me and I didn't exactly have any other suitors at the time, okay?"

Mikey smiled, tugging on my hair before he leaned in and kissed me again, making all the butterflies in my stomach take flight once more.

"Does it feel weird to you?" I asked when he pulled away.

"Kissing you?"

I nodded.

His mouth pulled to one side, his eyes on the sky before they found me again. "Strangely, not at all. I guess now that you mention it, it probably should, huh? But it doesn't. It feels… I don't know. It feels right. It feels natural." Then he smirked. "It feels like I want to do it all the damn time."

He leaned in, kissing me all over my face as I laughed and shoved him away.

"Does it feel weird to you?"

I shrugged. "Not weird, but…" I blew out a breath, trying to figure out how to explain. "It's just, I wanted you to kiss me for so long, and now you just… do it. So, it's kind of shocking. Exciting, but surreal, if that makes sense. It surprises me, I guess."

My stomach flipped and floundered with every word I said, like it couldn't believe I was being so honest about something so embarrassing. But it was Mikey. I didn't know how to lie to him, how to hide from him.

Especially ever since the only secret I ever *did* keep from him had been exposed.

He held me on top of that water tower, one hand playing with my hair while the other drew circles on the hand I had in his lap. His brows were furrowed as he watched me, his eyes flicking back and forth between my own.

"How long have you wanted to be more than friends, Kylie?"

I swallowed — or rather, *attempted* to swallow. "For a while."

"How long?"

I shrugged, but didn't look away. "I think the first time I really realized it was the summer after eighth grade," I whispered. "But... I don't know. I think I always kind of felt it. In some way."

He shook his head, frowning more like what I was saying was impossible. "Why didn't you ever say anything?"

I laughed. "Because it's *us*, Mikey. We're friends, and I didn't want to ruin that." I paused. "And, honestly, because I just thought..."

I stopped, my heart clenching hard in my chest, as if it was warning me to stop while I was ahead.

"You thought what?"

I forced a breath. "I thought there was no way it wouldn't happen. Eventually. When the time was right." I shrugged. "We were already best friends. I was just waiting for you to realize I was a girl. You know," I said, leaning forward with a cocked eyebrow. "With boobs."

He swallowed, eyes falling to where my t-shirt gaped a little now, giving him a peek at the aforementioned cleavage. "Yeah... *really* not sure how I missed those."

I chuckled, sitting upright again.

"We held hands all the time, and cuddled," I pointed out. "I guess I just thought things would kind of slowly progress... when the timing was right. But, when you and Bailey started hanging out..." My eyes fell to my lap. "Well, we all know that story."

His hands went still for a moment, but only a short breath before he groaned, shaking his head. "God, and I asked you to help me plan our dates and write her notes and pick out stupid flowers for her and shit."

"Yep," I confirmed, the word ending on a pop.

He tucked my hair behind my ear, waiting for me to look at him. "I'm sorry I never saw."

I shrugged. "It's okay. It is me, after all." I chuckled. "Not like there's much to look at."

He frowned, shaking his head and framing my face in his hands. He held me there for a long time, just looking at me, his eyes tracing every inch of my face — from my forehead to my nose to my chin and cheeks and eyes and back around.

"What are you doing, weirdo?" I asked, lifting a brow.

"Making up for lost time."

My heart squeezed, those damn butterflies in a tizzy again, and his eyes stopped their roaming when they found mine.

"For the record, there is a *lot* to look at." He swallowed. "You're the most beautiful girl I've ever known."

I wanted to roll my eyes, but I fought against it, though I couldn't fight hard enough to stop my knee-jerk reaction of word vomit that came next. "What about Bailey?"

He blinked, but his eyes never left mine. "What about her?"

Emotion surged through me like a tidal wave, so fierce and fast that I couldn't stop the tears that pricked my eyes. They weren't sad, and they weren't strong enough to fall — just powerful enough to let me know they were there, that I was feeling something.

That it was real.

Mikey leaned in, kissing me for a long moment before he pulled back and narrowed his eyes at something behind me. "Is that what I think it is?"

"What?" I asked, turning to look as he popped up and walked over to whatever it was he saw.

He bent down, picked something up, and then turned to me with a mischievous grin, holding a can in his hand.

"Spray paint," he said, shaking it.

I stood, walking over to inspect it with him. "I bet it doesn't work anymore."

"No?" he asked, still shaking it. The little ball inside it clicked and clacked. "Sounds like you're wrong about that one." He scanned the tower behind me. "But, only one real way to find out."

He brushed past me, popping the lid off the can and bending down toward the tower.

"Wait!" I hissed, bending down with him and snapping my hand down on his wrist. "You can't do that. It's vandalism."

"Kylie, look around us," he deadpanned. "It's tradition."

I swallowed, biting my lip as I read over the names and years and doodles.

"What are you going to write?" I asked.

He smirked, taking my question as permission and shaking the can once more before he started to spray.

I choked against the fumes, waving them away and standing to put more distance between myself and the cloud. Mikey's rounded back shielded whatever he was drawing from my view, but I watched the muscles of it as he moved. And when he stood, he turned, grinning at me before he stepped aside.

It was our names.

Ky + Mikey, it read — surrounded by a lopsided heart.

I rolled my lips between my teeth, shaking my head before I looked back at him. "You're insane."

"We left our mark," he said, dropping the can to the metal floor. "Now, let's make out."

I laughed, shoving against him when he advanced on me, but I didn't really try to keep him away. And when his lips found mine, and he wrapped his arms snug around me, I melted into him, into the moment, into the fact that our names were written together and framed in a heart on our town's water tower.

It was silly.

It was cliché and cheesy.

But it was something almost every girl in this town wanted — and I wasn't too proud to say I was one of them.

The longer he kissed me, the more my mind raced with questions I was too afraid to ask. What did it mean that he wrote our names on that tower? What did it mean that he put them in a little heart for all the town to see?

Those names were permanent — at least, until someone who worked for the city climbed up there to paint over everything. And judging by the years that still showed, my guess was that didn't happen very often.

It was something a couple would do.

Something a *boyfriend and girlfriend* would do.

My fists twisted in his shirt, pulling him closer, kissing him harder as if that could somehow stop my mind from overheating. And by some miracle, when he opened his mouth and slipped his tongue inside mine, caressing it with a roll that made my nipples harden under my sports bra, it worked.

Every other thought was gone, and all I could focus on was the way it felt to have his hands on me, his lips kissing my lips, his tongue touching my tongue.

Maybe we didn't need to talk right now.

Maybe we didn't need a stupid title.

Maybe, at least for now, those names on the water tower were enough.

Chapter Thirteen

Michael

The summer blazed by like a comet, and my entire universe was wrapped up in Kylie.

After the night at the water tower, we were as inseparable as we had been before I met Bailey. Every day after work, we met up at her house or mine, sometimes spending the night playing video games or watching movies, other times, checking off more items on her list of adventures.

And what I realized on top of that tower stuck with me long after I left it.

All summer long, I'd been all about me. *My* broken heart. *My* move to New York. *Me me me.* And all the while, Kylie had given herself over, put all her focus into making me happy — even when it seemed impossible to do.

It was my turn to return the favor.

We went fishing at the lake, even though neither of us knew how to rig up a pole, and Kylie nearly cried when I had to shove a hook through the worm we had for bait. All it took was one time of actually hooking a fish for her to *really* cry and for us to throw in the towel on fishing.

We drove around town late at night, eating ice cream from Blondie's and talking for hours. We sat by the fire in my backyard, me playing my new guitar while Kylie read or planned out her gap year road trip — one I was *making* her plan, because one way or another, I was determined to get her to actually go on it.

There were Saturdays at the nursing home pool and Sundays holding hands in the back of the church. There were Friday nights where I tried to teach her more line dances in her living room while her father laughed and laughed, and Sunday evenings drinking sweet tea on the porch with my mom, listening to her talk about how different our little town was thirty years ago.

And yet how much it was the same.

We spent the Fourth of July lighting fireworks down by the lake with her family and mine, and as the summer days got hotter and longer, so did our kissing. Every time I touched her, it felt like a fire scorching me from the inside out, and when I was brave enough to feel under her shirt or slide my hand a little farther up the inside of her shorts, the moans she gave me were the sweetest reward.

When I was at work, I texted her the entire time and thought about how I couldn't wait to see her after. When I wasn't at work, I was with her — period.

And all thoughts of New York were put on the back burner.

I knew I needed to be looking for apartments, for a job, for a moving truck. I needed to figure out what I was taking, what I would ask Mom to hold onto for me, what I would sell or donate. It was already July, and I didn't have anything more in my plan to leave than I did when I announced it at my graduation dinner.

And maybe part of that was because I knew I could separate the junk in my room, figure out what to keep and what to sell and what to toss in the trash.

But I couldn't do that so easily with Kylie.

Any time I *did* think about it, anxiety would creep in, hard and cold, and I'd immediately shake free from it before it could wrap me in its grasp.

I knew I was avoiding — not just what would happen when I left, but talking about what we were and weren't, too.

Because I didn't know.

And I didn't want to fixate on it when I could spend time with her, instead.

On Sunday, July eleventh — one week after Independence Day — Kylie and I were wrapped up in a flannel sleeping bag in the treehouse my father had built for me and my brothers when we were kids. Each corner of it was decorated based on our personalities, on what we loved. Logan's was filled with books, Noah's with sailboats and constellations, Jordan's with football legends, and mine, with music.

Of course, at that point in the night, my guitar had been abandoned next to my shelf of records and the old record player Dad had brought out there for me, because I was too busy putting my hands on Kylie to play a damn chord, let alone a song.

We were both breathless when I finally pulled away from her kiss, trying not to think about the way her hand was tucked into the band of my basketball shorts, and mine was wrapped around her, holding her small, perfect little ass. As much as I wanted to devour her, I had a more pressing subject to discuss.

"I need you to do something for me," I said, running my fingertip down the bridge of her nose before I tapped her swollen lips.

"What's that?" she asked, her eyes heavy and sated, cheeks rosy pink.

"Tomorrow after work, come to my place."

"Like always?"

"And bring your dad."

She frowned, watching me like I was insane. "Okay... why?"

"My mom wants to cook dinner for you guys," I lied — well, *partially* lied. "I know it's last-minute notice, but do you think you can make it happen?"

"Well, if I don't cook or bring home takeout from the diner, Dad doesn't eat. So, I think he'll do whatever I say when it comes to dinner."

"Good," I said, smiling and lowering my lips to hers again to end the conversation. I didn't want her asking too many questions and spoiling the surprise.

"Why do I feel like you're trying to distract me from whatever it is you have planned tomorrow?" she asked, smiling against my lips as I played with the hem of her tank top under the sleeping bag.

I slipped that hand under the fabric, splaying it flat on her stomach before I inched my fingers up, brushing the bottom of her bra. "Is it working?"

She let out a sharp gasp of an exhale and nodded, no longer able to speak.

I smiled wider, tracing the lacy edge of her bra with my fingertips, but not going even a little bit under the cups. She squirmed and moaned, and the way she ground her pelvis against my thigh had me rock hard under my shorts.

I groaned, adjusting myself before I pulled away and wrapped her in my arms to halt the kissing. "You're going to be the death of me, you know that?"

"You're the one who keeps stopping," she panted.

I smirked, kissing her forehead and running my fingertips through her hair. "We have time," I told her.

The truth was I knew without her having to say it that I would be her first — for anything I chose to do with her. If I was her first kiss, then I already knew I was the first to put my hand up her shirt, the first to grind against her while making out, and — if I made the move — I'd be the first to touch her, the first to finger her, the first to kiss her below the belt.

The first to be inside her.

My erection throbbed at the thought, and I inhaled a long, cleansing breath and closed my eyes, counting to ten in my head. As much as my teenage hormones protested against it, I knew I needed to wait, to slowly ease into all of that.

I couldn't go back in time and notice Kylie sooner. I couldn't take away all the pain I'd put her through while she watched me date Bailey. I couldn't go back and save myself for her, too.

But I *could* take it slow, and make sure every time I *did* touch her, she knew that I treated it like the goddamn privilege that it was.

And that's what I intended to do.

"So, you going to tell me what you really have planned for tomorrow?" she asked after a moment. "Or are we sticking with the *Mom wants to make you dinner* story?"

I kissed her hair. "Patience, baby. Patience."

She froze in my arms, and then leaned up, balancing on one elbow with the flannel sleeping bag falling off her shoulder as she looked at me. "You just called me baby."

I smiled, brushing her hair out of her face and tucking it behind her ear. "I did. Is that okay?"

The smile that bloomed on her face was the one I loved the most, the one that reached all the way up to her eyes, crinkling the edges of those nutmeg irises I loved to stare at so much.

She nodded, leaning down to kiss me. I thought it would be a peck, but she held it there, kissing me over and over until I opened my mouth and let her sweep her tongue inside. As soon as she did, the erection that I'd finally got to calm down sprang to life again.

"Woman," I groaned, grabbing her arms in my hands and holding her from grinding on me.

"Come on," she pleaded, nipping at my bottom lip. "It's just kissing. We can kiss, right?"

I sighed, shaking my head at her playful, *I'm-so-innocent* smile as she lowered her mouth to mine again. But I couldn't say no — not with her pouting and looking at me with those big eyes of hers.

So we kissed.

And we kissed.

And we kissed some more.

Until our lips were chapped and the night crawled slowly into early morning, I kissed that girl.

And I wondered if I'd ever be able to stop.

• • •

Kylie

All summer long, I'd been flying.

I'd lived in the clouds, in a place where my days were filled with volunteering and my nights were filled with kissing my best friend. I'd lost myself in weekends wrapped up together under blankets and surrendered all my thoughts to daydreams of Michael Becker.

But that all came crashing down on July twelfth.

I woke that Monday morning with my gut already sick and knotted, with my mouth dry, my eyelids heavy and swollen. I wished I could blame it on staying up too late in the treehouse with Mikey, but I knew better.

It was July twelfth.

And my mom had been dead for ten years.

As soon as I sat up in my bed, leaning against the white headboard with my floral-print comforter pooling around my hips, the loss hit me just like it did every year on that day. I blinked once, twice, a third time, and by the fourth, each new blink set loose a new river of silent, hot tears.

I wasn't sure how long I sat there in bed, staring at the wall, crying and surrendering to the aching loss I felt in the hollow part of my chest reserved for this day. All I knew was that eventually, the tears ran dry, and my stomach growled in protest that I hadn't eaten yet, so I climbed out of bed and padded down the hall to the kitchen to make something for breakfast.

Dad was already at work.

I knew he had been up all night, and that he'd probably gone into work early. If it weren't for me telling him we had plans at the Beckers that evening, he would have worked late, too.

I surrendered to my emotions on this day.

My father hid from his.

Ten years. Those two words were on repeat in my mind the entire day — as I made breakfast, as I got dressed, as I cried to Betty at the nursing home later that afternoon. It had been ten years without my mom, without having her there to lean on, to ask questions, to hold me when life got hard. Ten years without her bubbly laugh, without her homemade biscuits and one-of-a-kind sausage gravy, without her holding my dad's hand at the kitchen table.

An entire decade without her.

And for the first time, I realized I'd lived more life *without* her than I had with her.

That fact gutted me, and I couldn't seem to let go of it — no matter how Betty assured me that my mom had always been with me, and always would be. It didn't matter if I felt her presence, if, spiritually, I believed she still watched over my father and me.

Because in *reality*, she was gone.

As if it wasn't already the worst day of the year, I'd woken up to two social media notifications that had knocked the wind out of me.

Both from Bailey Baker.

She'd liked two of my posts — both from weeks ago, and both containing Mikey in them. One was the video I'd posted of him singing and playing the pink guitar with *My Little Pony* stickers all over it. The other was a selfie I'd snapped of us on top of the water tower, and in the background — just barely — you could see our addition to the graffiti.

She didn't comment, didn't message me, just simply *liked* each one of them — but something in my gut told me she didn't *like* it at all. She'd never wanted Mikey and I to be friends, especially not after they'd started dating. She was suspicious of me, and she had a reason. Maybe she saw what Mikey never did all along.

I warred with whether to tell Mikey about it or not. He'd unfollowed her on social media, but I was pretty certain he hadn't *blocked* her. If he had, she wouldn't have been able to see the pictures I'd tagged him in, at all.

And if he hadn't blocked her, that meant he'd likely woken up to the same notifications I had.

Maybe he didn't care. Maybe it wasn't as big of a deal as I felt like it was. But, that gut feeling that my dad said I got from my mother was churning like a locomotive, and I didn't know how to ignore it.

Still, today wasn't the day to address it — of that, I was sure.

Today was about Mom.

My eyes were so puffy and red by the time I started getting ready to go to Mikey's that I almost considered putting on makeup, but I knew it was no use. The minute he wrapped me up in a hug, I'd lose it again, and the mascara I bought at the drug store and never wore would streak down my cheeks. So, I opted for dressing in my favorite pair of yoga pants and an oversized Stratford High t-shirt, and I threw my hair up in a bun.

Dad was silent as I drove us to dinner, but he reached over and held my hand, squeezing it as supportively as he could for someone falling apart themselves. When we pulled in, he put on his best happy face, joking with Lorelei as soon as we were out of the truck and offering to help her finish up in the kitchen.

Mikey just stood on the front porch, waiting for me.

When our parents were inside, I walked slowly up the three wooden stairs, and then I stopped a few feet away from him. His sad eyes searched mine, and I shrugged, as if we both already knew there was nothing to say in that moment.

Then, he pulled me into his arms, and I broke again.

"I know," he said, rubbing the back of my neck as he held me. His arms were firm and warm, the embrace I'd found comfort in on this day ever since I was eight. "I know."

Maybe what made that hug so comforting was that he really *did* know. Just one month before, it had been him grieving a decade without his father, and I knew that Mikey understood like no one else in my entire life ever would. He wasn't just saying something to say something, he wasn't pretending to understand when he didn't.

We were tied together in that way, in a way we never would be with anyone else.

I sniffed, pulling back from his embrace and swiping the tears off my cheeks. "I'm sorry I look like such a mess."

He chuckled, kissing my forehead before he grabbed my hand and tugged me toward the front door. "You look beautiful. Like a model. A queen. A goddess."

I pinched his arm, but couldn't fight the smile tugging at my lips. "Shut up."

Dinner passed in a numb blur.

Lorelei made a southern buffet of my dad's favorites — barbecue ribs, corn on the cob, potato salad, and cornbread. We had fried pickles for an appetizer and hot apple pie with vanilla bean ice cream on top for dessert. All the Becker boys were there, along with Mallory and Betty, too. It was a feast, and the entire evening was filled with laughter and stories and we talked about everything *but* the fact that it had been ten years since my mom had passed away.

It was perfect.

Dad was actually laughing, and he loved Betty and her crazy stories just as much as the rest of us. Mallory gifted Lorelei a beautiful painting of the view from her backyard at the end of dinner, and we all clamored around to *ohhhh* and *ahhh* at it. She really was the most talented artist I'd ever known in real life, and by the way tears welled up in Lorelei's eyes, I knew it was a special gift to her.

By the time dinner was done and the dishes were cleared, I was ready to climb into bed and say goodbye to the day, but Mikey had other plans.

"I have a little surprise for you and your dad," he said, quiet enough for only me to hear. His brothers and Mallory were already out on the front porch, drinking and catching up while Lorelei and my dad washed the dishes in the kitchen.

I lifted one brow. "A surprise, huh?" I nudged him. "I knew there was more to tonight than dinner."

He smiled. "Give me ten minutes, and then bring your dad into the backyard. Okay?"

I frowned more. "Okay...?"

He didn't offer anything else to ease my curiosity, just squeezed my hand under the table and excused himself out the back door. I glanced at the front porch, wondering if they were talking to Jordan about what he'd found in his dad's journal. Curiosity about *that* had been eating away at me since we handed the hard drive over to him.

But I didn't have time to eavesdrop before Dad and Lorelei were back at the table with me, and just as instructed, I waited about ten minutes and then told Dad our presence was requested out back.

Lorelei smiled a knowing smile when we stood, and she grabbed me in a hug before I could leave.

"I love you, baby girl," she whispered, holding me tight. "I hope you know how special you are to our entire family."

If I hadn't already cried so much that day, I knew I'd be sobbing again. Instead, I squeezed her tight, nodding against her chest before we both pulled away.

"I love you, too," I said. "Thank you for dinner tonight, and for taking our minds off everything." I looked back at my dad then, who was watching us with a sad look on his face. "I know we both really appreciated it."

"Yes," he agreed with a nod, his eyes shimmering with unshed tears. "Thank you, Lorelei. Truly."

"Oh, don't thank me," she said, waving us both off. "Thank that passionate boy in the backyard. It was all his idea." She smiled, looking out the back door before she found my eyes again. "Speaking of which, I think he's ready for y'all."

Dad and I made our way out the door and down the back porch steps, but it wasn't the same backyard I'd hung out with Mikey in all summer long.

It had been transformed.

Strings of different-sized, white lights stretched from one end to the other, criss-crossing to illuminate the yard as if someone had reached up and pulled the stars down to hover just above us. There was a giant blow-up screen just in front of where I knew the fire pit was, and two giant bean bags set up in front of it, each of them covered in blankets and pillows. Two speakers sat on either side of the screen, and a bottle of champagne sat in a bucket on ice between the bean bags.

"What is all this?" I asked, shaking my head and looking around in awe.

Dad leaned down to whisper where only I could hear him. "I think that boy might love you, my dear." He stood then, frowning. "And I don't know if that makes me want to hug him or threaten him with a shot gun."

I laughed, looping my arm through Dad's as we made our way toward Mikey and trying to ignore what my dad had said.

Love.

My stomach tilted like a carnival ride at the thought, but I placed my other hand over it, as if to physically tell it not to get ahead of itself.

Mikey stood in front of the screen, hands in his pockets and a grin on his face, watching me and Dad as we made our way across the yard. When we were in front of the screen, he gestured to the two chairs.

"One for you, Mr. Nelson," he said. "And one for us, Ky. Go ahead, sit down."

"What's all this about?" I asked when we were both seated.

Mikey cleared his throat, popping the top on the champagne bottle before he poured three glasses. "Mr. Nelson, I hope you don't mind. I know we're underage, but I figured a glass or two of champagne wouldn't be too bad — especially in the safety of our own home. And, well, tonight… we're celebrating."

"Celebrating?" I asked, cocking an eyebrow at Mikey first, and then my dad as Mikey handed him a glass, too. Dad was suspiciously quiet, smiling, and not objecting to any of it, which made me narrow my eyes farther. "What do you know that I don't, huh, Pops?"

He just smiled wider, holding his glass of champagne toward Mikey. "Shhh. Michael's talking."

I glared at him.

"I know, maybe more than most people, how hard today is for both of you," Mikey said, calling my attention back to him. He seemed a little nervous now, his fingertips drumming on the side of his glass. "And I know that we all handle days like this in different ways. Some of us get sad," he said, looking at me. "Some of us hide from it all," he added, looking at my dad. Then, he raised his hand. "Some of us get angry. But, no matter how we handle it, we all have something in common." He paused. "We miss the one we lost too soon. And we wish they were here with us."

I sniffed against the sting those words brought to my eyes, and Dad reached over to squeeze my hand.

"Today marks ten years since you both lost someone very important to you. And I know it's a hard day, and that there will be more hard days to come. But, I thought, at least for tonight, we could shift gears a little. Instead of hiding from how we feel, or giving in and being sad, I thought we could celebrate — toast to the life you both had with Jocelyn — and look back on some memories."

Tears welled in my eyes again at the mention of her name — a name we barely said anymore, and that I suddenly was very ashamed of.

"So, if you'll lift your glasses," he said, holding up his champagne flute. Dad and I joined him, and he smiled. "To Jocelyn Nelson... an amazing mother, a devoted wife, one hell of a dancer, and a woman we will all hold close to our hearts forever. Cheers."

"Cheers," Dad and I echoed, and then we all took a sip, and Mikey sat down in the bean bag chair with me, putting one arm around my shoulders and holding me close.

He kissed my cheek, hit play on a small remote he had in his hand, and then, my mother's face filled the screen.

I gasped, hand flying up to cover my mouth as she looked up at the camera with a wide, tired smile. She held a small baby wrapped in a pink blanket in her arms, and she was rocking in her favorite chair — one we still had in the corner of our small apartment living room.

"Oh, my God," I whispered.

Mikey hugged me a little tighter but didn't say a word.

"*Say hello, Momma,*" my dad's voice said behind the camera. Mom laughed and shoved the camera away, but then her eyes were on me, and the camera zoomed in.

"*Hello, my sweet girl,*" she whispered.

The clip cut out, and then it was me and her in the backyard of our old house. I was in the swing, chanting, "*Higher! Higher!*", my hair tied up in a pink bow as she pushed me.

Next, it was me holding the camera, making a face before I turned it around and zoomed in on Mom and Dad sitting on our back porch holding hands. "*They're gonna get cooties!*" Six-year-old me said, and then my mom leaned over as if cued and kissed my dad on the cheek.

I looked over at my dad just in time to see his smile, and two tears slipped free — one from each eye — falling over the apple of his cheeks and into the laugh lines on his face.

Over and over, clip after clip, memories of my mother played out on that big screen. There were birthdays and Christmases, camping days at the lake and lazy nights at home. There were videos and pictures, smiles and laughs, all put together over the sound of some of her favorite songs.

Now I knew why dad had been so quiet. There was no way Mikey could have gotten all those videos and pictures without his help.

He'd been in on it, too.

I couldn't stop the tears that flowed from my eyes, but I also couldn't stop smiling, either. My heart swelled with an overwhelming amount of emotions as we watched the video, and Mikey held me close the entire time.

When the last clip played and the screen went dark, Mikey popped up to refill our glasses.

He held his up to me. "You once told me that your mom's favorite band was The Rolling Stones," he said. "Well, I found a recording of one of their concerts they played the year you were born. I figured Jocelyn probably wasn't going to any concerts while she was pregnant, so, if she's here with us tonight — and I believe she is — then it will be a treat for her to watch, too."

I laughed, and then there were chairs being set up all around us. Lorelei, Betty, Mallory, and all Mikey's brothers took their seats behind where Dad and I sat, each with a drink in their hand, too.

"I brought popcorn!" Lorelei announced, dropping a giant bowl of it on the same table that held the champagne.

"I'm only here to see Mick Jagger shirtless," Betty announced as she took her seat. "So, you better have picked the right concert, Mikey."

"Did he ever wear a shirt on stage?" Mallory asked.

Betty harrumphed. "It was a crime when he did."

We all laughed at that, and with everyone still talking and grabbing popcorn and calling out their favorite Rolling Stones songs, Mikey hit play and fell back into his spot next to me on the bean bag chair. The crowd at the stadium where the concert was filmed went wild, and the first notes of "Street Fighting Man" began to play, but all I could do was stare at the boy next to me.

"I can't believe you did all this for us," I said.

Mikey put his arm around me, pulling me into him with a smile. "You're my girl," he said — effortlessly, like I always had been, like it was so obvious I should have already known. "I'd do anything for you."

My chest squeezed with something so unfamiliar I had to bury my head in Mikey's chest to hide from it. I wrapped my arms around him and cuddled closer, covering us with one of the blankets, and for the next hour and a half, we had our own private Rolling Stones concert in that backyard.

I felt my mom there with us, like she was sitting in the bean bag with my dad and singing along.

I felt the anxiety over Bailey wash away as if it'd never existed at all.

And I also felt something strange tugging at my heart.

Something that felt a lot like what I always thought love would.
Something I hoped I'd never have to lose.
Something, I realized in that moment, that I had to tell Mikey.
And I knew just how I wanted to do it.

Chapter Fourteen

Michael

That Friday, Kylie showed up at the distillery gift shop thirty minutes before we closed.

"Hey," I said, catching her when she jumped into my arms behind the counter. She planted a kiss on me before I could say another word, and I chuckled, still holding her when she pulled back. "Well, hello to you, too. What are you doing here?"

"Can't a girl visit her..." Her voice faded, but her smile never slipped as she shrugged it off. "I have a surprise for you."

"You can say it."

"Say what?"

I smirked, tapping her nose before I released her. "Boyfriend. You can say it."

Her smile was timid, cheeks flushing as she looked down at her shoes. "Okay. Boyfriend."

"Okay. Girlfriend."

She chuckled, rounding the checkout counter to stand on the other side of it when a customer approached. She waited while I rang them up, and once they were gone, she leaned over the glass.

"We're going somewhere tonight."

"To the moon?"

"Something like that. But, you need to pack an overnight bag. And here," she said, sliding a folded piece of notebook paper toward me. "A packing list."

I quirked one brow, reading the top line. "*Wear something casual and cool, like if you were going out for a night on the town with your boys.*" I laughed. "When have I ever gone out on the town with *my boys*?"

"Stop being a nincompoop and get out of here on time so you can pack."

"Did you just call me a *nincompoop*?" I shook my head. "You've been hanging out with Betty too much."

"Finish up here and pack your bag," she said, ignoring me as she jumped up, leaning over the counter long enough to plant a kiss on my lips before she was backing her way up out of the shop. "We leave in two hours."

"Bye, girlfriend."

She shook her head, waving me off, but I didn't miss the way her cheeks tinged pink.

Two hours later — after she made me change a few times — we were in her truck, heading northbound out of town with our overnight bags in the back. Kylie had her eyes on the road, but I couldn't take my eyes off her.

"You're wearing makeup."

She smiled, her normally-nude lips painted a soft, watermelon pink. "I am."

I traced the edges of her face, noting how her lashes were darker and longer, her eyelids dusted with a greenish-gold eyeshadow that got darker at the edges — where she also had eyeliner drawn to a point. That shadow made little flecks of gold in her nutmeg eyes pop in the dusk glow coming through the windshield, and the sun also highlighted the blush on her cheeks, and the shimmer of the gloss on her lips.

The longer I stared at her, the more she blushed.

"Mallory helped me with it," she confessed, glancing at me before her eyes were on the road again. "Is it too much?"

"Not at all," I answered quickly and honestly. "You look amazing. I mean, you always do — without any makeup. But, you look..." I paused, wondering what it was. "You're glowing, I guess. You just look happy. And you still look like you, just... a little different."

She smiled.

"And this outfit," I continued, letting my eyes devour her from the neck down. She had on tight, black-washed jeans ripped down the thighs to the knees, a simple white tank top that showed the pleasant sweets of her cleavage, and a blue and green flannel tied around her slim waist. The necklace that hung from her neck was a delicate silver chain. It had the phases of the moon linking down her chest, dipping below the hem of her shirt and disappearing somewhere that made me a little jealous of it. "I like this style on you. Did Mallory help with it, too?"

"Nope, this was actually all me," she said proudly. Then she placed her left hand on top of the steering wheel, reaching for me with the other. She laced her hand with mine, glancing at me just as we reached the edge of town. "I figured if I had any shot of getting Brandon Flowers' attention, I needed to glam up a bit."

I chuckled, but then her words registered, and I froze. "Wait... did you just say... Brandon Flowers? As in, lead singer for The Killers?"

Her lips curled into a wicked smile.

"No," I said, shaking my head, mouth popping open as I stared at her. "Wait. Are you fucking serious? Are we going to see The Killers tonight?"

"We're going to see The Killers tonight."

"NO FUCKING WAY!" I screamed, staring at her like a wide-mouthed bass before I pulled her hand to my lips, kissing up and down her arm before I moved to her cheek, her neck, her ear.

She squealed and wiggled away from me, laughing. "You're going to make me crash!"

"I can't fucking believe it!" I sat back, still staring at her in disbelief. "Where?"

"Nashville."

"*Nashville!*" Excitement was pouring out of me, and I kept shaking my head, still holding her hand in mine. "I can't believe it. We're seeing my favorite band in one of my favorite cities."

"And, we're staying the night," she added. "I found a hotel that lets you book at eighteen. It's not the Ritz," she joked. "But, hey — it's a place to sleep." Her smile slipped then, and I noted how the chain around her neck ebbed when she swallowed. "It's just one bed. A king."

I smirked, bringing her hand to my lips again and kissing each one of her knuckles. "I get to see my favorite band in concert, *and* I get to snuggle you all night long?" I shook my head. "What did I do to deserve all this?"

"It was on our list of adventures," she said, but I knew it was a lie. I knew this wasn't just something she'd thrown together. It was something she planned, something to show me she cared.

My next breath was a little harder, the knot in my chest hard and tangled. Because when I looked at that girl behind the steering wheel, I saw so much more than I ever saw before that summer.

And I realized, suddenly and acutely, that I didn't want to know what it was like to live without her.

I swallowed, my throat sticky and dry as she cranked the volume on the stereo, singing along to a song off The Killers first album. But I just watched, not able to sing with her — not with three little words dancing around in my mind like flashing-neon billboard signs.

If I said them, everything would change.

If I said them, then how could I leave?

But I already knew the consequences didn't matter.

Those words were coming.

It was just a matter of when.

• • •

The elation I felt standing below that stage was both achingly familiar and completely unknown.

It had been so long since I'd been to a show, I'd almost forgotten the feeling — how the bass thumps deep within you, like a heartbeat, and the music transcends you to another place. I'd almost forgotten how screaming your favorite lyrics at the top of your lungs while surrounded by thousands of other fans doing the same thing was a spiritual experience. It lifted you, filled you from the inside out.

It was like church, like a holy Sunday morning in the middle of the darkest time of your life.

Jumping around in the pit with Kylie, I wondered how I'd ever lost the love for it. I wondered how a girl had somehow stolen that joy from me, and how another girl — the one with me tonight — had somehow brought that joy back.

She'd brought music back into my life.

No... she *was* the music in my life.

It didn't make sense to me, and I tried not to focus on it, reveling instead in the way it felt to watch Brandon Flowers and Dave Keuning up close and personal. Dave was one of my favorite guitar players, and for half the show, I stood dumbfounded as I watched him shred, and Kylie just laughed.

"They're amazing!" I screamed when they finished "Smile Like You Mean It." The crowd was still going wild, and I wrapped my arms around Kylie, pulling her to stand in front of me as we stared up at Brandon and waited for him to announce the next song. "Thank you," I said in her ear, kissing the skin below it. "You're the best girlfriend ever."

The stage lights illuminated her smile, and she leaned into me, resting her head on my chest as we watched the stage. It had to be nearing the end of the show — we'd been dancing and singing for nearly two hours now. And the whole crowd felt it, that anticipation of their biggest song, of the one that would end the night and send us all home on a concert high.

And without another word, the band members looked at each other, shared a knowing smile, and launched into the iconic first notes.

"Mr. Brightside."

Kylie and I both screamed, throwing our hands up in the air with the rest of the crowd. It was deafening once the first verse started, the crowd singing so loud I almost couldn't hear Brandon's voice at all. Everyone was jumping and screaming, dancing and laughing, throwing their hands up in the air and worshiping their music god.

When Dave stepped forward, transforming the usual guitar rift after the second chorus into an epic guitar solo, little white lights started popping up all around the venue. Fans lifted their phones, turning the flashlights on and waving them in time with the music. It was like a thousand little stars shining all around us, and I went to fish my own phone out of my pocket, but before I could, Kylie turned, reached up to grab my face in her hands, and pulled my lips to hers.

The music died.

I knew it was still there. I knew it wasn't possible that Dave had stopped playing, that Mark Stoemer had stopped keeping the rhythm with the bass guitar, that Ronnie Vannucci Jr. had ceased to drum or Brandon had stopped singing the iconic lyrics along with the thousands of fans singing with him.

But to me, right there in that moment, it was silent.

The lights from the stage and the phones being held up around us swayed, irradiating the lines of Kylie's face. The glimmer from her eyeshadow was the last thing I saw before I closed my eyes and surrendered to the feel of her in my arms, of her lips on mine, of her hair in my hands as I trailed my hands up and cradled her to me. It was like we were spinning, like the gravity that held us to the ground was fading, weakening, threatening to break at any moment and let us float up to space.

I'd kissed other girls before. Hell, I'd kissed Bailey probably a million times in the two years we'd been together. But nothing, *nothing* compared to the way I felt when I kissed Kylie.

There was something about the way her lips moved with mine, tender and timid, so unsure and yet so perfectly natural. It was the way she fit in my arms, the way her chin tilted up and mine tilted down, the way that when we closed our eyes, we still somehow saw each other — as if we traveled to another place together. It was the way we had history, the way I knew the girl I was kissing knew more about who I was than maybe even I did.

In the sea of screaming fans, singing and dancing and jumping around, we were still. We were silent.

We were in another universe, another time.

Kylie pulled back after an hour, or maybe only a minute — time was inconsequential. She pressed her forehead to mine, and when my eyelids fluttered open, I found her staring back at me.

"I love you."

I saw her lips move, saw the words outlined by that watermelon lip gloss, though everything still felt silent somehow. I'd heard her, and yet nothing had been said at all.

Gently, the music made its way back, the final rifts of the song floating into our private space there in the pit like someone was slowly turning the volume back up. Kylie pulled back, her eyes searching mine as her hands tangled in the hair at the back of my neck.

"I love you, Michael," she said again as the music crescendoed. "And if you love me, too — then I want you to show me. I want you to make love to me." She swallowed, eyes falling to my lips before they found my gaze once more. "Tonight."

Then, the song ended, the lights went out, and the crowd screamed for more.

Chapter Fifteen

Kylie

I noticed more than I should have about that tiny little hotel room off inter-state sixty-five, like that the walls were painted a soft, sea-foam green that seemed to cast a glow over everything inside. I noted that there were only two pieces of artwork — both of them indistinguishable as much more than some broad brush strokes over a canvas, and yet somehow, I saw entire lives in those abstract paintings. And I couldn't help but catalogue how cool it was, like some-one had cranked the air on in the heat of the afternoon and forgotten about it.

There was one bed — a king, covered in a textured white comforter with a gold runner at the feet. There was also a desk and an office chair, two bedside tables — one with a phone, one with a guide to Nashville, and a small dresser with a modest-sized television on top of it. The bathroom was small but clean, with a shower and a sign hanging from the door knob that encouraged guests to reuse their towels and *be green.*

It was all I could do as I sat there on the edge of the bed. All I could think about was what that room looked and felt and smelled like, because if I didn't focus on what I could sense, I'd be taken under by the wave of what I was feeling.

I avoided it for as long as I could, holding Michael's hand in the truck on the way back as we jammed to music, pretending like nothing was going to happen once we got to this room. We laughed and joked with the front desk attendant when we checked in, and we were still talking about the concert as we grabbed our bags out of the truck and made our way to our room — number two-oh-six, on the second floor in the back near the pool.

I focused on everything I could in that room so I could *not* focus on the way my hands were clammy, the way my breaths were too shallow, too weak, and the way my heart was beating just a pace too quickly, like it wasn't sure if it needed to be prepping me to fight or fly or if we were about to lie down to rest.

But as soon as Mikey connected his phone to the Bluetooth speaker in the room and Billie Holiday began to play, I couldn't hide anymore. I couldn't avoid or pretend or escape.

This was real. It was happening.

I was about to lose my virginity to the one man I'd always hoped I would.

Mikey sat his phone down, watching me from where he stood next to the desk, and my fingers curled into the comforter on the bed, as if it would somehow hold me steady through all this.

Excitement and anticipation swirled with fear and anxiety like the fiercest tornado inside me. I wanted to jump up and run to him, throw myself into him, kiss him hard and give myself to him fully. But, I couldn't move against the *other* half of the storm, the one that whispered doubts into my mind.

What if you're terrible?

What if it hurts?

What if he doesn't want to?

What if it's awkward?

What if he breaks up with you because there's no chemistry?

What if he thinks about Bailey?

My hormones battled with those thoughts, the pulsing between my legs already strong and heavy as Mikey watched me with his hands in his pockets, his jaw set, his eyes trailing over every inch of me slowly and purposefully. Until tonight, I'd been the only one to ever touch me. I'd been the only one to ever push a finger inside me, to ever play and explore and discover.

Now, I was about to let another person do the same.

Mikey took a few steps toward me, and when he did, a long, shaky breath left me unwillingly. My hands were still curled into the comforter under my thighs, and I gripped tighter, watching him until he was standing right above me.

I hadn't even noticed he had the condom in his hand until he set it on the bedside table, the blue packet all I could look at until he held his hands out, waiting.

I swallowed, placing my hands in his and tearing my eyes from the packet to look up at him, instead. He gently pulled me to stand, holding me steady at the elbows once I was on my feet. His fingertips slipped over the skin of my upper arms, hands gliding to cradle my neck, and when my eyes met his, he smiled.

"It's just me," he whispered, eyes flicking back and forth between mine. "It's just us. It's okay, you can breathe."

I blew out a breath on cue, smiling and shaking my head before I buried it in his chest. "God, I'm sorry. You can tell how nervous I am, can't you?"

He chuckled, pressing a kiss against the crown of my head. "A little."

He held me for a long while, fingers playing with my hair as I attempted to school my breathing.

"We don't have to… you know, we don't…"

"No," I said definitively, pulling back to look him in the eyes again. "I want to."

Mikey frowned. "Are you sure?"

"More sure than I've been about anything in my life."

The corner of his mouth tilted up, and he brushed my hair back, watching his hand as he did before those forest eyes locked on mine. "Before we go any farther, there's something I need you to know."

I didn't say a word, just waited, watching him as he watched me.

"I love you, too, Kylie," he breathed, a smile flashing over his lips before it was gone again, and he swallowed. "I always have, ever since we were kids. But, now... I am *in* love with you. I am, without a doubt, head over heels, can't get enough, want you every day, need you every night, stupidly and disgustingly in love with you."

A small laugh bubbled out of me, but my eyes were glossy, blurring his face as he smoothed his thumb over my jaw.

"And I'm in love with you," I whispered.

He nodded, lowering his forehead to mine, and then, he tilted my chin up with his fingertips, and we sealed our declaration with a soft, slow kiss.

There was something in that kiss that wasn't in any of the ones we'd shared before. It was a promise. It was arms outstretched to catch me as I free fell out of the clouds. It was comfort and warmth, and assurance, and more than anything, it was everything I needed to know I could trust him with my first time.

Slowly, hesitantly, the kiss deepened, Mikey rolling his tongue against mine as his hands slipped down to grip my waist. My breaths came quicker, shallow and hot, and every part of my body began to awaken under his touch.

"I've always wondered what it would be like to kiss you like this," I breathed against his lips. "To touch you like this."

"Am I living up to the hype?" he asked, kissing down my neck, his scruff tickling the tender skin as my head fell back.

I closed my eyes, mouth slack as I reveled in the feel of his teeth grazing my collarbone. "Surpassing," I managed on a breath.

Mikey smiled, kissing back up my neck until his lips were on mine again.

Then, he undressed me.

The soft, romantic crooning of Billie Holiday's voice and the heavy breaths leaving my lips were all I could focus on as Mikey's hands dropped to the flannel tied around my waist. He kept his lips fastened to mine as he untied the arms, letting the fabric fall to the floor. His hands slid up and under my tank top next, the warmth of his palms eliciting a wave of chills over my navel as he guided the fabric up, up, over my rib cage, my bra, until I had no choice but to lift my arms and let him tug the shirt over my head.

My hair spilled out from the neck and over my shoulders, and Mikey swallowed at the sight, his eyes dancing over my cleavage before he locked his gaze with mine again. In one fluid motion, he ripped his own shirt over his head, and I marveled at the valleys and ridges that made up the landscape of his abdomen.

Need pooled between my legs as he stepped forward again, his lips on track for mine as his hands slipped behind my back, unfastening my bra in one quick snap. I let the straps fall over my shoulders, down my arms, and then the bra fell between us, and Mikey broke our kiss, pressing his forehead to mine to look down between us.

He let out a heavy breath, hands skating around my rib cage until he cupped my breasts in each hand. I gasped, leaning into the touch, and when he looked into my eyes and brushed his thumbs over each nipple, I whimpered, shaking involuntarily and gripping onto him to hold me steady.

Mikey wet his lips. "You are so beautiful."

Each piece of clothing that we shed was like discovering a new world. We took our time, slowly stripping, each of us marveling at the other. Our shoes were kicked off, jeans peeled down our legs and shoved to the side, and then it was just a scrap of lace around my hips and a tight pair of briefs around his.

My fingertips roamed his shoulders, his abs, the deep valley that lined his hips and dipped down below the band of his briefs. I kept my touch there, trailing that gray band with *Calvin Klein* written on it, eyes locked on the bulge still hidden beneath the fabric. Mikey's hands discovered me, too — skating over the swells of my breasts, down over my hips, his thumbs hooking in the straps of my thong.

"I love that no one else gets to see you like this," he whispered, toying with the lace. "I love that you're mine."

I gripped onto his arms as he pulled me into him, one arm wrapping around to hold me close as the other hand slipped under my panties. His eyes locked on mine, both of our lips parted, and he kept my gaze as his finger dipped between my lips, gliding against the wetness, his fingertip brushing my entrance as his palm rubbed my clit.

I gasped, legs trembling so hard I nearly fell before he backed me up to the bed. The backs of my knees hit the mattress, and then Mikey lowered me down, kissing me from mouth to neck and back up again as we maneuvered into place.

The pillows were plush and cool against the hot skin at the back of my neck, and I let out a shaky breath, holding onto Mikey's shoulders as he posi-tioned himself on the side of me, his hand slipping back beneath my panties.

"Have you ever…" he paused, fingers wet as they stroked me under the lace. Each time his fingertip brushed my clit, my body involuntarily shook and writhed. "Is this the first time for *everything*?"

I swallowed, still holding onto him for dear life. "I mean, *I've* done it… you know… like…" I flushed, and a smile creeped up on Mikey's face. "I've done it," I said again. Stupidly.

He kissed me, sliding his finger down, down, into my folds, and gently — slowly — pressing just the tip inside me. "If it hurts too much, tell me, okay? Tell me and I'll stop."

I nodded, breathing hard against his mouth as he slipped his finger just a little more inside, and everything woke up all at once.

He was slow and calculated, tender and caring, but each time his finger withdrew and slipped in a little deeper, a searing pain burned through me. It started where he touched me and raced in a hot line up my core, to my chest, to my head, encompassing every part of me. I gritted through it, holding onto his shoulders tighter and squeezing my eyes shut against the feel of it.

I'd fingered myself before, but it was just a little bit. Mostly, I'd focused on my clit — which, I'd discovered, was what got me over the edge and into orgasm territory. I'd never used a toy or had an entire finger inside me, I'd opted for Thinx panties when on my period instead of tampons, and I was painfully aware of all of those facts as Mikey kissed me deep, and penetrated me deeper.

My back arched, pain ripping through me as my nails dug into his arms. He stopped, withdrawing his fingers a little as his worried eyes searched mine. "Are you okay?"

I nodded, blowing out a slow breath. "It hurts, but it's okay."

"Are you sure?"

I nodded again, pulling his mouth down to mine. "Just kiss me," I pleaded. "And go slow."

His lips melded with mine, his steady breathing helping to soothe my own as he slipped my panties down my legs, pulling them free from one and then the other. Then, slowly and gently, he pressed his finger inside me again.

Each time he entered me, I felt myself stretch a little more, and the pain — though still there — waned, something else creeping in its place. It was like a slow, cool liquid spreading from where he touched me out and up and all over, tiny tingles of pleasure and euphoria masking the burn.

"Oh, God," I breathed against his lips when his palm pressed down on my clit. He caught the clue, and kept his warm palm there, rubbing the sensitive bud each time he withdrew his finger and pushed it in again. My legs opened more, glutes tensing, thighs shaking as I reached for more of that feeling.

Intelligible moans came from my lips, moans I swore had to be from someone else as Mikey picked up his pace a little, kissing my lips, my neck, sucking my earlobe between his teeth. His hot breath in my ear sent chills racing over every inch of me, and I rolled my hips against his hand, the pain gone, overpowered by the need for something else.

It hit me — right there in that moment, and completely out of nowhere.

Michael Becker was touching me.

My best friend who I'd loved in secret for years was fingering me.

Something about that knowledge had me grinding my hips harder, faster, and I grabbed his hair in my hands, pulling his mouth to mine. He answered my plea with a deeper plunge of his finger, and he kept his palm pressed against me, moving it subtly against my clit as I gasped and panted and rolled my hips.

I nearly cried when he broke our kiss, but the urge was gone in the next moment when his lips descended on my breast. He licked and sucked the sensitive skin, his finger still working inside me, and when his tongue flicked over my nipple, I cried out, arching into the feel of it, black creeping in to invade my vision.

"Yes," I think I whispered, though I couldn't be sure, because in the next moment I was pulsing and racing toward the edge of a rollercoaster, each flick of his tongue propelling me forward, closer and closer, until I was right on the edge, waiting to drop.

Mikey curled his finger deep inside me, his palm hot and hard on my clit, and the combination sent me tumbling.

I curled my hands in his hair, pulling his mouth back to mine as I rolled down the coaster, surrendering to the hot waves pulsing through every inch of me. Every muscle tightened, my moans the only thing breaking our kiss as I hung onto him like a lifeline. My hips rolled, my glutes tightened, my thighs burned and shook until the euphoric waves slowly mellowed out.

And I collapsed.

Everything went lax, my legs falling even wider, hips opening, hands releasing my grip on him as they fell into the pillows under my head. I gasped for air, chest heaving, and when I finally creaked my eyes open, Mikey was watching me with a smirk.

"That was hot," he said, his finger still inside me. He withdrew it slowly, circling my clit with my climax on his fingertips before he entered me again.

I shook and writhed against the touch, everything ten times more sensitive than it had been, and my eyes fluttered closed again as I surrendered to the feel.

Mikey kissed my lips, withdrawing his finger once more. "Don't move," he whispered. "I'll be right back."

"Mmmm," I murmured, but my eyes stayed closed, my body melting into the bed like it was slowly enveloping me.

Somewhere in the back of my mind, I felt the dip of the bed as Mikey left it. I heard the water running in the bathroom and the padding of his bare feet on the carpet before the bed dipped with his weight again. But still, my eyes stayed closed, and another wave of pleasure rolled over me at the feel of a warm wash cloth dipping between my legs.

"Ohhhh," I moaned, stretching the word out as I shook beneath his caring touch. "That feels so nice."

I creaked my eyes open, watching a soft smile bloom on Mikey's face as he watched his hand between my legs. But when I looked down, too, I froze in horror.

The wash cloth was covered in blood.

"Oh, my God," I scrambled to sit up, knees snapping together.

"It's okay," Mikey assured me, keeping his hand between my legs. He brushed my hair back behind my shoulders, kissing the skin there before he kissed my lips. "It's okay. It's normal."

"I'm bleeding."

"It's *normal*, Kylie," he said again, this time tilting my chin up until I looked him in the eyes. "It was your first time. This happens."

I swallowed. "Is it done? Or will I... is it still going to happen when we..." I glanced down to where his erection was still rock solid in his boxer briefs.

"It might," he answered truthfully. "But if it does, it's okay."

"You're not grossed out?"

He wrinkled his nose, looking at me like I was crazy. "What? No, of course not." He shook his head, bending down to kiss me before he spoke again. "I'm honored to be the first to touch you, Ky. And if you can't already tell, I'm insanely turned on."

I chuckled, but then my hands trailed down his chest, over the fabric of his briefs to grasp the bulge beneath it. A needy breath left Mikey's lips and his eyes fluttered shut, his hand between my legs stilling.

"I want you," I whispered, glancing back up at him with my novice hands moving over his bulge.

He swallowed, nodding as he dropped the wash cloth on the bedside table and leaned back against the pillows. His eyes never left mine as he peeled his briefs down, his erection springing free as they slipped past his hips, over his knees, his ankles, until he was gloriously naked.

My heart tripled its pace as I stared at the impressive length standing at attention between his hips. Mikey and I had stayed the night together plenty of times. Even though we never talked about it, I'd seen his morning erections straining against his shorts when we were maneuvering puberty, and past that, it was impossible not to notice even his *resting* bulge when we were in his bed playing video games.

But now, seeing him in all his naked, hard glory, I couldn't breathe.

Mikey watched me as I scooted closer, and I reached out, grabbing him in a firm hold and timidly stroking him like I'd seen in the few clips of porn I'd watched. He groaned, the sound guttural and animalistic as his head dropped back against the headboard. He flexed into my hand, and I watched with fascination, my own desire already pooling again as I watched him moving.

"Michael."

"Yeah?" he managed, eyes still closed as he flexed into my hand again.

"Make love to me."

He stilled, eyes opening and finding mine. I rolled my hand over him again, playing with the pre-cum on his tip before I smoothed it over the rest of him. He groaned again, reaching for me until his hands were cradling my neck and he was rolling, flipping us over, his mouth hot on mine as he landed between my legs. The condom he'd placed on the bedside table was unwrapped and rolled over his length, and then he was hovering over me, and suddenly, everything stopped.

My breaths that were loud and hot and quick ceased altogether, my hands gripping his shoulders, eyes flicking back and forth between his. Mikey's lips were parted, but it was as if his breath had stopped, too, like everything in him was tied up in everything in me, and if I didn't move, he didn't either.

His chest was pressed to mine, his elbows balanced on either side of me, and I felt his erection hard against my stomach. I'd waited for years for this moment, to be with Mikey this way, and that reality slapped me so hard that my eyes stung, tears blurring my view of the golden-green irises I loved so much.

"I'm sorry," I whispered, shaking my head as the tears slipped free. "God, I'm being that girl. The virgin who cries."

Mikey smiled, kissing away the tears that had just fallen down my cheeks. He pressed his lips to mine next, and I tasted the salt of my tears mixed with the sweetness of his kiss.

"It means a lot to me, too," he said, as if he already knew what I was thinking without me even having to say it. Then, he balanced on his elbows, eyes meeting mine. "I love you."

"I love you," I echoed.

Those words brought our next breaths, steady and calm, and then Mikey reached between us, lined himself up with my entrance, and gently, slowly, pushed inside.

It was only the tip of him at first, but already, that searing pain I'd felt before was back. I winced, squeezing my eyes closed tight and holding onto him even tighter. He bent to kiss me, his tongue slipping inside my mouth, lips playing with mine as he withdrew and pushed a little deeper.

The lights in that room, in that city, in the entire world went out. Time morphed. Space ceased to exist. In the next breath, the next push, everything centered around me and him, around the places where our hips and mouths met, around the overwhelming emotion that was too powerful to have a name.

Just like when we'd entered that room, my senses heightened.

I felt every inch of him entering me, heard his breath in my ear and the sweet, sultry voice of Billie Holiday singing about being in a daydream with the one she loves. I felt him trembling in my arms, smelled his cologne and that familiar scent that had always been his — bonfire and cedar. I didn't just see his eyes, or the muscles in his arms, or the parting of his lips. No, I saw years with him, the days and nights we'd shared in the past and the days and nights I somehow knew we'd have in the future.

And I tasted him — the sweetness of his tongue, the saltiness of his skin, the warm, honey-glazed pleasure that manifested to life and transferred back and forth between us as we moved.

Time passed in a daze, in a blur of hands touching and breaths panting and hips moving and lips shaking. Mikey pressed up onto his palms, and my legs opened wider, and he quickened his pace, his eyes locked on mine. I watched his eyes flutter and close, savored the guttural moan that came from his chest, and memorized everything about the moment when he lost control inside me, his body stilling, muscles in his abdomen tightening and pulsing as he emptied into the condom.

And just like that, I was no longer a virgin.

And we were no longer in a non-defined space between *just friends* and something more.

I pulled him down into me, kissing him as he relaxed his body and let his weight cover me completely. Our skin was slick and hot, and Mikey rolled until we were on our sides, our legs tangling together as soon as he slipped out of me. We kissed and kissed, fingers tracing, hands still trembling as we pulled each other closer, as if even a centimeter of space was too much.

"Mikey," I whispered after a long while, when my lips were swollen and chapped and every muscle in my body ached.

"Yeah?"

I leaned up on my elbow, running my fingers over the scruff lining his jaw before my gaze found his again. "I'm hungry."

He blinked, watching me like he wasn't sure he'd heard me correctly, and then he barked out a laugh, reaching up to pull me into a bear hug. He kissed me all over as I laughed and squirmed to get away, though we both knew that wasn't really what I wanted.

"Well, then," he said, still laughing. "I think it's time I feed you." He released his grip a little, kissing my nose before he cocked one eyebrow. "Pizza?"

"Mmmmm," I moaned. "Pizza."

He grinned, assaulting me with another flurry of kisses before he hopped out of bed and crossed to the desk where he'd left his phone. I watched his ass the entire way, not even an ounce of shame, a yummy ache between my legs reminding me I'd just had him — in every way a girl could.

And maybe that was the best part about sleeping with your best friend.

There was no awkward silence after, no weirdness as each of us got dressed, no excuses about how we needed to go or dodgy questions about whether we'd call each other or not.

No, instead, it was t-shirts and underwear, and pizza straight out of the box, and our favorite movie rented off the hotel's pay-per-view, and cuddles and talking until both our eyes were so heavy that we fell asleep, wrapped in each other's arms, warm and comfortable and safe.

It was heaven.

And I never wanted to leave.

Chapter Sixteen

Kylie

We woke the next morning to a thunderstorm, and I guess that should have been my sign.

I should have known when the thunder rattled the hotel windows, when the lightning flashed bright and fast over Michael's sleeping face, when the rain poured so loud and hard that it sounded like hail, that everything was about to crash and burn. It was a bad omen if I'd ever seen one, but I'd been wrapped up in the sheets with my best friend, wrapped up in our own little paradise that I was sure could never end. I couldn't see it for what it was. Not then.

Not until that literal storm turned into a metaphorical one right before my eyes.

We woke up slowly, the room still dark from the storm raging outside making for perfect cuddle weather. Mikey held me close to his chest, running his fingers through my wild hair until it was an hour before check-out. Then, he ran me a bath so I could soak, and I didn't realize how badly I needed that until I sank down into the hot water and felt every muscle cry out in a mix of protest and thankfulness.

I was still sore between my legs, an unfamiliar but welcome ache that reminded me what happened the night before as we packed our bags and ran through the rain to my truck in the parking lot. The sky was dark and menacing, and Mikey insisted that he drive, since I wasn't a fan of driving even when it was sprinkling, let alone storming.

It still felt perfect — all of it. The night we'd shared, the slow and easy morning, his hand on my knee and the other on the steering wheel as we drove back down south toward home. The rain battered the windshield and shots of lightning illuminated the clouds, but the farther we drove, the more it weakened, the sun trying its best to break through it all.

We stopped at a gas station twenty minutes outside of Stratford to fill up the truck. While Mikey pumped gas, I ran inside to get us each a breakfast taquito and blue raspberry Slurpee — an admittedly gross tradition for us when we stopped at 7-Elevens together. The smile on my face seemed to be a new permanent part of my appearance that morning, and I was humming "Mr. Brightside" as I made my way back to the truck with our snacks in tow.

"Got the goods," I announced, setting Mikey's Slurpee in the cupholder while I took a big sip of mine. "Do you want your taquito now or later?" When I looked over at him for an answer, the smile I'd worn all morning finally slipped. "What? What's wrong?"

His shoulders were hunched, brows furrowed tightly together as he stared at his phone in his hands. The muscle in his jaw ticked, the ones lining his arms tense. The hair on the back of my neck stood on end like lightning was about to strike, and in a way I couldn't have predicted then — it was.

"Mikey?"

I glanced at his phone and then back at him, stomach churning. I worried it was his mom, or one of his brothers. I wondered if it was Jordan, if he'd found something on the hard drive, something bad.

I prayed no one was hurt.

I prayed the sickening wave rolling through me was wrong.

"What is it?" I asked again.

He swallowed, taking one long, deep breath with his eyes still on his phone. He wouldn't look at me. He wouldn't look at anything but that screen.

Finally, he let the phone drop into his lap, though he still clutched it with his hands as his head fell back against the headrest. He looked up at the roof of my truck like he'd asked a question out loud and that roof somehow had the answer.

"Bailey called."

Two words. Two words struck my paradise like a Mack truck at ninety miles per hour, completely obliterating it in an instant. The blood in my veins ran as ice cold as the cup in my hand, and I gripped that cup a little tighter, as if that would somehow change what he'd just said.

I thought of how she'd *liked* my video of Mikey, how she'd *liked* the photo of us on top of the water tower, and my stomach churned violently.

"Oh," I managed, my pulse ticking up a notch.

Mikey finally looked at me. "She's coming to Stratford for the Single Barrel Soirée next weekend," he explained, two lines forming between his brows as another swallow bobbed in his throat. "She asked if we could talk."

My next breath felt like I was inhaling black smoke.

I waited for him to say more, but he just sat up, tossing his phone in the center console and throwing the truck in drive. We pulled back out on the little highway that led into our hometown without him saying another word.

I faced the windshield, watching the little yellow lines separating us from the opposite lane flash by. The rain had stopped, but the clouds still hung heavy and dark overhead.

"So..." I said after a minute that felt like an hour of silence, setting my cup in the holder. Our taquitos were still in the bag at my feet.

That one word apparently didn't prompt him to say anything else, as he remained silent, so I swallowed my pride and asked the question I needed the answer to.

"Are you going to?"

"Going to what?"

I pressed my lips together, fighting against the urge to huff or scream or rattle him. "Are you going to see her?"

"Yeah," he answered easily — shrugging, nonetheless, like that answer was obvious. "I don't see why not."

"You don't see why not," I deadpanned, tonguing my cheek as I faced the front again. "I can give you a few reasons."

"She just wants to talk," he said, adjusting his grip on the steering wheel. "We were in a relationship for two years, Kylie. It's not like we don't have a friendship, or like I hate her or something."

I inhaled a stiff, cold breath through my nose, letting it out slowly to stop myself from crying. I didn't handle confrontation well — it had never been my strong suit. But, for some reason, Mikey knew all the right buttons to push to make me boil over.

And the worst part was that he didn't even realize it.

"Yes, you were in a relationship," I echoed. "*Were* being the keyword there. But, she left... not that I need to remind you of that," I added, throwing my hands up when he glanced over at me. "I'm just saying. She put you through hell, and you're just now getting back to yourself." I looked at him then, and our eyes met for just a flash before he was looking at the road again. "Why would you let her back in when you've done so much work to let her go?"

He shook his head, and I swore to God if he told me I didn't understand again like he had the night outside Scootin' Boots, I really would throttle him.

"I'm not *letting her back in*," he said, definitively. "I haven't even answered her, okay? She left a voicemail. But I don't see why I would say no to just talking. Maybe she wants to apologize. Maybe she wants to be friends."

"Friends," I snorted, crossing my arms.

"Why are you being so dramatic?" he shot at me, like a bullet to the chest.

"I'm being *dramatic*?" I scoffed. "Oh, I'm sorry I don't want my boyfriend hanging out with his ex who broke his heart less than a year ago. I guess a normal person would be completely fine with that."

Mikey shook his head, laughing through his nose at my passive-aggressiveness. "She wants to *talk*, Ky — not makeout."

"Yeah? So you'd be cool if, say..." I waved my hand in the air. "Parker Morris called me? And asked if we could talk and I said *sure, I don't see why not*?"

"That's not the same thing."

"It is *absolutely* the same thing."

"I don't understand why you're being so possessive right now," Mikey said loudly. "I've made it clear how I feel about you."

"Yes, which is why none of this makes sense. Why would you go see her if we're... if we're..." I was at a loss for words.

"It's not that big of a deal!" he hollered again, exasperated, his hands flying off the wheel before they clamped down again. "Going to see her, to hear her out, does not mean anything. Besides, I don't really see why you're getting all up in arms about it. I'm leaving soon anyway, it's not like we—"

He clamped his mouth shut, shaking his head, but I was watching him like he was a wildfire that somehow made it to my backyard without me even realizing I was in danger.

"It's not like we *what*, Michael?" I pressed.

He exhaled. "Nothing."

"No, not nothing. Finish your sentence."

A semi whizzed past us, rocking the truck, and Mikey gripped the wheel a little tighter.

"I'm just saying, I'm leaving soon. I'm going to New York, and..." He swallowed. "I just don't know what that means for us."

And there it was — the truth we'd both been avoiding ever since the night we first kissed. He was still leaving. He was going to New York, and anything else that he'd said or we'd done didn't matter past that.

"You don't know what that means for us," I repeated, enunciating each word slowly, like that would somehow make the sentence as a whole sting less.

My eyes flooded with tears, and I hated myself so badly for crying in that moment. I wanted to hold my head high, to be strong, to look him in the eyes when I said my next words, but I couldn't.

"Wow." The word bubbled out of me, my voice trembling as the first tear slipped over my cheek. I swiped it away, crossing my arms again. "You know what? You're right. You should go. Go to the girl who broke your heart and left you stranded, who built up a future with you and then decided on a whim to take it all back. Leave the girl who *loves* you," I choked on that last sentence, squeezing my eyes shut and setting free another wave of tears. "Who has *always* loved you, who has always been there for you. Leave that girl behind."

Mikey's hand folded over my knee, but I ripped it away, hugging the passenger door like he was poison. I turned on him, meeting him with narrowed eyes.

"You think you're so misunderstood," I cried. "That no one gets you. But I've known and loved you for *exactly* who you are since we were kids. I have always been here. I have always understood. But this?" I shook my head. "I do *not* understand this."

"Kylie..."

"No, you know what?" I threw my hands up, laughing a little. "This is actually kind of perfect. I mean, I don't know what I expected," I confessed, crossing my legs against the ache that was still there — the proof that my best friend had been inside me the night before.

He'd been inside me, but he never planned to stay.

I swiped away the new tears on my cheeks like they were flies.

"I've never been the girl who gets the guy," I whispered, more to myself than to him now. "I'm not the pretty girl, the talented girl, the fun one every girl wants to be friends with and every guy wants to date." I laughed, pointing my thumb into my chest. "*I'm* the girl who *reads* about the fairy tale ending — not the girl who gets one." My heart sank with the truth of it all, shoulders sagging along with it as I whispered, "I'm not the girl who wins."

The truck jerked then, and I grabbed the handle above my window with one hand and the center console with the other as Mikey pulled us to the side of the road — right in front of the large, wooden sign that read *Welcome to Stratford*.

Mikey threw the truck in park, turning in his seat and reaching for my hands. But as soon as he touched me, my stomach turned, tears blurring my eyes again as I recoiled from him.

"Kylie, please," he whispered, his eyes searching mine. "I didn't mean what I said. I just..." He pressed his lips together, swallowing hard. "You *are* that kind of girl. You're beautiful — and not in a fake way, or a way you have to try. You're effortlessly so. And you're funny, and smart, and giving, and kind. You deserve to be loved." He paused. "*I* love you."

My face twisted with emotion, and I rolled my lips between my teeth, looking out the window and away from him. "You love me?" I whispered.

"Yes," he said instantly. "I do, I love you. I'm sorry about what I said about leaving. We can figure it out. We can... I don't know. I can stay a little longer, we can make a plan."

As much as I wanted to feel relief, in that moment, it wasn't about New York. It wasn't about whether he would leave and I'd go with him or if we'd do long distance or if we'd even stay together at all.

Right then, though I hated it more than I could stand, it was about Bailey — and the fact that she was more important to him than I was.

"You love me?" I asked again, still looking out the window.

He nodded, reaching for my hands, and this time I let him hold them. "Yes, Kylie. I love you."

I turned then, locking my eyes on his. "Then choose me."

Mikey frowned, as if he didn't understand what I was asking, but as recognition settled in, his face leveled out. He swallowed, looking down at where he held my hands in his, and he rubbed his thumb over the skin stretched across my wrist, over and over, like he was trying to find some hidden message.

I waited, both of us silent — the entire *world* silent, save for the soft *whoosh* of the cars passing us every now and then.

When Mikey looked at me again, his brows were furrowed, but his jaw was set and sure. "She just wants to talk."

I closed my eyes, freeing two more tears — tears I swore would be the last ones I would ever cry over Michael Becker. I pulled my hands from his gently, not in haste, and slowly wiped my cheeks. My eyes traced the letters on the welcome sign, drifting to our little town and where it began just behind that mark, and somewhere deep in my chest, my heart splintered into two, perfectly jagged pieces.

"Get out," I whispered.

Mikey reached for me again, but I pulled away, facing him with as much resolution as I could manage.

"I said get out."

"Kylie," he warned, shaking his head. "Don't do this."

"*I* didn't do this," I said, voice trembling as I pointed a finger right into his chest. "*You* did. I'm not asking you again. Get out of my truck. You can walk or call for a ride or..." I waved my hands. "Whatever you want. I don't care. But I'm done giving you my time, my energy, my *heart*." That last word stung, but I swallowed it down before the tears could burn my eyes again, keeping my promise to myself as I faced him head on. "Get. Out."

Mikey swallowed, and suddenly, everything about him looked worn and tired, like he'd just lived twenty-five years in the last fifteen minutes. He opened his mouth to say something, but thought better of it. Then, like I asked, he reached into the back, grabbed his bag, slung it over his shoulder, and slipped out of the driver seat to stand on the side of the road.

I sniffed, making sure there were no more tears on my cheeks as I climbed over the console and settled behind the steering wheel. I shut the door without looking at Mikey, adjusting the mirrors and firing the engine to life.

"Please, Kylie," he said, his voice muted behind the window that separated us. "I love you."

But I ignored the lie, throwing the truck into drive and sending gravel flying with the tires as I sped back onto the highway. I didn't look at him in my rearview mirror, and I didn't cry a single tear more than I had in front of him.

He had his chance to choose me, and he didn't.

I might have missed the sign the thunderstorm was trying to give me, but I wouldn't mistake this one.

My chest ached, heart splitting more, and I pressed a hand over the bones, soothing them as best I could. I forced three long, burning breaths, and then I drove back into my little hometown with only one aspiration.

To leave it.

Along with the boy I wished I'd never met.

Chapter Seventeen

Michael

I didn't realize I'd escaped the numbness I woke up in the day after my high school graduation — not until I slipped back into it, like it was two open arms welcoming me home. And it only took four days for it to happen.

Four days without Kylie.

Four days of unanswered calls and texts.

Four days, and somehow, an entire summer had been erased.

In a way, it did feel like home — to be broken, to be numb, to be hopeless. Sure, I'd had a summer of warmth and sunshine, of long days and even longer nights with Kylie. But that was gone now.

She was gone now.

And I had no one to blame but myself.

Somewhere, deep down, I think I knew. I knew when I first kissed her that it was a mistake, that there was no way I could ever be the kind of man she deserved. I was too fucked up from Bailey, from just who I naturally was as a person.

Unlovable.

Unsaveable.

I hadn't seen Kylie coming, hadn't been able to predict what would happen between us — and how *fast* it all would happen. Blindly... that's how I had fallen into her. She was safe, and familiar, and somehow completely fresh and new, too. It all felt natural, like there was no other choice for either of us *but* to end up together.

Except that I'd ignored one very important thing.

I hadn't healed from Bailey.

It didn't matter that I hadn't thought of her in months, or that I no longer checked my phone and wished to see her name there, or laid awake at night wondering what she was doing in Nashville. It didn't matter that when Kylie and I *went* to Nashville, I hadn't even paused to realize I was in the same city as my ex. It didn't matter that when I saw that she'd liked the photo of me and Kylie, I hadn't cared one bit — not even enough to give the notification a second glance before I'd shut the app completely.

I was all Kylie's — heart, soul, and more.

All I cared about was being with her, singing with her, dancing with her, making love to *her*.

But when Bailey called, when I heard her voicemail, something in my dumb, broken brain short-circuited.

And as per usual, I fucked up.

A heavy and deep sigh was my next breath as I looked myself over once more in the bathroom mirror at the Scooter Distillery, deciding that no matter how I tried, I couldn't look like anything but shit. It was Thursday and I hadn't slept since Saturday, had barely eaten, had barely done anything other than stare at the lines of unanswered texts in my phone and wonder how I could have screwed up so royally.

Maybe it was because I didn't need to wonder. I already knew.

Bailey still had her hooks in me.

And even at the risk of hurting Kylie, I needed to see her.

I wasn't sure what I hoped for as I climbed into my car after work, hands shaking a bit on the steering wheel. Just a short drive into town would take me to the old diner, to the booth where I'd shared milkshakes and onion rings with Bailey, and to the place where she waited for me now.

Maybe I'll get closure, I thought idly as I drove. *Maybe she'll apologize, tell me she should have handled things differently.*

When Kylie and I had argued in her truck, those were the thoughts in my head. I wanted to hear Bailey out. I wanted to hear her say she was wrong. I wanted to hear her apologize.

And, though I hated to admit it, I wanted to see her.

She'd left my life so abruptly, almost as if she'd died. And now, I had the chance to see her resurrected, to get answers, to get... *something* I couldn't quite name but knew I needed.

I hadn't known that day in Kylie's truck what it would cost me to get the closure I so desperately wanted.

I blew out another sigh, shaking my head at the same anxiety spiral I'd found myself in all week. The truth was that it didn't matter what I'd done, what I'd do differently, because it was enough to push Kylie completely away.

She wouldn't talk to me.

She wouldn't see me.

And I couldn't blame her.

I had no other choice but to let her go, to accept what I'd done and move forward. *On.* To New York. To a new job, a new home, a new life — just like I'd planned.

That dream felt less like a fresh start and more like a prison sentence as I parked my car at the diner and got out, making my way toward the familiar red and white building. But all thoughts were erased completely when I looked through the window at the booth I'd sat in most of my high school years and saw Bailey there.

She smiled tentatively, waving at me through the glass. My feet stopped moving, stopped carrying me toward the door, and I stood in the parking lot and looked at her as if she were a ghost.

She might as well have been.

Her hair was different. Gone was the long, natural blonde hair she used to braid over one shoulder, replaced with a short, edgy haircut and locks dyed a bright, platinum blonde that was almost white. She wore so much makeup, I almost didn't recognize her, and even from the distance, I could see that she'd lost weight, that her arms were more toned, her skin darker, like she'd been spending all her days in the sun instead of on the stage.

But her eyes were the same — the almost-translucent, moss green — and they watched me with a familiar warmth that had my stomach turning.

I stuffed my hands in my pockets, crossing the rest of the parking lot and pushing through the diner doors. I smiled at the hostess, pointing back to where Bailey was sitting — to where nearly everyone in that diner was staring. She was a celebrity now, though she seemed oblivious to that fact as she stood and waited for me next to the booth.

"Hey, you," she said, as if we were best friends, as if we'd just seen each other a week ago. She opened her arms and stepped into me before I could object. Her nose nuzzled into my neck as she hugged me, and I held her, too — a sickening wave of nausea making me see stars at the scent of her familiar perfume.

"Hey."

"I'm so glad you came," she said when we pulled back, and she gestured to the booth. "I got us our old spot, can you believe it? And a milkshake to share, just like old times."

I managed something close to a smile as I took a seat, staring at the strawberry milkshake with whipped cream and a cherry on it. Bailey slid back into the bench seat across from me, her eyes shining in the slanted rays of sun coming in through the windows.

"You look so good," she said, smiling as her eyes roamed over me. Then, she reached across the table, running her fingers over my chin and jaw like it was completely normal and natural. "I *really* like this. Scruff looks good on you."

Someone at the bar had their phone trained on us, and when they realized I was staring at them, their eyes widened and they turned quickly, shoving their phone away.

I peeled Bailey's hand from my face, ignoring how much her fingers still felt like they belonged in mine as I let them go. Something cold was settling in, invading my veins, my bones. I suddenly didn't feel right being there, being around her. It was like a stomach virus had swept up on me, without warning, and now I couldn't think about anything but getting away from the source. "Why did you ask me to come here?"

She frowned. "I wanted to see you."

"Right. But why?" I shook my head. "You left almost a year ago and you haven't so much as texted or called. You haven't wanted to see me. Until now." I blinked. "Why?"

Her frown deepened, her eyes falling to her hands as she picked at her nail polish. I noted the rings that lined each finger — rings I'd never seen her wear. It was the same with the tight dress she wore, the boots, the choker around her neck. She was the same girl I'd loved and yet someone I didn't know at all — all at once.

"I *did* want to see you," she argued softly. "But, everyone told me I needed to leave you alone. To let you go, let you heal. And after that night you got drunk and you were texting me all that stuff... I knew they were right. I mean, it was my choice to leave early, to change the plan we'd had together, to..." She swallowed, and I noted the way her eyes glossed over. "To end it all."

I shifted uncomfortably in the booth, my chest on fire like it was warning me of an incoming mortar. *Run,* it urged. *You're in danger.*

"But... I can't do that anymore. I can't leave you alone, not with how I'm feeling... with how I've *been* feeling." Bailey lifted her eyes to mine again, rubbing her bow-like lips together. "Michael, I want you to come to Nashville."

My eyebrows shot into my hairline, heart stopping altogether before it kicked back into gear and tripled its pace.

"I know I don't deserve it," she said hurriedly. "But, I'm asking you for a second chance."

She reached across the table and took my hands in hers, and I was too numb to pull away, too shocked to do anything but stare at where she folded her fingers over mine.

"I was stupid to think I needed time and space to focus on my music, to think that I needed to do this without you for some reason. Heck, you *are* the music in my life. I mean, have you heard my single on the radio?" She squeezed my hands until I looked at her. "I know you have," she said with a smile. "And I know you know it's about you. You helped me write it. And that's the thing, Michael. *You* are my inspiration." She swallowed. "You're my everything."

I just blinked, unsure if I was going to throw up, or pass out, or both.

"I know it's a lot to consider," she continued. "But, I figured... you've graduated now. And we had this plan anyway, and I know saying I'm sorry doesn't fix everything that happened between us, but... we can work on it, right?" She smoothed her thumbs over my hands. "I mean... I know that *I* still love you. And I'd wager you haven't lost all your feelings for me, either."

My heart kicked painfully in my chest again at her words, and it wasn't from finally hearing what I thought I'd wanted to hear all this time. No, it was a wicked, gut-wrenching stop and thud that told me I didn't like hearing those words from her mouth.

Because what she didn't realize was that I'd since heard them from Kylie's.

And she was the only one I wanted to hear them from now.

My chest ached with the realization that I'd never hear them again, that I'd fucked it all up and, for what? To come to this diner and sit across from this girl and hear *this*?

Of course, she missed me. Of course, she wanted me back. I could hear everything she was saying and everything she *wasn't*.

She was dried up. Void of inspiration. Not a single lyric left in her, now that she didn't have me.

And here she was, looking for me to save the day, to take her back, to uproot my life and give it all up for *her* just like I'd agreed to do when I was in love with her.

But I wasn't under her spell anymore.

I pulled my hands from Bailey's, sitting back in my booth as the realization hit me. Bailey kept talking, like I was listening to her and digesting what she was offering, but the truth was that all my thoughts were on the girl I loved.

The girl I'd hurt.

The girl I'd lost.

And it wasn't the one I was sitting with now.

"I even talked to my agent, and we have a job for you," Bailey said excitedly. "You'll be my tour manager. I know you love music, and you know more about concerts than anyone I trust. You can do this." She leaned across the table. "*We* can do this." A laugh bubbled out of her. "I thought we could even make a big deal of it, sing a song together at the Single Barrel Soirée, announce that we're back together and that you're moving to Nashville. I mean, our family and friends would love it, the town would love it, the *press*," she added, shaking her head. "God, they'd have a field day. My PR team wants to film it, put it on the documentary we're working on detailing my *rise to fame*." She chuckled. "Isn't that crazy?"

I covered my mouth with one hand, shaking my head at my stupidity and effectively ignoring everything Bailey was saying, though she continued on. My only focus was on the cold shower of reality I was sitting in.

I didn't need closure from Bailey.

I didn't need to see her or talk to her or give her any part of me ever again.

What I needed was Kylie.

She'd brought me back to life that summer, and what I hadn't realized until that very moment in that very booth was that she'd *always* been the one to bring me to life. She was my first friend after my dad died. She was the first person I told all my deepest fears and biggest dreams to. She was the one my heart was drawn to, magnetically, like there was no other option — even if it'd taken me too long to realize it.

And I'd made her feel less than. I'd put talking to an ex above her feelings because of some selfish, pointless desire I'd had to hear all the things Bailey was saying now.

That she was wrong.

That she was sorry.

That she wanted me back.

But none of it mattered, because Kylie was the only thing I wanted. And in true *Michael Becker - Fuck Up Extraordinaire* fashion, I'd lost her.

I scrubbed my face down over my mouth, my jaw, shaking my head and cursing myself for always being the guy to learn my lessons too late.

"... And I'm so excited to get writing with you again. I mean, just think of the *angst*, the torturous yet pure gold breakup and get back together songs we can write." Bailey paused, smile slipping. "Michael, baby," she said, her voice soft as she reached for me. "Did you hear what I said? I want you back. I want *us* back."

I looked at her, at the melted milkshake between us, and then back at her once more. I wondered how to tell her, how to explain that I was in love with Kylie, that I had waited and longed for Bailey for so long but that over time, I'd let her go. Over time, I'd lost myself. And over time, I'd found myself again... with the girl I'd somehow always known was the one for me.

Then, I decided I didn't owe her a damn thing, least of all an explanation.

So without another word, I stood, and to the tune of her calling out my name and asking me to wait, I walked away from the girl who'd broken my heart and ran to the girl who'd pieced it back together.

• • •

Kylie

"Not that I don't love your company, but maybe you should go home," Betty suggested Thursday evening. "Get some real rest."

She was rocking in her chair, reading a gossip magazine, and I was sitting on her bed, laptop open and notebook in my lap as I mapped out my road trip. It was my sole focus over the last four days. I was far too busy planning my gap year and volunteering at the nursing home to be sad or heartbroken.

That was what I convinced myself.

"I'm getting fine rest here," I said absentmindedly, clicking through the campsites on my route in Virginia to find the best one in my budget.

"On the cot in the janitor's closet?" Betty challenged.

"It's more comfortable than you think."

"I'm sure," she mumbled. "But, you need a shower. And what about your dad? I'm sure he misses you."

My stomach tightened at that, because I hadn't been home in two nights, and I knew my dad *did* miss me. I missed him, too. But, when I was at home, I couldn't busy myself with other people and their needs, as opposed to thinking about my own mess of a life.

Dad wanted to talk. And when I talked, I cried. And when I cried, I got angry, because I promised myself I was *through* crying over Michael Becker.

So, I stayed at the nursing home to avoid the vicious cycle, and to ignore the aching in my heart for as long as I could.

"Maybe I'll go home for dinner," I conceded.

"No, you'll go home for the *night*," Betty corrected me, closing her magazine and resting it in her lap. "Baby girl, I know you're heartbroken right now, and I know it feels better to ignore that pain and throw yourself into whatever and whoever else to avoid it. Trust me, I used to handle my problems much the same way. But the truth of the matter is, you aren't going to move on if you don't first acknowledge that there's something to move on *from*."

I sighed, closing my laptop with a *snick* before I leaned back against her headboard. I didn't have anything to say to her very valid point, so I just looked at her, instead.

"Have you talked to him?" she asked.

"No," I answered quickly. "Not for his lack of trying. But there's nothing more to say."

"So, you're completely done, then?" she probed. "There's nothing he could do or say to make amends?"

I sighed, gathering my laptop and notebook and pen and stuffing them all into my messenger bag. "Betty, we've talked about this so much that I'm pretty sure you could recite what I'm about to say yourself. He doesn't love me. And no matter what he says, his actions proved that. If he loved me, he—"

"Would have chosen you," she finished for me on a huff. "I get that, I really do. And trust me, I'm so mad at that boy for what he did to you that I could wring his neck like a rubber chicken," she added. "I guess I just really liked you two together, and it's hard for me to imagine you giving up on someone so fast when you're always the last one standing in the corner, cheering and holding up the number one foam finger."

"That's just it," I said, standing and tossing my bag over my shoulder as I faced her. "I've always been there for him. *Always*. No matter what he did, it was never wrong enough for me to leave him. But I don't want to be that fool anymore. I don't want to be the one standing there waiting for him when it should be *him* in *my* corner, too." I shrugged. "So, I'm just going to focus on my gap year, on what comes next, and let him go. If *he* wouldn't choose me, then I have no other choice but to do it myself."

Betty's mouth pulled to the side, but before she could respond to my argument, there was a knock at her door. It was already cracked, and after the knock, it swung open slowly, and Michael stood on the other side.

Seeing him standing there knocked my next breath out of my chest like a hammer, and suddenly the air in the room felt cold and stiff, like I knew my next inhale would be painful before I even took it. So, I held my breath, instead, staring at him. Waiting.

He was still in his work uniform, his eyes tired and worn, the scruff lining his jaw more unruly than I'd ever seen it. He attempted a smile, but it fell flat. "Hi."

I didn't respond.

"Betty," he said next, turning to her. "It's nice to see you. I'm sorry I'm here so late, I was just..." He turned back to me. "I was hoping we could talk."

I crossed my arms, again — waiting.

"Maybe you two should take a walk," Betty suggested.

"Whatever he needs to say, he can say it here." The words were clipped, and I almost didn't recognize my own voice as I said them.

Michael swallowed, stepping a little more into the room, but I took an equal-distance step back. He paused at that, brows bending together before he shoved his hands in his pockets.

"I met with Bailey today," he said. "Just now, actually."

That next inhale burned like I knew it would, and I looked at the tile floor between us with my heart ringing in my ears.

"She said she wants me back. She wants me to move to Nashville."

My nose stung, the threat of tears building against my urgent plea with my body to *not* let them happen. I crossed my arms tighter, mustering as much apathy as I could. "Congratulations?"

"No, no," he said, moving toward me. "That's not what I..."

I stepped away from him, the backs of my knees hitting Betty's bed before he stopped.

He held his hands out, like I was going to dart around him at any moment and run out the door. And honestly, I was thinking about it. "What I mean is that she wants me back, but I don't want her," he said softly. "I want *you*."

My heart squeezed, and I hated the mix of hope and relief that washed over me before pain and anger seeped back in. It was almost enough to make me want to cross the room and melt into him.

But my pride stopped me, and I'd never been more thankful in my life.

"I want *you*," he repeated, taking a tentative step toward me. "Don't you understand? I don't care about Bailey, or Nashville, or any of it. I care about *you*."

I closed my eyes, shaking my head before I finally looked up at him. "But you still had to go to her to see it. You still chose her over me. Don't *you* see *that*?" I mimicked.

He gaped at me, speechless for the first time since he'd walked through the door, and a quiet part of me cried out in victory.

I sighed, adjusting my bag on my shoulder. "Look, maybe we were just better off friends. Maybe what I thought we could have was all just... just..."

I waved my hands in the air, searching for the right word, but Mikey cut me off, rushing toward me before I could back away. His hands reached for me, grasping me at the elbows, his eyes wild as he watched me.

"No, no, it wasn't just anything, Kylie. It *isn't* just anything." His tired eyes searched mine. "I love you."

I winced. "Please, stop saying that."

"But it's true. I—"

"If it was true, you wouldn't have gone to Bailey when I begged you not to!" The words came out rushed and pitched and urgent, my heart racing wildly and betraying the calm demeanor I was aiming for. "You would have picked *me*," I said, the word breaking along with my heart.

"Kylie..."

"You say you don't want her, but why should I believe you? You went running to her as soon as she called you, completely disregarding everything between *us*," I reminded him, gesturing to the space between us. "You chose her. Why wouldn't you do the exact same thing the next time she calls you up and crooks her finger and says *jump*?"

"If you give me the chance—"

"I *did*," I said, bottom lip quivering hard. "I did give you the chance. But I won't be second place. I don't deserve to be."

Pain washed over his expression, but before he could say another word, I held up my hands.

"Please," I begged, the tears breaking loose and rolling down my cheeks as I pulled away from his touch. "Please, just leave me alone."

Those words were the ones that broke him.

I watched it in slow motion — the slumping of his shoulders, the bend of his brows, the sorrow that seeped over every inch of him like a flowing stream of water. It covered him completely, and I watched him sink into it.

I wanted to both reach out and save him from it as much as I wanted to push him in deeper.

After a long moment, he nodded, his hands finding his pockets again. He opened his mouth, closed it again, and finally looked at me with years of regret and sorrow and pain swirling in those hazel eyes of his. Then, he whispered one, powerful, life-altering promise.

"Okay."

He turned, offering something close to a wave to Betty before he excused himself, and we both stared at the open door, listening to his footsteps until they rounded the corner down the hall, and the front door opened, and he was gone.

I closed my eyes, swiping the tears from my hot face before I dug in my bag for my truck keys.

"You know," Betty said from behind me. "It took a lot of strength for that boy to show up here tonight."

My chest tightened, but I ignored it, finally fishing my keys free. "Yeah, well, it took a lot of strength for me to say no to his bull crap, too."

"He's only human," she said softly. "Just the same as you and me. And while I can't speak for you, I'll say this — I've done a lot of stupid stuff in my lifetime. The only reason I've survived is that the people who love me have always known who I am at my heart. They've always seen the best in me, even when I wasn't showing it."

She paused, and I stood there with my keys in my hands, trembling for a reason I couldn't place.

"Maybe you can't be with him," she said, lowering her voice to almost a whisper. "But does that mean you can't ever forgive him?"

The question hit me like a ping pong ball, and it volleyed back and forth, rattling my brain as I straightened my spine. I didn't have an answer for it, so I just let it bounce, let it assault me as I moved for the door.

"I'm going to take tomorrow off, but I'll be back on Saturday," I said, avoiding her question.

"That's the Soirée," she pointed out. "You don't want to go?"

I didn't answer, because I didn't need to — she already knew the entire Becker family would be there, and therefore, it was the absolute last place I wanted to be.

"I'll bring some new magazines," I told her.

And with that, I shut the door to her room, and the door to what could have been with Michael Becker.

It was a door I swore I'd never open again.

Chapter Eighteen

Michael

The next evening, I sat on Mom's front porch, watching the sun set in the distance as I scrolled through endless apartment listings on my phone. It was one of those perfect summer evenings, when the katydids were humming softly, the breeze was gentle and cool, and the last bit of the sun sinking down over the horizon cast the yard in an otherworldly orange glow.

I rocked back and forth in one of the rocking chairs, one foot planted on the wooden porch and the other tucked under that leg. I'd click on an apartment listing, check out the price and the location and the amenities, then close it again, only to open up the next one and do the same thing all over again. The sun warmed my skin, but inside, I was as cold and dead as the arctic tundra.

Something clicked last night.

When I left Kylie, promising her that I would leave her alone, a new kind of heartbreak settled over me. It was the defeated kind, the kind that sat deep in my chest and reminded me every chance it had that there was no going back to what I'd lost, there was no happy ending in sight, and there was no one to blame but myself. That hollow ache served one purpose and one purpose only: to remind me over and over, as many times as it would take, that it was time to let go and move on.

Sleep still hadn't come, and my appetite was gone for the foreseeable future, so I threw myself into work at the distillery and, as soon as I got home, into what my next move would be.

Manhattan.

It didn't fill me with as much hope and promise as it had at the beginning of the summer, but it *did* give me something to do with my time. If there was anything I learned from my breakup with Bailey, it was that time was about the only thing that made anything better.

Time, and Kylie.

And I'd never have the latter again.

Every now and then, a sharp sting of pain would split my chest when I realized what I'd lost. And again, that hollowness would take over, splash me with water as if to call me back to the reality at hand. *No use thinking about the past, about what could have been*, it seemed to whisper. *All you can do now is move forward.*

My eyes were starting to blur from staring at my small phone screen when the screen door opened, and Mom joined me on the porch, setting a glass of sweet tea on the table beside me.

"How goes the apartment hunting?" she asked with a smile, one I knew was forced and a bit sad, because the last thing she wanted me doing was searching for apartments halfway across the country.

I sighed, closing my phone and scrubbing my hands over my face. "It's a little overwhelming. I mean, at least the job part of it all is figured out, but now, it's finding somewhere I can afford with said job's salary."

It turned out, Mallory had a friend from school working at a small art gallery in the city. It was right in the middle of the financial district, and it just so happened they were in search of a new gallery assistant, someone who would man the front desk, do some lifting from time to time, speak with guests, help organize events, and so on. Their current employee was leaving in a month, which was just the right timing for me to take over.

One phone interview had sealed the deal, and I now officially had a job waiting for me in New York.

I wished I could be excited about it.

"I imagine that's pretty tough in the big city," Mom mused. "Think you'll need a roommate?"

"That's what it's looking like. I guess I should get on Craigslist."

Her eyes doubled in size.

I chuckled, patting the chair next to me. Mom took a seat, and for a while, we just rocked silently, our eyes on the pinks and purples streaking the sky as the sun dipped lower.

"Does Kylie know you've found a job?" Mom asked, her not-so-subtle way of asking if we'd made up.

"Kylie doesn't want to know anything about me anymore."

Mom's mouth pinched to one side, and she reached over to fold her hand over mine. "I'm sure that's not true."

"Oh, trust me, it is," I assured her. "And honestly, after the way I treated her, the way I acted?" I shook my head, that iron-hot razor blade splitting my chest again. "I don't blame her one bit."

"Have you tried talking to her?"

"Yes."

"No, I mean *really* talking to her."

I sighed. "Yes, Mom. I've tried. She doesn't want to hear it. I've apologized, told her I was wrong, told her how she means everything to me, how stupid I was for thinking I needed to see Bailey again when I should have just told her to kick rocks." I swallowed. "How I love her."

Mom's hand squeezed mine, and I couldn't look at her for fear of what her eyes would look like, of the pity and sorrow I'd see in them.

"I bet she'll come around," she whispered.

"I know she won't," I argued in a whisper. "You know, I don't remember a lot of Dad."

I glanced at Mom, surprise settling over her face at the subject change.

"I hate admitting that out loud to anyone, but especially to you," I said softly. "But, it's true. A lot of my memories of him are from photos or videos, or from stories other people have told me." A different kind of sadness rang through me at the admission. "But, there is one very clear memory I have with him."

I looked out over the yard, smiling a little as the memory came to life in my mind.

"It wasn't long before he died," I started. "I was upset with Caden. Do you remember Caden? He was my first best friend, in primary school. He lived down the road from here."

"I remember," she said with a smile.

"Anyway, we were in a fight over something. And looking back, I know now how stupid that something must have been because I couldn't even remember what it was a year later when I told this story to Kylie."

I shook my head, her name on my lips a painful reminder of the loss.

"But, it didn't matter how stupid it was, Dad sat there and listened to me. I had snot and tears running down my face. I was so upset. And I'll never forget what he said to me. He said, *'Son, my biggest wish for you is that you learn when to hold onto something, and when to let it go. That you understand when to fight, and when to walk away.'*"

Those words hung in the air between us for a long while, neither of us speaking, her hand still holding mine as the clouds shifted from pink and purple to a gray kind of blue.

"I have heard those words so clearly in my mind, all my life," I explained. "I think it's why I fight so hard for what I want, for what I love — and also why I walk away when I need to. You know? Like... those words are why I held onto Bailey, thinking I could somehow get her back. They're why I walked away from a fight with Dustin Mannion at The Black Hole when he tried to get under my skin after Bailey left. They've just always been with me, sitting there, a constant reminder to know when to push and when to back off."

Mom nodded in understanding, but didn't speak, letting me finish.

I looked into her eyes — eyes just like mine — and ignored the pain ripping my chest open as I said, "Kylie and I have made many pinky promises in our lives. We've always been honest with each other, and we've always been there for one another. We get each other in a way that no one else could ever understand." I swallowed, nose stinging. "That's why when she looked me in the eyes and told me to *please* leave her alone... I knew she meant it. And I knew I had to honor that, that this was one of those things that fell into the *leave it be, walk away* category." I shrugged. "And it doesn't matter whether I want it to be this way or not. It just is. The only thing I *can* do is accept that."

Mom nodded again, her eyes floating over the yard a moment before she pulled her hand from mine and sat back in her chair. She rocked silently for a moment, thinking.

"Well, I agree with your father," she finally said. "I wish that knowledge for you, too — to know when to fight, and when to walk away. But, honey, I don't think you've learned the lesson yet."

I frowned. "What do you mean?" I laid out my hand, as if I'd just served her proof on a silver platter. "I literally just explained how I *have* learned that lesson."

"No," she argued. "What *you* explained was that she asked you to leave her alone, and you think listening to that is the right thing to do. And in many ways, I suppose you're right. I've raised you well, to know that no means no and to respect a woman and what she says." She held up a finger. "*But*, the weird thing about love is that sometimes, we ask for the exact opposite of what we want, just because we think asking for the let down and getting it will be less painful than asking for love and *not* getting it."

My frown deepened, and I sat back, crossing my arms as I tried to digest it.

Mom paused, turning to face me. "You can't just call and send a bunch of texts and show up *one time* to try to talk to her and consider that trying," she said, matter-of-factly.

"Mom, it's not like that," I tried to explain, splaying my hands out again. "I have done such a piss poor job of listening to her, to what she wants, what she needs. But I heard her loud and clear this time. And if what she needs is for me to leave her alone, then that's what I'll do — even if it's not what I want."

She shook her head. "But, that's just the thing. What Kylie *wants* is for you to put your money where your mouth is. She doesn't want all your lip service, all your words and promises and assurances that you've tried to give her." She tapped my knee. "What she wants is for your actions to match what you're saying, for you to *show* her that you love her — so that she doesn't have to wonder if your word is worth a damn or not."

My chest tightened.

"Look," Mom said, waiting until my eyes met hers. "If your father were here, you want to know what he'd say?"

I nodded, wishing more than I could ever explain to her that he *was* actually here. It killed me, living without him. He wasn't there to watch me play baseball, or watch me walk across the stage at graduation, or to help me find an apartment in New York. He wasn't here to give advice on girls or jobs or anything else.

It was the worst kind of pain to live with as a kid, and I was learning the pain didn't ebb as an adult.

"He would tell you not to walk away until you've done everything in your power to right your wrong with her, to show her who you are, and to make it clear what she is to *you*." She paused, eyes searching mine. "So, I'll ask you… do you feel like you've done that?"

I opened my mouth to answer, to remind her of everything I'd already said, but before the words could come out, I felt something inside me strangle them and snuff them out like a small match fire.

Because the truth was I hadn't — not really.

I'd texted. I'd called. I'd showed up at her work and hurriedly tried to convince her that I was sorry, and she was right and I was wrong and that we could make it past this.

But had I done all I could? Had I put every piece of me that loves her into action to save what we have?

The answer I was ashamed to admit was no, I hadn't.

"She doesn't want you to leave her alone, Mikey," Mom said softly. "If there's anything I know about that girl, it's that. She has been in love with you since you were kids, *way* before you ever realized it," she added, smirking. "Ya big dummy."

I chuckled.

"Right now, Kylie is shutting down. She's trying to protect herself. She's been hurt by being in love with you while you were in love with someone else, and then right when she gets you?" Mom snapped. "She loses you, just as fast. And in her mind, you chose Bailey over her — just like she always feared you would." She swallowed. "Just like you did, for two years straight."

I sighed, hanging my head as my hands raked back through my hair. "I don't know what to do," I admitted, shamefully and pathetically.

Mom reached over and squeezed my arm, making me look at her once more. "If you love her, if you want to have her in your life, then you owe it to her *and* yourself to really put your heart into it and try to save this relationship. *Show* her that you mean what you're saying." Her eyes softened. "If you can do that, and she still denies you?" A shrug. "Well, you can't control that. And then, at that point, you can let her go. But at least then you'll be able to say that you did everything in your power to keep her, first."

A smile found my lips as I looked at my mother, the woman who had brought me into this world, and was never afraid to remind me of my place in it. I wondered if she even knew how strong she was, how much I admired her for raising me and my brothers — especially after she lost her partner, the one she was supposed to go through it all with.

"How did you get to be so smart?" I asked her.

She chuckled, tapping my knee twice before she sat back in her chair. "Oh, I'm not smart at all — just well-seasoned. For starters, I married an idiot boy, who then helped me adopt an idiot boy, and then helped me give birth to three *other* idiot boys." She eyed me. "The good thing is that even though you

Becker boys keep me busy, you've all got good hearts, and good heads on your shoulders." She shrugged. "Makes it easy to love you and coach you through things when I know those two facts."

I smiled, standing and pulling her to stand with me before I wrapped her in a giant hug. I held her there for a long time, feeling how small she was in my arms, but how big her love was as it poured over me. I was convinced in that moment that *Mom* was just a coverup for all the real-life superheroes in the world, because I could never imagine being strong or wise or patient enough to do what a mom could.

"I love you, Mama," I whispered, squeezing her once more before I pulled back and held her arms in my hands. "Thank you."

She pinched my cheek. "Don't thank me. Just make me proud. And don't let that girl go without giving it the fight of your life," she warned. "Because I promise you, there isn't a single one in the world like her."

And I knew it was the truth.

Mom left me with my sweet tea and my thoughts as the sun made its final descent, the last bit of glow fading from the sky as dusk settled in. And with a new resolve, I racked my brain for my next move, for the last round in the ring, for my last chance to get back the girl who meant everything to me.

And for the first time that summer, I bowed my head, and I prayed.

To God, to my dad, to any angels who might hear my plea and have mercy on me. I closed my eyes and spoke the words over and over in my mind, hoping somehow, the universe would answer.

Please, don't let me lose her.

Please, let me be enough.

Please, help me show her that I mean what I say, that I am who I say I am, and that she is who I say she is to me.

I swallowed, eyes slowly opening as I finished.

"Amen," I said out loud.

Then, I got to work.

Chapter Nineteen

Kylie

Saturday evening somehow felt like Monday morning, sleep still in my eyes and the Tervis of iced coffee in my hand nowhere big enough to help me feel less exhausted. The bags under my eyes were large enough to pack for a two-week Eurotrip and I felt just as weak physically as I did emotionally — thanks in large part to lack of sleep and lack of appetite, a dangerous combination.

I knew it would fade. I knew, eventually, that the heartbreak would heal over and I'd start putting myself back together. If anything, I took solace in the fact that I had a road trip half-planned, and being alone on the open road sounded like the perfect way to get myself in order.

But I wouldn't leave until I had everyone *else* in order, first.

I was already working on my father, teaching him how to make his way around the kitchen and reminding him what days to pay which bills, even though he assured me he was an adult and could do everything just fine without me. After all, he'd reminded me, he *did* somehow survive before I started taking care of him.

But he had Mom, then.

I knew he would be okay, but it was the worrier in me, the caretaker and giver who couldn't be quieted. I needed to be sure he would eat a well-balanced meal and get out of the house and not just work and then go home to be alone. I even called Michael's mom and asked if she'd look after him in my absence, check on him from time to time, visit.

My stomach dropped at the thought of that conversation — one I asked her to keep private from Mikey. Lorelei had listened to my side of everything that had happened, just like I imagined my own mom would have, if she were here. But the best thing about Lorelei was that she didn't push or pry, she just assured me everything would be okay, and told me she loved me and was proud of me.

I'd held onto that conversation all week.

Still, I'd felt stronger on Thursday than I did that Saturday evening walking into the nursing home. On Thursday, I was four days clean. On Thursday, I was on my way to recovery.

But on Thursday *evening*, I saw him. I heard him beg for me to forgive him, to understand, to believe in us.

And that had cracked my heart right in half again.

Because I wanted him more than anything in my life, but I refused to be second place.

With another jolt of pain in my chest, I pulled the handle on the nursing home door, slapping on my best smile as I strode into the main hallway. Immediately, I noted that it was too quiet, too still.

Annie sat at the front desk as usual, and she smiled at me. "Hey there, sunshine. Don't you just look like a field of daisies today."

I rolled my eyes. "I'll pretend that was a compliment and not a passive insult." I swept my eyes down each hall, not finding a single soul. One glance out the back door behind her showed no one in the garden, either. "Is it universal nap time or something?"

Annie smirked. "Oh, you didn't hear? A gracious donor paid for a tour bus to take all the residents down to the Single Barrel Soirée," she explained. "They've been gone about an hour now."

My shoulders sagged. "Oh."

"It's okay," Annie said, patting my hand when she noted my disappointment. "I think you'll find you're still needed around here today."

I quirked a brow. "Do you need me to clean or something?"

Annie said nothing, just smiled her classic rosy-cheek, gap-toothed smile before she opened the little drawer under her computer. There was a small, gold envelope in her hands when they emerged, and she placed it on the counter, sliding it toward me.

"For you," she explained. "From the donor."

I frowned, shaking my head. "I don't understand."

But Annie was already gathering her purse, her lunch box, and she paused with both in her hand before she looked at me again. "It's my dinner break. I'll be back in an hour. Hold down the fort for me?"

"But, Annie—" I tried, but she was already striding toward the door in her butterfly-covered scrubs. She threw up a hand in a wave behind her, slipped out the front door, and then it was just me.

Alone.

Silent.

I looked down both halls again, heart unsteady as if it could already sense something I wasn't aware of. Then, I looked at the envelope in my hands.

Slipping my index finger under the flap, I pulled gently until it gave way, revealing a small, folded note inside. As soon as I opened it, my heart stopped.

It was Mikey's handwriting.

Kylie,

I want to start this letter off by telling you that I heard you loud and clear when you asked me to leave you alone, and as you should know from years of being my best friend, I am nothing if not true to my word.

But before I can do what you asked, I have to do what my heart is asking of me, first.

This summer, you made a list of epic adventures for me. You took me all around town in an effort to remind me why Stratford was my home.

Well, now it's your turn for an adventure.

If you hate me, if reading these words makes you so angry your eyes are crossing in that adorable way they do when you're pissed, and if you would rather jump off the water tower than hear one more thing I have to say — I understand. You can simply light this note on fire and walk right out the door, and I will do as you asked. I'll leave you alone.

But, if there's even one small part of you that's filled with hope right now, if your chest is light and fluttery, if your heart is beating faster and urging you to take the adventure route... then follow this first clue to start your scavenger hunt.
Your idiot,
Mikey

A smile found my lips at the signature, but I frowned again at the clue written beneath it.

To start again, you must go back to the beginning.

I folded the note, holding it in my hands as I looked around me. There was still no one in sight, and as much as I wished it, there was no neon sign with RIGHT ANSWER flashing on it, either.

I was alone.

And the decision was mine.

I bit my lip, opening the note again to re-read what he had written. My eyes stuck on the part about walking out the door, about his promise to truly leave me alone, if that was my move.

But my heart pounded furiously in my chest at the thought.

The truth was I *couldn't* walk away from him — not now, maybe not ever. And certainly not before I figured out what that damn clue meant.

My competitive side kicked in, and I dropped my bag and Tervis of coffee on the counter before I read over the clue again, frowning. "Back to the beginning..." I said out loud, looking around as I tried to decode the meaning.

The front door?

I looked behind me, making my way down the short hall and looking around the entrance.

Nothing.

I hung a hand on my hip, brain practically smoking as the wheels turned. Then, I remembered my orientation, the story of the nursing home's founding mother — a woman by the name of Gertrude Heisentower, who had built and opened the nursing home in 1982.

There was a plaque in her honor in the garden.

My feet moved quickly, hands pushing the garden doors open, and as soon as I was surrounded by the walls of ivy and beds of flowers and vegetables, I saw it.

A gold paper-covered shoe box — right under the plaque.

I shoved the first note in my pocket, carefully removing the top of the box as if opening it too quickly would set off an alarm or cause a bomb to explode. But neither happened, and instead, I was greeted with an old, worn photo of me and Mikey.

We were eight years old.

I covered my mouth, eyes scanning the photo as my heart did backflips in my chest. It was taken on school picture day by the teacher in charge of the yearbook, and I remembered it being taken like it had only happened moments ago. Mikey was the same height as me then, but his arm was slung around my shoulder like he was taller. Mine was around his waist. Both of us were crossing our eyes, and I had my tongue stuck out as we waited in line for our official school photo to be taken.

The smile that bloomed on my face was effortless as I reached for the photo, revealing a rainbow-colored, broken bracelet and another note underneath it. I picked up the bracelet first, giggling as my fingers smoothed over the worn thread. Then, I read the note.

You are my best friend.

I never could have known that first day we met on the playground just how much you would mean to me, but I think a part of me felt it on the day you gave me this bracelet. You'd stayed up all night making it — using a flashlight under the covers, just in case, so your dad wouldn't ground you. This picture was taken on the first day I wore it, and I wore it every day after until four years later when it broke and I tucked it into my desk drawer at home, keeping it safe.

I love that about you.

I love that you are always thinking of others, that you make homemade gifts and cook for your father and volunteer any spare time you get and pay for strangers' ice cream.

I chuckled, emotion swelling in my chest.

There is no one in this world more giving than you.

Now, ready for your second clue?

I set the photo and bracelet back in the box, reading the clue on the note out loud. "You are just as sweet as your all-time favorite treat." I rolled my eyes. "Michael Becker with the cheese, ladies and gentlemen."

But I was already smiling as I made my way back inside, on track for the row of vending machines just outside the cafeteria. They were the only place you could find a Kit Kat — and since my favorite caramels from the next town over weren't anywhere near the nursing home, I knew my second favorite candy had to be what the clue was referring to.

As soon as I rounded the corner of the hallway that led to the café, I stopped dead in my tracks.

"Oh, my God…"

The vending machines had been transformed, the glass of all three completely covered with old notes and photos of the two of us. My feet moved slower, eyes trailing each photo, each memory as I made my way down the rest of the hallway to the machines. I laughed out loud at one of the photos on the left one — a picture of me and Mikey sitting in his bed, playing video games, wrappers of candy and chips littered around us. I had my hair in a messy bun, Mikey looked like he hadn't showered in weeks, and I was a mouth full of braces smiling up at the camera where his mom was snapping the photo.

It was the day we had a video game marathon, a rainy Saturday that we were supposed to spend at the lake.

Inch after inch, photo after photo, all three machines told our story. There were freshman homecoming photos, the tie of his tux matching the ugly coral dress I'd thought was a great idea at the time. We ditched that homecoming, but not before we got a few horrible photos, first.

There were shots of us down at the lake, camping with my dad, continuing the tradition he'd started with my mom. There were pictures of us when we were ten, laughing as we slid down the home-made slip-n-slide we'd built in his backyard that summer, and ones from when we were thirteen, each of us lanky and awkward, our skin broken out and smiles uneasy on the first day of eighth grade.

I found the notes next — dozens and dozens of old, faded notebook paper with our handwriting scrawled in different color ink. The pages were ripped and worn from being folded over and over, and it switched back and forth between his handwriting and mine. They were the notes we passed between classes, sometimes *in* class, the timing of them ranging from that first year we met, all the way up to our last year in school. I chuckled at the one sheet of black notebook paper with white and green gel pen ink lining it — an obsession I'd had when we were in fifth grade.

Right in the middle of it all was another golden envelope, and I peeled it off the glass, sliding my thumb under the flap to reveal the note inside.

If you'll notice, there is a theme to the photos here — they are all awkward as fuck.

I laughed, glancing up at the myriad of photos again before I continued.

We grew up together, Kylie. From braces and puberty to homecoming dances and high school graduation, we've been through it all. And no matter what stage of life we were in, you were always so unapologetically you.
I love that about you.
I love that you burp louder than me, that you never worry about putting on makeup before we go somewhere, that I was the first person you called when you got your period and that you were the first person I confessed an inconvenient teenage boner to. By the way — I still shiver when I think of walking down the hall that day, holding my science textbook over my crotch like I could hide it.

Another laugh bubbled out of me, and my eyes filled with tears from the hilarious memory.

I love that you're the only person in the world who was sad to get your braces off, and that you had absolutely zero shame in Googling "How to shave pubic hair" on my mom's computer. As embarrassing as all these photos and notes and memories may seem now, they were a part of us, of our journey, and I love that I got to experience every single awkward moment with you.

Emotion strangled my throat as I let the note fall, eyes rolling up to the ceiling to stop myself from crying. Then, I read the next clue, and away I went.

The scavenger hunt covered the entire nursing home, from the game room to the music room and back again. And each new stop held new memories, new photos, new remnants of our life together. He'd even covered Betty's room — hanging pictures from strings attached to the ceiling so they appeared like they were floating.

Each new clue led to a new time in our life, and each new note relayed something he loved about me — about us.

I love that you never take no for an answer.
I love that my mom loves you more than she loves me.
I love that you know every word to Greased Lightnin'.
I love that you dressed up as Baby Groot for Halloween last year.
I love that you don't see how devastatingly beautiful you are.

By the time I made it to the final clue — one that was taped under a chair in the theatre room — my cheeks were stained with dried tears and my stomach hurt from a mixture of laughing too hard and feeling like I wanted to throw up. I couldn't place the emotion swelling inside me, only that it was powerful, and that it was one-of-a-kind.

It was the emotion only he could pull from me.

I swiped my cheeks before I read the last note.

Do you remember when I got so mad at you for beating me over and over in Halo that I grabbed your Razor flip phone and broke it in half? You were so furious with me… for about three seconds, and then you laughed and teased me for being a sore loser and, most importantly — you forgave me.

I love that about you.

I love that no matter how many times I prove to you that I'm an idiot, you somehow see past my stupidity to who I really am. You know me better than anyone else in this world, and for that reason alone, you forgive me.

I know I don't deserve it. I know the way I treated you, the things I said to you last weekend firmly fall in the do not forgive *category. But, I'm praying you will, anyway.*

I'm praying you'll find it in your heart to remember who I am, to trust what your gut tells you about how I feel about you, and how I feel about us.

And more than anything, I hope that you'll give me one last chance to prove to you that I mean what I say, that I'm not just a mouthful of words and empty promises.

Let me show you this is real.

Come to the pool.

My throat tightened as I lowered the note, still clutching it in my hands as my eyes rolled up to the ceiling. Every muscle in my body was tense and tight, my chest aching, broken heart somehow beating faster as if to warn me.

Or maybe, to urge me.

Because in that moment, there wasn't a single cell in my body that told me to run.

There wasn't a single thought or feeling other than *go to him, find him, be with him.*

And so, I listened.

Wads of notes and clues stuffed in my jean pockets, I tore through the nursing home, practically running to the back door that led to the pool. The closer I got, the more I heard the faint sound of music, and when I pushed through and emerged outside, I heard it clear as day.

I followed the sound of Rascal Flatts, sneakers hitting the concrete faster with each step until I reached the wooden gate. I unlatched the lock, shoved the gate door open, and froze.

The sun was starting to slowly set, the sky a mix of purples and oranges and pinks. Those colors reflected in the pool, which was illuminated by a maze of hanging white lights strewn above it — the same white lights he'd hung in his backyard on the anniversary of my mom's death. Each strand criss-crossed from one end of the fence to the other.

"Bless the Broken Road" played from a speaker propped on one of the lounge chairs, and the photos that hung from strings tied to the lights over the pool seemed to dance in the breeze to the tune, little pictures of us at all ages, hundreds and hundreds of memories.

And then, there was Mikey.

He stood at the opposite end of the pool, dressed in the same tuxedo he'd worn to junior prom, one hand in his pocket and a bouquet of my favorite flowers in the other.

Daffodils.

His eyes pinned me to where I stood, the green and gold of them shining in the warm lights he'd hung above us. He wore a soft, tentative smile, and his heart on his sleeve.

Slowly, I let the gate door close behind me, and I kept my eyes locked on his as my feet carried me blindly toward him. My heart raced more with every step, palms damp where they folded in on themselves at my side, and when I stood just a few feet from him, I stopped, watching him.

Waiting.

It was truly unfair how handsome he looked in that moment. Maybe it was the lighting. Maybe it was the tux. Or maybe it was just him — his messy hair, his unkept scruff, his bent nose and square jaw and soft smirk that tugged his lips to one side. But when I looked closer, I saw the bags under his eyes that matched mine, and the proof that he hadn't been sleeping either.

He swallowed, holding the bouquet of flowers toward me. "Your favorite."

I managed a smile. "Thank you."

Silence stretched between us, save for the new song that was playing now — George Strait, "I Cross My Heart" — and Mikey grabbed the back of his neck nervously, cringing a little as he looked around us.

"This is all a little cheesy, huh?"

I chuckled. "Maybe a little."

"Like, that fake nacho cheese they put on tortilla chips at the football stadium concession stand? Or, like the amazing cheeseball your dad makes for Christmas every year?"

"Maybe like the squeeze-out-of-a-can cheese your mom puts on Ritz crackers," I said. "You know, like it *seems* weird, but actually tastes pretty delicious."

His smile bloomed, and my heart did a flip.

"Kylie?"

"Yes?"

"Come to New York with me."

My smile fell, along with my stomach and my jaw. I gripped the flowers in my hands tighter, as if they would somehow assure me that I hadn't just heard what I thought I had.

Mikey took a step toward me, reaching out to peel the flowers from my hands and set them on a lounge chair beside us. Then, he grabbed both of my hands in his, locking his gaze on mine.

"This summer, you were on a mission to remind me why I love this town. And it worked. I *do* love Stratford," he said. "But what you might not have realized was that in the middle of all our adventures, you lifted a veil I never knew was hiding the truth I'd known all along." He paused, smoothing his thumbs over my wrists. "It's *you* I love most about this town." He smiled. "About this *life*."

My hands trembled in his, and he held them tighter, stepping even closer, until I felt the heat of his breath on my lips.

"I know there are no words that could ever make up for the mistake I made last weekend. And that's what it was — a mistake. When Bailey called me…" He frowned, brows bending together as his eyes searched mine. "I can't explain it, but it was like my brain went haywire, like nothing I said or did after that voicemail showed up on my phone made any sense and I *knew* it… but was powerless to stop it. It wasn't until I actually saw her, until I actually looked the ghost that had haunted me for months in the face that I was able to snap out of the spell."

My chest threatened to split open, but for some reason, the way he held me in that moment held every part of me together, too. It was something about the sincerity in his eyes, about the way he touched me — like it was natural and pure and inevitable.

"I can't go back and undo what I did, just like I can't go back in time and realize that I loved my best friend long before I even knew what love was. I can't go back and be the first guy to kiss you," he said, one brow quirking. "Although, I hope I at least hold the title for *best* kiss."

I laughed, the tension wrapping my chest in a vise lock shaking loose with the movement.

"I can't go back and take you to prom, or drive you out to make-out creek and do dirty things to you."

I scrunched my nose at that, and he chuckled.

"But you know what?" he added after a moment, his eyes searching mine. "I wouldn't — even if I could. Because somehow, some way, all those moments we missed," he said, looking up at the photos hanging around us. "All *these* moments we had — they somehow led me right here, to you. To us."

My heart squeezed in my chest, and he squeezed my hands as if he knew.

"I can't go back," he said again. "But, I can go forward. And I want to go forward — to a new place, a new life, a new future with you."

I blew out a breath, one that felt a little like smoke as it burned its way out of my lungs. "To New York?"

He grinned. "To New York."

I shook my head, biting my lip as I considered it. "We don't know anyone there," I pointed out. "Neither of us have a job, or a place to live, or a clue in hell of what it's like living in a big city."

"Well, *technically*, I have a job," he corrected. "Which we can talk about later. But yes, you're right. It's big and scary and new and nothing like Stratford. But... I can't imagine going without you. And I thought, with it being your gap year, and how we found out that your mom spent some time in the city, too..."

"I could follow in her footsteps," I whispered.

He nodded.

"And we'd be together."

Mikey's smile widened. "We'd be together. Making more memories. At least, if you'll have me. If you'll forgive me for being the dumb oaf that I can sometimes be."

"Sometimes?"

"Hey, now..." he warned, but his arms were already opening, and I was already sliding into them, letting him hold me to him as I rested my head on his chest. Warmth and comfort washed over me like a gentle waterfall, and I sighed, leaning into the boy I knew I could never truly walk away from.

"You really hurt me," I whispered, but my fingers curled in his tuxedo jacket, holding him close. "I've never felt like this before in my life."

"I know," he whispered, kissing my hair. "I've been an absolute wreck, too. But I promise, I will make it up to you. I'll show you what you mean to me, what you've *always* meant to me." He pulled back, looking down at me. "If you'll let me."

I smiled, narrowing my eyes a bit. "Hmm... I don't know. What's in it for me? I mean, I have this whole road trip planned now, and you just want me to abandon it and move to New York with you?"

"Wait," he said, searching my eyes. "You did it? You planned your trip?"

I chewed my lip, nodding.

"Well, then," he said, a smile spreading on his face. "New plan: take your road trip. And take me with you."

I laughed. "That's presumptuous."

"Don't act like you don't want me there," he teased. "Or like you don't need someone to drive, since you fall asleep at the wheel on any trip that's longer than two hours."

I grimaced. "You've got me there. But... what about my gap year? And what about school?"

"I don't want you to give up any of that," he said. "That's not what I'm asking. Travel, study, research the schools in the city and if you hate them all, then go somewhere not in New York and I'll follow wherever you go."

My brows bent together. "Really? You'd follow me?"

"Are you kidding?" He chuckled, brushing my hair behind my ear before his thumb smoothed over my jaw. "Anywhere."

I leaned into the touch, heart racing, mind spinning as I considered his offer. "This is insane, you know."

"Oh, trust me," he said on a smirk. "I know." His eyes flicked back and forth between mine, his hand still holding my face as he watched me. "But you know what? We're young. And I think we're allowed to be a little crazy." A pause. A smile. "Spend your gap year with me," he whispered. "And then, maybe spend forever with me, too."

Something between a laugh and a sob broke free from my throat, and as tears pooled in my eyes, I nodded — over and over, again and again, a whisper of *yes* on my lips and in my heart as Mikey pulled me into him. His lips pressed against my hair, my forehead, each cheek and up and down my neck as I giggled. Then, he pressed those lips to mine, and we melted into that kiss like it was our first and last breath all at once.

"How the hell are we going to pull this off?" I asked, breaking the kiss as I framed his face in mine and shook him like he was a maniac — which in that moment, I knew he was. "We're moving across the country," I pointed out. "To, like... the biggest city in the nation."

"I know."

"We're eighteen," I reminded him, panic rising in my chest. "We don't have degrees or anything."

"I know."

"We've been in the same town our entire lives."

He chuckled, peeling my hands off his face and kissing each one before he wrapped me in his arms again. "I know. But you know what I also know?"

I shook my head.

"We're going to be okay. No... more than that. We're going to be *amazing*. Because it's a new adventure. And it's us. And if there's one thing I know for sure, it's that there is no more winning combination than that right there."

"You're so sure," I said, still shaking. "How?"

Mikey shrugged, as if the answer was obvious. "Like I said — because it's us." Then, he lowered his forehead to mine, inhaling a deep breath. "You're my girl, Kylie," he whispered. "You always have been. And as long as that's still true, I know everything will be okay."

My heart swelled, threatening to pop out of my rib cage and float up to the lights that hung above us. I wrapped my arms around his neck, stepped onto my tiptoes, and pressed my lips to his, knowing that what he said was the truth.

It was us.

And as long as we had each other, we had it all.

"I love you," he whispered against my lips, and through the tears in my eyes, I whispered that I loved him, too.

Everything else disappeared in that moment, with his lips on mine, his arms around my waist, mine hanging onto his neck. What happened with Bailey was in the past, along with every other bump in the road that had led us to this moment. All that mattered now was that he was mine, and I was his, and that list of epic adventures that I thought had ended had only just begun.

"So," I said, pulling back, my eyes finding his. "Manhattan?"

He grinned. "Manhattan."

I shook my head, but every part of me screamed *yes* as I grabbed that boy's hand in mine.

Then, with a smile and a kiss, a new adventure was born.

And two small-town kids were big city bound.

Epilogue
Michael

One month later, Kylie and I sat on the floor of a tiny, studio apartment in Manhattan.

Our tiny, studio apartment.

We'd managed to find a shoe box of our own in Greenwich, and it was — no exaggeration — only slightly larger than my old bedroom had been. It was dorm style, the kitchen small, bathroom even smaller, living area just big enough to cram our family into and the bed situated in a loft *above* the little kitchen. Every piece of space in that apartment was utilized for some sort of appliance or storage, and it felt a little like something out of a storybook, a room with too much and yet nothing at all.

But it was ours.

A buffet of traditional New York food favorites made up a picnic on the only piece of furniture we had in the ten-by-ten space designated as the "living room" so far — a coffee table, given to us by her dad since it had been in storage for years. We figured we'd be lucky to fit a love seat in behind it and mount a TV on the wall, especially since Kylie was avid that we *make* room for a bookshelf.

For now, it was just food and plastic plates littering that table, and our entire family sitting on the floor around it with us.

Our first dinner in our new place.

Mallory peeled back the first slice of greasy, New York-style pizza, plopping it on her paper plate with a satisfied smile. "Oh, yeah. I could totally get down with eating like *this* every night."

Logan grimaced, handing her a napkin immediately as he eyed the spread of food. "Why did we not get *anything* that requires a fork or spoon to eat?"

"Because that's the way it is here," Noah said, unwrapping one of the foil-covered hot dogs we'd grabbed from the street car downstairs. "Everyone's on the go. No time for silverware, little bro."

"I like it," Mr. Nelson chimed in, grabbing a churro with his bare hands. "And before any of you say a word, life's too short to not eat dessert first."

Kylie smiled, reaching over to grab a churro of her own, and everyone else worked on filling their paper plates with the street food of their liking.

Everyone, that was, except for Mom.

She was still looking around our small space, notebook in hand, writing down things we'd need as she thought of them.

"I still think we should go to the market after dinner," she said, adding three more items to the list.

Trash can.

Dish soap.

Laundry detergent.

"Just to get the essentials," she said.

"We're going to go tomorrow," I told her. "I promise."

"But, what if you need something tonight? You don't have bottled water or toilet paper or *anything*."

Kylie held up her napkin, one out of the giant stack we'd snatched from the falafel truck. "We have these."

Mom's bottom lip quivered, and she looked back at the notebook in her hands like it was a puppy she was about to have to give up for adoption.

I chuckled, fixing her a plate and setting it on the table in front of her before I took the notebook. "Thank you for making this list, Mom. It's really helpful. And I promise, you can help us shop tomorrow."

"Really?" She sniffed.

I nodded. "Of course. We can't do this on our own."

That seemed to appease her, and she ruffled my hair before taking a deep breath and moving in on her plate.

Kylie reached over and swept her hand into mine, giving it a gentle squeeze. We shared a knowing glance, because although we both *wanted* to do it on our own, we knew it'd break our family's hearts to not be there for all of it. Hell, even Ruby Grace had flown up, meeting us in New York as soon as her contract with AmeriCorps was done.

We'd all stayed in a hotel last night, moving in what little we had today. It all fit in the back of Kylie's truck that we'd driven up, mostly because we knew the size of the apartment wouldn't allow much more. And Kylie's dad would drive that truck back to Stratford, our need for a car gone.

A buzz of excitement filled that small space as everyone ate and chatted, and I looked at my favorite girl, at the place we'd now call home. It was just a few short blocks from my new job at the art gallery, and less than half a mile from NYU — which, if my gut was right about my girl, would be her university of choice after her gap year was up.

We'd spent the last few weeks cramming as much as possible into the time we had. We secured the apartment just three days after we made up — thanks in large part to our parents co-signing for us — and then we packed as quickly as we could, stored what we wanted but couldn't bring with us in

Mom's garage, donated what was left over, and then hit the road for a three-week road trip that ended right here in Manhattan.

Every morning and every night, my life had been wrapped up in Kylie.

We'd taken that road trip just like we did any adventure — with a plan and a promise to break it. We camped and hiked, ate more food than either of us thought possible, stopped at spontaneous concerts in every city we could, took our pictures with all the cheesy, touristy pit stops on the side of the road, made a few mistakes along the way and a whole lot of love, too.

And through it all, I was in the driver seat, and she was right there beside me, her hand in mine.

As we'd made our way into the city, crawling with the rest of the traffic on the bridge as the Manhattan skyline stretched out before us, she'd looked at me and said, *"This is it. This is where our life begins."*

When I'd first made the decision to move to New York, I'd imagined it, what it would feel like once I finally got here. I imagined a small apartment just like the one we were in, and boxes just like the ones all around us, and the exciting promise of a fresh start, just like the one building in my chest now.

But I had imagined it alone.

And being with Kylie made it a thousand times better.

"So, when do you start at the new gig, little bro?" Jordan asked around a mouthful of grilled cheese.

"Wednesday," I answered. "So, we have a few days to get settled."

"And what about you, missy?" Ruby Grace asked Kylie.

"Well, I'm going to start researching schools, and I'd like to check out New York Cares," she said. "See how I can get involved in the community."

"That's my girl," her dad said with a proud grin.

"That being said, I'll be on the job hunt Monday. One salary alone isn't going to pay rent on this shoe box."

Everyone chuckled, but I didn't miss the worried expression on Mom's face as she unwrapped her hot dog.

"We have a pretty good savings to get us by for a while, though," I said to the room, but namely, to ease Mom's anxiety. "Anyway, what I *really* need to know is how much time I have to save for a flight back to Tennessee for my big brother's wedding."

We all eyed Noah, and he smiled at his bride-to-be, resting his hand on her thigh under the coffee table. "You want to do the honors?"

She blushed, and though she answered us, she never took her eyes off him. "November twenty-sixth," she said. "The Saturday after Thanksgiving."

"November," Mom echoed. "That's so soon!"

And it was. We were already more than halfway through August.

"We know," Noah said, grabbing her hand in his. "But, we want something small, intimate. Neither of us wants to stress out about the planning. It'll be casual."

Mom dropped her hot dog back on her plate without taking a bite, blinking several times with her mouth ajar. "Casual."

"I'll still wear a tux, Mama," Noah assured her. "I promise."

That seemed to appease her a bit, and she picked up her hot dog again, but before she could take a bite, Logan cleared his throat.

"Uh... before you do that, we have some news," he said, glancing at Mallory. "And I think it might be best to not have any possible choking hazards around."

"Oh, my God. If you proposed and Betty isn't here to gawk at the ring, we're all in for it," Kylie joked. The table chuckled in agreement, but Logan didn't join in, and Mallory looked as pale as a ghost.

"Did you?" Mom asked, her eyes bouncing back and forth between the two of them. They looked half lit up with excitement, and half panicked — and I had a feeling it was because Mallory's last name belonged to the family ours had been at war with for decades.

"Not exactly..." Logan answered.

We all waited, eyeing each other with equally as confused looks. I shot a glare at my oldest brother, the one I was sure Logan would tell a secret to first, but he just shrugged.

"I'm pregnant."

The words flew from Mallory's mouth, her eyes on Logan's before she turned to the rest of us and smiled hesitantly. "Surprise?"

My heartbeat traveled up through my throat to my ears, and I focused on the pulse of it as an awkward silence fell over the table. We all just sat there, shell-shocked, looking at Mallory before one by one, our attention turned to Mom.

Her lips were pressed together, eyes wide, hands still holding that damn hot dog which surely had to be cold by now. Mr. Nelson cleared his throat like he was about to say something, but Kylie nudged him, warning him not to — not yet.

Not until Mama had the first word.

She looked down at the hot dog in her hand, as if she'd only just then remembered it was there at all. She set it down, wiped the corner of her mouth with her napkin — which didn't make sense, since she hadn't taken a bite yet. Then, she looked at Mallory again.

This time, she had tears in her eyes.

"That is..." she whispered, shaking her head as the tears pooled and began to run down her cheeks. "The most *wonderful* news."

The whole room let out a breath in sync, my brothers and I sharing looks of relief as Mallory's shoulders deflated. "Really?"

Mom nodded, swiping at her tears. "Really. A *grandchild*," she said, shaking her head. "I can't believe it. I'm going to be a grandma!"

Jordan started clapping, which led us all to join in, and before I knew it,

Mom, Logan, and Mallory were on their feet, hugging each other while Mom blubbered. I didn't miss how Kylie dabbed at the corner of her own eyes, and I pinched her side, teasing her.

"Softie."

"Bite me," she said, but smiled all the same.

The room became a flurry of tears and congratulations, everyone taking their turn to stand and hug the soon-to-be parents. When it was my turn, I hugged Mallory tight, telling her I *knew* she was glowing, which earned me a hard eye-roll from her. Then, I turned to my older brother, hugged him with a hard clap on the shoulder, and told him the truth.

"You're going to be the best dad."

He smiled, socking my arm. "Thanks, but I think that title already belongs to someone else in our family."

"Maybe," I said. "But, if I had any money to bet, I'd bet that you're going to be just like him." I frowned. "With a touch of OCD."

Mallory laughed at that. "Oh, yeah. I can already see how fun this is going to be. Who wants to take bets on how many baby wipes and bottles of hand sanitizer he'll stock up on before the due date?"

Jordan and Noah started calling out numbers as Logan flicked us all off, and after a few more jabs, we were all seated again, the conversation alive with wedding and baby details.

I eyed my oldest brother at the end of the coffee table, who was typing something on his phone, and was otherwise quiet. His brows were furrowed, lips tight.

"Everything okay, Jordan?" I asked.

The table quieted, which wasn't my intention, and I could feel my brother's uneasiness at the attention as he tucked his phone away. "Fine. Just got some staff news, that's all."

"They fill the new trainer position?" Mr. Nelson asked. Even though he never had a son, he was at every single Friday night football game in Stratford, and had been as long as I could remember.

"Seems so."

"Anyone we know?" Logan asked.

Jordan nodded. "Sydney Kelly."

I didn't miss how Mallory stiffened, or how Logan quickly grabbed her hand in his without taking his eyes off our oldest brother. "As in, Police Chief Kelly's newly ex-wife?"

"The very one."

Silence fell over the table.

"Well," Noah said after a long pause. "She used to work at the hospital, didn't she? Before their kid was born. I'm sure she'll do a good job."

"Maybe," Jordan said, noncommittally. "It's just... it's the first staff change I've had in the years I've been head coach. I'm not sure how the team will react."

"Hey, with you as their coach, they'll react however you want them to. They look up to you," I reminded him. "You set the tone."

Mom nodded. "I agree. And I think having a woman on the staff will be a nice change."

"I'm sure the players won't mind," Kylie added. "Sydney Kelly isn't exactly hard on the eyes."

"Yeah, I bet the biggest problem you'll have is keeping them from getting purposefully injured, just to have her hands on them," Noah teased.

Jordan chuckled, though he still seemed worried, and Mom must have picked up on it, because she asked Mallory if they'd thought of any baby names, effectively changing the subject.

"Hey," I said, lowering my voice and leaning across the table so it was clear I was talking to Jordan. "Take a walk with me real quick?"

A short ride down the elevator, and we were on 11th Street, Jordan visibly more relaxed as soon as the fresh air hit him. I walked beside him in silence until we hit the end of the block and turned right, rounding past one of the food stands we'd raided.

"Big change, adding a woman to the staff, huh?"

Jordan sighed. "Yeah. I'm not worried about the fact that she's a woman, just that she's never worked with football players before."

"Think you can teach her all she needs to know before the season gets in full swing?"

"Guess I'm going to have to."

I nodded, stuffing my hands in my pockets. "Have you been reading Dad's journal?"

Jordan looked at me, watching me for a moment before his eyes grazed the buildings around us. "Yes."

"And?"

"Nothing to tell yet."

I sighed. "Look, I know if it was important, you would have said something. But... isn't there *something*? Even if it doesn't feel like a big deal to you." I lowered my voice, like anyone in that big city gave a rat's ass about the drama in our hometown. "I've been going crazy, wondering what you've found. I mean, Kylie and I spent months trying to crack that hard drive open, and then we do, and I hand it over, and I've been so caught up with everything, and I just..."

"I know," he said, cutting me off with a sigh. "I know." Then, he looked around, too, lowering his own voice as we rounded the next corner. "For the most part, it's been boring. Daily logs of what he was working on, meeting minutes and notes, lists of stuff he needed to do the next day. But... there is something."

I perked up. "Yeah?"

"You know how he was tasked to clean out that office, right?"

"Yeah…" I said, slowly, because that wasn't a secret to anyone. It was the whole reason he was the one and *only* one to perish in the fire that day. "And?"

"Well, he found something I don't think he was supposed to find."

"What?"

Jordan stopped walking, and I did, too, turning to face him as his eyes locked on mine.

"A will."

"A *will*?"

Jordan nodded. "Robert J. Scooter's will."

My jaw dropped. "I thought he didn't have one."

"That's what that whole town thinks," Jordan said, then he shook his head and started walking again. "He hasn't written about anything more, yet. And it's been a dozen entries since the one that mentioned he found the will. All the ones I've read after it are talking about the new brand launch, which I guess he got tied up in."

I shook my head, confusion throbbing in my head. "That doesn't make sense. If he found a will, why didn't he tell anyone? And what happened to it? What did it say?"

"All things I'm hoping we'll find out, baby brother," he said. "For now, that's all I got. And I'd like to keep it between us."

I nodded, and the conversation ended there, but the wheels inside my head spun on for the rest of the evening.

A few hours later, when the leftover food had been stored in our small fridge and the trash cleared from the table, I hugged my brothers goodbye — all of them and their significant others flying back home the next day. I hugged Mom, too, and kissed her head, promising that we'd text her first thing in the morning so she could come over and we could get to shopping.

"Now, I mean it, Dad," Kylie said, wagging her finger at her old man. "I'm coming home in just a few months for that wedding, and if I come home and that apartment is filthy or there's evidence that you've only been eating food that you can pick up at a drive-thru on your way home from work, you're not going to like what happens next."

Mr. Nelson chuckled, one eyebrow lifting as Kylie continued.

"And there's a note on the fridge with all the bills and their due dates. And don't forget to water the plants on Wednesdays. Watering Wednesdays, just like that guy said at the flower shop we stopped in at today."

"Longbourne," I said.

She pointed a finger at me. "Right. Just like the man at Longbourne said. And if you change your mind about the cleaning service, their number is on the fridge, too. They can come every couple of weeks to give the place a real scrub down. Oh, and don't forget to check on Betty. It'll be good for you to volunteer at the nursing home every now and then, get you out of the house for something other than work."

I chuckled, placing my hands on her shoulders with an apologetic smile at Mr. Nelson. "I think he's got it, babe."

She deflated under my hands, then broke away from them completely, wrapping her dad in a fierce hug. "And most of all, don't forget that I love you, and I'll miss you. Every day."

"I'll miss you, too, Smiley," he said, kissing her head on a chuckle. "Why don't you walk me downstairs and help me call a cab?"

"Deal."

They disappeared through the door, the parade of my family following after, and then, I was alone.

I looked around the space, somehow empty and crammed all at the same time. Part of me was exhausted, but the other part of me was too excited to even think about sleep. So, I turned on my Bluetooth speaker, hit play on my favorite playlist, and cracked open the first box that needed to be unpacked.

I was humming along to a Florence + The Machine song when Kylie came through the front door, eyes red and puffy, a folded piece of notebook paper in her hands. I dropped what I was unpacking at the sight of her, sweeping her into my arms as she wiped her nose on the back of her wrist. She leaned into my touch when I held her, letting out a long sigh.

"It's okay, baby," I said, running my fingers through her hair. "We'll see him soon."

"I know," she said. "It's not that. It's this." She held up the notebook paper.

I frowned, pulling back to study it with her still in my arms. "What is it?"

"A gift," she said with a wobbly lip. "Every single one of my mom's favorite places in the city is on that piece of paper. He said he thought it could be a new list of adventures for you and me to check off together."

My heart squeezed, and I pulled her back into me, holding her tighter as she curled her hands in my t-shirt. "He's an amazing dad."

"The best there is," she agreed. Then, she let out a groan, pulled back, and swiped her hands over her face. "Okay. Let me go wash all these salty tears off my cheeks and then let's get to work unpacking, shall we?"

I chuckled, kissing her forehead before I released her. "Deal."

For the next couple of hours, we unpacked, box by box, bit by bit. We didn't have much, but we didn't need much, and the more we filled that tiny apartment with little things that made us, *us* — the more it felt like home.

When most of the work was done, I pulled Nelly out of her case, tuning her up before I sat on the edge of the coffee table and began to play.

"Mmm," Kylie said, sitting on the table behind me. She wrapped her arms around my middle as best she could without interrupting my playing. "I like the sound of this one. What's it called?"

"That's for me to know and you to find out."

She crooked a smile. "You writing a song for me, Michael Becker?"

"What can I say?" I shrugged. "You're my muse."

"Cheeseball."

I smirked, dropping my guitar carefully into the case before I turned quickly, tickling Kylie before she could escape. She laughed and writhed in my arms, and when she was breathless and maybe two tickles from kicking me, I stopped, holding her with my eyes searching hers.

"I was thinking…" I said, swiping her hair out of her face. "Maybe we could carry on one of my family traditions in our new home."

"Oh, yeah? And what tradition is that?"

I kissed her nose, releasing her long enough to cross the room to where my phone was, and then I put on a familiar song — one I knew would need no explaining.

As soon as it started, recognition hit Kylie's eyes, and she smiled, watching me as I made my way back to her. I held out my hand for hers, and when she stood, she wrapped her arms around my neck, and mine found her waist.

"Same song and everything?"

"Same song and everything," I echoed.

"Why's that?"

"Because it meant something to my dad, and still means so much to my mom, to my brothers, to me," I answered honestly. Then, I smirked. "And, because it's true. You *do* look wonderful tonight."

Kylie smiled, lying her head on my chest as we swayed, the soft melody of the Eric Clapton song I'd listened to my whole life making it feel a little more like home. "I love you, Mikey."

I tilted her chin, waiting until her eyes found mine before I answered. "And I love you."

We danced until the last note played, until I swept her into my arms and up the ladder to our loft bed. Then, I spent the night reminding her in every single way I could that she was mine, and I was hers, and that those three words I'd said were true.

And in that little New York City apartment with my best friend, a new adventure officially began.

I knew it'd be the best one yet.

Old Fashioned

To the ones who won't back down,

who won't go quietly,

who won't give up.

To the fighters.

This one's for you.

Chapter One

Jordan

Ever since I was twenty-three years old, there had been a fire burned into my memory.

I wished it was a metaphorical fire, one that drove me to excel and succeed and filled me up from the inside. I'd even settle for a bonfire that was memorable, one my friends and family had gathered around on an evening when everything felt right in the world. But for me, the fire was a living, breathing monster, seemingly small where I viewed it against a pale blue evening sky as it devoured a corner office in an old whiskey distillery on the edge of town.

A corner office, and nothing else.

A corner office I didn't know held my father inside it.

I'd been the only one of my family to see the actual fire, to watch the smoke billow and what was left of the flames lick at the roof of the building through the busted windows of that office. I hadn't thought twice about it, other than to think it was a small annoyance that had traffic backed up heading into town. I was on my way to Mom and Dad's for dinner.

It was such a small fire, already in control when I drove past it. The fire department had it surrounded, water spewing from their truck, the flames already weakening. I didn't know much about fires, but even I could tell that it was in no danger of spreading, that it was tamed, and I drove past it wondering if Dad would be called back up to the distillery to fill out paperwork, since he was on the board.

When I had opened the screen door from Mom and Dad's front porch, all three of my brothers were in the living room, playing video games and talking over each other at a volume that was always too loud for my taste.

None of them looked like me. My skin was darker, an umber brown that was light in the winter months and dark from the sun during the summer. Compared to their olive tan, it stood out, a reminder of our differences that we never really acknowledged. My onyx hair that curled tightly to my scalp was also a contrast to their sandy brown, straight locks.

But, the fact that the blood that ran through my veins was not the same as that which ran through theirs didn't matter. My *adoption* didn't matter. It never had.

We were brothers, an impenetrable force, a team forged in bad times and in good.

Mom had smiled when I arrived, wiping her hands on her apron before she crossed and kissed my cheek.

"Can you help me set the table?" she'd asked, hanging a hand on her hip as she gestured to the rest of my brothers with the other. "As you can see, this motley crew is useless. And your father had to stay late at work, something about exciting news." She rolled her eyes a little, because we all knew that *exciting news* to my father could mean anything from a promotion to him finding a washed dollar in his jean pocket.

I'd never forget that smile she wore when she turned back to me, the one that crinkled the edges of her eyes and spread from cheek to cheek. Because less than thirty seconds later, the home phone rang.

And I never saw my mother smile like that again.

I blinked, the memory of that summer night ten years ago fading as my laptop screen came back into focus. A dated software system filled the screen, Latin words on an old word processor file, a journal my father had kept for years before he passed.

A journal my brother had found on a hard drive not meant to be discovered.

A journal I was now trying to decode, as if it would somehow reveal all the answers to every question my family and I had asked since that fateful day in June.

I'd gone through months of entries before I'd discovered that my father had found a Last Will and Testament of the founder of the distillery. That had shocked me, since this entire town was rocked with surprise when Robert J. Scooter died and a Will *hadn't* existed.

It turned out one had, at least, according to Dad's journal.

But he hadn't mentioned it since that first entry.

I sighed, cursing under my breath when I checked my watch and saw it was almost one in the morning. I wasn't going to find anything more tonight — especially with so much on my mind. I safely ejected the hard drive and tucked it into my top desk drawer, the screen of my laptop modernizing again before I put it to sleep. I had to do it quickly, before my fingers hit the keys that would open my lesson plans for the week or, even more risky, my practice plans.

Tomorrow was the first day of high school for our small town of Stratford, Tennessee — and I had a team of football players to whip into shape.

I scrubbed my hands over my face, body aching as I lifted it from the chair I'd been living in all evening. It was normal for me to be anxious before the first day of school, the first day of *football*, but I was even more wired than usual.

Maybe it was the pressure of walking into a new season with two state championships under my belt. This entire town expected our team to keep winning, expected *me* to keep winning, which was a completely different kind of pressure than when you were the coach taking a team that rarely ever won all the way to state. That had been a driving kind of pressure.

This, however, was more on the crippling side.

Maybe part of my anxiety came from my youngest brother, Michael, moving across the country to New York City with his girlfriend. We'd all flown up to help get him settled, and while I knew *he* would be okay — mostly because Kylie would make sure of it — I worried about our mother, who was now in the house alone for the first time.

The same house she bought with my father.

The weight of responsibility I'd always felt for my mother pressed heavy on my chest, but I forced a deep breath, going through my nightly routine of brushing my teeth and flossing and lotioning from head to toe. When all that was left to do was crawl into bed, I splayed my large hands on the bathroom counter instead, staring at my reflection.

I didn't know the two human beings responsible for making the man who stared back at me.

I didn't know if I had my mother's eyes — gray-blue, with a brown burst surrounding the iris — or if I had my father's nose, the bridge slightly bent, nostrils wide. Was it his scowl that mine mirrored, thick eyebrows forever in a bent state of determination? Was it her freckles that broke through the dark complexion of my cheeks in the summertime?

Which one was black, and which one was white?

How did they find each other, and where were they now?

They were questions I'd asked myself hundreds of times throughout the course of my life, questions I knew I'd never have answers to. But one thing I *did* know was that I wasn't anxious about the first day of school because I felt pressure to win, or because my little brother was in New York, or because my mom was sleeping soundly on her own across town.

The truth was my anxiety was rooted in the newest addition to my staff.

A woman.

A very attractive, very distracting to young, hormonal boys, very newly divorced woman.

She would be the *first* woman on our staff, and the first new blood to come onto our team since I took over as head coach.

Everything I'd worked for, all the synchrony I'd developed over the years, all the trust and rhythm and comfort we'd grown accustomed to was about to be shaken up.

By the police chief's ex-wife.

Before I could fall into another spiral, I shook my head, pushing off the counter and swiping the bathroom light switch with my palm. I peeled my shirt off, stripped my sweatpants off next, and climbed into my flannel sheets in my boxer briefs, setting an alarm on my phone before I plugged it in and turned it face down on my nightstand.

Then, I laid awake for hours, tossing and turning, pretending that I was still in control and everything would be fine.

By the time I finally fell asleep, the alarm rang.

• • •

Stratford, Tennessee, was a small map dot southeast of Nashville. It had a population of two-thousand-one-hundred-and-seventy-two people, according to the most recent census — and almost half of those residents worked at the Scooter Whiskey Distillery on the edge of town. It was where my grandfather had built his career, where my father had worked his entire life, and where two of my brothers worked still.

Noah was a barrel-raiser, with skillfully quick hands and muscles lining every inch of his arms. Logan was a tour guide, the face of our town to the tourists who passed through. And, before he left, Michael had worked in the gift shop.

It was a family tradition.

And though I was the oldest, and perhaps the one Dad *most* expected to follow in his footsteps, working at a whiskey distillery was the last thing on my mind growing up.

For me, it was all about football.

Mom had always told me that the first time I held a football, I couldn't even walk yet. Dad had been tossing one in the backyard with a friend of his, and when he missed a catch, it rolled over to where I was sitting on a blanket with Mom. She said I picked it up with both hands, stared at it with both brows bent, and then I looked up at her and smiled.

She said she knew right then that I'd play football.

What she *didn't* know was that I wouldn't just play it, I'd become *obsessed* with it. From the time I was on my first Little League team, football was my life. I couldn't wait for practices and games. I watched football whenever I wasn't playing it. I followed ESPN football stories like it was my job. I collected cards, ran drills on my own when the season was over, and was always looking forward to the next time I'd get on that field.

But where my teammates in high school dreamed of being scouted to a college and drafted into the NFL, my heart drew me to the behind-the-scenes work of it all. I wanted to dissect every play, watch every game, replay every tape, draw up my *own* plays, and — perhaps more than anything — I wanted to coach.

I never took for granted that my dream had come true, that I was doing what I loved most in the world and somehow managing to get paid for it, too.

That's why a familiar buzz of excitement crawled under my skin as I pushed through the doors of the stadium locker room, eyes on my clipboard, words I would say to the team repeating in my head. It was only an hour until our first practice, and nothing compared to that feeling of starting a new season — not the ten days of summer camp, not the energy that coursed through every kid at tryouts.

Nothing.

It'd been a fast first day of school, my regular day filled with introducing myself to freshmen who were in my physical education class and catching up with the athletes in my weightlifting classes. I enjoyed teaching both for very different reasons. The freshmen were nervous, and I always jumped at the opportunity to make them feel welcome and comfortable in their new atmosphere — mostly by encouraging them to join a sport. And when the students I'd worked with came to me in weightlifting, athletes of all backgrounds with issues ranging from golf swings to softball pitching, the excitement that rang through me was palpable.

I *lived* for this, for discovering a physical limit and making a plan for how to overcome it.

But as much as I enjoyed teaching throughout the day, it was the first day of football practice *after* the school day let out that my heart really pounded for.

My head was still down when I pushed through the door to my office, using my back to open it. I kicked the door stop under it with my foot to prop it open, still not taking my eyes off the notes on my clipboard. I didn't realize my office wasn't empty, even after I sat down in the familiar, worn chair, the old leather splitting under my hamstrings, a soft *whoosh* of air from the cushion.

It wasn't until a soft clearing of a throat hit my ears that I looked up from my work and saw her sitting across from me.

Sydney Kelly was not the kind of woman you could pass by without noticing — she never had been.

I hadn't known her well in high school, but even then, every head would turn when she walked by, regardless of their sex or sexual orientation. She was riddled with unique features, from her jet-black hair — which was pulled into a high and tight ponytail right now — and almond-shaped eyes to the curious complexion of her skin. It was a golden brown, darker than the tans my brothers could achieve in the summer but lighter than my own. She never covered that complexion with anything but sunscreen, not in all the years I'd seen her around town. Makeup seemed to be nonexistent in her universe, which made the dusty pink of her plump lips and the severeness of her high cheek bones and the length of her black lashes that much more mesmerizing.

She was beautiful — dangerously so.

And she had *team distraction* written all over her.

I mentally cursed Principal Hanley, wondering how he didn't see this as an issue when he hired Sydney as our new athletic trainer. Of course, I'd voiced my concerns when we were reviewing applicants, but Dustin Hanley was close friends with Sydney's older sister, Gabriel. Dustin and Gabby had been in the same college when the Clarks first moved to Stratford. Apparently, the bond they'd formed in school had carried through.

What I had to say on the matter didn't seem to be a factor in the decision at all.

Not that I thought discrimination in *any* form was okay, but the truth of the matter was that teenage boys with raging hormones were hard enough to wrangle with a staff full of stalky, grumpy men.

With Sydney on the field, it'd be damn near impossible.

I stood abruptly, dropping my clipboard on my desk as I rounded it. "Mrs. Kelly, I apologize. I'm afraid I didn't see you there," I said, reaching out my hand for hers as she stood, too. She wore modest black leggings and a loose-fitting polo in our school's shade of red, but I realized in the moment that she could have been wearing a potato sack and she would still be a complete knockout.

I kept my eyes trained on hers to avoid the length of her toned arms, or the way her hips filled out those leggings, knowing full well that I'd be the *only* one on this team capable of doing so.

"Coach Becker," I said with my hand still extended. "Welcome to the team."

"No need to apologize, *Jordan*," she said my name with a smirk that set my nerves at attention, her eyes playful. "I'm glad to see you work just as hard as you did in high school. I don't think I'd ever seen that kind of focus before my first group project with you our junior year."

I chuckled as her soft hand slipped into mine, but she shook it firmly.

"And it's Sydney *Clark*, now," she added, her smile faltering before she snapped it back into place.

Clark.

Her maiden name.

Embarrassment flittered through me, along with a recognition. I couldn't believe I'd let her married name slip, especially after the scandal that *was* her divorce with Police Chief Randy Kelly. But, they'd dated ever since I'd known them — in high school and beyond. It was difficult to separate one from the other, anymore.

"Of course," I said, shaking my head as we released our grips. I slid my hands into my pockets, changing the subject away from her recent name change. "I didn't expect you so early."

"An hour before practice?" she asked, quirking one eyebrow. "I'd say that's more *punctual* than early. I figured you'd want to show me my office, let me get my table and supplies set up." She tapped the large duffle bag hanging off her shoulder.

"I guess I'm just used to the rest of my staff who like to roll up here ten minutes before the team starts showing up."

She smiled. "Well, then, let's just say I'm not like the rest of your staff."

You can say that again.

I motioned toward the hallway, guiding her out of my office and past the rows of lockers to the athletic training station. Once I flicked on the light, I stood at the entrance with my hands in my pockets. "We got a pretty decent amount of money from the boosters last year," I explained as Sydney dropped her duffle bag on the examination table, looking around her new space. "So, lucky for you, you're walking into an upgraded version of the mess that was here before." I pointed. "New ice bath, new whirlpool, extra storage, nice table for soft tissue work. We even got those fancy boot things."

"NormaTecs," she mused, crossing her arms as her eyebrows crept up. She eyed me with a smirk. "I didn't realize I was working for a team of professional athletes."

I grabbed the back of my neck with a shrug. "What can I say? When you win two state championships, you get a lot of money thrown your way. We had all new pads, new jerseys, new staff gear, end zone cameras, new iPads and screens for reviewing tapes. I was running out of ways to spend it."

She chuckled. "You poor thing."

I wanted to smile, too, but I was still rubbing my neck, staring at what I knew would be the source of every headache I'd have in the next few months.

"Sydney, listen," I said on a sigh, letting my hand fall. "I don't know how else to say this but to be frank with you."

Her smile fell, expression flattening as she straightened her spine.

"I'm worried about you being our athletic trainer."

Her eyebrows dipped, lips pursing. "Let me guess — because I'm a woman?"

"No," I said quickly, but then I rolled my lips together. "Well, honestly? Kind of." I held up my hands when she rolled her eyes. "But not because I don't think you're capable. It's just that... we're dealing with teenage boys here. They're rowdy, and — God help us — dominated by hormones that they can't control yet."

Sydney folded her arms over her chest, listening, her expression unreadable.

"I'm just saying," I continued. "There's a lot riding on this season. We've won two state championships in a row, and we have a lot of eyes on us."

"Meaning, you have a lot of eyes on *you*."

I swallowed. "Yes."

"And you think I'll be a distraction."

"Honestly? I know you will be."

Sydney smiled, shaking her head and looking around her new office before she took two purposeful steps toward me. "I understand your concern, but here's my side of things."

She paused, and I realized I'd never been this close to Sydney — not in high school, not in any of the years since. And there was an energy pulsing off of her, one that hit me like a wave of electricity low in my gut.

"If your players are distracted by a woman on the sideline, that is on *them* — not on me. If their parents didn't teach them that, then I'd wager that's *your* new job. I'm an athletic trainer, and a damn good one, which is why I got this job in the first place. I'm here to *do* that job, and the last thing I need is for my new boss to tell me that I might be *too pretty* to do it effectively."

"I didn't say you were…"

"Then what exactly *are* you saying?" she probed, taking another step. She didn't raise her voice, but the intensity between us shot up three levels. Her chest was a few inches from mine now, her eyes cast up, chin held high, jaw set. Those dark lashes brushed her cheeks when she blinked, waiting.

I catalogued every feature.

"What I'm saying is that you are the first new member to our staff since I became head coach seven years ago, and I'm making sure you understand that we set the standards high on this team."

"Great. Your expectations have been made clear. Can I have a while alone to set up my office now?"

I narrowed my eyes. "Do you have a problem with authority, Ms. Clark?"

"Only as much as you seem to have a problem with equality, *Coach*."

I blew out a frustrated breath, eyes rolling up to the ceiling as I debated whether it was worth fighting her over. I wanted to. *Oh*, how I wanted to. But the truth was I knew I'd already put my foot in my mouth, that I hadn't explained my concerns properly.

I *did* sound like a sexist asshole, and no verbal argument could win me out of that perception in this moment.

The only way for her to see that my concerns were valid was to witness them play out.

And I had no doubt they would — in less than an hour when that locker room filled with boys.

"Let me know if you have any questions as you get set up," I said, forcing a calm breath. "After practice, I'll get your sizes so we can order you staff polos and jackets for the games. The team should start showing up in about forty-five minutes."

I didn't say another word, nor did I wait to see if she had a last one to get in, either. Instead, I moved swiftly back down the hall, resisting the urge to slam my office door. I swiped my clipboard off the desk, attempting to focus, but I read the same line over and over again, all the while stewing on what I'd said, how I'd said it, and what she'd thrown back at me, in return.

It was less than an hour before the first practice of the year, and one thing was already abundantly clear.

It was going to be a long season.

Chapter Two

Sydney

Thirty boys and three grown men stared at the giant, square trophy in Jordan Becker's hands as he carried it silently through the locker room. He sat it gently on the folding chair he'd propped in the middle of the room, placing his hand on the large, golden football that adorned the top of it. For a long while, he just stared at that trophy and didn't say a word.

The entire locker room was silent, too.

As much as I wanted to hate him for his rather rude welcome to me on the team, I couldn't deny that I respected him in that moment. He commanded attention — and he'd always been that way. I remembered him having the same presence in high school, though we weren't in the same crowd. One thing I'd learned was that he didn't speak often, so when he did, everyone knew it was important, and valuable, and necessary.

So many people filled the world with hot air, speaking before thinking, talking about nothing at all.

Jordan Becker was the exact opposite.

He was purposeful, severe — like the flood God cast down to cleanse the earth.

I stood straight in my little corner of the room, trying to blend while also knowing it was impossible. Until Jordan had waltzed that trophy into this room, I'd been about the only thing anyone could stare at. Eyes of each member of that staff widened when Jordan introduced me to them, and as the boys filed in one by one, their eyes stuck on me, too. They whispered to each other, smiling and elbowing each other in the ribs, and I could only imagine what they were saying.

Thank God, because imagining was still better than hearing it for real.

In retrospect, I knew Jordan wasn't wrong about the way the boys would react to me. The fact that it was sexist and *not* my fault didn't matter — boys would be boys, as they say. Still, this was my first day of work after years of being a stay-at-home mom — a job I didn't choose, but rather, was selected *for* me. If it wasn't for my sister's friendship with Principal Hanley from when they were in school together, I wasn't sure I would have been able to find a job as an athletic trainer after all the time I'd taken off. Before my daughter was born, I had been primed and ready to start my career, and I had offers waiting.

But things changed.

And no one in that locker room saw me as anything but someone new to the team. They had no idea that that day symbolized freedom for me. To them, and to most of that town, I was the bitch who divorced the sweet, amazing hero who kept this town safe. What they didn't know is that I'd been anything *but* safe in my marriage with him.

But in a small town, when the Police Chief is beating you with his words and his hands, you have no one to run to.

And you believe him when he says you're crazy, and that you deserve it.

I swallowed, shaking those memories off before they could slide in to ruin the first day of my new chapter. It didn't matter if no one else knew it, *I* knew it.

It was a new beginning.

A new era.

A tiny smile curled my lips at the realization, but as soon as Jordan lifted his head, I straightened again.

"Anyway."

It was the first word Jordan spoke, and I watched as confusion swept over the faces in the locker room — mine included. The boys glanced at each other, wondering if they'd missed something, while the staff of coaches stood behind Jordan with similar gazes.

"The past five years, this team has had a word of the season. Every day, we come back to that word. When we lose, when we win, when we practice, when we're on this field, and when we're off it — that word is our guide," Jordan explained.

His eyes were a storm in and of themselves, a swirl of gray-blue like an ominous sky with a burst of golden-brown around each iris. They locked on each of the boys looking up to him, as if he wanted to ensure they each felt seen. The way he stood next to that trophy, with his bicep muscles bulging out of his polo, his broad shoulders square and straight, his chin high, brows bent and determined, jaw square — he looked like he was about to take these boys into battle rather than onto a football field.

And with the way they looked at him, I knew they wouldn't hesitate to go to war for their sergeant.

"Our first year, the word was *work*. Then, *growth*. We took *growth* to *perseverance*, and then to *discipline*, and last year, to *determination*."

That last word fired up the boys who I assumed had been on the team last year, and they chanted the word three times in different cadences before giving a deep-chested *ooah!* that echoed through the locker room.

Jordan smirked, but the curl in his lips faded as fast as it had come. "This season's word is different. It doesn't look motivational if you slap it on a poster and it probably won't make sense to anyone outside of this room. And that's exactly why I picked it. Because the truth of the matter is this: *we* are the unit. *We* are the team. And *we*, alone, are responsible for what happens this season."

There were a few nods, an unspoken understanding, the locker room so quiet you could hear my sneaker squeak against the floor when I shifted my weight.

"This season is going to be hard, but we're going to persevere, anyway," Jordan said after a while, glancing around the room. "Practices are going to be long and hot, but we're going to show up, anyway. There's a lot of pressure on us to perform, but we're going to excel, anyway. There are going to be days we all want to grumble or scream or throw our helmets or quit, but we're going to stay here and fight, anyway."

The more he used the word, the more fired up that locker room became. I watched the boys hold their heads higher, their brows furrowing deeper, their chests puffing out more and more with every word. I'd sat in the bleachers behind this team for years, every Friday night that we had a home game, watching Jordan lead them to win after win — but I'd never seen the *inside* of the machine, the one we watched work so effortlessly together on the field.

This was the making of a team.

This was magic.

Jordan left his perch by the trophy, walking around the room now. "You're going to mess up," he said, nodding. "Oh, trust me — you are. You're going to miss catches and tackles and run the wrong plays and look back on tapes wishing you'd done it all differently, but you know what?" He pressed his finger into one of the kid's chests. "You're going to get your ass back on that field on Monday, anyway."

There was a shuffling, a few kids rising to their feet with cries of *yeah!* and *that's right!*

"Your body is going to ache," Jordan said, raising his voice. "Your muscles are going to scream and beg you to stop and you're going to be pushed past your limits and everything inside you is going to tell you to quit. But you're going to keep going, anyway."

More standing, more cheers.

"Everyone out there," Jordan said, all but screaming now as he pointed to the locker room doors. "Is going to expect you to fail — expect *us* to fail. They're going to wait for us to crack under the pressure, to mess up, to fall short. But what are we going to do?" He looked around that room, and while I expected someone to answer, they all stood and waited, apparently well aware that it was a question Jordan would answer, himself.

And he did.

He smiled, shook his head, and thumbed his chest. "*We* are going to win, anyway. Can I hear you say it?" He held out his hands. "What are we going to do?"

"We're going to win, anyway," the room echoed back to him, softer than he wanted.

"What's that?"

"We're going to win, anyway!"

"When they tell you we lost our best players to graduation, what are you going to say?"

"We're going to win, anyway!"

"When they tell you there's no hope of us getting another state title, what are you going to say?"

"We're going to win, anyway!"

"This is not going to be an easy season," Jordan said to the humming room, all the boys on their feet now, shuffling, some of them clapping or stepping side to side. "We're going to have to work, and work hard. We're going to have to rise up against the odds. This town is supporting us, but the rest of this state can't wait to watch us fail. So, when the doubts creep into your mind, when your body hurts, when the scores don't look good or the fear strangles you, I want you to show up here, anyway. I want you to believe in yourself and in this team, anyway. And I want you to—"

"Win, anyway!"

Jordan smiled as the locker room erupted into cheers, and he clapped one of the boys on the shoulder. "Damn straight."

More cheers rang out, and I couldn't help but smile from my little corner of the room. It was the first day of practice and he'd already fired them up for the entire season.

That was a sign of a great coach.

"He's something out of this world to watch, isn't he?"

I followed the voice to my right, where the defensive coordinator had slid up beside me. Coach TK, as Jordan had introduced to me. He was a white man, with kind, hazel eyes and a smile that reminded me of my ex-husband's father. Coach TK was just as tall as Jordan, his stocky figure hinting that he, too, had played football in his youth, and he wore a baseball cap to cover his balding head.

"He's something, alright," I mused with a smile, eyeing Jordan with a mixture of annoyance and appreciation. I couldn't deny that he deserved to be where he was, that there was no better man to lead our town's team to victory.

But I could still be upset with him for his presumptuous welcome.

"Now, before we hand out equipment and get our first day of practice under way, we have a new member on our staff," Jordan said, and as soon as the words were out of his mouth, all eyes were on me.

I smiled, pushing off the wall I was leaning against to stand straight.

"Please help me welcome Sydney Clark, our new athletic trainer."

Someone whistled, someone else yelled out, *"Oh, I'll welcome her, alright,"* and then the room filled with a mixture of laughter and cheers.

I frowned.

Jordan walked purposefully toward me, his eyes locked on mine, and that moment seemed to lengthen and stretch. There was something about that man's eyes, about the way he held himself, the confidence he exuded and the respect he demanded.

It left me breathless, awakening a part of me I thought had died forever, before he swiveled and faced the room of boys.

"I'm going to say this one time and one time only, and if it doesn't sink in, you will all run suicides for every time I have to repeat myself."

That shut them all up.

"You will respect Ms. Clark just as you respected Mr. Perry when he was in the position. There will be no foul remarks, no whistling, no slanderous talk, and no other behavior that your mother would classify as disrespectful and skin your hide for. If any of you fake injuries to get time on her table, or pull any kind of crap that makes her uncomfortable, you will have me to answer to — and trust me when I say the punishment will not be pretty. Am I understood?"

There were mumbles of *yes, coach* in response.

Part of me wanted to be annoyed that this even had to be a conversation, but the other part of me was glad he was setting the standards for his team from the start. He didn't allow it to get past those first remarks made, and he was making it clear what was expected.

More than anything, it was a sign of respect for me.

One I appreciated.

"Good," Jordan said, nodding once. "Ms. Clark has studied sports medicine in depth and had past offers to play with college teams."

His eyes found mine then, and my brows folded. *How did he know that?*

"We're lucky to have her," he finished, with his eyes still on mine. I could feel the sincerity in them, the belief he held for the words he'd just spoken.

And something else.

Something else I couldn't quite place.

But before I could dissect it further, he clapped his hands, barked out an order, and the team fled out of the locker room and onto the field.

• • •

They don't tell you anything about motherhood.

When you're pregnant, you *think* they're telling you everything. You think the baby books and the unsolicited advice from family members and older mothers in town cover just about everything you'd need to know — and everything you *never* wanted to know, too.

You think you're prepared. You know that it will hurt, that the pain won't matter once that child is in your arms, that your life will never be the same. You know not to expect sleep, and that your breasts will swell until you feed, and that your priorities will shift to completely center your world around this new, tiny human you've created.

But what no one tells you is that from the moment that first cry rings out in the hospital, you will be terrified.

They don't tell you that you'll worry if you're breastfeeding long enough, or if you should breastfeed at all, or if you fed them the right food once they were able to eat solids. They don't tell you that as much as that kid's first steps will amaze you, they'll also make your stomach drop in fear. They don't tell you that for the rest of your life, you'll wonder how your actions affect that little human you made — are you screwing them up? Are you giving them a complex? Are you going to be the subject of their future therapy appointments?

Will they end up like their father, angry and impulsive and vindictive?

Or is there more of *you* in your child?

And if so, is that even a good thing?

It was enough to drive a person mad — which, I was convinced, was a permanent state of being for most mothers. We just knew how to *handle* our insanity, how to live with it and somehow get our shit done. You had to learn to quiet the fears and anxieties, to *fake it till you made it*, to do whatever it took to make ends meet and keep your home a safe place for your child.

Some days it was easy.

Some days it was impossible.

And every day, as a newly single mother, I worried.

"This is gonna be our year, Mama," Paige said, splaying her tiny hands over the laces of the football in her hands as she watched the Tennessee Titans press conference. They were her favorite team, and she idolized Mike Vrabel like he was her father.

In a twisted way, I wished he was.

"You think so, huh?" I asked, smiling at her from the kitchen where I was browning hamburger meat for dinner. I hadn't had the energy to do more than whip up a box of Hamburger Helper that evening, not after my first day of work. And it wasn't that Paige would mind — she was a kid, she didn't care. But it seemed I was always on a cycle of mom guilt, thinking I should be doing *something* better.

Or everything, really.

So, the fact that I hadn't come home and made a fresh, balanced dinner weighed on me a bit as I stirred the meat.

"I know so. Look at coach," she said, gesturing to the TV before her hands were on the football in her lap again. "He looks..." She stopped, struggling for the word.

"Confident?" I suggested.

"Yeah! And the rookies we drafted, the way the team worked together last season." She looked back over her shoulder at me with her crooked smile. "I can feel it."

I smiled back, tracing her features. I knew all mothers thought their child was the most beautiful kid in the world, but with my Paigey, it really was true. She had a full head of bouncy curls that would have made me and my sister both hate her and love her had she been our friend as kids. Her skin was a smooth tawny, her cheeks peppered with freckles that were like stars under her almond-brown eyes. She had a gap between her two front teeth that grew back in fully last year, and somehow it only made her cute factor go up.

She was only nine years old, and still, I knew I'd be in trouble once she started dating.

Another flare of anxiety over her having her heart broken seared through my chest, but I subdued it, draining the pasta noodles in the colander in the sink. "Well, if you believe it, then I do, too."

I *also* knew that all mothers thought their child was the smartest kid to ever exist, and once again, I was no different. Of course, with Paige, it was only pertaining to one subject: football. She watched games and listened to podcasts and studied football terms like it was her full-time job. She learned words that most kids her age couldn't pronounce, let alone understand, all in the name of being an expert in the sport she loved.

"You'll see, we're going all the way this season," she said, turning her attention back to the television. Then, a long sigh left her chest, and she whispered so low I almost didn't hear. "I can't *wait* to play football."

I furrowed my brows, torn as always with how I would explain to her that the likelihood of that happening was slim to none. She'd been watching football with her father every Saturday, every Sunday, and every Monday night since she was born. Somewhere around four years old, she started saying she wanted to play football. At the time, I thought it was cute, something she'd grow out of, but it turned out football would be one of the staples my daughter was built on.

She was hell-bent on playing football someday, and as a mother, that terrified me.

Again — normal.

Before I could decide if I wanted to respond encouragingly or realistically, my cell phone rang.

"Hello, sister," I answered, putting her on speakerphone as I mixed the fake, processed, powdered "cheese" with the noodles and hamburger meat. "Paigey, come sit at the table for dinner."

"But, Mom! Can't I just eat it in here? Coach is still talking!"

"Yeah, Mom," my older sister teased. "Coach is talking."

"Hush," I told her on a laugh, but when Paige hopped up and clasped her hands together, begging me with her signature pouty lip and big eyes, I was helpless.

I sighed.

"Fine," I said, scooping a good helping into a bowl for her. Paige hopped up and down in victory. "Set up the TV tray though, and use your napkin, Paige Marie, *not* your jeans." I gave her *the mom look* when she bopped into the kitchen, making sure she knew I was serious before I handed her the bowl. Once she was set up in the living room, I took my sister off speakerphone, pressing the device to my ear, instead. "Gray hairs, Gabby. I swear I'll have them before the year is up."

My sister chuckled. "Oh, come on. So your daughter is obsessed with football. It could be worse. She could be obsessed with boys like we were."

"Don't jinx it," I said, smiling when Paige tossed the football up in her hands between bites, her eyes fixed on the press conference. "How are you?"

"Oh, same old same here. It was a long night at the hospital, we had a three-car accident that was pretty nasty. I was dead on my feet by the time I got home this morning."

My sister, Gabriela, was older than me by five years. It was just a wide-enough gap to keep us from ever being in the same school together, but not too wide to where we couldn't share clothes. She was my best friend — thanks to our life traveling around with a mom in the military. Where the few friends we *did* make were left in the dust each time we were re-stationed, our bond never died. It only got stronger throughout the years, and Gabby was the only person I ever felt comfortable talking to about anything deeper than the weather.

Besides Randall, but I'd learned my lesson the hard way that not even he could be trusted.

"If you still lived here, I'd make you a glass of my famous sangria."

"Ugh," she dragged out the groan. "Don't tease me like that. It's not fair."

"What's not fair is that I can't walk two doors down and plop on my sister's couch anymore."

"You could," she argued. "If you moved here with the rest of us."

I grew silent at that, casting a glance toward my daughter before I made myself a bowl of Hamburger Helper and stepped out onto the back lanai. I still kept an eye on her through the sliding glass doors.

"You know it's not that simple," I said once I was outside.

Gabby sighed. "I know, I know. I wish it were, though."

I didn't have to elaborate, because Gabriela was the only one I'd ever opened up to about *everything* that had happened between me and Randy. Mom and Dad knew we were divorced, but they thought it was just because the love had faded over time and we'd been fighting a lot.

Gabby knew the truth — the bruises, internally and externally, that prompted my final decision.

The only reason Randy had even granted me the divorce I'd asked for was because he didn't think it would last, and because it happened on *his* terms. I'd threatened to hire a lawyer, to get my parents involved, to show people the photos I'd taken with the marks he'd left on me. So, to keep his reputation safe, he agreed to the divorce.

On the condition that I would never leave Stratford, so that Paige would be close to him.

So that *I* would always be in reach.

My heart squeezed. Growing up, Gabby and I were all each other had. With Mom in the Army and us moving every few years, we had grown up changing schools like most girls changed which Barbie doll was their favorite. After Mom retired, we came to Stratford.

I was a junior in high school at the time, and Gabby was just starting college after taking some time off. For a while, we called this town home, but when Gabby got into nursing school in Texas, our parents moved with her — mostly because Mom had been offered a full-time Army Policy Analyst position in Austin.

Under different circumstances, I would have gone, too.

But when it all happened, I was newly married, starting a new life of my own.

And I was pregnant.

That's another thing they don't tell you — how when you start a family of your own, the family you grew up with suddenly shifts to second place.

"So, how was your first day?"

I blinked, shaking free from my thoughts as I shoved a bite of our cheap dinner in my mouth. "It was... something."

"That bad, huh?"

"Not bad," I clarified, taking another bite and speaking around it. "Just... interesting. It felt good to be at work, to feel that part of my identity come back, but... well, let's just say my boss gave me a less-than-stellar welcoming."

My sister's voice hardened, and I could picture her brows folding together. "Who do I need to kill?"

I chuckled. "Easy, no need to bust out the nunchucks," I teased, referring to the time in sixth grade when she'd handed a kid his ass after he tried to put his hand up her skirt. She'd ripped his stupid toy nunchucks from his other hand and knocked him upside the head with them. "He was just predictably sexist with the intro, that's all."

"What do you mean?"

I rolled my eyes. "He went on about how he's worried about me being the new trainer because I'm a woman. He thinks he'll have trouble with the team being distracted."

"He said that?"

"In not so many words, yes."

"Well... don't hate me, sis, but... he's probably not wrong."

I sighed. "I know he's not, but the point is that it shouldn't be *me* he talks to about that. It's not my fault I'm a woman, and I shouldn't be held responsible for the teenage boys on his team getting distracted."

"Did he say anything to them about it?"

I shifted, poking at the noodles in my bowl until I had five of them stacked on my fork. "Well, yes, actually. He did. He set his expectations for how they should treat me before practice."

"Was he condescending then?"

I frowned. "No," I admitted. "Actually, he spoke about my accolades, and said they were lucky to have me."

"Wow," she said, mockingly. "What a jerk."

"*Anyway*," I said, ignoring her. "After that, it went fine. No injuries during practice, but I did meet with a few of the players who had injuries last season, to see where they're at in recovery. And I got my tables all set up. You wouldn't believe the equipment they have, Gabby," I added. "It's like a professional football team rather than a high school one."

"Well, that's what happens when you win two state championships in a row." She paused. "Who's the head coach again? Anyone we know?"

I flushed, though I couldn't be sure why, and I was *damn* sure happy my sister couldn't see it. "Jordan Becker."

"Becker..." my sister repeated. "I don't think I knew him."

"He was in my grade, younger than you," I explained. "But, his dad is the one who died in the fire at the distillery."

"Oh, shit..."

I frowned. "Yeah."

"No, I mean, *yes*, that's terrible, but what I said *oh, shit* to is his head-shot." My sister whistled. "I just Googled him. Hot *damn*, sis. Your new boss is hotter than a Texas parking lot in July."

I snorted. "You're ridiculous. Although, I will say, you're not the only one who thinks so. You should have *seen* the Mom Parade at practice." I rolled my eyes, popping another bite of hamburger in my mouth as I thought back to practice that afternoon. "There's not even a reason for any of them to *be* at practice, but they're all right there in the bleachers, offering coach lemonade and telling him what a great job he's doing after every drill. One of them even dunked a towel into their ice chest and offered to put it on his neck."

Gabby laughed. "I don't blame them. Hell, I don't even have a kid and I'd find a way to fake it so I could be there to watch that man sweat."

"Gross."

"Don't act like you don't want to lick his chest."

"Again, gross," I said, but my cheeks flushed in betrayal. "He's my boss, Gab. And not that there are any official rules against it, but it's a *very* clear, unwritten rule that the head coach doesn't date anyone on his staff. Plus..." My voice faded, eyes finding my daughter through the sliding glass door. "You know my feelings on men. One psychopath in my life was enough. I have zero intentions of ever dating again." My voice faded. "And even if I did..."

Again, words were lost, but I knew Gabby understood. With Randy always around, watching me the way he did, the possibility of me dating anyone again was so close to impossible that I didn't even consider it.

He still felt like he owned me, and I knew better than anyone that if someone tried to play with his toy, they'd pay the price for it.

Inside, Paige took her own dishes to the sink and rinsed them, putting them in the dishwasher before she went back to continue watching the conference.

I smiled, the only piece of my heart left swelling at the sight. "It's just me and Paigey now."

My sister was quiet for a long while, and I knew she wanted to argue with me. She'd wanted me to join a dating website as soon as the divorce between me and Randall had been finalized. But she knew as much as I did that there was no use trying.

I was permanently broken, permanently turned off from love, and permanently happy being single.

"You know, you could go for full custody," she whispered. "Bring Paige here to be around her awesome aunt and amazing grandparents."

"In a normal situation like this, maybe," I conceded. "But, he's the Police Chief of a tiny map dot, Gab. Everyone loves him — including highly influential people, like Patrick Scooter, and the Mayor. You and I both know the power he has..."

She sighed, though it sounded more like the huff of a bull about to buck a cowboy off at the rodeo. "I hate him."

"That makes two of us."

"I have to get going," she said, a long pause hanging between us. "I love you, sis. Don't be too hard on the guys on the team. You're the first woman to be on the staff, in a small southern town, and in a sport dominated by men. Baby steps, okay?"

I smiled. "Okay. I love you, too, sis. Thanks for calling."

After she hung up, her words echoed in my thoughts, and I glanced once inside at Paige before I pulled up Google on my phone. I typed in my new boss's name, and when his stern face filled the screen — along with a Wikipedia article populating with all his stats — my stomach tightened.

Those eyes...

"Mom!"

I jumped, exiting out of the browser and shoving my phone in my pocket as my daughter bolted out into the yard.

"Can we go to the park and run drills?" she begged, holding up her football. "Pleeeease?"

"Maybe this weekend, okay? It's a school night."

She was tempted to pout, but knew better than to try that with me. Instead, she nodded. "Okay."

"Why don't you go run a bath and I'll braid your hair after."

Paige nodded, bounding back inside. My phone felt like a hot brick in my pocket, begging me to pick up where I left off, but I ignored it, taking my empty bowl inside to clean up the kitchen, instead.

As I ran the hot water, a pair of stormy eyes still burned in my mind.

Chapter Three

Jordan

Ten days blew by in a whirl, as they often did when the school year started. For me, it was always a blur of practice and plays and drills and tapes. It was school days filled with working my players in their weightlifting classes, and evenings spent getting them ready for the first game.

It almost seemed like I'd stepped in a time warp, because here it was, Friday night.

The first game of the season.

This was what I lived for — the smell of the turf, the energy of hungry athletes buzzing in the locker room before it exploded out onto the field, the hum of the crowd anticipating what will happen. It felt like coming home to me, pacing the sidelines as I watched my team, clipboard in hand and a piece of gum in my mouth for me to chew on when what I really wanted to do was scream like a maniac.

I had learned that trick after my first three games as head coach.

Still, tonight's game felt different than any game ever had before. Because as much as everything familiar and comfortable greeted me on that field, there was something else there, something quiet but menacing, soft but blatantly apparent.

Pressure.

The stadium lights felt like spotlights, all of them pointed at me as the residents of Stratford filled the bleachers. Everything in our town shut down on Friday nights during football season. You couldn't find a place open to get groceries or grab a bite to eat because customer or shop owner — everyone was right here.

I crossed my arms on the sideline, clipboard in hand as I watched the team warm up. My assistant coach and defensive coordinator were on oppo-site sides of our half of the field, running drills, while the Red Rock Raptors swarmed the other half. I watched them just as much as I watched my own team, wondering if they would be contenders this year. They had given us a run for our money last year, with a group of juniors growing stronger — juniors who were now seniors and ready to lead their team to victory.

"Your boys look good out there tonight, coach."

I smiled at the familiar voice coming from behind me, and when I turned, I was greeted by a crooked yellow grin.

"Let's hope they play good, too, eh?"

Elijah Braxton was the town fixer-upper. Any kind of maintenance job that needed done, he could do it. He knew plumbing, electricity, woodwork, and more. Whether it was a broken refrigerator or a tree falling on your house — he was the man to call. He was known for being a bit of a grump — except for when it was Friday night football, of course — and a bit crazy, too. He always wore the same fedora hat, one he'd owned presumably all his life, and he talked to himself while he worked.

Perhaps what *really* made him crazy was that he only charged what the person could afford for his services. If you were elderly, poor, or just going through a rough time, you could pay him in hugs and a fresh batch of snickerdoodle cookies, and he'd still fix your toilet.

He was a man with gumption, and I happened to like him very much.

I first met him when I played on this very field in high school. It was hard for me not to notice him, especially since there were very few black residents in our small town. I knew, because I was one of them, and especially as a child, I'd noticed the difference in my appearance compared to the other kids I played with in town.

And compared to the kids I watched on television.

And compared to pretty much every source of my cultural exposure.

I didn't know my exact genetic makeup, didn't know who my parents were or why my skin was caught somewhere between being as black as Eli's and as white as my adopted father's, but I knew I was different.

For a long time, I felt caught in the middle of something I couldn't quite put a name to.

I stopped trying to figure it out somewhere in my late twenties, deciding instead to just be me and let others put labels on me if they felt it was necessary.

I didn't need labels.

And I wouldn't live within the confines of them, either.

The point was that since the day I first saw him there, Eli had stood out in a sea of white in those bleachers. He was a little like me in a way that most other residents in that town weren't.

Ever since I'd been head coach, he'd been at every home game, and some of the away games, too. He was one of our biggest fans, and he was never shy to tell me what he thought of the team — or of my coaching.

The way our stadium was set up, there was a fence separating the track and field from the stands. Eli stood behind it, elevated just above me.

A few of my players' mothers interrupted me and Eli before he could say anything else, offering me words of *good luck* and inviting me to their house for a party after the game. I politely declined, and rolled my eyes at Eli's knowing smirk before turning back to my players.

We were the Stratford High Wild Cats, and Eli always called the moms who blatantly hit on me *The Stratford High Cougars*.

"Lost quite a few seniors last year," Eli said when we were alone again, his eyes on the field now. "You think you got boys who can step up and take their spots?"

"We'll find out soon enough," I murmured, leaning against the gate that separated the bleachers from the field.

He hung his arms over the top railing. "You got a lot of eyes on you this year."

I nodded, and to anyone who looked at me, I imagined I appeared calm and collected.

Inside, I was a tornado.

"Hope you did a better job working with the offensive line in this first week of practice," he said. "Even I could have sacked Rodgers in that first game last season."

I smirked, because this was always Eli's game. He'd play nice, give a few compliments or offer up a few generalized statements, and then he'd tell me what he was really thinking.

"Well, I tell you what. If Rodgers gets sacked tonight, consider yourself welcome to practice Monday morning to whip that O-line into shape."

"Famous last words, Coach."

I smiled over my shoulder at him, tapping the top of the fence twice before I made my way toward the water table. Sydney stood beside it with her thumbnail between her teeth, a giant bag of athletic training supplies on the ground at her feet. Her eyes were like cars on the highway, speeding back and forth, watching the players on the field like she was ready to grab that bag at her feet and sprint onto the green at a moment's notice.

She'd worked hard over the past week and a half, especially when one of our linebackers had a pretty severe turf toe injury. And, blessedly and most importantly, she'd stayed out of my way. Sydney showed up, did her job, worked with the guys who needed her and handled the ones who gave her a hard time without needing help from me.

I knew the twins on our defense — Bradley and Boone — would give her hell. They were by far the most girl crazy and tended to feed off each other as the team clowns. But, to her credit, Sydney was unfazed by them, and in just ten days she had a reputation with the team.

She was knowledgeable. They could trust her with their injuries.

What's more, they respected her — and they knew she took no shit.

I still felt a little guilty for the way I'd welcomed her onto the team, but it seemed to be all but forgotten between us. We didn't necessarily apologize or forgive, but we'd had civil conversation, and we'd done our jobs in the vicinity of each other for a week and a half now.

We were finding a rhythm, even if it was a little off tune to start.

"Nervous?" I asked, grabbing one of the plastic cups on the table and filling it with Gatorade.

"No," she answered quickly. "Just alert."

Her eyes never left the field, and I smiled, leaning against the table beside her as I took a drink. "I'm a little nervous."

Sydney snapped her attention to me, all but breaking her neck in the process. "You? Really?"

I nodded. "If you tell anyone, I'll deny it and fire your ass."

"You can't fire me," she shot back, but a small smile bloomed on her lips. "But I won't tell."

"Thanks," I said, watching our players on the field. "Two state championships... it's a lot to live up to. I mean, look around us," I said, but my eyes stayed put. "The entire town is here, and it's only the first game and already scouts are showing up, too."

Sydney glanced at the bleachers behind us. "It is a lot," she admitted. "The energy is palpable."

"Just wait until kick off."

Sydney looked at me, and my eyes found hers, and for a moment, it felt like an olive branch had been extended between us. In the lights from the stadium, her soft brown eyes were aglow, and I let them suck me in for the briefest second.

The corner of her mouth curled, and mine did, too.

"GIVE 'EM HELL, COACH!"

A roar of applause erupted behind us, and we both turned to find my brothers, Noah and Logan, banging on the fence and hooting and hollering like they were teenagers instead of grown ass men. They'd fired up the section of fans in the bleachers behind them, too. I smiled, waving to Mom as she passed behind them, shaking her head with flushed cheeks at her outlandish boys.

"I see the Becker brothers haven't grown up a bit," Sydney commented.

"We have too big of a reputation to live up to for all that."

She chuckled. "It does look like they're settling down, though. Bet that feels kind of weird, huh?"

I followed Sydney's gaze to where Noah and Logan were leading their significant others up the bleacher steps. Noah held Ruby Grace's hand — the hand that donned an engagement ring, and in just a few months would have a wedding band on it, too. Logan had his arm around Mallory, holding her at the hip, as if he was afraid she'd tumble backward down the steps if he let her go. I had a feeling it was the growing bump of a belly she had that made him so protective.

And though he wasn't there that night, I knew my youngest brother, Mikey, was building a new life with Kylie in New York City in that very moment, too.

"Yeah, I guess it is a little," I admitted, voice soft as I watched them. "But, they're happy. That's all that matters to me."

A longing for something unattainable sent an ache through my chest, and the way Sydney's eyebrows tugged together where she watched me, I was afraid she'd somehow seen it.

"What about you?" I asked, turning the attention away from me. "You have family here?"

Her eyes shot somewhere behind me, but then she pulled them back to the players on the field. "Yeah."

It was all she said — no explanation of who or where. But when I glanced over my shoulder, I didn't need another word. My eyes connected with our Chief of Police — Randall Kelly — who stood at the far edge of the bottom bleacher.

And their daughter stood next to him, her eyes wide with glee as she watched the field.

Randy didn't look as pleased. He wore a permanent frown, and his uniform, the black threads over bullet-proof vest and shiny gold badge over his heart giving him an air of arrogance and power. He watched me as if I had somehow offended him, so I offered a nod in acknowledgement.

He didn't nod back.

My brothers and I had our shares of run-ins with the law in this town — mostly over stupid bar fights or fights between ourselves. We were a rowdy crew, I'd admit that, but I'd never had Randy stare at me like that before.

Behind me, a whistle blew, and the sideline flooded with everyone but our team captain, who was already jogging to the fifty-yard line for the coin toss.

With one last glance at the town that came to watch us, I jogged out, too.

The coin was flipped.

And the game began.

• • •

Three minutes before the end of the third quarter and our team down by three, my star running back limped off the field with what looked like a hamstring injury after a long run.

My heart tripled its pace as he hobbled in, and I sent in our backup for the next play. There wasn't enough time on the clock to assess his damage before the next play would take place. I nodded to Coach Pascucci, my assistant, letting him know to take over as I rushed to where Sydney was already bent over our player.

"Where'd you feel the pull?" she asked as I bent down next to her. She ran her hand along the hamstring of his left leg, which was in a bent position, cleat planted on the grass. "Here?"

He shook his head, swallowing as he reached down with his own hand and brushed the inside of his thigh.

As in, his fucking groin.

"I think it's more... here," he said, and his eyes flicked to mine before he laid back again, closing them altogether in a wince of pain.

I narrowed my gaze, standing again with a shake of my head. "Parker, get your ass up and get ready to go back on that field."

His shoulders deflated as he looked up at me, but before he could speak, Sydney's head whipped around, her eyes on me like lasers.

"Excuse me?" she hissed. "He will do no such thing, not until I properly assess the injury in the locker room."

"He's fine," I growled, barely glancing at her before I was barking at him again. "Parker. Up. Now."

"Do not move a muscle," Sydney said to him through her teeth, then she stood, jutting her chin up to face me. "I'm taking him back to do a full examination. If he's fine, I'll—"

"He *is* fine," I snapped. "He's being a smart ass and faking it to get time on your table. And he *will* pay for it in practice," I added, glaring down at a shrinking Parker.

"How do you know he's faking it?" she challenged. "It could be serious. It could be a strain or a stress fracture or—"

"You're kidding, right?" I folded my arms as I assessed her. "He limped off the field in a way that indicated a hamstring injury, now he's pointing to his groin." I blinked. "His *groin*, Sydney."

"Groin injuries are common in football," she pointed out, flatly. "I'm not clearing him to play again until I do a full assessment. So how about I do my job, and you do yours. Game's not over, in case you didn't realize."

I blew out a breath like a dragon, so hot I was surprised little flames didn't shoot out of my nose, too. But Sydney didn't allow me to argue further. Instead, she signaled for two of our players on the bench to help her, and as a group, they got Parker off the ground and on his feet, supporting him to the locker room.

I watched them go, grinding the gum in my mouth between my teeth before I let out a growl and snatched my clipboard off the bench in time for the next play.

Everything went downhill from there.

We were down by three when Parker limped off the field, and it was as if our offense couldn't get their shit together once he was gone. He was a natural leader, a key player, and without him, we suffered.

It didn't matter how hard the defense worked to keep the Raptors' score from climbing higher, our offense couldn't score. Hell, they couldn't even get us close enough for our kicker to get us into overtime with a field goal. I watched the clock run down on the last minute in the fourth quarter without Parker or Sydney returning to the field, and when the final whistle blew, I saw red.

We'd lost our first game.

At home, nonetheless.

It took every ounce of willpower I had to make it through shaking hands with the Raptors's coach and each of the players on their team before I was sprinting toward the locker room, ignoring the calls of my name and unsolicited advice from the bleachers. The team was still gathering their equipment off the sideline to limp their sorry, losing asses into the locker room when I pushed through the doors, full steam ahead until I was standing inside Sydney's office.

"We lost," I said, waiting until she brought her gaze to mine before I continued. "So, tell me. What's his big injury?"

Sydney blinked like she was bored, checking something off the clipboard in her hand. It was a bad time for me to realize that the red of our team polo blazed against her dark skin, or that the leggings she'd paired with it hugged her in all the right places, but I realized it.

And clearly, I wasn't the only one.

"He's fine," she said, checking something off on the clipboard before she set it on her desk. "I did my full assessment and had him work through a few exercises to make sure. He should be good to go for practice Monday."

"Well, isn't that great? He couldn't get back to finish out the game and get us a W, but at least he'll be okay for practice!"

I was blowing my top.

I was being irrational.

I knew it, but I couldn't stop it.

I was the calm one in my family, the sensible one out of all my brothers, no matter what was going on.

But when it came to football, my fuse was as short as my fingernails.

"Coach, this is my fault, not Sydney's," Parker said, raising his hand like he was in class. "I... you were right, I faked it. A few of the guys on the team dared me to. I waited until close to the end of the game because... well, I know we were down but... I guess I still thought we were going to win. I didn't think... I'm sorry."

Sydney's mouth popped open, and I couldn't help the smug smile that bloomed on my face.

Parker hung his head, staring at his hands in his lap as I stared a hole into his head. I *would* find out who made the stupid bet with him, and all parties would pay.

For now, I had a bigger fish to fry.

"Get out, Parker," I said simply, calmly — which should have scared him more than if I had yelled.

He glanced at Sydney apologetically, then back at me.

"*Out,*" I hissed through my teeth. "And you better enjoy your weekend, because this field is going to be your own personal hell on Monday."

I didn't have to look at him to put the fear of God in him. He tucked his tail between his legs and hobbled out of the training room, as if he really were injured, and all the while, I kept my smug gaze on Sydney.

She inhaled a stiff breath, closing her mouth like she'd just realized it'd been hanging open this entire time. When her eyes met mine, there wasn't an ounce of apology in them.

"Got anything to say for yourself?"

Her head popped back like I'd slapped her. "Um... you're welcome for doing my job?"

"Your job." I snorted. "I told you he was faking it."

"And I told *you* that until I did a full assessment, I wasn't able to say whether that was true or not."

"We *lost,* Sydney," I reminded her, taking a full step into her space. Her chest puffed, but I puffed mine right back. "Because of you babying one of our star players."

"This is not *my* issue," she shot back. "Do not blame your loss on me because your so-called *star player* thought winning a bet with his buddies was more important than playing tonight. I did my job, and I will not apologize for it."

I didn't realize she'd been walking toward me until our chests brushed, the heat of her breath hitting my nose as she glared up at me. Anger rang in my ears, my fists clenching at my sides as I glared back. Our chests heaved, neither of us backing down, both of us sure in our stances.

Sydney's dark hair was pulled into a sleek ponytail, leaving nothing to distract me from the depth of her dark eyes. Time stretched between us in an immeasurable way as I fell into those pools. Her breathing softened a little, and without warning, my gaze fell to her lips.

They were nude, and smooth, and even when they were flattened into a frown, they were still somehow plump and full. I let my eyes focus on those lips for longer than I meant to, longer than was appropriate, and when they parted slightly, a hot breath slipping between them to assault my senses, I ripped my gaze back to her eyes.

Her dark eyes watched me in a completely different way now.

The step back that I took next came too late, and with it, each of us drew in a long breath. The air in that training office felt heavy and wet, like it was liquid instead of oxygen, and suddenly, I felt I'd drown if I stayed even one minute longer.

I glanced at Sydney once more before I turned, storming out of her office with anger still rolling off me in plumes. It took me ten steps to clear the hallway and step into the locker room — where a team of thirty boys and three coaches watched me with weary eyes and their heads hung, waiting to hear what I had to say.

And oh, were they in for a mouthful.

Chapter Four

Jordan

My throat was sore, voice hoarse by the time I got to my mom's house. And when I slammed the door to my truck, still fuming as I made my way up the drive to Mom's front door, I was shocked to see Mary Scooter walking out of it.

Mary was Patrick's wife, and other than seeing her playing her role as the dutiful wife behind him all these years I'd grown up in Stratford, I didn't know much about her. One thing I *did* know was that since the fire, she hadn't set foot near my mother — probably because Mom was horrified that Mary didn't take her side on it.

Patrick, Mary, Dad, and Mom used to run in the same circle in high school. They were close friends, from what I'd picked up in passing conversations between Mom and Dad, but somewhere along the way, that had changed.

Still, Mary knew my Dad didn't smoke, yet she'd looked at my mom with the same sympathetic eyes the entire town did after the fire — like she felt sorry for her, like Mom was in denial.

Mary's eyes looked like she'd been crying, and she sniffed, nodding at me as she passed. "Jordan," she said.

"Mary," I replied, still confused.

"Good game tonight. Sorry about the loss, but you'll get them next time."

I forced as close to a smile as I could muster, and then she got in her car I hadn't even noticed parked among the others, and she was gone.

Mom was on the porch, and she pulled me in for a hug with a knowing look as soon as I was standing with her.

"Tough loss," she said.

I nodded. "What was Mary Scooter doing here?"

Mom's expression was unreadable, but she patted my shoulder — reaching up high, since she was so short in comparison — urging me inside. "Oh, no reason, really. She's just going through some things. We used to be best friends, you know."

"I know, but..."

"It's nothing," she assured me. "And please, don't say anything to Mallory about her being here. Okay?"

Mary was Mallory's mom — and ever since the big fallout between her and her family after she and Logan made their relationship official, they hadn't talked. At least, not to my knowledge.

Even when Mallory told them she was pregnant, there had been no reciprocation.

I nodded, though I didn't like keeping secrets. For Mom, I'd do anything. And if she was saying it was nothing to worry about, I believed her.

We made our way inside, Mom heating up leftovers from dinner while I made a drink. Everyone was gathered at the house — Noah and Ruby Grace, Logan and Mallory — but thankfully, everyone was leaving me alone for now.

It was a family tradition of ours, to have dinner at least once a week at Mom's, and any time that dinner fell on a Friday night during football season, they'd have dinner without me, come watch the game, and then we'd all gather here again after the game for me to heat up leftovers and for all of us to catch up.

Tonight, though, my appetite for anything that wasn't whiskey was nonexistent.

Later, Mom stared at the untouched plate of food in front of me, worry in her eyes as I sipped on the old fashioned I'd made. It was a bit strong, but already I felt myself cooling off, my temper settling.

It was me, Noah, and my mom at the table. Logan and the girls were in the living room, all three of them watching a documentary on Mars that Logan had been waiting on to air for weeks. I watched the screen from the dining room table in a numb state of being, all the adrenaline draining from my body to leave me feeling completely wiped.

"So," Noah said, sipping on his own glass of whiskey. He swirled the ice cubes around in it before setting it back on the table. "You wanna talk about tonight?"

Noah was the oldest of my brothers, but still four years younger than me. I remembered being wide-eyed and fascinated by him growing in our mother's stomach, back when I was the only kid in the Becker household. I had no idea what would come with being an older brother, only that my father had told me I would be responsible for him, that I would have to look after him, protect him, have his back.

And I had, from the very minute he was born.

Noah and I had our differences, though, and of all my brothers — I'd fought with him the most. He was bullheaded and always felt like he had something to prove. Especially after Dad died, he was hell-bent on being *man of the house*. I had to literally wrestle him to the ground and kick his ass for him to calm down and see that we *all* had that title — and that it would take the entire team.

He was also the only one of us who really looked like Dad.

He had the same blue eyes, the same reddish-tone to his bronze skin. He was stout like Dad had been, where Logan and Michael were both lean and tall. They had Mom's eyes, and her smile, too.

"Not particularly," I answered after a minute.

Mom reached across the table and squeezed my hand. "It's one loss. One loss does not a season make."

I softened, squeezing her hand in return before I forced myself to take a bite of dinner. I knew if I didn't at least make an attempt, I'd break my mother's heart, and if anyone had a soft spot in me — it was her.

"I agree," I told her, taking a bite of sweet potato. "But, we should have won. We *would* have won, in my opinion, had a certain situation been avoided."

"You talking about Parker getting hurt?" Noah asked.

"He wasn't hurt."

Mom frowned. "He limped off the field. I saw the new trainer take him back to the locker room."

I ground my teeth together, forgoing my next bite and reaching for my glass, instead. "I know. But I saw it in his eyes even before he was taken back. He wasn't hurt, he just wanted to be rubbed down by Sydney. And like a fool, she fell for it."

Noah and my mom exchanged glances.

"I know I sound like an asshole," I admitted. "But, I told her not to take him back, to put him back on the field, and she refused. She dug her heels in like a stubborn woman."

"Jordan Solomon," Mom chastised.

"Sorry, Mom," I said quickly. "Male or female, it was a stubborn move and a blatant disregard for authority. She took him back, anyway, insisting she needed to assess the full injury, and then after the game, wanna know what happened?" I grinned, though I was far from happy about it. "He admitted it. A few of the players had dared him to fake an injury to get her to rub down his groin, and she fell for it."

Noah snickered and Mom swatted him across the chest.

"This is nothing to laugh about. First of all, that's awful that they did that to her. But, Jordan," she said, shaking her head as her eyes found mine. "Sydney doesn't know these boys like you do. If Parker had truly been hurt and she let him go back into the game, that would have been on *her*."

Mom looked older in that moment, as if the story I'd just told had somehow aged her. I knew the reality was that the last ten years had — ten years of raising four rowdy boys without her life partner to help. She'd recently cut her hair even shorter, the edges of it curling over her ears, and almost all of the soft brown was replaced by a silvery-gray. Her eyes were still a bright hazel, though — a swirl of green and gold.

"It's kind of funny," Noah argued after a moment.

"Regardless of whether it's funny or awful, it cost us the game. And I hear what you're saying, Mom, I really do," I said earnestly. "But, I have to figure out how to handle it and establish my expectations when I walk into that locker room on Monday."

"Hey now," Mom said, pointing her finger into my chest. "You don't know if you would have won that game had that Parker kid gone back out onto the field. For all you know, he could have fumbled the ball and made the score worse. There were other errors made far before he got hurt, like Rodgers throwing that interception that gave the Raptors their first touchdown. And *that* was probably caused by your offensive line not giving him time to make a smart throw."

A genuine smile found my face for the first time that night, because I could remember a time when Mom knew nothing about football and couldn't have cared less what the score was at the end of the night. But when I told her as a junior in high school that I thought I wanted to become a coach, she took a serious interest, and she was at every game, learning the rules, cheering me on, and — on my favorite nights — giving coach an earful of what she thought should be done to win.

Mom was our biggest fan, no matter what we did. And I knew it was a rare and special gift.

I sighed, still smiling, because her words were sinking in as they always seemed to do. "Do you ever get tired of being right?" I asked her.

She smirked. "Never."

Noah ran his finger over the edge of his glass, brows furrowed as he thought. "You know, I see where your frustration comes from. You saw what Sydney didn't see, because — like Mom said — you know those boys better than she does. Keep in mind, this is her first year on the team."

"It's also her first year back at work after being a stay-at-home mom for years," Mallory added, joining us at the table.

"What's wrong? Not interested in how we got a robot to Mars?" Noah asked.

Mallory rested her hand on her small, but rounding, belly. "All the orange makes me nauseous."

"Trust me, sweetie. *Everything* is going to make you nauseous for about another month, at least," Mom chimed in. "Let me make you some tea."

Before Mallory could argue, Mom was already up and in the kitchen.

"Seriously, though," Mallory said, her attention on me. "I don't know if you know Randy Kelly, but he's a prick. And she was *married* to him. Don't you remember that she was one of the smartest girls in school? She was *years* ahead of me and even I remember her sweeping the award ceremonies. She already had college credits when she graduated high school, and she graduated with her master's degree at twenty-two."

"What are you saying?" Noah asked.

Mallory shrugged. "I'm just saying. She wanted a career, and yet she never had one. She got pregnant before she ever had the chance to be a trainer like she'd wanted to be. And now, she's finally working, finally has the chance to prove herself — and all that after a divorce where you guys know as well as I do that she was painted as the villain." Mallory's eyes caught mine just as Logan came up behind her and squeezed her shoulders. She placed a hand over his. "Wouldn't *you* feel like you had something to prove — not just to the team full of boys you work with, and not just to this town, but to *yourself*?"

It wasn't a question she expected me to answer, and thanks to Mom delivering tea, I didn't have to. Ruby Grace joined us at the table and the conversation turned fully away from me and onto the upcoming wedding.

I sat quietly the rest of the evening, chewing on what Mallory had said, considering Sydney in a way I hadn't until that moment. I'd known she was married to Randy, of course, and that she had a kid. But I'd never considered the sacrifices she'd made — just like the ones my own mom had — nor had I considered what she must feel like as the only woman on a staff of men.

I'd pointed out that she could be a distraction, and now, I wanted to laugh at myself because I realized that was far from news to her.

She *knew* she'd be dealing with boys, that she'd be proving herself to men, that she'd be fighting an uphill battle from the moment she walked through those locker room doors.

And I'd been the General of the opposition.

More than that, what Mom and Noah had said sank in more and more the longer I sat there sipping on my whiskey. Sydney *didn't* know those boys as well as I did. And if Parker really had been hurt, she would have been responsible for letting him back on the field — even if it had been my call.

I sighed, disappointed in myself, and more than that, frustrated with where to go from here. I understood why Sydney took Parker back to do a full assessment. He was limping. He was claiming he was hurt. He was showing all the signs of not being okay to go back onto the field. It didn't matter that he was faking, to a responsible and professional athletic trainer, he was hurt.

And had it been our previous trainer, Perry, who'd done what Sydney had tonight, I would have appreciated him taking his job and the safety of our players seriously.

I'd judged her too harshly, and placed blame on her for something that was entirely Parker's fault.

And, maybe, partially mine, too.

"It'll all work itself out, Son," Mom said, leaning down to kiss my cheek as she passed by me and into the kitchen. I could tell when I glanced up at her that she saw the warring thoughts in my head even when I didn't speak them out loud. "Now, eat up. You're not allowed to leave that table until that plate is empty."

She patted my shoulder and continued into the kitchen, and I stared down at my full plate of lukewarm food as if it could somehow solve my problems.

I knew I, alone, was responsible for that.

I just had to figure out how.

• • •

Later that night, home alone with the glow of my laptop screen the only light in my living room, I felt another rush of adrenaline.

It had been more than a month of entries in Dad's journal since he'd mentioned the Last Will and Testament he'd found while cleaning Robert J. Scooter's office. Every night, I'd translated an entry from Latin to English, just to be disappointed that it spoke only of the new branding initiative or some other boring board discussion. It was frustrating, and more than one night of work on the journal had left me feeling deflated, like I was wasting my time looking for something that didn't exist.

But that Friday night, knowing I wasn't ready to sleep, I'd translated two more entries.

And what I found in the last one stole the last shred of hope I'd been holding onto that I'd get any sleep at all.

Something has been eating at me.

It's been over a month since I found Robert's will. I should have told Patrick about it, but I didn't. The truth is, I haven't told anyone — not even my wife.

The scary part is that I'm not sure why.

All I know is something is telling me to hold onto it, and — against every moral code I'm built on — I'm considering reading it.

I know it would be wrong. I know what is inside that sealed envelope is private and important. I should hand it over to his family, over to Patrick for him to read with their lawyer.

But... curiosity is eating me alive.

And something else.

It's hard to explain, which may be why I've kept it all to myself, but... I feel drawn to this document, like I found it for a reason.

It's as if a ghost is whispering in my ear.

But maybe it's just the devil.

Chapter Five

Sydney

It was an awful thing, to look around the park in search of blunt objects that could knock my ex-husband out, but it was all I could do in that moment.

It was all I could focus on to get me through the bi-weekly bullshit parade I had to endure with him, where he told me all the ways I'd fucked up by leaving him, and I sat there and pretended to listen, all the while counting down the minutes until he was gone and it was just me and Paige again.

I longed for sole custody of my daughter just as much as I hoped it would never happen. I never wanted to have to speak to Randy again. I wished so badly to leave him in my rearview mirror as a mistake I wished I'd never made.

But the truth was, I wouldn't even if I could.

Regardless of what we had been through, if it weren't for him, my daughter wouldn't exist — and I couldn't imagine a life without her.

I also knew it would *kill* her to be told she'd never see her father again, because as much as he was a class-A prick to me, he was a damn good father to her and always had been.

And so, twice a week, we met in a public space to trade Paige back and forth, and I endured my ex-husband's crap in the name of my daughter.

"Mayor Barnett approved a nine-percent raise for me," Randy bragged, puffing out his chest as he assessed my reaction.

Of which, there was none.

"I knew he would, of course," Randy continued, eyes skirting over the park a bit as if he was still on duty before they found me again. "I mean, after all the trouble he'd found himself in with the Scooters... all the drama with his daughter not marrying that politician..." Randy clicked his tongue. "It's been a mess to clean up."

I blinked, tracing my ex's features and remembering a time when I found him attractive. I could close my eyes and go back in time to high school, to the older, more-popular boy noticing me. And though it was a bit foggy now, I could still remember when he'd flash that smile of his — a dimple on each cheek — and I'd melt into a puddle on the tile floor. I used to look into those eyes and find safety and warmth. I used to run to those arms bulging out of his uniform as if they were put on this Earth only to protect me and hold me and make me feel loved.

I used to look into those green eyes and see my soulmate. I used to run my hands through that dark, coarse hair and get so turned on I could barely wait to get him home and undressed.

There was a time when I didn't even notice that his skin was white where mine was brown, a time when I thought it didn't matter.

Now, when I looked at that man, I didn't see a man at all.

I saw a monster.

Randy had never been obtuse in the years he abused me. The times he did hit me were few and far between, and usually spawned by a fight that I could easily look back on later and say I'd played a part in. It was the control he'd exercised over me that had been the real abuse, and my skin crawled the longer I stood next to him, knowing that as free as I felt, I'd never truly be free of that control he had.

"I'm sure it has been," I finally responded. "Especially since the police department is having *such* a hard time shutting down Patrick Scooter's little underground casino. Seems like if y'all could just do that, all of this mess would be gone." I tapped my finger to my lips. "But I'm sure it's not that easy, though, huh?"

Randy's mouth flattened. I was mocking him, and he knew it. My ex-husband was so elbow-deep in the dirty political shit of this town that he had proverbial flies hovering around him in a cloud — and it had been that way since he first joined the department.

It was always my theory for why he'd moved up so quickly in rank.

They knew he'd play dirty for them.

Patrick Scooter was the son of the founder of the whiskey distillery that Stratford, Tennessee, was built on. His father, Robert, had apparently been a stand-up guy. But Patrick? Well, I had my opinions about how he ran his business — how he ran this entire *town*. And the saddest part was that he didn't work alone, because he *couldn't* work alone. If Mayor Barnett and my ex-husband would have joined forces, they could have easily taken him down.

But to them, money and reputation talked.

Everything else was null and void.

"You know, it's a shame we're not together anymore," Randy said. "We could finally get that boat you've always wanted, take Paige out to the lake for long weekends in the summer..."

"Yep, it's sure too bad," I said, not feeling bad *at all*. If Randy should have known anything by now, it was that his money didn't mean a damn thing to me. I'd even told the judge I didn't want alimony, though it was owed to me. All I asked for was child support — and even *that* was nothing, in the grand scheme of things.

"How's your little *job* going?" he asked next, changing the subject away from his unethical nature. "I heard you pulled a kid out of the game for no reason and that's why the team lost last night."

I resisted the urge to grind my teeth together or scream or shove him backward so hard that he hit his ass right on the pavement. Instead, I blinked, took a long breath, and smiled.

"Parker is one of our best running backs. It was unfortunate that he was injured in the third quarter, and I'm sure the team missed him once he was gone, but his injury was one that needed closer assessment before he could be cleared to play again. As for why we lost, I have my own opinions about that, but I recommend you talk to Coach. He's the expert."

I chuckled internally at my sass on that last comment, but when I turned to my ex, he was watching me with disdain.

Randy *hated* that I divorced him, but I knew he hated even *more* that I was working. When I got pregnant, he made it very clear that I was expected to stay home and take care of Paige and the house. *They* were my job, now. It didn't matter that I had a passion for school, for learning, for the human anatomy and the way we push our bodies past their limits in athletics. It didn't matter that I'd already had an internship at the hospital two towns over, or that there was a junior college baseball team talking to me about coming on as their athletic trainer after Paige was born.

Honestly, *I* didn't matter to him — not really. He'd made me feel that way, made me feel precious and special and doted on, like I was his entire world. The moment I said yes to being his wife and that ring was slipped onto my finger, his true colors came out.

And I was already pregnant.

I shook off the ghosts threatening to join us in that park, turning my attention to where Paige was asking yet another little boy if he wanted to play catch with her. She held her football hopefully, her eyes wide.

"Oh, trust me, I plan on talking to Jordan. I'm sure this whole town does," Randy replied. "Last night's game was a mess, and if he has any hope of bringing another championship home, he's got a lot of work to do."

"Mmm," I answered, exhausted by trying to be nice to the man who'd been my own personal hell for years. My eyes flicked to where a gaggle of women were watching me and Randy more carefully than they were their kids, and I knew without a doubt they were gossiping about the divorce, likely painting me as the villain this town wanted to believe I was.

How could anyone leave sweet Randy Kelly?

He's such a great officer, and an amazing father.

She had nothing going for her. She was lucky to have him.

Why is she even staying in Stratford if she doesn't want to be with him?

But they didn't know me.

They knew nothing.

"Well, thanks for meeting up," I said dismissively. "I'll text you on Wednesday after practice to figure out where you want to meet."

"I could just come by to pick Paige up," he offered.

"No."

He frowned. "I used to live there, too, you know. That's my house, too."

"Not anymore. Public places, Randy," I said, a warning in my eyes. "Court's orders."

An evil smirk bloomed on his face, like he knew something I didn't, but instead of revealing his secret, he just offered me a wave and headed toward his truck in the parking lot. That smirk of his was one I knew well, and it elicited a deep wave of chills that cooled me to the bones.

As soon as he pulled out of the lot, I took what felt like my first breath since he'd shown up. My body was always tense when he was near, senses on full alert — as if I might need to run or fight at any given moment. I rubbed the back of my neck with a sigh, turning to find Paige on the playground.

When I did find her, my body tensed right back up.

"Shit," I said out loud, already jogging toward where she was standing at the opposite edge of the park. She still held tight to her football, but instead of pestering some kid her own age to play catch with her, she was talking animatedly to a very tall, very shirtless, very muddy Jordan Becker.

He wore an amused smile as he listened to my daughter, huge biceps crossed over his bare chest. His eyes flicked to me when I was ten yards away, and he smiled even wider before he turned his attention back to Paige.

"... You know what I mean? And, don't even get me started on the cornerback. The twin. What's his name?"

"Boone Parson."

"Parson!" Paige said, snapping her fingers together just as I came to a stop beside her. She glanced up at me with a grin. "Hey, Mama." Then, her attention was right back on Coach. "So, yeah, Parson. Does he butter his hands before the game? Because *honestly,* there were two times during the game last night where he could have had an interception if he'd just held onto the ball. *Two times,*" she repeated, holding up her fingers in a peace sign as if it wasn't sinking in yet. "Can you imagine what that might have meant for the final score?"

"Paige Marie, what on Earth are you doing?" I asked, grabbing her hand in mine until she looked up at me. "After all the *stranger danger* drills we've had, and you run up to a grown man on the playground?"

Paige's face screwed up in confusion. "Coach isn't a stranger," she argued, looking at Jordan before she glanced back up at me with her hand stretched toward him. "It's *Coach.*"

I pursed my lips — my classic *Mom Look* — and Paige shrunk an inch.

"Yeah, Sydney," Jordan said, tapping his chest with both hands. "I'm Coach. I'm not a stranger."

"You do not know Jordan personally," I said to my daughter, ignoring Jordan completely — mostly because he was still *very* shirtless and I did not know how I felt about that. "I understand that he feels safe because he is in a position of power in a sport that you love, but you still need to be safe, okay? You do not run up to an adult that is not your family without talking to me first. Understand?"

Paige dropped her gaze to her sneakers. "Yes, ma'am."

My heart ached a little at the sight, mom guilt sneaking in as it always did. I grabbed her shoulders and squeezed, moving her in front of me. "Now, go ahead and finish telling Coach how to make the team better."

Paige threw her head back, grinning up at me as Jordan barked out a laugh. For the next ten minutes, I listened to my daughter give every opinion she had on virtually every position on the team, as well as the plays that were run and the errors that were made in last night's game.

I had to fight back laughter when she said things like *buttered his hands* and *couldn't block to save his life*, knowing full well that she picked those phrases up from watching player discussions on ESPN. And when she struggled for the right words, Jordan helped her through them, suggesting what he thought she was trying to say. I knew she'd be cataloguing this conversation, adding it all to her football talk arsenal.

When she finally paused for air, I told her to go find someone to play with while I talked to Jordan, and that we were going to head home for lunch soon.

Like a bullet, she was off.

Jordan and I watched her sprint to the jungle gym, and I hung my hands on my hips, shaking my head. "I would apologize, but I love that little girl — quirks and all."

Jordan chuckled. "I would have been offended if you did apologize. That was the best football conversation I've had in years."

I smiled, glancing over my shoulder at him. The minute our eyes met, I remembered all too well the last time they had — when we were chest to chest and breathing fire at each other in the locker room, and when his eyes had stared at my lips...

I swallowed, but immediately after that tightness in my throat, I remembered what he'd said, how he'd blamed the entire loss on me. Judging from Randy's comment, the entire town now thought the same thing.

I frowned, clearing my throat before I turned back toward the playground. "Well, I better—"

"She said she wants to play," Jordan interjected before I could excuse myself. "Did you know that? That she wants to play football?"

I sighed, watching my daughter tuck the football into her chest and run with her hand out like she was blocking a defender. "I am very aware."

"You don't seem happy about it."

"I love that she's found something she's passionate about," I explained.

"But... as her mother, I worry. If you haven't noticed, there aren't many girls playing football, and there isn't a single female player in the NFL." I turned to him with a frown. "How the hell do you tell your nine-year-old daughter that her dream of playing football professionally has practically zero chance of ever happening? How do you tell her that the sport she loves is *a man's sport* and she should try something else, like basketball or softball? And, that even if she *does* try one of those and happens to fall in love with it, she *still* has a very slim chance of ever doing it professionally, because female sports are not revered in America the way male sports are?"

Jordan's face changed several times as he listened to me, and when I finally stopped talking, he shrugged. "You don't."

"What do you mean *I don't*?"

"I mean, you don't tell her any of that."

I scoffed, crossing my arms as I found Paige on the playground again. "You're not a parent. You don't understand."

"No, I'm not, and I agree that I don't fully understand what it's like to be in your shoes," he said, moving until he was in my view. I let my eyes flick to his, but the rest of him was so distracting that I ripped my gaze away as soon as it had connected. "But, what I *do* know is that there's nothing in this entire world like that feeling when you're a kid — that feeling where you can do anything, be anyone, if only you work hard enough. There may not be any precedent set, not yet, but does that mean she can't possibly be the one to set it?"

I chewed my lip, watching my daughter laugh uncontrollably as she played football.

By herself.

"What if she were the first girl to play high school football for Stratford? Or the first to play for an NFL team? Hell, right now, there are girls playing football in college. Who's to say one of *them* won't be the first to play professionally, and suddenly, those doors you thought would always be closed for Paige open up."

I allowed myself to face him fully then, searching his eyes and smirking a little when I found nothing but sincerity there. "You really believe all that, don't you?"

"I do," he said confidently. "If there's one thing I've learned from watching my mother endure what she has, it's that women are a hell of a lot stronger than anyone gives them credit for. And if Paige has her heart set on playing football?" He shrugged. "I would never be the one to tell her that she couldn't do it." He paused. "Mostly, because I hate being wrong, so I wouldn't take that chance."

I scoffed, shaking my head and letting out a long breath. "I'm scared," I admitted. "She asked me if I'd let her play next year. She turns ten in March, and for her birthday, all she wants is to go to football camp next summer and play little league."

"I think you should do it."

I swallowed, all my mom senses prickling to life under my skin. "What if she's bullied? What if she gets hurt? She's never done more than toss a football around with her father, and he hasn't even taught her much but how to line her fingers up on the laces." I looked at Jordan. "I want her to have an equal opportunity, but you and I both know that's not usually how it works."

Understanding settled in his eyes, and he nodded, lips pressed together. "Well... I understand your concern, and I can't say that none of that will happen. She will probably get bullied. And as someone who has played football all his life, I'd say chances are pretty good that she'll get hurt, too." He paused. "But, isn't that the risk we take with everything? If all we did was play it safe... would that really be living at all?"

I'd never heard so many words out of Jordan Becker's mouth than I did in that park that morning. He was always a man of quiet reserve, but it was like I'd found the secret to splitting him wide open.

Football.

My eyes trailed from where his gaze held me, down his chest, bare and glistening and smothered with a reddish, clay-like mud. His body was that of a Greek god — broad shoulders, narrow waist, calves that were bigger than my head. I used the mud as an excuse to catalogue every hard ridge and deep valley of him, all the while pretending like I wasn't suddenly aware of how hot the mid-morning August sun was.

Mud covered him in patches on his abdomen and arms, and almost every inch of the skin on his legs. It specked his cheeks and forehead, matted his short hair, even peppered the inner canals of his ears. I let my eyes stray to his basketball shorts, which I would *hate* to be responsible for cleaning, before I found his eyes again.

His stormy eyes.

"So... did you have to fight your way out of the jungle last night or something?" I cocked a brow.

Jordan chuckled, grabbing the back of his neck. "Uh... I like to run in the mud."

I blinked. "I'm sorry, you what?"

He nodded behind where I stood, and when I turned, I found his Bronco just as dirty as he was. There was a bucket of soapy water and a large sponge next to it, along with a hose from the park's free car wash station.

"I don't know," he said when I turned back to him. "I went mudding with a friend in high school when I got my first truck at sixteen, and I guess that's where it all started. I used to take my little brother a lot, and then I started going by myself. And... well... one time when I was out there, I got stuck, and I had to run back to the main pit to find someone to come dig me out. At first, it sucked. But, then... something happened. It was like... I don't know, like I had this moment of total clarity, of a complete clearing of my mind. It was just me and my body, and even though I was sore as hell the next day, it was like I'd taken a hit of some magical drug rather than gone for a run." He smiled sheepishly. "Been addicted ever since."

I smiled, and for a long pause, our eyes connected the way they had in the locker room the night before. Only this time, there was no anger, no accusation. We were standing in an open park, and yet somehow it felt like we were in the smallest room, like the oxygen we shared was limited.

"Sydney," he said, swallowing. "I—"

"Mommy!"

Before Jordan could say whatever it was he had to say, Paige flung her arms around me, panting after the sprint she'd just made toward us.

"I'm hungry," she said. "Can we go eat lunch?"

I glanced apologetically at Jordan, but he waved me off.

"We sure can. What do you feel like having?"

"Hmm..." she tapped her finger to her lips, just like I'd done earlier, and my heart swelled. I loved little moments like that, when I saw pieces of me in her. "Macaroni and cheese!"

"And how about some chicken nuggets, too," I offered.

"Yes!"

"And broccoli."

Her nose wrinkled, shoulders deflating. "*Broccoli,*" she repeated, dragging the word out. "Yuck."

I chuckled, tugging on one of her braids before I steered her toward our car. "Greens make you strong, baby girl." I tossed a look back at Jordan. "See you on Monday."

"See you," he said, then he hollered at Paige. "I'll be sure to get onto Parson for you, Paige."

"Tell him if he wants anyone to draft the defense team he plays on for their fantasy football team in the future, he better get his act together."

That made us all laugh, and with one final wave at my boss, Paige and I climbed in the car, leaving Jordan with his mud.

And me with a burning curiosity over what he was going to say before my daughter interrupted.

Chapter Six

Sydney

There was a different energy in the locker room that following Monday. Gone were the smiles and the rambunctious boys from the weeks prior. No one looked excited as they tugged on their cleats and wrapped their wrists. No one was telling a loud story about a girl or making a joke about another player's mom. Instead, each boy filed in quietly, one by one, and got dressed without much of a word to anyone else.

They weren't exactly *defeated*, either. They didn't seem sad. No, it was more of a determined silence, as if they knew before Coach said anything that they had a lot of work to do, and they'd all shown up ready to do it.

I found the quietness welcoming as I worked, helping players with their bandages and doing some soft tissue work on those who needed it. I even checked in on Parker, who was sheepish and blushing when I approached him. He apologized and seemed sincere in it, so I dismissed him, deciding to let Jordan determine what his punishment would be.

When Jordan finally made his way into the locker room to stand in the center, I found my usual corner, trying to all but disappear and just observe.

He wore a permanent frown that day, his eyebrows folding so low I wasn't sure he could see at all. The quietness somehow silenced altogether when he stood in the center of the room, as if everyone were afraid that even a sneaker squeak would set him off like a ton of missiles.

I expected him to roar and growl and put the fear of God into those boys. At the very least, I expected an epic pep talk like the one he'd given the first day we'd all walked into this place. Instead, he looked at his clipboard, flipping through pages with all eyes on him for what felt like an eternity before he lifted his gaze and said three simple words.

"On the field."

Immediately, there was a shuffle of cleats and pads and heads hung as the boys made their way outside. And I learned that afternoon what all of them already knew.

If coach was quiet, there would be pain.

Suicides. Burpees. Bear crawls. Gut busters. Snakes.

Every football player's most-hated drill was called on that day, and I watched from the sidelines with a grimace as those boys sweated and screamed and cried and fell and threw up and still, every time, they got up and got back to work.

Not a single one complained.

Not a single one asked to stop.

Jordan didn't say another word after those first three in the locker room. The other coaches led the torture, with Jordan on the sideline watching like a king over his subjects. When more than two hours had passed, he found my gaze on the sideline, and he must have seen the worry etched in my features because he finally blew the whistle that signaled the persecution to stop.

I breathed out a silent sigh of relief along with the boys, who all hit the ground in sync, panting and groaning and catching their breaths. Jordan didn't say another word before he was heading back toward the locker room, and slowly, the rest of the coaches and players did the same, shuffling in with their helmets in hand and their heads held a little higher than they had been on the way out.

When we were all settled in the locker room, I checked in with each group of boys, making sure no one needed me before I found my corner again. Jordan seemed a little less tense, but not enough to make anyone in that room feel safe yet.

"We don't get time to rest in football," he said after a while, looking around at each player. "We don't get time to recover from a loss or come down from the high of a win. Because in four short days, we'll play our next opponent, and we have to be ready."

He paused, rolling his lips together.

"I'm not angry with your performance on Friday," he started. "I'm disappointed with the attitude you all had when you walked onto that field. You thought it would be easy. You thought that win was yours, like you'd already earned it before you'd even laced up your cleats. The Raptors?" He tongued his cheek. "They went out there ready to fight for that win, and they did, and they got it. And you know what else? *They* deserved it."

A few boys shook their head, and I wasn't sure if they were disagreeing with Coach, or if they were feeling the same disappointment he was.

"Regardless of how sore you are tomorrow, we have a lot of work to do, anyway," Jordan said quietly. "Regardless of how poorly or how well you feel like you played Friday night, we have to start all over tomorrow, anyway. And regardless of how entitled you may think you are to another championship, we have to fight like we've never had one, anyway. Because that's how this game goes. No one is promised a damn thing, and whoever is the hungriest takes the W. Understand?"

Nods across the room.

Jordan sniffed, looking around at his team. "We may be disappointed, but what are we going to do on Friday?"

At first, there was no answer, but then the kicker gently said, "We're going to win, anyway."

Jordan nodded, and then he said, "We may be embarrassed, but what are we going to do on Friday?"

"We're going to win, anyway," a few more players chimed in.

The energy started as a buzz, a soft flap of bee wings, and with every new question Jordan threw at them, it grew into a thunderous roar.

"We may be beat down!"

"We're going to win, anyway!"

Jordan stood, circling the room as his voice rose. "We may have a thousand eyes on us, waiting for us to fail!"

"We're going to win, anyway!"

"We may have an opponent ready to gobble us up and spit us out and show us we ain't shit!"

"We're going to win, anyway!"

Jordan started beating a rhythm on his chest, and the boys joined in, until it was a room of bodily percussion and a hum of energy so strong I felt it in my core.

"Tomorrow, we turn it around. Tomorrow, we get back to work." Jordan pointed his quarterback and team captain directly in the chest. "Tomorrow, we fight."

A roar of cheers, every player on their feet, and then in a circle where they chanted something I couldn't quite make out. When they threw their hands up in the air, Coach called practice, and every single player walked out of that locker room a completely different kid than when they had walked in.

I couldn't hide my appreciation.

"Sydney," Jordan said as he walked past me with his eyes on his clipboard. "A word in my office?"

He'd posed it as a question, but I knew it wasn't a request at all. There was something deep and demanding in that voice, in the way he said my name. I followed him without a verbal response.

My heart raced more with every step, neck heating as I prepared all my defenses for the lashing I was sure I was about to receive. If he tried to blame that loss on me again, I had a full list of errors to throw back at him.

Mostly thanks to my daughter.

When I stepped into his office, Jordan closed the door behind us, leaving his eyes on his clipboard as he motioned for me to take a seat in the chair in front of his desk.

I swallowed, doing as he asked, and once he was seated on the other side, he abandoned his clipboard on the desk and folded his hands together, his raging eyes somehow peaceful when they found me.

"I owe you an apology."

The breath I'd been holding blew out in a sharp exhale, my defenses easing, heart calming. Jordan watched me with a wrinkle between his brows, his jaw set.

I didn't say a word.

"I don't get riled up over much," he started. "If you ask anyone in my family, anyone on this team, they'd tell you that. I am generally calm, but when it comes to football, I'll admit that I tend to lose my good senses."

Still, I stayed quiet.

"You did nothing wrong on Friday night."

I couldn't help but scoff at that, because *obviously*.

Jordan smirked. "I know you already know that, but I couldn't see clearly until later that night. All I *could* see in that moment was our loss, and I felt the pressure of the entire town's weight on my shoulders, and I am ashamed to say I crumbled beneath it."

My own shoulders softened at that, and I opened my mouth to speak but he beat me to it.

"I'm sorry for blowing up on you, for questioning your decision and trying to assert authority in a space where I hold none. This is your area of specialty, and that's why we hired you. If I ever question your decisions again, feel free to kick my ass, and I know you probably could."

I laughed out loud at that, relaxing.

Jordan smiled, too. "Seriously, Sydney. I'm sorry. Not just for that night, but for my general attitude since you walked through those doors. You've done nothing but prove yourself, and still I have this urge to... protect you, or stick up for you."

A completely new heat crept up my neck at that, and I felt it tinge my cheeks, rendering me speechless once again.

"Which is stupid, I realize," he continued, holding up his hands. "But, I think it's part of how I was raised, and just part of who I am, in general. Regardless, I've made an ass of myself, and I was hoping we could start over. Call a truce."

I smirked. "I didn't realize we were at war."

"Well, this is me throwing the white flag, anyway."

A silence fell between us, and I sat forward, finding his gaze. "Thank you for apologizing. I think it takes a great man to do so in situations like this. And, if I'm being honest and fair, you were right."

His left eyebrow shot up at that. "I was?"

"Not about everything," I clarified. "I did my job, and there was no way for me or you or *anyone* to know that Parker was faking it, but... he was. And I couldn't see past his façade. I still think I would have done everything the same, but now that I know what these boys are capable of?" I smiled sheepishly. "Let's just say I won't be so easily fooled next time."

Jordan chuckled. "They are nothing if not a handful. Still," he continued. "I wasn't right. *You* were right. Yes, I know these boys, but regardless, you did exactly what you were supposed to do. We can't take injuries lightly, and I needed you to remind me of that. Parker took responsibility for his part, and he paid for it today on the field, but in the end, you did the right thing. So, don't consider yourself as easily fooled. Consider yourself as a professional trainer who I'm glad to have on my team, and thankful you put me in my place."

We shared a smile, and with that white flag waving between us, the truce was signed.

I stood, taking that smile as my cue that our conversation was over and I needed to wrap up work, but before I could take a step, he spoke again.

"I've been thinking," he said, standing with me. "About Paige. And... if you'd be open to it... maybe I could work with her. Teach her a few things, so that when she walks into summer camp next year, she'll be prepared."

My heart swelled and then fell into the pit of my stomach so fast that I was confused as to whether I thought that was the sweetest thing I'd ever heard, or the most terrifying.

"I'm trying to turn her *off* from football," I reminded him with a smile I hoped seemed casual and non-affected, crossing my arms. "Not provide her with a personal coach and source of encouragement."

"It's your call," he said with a shrug, sliding his hands into the pockets of his shorts. "But, one thing I've figured out with kids like her? Once they decide something and set their mind to it, there's no stopping them."

My smile slipped, lips pressing together as worry flittered through me like the wings of a thousand birds.

"You can either fight her on it, or you can embrace her dream and support it. Whether it hurts her or not, I can tell you just from hearing her talk on Saturday that she's not giving up on football — no matter how much you may wish she would."

I bit my lip, and Jordan rounded the desk as soon as he saw the anxiety I could no longer hide. His strong hand reached out, touching my elbow and holding it as he offered me a smile.

"No pressure, okay? Just think about it."

His thumb rubbed my forearm where he held me, and I looked down, marveling at the tenderness concealed in those calloused hands before he pulled away.

He swallowed when I looked up at him, and the energy shifted in the same way it had Friday night. But before I could latch onto it to dissect it, he stepped back, picking up his clipboard and effectively dismissing me.

"See you tomorrow," he said.

And I walked in a daze back to my office with every warning bell in my system ringing in sync.

Chapter Seven

Sydney

The week flew by in a cyclone of work and practice and evenings spent with Paige. I didn't even mind meeting up with Randy on Wednesday to swap, because all my energy and emotions were tied up in the team and the upcoming away game against the North Valley Hornets.

Monday's practice and talk from coach had changed everything, throwing the team into a new orbit that I couldn't help but marvel at. Every single player was fired up and ready to work when we met back in that locker room on Tuesday, and all week long, I watched with timid fascination as they somehow worked twice as hard as they had the first week and a half that I'd watched them before our first game.

Something had clicked, and no one was messing around anymore.

Of course, with harder work came more injuries.

I found myself busier and busier with each passing practice, and I had my eyes on almost every player for something or another. There were ice baths and compression boot treatments and soft tissue sessions and all the while, I was urging the players to rest as much as they could, knowing they wouldn't for a single second. I'd given out so many ice packs that our ice machine couldn't even keep up, and I had to run to the store to grab as many twenty-pound bags as our local grocery store had on hand.

So, when we loaded up on the bus to head to the game Friday night, I felt just as fired up and determined as the players and coaches did.

I sat in the front seat behind the driver, smiling to myself as I listened to the players talk about girls and cars and sports and video games and all the things that made high school boys tick. I smiled because I could easily remember a time when my worries had been as simple, too, and part of me yearned for that innocence.

Once everyone was accounted for and coach gave his speech, reminding the boys that we still had a game to play and they needed to be focused for our short, thirty-minute bus ride, we were off.

TK and Coach Pascucci sat together in the front seat opposite mine, already huddling over their clipboards and murmuring softly about plays, so Jordan took the open seat next to me. He let out a breath as we pulled out of the school's parking lot, dropping his clipboard between us and rubbing his eyes.

"Nervous?" I asked with a smile.

"More like *exhausted*," he said. "Is this what parenting feels like? Because if it is, I'm thankful I never went down that road."

I full-on laughed at that. "Oh, this is *nothing* compared to being a parent. Trust me."

"How do you handle it?"

I shrugged. "Yoga, gardening, running — anything where I can be alone with my thoughts and relieve stress. And I try to keep as much of myself present so that I don't lose who I was before I became a mother, if that makes sense. It's a big reason why I was excited to get back to work."

Jordan nodded. "Why didn't you work before?" Immediately, he paled. "I'm sorry if that was rude to ask. I just mean... did you want to wait until Paige was a certain age before you worked, or...?"

I attempted a smile, though my insides were on fire now with flashes of Randy striking like lightning in my veins.

"It wasn't exactly my choice not to work," I said, carefully.

Jordan's expression hardened, the gold around his irises catching the rays of sun as they filtered in the bus windows through the trees we passed.

Everything inside me begged him not to press, and without a word exchanged, he seemed to understand.

"Yoga, huh?" he asked instead, crossing his ankle over the opposite knee. He was dressed in black athletic slacks and a red polo with STRATFORD FOOTBALL embroidered on the pocket. The sleeves of it hugged his biceps, the hem of it tucked into the band of his pants where a belt was fastened.

He looked professional and somehow dangerous, too.

"Yep," I answered, nudging him. "Not as fun as running in the mud, I'd wager, but it's my own brand of release."

"I've never tried it," he confessed, popping a piece of gum into his mouth. I'd learned it was his game ritual, to chew gum, and I wondered if it helped him keep from blowing his top. He offered me a piece, too, but I declined. "Maybe we could do it with the guys during a Thursday practice sometime, if you'd be willing to lead us," he suggested. "Lord knows we could all learn to relax a little more."

"Maybe," I agreed with a smile, and then I turned to look out the window, because emotions I worked hard to keep down were bubbling up like a spring.

Jordan left me to gaze and think, pulling his iPad out and leaning over the aisle to talk to the coaches while I watched our little town disappear and fields of nothing take its place.

I loved the country.

Occasionally, we'd pass a house or a barn or a little fruit stand, but for the most part, there wasn't much between us and North Valley, and I surrendered to the solemn depths of my mind as we drove. Because it hit me in that very moment with Jordan's question that I was finally here, I was finally on the other side of the hell I'd endured, standing on my own two feet.

I was working.

I was taking care of my daughter.

I was remembering who I was.

I was living.

And, for the life of me, I couldn't decide why that made me want to scream in joy as much as it made me want to cry.

Thankfully, I didn't have time to dwell on it. As soon as we pulled up at North Valley's field, that same energy I'd felt in practice all week swept over us like a strong summer wind, and we got down to business.

There was something about Friday night football in Tennessee, an energy unlike any other in the entire world.

It was almost impossible to explain it to anyone who hadn't experienced it themselves, that cocktail of anticipation and excitement with a twist of anxiety. The passion for these teams ran deep in the blood of not just the students, but the entire town. There were painted faces and giant handmade signs and whistles and cowbells and synchronized cheers.

When it was game time, nothing else mattered.

Not for any of us.

I scanned the stands for my daughter, and when I found her sitting next to Randy with her wide eyes scanning our players as they warmed up, I smiled. She was pointing to each one of them and rambling on and on to her father — likely about who she thought should play, what their stats were, what part they played in last week's loss, and what they would need to do to turn it around.

Randy nodded and listened, but I didn't miss how much his eyes watched *me* instead of the players.

I was glad I took that moment before the game to find my daughter in the crowd, to watch the excitement on her face, because from the moment that first whistle blew, I didn't have another spare minute.

The boys played hard.

They had something to prove.

And there wasn't a single moment of that game that I wasn't wrapping or icing or working on sprains or joints or helping someone stretch out or checking them for concussions or watching a loud collision from the sidelines while I silently prayed nothing was broken in the process. I ran on and off the field more times than I could count, players on the ground with the stands silent until we both stood in unison and I got them to the sidelines.

It was a long and grueling game.

But when the final seconds on the scoreboard ticked down, we had twenty-eight points, and the Hornets had twenty-five.

We won.

It was an explosion of excitement from our sideline, benched players and all the coaches running out on the field to meet the team. I laughed from beside the bench, watching the high fives and hugs — not just with our own players, but with the other team's, too. It was perhaps my favorite part of football, that camaraderie that was shown to the opponent at the end.

"Mama!"

I turned to find Paige leaning over the railing of the stands, and I rushed to her, jumping up to high five her outstretched hand.

"We won, we won!"

I chuckled. "We did, didn't we?"

"If you ask me, it's because Coach and I had a talk." She looked up at her dad then, who was narrowing his eyes at me. "I know what I'm talking about when it comes to football, don't I, Daddy?"

"No one knows more, munchkin," he said, but his eyes still bore into me. I stood straighter, which I knew he hated.

He was so used to me cowering under that gaze.

"She told me you guys ran into Jordan at the park after I left," he mused. "How convenient."

I had to fight so hard not to roll my eyes, I barely had enough strength to respond. "He was there washing his car. Paige saw him and ran over to light into him about the game." I turned my attention back to her. "Which worked, apparently."

Her smile doubled, and she bounced a little, her wild curls hopping with her. "Can we stick around to talk to Coach, Daddy?" She tugged on his sleeve. "Please, please, please!"

"They've got to load up on the busses, sweetheart," he said to her, rubbing her head to pacify her as she pouted. "And we've got important business, too."

"We do?"

He nodded, lowering himself nearer to her ear and whispering, "Ice cream."

Paige lit up at that, squealing and bouncing for a new reason. Randy chuckled and I couldn't help but laugh, too.

When our eyes met, we shared a brief moment of understanding.

A brief insight into what it felt like to look at each other *before*.

But as soon as it had come, it was gone again.

I hardened my gaze, his laugh slipped off, and with a quick hug and instructions to *be good*, Paige grabbed his hand and they were gone.

It was complete chaos for Jordan after the game ended. He was talking to local news reporters and shaking hands with administration and doing business with scouts and stealing players away for brief moments of either criticism or praise or both. It wasn't until we were back on the bus that he had a moment to himself, and as soon as he sat down next to me, he blew out a breath.

This time, it was with a smile.

"Congratulations, Coach," I said, nudging him with my elbow. "Looks like our year isn't hopeless yet."

"It's just one game," he said, falling back into the seat like he was wiped. "But *damn*, does it feel good to win."

He turned to look at me as the bus pulled out of the lot, and the stadium lights played with the shadows on his face until we slipped into darkness on the country road. I expected him to turn away, to give me a high five and lean over the aisle to talk to the other coaches about the game, but instead, he just stayed that way.

Watching me — like he was waiting for something, or like he was on the cusp of discovering something he'd missed all along.

"You're damn good at your job, did you know that?"

His words surprised me, and I couldn't fight off the blush that shaded my cheeks. I shrugged. "Just doing what needs to be done."

"No," he said, shaking his head. "Don't do that. Don't downplay what you did out there like anyone could do it. This is only your second game, and already, the boys on this bus feel more comfortable with you than they ever did with any other trainer we've had. Do you understand what that means?"

"Maybe it's because I'm a woman," I offered as a joke. "I give off those motherly, nurturing vibes."

"You do," he agreed. "But, that's not why they trust you. They trust you because you know what you're doing, and you prove it time and time again when you take them back for treatment. They know that if you say it's not safe to play, it's not. And if you say they're going to be okay, they will be. And if you say to rest or to ice or to do therapy, they know it's not just bullshit talk to fill the space. It's necessary." Jordan paused, frowning a bit. "You are a very impressive trainer, Sydney."

Emotion swelled in the middle of my chest like a lotus flower, sprouting up from the sticky mud that had stifled my self-pride for years. I hated how hot my ears were in that moment, but I loved the way it felt to have my hard work and talent acknowledged.

"Thank you, Jordan," I said — softly, almost a whisper. My eyes found his. "Really."

One corner of his mouth tugged up a centimeter, but otherwise, his expression remained the same. He nodded, still watching me, his eyes flicking back and forth between mine.

Those eyes that were too mesmerizing not to watch in return.

The air on that bus liquified, as if I could reach out and touch it and send a ripple flowing between where I sat and where Jordan was next to me. I felt it weighing in on me, warm and heavy, my breaths labored under the pressure.

I cleared my throat, ripping my gaze from his. I picked at my chipped nail polish a moment — polish Paige had painted on the night before I took her to her dad's. I'd found it funny and endearing that my football-obsessed little girl wanted to paint our nails together, and I smiled at the memory.

"You know," I said, picking a fleck of the red off before I looked at Jordan again. "Paige insinuated that you have *her* to thank for tonight's win."

"Did she now?" Jordan barked out a laugh, crossing his ankle over his knee. "Well, she was definitely part of it. You know, it was her idea to try Ingram at running back. She saw his speed and protection of the ball when he was warming up for last week's game." Jordan shook his head, as if he couldn't believe he'd missed it. "He's so young, you know. Freshman. I just didn't think he could handle that kind of pressure yet."

"And then he gets two touchdowns in his first game as a starter," I mused with a whistle. "Damn, my girl is smart."

Jordan chuckled. "That she is."

Darkness fell over both of us as we slipped past the last little part of North Valley, and I knew even though I couldn't see it, that same country I'd stared at on the way over was outside our windows now.

"I've been thinking," I said, biting my lip just in case I wanted to change my mind before I continued. "About what you said. About Paige."

"Yeah?"

I nodded. "I was wondering... would you possibly like to come by for lunch tomorrow? I hoped maybe you could sit her down, *really* explain what it would mean for her to play football. And I mean *really* explain it — the good, the bad, the ugly. I want her to understand everything she's getting herself into." I swallowed, the instinct I'd gained as soon as I became a mother flaring in my gut. "And if she's still serious after that... well... will you help her?"

Jordan smiled, but I balked instantly.

"I mean, if and when you have time, of course," I said quickly. "I know it's football season and you've got classes and practices and games, and a social life, I'm sure. I just... the other day, in your office, you had mentioned —"

"I'd love to."

Jordan was still smiling as I blew out a breath. "Yeah?"

He nodded with his eyebrows pinched together, like it was obvious. "Are you kidding? That girl's got grit. If she can play even half as well as she can chew my ass, I think she's got a real shot of making some serious moves in football."

I laughed a little too hard, covering my mouth with my hand as I shook my head. "I'm scared," I admitted.

"That just means you're a good mom," he said, and as if it was normal and casual and damn near instinctive, his hand reached over and wrapped around my knee with a squeeze.

It was a friendly touch, one of admiration and assurance, which was why I nearly squeaked out loud when a bolt of violent heat sprang from his touch up the inside of my thigh.

We both looked at where he touched me, then at each other, and in the same breath, he pulled his hand away and straightened while I tucked my hair behind one ear and looked out the window.

I squeezed my eyes shut, knowing I should respond, that I should say something — *anything*. But when I finally turned back to him and opened my mouth, he was already leaning over the aisle, a clipboard between him and Coach Pascucci as they discussed the game.

I internally groaned, letting my head fall against the window. The glass was slightly cool, a sign that fall was approaching — slowly, but surely.

My skin that touched it, however, was still burning hot.

Chapter Eight

Jordan

One thing I had learned about Sydney in her time on the team was that she was tough.

She wasn't one of those people who had to try hard to give off that vibe, either. It wasn't as if she walked around scowling all the time, or puffed out her chest, or showed her scars and told battle stories. She didn't bark at anyone who came near her, and she didn't use force to get her point across when she had one to make.

She was effortlessly strong, in a way that was natural and pure.

I knew it from the moment she walked into my office. I saw it in the way she held her chin high, in the way her stoic eyes held mine, in the way she spoke — calmly and evenly, always. She didn't have to tell me that she'd been through shit for me to see it, and she didn't have to prove to me that she could handle herself.

Somehow, I knew that, too.

Last night, I watched her run on and off the field, her demeanor serious as she assessed each injury and determined next steps. She did it so quickly and confidently, and the players trusted her implicitly.

When I thought of Sydney, I thought of everything hard and resilient — rock, stone, iron, maybe even diamond.

Which was precisely why I was surprised on Saturday when I parked my Bronco in the driveway of a very soft, very feminine, very welcoming and modest two-story house on the north end of town.

It was a gray house with a yellow door and white trim. A colorful variety of stones paved the way from the driveway to the front porch, which was surrounded by a stunning garden of flowers and plants. I smiled at the three rocking chairs on the porch — two that were much like the ones my mom had, and one that was the same yellow as the door and about half the size of the other two.

It was exactly the right size for Paige.

There were remnants of a chalk drawing on the porch, too — a dragon and a castle, I thought. And as I lifted my fist to knock, I chuckled at the handmade Tennessee Titans wreath on the door.

"I'll get it!" I heard a tiny voice yell before there was the distinct sound of bare feet barreling toward the door. In the next moment, it flew open, and Paige grinned up at me with a crooked smile.

"Hey, Coach!"

"Hey, yourself."

"Mama said we're going to play football today!"

"That's not what I said," I heard from somewhere in the house, and I smirked, bending until I was level with Paige.

"We're going to *talk* about football, yes," I corrected, but before she could pout, I lowered my voice to a whisper. "But, I'd wager we'll end up playing some, too."

"I can already see you two will be the death of me," Sydney announced as she swung around the corner behind Paige — who was snickering now, like we had a secret.

My smile faltered at the sight of *Sydney at Home*, who looked *nothing* like *Sydney at Work*.

Her hair that was normally pulled into a bun on top of her head was wavy and unruly, pulled out of her face by a bright orange headband tied at the top of her forehead. It wasn't curly like her daughter's, but it was wild in its own way, barely tamed by that scrap of orange fabric. And the way she carried herself was different somehow, as if she were strolling in the park with nowhere to be. That guard she always hid behind, that shield that was always up seemed to not even exist at all.

She smiled at me as she wiped her hands on a rag, a tired smile on her face — along with a few smudges of dirt. I did a double-take at her overalls and gardening belt, my curiosity climbing as I noted the dirt stains on her knees.

"It looks like *you're* the one who's been playing football," I teased.

Sydney chuckled, opening the door wider so I could step inside the foyer with them. Paige was staring up at me with a giddy smile, bouncing slightly.

"I've been working in the vegetable garden out back," Sydney said, leading me through the foyer and into an open space that seemed to serve as the living room and dining room, both. College Game Day was on the television, and in the kitchen just off to our right, there sat a basket full of the evidence of that garden's existence. It was on the counter next to two dirty gardening gloves and a sheer.

"Wow," I mused, walking straight to it and picking up a carrot from the top. "Carrots, cauliflower, Brussel sprouts..." I paused, picking up a familiar herb. I turned to her. "Basil?"

Sydney nodded, folding her arms where she watched me. "You didn't call it a pile of leaves," she commented. "I'm impressed."

I chuckled, but before I could ask another question about her garden, Paige sighed, flopping down at the dining room table. "Mom's got a garden. There are carrots and stuff in it. Yeah, yeah, yeah, okay, we've covered it now, can we *please* get down to business here?"

She clasped her hands together in a plea, eyes wide and little feet dangling under her chair.

"Paige Marie, that was rude," Sydney said at the same time I burst into laughter.

"No, no, it's okay," I assured her, taking a seat across the table from Paige. "I like the excitement. You really do love football, don't you?"

Paige's face leveled, the most serious I'd ever seen her. "More than anything in the *world*, Coach."

"Except her mother, of course," Sydney said, kissing her daughter's hair — which was presently a wild fluff of half curl, half wave.

Paige waved her off with a groan, but smiled, too, and Sydney hung her hands on her hips.

"I'll pour us some lemonade and start working on lunch while you two *get down to business*," she said, offering me an apologetic smile before she made her way to the cabinet next to the sink. My eyes followed her up until the very moment she stepped on her tiptoes to reach the glasses, and I noticed the smooth, brown skin exposed between her tiny tank top and the overalls she wore over them. That gap between them gave me a view I'd never had before of her slim waist, and her hips as she wiggled to reach the top shelf.

I swallowed, tearing my eyes away and back to Paige.

Who was watching me with a smirk.

"So," she said, glancing at her mom and back at me pointedly. "*Football.*"

"Football," I echoed, ignoring her smile that said she knew something I was trying to hide. "Let me ask you something, Paige — do you get your feelings hurt easily?"

"Nope," she answered quickly, nodding once before she sat up straighter in her chair. "I'm tough, Coach. I can handle anything."

"Anything?" I asked, leaning toward her as Sydney dropped off two glasses of lemonade on the table. She smiled at me before making her way to the basket on the counter, and again, my eyes followed her, watching her unpack each ingredient with care.

"Anything," Paige said, knocking on the table to pull my attention back to her.

"So, if you show up at football camp next summer, and all the boys on the team make fun of you and call you names and shun you out of their groups and make you feel like you don't belong, you can handle it?"

Paige rolled her eyes. "Please. I'm only nine years old and I know that boys are stupid and their opinions don't count for anything."

Sydney high-fived her daughter as she walked past to turn the volume down on the television.

I chuckled. "And if you go out there and work twice as hard as those boys who are teasing you, and end up being twice as talented, and yet, your coach still doesn't give you the same playing time as they get... can you handle that, too?"

Paige's confidence slipped. "That doesn't sound fair."

"It's not, but it's a very real possibility that could happen," I said, honestly. "And there's also a very big possibility that not only would you isolate yourself from having many friends by being a girl playing football, but that you could make a lot of sacrifices, work really, *really* hard, and still not be able to play past high school. And, even if you do get to play in college, as of this very moment, there is nowhere for you to advance to play football professionally."

Paige's eyes widened with every word I said, her little eyebrows tugging inward. It broke my heart to see it, and I could tell by the way Sydney watched us over her shoulder where she was cutting up the carrots that it worried her, too.

But, this is what she wanted. She wanted me to be real with Paige.

And I would be.

"I'm giving this all to you straight, Paige, because I believe you can handle it," I said, folding my hands on the table. "You want to know what else I believe?"

Paige didn't respond.

"I believe you *will* be better than a lot of boys on the teams you play on, and I believe you *will* excel in football. I think you will learn some of life's biggest lessons from it, and that it will become a part of you — a *permanent* part of you, one you'll never be able to erase. I think you'll breathe it in like it's the only oxygen that keeps your lungs working, and I think that no matter what challenges you face, you'll overcome them."

I leaned closer, leveling my eyes with hers.

"And more than anything, I believe you can have a happy and amazing life playing football. I believe you *could* play in high school, and college, and — truly — maybe even in a professional league. Now, I don't know what that would look like — not yet — but I believe just by your passion alone that it could happen. And if it doesn't work out that way?" I shrugged, smiling as I tapped her nose. "I know for a *fact* that you'd make a damn good coach."

Paige giggled at that, but as soon as her smile had appeared, it slipped away again. "Why can't girls play football professionally?"

Sydney and I exchanged glances, and she wiped her hand on her apron before walking over to her daughter. She bent down, swept her hair out of her face, and looked her in the eyes. "There are many reasons, Paigey. Some argue that women would get hurt, and it's a very valid argument. As you know from watching, there's a lot of danger with concussions and other life-altering injuries — whether you're a girl or a boy." Sydney sighed, glancing at me before she addressed her daughter again. "But, there are no rules that say a woman *can't* play in the NFL."

"Really?" Paige lit up.

"Really," I chimed in. "And, there are already *many* women working for the NFL as coaches, advisors, agents, trainers — like your mom — and more. There are a lot of ways to make a life in football."

We both watched her as she digested it all, and I resisted the urge to say more. It was a lot to throw on a nine-year-old. Hell, most kids her age had no *idea* what they wanted to do with their lives, and even if they *thought* they knew, they were likely to change their mind down the road.

But, I knew that look in Paige's eyes when she talked about football. It was the same one I'd seen reflected in my own growing up.

This wasn't just a phase for her.

It was everything.

After a long while, Paige looked at her mom, and then at me, and with determination in her eyes, she nodded. "I know it's going to be hard, and I know the boys are going to be tough on me, but I don't care." Her little hand balled into a fist on the table. "I want to play football."

I smiled, glancing at Sydney who looked over her shoulder at me with a mixture of pride and anxiety. I nodded slightly, locking my gaze on hers with a silent promise that I would help Paige, and that I would take care of her. And Sydney nodded back, as if she understood.

As if she trusted me unreservedly.

For reasons I couldn't grasp, I wanted to hold onto her gaze, to memorize the trust in her eyes and analyze the depth of it.

But, I tore my eyes away and looked at her daughter, who was watching me without so much as a single ounce of hesitation or concern for what she'd just decided.

"Okay, then," I said, standing. "Let's play."

• • •

Paige was just as tough as her mother.

She was also just as talented.

We spent every hour of sunlight in Sydney's backyard with a football, breaking only to eat lunch and to run in for bathroom breaks. From the moment we stepped foot on the grass and Paige showed me how she learned to line up her fingers on the laces of the ball and throw a perfect spiral, I knew I hadn't been wrong in my assumptions about her.

Football was ingrained in that little girl. It was already a part of who she was, and I knew without a doubt it would be a part of who she'd become, too.

Regardless of that belief, I didn't go easy on her.

We ran drills just like the ones I knew she'd run in football camp. I pushed her to her limits, testing her in everything from agility and speed to stamina and strength. When I asked what her top three desired playing positions were, she answered with quarterback, wide receiver, and kicker.

Three very different positions with very different sets of challenges.

Still, I gave her a crash introduction course in each, running throwing drills and catching drills and making her kick over and over until she started to complain that her foot was sore.

Sydney worked in her garden, did yoga on the porch, read over her notes in her training binder on our players, and read a thriller I recognized from Logan's bookshelf — all while keeping a close eye on us. When the sun began to make its descent, casting Paige's brown curls in a golden light, Sydney finally called it.

"Alright, you two," she said, standing as she slipped a bookmark between the pages of her book to hold her place. "I think that's enough for today."

I expected Paige to whine and beg for more time, but she put her hands on her knees, panting for a long moment before she stood and smiled at me victoriously.

"How'd I do, Coach?" she asked, squinting against the setting sun.

I ruffled her hair, the roots of it damp with sweat. "Killed it."

"Can we do this again?" she asked with wide eyes.

I glanced at Sydney, who worried her lip a little before nodding.

"Of course," I answered Paige, holding out my hand for a high five. "But you better work on these drills by yourself, too. Don't wait for me to get you going."

"I will! I promise!"

Sydney joined us from the porch, resting her hand on her daughter's shoulder. "Alright, Paigey. Go get washed up for dinner."

"Are you staying for dinner, too?" Paige asked me, folding her hands together. "Oh! And maybe to watch the Vols game, too?"

"Paige..." Sydney warned.

"Oh, Mama, *please*," Paige said again, turning her begging eyes to her mother.

Sydney pulled on one of Paige's curls, letting it bounce back into place before she spoke. "Jordan has been with us all day, sweetie. I'm sure he wants to get home."

"I don't mind."

The words came out too quickly, too honestly, and Sydney's eyes locked on mine as Paige tugged on her overalls.

"See? He *wants* to. Pleeeeeeease." She folded her hands together again and bounced, eyes hopeful and bottom lip protruded.

Sydney watched me for a moment longer, a question in her eyes I couldn't decipher before she addressed her daughter again with a sigh. "You're too cute for your own good."

"Yes!" Paige said, knowing without an affirmative answer that she'd won. She bounded off into the house without another look. "I'll shower fast and put the game on!"

She was gone before I could answer, and I chuckled, sliding my hands into my pockets. "I'm sorry about that," I said to Sydney, a little embarrassed. "I should have pulled you aside to ask you if you wanted company before I agreed like that."

"No, it's okay," she said just as quickly as I had, and I smiled at the sight of a blush on her cheeks. "I don't get the chance to cook for guests very often. I like it."

"Yeah?"

She nodded.

For a long while, we stood there, toe to toe, in her backyard as the sun lit up the sky with vibrant pinks and violets, her eyes on mine and mine watching her, in return.

"Need some help in the kitchen?" I finally offered.

At that, she gave a short laugh out of her nose. "I'd love that," she said, but one brow quirked high as she let her eyes roam down the length of me. "But you need a shower first, too."

"What? Am I a little sweaty?" I asked, inching toward her.

Sydney's smile flattened, her eyes wide before they narrowed in warning. "Jordan... don't you dare."

"Oh, come on," I teased, reaching out for her before she could escape. She squeaked and writhed in my grasp as I crushed her in a hug. "See? I'm perfectly dry!"

"Ewww," she dragged out, swatting at me in laughter until I let her go. She shook her head, shoving me toward the door. "Shower. Now. Before I change my mind and kick you out."

I was still thinking about the way she felt in my arms, about her eyes, and her smile, and about the way that smile filled her entire face that afternoon as I washed away the day in her shower. I had to wash with her shower gel, which smelled like her, and dry with a towel that did, too.

And it was when I had my nose in that towel, when I took a deep inhale and soaked in her scent, that I realized what I was doing.

My eyes shot open, and I saw myself reflected in the foggy mirror in her bathroom.

What the hell are you doing?

You shouldn't stay for dinner.

You shouldn't have been that close to Sydney.

You should leave.

Now.

I knew why I wanted to stay for dinner, regardless of whether I was ready to admit it to myself or not. It was because I didn't want to leave *Sydney at Home*. It was because I'd had a glimpse inside her life, and now I wanted to know more.

I wanted to know *everything*.

It was because I liked the way she felt in my arms, and the way she smelled, and that she had a garden and that she did yoga on her back porch.

It was because I found her beautiful, in every way possible, and I wanted to be with her for as long as I could be.

My expression hardened at my reflection in the mirror. Everything about the man staring back at me screamed question after question, warning after warning, accusation after accusation. It was a dangerous line I was tiptoeing on. There didn't need to be a written rule for me to know that there were lines between me and Sydney that couldn't be crossed — not with me as head coach and her as the athletic trainer.

But who said it had to be more than a friendship?

I could stay for dinner. I could get to know Sydney, admire her beauty and loveliness without acting on it.

I wasn't doing anything wrong.

I searched the eyes I'd searched my entire life for a long moment, something between shame and stubborn denial washing over me the longer I did.

But before it could permeate my skin, I ripped my gaze away.

I finished drying quickly, ignoring the voice inside me that always warned me when I was on the precipice of doing something stupid. I told myself I wasn't breaking any rules, that I had no intentions other than to be helpful and polite. I told myself I was a welcome guest, that Sydney and I worked together and could be friends, that I was here to help *Paige*.

Surely, that was okay.

I repeated my excuses over and over as I dressed in a pair of basketball shorts and a t-shirt I always kept in my car just in case — namely for when I went to Mom's straight after practice or a game and showered there.

Then, I threw my towel in Sydney's dirty hamper and joined her in the kitchen, ready to help.

I didn't look at my reflection again.

Chapter Nine

Sydney

It was nine-oh-eight when I popped the cork on a bottle of red wine, and I sighed out loud at the sound of it, filling my glass a little past the line of what was ladylike before I held up the bottle with my eyes on my guest.

"Wine?" I asked.

Paige was finally in bed, conked out cold after what was likely the most exciting day she'd had in her young life. She was still talking animatedly about football and how her day with Jordan had gone when I'd tucked her in, and I'd listened to her intently, even as she spoke through her yawns. When I'd paused at her door to tell her I loved her before turning out the light, she'd taken the opportunity to melt my heart.

"This was the best day ever, Mom," she'd said before she closed her eyes and rolled over. "Thank you."

I couldn't help the smile that little girl brought out in me with that statement, nor could I disagree with her that it had been a good day.

But, I was still exhausted — physically and mentally — and my anxiety had worked my nerves to the point of being nearly shredded.

Mama needed a drink.

Jordan smirked at my offer, leaning his elbows on the counter from where he stood on the other side of it. He still looked freshly showered even a couple hours later, his hair slightly damp, skin clean, the faint scent of my bodywash wafting off him. I flushed a little bit at the thought of him naked in my shower, but turned my attention back to the bottle in my hand and away from my boss's nudity.

"Any chance you have something a little stronger?" he asked.

I gave him an incredulous look before I set the bottle of wine down and pressed up onto my tiptoes to reach into the cabinet above my sink, retrieving a bottle of Scooter Whiskey.

In this town, *everyone* had a bottle somewhere in their house.

Jordan's smile climbed at the sight. "That's more like it. Now," he said, rounding the counter to join me in the kitchen. "What are the chances you've got an orange, some cherries, some—"

"Simple syrup and some bitters?" I chuckled, retrieving two glass tumblers from the cabinet next. I shoved the cork back into the bottle of wine I'd just opened as best I could. "I knew I liked you for a reason. Two old fashioneds coming right up."

His mouth dropped. "I was totally kidding. You really have everything to make one?"

"It's one of my dad's favorite drinks, too," I explained with a shrug. "I don't know when I started doing it, but I always have the ingredients on hand — just in case."

Jordan watched me silently as I made our drinks, and when the final garnish of the cherries were dropped into the glasses, I handed one to him and held the other up in a toast.

"I can't believe I'm saying this," I said with a sigh. "But, to football."

"To football," Jordan echoed, holding up his own glass. "And to you — may God give you the strength to keep up with that little girl in there."

"And send me a few angels to help, too."

We clinked our glasses together with soft laughter, each of us making our own noises of appreciation after the first sip.

A moment of silence fell between us after that, and I kept my eyes on my glass, but could feel Jordan watching me.

"You really are a great mom, you know," he said. "I should know. I have a great mom, too."

I smiled. "I'm just trying to keep my head above water."

"Do you feel a little better about her playing football after today?"

"No," I answered quickly and honestly on a laugh. My eyes found his, then. "I mean, I guess I feel *marginally* better, because I know she has you to help, and I feel like she at least understands what she's getting into. But... I don't think she'll *really* understand until she's in it. You know?"

Jordan nodded.

"I mean... I don't have to explain this to you. But, it's already going to be tough for her in ways that aren't fair or reasonable. She has hair that doesn't straighten and skin that's too dark to be white but too light to be black." I swallowed, picking at what was left of the polish Paige had painted on my nails. "In this town, and sadly, in a *lot* of towns, that's something that will create hurdles for her."

Jordan let out a long exhale, his eyebrows pinched together as he chewed on what I'd said. "I understand what you're saying. Trust me, I grew up in an all-white family in practically an all-white town. I get it." He stood a little straighter, tilting his head before his eyes found mine. "But, she will persevere through any challenges she faces. And I do mean *any* of them. I know that just after spending one afternoon with her, and I'd wager you know it, too."

Warmth spread through my chest like a spring on a summer day. "I will never understand how she got so tough."

Jordan scoffed. "That one's easy. You're her mother." We shared a smile. "So, since we're on the topic, what exactly *is* your nationality?"

I chuckled, because it was a question I got with everyone's eyes when they first saw me. They didn't understand the color of my skin or the shape of my eyes and most of all, how they existed in the same human.

I nodded to the dining room table behind Jordan, where we both took a seat before I answered. "Well, my mother is Filipino," I started. "My father is a mut, as he always liked to put it. His father is African American, his mother is a Caucasian woman from many different descendants." I shrugged. "So, I'm somewhere between all of that. What about you?"

Jordan was smiling as he listened, but the curve faded when I asked him to tell me his background. He scratched his neck, looking out the sliding glass door at the dark backyard. "I wish I knew."

A long, quiet moment stretched between us, and I glanced at where his hands rested on the table — one wrapped around his drink, the other beside it with nothing to hold. I debated reaching out to let him know I was there, but thought better of it, standing to make my way over to the Bluetooth speaker in my living room, instead. I put on a mellow playlist before rejoining him at the table.

"How old were you when the Beckers adopted you?"

"I was a baby," he answered quickly, and I noted the way his shoulders relaxed now that the conversation was on the family he'd been with all his life instead of the one that created him. "I don't remember anything before I was with them. Honestly, I didn't really understand that I *wasn't* truly their son — not until we went to the lake for the first time."

I tilted my head, confused.

"I was five. It was the summer before kindergarten. I don't remember a lot, but I do remember that Noah was only a baby, one or so, and we went out to the lake with Mom and Dad. I was swimming with some other kids, and one of them pushed me into the water and was making fun of me. He asked me where my parents were so I could run and cry to them, and I pointed to where Mom and Dad were on the shore with Noah, and the kids all laughed. They said, '*That can't be your parents. They're white!*'"

My stomach knotted so tightly I placed a hand over my gut to soothe it.

Jordan just shrugged, wiping the sweat from his glass before he took a sip. "So, on the ride home, I asked Mom why I looked so different from her and Dad and Noah. And I'll never forget that look they shared, the one that told me I'd missed something, that there was something being hidden from me."

Jordan paused for a moment, and I took a sip of my old fashioned, waiting.

"They told me everything that night, and from that moment on, I understood. And it didn't make me feel like any less a part of the family," he clarified, but then his eyes found mine, the gray-ish blue that surrounded his brown iris glowing in the low light of my kitchen. "But, it did open a new door in my mind, one I didn't even know existed. I realized I was theirs, but not really *theirs*. They were my mom and dad, but I had *another* mom and dad, too."

I nodded in understanding.

"So, yeah. It opened a new door. And I've walked through that door frequently ever since that day, looking for answers that I know will never come."

My heart ached with the desire to hug him.

It hit me so fiercely and unexpectedly that I nearly followed it. I uncrossed my legs and made to stand before I realized what I was doing and stopped myself, taking a deep breath, instead. There were no words to say in that moment — none that would be anything other than hot air to fill the space. So, I didn't say a word. I just sat there with him and let him know he wasn't alone.

"It's strange, because I had a similar awakening when we camped when I was a teenager, too. Only that time, I had been hanging out with a brother and sister who were black. But, they treated me differently, like I didn't actually belong with them." His eyes found mine. "It's like you were saying with Paige, and I'm sure you've been there, too. It's like I'm stuck in this strange in-between of not being black enough, but not being white enough, either."

I nodded, a grim understanding. "I know that feeling well."

"I couldn't have asked for a better family, though," he said after a moment with a small smile. "I'm proud to be a Becker."

I laughed softly. "You boys are as thick as thieves. Always have been. I think I'd heard of every single one of you before I even started my first day of school here."

"Hey, to be fair, I'm usually the one *wrangling* those trouble-makers — especially Noah. Lord knows Ruby Grace couldn't have come a moment sooner to settle that hothead down."

The mood lightened with the mention of his brothers, and we chatted about each of them. A big part of me was curious about the fire that had taken his father's life, but after having one already-heavy conversation, I skirted around my curiosity and stayed firmly in the friendly territory.

"Speaking of siblings, how's Gabby doing?" Jordan asked after a while.

I smiled at the mention of my sister, who I knew would likely lose her mind if she knew Jordan was in my kitchen at this hour of the night. "She's really good, loving the nursing life — though I'll never understand it. She works all night, long hours, dealing with people who usually treat her like she's a problem rather than a help." I shook my head. "Makes me appreciate people who work in healthcare more."

"Where's she at now?"

"She and my parents are all in Austin," I said, frowning as my finger traced the top of my glass. "Mom got a civilian job there working as an analyst, and I guess since we were all moving around together growing up, Sis just wanted to go with them."

"You didn't?"

I shrugged in lieu of an answer, my heart screaming *I did*.

Jordan was quiet for a while before he asked, "Was it hard, moving around like that when you were younger?"

I tilted my head, considering. "Yes, and no," I said honestly. "It was hard not staying in one place long enough to have real friends, but... my sister and I were so close, you know? And it always felt like an adventure, moving from place to place, always having something new to discover."

"I can't even imagine," Jordan said. "I've been in this town my whole life."

"There are worse places to be."

Jordan leaned back on a nod, watching me with a tired smile.

Conversation flowed easily between us after that, and so did the whiskey. As we talked, we went through two more old fashioneds, and the more we sipped, the easier it was to open up. I told him more about my upbringing, about the trouble I would get into with Gabby, a little about my parents. He knew about my mom's military job, but had no idea that my father built and sold custom furniture made of solid wood wherever we were stationed. So, we talked for nearly an hour about the places I had lived and traveled to growing up, about Mom's deployments and various job duties, and I even showed him pictures of my father's favorite projects.

I'd just finished sharing a story about me and my sister getting in trouble for swimming in an old quarry in Alabama when I glanced at the clock and realized it was almost midnight.

I sighed, opening my mouth to tell Jordan it was probably time we both get some sleep, but then the song changed, and he closed his eyes and smiled, letting out an appreciative noise through his nose.

"Wow," he said, shaking his head before he opened his eyes. They found mine instantly, and he stood, reaching one hand down to where I sat.

I stared at his hand, quirking a brow before I glanced back up at him like I had no idea what I was supposed to do with it. But he curled his fingers with a smile, nodding behind him to the living room like it was a dance floor.

"What?" I asked, feigning ignorance.

"Dance with me."

I laughed.

"Seriously," he said before I could call him crazy. "There's a great story that goes along with this song, and I want to tell it to you."

Well, shit.

That got my attention, and I took one last sip of my drink before I slipped my hand in his, ignoring the way it covered mine easily with warmth as he tugged me to the living room. When we were in the space between my couch and love seat, he twirled me, pulling me into him with ease before I had the chance to stumble or fall.

Jordan Becker.

A good dancer.

Who the hell would have guessed *that*?

For a moment, we just swayed — one of his hands on my waist and the other covering my hand where it rested on his chest. I held my other on his shoulder, listening to the song. It was one I didn't really know. I recognized it, and vaguely recalled my parents listening to it when I was younger, but past that, I had no idea why this song had made Jordan Becker pull me into my living room to dance.

"Do you know who this is?" he asked.

I shook my head.

"Eric Clapton," Jordan said with another smile. He was like a completely different man in that moment, one I'd never met before. The coach with the clipboard didn't exist, not in that living room. He was somewhere else, sleeping or planning plays, and the man who swayed with me was the *real* Jordan Becker. It was like spotting a Siberian tiger in the wild.

I wondered how many people had ever seen him with their own two eyes.

"Wonderful Tonight," Jordan said, just as the chorus began to play. "This was my mom and dad's wedding song."

I smiled, my heart squeezing as he twirled me out and back in. "It's beautiful."

Jordan nodded. "It is. And they didn't just dance to it at their wedding. Every night after dinner, Dad would help Mom clean up in the kitchen, and then he'd pull her into the living room, put on this song or sometimes another one that they loved, and dance with her."

I stopped swaying, gaping at him. "You're kidding."

Jordan didn't miss a beat, sweeping me back up in the rhythm with him. "Dad was a smooth cat."

"I can see that," I said, chuckling. "So, *every* night after dinner?"

"Every night," he repeated, and his smile slipped, ghosts dancing in his eyes just as much as we danced in that room. "When he died, I think that was the hardest part for her." He had a far-off look as a moment passed between us. "I mean, my brothers and I, we were dealing with our own shit, you know? Noah was on this kick about who would be the man of the house. Logan was going crazy trying to figure out where he should step up and take Dad's place in running the house, paying the bills, cleaning, caring for the lawn, doing taxes, all that. Mikey was so young… he was just trying to hold on, to understand that he'd lost his father."

I squeezed his shoulder where I held him.

"And then one night, after dinner, Mom was in the kitchen cleaning up, and she had these big tears in her eyes that she was trying so hard not to let fall. My brothers and I sat at that table feeling helpless and run down. It was the first time I think we'd ever really felt off-kilter as a family."

I nodded in understanding.

"And then, Logan got up from his chair, went into the living room, and put on this song." He smiled. "I'll never forget the way Mom froze in the kitchen, her eyes widening at the sound of it. And Logan went in there and reached for her hand, and took her back to the living room, and he danced with her."

Tears welled in my own eyes, and I rolled my lips together to keep them from falling.

"And I swear, it was that dance that brought us back together as a family," Jordan said, his voice softening to a whisper. "Every time we have family dinner at her house now, we take turns dancing with her after. And it's like Dad is still alive, like he's there with us, like *he* was the one who pulled us all together that night, as if to remind us that we always have each other, and he's never really gone. And you know what?" He chuckled. "This song never gets old."

My heart broke at the same time it surged with emotion. I didn't know how to react to Jordan opening up to me. I didn't know how to feel with his hand on my waist, with his other hand holding mine over his chest, with his stormy eyes searching mine as the music played between us.

But I leaned into him.

I leaned into his life, into his story, into everything and every person who made him who he was today. I leaned my body into his, leaned my heart into this soft man with the hardened edges. And when we both stopped swaying, when the music seemed to grow so loud it permeated our skin, when his fingers trailed their way up my ribs, over my arm, and framed my chin before tilting it up toward him, I leaned up on my toes.

His exhale was shaky when it touched my lips, but then my eyes closed, and his mouth found mine, and my living room exploded into a universe of stars.

The kiss was timid at first, our lips barely touching, sticking together in a hesitant embrace before we pulled away again. It was like we were each testing the other, giving them the chance to back out. My heart tripled its pace in my chest when our eyes met, and then, he kissed me again.

This time, his mouth was harder when it found mine, and more sure, his arms wrapping around me as he pulled me into him and kissed me like he was always destined to do so.

We both inhaled — the kiss, the night, each other — and his hands framed my face, holding me to him as if he was afraid I wasn't real, that I'd fade in an instant if he didn't hold onto me for dear life. He kissed me long and tender, and yet feverishly, too. We were lips and breaths and moans and then our mouths opened at the same time, and his tongue found mine, and an electrifying heat I hadn't felt in years zipped violently from where we touched through every nerve in my body, ending at one point of contact between my legs.

It was that rush of heat that kicked my brain into gear, and I realized with freezing cold awareness what I was doing.

I was kissing Jordan Becker.

I was kissing Jordan Becker — my *boss*.

I was kissing someone.

Period.

I broke away as if his kiss was a knife in the gut rather than the sweetest ecstasy. Before he could even frown, I was already out of his grasp, backing away with my hands over my mouth, eyes wide.

When he registered what he was seeing, his eyes went wide, too.

"Shit," he muttered, holding up his hands and taking a step toward me. I backed away just as much. "Sydney, I'm sorry. I—"

"It's late," I interrupted, turning away from him and bolting toward my dining room table as I cleared my throat. I immediately picked up our glasses, dumping what was left inside them into my sink and tossing the garnishes in the trash. I kept my eyes on my hands as I washed the glasses, as if I couldn't have tossed them into the dishwasher, instead.

"Sydney," Jordan tried from behind me.

"Thank you for today," I said, heart racing, mind blurring. I didn't know why it was happening, and I *hated* it, but in that moment?

All I thought of was Randy.

All I thought of was that Jordan and I couldn't happen, that Randy would never *let* it happen, and that perhaps more than anything, I wasn't ready for it to happen.

"I'm pretty tired," I continued, still washing. "I think we both better get some sleep."

The water was scalding hot on my hands but I didn't move to change it. I just scrubbed and scrubbed until the soap was a frothy foam of bubbles on the sponge and the glass in my hand was clean enough for the Queen herself to drink from.

I could still sense Jordan in my home, hear his breaths, feel the mixture of longing and regret swirling inside him the same way they moved in me. But slowly, without another attempt to speak to me, he gathered his belongings, and with one last look in my direction that I didn't return, he let himself out my front door.

And I fell to the floor, the water still running as I backed myself into the cabinet and squeezed my eyes shut, running my hands through my hair.

What have we done?

Chapter Ten

Jordan

Was it possible for a hangover to last forty-eight hours?

If anyone would have asked me on Monday afternoon thirty minutes before football practice, I would have responded with a resounding *yes*.

My head still pounded, gut churning like I was in danger of forfeiting what little I'd been able to eat at any given moment. I knew there were bags under my eyes and that I was in rough shape as I ran over my plans for the day's practice.

And I also knew that *none* of it had anything to do with the alcohol I'd consumed.

I hadn't been drunk — not at Sydney's, not in the car on my way home, and not the next morning. If anything, I'd nursed those drinks to make them — and the conversation with Sydney — last.

I wasn't hungover from the whiskey.

I was hungover from her kiss.

I'd been in that state of absolute worthlessness since I left Sydney's house on Saturday night, spending the rest of the weekend ruminating on my actions, and even more on her *reaction*.

I'd kissed her.

Like a damn fool, I'd kissed her.

And she'd torn away from me like I was the devil himself.

Here I'd been chastising my team the past few weeks, telling them to be respectful of Sydney, and it had been *me* who had crossed the very line I'd put in place. She'd trusted me — not just here on the field and at the school, but in her home, too. I was there to work with Paige, to reassure Sydney that it was all going to be okay, and instead, I'd put her in the worst-possible situation.

I felt like a predator, and even more, like a joker.

Because the worst part of it all was that I really did think she wanted to kiss me, too.

I'd thought I'd read the signs right, that she'd leaned into me and looked up at me with eyes that silently pleaded for me to break the rules and lower my mouth to hers. I thought she'd opened up to me, and that I'd opened up to her, in return, and that we'd crossed into a new territory that could no longer be defined by our roles on the Stratford High School football team.

I'd thought we'd shared something that night — hell, that entire *day*.

What. An. Idiot.

I'd run over my mistake in my head for the rest of the weekend, and nothing could save me from my thoughts. Not even taking the Bronco out mudding or dinner with my family on Sunday night brought me relief. Mom commented on how I was even quieter than usual, but I couldn't even open up to her about what had happened — *that* was how stupid I felt.

More than that, I felt irresponsible.

I decided long ago that relationships were not for me. I knew too well how they could fail, how one partner could be left behind, how the pain that came with love almost always outweighed the pleasure. I never wanted to be in that line of fire, and more than that, I never wanted to be responsible for someone else's demise, either.

Football was the love of my life, and I was happy with that.

So, when I'd crossed that line with Sydney, I'd done so not with the intention to hook up with her, to have a one-night stand, to have something *casual*.

I'd done it with the knowledge that I didn't *do* anything half-assed.

I wanted her. I wanted to court her and date her and take things slow and worship her and eventually call her mine.

I wanted all those things knowing that she'd already been through hell once, judging by the ugly breakup with her and Randy, and that I would likely put her through it again, because that was just the way love worked.

Round and round and round these thoughts went in my head, all weekend long, like a carousel of torture that ran on its victims screams — of which there were plenty. Even working through more of Dad's journal entries hadn't distracted me from what I'd done and what it would mean.

And all along, I'd been dreading this very moment — when we'd have to be at work together, and it wouldn't be the same as it was when we worked together just three days ago.

Another heavy sigh racked my chest as I tried to soothe my anxiety with a deep breath, and at that very moment, my office door swung open and slammed shut again before Sydney plopped her ass down in the chair on the opposite side of my desk.

"Alright," she said, tying her hair up in a knot on her head before her eyes locked on mine. "Let's get this awkward conversation out of the way now, shall we?"

It was unfortunate that I'd just exhaled instead of inhaled, because I held my breath from the moment she sat down, waiting for her to continue.

"So, we kissed," she said, as if we were discussing a player who got hurt on the team and what to do about it instead of everything I'd worried about for the past forty-eight hours. "I think we can both agree that we were tired, it'd been a long day, we had been drinking and we were talking about some pretty heavy things and neither of us were thinking clearly."

I kept my mouth shut, because while I *could* agree with some of that, I didn't agree with the last part.

I was thinking *very* clearly when I pressed my lips to hers.

"The first thing I want to address is..." She paused, rolling her lips together. Her eyes that had been so fiercely on mine fell to something on my desk — an object serving as a focal point, I imagined. "I just don't want you to think that you did anything wrong, because you didn't. I..." She swallowed. "I also took part in what happened, and it was not one-sided or anything."

Her eyes flicked to mine, but they didn't stay there long.

"That being said, I have a lot on my plate right now with my recent divorce, and with Paige, and I just..." She sat a little straighter, finally looking at me again. "Frankly, I do not have the capacity to be... like *that*... with anyone right now. And I think we both agree that even if I did, it shouldn't be my boss. I know there are no written rules or anything, but you and I both know that I can't... *we* can't..."

I remained silent, though I was very aware of how tight my chest was at those words.

"Anyway, I wanted to come directly to your office this afternoon so we could just put this all behind us. What do you think?"

My eyes bulged, because it was my time to speak and I hadn't even *breathed* since she'd walked into my office.

I started there, inhaling a stiff breath before I nodded, schooling my features. "Yes. Of course, totally."

"So, we're in agreement, then?" she asked. "We can just pretend like it never happened?"

"Like what never happened?"

Her jaw dropped a little, but then she let out a relieved sigh on a smile when she realized what I'd done. "Exactly."

I faked my best smile in return while my stomach continued to tie itself into knots. But, the longer I watched her, the more I knew I had to say. "Sydney... I really am sorry."

She held up her hand quickly. "Please, don't. You don't need to apologize. It never happened. Okay?"

I frowned, but nodded, nonetheless.

"Does this mean..." I started, but then paused, reframing what I wanted to ask. "I was hoping... just because I know she was excited about it, and I don't want her to think I bailed on her or anything... would it be okay if I still worked with Paige from time to time?" I held up my hands. "Not all the time," I clarified quickly. "Just... you know, whenever it works out. I just would love to keep working with her and help her get ready for camp next summer."

Sydney smiled, letting out a long exhale that was calmer than any breath had been in that room since she walked into it. "Of course," she said. "You're always welcome."

I returned her smile, and though there was still something new and uncomfortable that existed between us now, at least the conversation was had, and we could begin to put it all behind us.

My chest tightened again, as if it was protesting that I had just agreed to forget what was honestly the best kiss of my life, but I ignored it, standing instead.

"Welp, I'm going to go get these boys fired up for another week of practice."

Sydney stood abruptly, too. "Yep, I'm going to go get my tables set up and ready. I've got a few injuries to follow up with today and I'll give you a report of who we need to keep an eye on by the end of practice."

"Sounds good," I said with my eyes on my clipboard as we made our way out of my office. "Oh, and can you do some soft tissue work on Martinez's right shoulder?" I added. "He's been rubbing it after almost every throw, and the last thing I need is a second-string quarterback who can't perform if he's subbed in."

"I'm on it," she assured me, already heading down the hall toward her office.

And just like that, it was back to work.

Like nothing ever happened.

• • •

And so the week went.

Everything was back to normal, in the sense that they were *far* from normal, but at least we were pretending. My days passed with teaching my P.E. classes and weightlifting, evenings passed at practice with me and Sydney dutifully dancing around each other, all the while being "normal," and at night, I fell back into my routine, meal prepping and running and working through entries in Dad's journal.

Part of me wondered if it really was only me who felt like we were pretending. Sydney seemed fine, as far as I could tell. She was focused on the field and in her office, not skipping so much as one beat after our conversation on Monday.

I wondered if anyone could tell that I was on the opposite end of that spectrum.

It drove me mad that I couldn't drop it, but I tried my best, reminding myself of our conversation.

It was a mistake.

We were tired and tipsy.

It's not a big deal.

It never happened.

On Thursday night, I was successfully distracted, my nose buried in my playbook as I mapped out my strategy to take on the Conway Chargers. It would be another away game for us, and though the team was on a high from the win the week before, I knew it would be important to keep them focused and run the plays that we were nailing over and over in practice.

I wanted to play this game safe and bring home another win without any fanfare. That was my goal.

My eyes were starting to blur with all the x's and o's when my phone buzzed on the coffee table where my feet were propped. I scrubbed my hands down my face, moving my playbook to the side and smiling when I saw my baby brother's face on the screen.

"Well, if it isn't the city slicker," I answered, kicking back on the couch again.

"Hey, old man," Mikey teased back. "I was worried I might not get an answer, what with it being eight o'clock and all. I know that's past your bedtime."

I smiled, though my chest ached a bit, too. Mikey was the first of us to move away from Stratford — likely, the *only* one who ever would — and the Becker clan felt a little unsteady without him here.

"How are you?" I asked.

"All is good over here, just getting settled in still. The art gallery is pretty cool, and Kylie has been volunteering. She got a job helping out at the hospital, too. When we're not working, we're exploring the city. Kylie's dad put together a list of all her mom's favorite places from when she lived here, so we've been working through that."

I smiled. "That sounds fun. And you sound good."

"I am good," he replied, and I could hear the smile even though I couldn't see it. Then, I heard a faint *hi, Jordan!* in the background, and my smile grew. "Kylie says hi, by the way."

"Tell her I said hi back, and to keep you in line up there."

"Like you even have to tell me, that's my number one job," I heard her reply, like she'd stolen the phone from Mikey altogether.

I chuckled.

"What about you?" Mikey asked. "How's the season going? You ready for tomorrow night's game?"

I blew out a breath, tapping the playbook beside me with a longing look. "Working on getting ready, anyway. I mean, the team seems pumped, coming off a win last week, but with that giant L from week one still fresh in everyone's mind, I don't think anyone is unaware of the fact that this is an important game."

"One loss doesn't make a season, Big Bro."

"You sound like Mom. And I know," I agreed. "But, it does serve as a pretty heavy weight on our shoulders."

"How's it working out with the new trainer?"

My throat constricted, heart stopping before it took a nose-dive into my gut and resurfaced again, beating faster. "It's fine, everything is fine, why would you ask?"

There was a pause. "Uh… well, because you seemed kind of worried about it when you were here? I mean, when you found out about her joining the team and all. I just was curious if it had been an issue."

"Oh," I said quickly, and my next breath came easier. "Yeah, she's been great. I made a bit of an ass of myself when she first joined, basically saying in not so many words that I was worried she'd be a distraction on the team."

"Jordan…"

"I know," I said before he could continue. "Not my proudest moment. But, I was stressed coming into the new season, and to be honest, I *was* worried that the guys would be distracted by her. And, to be clear, they are — but that's not her fault. She's doing her job, and doing a damn fine job of it, too. At first, the guys were all gaga for her, but they respect her now. She feels like part of the team already."

"That's awesome," Mikey said, but there was a hesitance in his voice. "Now… are you going to tell me why you reacted like a kid getting caught with his hand in the cookie jar when I asked you about her?"

I opened my mouth to argue, but he cut me off before I could speak.

"And don't pretend like it's nothing, because I know you better than that, and to save us both time we should just skip the part where I have to beat it out of you."

I wanted to be annoyed that my brother knew me so well, but I couldn't help but smile, because I was this way with all of them, too.

We could see through the bullshit when it came to each other, and that was part of what made our bond so strong.

I sighed. "I don't even know where to begin."

"How about you start with whatever is on your mind right now."

I worked the inside of my cheek. "I kissed her on Saturday night. She freaked out and basically kicked me out of her home. Then on Monday, she stormed into my office and said it was a drunken mistake and we should forget it ever happened."

"Ouch."

"And I agreed," I continued. "Even though I don't *actually* agree."

"I see."

"And I hate it," I added, chest aching with the realization that I really, really *did* hate it. "Because we had a friendship, you know? I felt like… like I could talk to her, and like she was opening up to me. And we would joke with each other, and we worked well together, too… and now?" I sighed again. "We're just dancing around each other, pretending like I didn't cross the line and that everything is back to normal, when we don't even *have* a normal, anymore."

Mikey was quiet for a long time, then he asked one simple question.

"Do you still want to kiss her?"

I frowned. "It doesn't matter if I do or not."

"I guess what I mean is — when she said it was a mistake and you guys should forget about it, did you take that opportunity to tell her that you *didn't* feel like it was a mistake, and that you'd like to try being more than friends?"

"Mikey, she told me we should forget about it."

"I realize that," he said. "But what I'm asking is does she know you feel this way?"

"It doesn't matt—"

"It does!" Mikey's voice was loud and firm, and I shut my mouth in response. "She told you it was a mistake, that you both were drunk, and you agreed and said yeah, let's forget about it. What if there was a little bit of hope in her that it *wasn't* a mistake? What if she was waiting to see what *you* said?"

I frowned.

"Look, I know you, Big Bro, and one thing I know is that you don't misread signs when it comes to women. You are not an asshole, and you wouldn't so much as *think* about making a move on a woman unless there was a real connection and consent. You've always been the gentleman, and you've always taken things slow with the women you've dated — and what's more, there haven't been many. So, if you crossed the line and kissed Sydney, I know for a fact that it was because you felt something, and you wouldn't have felt something if *she* hadn't felt it, too."

A little balloon of hope filled in my chest, but I popped it quickly. "It's not that simple."

"It could be."

"I can't just…" I threw my hand out, as if to show him all the reasons why. "*Confess* that I wanted to kiss her and that I *still* want to kiss her and that I think about her every damn minute of every day. This isn't high school. We *work* together, Mikey. She technically works *under* my supervision, which makes me her boss, in a way. She's already working against the odds as the only female on an all-male staff in a male-dominated sport, *and* she's back to work for the first time in years. *And,*" I continued, running out of breath. "She has a daughter, and an ex-husband, and there are just a lot of complications at work here, okay?"

My little brother didn't respond for a long time. It was just me, breathing heavily, waiting for him to argue with me so I could fight him some more on the topic. But instead, after a long pause, he made a noise of understanding.

"Well," he said. "It sounds like you have your answer."

My chest was still rising and falling at a rapid rate, but when the urge to fight him left me, I was left in a hollow sadness wishing he would keep going, keep telling me reasons I was wrong.

"Just pretend like it never happened and things are back to work as usual," he continued. "She forgets about you, you forget about her. No harm, no foul. It was just a kiss, right?"

A long, slow exhale left my chest. "Right," I agreed, though my voice was soft and unsure.

Mikey didn't say anything, letting the silence sit between us, and I chewed on everything he'd said and every point I'd thrown back at him for the rest of our phone call. When we were all caught up and promised to talk again soon, I hung up the phone and stared at the blank screen of my television.

"It was just a kiss," I repeated out loud, to no one and to whoever might be listening — myself, included.

Then, I picked up my playbook, and got back to distracting myself from all the lies.

Chapter Eleven

Sydney

Fall began to make its descent on our little Tennessee town over the next two weeks. The days cooled to a beautifully perfect seventy to seventy-five degrees, and the evenings welcomed us with a crisp wind that brought chilly nights. It wasn't quite cold enough to get the fireplace going yet, but it was getting there, and I reveled in the fact that I could wear leggings and a long-sleeve shirt without sweating.

Margaret's Bakery boasted the arrival of pumpkin bread and apple cider, Charlie Warren was already setting up his pumpkin patch on the edge of town, and I knew the corn maze wouldn't be far behind.

And most of all, football season was in full swing.

It was our first home game since the one we'd opened the season with, and the Stratford stands were packed. We'd won all three of our away games since then, and our fans were anxious to see if we'd deliver a W at home to-night. Winning in any capacity was great, but winning in your own house was another level of high — and I could feel the pressure our players were putting on themselves to deliver.

"Alright," I said after wrapping our quarterback's left ankle. I tapped the toe of his cleat. "Try not to get sacked, and I'll re-wrap at halftime, if neces-sary."

Rodgers smiled, thanking me as he hopped up from the bench and jogged out to join his team warming up on the field. I packed away the tape in my training bag, looking over my notes on all the players to make sure I hadn't forgotten anyone. My pre-game responsibilities felt natural to me now, and I loved that I had a routine.

"Coach!"

I followed the sound of someone calling out to Jordan, smiling curiously when I found an older man I recognized from when he'd helped Randy work on our busted pipe in our kitchen one afternoon years ago. He had dark brown skin and soft, kind eyes — and a crooked yellow grin that widened the longer he stood there. He wore a fedora on his head, one that matched the suspenders he wore, and he tipped it at Jordan as he made his way over to the sideline, leaning over the railing that separated us from the fans in the bleachers.

"What say you, Eli?" Jordan asked, pressing his back to the gate next to where Eli stood. It made it where they could stand next to each other and talk, but he could still keep an eye on his team, too.

"I say I'm looking forward to you bringing all those W's you've gotten on the road home tonight."

Jordan raised his eyebrows, gaze following the throw Rodgers had just made to Smith on the field. "If all goes according to my plan, that's exactly what you'll see." He glanced up at Eli before his eyes were on the field again. "Missed you at last week's game."

Eli grumbled. "Yeah, well, they had a plumbing emergency down at the nursing home Friday evening. I couldn't very well leave Ms. Betty Collins without a properly working toilet, as I'm sure you well know."

Jordan chuckled at that, and I found myself wondering who Betty Collins was, and my curiosity climbed the more I watched them together. That was, until the Mom Parade made their way to the fan side of the fence.

I rolled my eyes at the way they leaned over it, giving glimpses of their cleavage, their eyes light and playful as they talked to Jordan. They asked if they could get him anything, if he needed a shoulder massage before the game, if he wanted to hang out *after* the game — and any time Jordan gave them an incredulous look, the women hid their intentions under a flurry of laughter, as if they were joking when we all knew they'd jump at the chance to have Jordan in their bed.

I didn't like the way my stomach soured at that thought.

I couldn't stop watching, and I wondered if he felt it, because as soon as the parade moved on, Jordan's eyes met mine, and I tore my gaze away like I'd been caught.

After that, I kept my focus on my own tasks, working through my pre-game checklist as the clock wound down toward kick off. Just beforehand, Jordan sidled up beside me.

"Ready to go?" he asked.

"Yep," I answered, eyes still on my notebook. "Everyone is wrapped up and massaged and iced and ready to rock."

"Good," he answered, watching the field.

I glanced at him, feeling like he was a complete stranger. That's what it had felt like ever since... well, since the night we both pretended never happened. We worked together the same as we had before, and to everyone else, I imagined we looked just fine.

But it was different.

We didn't joke, we didn't talk about anything of substance, and we definitely didn't spend any time getting to know each other better. He'd come over to help Paige twice since that night, and both times, he'd avoided me like the plague, and I'd done the same, leaving him to work with her and asking him to stay for dinner knowing full well that I didn't actually want him to and he wouldn't out of respect for our agreement.

We were putting it behind us, acknowledging it as a mistake and pretending like it never happened — just like I'd suggested.

And still... I longed for the version of us that existed before that night.

I also longed for a day when I wouldn't accidentally find myself staring at his mouth, remembering the way it felt pressed against mine.

A blush heated my cheeks as that thought found me, and I cleared my throat, glancing at the stands behind us and back at him. "Was that Elijah Braxton you were talking to?"

Jordan smirked, but didn't take his eyes off his players. "Indeed. He's a big football fan, comes to every game — even the away games, when he can." One eyebrow climbed as he faced me. "And believe me when I say that when we lose, he's the first one to let me know what he thinks about it."

I chuckled. "Well, at least if we *do* lose, you'll also have plenty of... *support*, too." I nodded to where the women who were just talking to him were gathered in the front row of the bleachers.

Their smiles grew when Jordan looked at them, and he had a brow cocked when he turned back to me. "I don't think I want the kind of support that crew would offer."

I bit my lip against a smile, not sure why his reaction to them made me happy. "Anyway, you better get out there," I said just as the referee blew the whistle signaling that it was time for the coin toss.

Jordan watched me for a long moment with a curious gaze, but then he nodded, jogging out onto the field without another word.

And the game began.

It was a wondrous sight to behold, the way Jordan could hold his shit together through one of the most nerve-racking games I'd ever witnessed. There was a lot on the line in this home game, and we volleyed back and forth with the Salem Serpents, scoring a touchdown only for them to answer with one, in return.

We'd go up by three, then down by three, up by seven, then down by three again. Back and forth, over and over through every single quarter of the game.

And all the while, Jordan paced the sideline calmly and coolly, chewing his gum, a permanent scowl on his face as he talked to the other coaches behind his clipboard and pulled players to the side to whisper in their ears each time they came off the field.

Me, on the other hand?

I was a mess.

My knuckles were white from how hard I gripped my notebook all game, and though I would never wish for a player to get injured, not having anything to take my focus off the field put me even more on edge. I would check in on the players I was working with from time to time, but for the most part, I wasn't needed — not for anything other than support.

When the two-minute warning came at the end of the fourth quarter, coach huddled up our offense, speaking with a low, firm voice in the middle of the circle. I couldn't hear what he said, but when the players ran back onto the field, I saw the fierce determination in their eyes.

We were down by three with the ball on our twenty-seven-yard line, and two minutes to score.

I didn't breathe for those two minutes — not when we made a forty-yard pass in a third and eleven situation and not when our offense was a wall against their defense, trying to push the last few yards into the end zone with less than forty seconds left to play. But when we finally broke through and scored, I gave my burning lungs the oxygen they needed and screamed like a banshee, jumping up and down on the sideline.

I could hear Paige going wild behind me, too, and I found her in the stands, giving her an air high five. Randy was there next to her, but he didn't seem in a celebratory mood. Instead, his eyes were hard on me, disapproving.

He didn't like that I was happy.

Nothing could get under my skin at that moment, though — least of all him. And I blew a kiss at Paige just as our boys lined up for the extra point kick. It was good, and then we were up by four.

But the Serpents still had thirty-two seconds to play with.

It was the longest thirty seconds of my life, watching them make conversion after conversion, lining up quickly after each play to get the next one in before time ran out. They were on a mission to win in the last stretch, and our defense was on a mission to stop them.

When they snapped the ball with four seconds left to play, their quarterback launched it long, eyes on their best receiver who was just ten yards from their end zone.

But he didn't catch the ball.

Boone Parson, our cornerback, did.

Every player on our sidelines jumped in the air when the interception happened, the stands going crazy behind us as we all rushed the field. The rest of the defense hoisted Parson up onto their shoulders, and he held the ball over his head in victory.

I was all smiles and laughs and cheers and a racing heart as I watched. Jordan remained calm until he shook hands with the other coach, and then, for the first time all game, emotion showed on his face. He thrust his fist into the air, joining in on the celebrations as the entire town of Stratford roared their approval.

We'd won four games in a row, and our first one at home.

The Stratford Wild Cats were on fire.

It was a high unlike any I'd ever known, winning a home game — especially one that close. The energy was still buzzing through me when my job was done in the training room and the players had all gone off to celebrate their win. The other coaches were still laughing and reminiscing over their favorite moments of the game when I rounded into Jordan's office.

"Okay, I have a serious question," I said, plopping down into the chair across from his.

He glanced up, smiling when he saw me as he kicked back in his chair. "I'm sorry, but I'm not signing autographs at this point in time."

I stuck my tongue out.

"What's up?" he asked, still smiling. I had a feeling that smile would be glued to his face all weekend.

"How the hell do you go to *sleep* after a game like that?"

Jordan barked out a laugh.

"I'm serious," I continued, shaking my head with my hands extended toward him. "I mean, my heart is *still* pounding."

"It was amazing, wasn't it?"

"Absolutely unreal," I agreed. "Paige is staying with her dad tonight, and I just cannot imagine a scenario where I go home, make some tea, and go to bed. Like... I feel like I could run a freaking marathon right now."

Jordan smiled as he took in my enthusiasm, but the longer he watched me, the more that smile fell. His eyes flicked back and forth between mine like he was warring with something, and he opened his mouth, shut it again, then finally spoke.

"Maybe you don't go home then," he suggested. "At least, not yet."

"And where the hell should I go?" I asked on a laugh.

But when Jordan's expression sobered, the storm swirling in his eyes, my own smile fell, too. There was a new energy in the room, one that had snuck in without me noticing, but now, it was all I could feel.

The air was hot.

The office was smaller somehow.

Jordan's eyes pierced me like the blade of a knife, and without rhyme or reason, I leaned into the edge.

"Come with me," he said — and it wasn't tentatively or hesitantly, but confidently, like there was no other choice but for me to agree.

My heart that had been racing stopped altogether, chest tightening as if to warn me this was a bad idea. And I knew it, too — I knew by the way it was suddenly difficult to swallow, and the way my neck heated the longer he watched me that way.

But no matter how bad of an idea I told myself it was, I couldn't suppress the louder voice inside me that said *go*.

So, I stood, and with that buzzing, electric energy still hanging like live wires between us, I ignored the danger and submitted to temptation.

"Let me grab my bag."

• • •

Jordan

"OH MY GOD, OH MY GOD, OH MY GOD!"

I couldn't stop laughing at Sydney's outbursts as we tore through the Tennessee mud in my Bronco, the full moon above us and my headlights lighting the way. She held on to what I referred to as the, *"Oh, shit"* handle with one hand and gripped the center console or the dashboard with the other — depending on which way the Bronco was moving.

My abs were on fire like I had been doing crunches instead of just laughing, but I couldn't stop, and I reveled in the sound of *her* laughter the longer we were in those woods.

Sydney went from screaming in terror to cackling in uncontrollable laughter and back in the span of sixty seconds. I focused on keeping us steady and safe, flooring it over the ramps and spinning my tires to fling up mud, all the while ensuring we never got deep enough to get stuck. When I finally pulled us onto one of the dirt trails for a break and the Bronco evened out, Sydney slumped in her seat, breathing like she'd just run for her life.

"Oh, My-Lanta," she said on a long breath when I pulled over, putting it in park in one of my favorite meadows. "Is it possible to be sore from mudding?"

"Hey, you said you had a lot of energy to expend. Tell me that didn't do the trick?"

"It did," she agreed, shaking her head. "But, it also maybe gave me a heart attack or two."

I chuckled, turning the keys in the ignition until the engine ceased, and then all the noise was gone and we were blanketed in a silence only nature could provide. Slowly, as my ears adjusted, the faint sound of the few katydids still hanging around in the cooler nights made their way through the silence. In the summer, the music they made together was deafening, a sign of warm weather. But in the fall, hearing them was rare — especially once it actually got cold.

I grabbed my jacket from the backseat, shrugging it on and climbing out of the driver seat as Sydney watched me curiously. There were other creatures talking to each other all around us — maybe birds, maybe coyotes, maybe insects. I couldn't be sure of all of them, but I knew they made up my favorite symphony.

When Sydney joined me outside the truck, I walked over to her side, offering my hand and nodding to the front tire.

She cocked a brow. "What?"

"Hop up," I answered easily.

She looked at the wheel, at the muddy hood, and back at me with her brows drawn together. "On the hood?"

I smiled, grabbing her hand in mine and giving her a boost as she lifted herself up. "Trust me, you won't hurt it."

She still seemed a little hesitant, even when she was sitting on the hood, but when I climbed up on the other side and sat next to her, leaning back against the windshield with my eyes on the clearing ahead of us, she relaxed, reclining until her back hit the glass, too.

It was chilly — not so cold that it was uncomfortable, but enough so that I was glad I had my jacket. Sydney wore a Stratford High Football hoodie, and she pulled the hood of it up, tucking her hands in the pockets and crossing her legs where they splayed out in front of her.

"This is beautiful," she said, eyes wandering over the meadow. It was a phenomenon I didn't really understand, how in the middle of mud and trees and a forest there could be a break in all of it where the grass and plants and flowers bloomed freely.

"You should see it in the springtime," I said, letting my eyes travel up to where the stars peppered the sky. On a dark night, you couldn't count them all to save your life. But tonight, the moon was full and bright, its glow stealing the show in the sky. "There are all these wildflowers, and if you sit here long enough and are quiet, you'll see deer and rabbits and warblers and all kinds of creatures. I even saw two foxes once." I smiled at the memory. "You ever see a gray fox before? Bastards are too cute for their own good."

Sydney laughed. "I take it you come here often, then?"

"It's my spot," I said comfortably, proudly. "I love mudding in the truck, and I love to get a good run in to burn off any frustration or stress, but this? Sitting here and being still for a while?" I shook my head. "There's nothing more peaceful."

We sat there on the hood of my truck, the damp coolness of the forest on our skin and our eyes cast upward. For a long time, neither of us said anything, and somehow, it was the best conversation we'd had in weeks.

"I'm sure you don't need me to tell you this," she said after a while. "But, you're a really great coach, Jordan. Those boys... hell, this whole *town*. We're lucky to have you."

I shrugged, humbled, but my chest filled with a sense of pride hearing those words from her. "Thank you," I said. "I just love football, and I care about my team. And I think when those two things are true, anyone can be a good coach."

"False," she said quickly, rolling onto her side. She propped her head up, elbow on the windshield and hand cradling her cheek. "It's more than just loving the game and you know it. You're talented. You see things that others don't. You know a player's weakness before they do, and what's more, you know how to *conquer* it. You command respect, and you know what to say when they're down and defeated and what to say to keep them focused when they're on a high, too. You make tough decisions when it comes to who to play where and when to take someone out, and you don't apologize for anything — not even when you lose — because you know you have a plan, and you believe in it."

I let my head fall to the side until my eyes met hers, and I swore I'd never felt so exposed in my life. I'd been given compliments on my coaching before, but no one had ever put it into words the way she just had.

"They're like family to me," I told her. "Not just the players we have now, but any player who I work with." I paused, wetting my lips as I tried to find the words to explain. "I've always wanted to coach, and I got started as soon as I could after high school. I wanted to make a difference — not just for our school and football, but for these boys — individually, you know? We're in a small town, and some of these kids don't exactly have the best role models at home. I want to be there for them to remind them what they are capable of, what they have inside them, to push them when they need to be pushed and encourage them when they need to be encouraged. And to tell them I'm proud of them," I added. "Because I might be the only one they ever hear it from."

Her eyes softened, brows folding together.

"But as much as I want to make a difference, I'm also fucking *terrified* of messing it all up — of messing *them* up."

"You have no reason to be scared," she assured me. "You're the best coach I've ever known."

"How many have you known?"

"That's not the point."

I chuckled, letting my eyes wander back up to the sky. "What about you?" I asked. "How did you end up in athletic training?"

"Oh, that's easy," she said quickly. "I love bodies."

I snorted.

"No, but really, I have always had an interest in the way we push ourselves as humans, especially in sports. I knew I had an interest in anatomy and the medical side of things, but I didn't really want to be a *doctor*, you know? So, when I went to college, I focused on sports medicine and fell in love."

She paused, and I turned toward her again, sobering a little at the distant look in her eyes.

"When I was finishing my master's, a small junior college baseball team asked me to come on as their trainer. Fresh out of school." She smiled, but her eyes were sad. "I couldn't believe it. But it was the first time in my life that I felt like everything I'd done was right, like it had all led to that moment."

"That's amazing, Sydney," I said earnestly. Principal Hanley had told me a little about her background, about her previous offers to work with a college-level team, but this was the first time I heard it from her.

She swallowed. "Yeah, well... I never accepted the job, so..."

"Why not?"

Sydney's eyes found mine, and she shrugged with the smallest, most innocent smile on her face. "I got pregnant."

My heart squeezed.

Part of me considered reaching over to grab her hand, or pull her into me, to hold her and let her know I understood. But the truth was I *didn't*. I didn't know what it was like to have a child, to give birth to another human, to have something happen like that where every priority in life shifted.

"They said they'd wait," she continued, her voice soft. "They said when I had Paige, I could come work for them whenever I was ready. They'd hold the spot. Do you know how unheard of that is?" Her eyes welled with tears. "But Randy insisted we get married, and what I didn't realize was that when I agreed to be his wife, I also agreed to live by his rules."

My face hardened. I didn't know a thing about Randy other than what he did for a living, but in that moment, watching the look in her eyes... I knew he'd hurt her.

That was enough for me to be pissed.

"That's bullshit," I said after a moment. "That's not how marriage is supposed to work."

"It was how it worked in his eyes," she said, sniffling. "And I was so young... so afraid. I was going to be a mother and I could barely take care of myself, you know? But Randy was there, saying he could take care of everything. I could just focus on Paige, be a mom, and he would take care of us both. And I loved him, and it all sounded so nice," she admitted, and then she bit her lip and let out a bitter laugh. "And it was. Until it was hell."

This time, I couldn't resist the urge that overcame me, and I reached for her, pulling her into my chest and folding my arms around her as if I could shield her from something that had already happened. I didn't even know what *it* was, what the hell she referred to entailed. All I knew was that I wished in so many ways that I could somehow snap my fingers and go back to high school and grab her in the hallway, pull her into a closet, warn her of the choices she was about to make.

But then, Paige wouldn't exist.

And Sydney wouldn't be the woman she was today.

As much as life hurt like hell, those painful lessons somehow seemed to have beautiful ramifications, like everything that happened was for a reason we could never fully see or understand until years down the line.

Sydney was stiff and hesitant in my arms at first, but then she relaxed, exhaling a long breath and letting me hold her. She was so small in my arms, and everything inside me ached to keep her safe.

We laid there with her wrapped in my arms and my chest tight for a long while, the soft sounds of the night surrounding us. I didn't dare speak, not for the fear of spooking her out of my grasp with the mere sound of my voice. It was just like all those other times I'd sat in that meadow and tried to be perfectly still and quiet so as not to scare away the fauna.

She relaxed more and more into me as the minutes passed, and I held her tight, rubbing my hands over her back to soothe her. Then, out of nowhere, a soft and low *hoot, hoot* broke through the silence.

Sydney lifted her head, looking at me before she looked up at the trees behind us. "What was that?" she whispered.

It came again, and I smiled, sweeping the mess of hair that had fallen from her bun behind her ear. "I think it might be a saw-whet owl," I answered, just as soft. "They're rare, I've only ever heard one once before."

Sydney smiled, laying her head back on my chest, and we listened to the owl until it quieted or left us, though we couldn't be sure which.

"You know... I had a huge crush on you in high school."

My eyes shot open at her admission, and I peeked down at her. "You're shitting me."

She laughed, shaking her head. "Nope. I thought you were soooo cute." She dragged out the syllables. "My friends did, too. But, you were so quiet, so elusive."

"You make it sound like I was some broody bad boy."

"To us, you were."

I laughed through my nose. "I was just minding my own business."

"Rare in this town."

"I had a crush on you, too, for whatever it's worth."

"Wait, really?" She looked up at me, a pleased grin on her lips. "I wasn't sure you even knew I existed."

"Are you kidding? Have you *seen* you?" I shook my head. "Besides, you were new in town. You know as well as I do that you can't be new in town and everyone not find out who you are."

"Why didn't you ever say anything?"

"Why didn't *you*?" I shot back. She stuck out her tongue, then laid on my chest again, her breaths coming easier now that we'd moved off the topic of her ex-husband.

We laid there silently, the night getting cooler around us. And with her wrapped up in my arms like that, I found myself thinking about the night I promised her I'd forget about, about the kiss we tried to swear never happened.

"I like this," Sydney said after a while. "Talking to you like normal again." She leaned up to look at me. "It's been kind of... awkward, hasn't it?"

I didn't answer, though my heart leapt into my throat.

"It's just nice to not feel like there's something weird between us," she continued.

"But there is."

Sydney stiffened, and my heart beat hard in my chest — once, twice, faster and faster, as if urging me not to stop until I'd said what I'd needed to.

"There *is* something weird between us," I said again, leaning up until my chest was even with hers, until our eyes were level and she could see the sincerity I hoped I was conveying. "That's why you feel it. And it's not just weird, it's rare, and unique, and intoxicating and terrifying, too."

Sydney's throat constricted, her mouth parting as she listened.

"We're both trying to pretend like I didn't kiss you when I did," I said, though my heart was so heavy in my ears I couldn't be sure I'd actually said it loud enough. "Like I didn't *want* to kiss you. But I did."

Her eyes flicked between mine.

"Like it was a drunken night or a mistake," I continued. "When we both know the truth is that I kissed you because I wanted to, because I *needed* to, because it felt like the only thing I could do in that moment."

"Jordan…" Sydney whispered, but it wasn't a warning — more like a plea.

"And I've wanted to kiss you every day since then, too."

Her lips trembled as she pressed them together, and I hadn't realized her hands were on me, not until I felt her fist twist in the fabric of my jacket, like she was in danger of falling off the hood of my truck if she wasn't latched onto me.

"Sydney," I said, soft and low. "It wasn't a mistake for me. It wasn't an accident. And I don't want to keep pretending like it is. But," I added, swallowing. "I *will* respect if that's the way you see it. If you truly want me to forget it ever happened, I… well, I'll find a way. But only if you can look at me, right now, look me right in my eyes and tell me that's what you want."

Her face crumpled, and for a moment I was worried she was about to cry, that I'd pushed too far, that I'd listened to my baby brother's advice like a fucking idiot and was about to pay the ultimate price.

"Was our kiss a mistake?" I asked again.

And with her eyes still welled up, she shook her head.

My heart slammed in my chest. "Do you want me to forget it ever happened?"

She shook her head again, and already, our hands were reaching for each other, our lips parting, closing the distance between us.

"Can I kiss you again now?" I whispered.

She nodded, and I tilted her chin up, taking her mouth with mine like it had always belonged to me.

And in a snap, all the energy in that forest rushed to the point where our lips met.

Chapter Twelve

Sydney

Everything that had been dead inside me came to life when Jordan Becker's mouth claimed mine.

It happened in a rush, in an instant, in a shock so violent and powerful that I felt it like an earthquake in my soul. Desire that I hadn't felt in years pooled heavy and hot in my gut. My heart that had only beat in fear and suspicion began to beat in urgent want, instead. My hands that I thought had forgotten how to touch a man reached for Jordan like he'd always been mine.

And in the midst of it all, the way he kissed me made me realize I'd never really been kissed before.

I'd never had strong hands holding my face like that — in a way that commanded I was his but also ensured I was cared for. How was it possible that his lips were hot on mine, that his teeth sent sharp pangs of pleasure and pain through me each time he bit down on my neck, that his hands gripped me hard enough to leave bruises and yet *still* he was somehow tender, somehow hesitant, somehow gentle and sure all at once?

I pressed my hands into his chest as the night came alive around us, feeling its energy as I straddled him on the hood of his Bronco. The more we moved, the more we both became covered in the fresh mud he'd conjured up on our ride out to the meadow, but I couldn't find it in me to care.

My kisses grew harder, more insistent as I rolled my hips, and when the heat of me met his growing erection, I smiled in satisfaction.

In two quick and fluid movements, I broke our kiss and stripped my hoodie over my head, letting it fall somewhere on the ground behind me. I already had my long-sleeve shirt up and over my head when Jordan's hands gripped hard on my waist, stilling me where I was grinding against him.

"Sydney," he panted just as I lowered my mouth to his again.

I stole his next words, and he moaned, holding me tighter as I kissed him and rubbed the seam of my leggings against the growing bulge in his pants.

He cursed into my mouth, breaking our kiss with his hands grabbing my wrists and holding me away from him.

"Syd," he said again, and for some reason, that little shortened version of my name made the urge to kiss him even more intoxicating. "Maybe we should slow down."

"Shut up and kiss me," I said, breaking the grip he had on my wrists and wrapping my hands around his neck.

My fingers gripped at the base of his head, pulling him into my kiss, and he bit down hard on my lip, releasing it with a pop before he held me away again.

"Woman," he warned, but he was smiling, panting. "I'm serious. I don't want this to be just…" He frowned. "I want to court you, get to know you, take you on a date."

"You can take me on a date later," I said, rolling my hips against him. It was the only place he wasn't holding me still, and his eyes rolled up toward the full moon above us with the friction I created. "Right now, I want you to *touch* me."

I couldn't believe those words came from my mouth, that the desire breaking free had been bottled up in my cold, lifeless heart. It was like I'd been broken and sewn together with a thin piece of yarn, and all Jordan had done was tug one end of it, but it'd been enough to unravel me completely.

With my request, Jordan gave up resisting, and his mouth claimed mine again, both of us panting and moaning, licking and tasting, rolling and flexing until the need inside us was so fierce we nearly died beneath the weight of it.

"Wrap your legs around me," Jordan said, lifting my ass like I weighed nothing. I did as he asked, and in a feat of strength that he made look easy, he held me to him as he hopped down from the hood of the truck.

His lips were still hot on every inch of me he could reach, kissing my lips and neck and chin and jaw as he walked us to the back door of the Bronco. He felt for the handle blindly, and then the door was open and I was on my back, Jordan sliding into the space between my legs with the door still open behind him.

When he lifted to take off his jacket, he thunked his head hard on the ceiling, and I laughed, loving the smile that bloomed on his face, too.

"Think it's funny when I get hurt, huh?"

"No," I answered, leaning up on my elbows. "Think it's funny that we're about to fuck in the backseat of your truck like a couple of high schoolers."

"How do you know I'm going to fuck you?" Jordan asked, slowing his movements as he tugged his t-shirt up and over his head.

I didn't even try to hide my hungry gaze as I devoured every newly exposed inch of him, remembering when I'd seen that chest and abdomen speckled with mud in the park.

"What if I'm just going to touch you?" he continued, trailing a fingertip over the swells of each of my modest breasts where they were pushed up in my bra. "That's what you want, right?"

He made a path with that finger up my neck and over my chin, running it along my bottom lip before I sucked it into my mouth and released it with a pop that had his eyes rolling.

"If you can resist fucking me right now, I'll wash your truck tomorrow."

He smirked. "Is that a bet?"

"I don't know," I asked, sitting up fully. I reached back to unfasten the clasp on my bra, letting my breasts spill out as I tossed it on the floor of the truck. "Is it considered a fair bet if you know you're going to win?"

I tilted my head, leaning back on one hand and tracing my nipples with the other. They each puckered under the touch, and Jordan watched with his mouth parted, stormy eyes snapping to mine.

In an instant, he was on top of me again.

His kisses were slow but hard, purposeful and breathtaking. He sucked the skin on my neck on his way down to my chest, and then he palmed my right breast in his hand, appreciating the weight of it with a groan before his lips closed over the peak.

I arched into the touch, into his mouth, into *him*, and slowly, subtly, as if we were in a movie or the pages of an epic novel, time slowed, and every sense awakened to that man and that moment.

His pace softened, and he took his time with each of my breasts, sucking and licking and kissing and touching. I was so heavy with need when he finally backed off of me to stand again, and he kept his eyes on mine as he unfastened his belt, slowly stripping out of his sneakers and then his pants.

The bulge in his boxer briefs had me biting my lip, and I fell back into the seat, lifting my hips until I could shimmy out of my leggings, too. I pooled them at my ankles before I tugged off my sneakers and socks, then I peeled the leggings the rest of the way off — just in time to watch Jordan grip the band of his briefs and tug them down in one swift motion.

Then, he stood, his erection springing to life between us.

My lips parted as I squeezed my knees together, suddenly shy. It wasn't that I was naked physically in front of my boss, it was that he'd already stripped me bare emotionally before a single article of clothing had been removed.

Jordan seemed to sense the shift in energy, too, as he slowly climbed back into the truck with me. He settled between my legs, and each inch of my skin he touched on the way fired shots through my nervous system until he hovered over me, our bare chests somehow hot and slick in the cool night.

For a long moment, his gray-blue eyes searched mine, and in that light, I couldn't even see the burst of brown around the iris. They were just two icy pools sucking me into his depths.

He swept my hair away from my face, still marveling at me like I was the most beautiful creature in the entire universe. "Where did you come from?"

His voice was just a whisper, and yet I felt it deep within me like he'd screamed to the world.

"Just finished my walk through hell."

"Does that make this purgatory?" he asked on a smirk.

I smiled, too, reaching up to press my lips to his. "I think that makes this heaven."

He frowned, leaning into my kiss with purpose, one arm holding him balanced over me while the other gripped my hip with force. I bucked my hips, and with the motion, the slick heat between my legs coated his shaft, eliciting a sharp breath from us both.

"Syd," he said, panting and pressing his forehead to mine as he stilled. "I..." He swallowed. "As much as you're right about me not being able to resist fucking you right now, I don't have a condom."

My heart stopped for a second, but it kicked back to its quick pace in the next breath. "Are you clean?"

"Yes," he answered automatically. "But..."

I swallowed, each half of me warring with whether I was ready to expose the next bit of information. But the desire pulsing through me won over the part of me that was somewhat ashamed.

"I can't get pregnant," I assured him with a soft shrug. "After Paige, I..." I swallowed. "I had a surgery..."

I didn't have to tell him what kind of surgery for him to understand.

Those words hung heavy between us, and the fact that no one knew that about me — not even my ex-husband — was written in my expression. I knew it, because without me even having to say it, I could tell *Jordan* understood that no one else knew. His brows bent in a sad understanding, and he kissed my forehead before his lips trailed to each of my cheeks and back to my mouth.

The tender moment lasted only a moment before it was replaced with urgency again, and I felt myself open to him — my mouth, my heart, my legs — until the tip of him was at my entrance and all it would take was a nudge of my foot in his backside, or a flex of his hips, to answer all my needs.

Jordan's breaths were shallow, his shoulders shaking where he held himself above me, and he broke our kiss, his mouth hovering over mine.

Then, on an excruciatingly slow roll of his hips, he entered me, and everything that wasn't Jordan Becker faded to black.

Pain ripped through me in a flash, the sensation of being spread open after having that part of me empty for so long. I cringed against it, and Jordan kissed me, distracting me as he slowed his movements and made his way deeper inside me as gently as he could.

Each moment brought more ecstasy and less pain, until I was denting his flesh with my nails, bucking my hips to meet his, my kisses hungry and desperate and hot. I reveled in the way his back arched with every thrust, in the way his glutes tightened with each flex inside me. It was animalistic, the way he held me to him, the unbridled passion that flowed between us as he took me in the back of his truck. The rough fabric of his seat scratched my back as

I scratched his, and pain danced with pleasure in equal measure with each passing minute.

Before I realized what I was doing, I'd pressed my hands into his chest, pushing him off me long enough to have him sitting in the seat and me climbing into his lap. He was barely out of me before I sat on top of him again, the length of him sliding in deeper, making both of us pause when he was all the way in as if we'd lost all breath completely.

The windows of that old Bronco were steamy and hot, but every now and then, a cool breeze would reach us from the forest, and I'd shiver and shake, the combination exhilarating.

Slowly, I began to move, my thigh muscles burning as I grabbed his shoulders and rode him. His hands were free to roam, and roam they did, gripping my waist and my hips and my breasts before they were cradling my face to his again.

I threw my head back on a gasp when he bucked into me, realizing that when he worked his hips in time with mine, a depth I never knew existed was reached. Each new thrust pressed a spot deep inside me that sparked my orgasm, like two rocks slicked together over a bundle of straw, just waiting to catch fire.

Jordan's mouth latched onto my neck, sucking and licking his way down to my breast, and when he sucked my nipple between his teeth and bucked his hips at the same time, I cried out in a moan I was sure couldn't have been mine.

"Oh, *God*," I groaned, and the muscles in my body ceased to work. I sat there on top of him without moving, completely useless, but Jordan kept working.

He wrapped his arms around me, hugging me to him so that every new thrust of his hips didn't just make him penetrate me deeper, but also had my clit rubbing against his pelvis, that fire closer and closer to catching with each flex.

"Jordan," I whispered.

"Oh, fuck, *Sydney*," he answered on a breath, my name long and desperate on his lips, and then he was pumping harder, faster, and I knew he was close, too.

His desire fueled mine, and I exploded, thighs clenching around him as I let my orgasm take me under. The spark that finally caught was more like a nuclear blast, one so powerful that I trembled and moaned like I'd left my body entirely in that moment. I floated above it, feeling everything and nothing at all, a powerful sensation of every nerve being ignited at the same time everything inside me numbed.

Jordan came right behind me, burying his head in my chest with a groan and gripping me so tight I could barely breathe as he stilled. I felt his hot release inside me, and I somehow found the strength to move when he couldn't anymore, riding him until we were both spent, collapsing into each other in a panting tangle of limbs.

The symphony of the forest came back to life, insects and birds singing in the night as our breaths evened out, our bodies hot and slick but still wrapped up in every possible way.

When I finally mustered the energy to peel myself away from him enough to look into his eyes, Jordan ran both hands back through my hair, tugging on it slightly until my chin lifted and his mouth met mine.

"Alright, you little devil," he said, kissing me hard before he pulled back on a smile and ran his thumb across my bottom lip. "Now that you've had your way with me, let's talk about that date."

Chapter Thirteen

Sydney

"OH, MY GOD, YOU KINKY LITTLE FOX!"

I covered my mouth to suppress my laughter at my sister's outburst the next day, casting a glance at Paige in the living room to make sure she hadn't heard anything. College Game Day was on, so of course, I was invisible to her.

"I can't believe you hooked up with your boss," Gabby continued, whisper-yelling at me. She was at Mom and Dad's for the day, and I'd told her to find someplace private when we got on the call. "In a friggin' *Bronco* in the damn forest, for God's sake."

I bit my lip against my smile, both loving and hating the giddy feeling inflating my belly like a hot air balloon. I loved it because it was fun and exciting, but I hated it because I knew as soon as it took over, anxiety would sweep in to knock me out of breath.

"You're ignoring the pressing question, dear sister, which is..." I glanced at Paige, making my way through the sliding glass door and onto the back porch before I continued. "What the hell do I do now?"

"What do you mean?" Gabby asked. "You bang him again — preferably in a bed this time, but hey, no judgment if exhibitionism is your thing."

I wished she was in the vicinity to smack her.

"Gab, be real. Do you not see every single thing wrong with this scenario? Because they're like flashing neon lights to me."

"So what, he's your boss," she said, as if that didn't matter. "First of all, there aren't any *official* rules that say you can't date."

"No," I agreed. "But it's *very* much implied. And could you imagine? I'm the first female to ever be on this staff, and rumor gets around that I'm sleeping with the head coach? And, on top of that, I'm already the villain in my divorce with Randy."

I lowered my voice on that last part, as if someone would hear me and the gossip that Stratford was so well known for would begin before I had the chance to thwart it.

Gabby sighed. "Yeah... I guess you have a point. What if you kept it on the down low? I mean, do you think it's serious?"

Her question made my stomach tie violently into a knot the size of a basketball. "I don't know," I answered honestly. "I mean... I guess I'd probably be naïve to believe it is, wouldn't I? I'm a single mom with the Police Chief as an ex-husband." I scoffed. "Pretty sure *no one* is lining up to enter into a relationship with me."

"First of all, Paige is not baggage. If anything, she adds to your hot factor because she's adorable and sassy and fun," Gabby said, and I could picture her holding up her stiletto-nailed fingers as she counted off. "And secondly, *you* are a catch. Your dumbass ex-husband is in your past, and he has no effect on who you are now."

I sighed, flopping down into one of the lounge chairs that was usually in the sun. Today was an overcast day, though, as fall as it could feel, and I wrapped myself up in my long cardigan sweater against the cool morning air. "Maybe it's me who's scared," I admitted. "Maybe the thought of opening myself up to a man again makes me shrink in terror."

"That breaks my heart, sis."

I shrugged, though she couldn't see me. "It's true."

A long silence passed between us before Gabby spoke again. "Well, I hope that one day you open yourself up to the possibility of letting yourself be happy again. But, if this is really how you feel, then I say keep it casual. Have the conversation with Jordan and let him know where you're at."

"Casual..." I repeated, testing the word on my lips. "As in, a booty call, a hookup, a friend with benefits that no one knows about."

"Exactly."

I wrinkled my nose. "Why does that make me feel dirty?"

At that, Gabby barked out a laugh. "Welcome to the modern world of dating, where no one is happy and everyone pretends to be fine with no strings attached."

My stomach soured, but I didn't know what other option there was. Jordan couldn't possibly want something serious with me, and even if he did, we couldn't possibly *be* serious. We worked together, I had a kid, and my ex was a psycho.

Three strikes, as they say.

"You also don't have to make any decisions right now," Gabby added. "You know?"

"Yeah..." I agreed, but my chest tightened as if to say *you better make some decisions before we have a panic attack, bitch.*

Suddenly, Paige jumped up from the couch inside and ran to the front door, voice loud and boisterous as she greeted Jordan. He was smiling down at her, giving her a high five for something she was telling him.

In the other hand, he held a bouquet of flowers.

"Shit…"

"What?" Gabby asked.

"Jordan just got here. He's working with Paige today."

"Yeah… you told me that. But why the curse word?"

"He brought flowers."

"Shit…"

We were both silent for a moment, and Jordan's eyes found mine through the window. The way the sunlight shined through the thick clouds that day illuminated those blue eyes of his, and the brown around his iris looked almost gold.

He crooked a sideways smile, and I melted.

"Wish me luck," I told her, and as soon as she did, I ended the call.

"… and I've been working on kicking. I really like it, actually. I always thought I wanted to be a quarterback, but you know, *so* many games come down to whether or not the kicker can make a field goal or an extra point, you know? And I was just thinking, *man*, I'd love to be that person who wins for my team."

Paige was still rambling on as she and Jordan joined me in the backyard, Paige circling Jordan with a football in her hand, hair a wild mess.

"I think you'd make a great kicker," he said, listening attentively.

"Really?"

He nodded. "We can work on more drills that will help you get strength and accuracy today. Sound good?"

"Yeah!"

He smiled, but then his gaze was on me, and the heat that came from it had me sweating instantly.

"Paige, why don't you run inside and braid your hair," I said with my eyes still on Jordan.

"Mom," she complained.

I snapped my eyes to hers. "No whining, Paige Marie. If you're going to be outside playing, you'll want it out of your face, anyway."

"But it takes *forever* to braid."

"Jordan and I need to talk about some work stuff real quick, anyway. Now, go braid your hair and then you can keep watching Game Day until he comes to get you."

Paige pouted, but did as I said, and Jordan's smile climbed a little when we were alone.

Just being near him had my body reacting, like every nerve was waking and reaching for him instinctively. The memory of his lips on mine, of his hands on my hips, of his thighs — big and strong beneath me as I rode him… it all came back to me in a series of flashes, and I blushed so furiously I thought my face would ignite.

"I know you already have plenty of flowers in your garden," he finally said, taking a few steps toward me and holding out the bouquet. "But… well,

I was brought up to bring a woman flowers when you care about her, and for no reason at all. So..." He shrugged, grabbing the back of his neck with his free hand. "I hope you like daisies."

I smiled, taking the bouquet when he offered it to me and inhaling the sweet scent. It was a beautiful gathering of Michaelmas daisies, all in rich purples and mauves, with little pops of yellow Goldenrod surrounding them.

"They're beautiful," I said.

Jordan smiled, reaching down to take the bouquet from me and setting it on the table. Then, he grabbed both of my hands, pulled me to stand, and without a single hesitation, pressed his lips to mine.

It was a soft and sweet kiss, his hands cradling me to him as he inhaled me like it was his first breath since he'd dropped me off back at the stadium after two o'clock this morning.

My breath was deep and long, too, and I melted into his touch, into that kiss, into the sweet feeling of having a man hold me and want me and bring me flowers.

But then my anxiety poked me hard in the ribs, and I pulled back quickly.

Checking inside to make sure Paige hadn't seen us, I quickly put space between me and Jordan, blushing as I gestured for him to sit.

"Uh, we should talk."

Jordan smirked, but sat in the chair that was a bit too small for his six-foot-whatever frame, anyway. He crossed one ankle over the opposite knee and folded his hands over his abdomen, kicking back in a relaxed fashion. "Okay," he said. "Let's talk."

I frowned. "Do you have to do that?"

"Do what?"

"That," I said, waving my hand at him as I took the seat opposite where he sat. "Look all effortlessly handsome and casually relaxed."

He chuckled. "I am relaxed. I'm happy to see you," he said easily. "Should I not be?"

I frowned again, a deep sigh leaving my chest as I leaned my elbows on the table. I stared at my hands as I spoke. "Look... last night was..." *Amazing. Incredible. The best sex of my life.* "Fun. But, I think we should talk about what we do from here."

I chanced a glance at Jordan, who cocked a brow.

"So... we should just keep this between us, I think. I'm sure you agree. With our jobs and everything... well, it's complicated. Plus, there's Randy..." I didn't elaborate there. "And I think we both know it's nothing serious, and we can have fun without anyone knowing, right? So..." I swallowed, because the more I talked, the more Jordan's smirk climbed. "Yeah. Casual."

I waited, and Jordan tilted his head to the side, assessing me before he leaned over the table toward me. His hands reached for mine, and they covered mine completely, his thumbs smoothing the skin on my wrist as his eyes found mine.

"Sydney, while our first time together being in the back of my Bronco might not insinuate it, I'm an old-fashioned kind of guy," he said, licking his lips as a soft sort of laugh came from his nose. "I don't know *how* to do the whole casual hook-up thing."

I sighed. "That makes two of us."

His smile grew a little at that, but then he was serious, his hands squeezing where he held mine. "This isn't a *keep it on the down low, let's just have sex and not tell anyone* kind of thing for me. I like you, Sydney. And I told you this last night — I want to get to know you. I want to *date* you." Jordan's eyes were sincere when he tipped my chin up so I'd look at him again. "If you're mine, you're mine. And I'm going to make sure everyone knows it."

My stupid heart shattered into a million butterflies, each one of them tickling my ribs as they fluttered about. But I herded them all back into their cage, brows bending together as I squeezed Jordan's hands in return.

"As much as I want to say the same, I think we both know this is more complicated than that."

"How so?"

"Well, for starters, I have a kid — a kid who *just* survived the divorce of her parents." I shook my head. "I'm not ready to tell her about us, because I don't think she's ready to hear it. Especially because she's grown so close to you in her own way, and I don't want her to worry about that being broken."

Jordan frowned, but nodded. "That's fair."

"And," I continued. "You're my boss. And before you even make the argument that neither of us signed a contract saying we wouldn't date," I said, holding up my finger to halt where he'd started to speak. "It doesn't matter. The fact still remains that I'm your employee, and the first female on this staff, and if word got around that we were intimate, I would be judged for it, and you would not be."

The more I talked, the more Jordan scowled — but it wasn't in anger, rather in a deep, unsatisfying understanding.

"Plus, Randy..." I started, but shook my head, not wanting to dive into it. "Well, let's just say I know he wouldn't be okay with me having a boyfriend, and I don't want to deal with that right now. Not when I'm just settling into being free of him."

Jordan blew out a long breath, squeezing my hands. "I understand."

He looked so hurt, so defeated, and it killed me.

I leaned into him, looking him in the eyes as I said, "I like you, too, Jordan. And I'd love to get to know you more, to see where this goes... but, I have to be realistic, and we have to go slow."

"I don't know how to not treat you the way you deserve to be treated."

I smiled, heart swelling. "You can, just... can you also live with knowing I'm yours, but keeping it between us for now?"

His lips twitched into a smile when I said the words *I'm yours*, and I smiled in return.

"So, dating on the down low."

I nodded. "As secret as if it were an affair."

His mouth screwed to the side at that, but he considered, nodding after a moment. "Okay. But, I have one condition."

"State your condition, Coach."

Jordan chuckled. "You have to come to my brother's wedding," he said. "As my date."

"Jordan..."

"It's not until November twenty-sixth," he said before I could argue. "That's a full two months away. By that time, playoffs will be over and we'll be in the offseason, so you won't have to worry about the team for a while. That gives us two months to warm Paige up to the idea of us."

"But Randy—"

"Randy is your *ex*-husband," he reminded me in earnest. "He doesn't get to hold power over you anymore."

My heart squeezed — both in warmth and in warning — and I chewed my lip, considering his proposal.

"What do you say," he asked after a moment, peeling his hands from mine before he extended one. "Do we have a deal?"

I fought against my growing smile, shaking my head. "You're ridiculous."

"I'm serious when it comes to making promises and keeping my word," he amended for me. "I'll agree to your half of the deal, if you agree to mine."

My mouth pulled to one side, but I reached for his hand anyway, and he shook it firmly as if he'd just sold me a car.

"Fine, I'll be your wedding date," I said, but I quickly held up a finger at his victorious smile. "*But*, I still want to have a discussion before we tell Paige. Or anyone else, for that matter."

"Tell me what?" Paige asked, bounding outside with her hair braided and football in hand.

"I told you to wait inside," I warned her, standing with Jordan, already missing the warmth of where his hands had been in mine.

"It was a commercial break, and you guys were taking *forever*," she said, dragging out the word.

"Well, let's get you warmed up, Miss Impatient," Jordan said, holding up his hands for the ball. "Hit me."

Paige grinned, tossing him the ball before she ran out into the backyard, and just like that, they were in practice mode and she'd forgotten what she'd heard when she'd walked outside — that was the blessed attention span of a nine-year-old in all its glory.

I made my way back inside, cleaning up the dishes from breakfast as I watched Jordan run drills with my daughter under an overcast sky. Every now and then his eyes would find me, too, and he'd smile, and I'd smile, and my heart would race in an exhilarating stampede of excitement and fear.

Autumn was upon us, alright.

And I had a feeling the leaves wouldn't be the only things falling in the upcoming months.

Chapter Fourteen

Jordan

Up until that point in my life, each month had fit into a category. When I was younger, they were separated by school months and summer months.

When I graduated high school, things blurred a little, and I began to measure them by the seasons, noting the different weather each month could bring.

When I got the coaching job at Stratford High, and every year since, the months had simply been divided into three: football season, off season, and summer training.

October, in my old life, would have fit right into the middle of football season. I would have greeted it with a nod and an otherwise non-affected state of determination to keep doing what I'd done in September and drive my team closer to the championship.

But now, it wasn't just October, the last month of football before we found out if we were going to the playoffs or not.

It wasn't just October, cool weather and colorful leaves and homecoming and Halloween.

Now, it was October, the first full month of Sydney Clark being mine.

It didn't matter that no one knew it but me — which was surprising, because it wasn't my usual game to play. But after our discussion at her house the morning after our game against the Serpents, we fell into a rhythm, into a sort of dance where we kept our distance and remained professional at school and around Paige, but blurred those lines when we were alone.

We had a secret, and I found no one really needed to know that I was kissing her lips each night — as long as that fact remained true.

Currently, on the Monday night after our homecoming game against the Ranchwood Rockets — whom we absolutely *crushed* — Sydney was on my couch in an oversized t-shirt and a pair of boy shorts, her hair loose and wavy where it framed her face, and she was popping candy corn into her mouth. She had her legs outstretched, feet in my lap, and I rubbed them as we finished the second movie in our Halloween movie marathon that night.

First was *Casper: The Friendly Ghost.*

And now, *Hocus Pocus.*

Turned out neither of us were big horror fans.

I tried to keep my attention on the movie, chuckling as the kids tricked the witches and the parents were put under a spell to dance all night. But I was more focused on my hands moving over her arches and pads, on the little groans of approval that she let slip from time to time, and on the unbelievable four weeks I'd had with that woman on my couch.

I wondered if she realized it, too — that one month ago in her backyard, she'd said she'd be mine.

Or maybe I was just a lovesick fool and should be ashamed that I even *cared* that it had been one month.

Still, though, I'd held my stern outward appearance at school and kept quiet around my family as per usual, when I was with her?

I couldn't pretend.

I massaged up her calf a little, smiling as I recounted the time we'd spent together. I didn't know which I'd loved more — watching her work with appreciation from a distance, sneaking kisses when the other coaches had yet to show up to the locker room, learning her as a woman on the nights Randy had Paige and I got Sydney to myself, or marveling at the role she played in Paige's life as her mother when I spent afternoons practicing with that little girl in their backyard.

I was learning her favorite flowers and memorizing the look of determination she wore when she worked in the garden. I was learning about her childhood, about her parents and her sister, about her life traveling before finally settling down in Stratford just in time to finish high school. I was learning who she was when she was with Randy, how she'd changed since, and the ways in which she would *never* change — like the fact that she was, had always been, and always would be a woman who was curious about the way things worked, like the bodies of the players she worked on and the vegetables she tended to in the garden and her daughter, who threw her for a loop because she changed and grew each day.

It was like slowly peeling off buttery flakes of a pastry, discovering new tastes with every layer, and I cherished each morsel.

The more I got to know her, the more I struggled to understand Randy — who, up until that point, I had respected. It wasn't that Sydney ever spoke ill of him, but she didn't need to. I knew all I needed to know about him, the way he treated her, and their relationship by how she responded to being treated the way she always should have been.

Every game he came to with Paige by his side, I would chance a glance at him, wondering how he could have been so stupid as to let her slip away.

He always met my gaze with the same intensity, as if he knew something I didn't.

As I became more familiar with Sydney, I revealed my own layers to her, too — letting her pass through walls I never realized I had built and fortified.

My smile faltered a bit as that thought settled in, because I realized one subject I'd yet to even broach with her was the death of my father — specifically, the hard drive and the journal and my discoveries so far.

And I knew it was on purpose.

That part of me — the young man who was left without a father, with questions never answered — he was tender and raw and I did everything I could to never expose him. The need to protect my father's legacy and my brothers and my mom and *myself* was so deeply sewn into my being that it had sprouted roots.

But, something in my throat tightened that Monday night on my couch when Sydney leaned up, kissing my cheek before she scampered off to use the restroom down the hall.

I paused the TV, grabbed my laptop, plugged in the external hard drive, and opened the journal I'd been neglecting since Sydney had stolen my time and attention.

Not that I'd complained.

"Uh-oh," Sydney said when she plopped back down on the couch beside me, leaning on the arm of the couch with one elbow. "Don't tell me you got another new trick play idea or the sudden urge to watch defense tapes. We were just getting to the good part."

She smirked, nodding toward the TV where the witches were paused on the screen, and I reached over to squeeze her knee.

"I want to show you something."

Sydney rolled her eyes, but scooted closer, wrapping her arm under mine and reaching for her phone. "*Fine.* But I'm setting a timer, and after twenty minutes, no more football talk until the movie's over. I don't care how close we are to playoffs."

"It's not football-related."

Sydney paused where she was reaching for her phone, her little mouth popping open into a soft *o*. "I'm sorry, I don't know how to hide my shock."

She was teasing, but when she saw the sincerity on my face, her brows tugged together.

"What is it?"

My heart stopped altogether on my next breath, and I held it, turning my laptop until she could see the screen.

I watched as Sydney's eyes roamed, her frown deepening the more she looked. "I don't understand... what am I looking at? It's like..." She reached for the computer, pulling it into her own lap for a closer look. "It's like an old processor or something. Is this Windows Vista?"

"Mm-hmm."

She frowned more, shaking her head at the document I had open. "And this is... well, part of it is in Latin, I think? But..." Her eyebrows softened, lips parting. "It says your father's name. It says... it's talking about the distillery." Sydney's eyes slowly found mine. "Jordan, what *is* this?"

I swallowed, realizing the jolt of nerves in my stomach wasn't because I was afraid to tell Sydney about what my brothers and I had found.

It was because I'd found someone I *wanted* to share it with.

"It's my dad's journal."

The tension between her brows released, her eyes widening. "Your... your dad's *journal*?"

I nodded, pointing to the hard drive plugged into the side of my laptop. "It's a long story, but... well, essentially, Logan and Mallory found this old, burned up, useless computer when they were tasked to clean out a storage closet at the distillery. He managed to get the hard drive out of it, and used this external hard drive," I said, tapping the large silver square. "To host it, I guess. It pulled up dad's computer as if we were logging onto it, but the problem was... it was password protected."

Sydney listened intently, her eyes ever-widening.

"Mikey's girlfriend — well, she was his friend at the time, but that's another story — she's smart, and has always had a fascination with coding and such. So, the two of them worked on trying to break into it. One day... they did."

"Whoa..." Sydney looked back at the screen. "And they found this?"

"Among other things. It was mostly work files and emails and such, when they first started looking, but then Mikey found the journal. And see," I said, reaching over to scroll on the mousepad until the beginning entries were on the screen. "At first, it's just a normal journal — and really, it's more like a daily log. Boring stuff. Him going to meetings, notes on what he needs to accomplish that week, random reminders. But then, something strange happens."

"He starts writing in Latin," Sydney finishes for me, scrolling down to the first entry in the old language.

"He starts writing in Latin," I echo. "My brothers were confused, but I remember when Dad got on this kick about how so many of our words are based in the Latin language, and how he read an article that if you learn Latin, it's a gateway to learn pretty much any other language in the world. I remember him listening to the tapes and studying this giant book he'd bought on it. And I got into it, too," I added with a shrug. "It was kind of fun. Challenging. And it was time with my dad, you know?"

Sydney's mouth pulled to one side, and she reached over, grabbing my hand.

"Anyway, I told my brother's that with some time and some online translation tools, I thought I could go through and figure out what he was writing... see if it was anything important."

"That's what I guess I'm missing here," she said, glancing at the screen and back at me. "I mean, I think it's cool that you found your dad's journal, but you're just... reading it? Kind of seems like an invasion of privacy. Don't get me wrong," she said quickly. "I'm sure it feels good to be close to him in a way again, and have access to what he was thinking each day, but..."

"It's not about that," I explained. "Think about it, Sydney. When Logan found the laptop, it was in a box that had been stuffed in a corner, covered by other tubs and boxes, in an old storage room that *no one touched* for almost ten years. And in that same box, there were charred things from my dad's desk — a picture of our family at the lake, a paper weight with a favorite quote of his, and some other things."

"Well..." Sydney looked like she was afraid to say her next words. "I mean, that makes sense, doesn't it? With the fire..."

"The fire was in Robert J. Scooter's old office. Why would my dad's things be burnt, if they were in *his* office? And why, when the Scooters cleaned out my dad's office, did they not give any of the things in that box to our family?"

Sydney's expression went blank, and she gripped the edges of the laptop harder as she sat back on the couch. "You think you'll find answers in the journal."

"Honestly, I don't," I confessed. "But... I guess there's a part of all of us that hopes."

"Have you found anything yet?"

I chewed my lip, taking the laptop from her long enough to pull up the entry where dad had mentioned he'd found Robert J. Scooter's Last Will and Testament. I turned the screen back to Sydney, watching as she read over what I'd translated.

"Jesus Christ..." Her eyes found mine. "I thought there wasn't a Will. I thought..." She shook her head, glancing at the screen and back at me. "There wasn't a Will. That's what the Scooters always said. I remember my dad telling me the story of the distillery when we moved here, and telling me about Patrick Scooter and his father and how he died from a random infection on a seemingly harmless injury and... and... *there wasn't a Will.*"

I cocked one brow on a sigh. "Well, it seems there *was* a Will... which leads me to believe that maybe there is something to be found in this journal, after all."

Sydney stared at the laptop for a long pause. "Does your mom know?"

"No one knows except me and my brothers," I said. "Maybe their significant others, at least Michael's girlfriend, Kylie, for sure. And, now... you."

She looked at me then, her almond eyes wide and glossy, lips parted, chin quivering.

Anxiety flickered like a lantern in my chest. "I'm sorry," I said quickly, shutting the laptop. "Was that too much? God, you probably think we're crazy, all the conspiracy theory bullshit—"

"I don't think you're crazy," she said quickly, turning to face me completely once the laptop was on my coffee table. Her eyes were sincere, her hands slipping into mine. "I think you're right."

I squeezed her hands in mine.

"Thank you, Jordan," she whispered, gaze searching mine. "Thank you for telling me, for trusting me."

I nodded, heart pounding slow like a fist was wrapped around it as she crawled into my arms. She kissed my neck, my chin, my jaw, all over until our lips fastened together and I pulled her tighter into my chest.

In that moment, I felt it — our hearts fusing together, our souls opening the door to each other's, finding a room, making it home.

And in the same breath that I found relief and warmth, I was also overwhelmed with a sickly cold terror.

Because suddenly, it was real.

We were real.

And I couldn't decide why, in the pit of my stomach, there was the gnawing notion that none of it could possibly last.

Chapter Fifteen

Sydney

"I'd like to make some toast," Paige said, holding up her champagne flute filled with Welch's grape juice and holding her chin high.

Jordan barked out a laugh, but lifted his glass, anyway, and I did the same, smiling at him from across my dining room table.

It was Saturday night, and less than twenty-four hours before, the Stratford High Wild Cats had clenched our spot in the Tennessee Division I High School Football Playoffs.

"To Coach," she said, addressing Jordan. "You were a loser at the beginning of the season, but that didn't stop you, and just like I heard Mom saying when she was making fun of you to Aunt Gabby one night, *you found a way to win, anyway!*"

Jordan laughed again, cocking a brow at me as I kicked Paige under the table. "You were making fun of my word of the season, huh?"

"Shh, I'm not done," Paige said before I could defend myself. "To the players, who have worked their butts off."

"That's right," Jordan said, pride beaming off him like a ray of light.

"And to my mom."

Paige turned to me, then, her little eyes that looked so much like mine crinkling at the edges as she lifted her glass toward me.

"The strongest woman in the whole wide world, and the best athletic trainer Stratford has ever seen."

Jordan held his glass toward me. "Hear, hear." Our eyes met, and he smirked, making me blush.

"Thank you, sweetheart," I said, heart squeezing as we all met glasses in the middle of the table.

"Here's to winning not just our first playoff game, but *all* of them, and bringing another trophy back to Stratford!"

We clinked our glasses to the tune of a little *yeehaw* from Jordan and some giggles from me and Paige, then we all took a sip, setting our glasses back down and digging into the celebration dinner I'd made for us.

"That was quite a speech, Paigey," I said, leaning over to help her cut her steak.

"I've been practicing." She sat straighter, turning to Jordan. "Now, before we get too much into the celebrations, we need to talk about that defensive line and their low sack record. Jones is too big and powerful for him to not have *at least* ten this season."

Jordan smiled, listening intently as Paige continued on, offering her suggestions and advice on virtually every single player and coach and play by the time we'd finished eating. I couldn't get a word in edgewise — not that I minded. My heart was full sitting at that table with my animated, passionate daughter and my kind, patient...

Whatever he was.

My stomach flipped, and I sipped down the last of my champagne before I stood, starting to clear the table.

"Cake?!" Paige asked excitedly, clapping her hands together and bouncing in her chair as she looked up at me.

I laughed. "In a little bit. Why don't you go play in your room for a while."

"But, Mom," she groaned, her little nose wrinkling as she thrust a hand toward the television. "The Vols are playing Alabama. This is like the most important game of the season."

I hung a hand on my hip, balancing the stack of plates in the other. "Jordan has spent the entire day playing football with you," I reminded her. "Ever think that maybe he needs some adult time? You can watch it in your room."

"Actually..." Jordan said, raising one finger up. He grimaced when I looked at him. "I really want to watch this game, too."

"See?" Paige said, dragging out the vowels. "Come on, Mom. We're celebrating tonight, remember? Football and cake and then I *swear* I'll leave you guys alone." She clasped her hands together. "Pleeeeease."

Jordan mimicked her, poking out his bottom lip until I rolled my eyes and tossed one of the dirty napkins at each of them to the sound of their laughter.

"I am so outvoted in this party of three and I am *not* okay with that."

"Thank you, Mama!" Paige stood on the chair to kiss my cheek before she leapt down off it and scampered into the living room, calling for Jordan to follow.

He stood, helping me carry the rest of the dishes to the sink, and when he glanced over my shoulder and found Paige glued to the television, he wrapped his arm around my waist, pulling me into him subtly.

"For the record," he said, whispering in my ear with his hot lips brushing my neck. "I really *am* looking forward to adult time."

His hand slid down, cupping my ass and squeezing it before he released me, and a flush burned through me as I bit my lip and swatted him away. He just grinned at me over his shoulder, and then he plopped down on the couch next to Paige, both of them kicking their feet up on the coffee table.

My hands were on autopilot as I washed the dishes, throwing some directly into the dishwasher after I rinsed them and spending time scrubbing the others. I found comfort in the warm, soapy water, glancing at Jordan and Paige in the living room from time to time, my thoughts wandering.

It melted my heart to see them together.

Jordan had been so comfortable with Paige from the start, and she was the same with him. It was like they were best friends from the very moment they spoke in the park. Paige counted down the days until she could spend an afternoon in the backyard running football drills with Jordan, and he never seemed to mind her stealing a Saturday of his. In fact, if I had to put money on it, I'd say *he* looked forward to it just as much as she did.

My stomach soured as Randy floated into my mind, as he still tended to do, this time as I compared his relationship with Paige to the one Jordan was building. It wasn't that he and Paige weren't close, or that Paige didn't look up to him and love him dearly, but I couldn't help but note that they'd never spent time together the way she and Jordan had. Randy had always put work first, from the very moment he was promoted to Chief of Police, and Paige and I had taken the backseat willingly, lovingly, with understanding and grace.

I wondered what they did when he had her for half the week.

I always did my best not to pry, not to ask her about her father when I already knew we'd put her in a tough position being the daughter of divorce. And, to Paige's credit, she never volunteered what they did. It made me wonder if she ever talked about *our* time together, or if she kept that between us, too.

She was a tough kid, and though I *knew* the divorce had affected her, she was the kind who wanted to handle it on her own. We almost never talked about it, or about her dad, or about how things used to be.

Paige was a survivor, and she looked forward, with her eyes on the brighter horizon, always.

My mind was still spinning when I sat next to Jordan on the couch, eyes blurring on the television screen with a football game on that I really couldn't have cared less about. Instead, I sipped the wine I'd traded in my champagne for, thinking about Randy, about my own father, and eventually, about Jordan's.

When I'd been at his house Monday night, not even a week ago, he'd revealed a secret to me that no one else in this town knew — one only he and his brothers shared. I hadn't had a good night's sleep since then, because while I was digesting what he'd told me about what they'd found at the distillery, I was also digging through my foggy memory, straining to recall what *I* had heard that night.

It had been late by the time Randy had come home — to *this* home, our new home at the time, one we'd bought with the help of his parents and my own when I'd come home from college earlier that summer. I wasn't even a full two months' pregnant with Paige, but I remembered holding onto my belly when I tiptoed down the stairs, pausing when I heard his hushed voice on the phone with someone in the kitchen.

The fire had been all anyone could talk about, all the local news could show that evening, and there was little information getting out. To this day, I'd never known what made me stop and listen at the foot of those stairs for a while before I made my way down the hall and into the kitchen.

Randy had ended the call quickly, and though he'd tried to smile and be gentle with me at first, his anger showed the more questions I asked.

He assured me it was an accident, that I was crazy, that it was started by a cigarette and they'd be closing up the case easily. He growled at my questions, when I asked how a cigarette could have started such a fire without John Becker noticing and being able to get out. *Was he sleeping?* I'd asked. *Was the door locked? How was he the only one to perish?*

That hadn't been the first night my husband had raised his hand to me.

But it had been the first time he'd let it fall.

He'd told me to mind my business, reminded me that I knew nothing about what was going on and that I was better suited to tend to our *home life.*

He'd said I was crazy, and I remembered that clearly because it was the first time he'd said it, but it wouldn't be the last.

What I *didn't* fully remember was why he'd said it in the first place, why he was struggling to explain himself, getting angry with the more questions I asked.

The memory was foggy, but every now and then, when the smoke cleared, I swore I remembered holding my daughter where she slept in my belly, my heart racing out of my chest.

And my husband's hushed voice in our kitchen whispering something about *homicide.*

• • •

Jordan

On the Thursday before our final playoff game — *the* game that would determine if we went to fight for the championship — I rallied up the boys, got them ready for practice, and sent them out on the field to work drills with Coach Pascucci and Coach TK.

"Sydney," I said, eyes on my clipboard as I made my way to my office. Everyone else was making their way outside. "A word in my office?"

I kept my face neutral, though my neck was hot, and no one suspected a thing as I continued on to my office without checking to see if she followed. The coaches were already on their way out, and the boys shuffled out behind them, their energy palpable with so much riding on tomorrow night's game.

I sat in my chair, and when Sydney entered the office, I told her to close the door behind her without looking up.

When she did, and we were alone, I dropped my clipboard, stood, and rushed to her.

She was in my arms in the next breath, giggling and whispering for me to get off her as I kissed up and down her neck, over her chin and jaw, her cheeks, before I claimed her lips and silenced her protests.

"Are you mad?" she whispered, but she was still smiling.

"Crazy about you, that's for sure."

I continued my assault of kisses, but she pressed one hand into my chest and shoved, putting space between us.

"Do you actually have something you need to see me about, or did you just interrupt work to make out?"

"Is *both* a reasonable answer?"

She rolled her eyes, but her smile was light and playful.

I gestured for her to sit, and then I leaned my ass on the edge of my desk, folding my hands in my lap as I looked down at her. The longer the silence passed between us, the more my heart raced in my chest.

"What?" she asked when I didn't say anything. Then, her smile slipped. "Oh, God. Did something bad happen?"

"No, no," I assured her, shaking my head, but the words were still lodged in my throat. I was equal parts excited and terrified over what I wanted to ask her. "Do you have plans for Thanksgiving next week?"

Sydney blinked, brows folding together in confusion. "Um… well, I have Paige. But, we're not going anywhere, just staying home, doing a little dinner with the two of us."

"Come to Thanksgiving at my house, instead." I paused. "My *mom's* house."

Sydney's eyes shot wide, her skin paling, lips parting in shock.

"Hear me out," I said before she could answer. "Mom loves having a big Thanksgiving, and everyone will be in town since the wedding is the Saturday after. Paige will have me and my brothers to watch football with, and you could meet everyone before…" I swallowed. "Noah knows I have a plus one to the wedding, but I haven't told him who it is yet. And I just thought…"

Sydney's expression morphed slowly into a soft smile. "Jordan, I'd love to join you and your family for the holiday."

"Really?" I let out a long, relieved breath.

She nodded. "Yes. But… can we just…"

She paused, standing and moving until she was between my legs, and my hands moved to her hips instinctively while her own pressed into my chest.

"For now… can we just tell everyone we're friends?"

My shoulders sagged.

"Not for much longer," she said quickly. "I just… I want to talk to Paige first, and with playoffs in full swing right now, and the holiday, and the wedding... it's just a lot." She swallowed. "I also think I need to tell Randy. He needs to hear it from me."

"You don't owe him anything."

"I know, but... it might save some drama in the long run." She shook her head. "I'm scared, for many reasons, and I know it's asking a lot of you, I know this was my part of the deal, but... I'm asking, anyway. I need a little more time. Okay?"

The next breath that came through my nose was short and hot, but I nodded, though my chest was tight. "Okay," I agreed. "But, if I'm being honest, I don't think my family will buy it."

She smirked at that, lacing her arms around my neck and pressing a kiss to my chin. "I don't think so, either. But, I appreciate you letting me do this the way I need to. I'll talk to Paige as soon as we make it through this busy time, okay? And then..."

"And then you'll be mine."

Her brown eyes searched mine, and she shook her head, pressing up on her toes to kiss me long and slow before she whispered, "I already am."

Chapter Sixteen

Jordan

"No, Betty, you're supposed to break the wish bone *with* someone," Ruby Grace explained to Betty Collins, who was holding both sides of a broken turkey bone in her hands. "And whoever gets the bigger piece is the one who gets the wish."

"Exactly. That's why I broke it on my own — better odds that way." She pointed the bigger piece of the bone at Ruby Grace. "That's just simple math, sweetheart."

Betty was a feisty old woman who'd been brought into our life courtesy of Ruby Grace and her time at the nursing home. She and Mom had become fast and furious friends, and she quickly became part of our family.

Ruby Grace rolled her eyes, but smiled still, taking the pieces of bone from Betty to toss out before she continued working on the stuffing she was making.

Mom had been trying to shoo her out of the kitchen all morning, repeatedly pointing out that Ruby Grace was a bride-to-be and should be relaxing two days before her wedding — not cooking. But Ruby Grace insisted she wanted to be in the kitchen, and Mallory and Kylie were helping, too.

I'd never seen Mom so frazzled at a Thanksgiving before. The poor woman didn't know what to do when she had actual help in the kitchen.

"Can I help with anything, Mrs. Becker?" Sydney asked, already reaching for a knife where sweet potatoes were waiting to be diced up for the casserole.

Mom swatted her hand away, and then instantly reddened, covering her mouth with wide eyes. "Oh, dear. I'm so sorry. I just…"

I chuckled, grabbing my mom by the shoulders with a tender squeeze. "Why don't you come hang out with your sons in the living room and let the ladies work? I can't remember the last time you took a Thanksgiving off."

Her bottom lip trembled, and Sydney glanced at me with caring concern before she smiled at my mom. "You know what? I would actually *love* a little tour of your garden, if you wouldn't mind? I saw the beautiful violas and pansies out front, and Jordan said you have a garden in the back."

Mom shifted her weight, glancing up at me before a small smile bloomed on her face. "That's where all the squash came from, and the pumpkin."

"You have a pumpkin patch?" Sydney shook her head. "Now you *have* to show me."

At that, a genuine smile found Mom's lips, and she patted Mallory on the back. "Alright. You ladies let me know if you need me, I'm going to take Sydney for a garden tour."

They all smiled at her, and I mouthed *thank you* to Sydney as they passed by me, headed out the front door.

As soon as Sydney was gone, all four pairs of female eyes were on me.

I inwardly groaned, knowing this was coming. Mom hadn't said much when I asked if Sydney and Paige could join us for the holiday. I'd proposed it under the pretense that it was Paige's first Thanksgiving since the divorce, and that Sydney's family lived in Texas, and that we had grown a friendship since she started working for the school. I'd mentioned how I'd been training Paige for football camp next summer, and that I knew they'd fit right in.

I knew Mom didn't buy my story, but she'd smiled knowingly and not asked a single question — bless her.

My brothers' significant others and Mrs. Betty Collins on the other hand...

"So," Kylie said, one eyebrow cocked. "Seems Mikey and I have missed a lot since our move to New York. Care to fill us in?"

Mallory and Ruby Grace exchanged looks before their smiles grew, Betty tapped a dirty spoon on the palm of her hand, and all of them waited for me to answer.

Just then, a roar of cheers and groans came from the living room.

I hooked a thumb over my shoulder. "Sounds like the game's getting good, I better go see."

"Jordan Becker!" Ruby Grace chided, throwing the top of a cut up celery stalk at me. "Don't you dare leave without spilling the tea."

I dodged the greenery and smiled, making a notion like my lips were sealed before I ducked out of the kitchen to the tune of four dramatic huffs.

I chuckled, knowing they would all be in there going crazy trying to figure out what Sydney and I were, but they knew by now that I was not the kiss-and-tell type. I wasn't the *anything*-and-tell type. I preferred to keep my private life just that — private.

At least, that's what I kept telling myself.

I rounded into the dining room, glancing out the front door where Sydney stood in the front yard with my mom. Mama was bent down, showcasing something as Sydney leaned over and nodded, her brows pinched in concentration.

And my heart pinched at the sight.

That's when I realized that while it wasn't out of the ordinary that I didn't want to talk to the girls about Sydney, that wasn't what had my chest tight.

It was that I *wanted* to talk about her.

Hell, I wanted to talk to *everyone* about the woman, and that was completely opposite of who I'd always been. The truth was if I had it my way, I'd likely talk more than I had in my entire life if I had the chance to tell someone, *anyone,* about the time Sydney and I had spent together.

But here we were, two months in, and the truth was I didn't know where we stood.

Until I met Sydney, I'd avoided dating with the general consensus that love was dangerous, and when you engaged in a relationship with someone, you put yourself and, maybe more importantly, *them* at risk. I'd watched my friends' parents go through divorce, watched my brothers break hearts and even get theirs broken in return, and above it all, I'd seen the unbreakable love my parents shared shattered by tragedy.

And maybe deep down, I'd always been afraid *I* wouldn't know what to do if I ever found "the right woman." I didn't know if I could treat her the way my father had treated my mother, if I could put her first, be patient and caring and kind.

With Sydney, it was effortless.

I treated her like gold because in my eyes she *was.* I didn't have to try to care about her, to put her first, to love her.

I did it all because it was as if there was no other choice, and all my life I'd been preparing for this moment with her.

My chest tightened again, because though I was fairly certain that *I* wouldn't be the one to hurt her, I didn't have a shred of assurance that she wouldn't do the same to me. Not because she wanted to — but because I swung into her life when I knew things were complicated, when I knew she wasn't ready, and when I knew we had an army of circumstance working against us.

That afternoon in her backyard, she told me what she could give me, and what she couldn't.

When I asked her to join us for Thanksgiving, she'd asked me for more time.

And now, it was two days before Noah's wedding, and we hadn't come back to that conversation to discuss *her* part of the deal.

I'd done what she needed me to do — stayed quiet, kept our relationship a secret, respected the boundaries she'd put in place. She assured me the time was coming, that she needed to do it *her* way, and I believed her.

But I wanted her so badly I couldn't bear the weight of not knowing if she felt the same way I did any longer.

And I knew I had to ask her tonight — before the wedding, before I had the chance to fall any further.

Though I knew in my gut it was already too late.

Another roar came from the group in the living room, and it shook me out of my daze. I chanced one last glance at my mother and Sydney together before I leaned over the back of the couch where Noah and Mikey sat. Logan was in Dad's old recliner.

And Paige was smack dab in the middle of the floor, sitting on her knees, eyes glued to the television.

"I *told* you the Cowboys didn't have a chance against the Bills' defense," she said, looking pointedly over her shoulder at Noah. "This isn't 2007."

"Were you even *alive* in 2007?" Mikey asked.

Paige turned back to the TV with a flick of her wild, wavy hair that had me stifling a laugh. "Doesn't matter if I was or not. I clearly know more about football than any of you do."

Noah's mouth popped open, him and Mikey exchanging glances before they looked over their shoulders and up at me.

Logan chuckled. "I like this kid."

"Me, too," I said, and Paige smiled back at me with pride.

A battle of emotions roared on inside me as the cheers roared on at the AT&T Stadium. I both loved having Sydney and Paige at my mother's house for Thanksgiving and loathed it, because I'd never brought anyone home with me before, and because they fit in like they'd always been here, and because I knew without having to ask that my mom was already falling in love with Sydney — her heart easier to win than my own — and that my brothers would already go to war to protect Paige, if they had to.

It was the weekend before my brother's wedding, and we were all gathered in the same place for the first time in months — Mikey and Kylie home from New York, Ruby Grace no longer separated from Noah with her AmeriCorps contract, and Mallory and Logan closer than ever with a baby on the way. Mom was at the head of it all, watching her family grow, and all the while, I thought I'd been flying under the radar, watching from a distance with nothing to add but a hug or a small piece of advice from time to time.

But I was here with someone I loved, too.

Even if she had no idea.

And maybe what scared me most was that having her and Paige here was a reciprocation, the missing piece I didn't realize I'd wanted so badly. For months, I'd spent days and nights in their home, learning who they were as a family.

The fact was that Sydney and Paige already felt like *my* family, too.

My stomach rolled more with every minute, and I wondered how I'd be able to eat. I was just about to make my way into the kitchen to pour an old fashioned that I hoped would settle my nerves when Mikey threw one arm over the couch to look at me again.

"So," he said. "One week from tomorrow, you'll be fighting for that trophy again. How you feeling?"

I blew out a long breath, leaning over the couch again and clasping my hands where they hung between my brothers. "The team is ready. They're strong, talented, and thanks to Sydney, all in a pretty healthy shape, too. But,"

I added, scratching my jaw with my eyes on the television. "Pressure gets to them. I saw it in the first home game, and again twice after when we played our biggest rivals. They get sloppy, and don't play smart. If that happens next week, we don't have a chance."

"You know what *I* think?" Paige said, standing and flopping down in the middle of the couch between my brothers, her chin turned up toward me.

"No, but I bet you're gonna tell me."

"You need to ask Rodgers to get them in the zone before Friday."

I cocked a brow, waiting, because I knew she wasn't done.

"What I mean is, he's the quarterback, right? And the team captain. But, he's a quiet guy — kind of like you, Coach. And I think that's why the team respects you so much. They know that when you say something, it's because it's important. And, well, I think it's like that with Rodgers, too. I think if you pulled him aside and asked him to step up this week, and suddenly their leader was speaking out, telling them the errors he sees, suggesting what they need to pay attention to?" Paige shrugged. "We'd win for sure."

"That right?"

Noah shook his head from beside her. "You're going to be president one day."

"Nuh-uh," she said, looking at him matter-of-factly before she smiled up at me. "I'm going to be a football player."

It wasn't long after that that the girls announced that dinner was ready. We called Mom and Sydney in from the garden, tore my brothers and Paige from the television, and all gathered around a feast that could feed at least three times the amount of people in attendance.

When we were all seated, Mom held out her hands, and I took her left while Noah took her right. Sydney was next to me, Paige across from us, and we all linked hands, connecting to each other around the meal that brought us together.

"I'd like to say grace, if that's alright," Noah said.

Mom smiled and squeezed his hand, and we all bowed our heads.

"Heavenly Father, thank you for the blessings you have bestowed upon this family. We are so blessed to be able to be here together in this way, to share a meal and spend time together when life can so easily slip away from us."

I swallowed, my throat tightening with emotion.

"I know I speak for everyone when I say we're missing a big piece of our puzzle today, but we know Dad is up there with you, probably watching the games and yelling at the big HD screens they got up there."

We all chuckled.

"So, give him a big hug for us, and tell him we love him and we miss him. And Lord, I want to thank you for our amazing mother, who has filled this home with love and wrangled us rowdy boys for our entire lives, and for my brothers — who I can always count on."

That emotion I'd felt before surged through me again, and I cleared my throat to ease the swell.

"I want to thank you for Kylie," Noah continued. "Who has put up with us for years and still manages to like us."

Kylie giggled.

"And for Mallory, who put up with us all being jerks to her because of her last name, and somehow still manages to love us and forgive us, anyway."

"And for *y'all* seeing past that last name, seeing me for who I really am, and loving me, too," she added.

"We pray you will keep her and Logan's baby safe and healthy inside that little oven of hers," Noah said. "And deliver him or her safely to us."

"Her," Logan whispered, and at that, all of our eyes popped open and locked on him, though he was looking at Mallory, who smiled and squeezed his hand.

"*Her?*" Mom cried out, her eyes flooding with tears.

Logan nodded, and the whole table buzzed with a mixture of congratulations and excitement.

"Shhh," Noah said, calming us. "Still praying here."

We laughed, closing our eyes and bowing our heads again.

"I want to thank you for Betty Collins, and for bringing her into our family when we needed her most."

"You're welcome," she chimed in, and we all chuckled again.

"And for our new guests, Sydney and Paige, who fit in like they've always been here, and already bring us joy, and make our oldest brother smile — which is honestly really weird and kind of unsettling, but we'll get used to it."

"I *told* you to stop being so grumpy all the time," Paige said to the tune of another flurry of laughter, but my throat was so tight I could no longer swallow, and I blinked my eyes open, looking at the place where my fingers intertwined with Sydney's.

"And Lord, I want to thank you for my incredible fiancée, who will be my wife in less than forty-eight hours from now. I have waited my entire life to find a woman like her, and you delivered her just like I always knew you would. Thank you for making me a patient man, for helping me see why it never worked out with anyone before, and comforting me in those dark times to know that the light was on its way. It wasn't easy," he said, and there was a murmur of agreement, but my eyes were floating up to Sydney's.

And hers were open, too — staring back at me.

"But it was so, so worth it. If there's anything this family has taught me, it's that love is the most important thing, and it's worth fighting for — no matter the risk."

Sydney's eyes were wide and glossed, a little pinch between her brows as she watched me and I watched her, nothing being said, but everything spoken just the same.

"Thank you for our blessings, Lord. And thank you for this meal. Amen."

"Amen," we all echoed, and while my mom instantly went into how great Noah's grace was and then began peppering Mallory with baby questions now that we knew the gender, Sydney and I continued watching each other, and I wondered if she felt what I felt in that moment, too.

I couldn't wait any longer.

I needed more from her. I needed her to claim me, to assure me that I wasn't crazy or alone in what I was feeling, to make what we had between us *real*.

And I would ask for it.

Tonight.

• • •

Sydney

After dinner, everyone helped clear the table, and then we all separated into little groups without really noticing it.

Jordan and his brothers were watching football in the living room with Paige, who I imagined was in hog heaven with so many people around who loved the game like she did. Before he retreated there, Jordan had pulled me to the side, asking if we could talk after I put Paige to bed tonight. My stomach was in knots wondering what it was about, but he assured me it was nothing bad, so I tried to trust him in that.

Jordan's mom, Laurelei, along with Betty and Ruby Grace were gathered at the dining room table, now filled with the contents of Ruby Grace's wedding planning binder. They were drinking wine and laughing as they went through last-minute preparations.

Mikey and Kylie were in the backyard, sitting together at a little bonfire they'd made while Mikey played the guitar.

Mallory and I were in the kitchen cleaning up, and we cracked the window so we could hear what Michael was playing. He was actually quite good, and I wondered to myself if he would ever consider making a career from music.

He and Kylie were so young, just nineteen years old, and I smiled from time to time thinking about how everything felt so possible at that age, and yet it also felt like nothing had to be figured out at all — not yet.

When I was nineteen, I was in college, with my eyes set on the future. I envisioned working with athletic teams across the country, learning more about the human body every day, and more importantly — how to keep athletes healthy and on the field or court where they wanted to be.

My stomach sank, as it often did when I thought about what could have been. Then I shrank from guilt, knowing that if it had turned out that way, I wouldn't have Paige.

I blinked the thoughts away as Mallory handed me a freshly cleaned casserole dish covered in warm soapy suds. I ran it under the cool water from the faucet, rinsing it completely before I set it to dry on a towel we'd laid out on the counter.

"I can handle this, Mallory," I offered for the second time since we'd started cleaning up the kitchen. "If you want to go help the other ladies with the wedding plans."

She scoffed, cocking an eyebrow at me before she got to work on the next casserole dish. "I know you don't know me very well, but trust me when I say wedding planning is nowhere on my list of things I'd like to do in my spare time."

I chuckled. "Not your cup of tea?"

"Let's just say the only time I like to get serious about what colors to pick for something is when it comes to dying my hair. At least, it *was*, until this little gal decided to start blooming and I started thinking about what color to paint her room."

She patted her stomach with a soapy hand, smiling at me before she was back to work on the dish. I took her in then, noting the fading pink and orange at the tips of her dirty blonde hair, the septum piercing in her nose, the fierce and beautiful makeup she wore on her white skin, the sliver of tattoos peeking out from where she'd shoved the sleeves of her sweater up to her elbows along with the lotus flower right behind her ear. She was unlike any girl I'd seen around this town, and I kind of loved it.

"Besides, you can't get rid of me that easily, not when we're all dying to know more about you — specifically, you and Jordan."

The blood rushed from my face, and I took the dish from her hands, rinsing it without responding. My heart was racing as I tried to find the *right* words to say — or really, any words at all. If only she knew I'd been asking *myself* questions about me and Jordan for the last two months, and especially the last week, wondering more and more every day what we were, how we could be *anything at all* considering our circumstances.

The gravity that pulled me into Jordan — effortlessly and completely — also sent me spiraling in the next minute, down a rabbit hole of uncertainty and warning. Nothing had changed since we first made our agreement. He was still my boss. I was still the first and only female on a staff of men in a small town. I still had a daughter who was fresh off my and Randy's divorce.

And I still had Randy, though I wish I could be severed from him forever.

If anyone would understand that, it would be Mallory, I realized sickly.

I didn't know her very well, as she had just pointed out, but thanks to Randy getting drunk one night and bragging about it, I knew that he'd made a move on her when she was younger.

Too young.

And that he'd embarrassed her in front of a room of men.

I shivered at the thought, lost in another time, and when I didn't answer, Mallory smiled, bumping my elbow with hers. "Hey, don't sweat it. I know what it's like to want to keep things private for a while." She handed me a plate before working on the next one in the stack beside her. "Logan and I, we couldn't tell anyone when we were together — not when there were so many... complications. And things were so messy for a long time. I hurt him," she admitted. "Badly. But we found our way, eventually."

I still didn't say anything, not wanting to own up to me and Jordan being more than friends, even though I *knew* it was silly to think everyone in that house didn't know.

Except for Paige — at least, I hoped.

Besides, my mind was on another topic now, one that I couldn't ignore.

"Oh," Mallory said, dropping the plate she was washing into the sink of soapy water and bending at an awkward angle, her hand on her lower back.

"Are you okay?" I asked, drying my hands like I was about to have to spring into action.

Mallory waved me off. "Fine. I've just been getting some back pains recently. But honestly, compared to the first trimester?" She shook her head. "This is heaven. I have more energy finally, and the nausea is gone — at least, for now. I've been craving some really strange food combinations, like — have you ever had French fries dipped in a malt from Blondies?" She mouthed *oh my God*, her eyes rolling up to the ceiling. "And it seems to feel better when I'm standing or moving around rather than sitting. But, otherwise? I'm feeling dandy."

I chuckled, placing a hand on her shoulder. "I really hate to be the one to burst your bubble, but this is the honeymoon stage of your pregnancy. Enjoy it while it lasts, because around the next corner is a whole lot of *fuck this shit*."

She burst out laughing, returning her hands to the soapy water as I readied myself beside her to continue rinsing.

We were quiet for a pause, and I frowned, my rib cage shrinking in on my lungs as I considered what I was about to say to Mallory. I couldn't explain why I wanted to, or why I felt comfortable enough to. Honestly, I *didn't* feel comfortable.

But I *needed* to talk to her.

I needed to get this out.

"Mallory," I said, keeping my eyes on my hands as I rinsed a plate and she handed me another one. "I owe you an apology."

Mallory paused. "What for? I told you I *want* to be in here doing dishes. Please don't make me go talk about ribbons and seating charts."

I couldn't find it in me to smile. Instead, I pinched the bridge of my nose with my wet fingers, leaning a hip against the counter. "No, no... it's not about now. It's about..." I sighed, looking at her with remorse. Suddenly, I didn't have the words.

"What is it?" she asked, her brows bending together.

My stomach fell to the floor before settling again, and I forced a breath. "Mallory, I am not proud of how long I put up with Randy's shit. Our relationship turned sour so early, early enough that I should have known it would never be okay, but I stayed, anyway."

Mallory's face went blank at the sound of Randy's name, and she'd turned back to the water, working on scrubbing the spatulas and serving spoons. She handed them to me to rinse without looking at me again.

"I was young," I said. "Not that that's an excuse, but... I... I didn't know how bad everything was, how much he was hiding from me. I had clues, but..." I was stumbling, and I shook my head, trying to clear the fog. "What I'm trying to say is though I am ashamed of how long I stayed with him, and what I put up with, I am the most ashamed of the fact that I knew he disrespected you, and I did nothing about it."

Mallory's hands went shock still in the water, and she slowly withdrew them, still not looking at me.

"I don't know everything," I said, lowering my voice to a whisper as I checked over my shoulder to ensure no one was listening to us. "But I heard him talking to his friends about that night in your dad's casino. He said... *awful,* inappropriate things about you, and about other girls who were far too young for him. And I..." I teared up, shaking my head as I lowered it in shame.

"It wasn't that bad," she said softly, but her eyes said differently. "He pulled me into his lap, made some lewd gestures and pretty much said I should call him when I turned eighteen."

"How old were you when it happened?"

She swallowed. "Fourteen."

I shook my head, my stomach rolling with the threat to overturn the dinner we'd eaten. "I did nothing," I whispered, ashamed. "I *stayed* with him and I didn't come to your defense and I... I was young and scared and confused," I tried to explain, but it all felt weak and pathetic. "I am so sorry."

In a flash, Mallory had dried her hands on a dish towel and framed my shoulders with them, bending her neck until I looked her in the eyes.

"Listen to me," she said sternly. "You do *not* apologize for him. You understand? It is not your fault. What he did to you, what he did to me, what he did to anyone — it is on *him*, not on you."

My eyes welled with tears, but I sniffed them back, unable to respond. It was true what I'd said about not knowing everything. I only had pieces of the puzzle I tried to put together for years. Randy was good at hiding things.

He was good at manipulating me to think I was crazy, too.

But I knew he'd done something inappropriate to Mallory, something that had made everyone in that underground casino that Patrick Scooter liked to run out of his house laugh and jeer and encourage him to push more. But I didn't know how old she was — just fourteen.

He was twenty-one at the time.

"You are not responsible for his actions. Do you hear me?" she said, pulling me back to the moment with her.

Mallory waited until I nodded, though I wasn't sure if I agreed.

"I know we have both been through a little bit of hell with that man — you much more than me, I'd imagine. But, as sick as this sounds, I'm not sorry for what he did to me. He opened my eyes that night, Sydney. He gave me a backbone, and for the first time in my life, I started standing up to what was wrong, and standing up for what is right. And look at you," she said, shaking me a little. "You are an incredible mother, and a bad ass athletic trainer — *on a team of men*, might I add. I can tell just by looking into your eyes that you are stronger because of what you have been through. Am I wrong?"

I rolled my lips together. I didn't have to answer.

"You and I?" Mallory whispered. "We are fighters, Sydney. We are warriors. Survivors. You *never* have to apologize to me, okay? You just have to keep fighting. *That* is what you owe me — not an apology, but a fight. Because if we don't fight? Then he wins."

I swallowed, and Mallory glanced over my shoulder at the dining room before she forced a smile and pulled me in for a hug.

"Now, pretend we were talking about baby stuff," she whispered through that smile, pulling back on a chuckle. "God, thank you. It feels good to talk to someone who's been through this stuff."

"Uh-oh," Jordan said, grabbing for the whiskey on the counter to refill his glass as he smiled at us. "Baby talk, huh?"

"The good, the bad, and the *very* ugly baby talk," Mallory confirmed, and she winked at me as I tried to school my features.

When Jordan's eyes met with mine, I knew I was doing a terrible job.

I somehow managed to get through the rest of the evening, but when Paige had had her pie and it was halftime on the late game, we took the opportunity to leave — much to her dismay. Jordan could sense that something was off, and I could feel how badly he wanted to touch me, to hold me, to reassure me.

And I wanted the same.

I hugged everyone goodbye — getting an extra-long hug from Jordan's mom — and Jordan promised to be back bright and early in the morning to help with wedding set-up and final preparations. And of course, the guys would be going out for what Noah claimed would be a "tame" bachelor party tomorrow night.

When we were piled into the car, Jordan and I listened to Paige go on and on about the football games and about every one of Jordan's brothers and the girls and his mom, too. She talked a lot about Betty, who she wanted to hang out with more, and I smiled and asked questions when appropriate, letting her run the conversation until we pulled into the drive, with Jordan watching me with worry in his eyes the entire way home.

When we got there, I took Paige upstairs and got her ready for bed. She was already softly snoring by the time I shut out her bedroom light after reading to her for not even ten minutes, and I tiptoed down the stairs, finding Jordan on the couch.

He stood when he saw me, his brows folding together, mouth in a thin line.

But I said nothing.

I just crossed the room and collapsed into his arms, knowing that as much as it would hurt, I had to tell him what I knew about Randy and Mallory, too.

When he wrapped me in those strong, warm arms of his and kissed my hair, rocking me gently, I struggled against the urge to cry.

And I prayed he would understand.

Chapter Seventeen

Sydney

Jordan didn't speak for the longest time.

I'd lit a candle — one that smelled like lavender and made me feel slightly better — before launching into what had happened with Mallory in the kitchen. I'd told him about what I'd known about Randy, what I wasn't sure I'd known, what I'd questioned.

And I felt ashamed, knowing that Jordan now knew how weak I had been, what I had put up with, what I had let happen to me and my daughter before I'd found a spine and left.

The candlelight flickered across his face, which was severe, his brows nearly touching in the middle of his forehead and making a wrinkle so deep I wondered if it'd stick forever. I wondered if he was judging me, deciding he didn't like what I'd uncovered. The only source of comfort I had that that was *not* the case was that he still rested his giant hand on my leg where I sat next to him.

After a long while, he swallowed, letting out a long breath. "So... did he..." He frowned even more. "Did he assault her?"

I shook my head. "No. At least, not that I know of. But he made her uncomfortable. From what I gathered, he basically pulled her into his lap and made some comment about them having sex when she turns eighteen."

"Jesus fucking Christ," Jordan said, and he finally stood, no longer able to sit still with what he'd just learned. He paced back and forth in my living room while I sat on the couch, watching him. "I wonder if Logan knows."

"I'm sure he does."

"Then I'm surprised Randy is still breathing."

I didn't have anything to say to that.

He continued pacing, and my heart had stopped beating altogether before I finally reached for his hand, pulling him to a stop. He looked down at me with that same severe look he gave the team when he was pissed.

"Are you mad at me?"

At that, his face crumbled, and he collapsed into the couch next to me and immediately pulled me into his chest.

"What? Of course not," he said, blowing out a hot breath and shaking his head as he rocked me. I clung to him like he was the only thing holding me to the Earth. "You didn't do anything wrong, Sydney. This is all on him."

"But I didn't tell anyone," I pointed out. "I didn't fight him on it or question him more when my gut *knew* something was off. I was scared, and he *was* the police, so I didn't know where to go... and I just... I feel so awful."

I buried my face in his chest as he gently quieted me, holding me tighter.

"Sydney," he said after a long while, pulling back until he could look me in the eyes. "Do not feel guilty for his actions. You did not play a role in what he did to Mallory or anyone else. You were a victim, too."

I sniffed, still feeling like he was wrong but not wanting to argue it.

"There were so many things I heard over the years," I confessed on a whisper, searching his eyes as that foggy memory from the night his father died flittered in like a wisp of smoke. "But nothing that was ever concrete. Nothing that I couldn't dismiss with just a few questions of whether I was crazy or not, of whether I had really heard what I thought, or if I was being dramatic."

Jordan swept my hair from my face. "He knew what he was doing. He knew his power."

I swallowed. "The night of Mallory's grand opening of her art studio last year... do you remember that?"

He nodded.

"That was when I knew," I said on a shaky voice. "We went to it, and Mallory saw him and I saw the look in her eyes and I *knew* I was right, that he had done her wrong. And then when I came back from the bathroom, I overheard him and one of his officers making a joke about it." I shook my head, tonguing my cheek. "He said something about how he wished she would have been down for the deal, because judging by her piercings and tattoos, he bet she was a freak in the bedroom."

Jordan's jaw clenched shut, and he looked away from me briefly, as if he needed to look at something else to calm himself and keep from shooting off that couch and flying across town to confront Randy right now.

"I told him I wanted a divorce the next day," I said. "Not to his face. I didn't stay, because I knew he wouldn't let me go if I did. I got a lawyer, made sure everything was on paper just in case anything happened, you know? And I wrote him a letter and got on a plane with Paige to go see my parents and my sister for Christmas." I shook my head. "My dad called Randy, and I don't know what was said, but honestly, Jordan, I think the only reason he signed the papers and granted the divorce was because I agreed to stay in town, to not move Paige away, and he knew..." I sniffed. "He knew that if I stayed, he'd still have power over me."

Jordan softened, pulling me into him again on a sigh and resting his chin on the crown of my head. "He will never hurt you again. I promise."

Tears finally broke free at his words, because I knew that he meant them with every fiber of his being. I knew that if it came to it, Jordan Becker would go to war for me, for Paige, for us.

And I wasn't sure I deserved it.

He held me for a long while before I sat up straight again, swiping the tears from my face and letting out a long, slow exhale. "Anyway, enough of this," I said, forcing a smile. "You wanted to talk about something."

"Sydney..."

"Please," I said, nearly crying again. "I really don't want to talk about this anymore."

He frowned, but nodded in understanding. "Well, what I had to talk about can wait, too."

"No, please, you wanted to talk first, and then I sprung this all on you, and—"

"Hey," he said, his knuckles finding my chin. He tilted it up, those blue eyes searching mine while I traced the rim of gold around his iris. "I am always here for you. Okay? Always. You are not a nuisance, and I *want* to be this person for you." He swallowed. "I want to be your everything."

My chest tightened, a mixture of the most intense longing and desire I'd ever felt swirling in a tornado with all the anxiety and warning sounds my body could release all at once.

"Jordan..."

But before I could speak, his lips were on mine, the warm swells both comforting and demanding as he took the words I was going to say and swallowed them whole.

I pulled back, breathless, fingers trailing down his chest before I grabbed his hand and stood. He followed me down the hall to the guest room, where we could be alone without the possibility of waking Paige since my room was next to hers.

When I closed the door behind us, the only light came from the horizontal slits in the closed blinds, and they cast streams of white across his face, his chest, his arms, his hands where they reached for me and pulled me in again, the next kiss tender and sure.

Just like that, we were done talking.

• • •

Jordan

Something about the way the night settled over both of us in Sydney's dark guest room was different than any time we'd been alone before.

The moment that door closed behind us with a quiet *snick*, the moment her hands reached for me in the dark, and mine reached for her, and our mouths connected, comfortable and instinctively, it sent a charge through me like an electric current. I felt that energy spread like warm oil, slicking up every joint, seeping into every crevice, filling me up whole.

I cradled her face in my hands, my eyes closed as I tasted her, memorized her, my heart aching from what she'd confessed in the other room. The urge to protect her and keep her safe tore through me in the next moment, and I pulled her into me, crushing her in my embrace as I strengthened the kiss.

Sydney gasped, and as soon as her mouth opened I was walking her backward, kissing down her neck and over her collarbone until the back of her knees hit the bed.

"Lie down," I whispered, and she reached blindly back, hands finding the bed as she sat and stared up at me, her chest heaving.

Without a word, I reached down for the hem of her sweater, peeling it up and over her head as she lifted her arms to let me. Then I kissed her, pushing her back until she was flat on the bed, and I kissed down, down — over the swells of her breasts, the muscles of her abdomen, the smooth skin above the band of her leggings.

My fingers dipped beneath that band, and Sydney lifted her hips, helping me peel them down her thighs and calves until they rested at her ankles. I kept my eyes on hers as I pulled them the rest of the way off, letting them fall to the floor.

She hadn't been wearing anything beneath them.

The urge to groan in approval ripped through me, but I suppressed it, because though she was nearly naked now and my erection was so strong it pitched a tent in my pants, there was something more to this moment than lust, something more than my hands on her thighs spreading her legs as I kissed a trail from her ankle to the sweet spot at the apex of them.

I couldn't take away what she'd been through. I couldn't go back in time and steal her away from Randy before he had the chance to make her his, before he took that chance and used it to fuck her up instead of cherish her. I couldn't *unhurt* her.

But I could show her what she meant to me.

My heart thumped hard in my chest — once, twice — reminding me that I had things I needed to tell *her*, questions I needed to ask, answers I had to have. But I quieted it with a soft kiss on her clit, one that elicited a gasp from her lips and an arch of her back off the bed.

It could wait.

Knowing what we were and what we weren't, hearing her claim me, explaining that I needed to claim *her*, that I needed more, that I needed all of her — it could all wait.

Tonight, I would *show* her what I felt.

And when the time was right, I'd tell her, too.

My hands grabbed at the creases where her hips met her thighs, and I tugged her down until her ass was half off the bed, the weight of her in my hands as I paid homage to her pussy. I ran my tongue flat and hot from bottom to top before sucking her bud between my teeth, gently sucking, just enough to make her squirm before I released it again.

Sydney's hands found my hair, and I buried my face more, letting her guide me where she wanted me. I listened to the words she wasn't saying, to the way her hands tightened in my hair or loosened, to the way she moaned or stayed silent. My tongue was the student, eager and devoted, and her body language taught all it needed to know.

She was panting heavily and squirming so much she'd nearly fallen off the bed when I adjusted her, making sure she was secure before I removed one hand from where I held her and tickled her entrance with my fingertips. She groaned, leaning up on her elbows, her eyes hooded from where she watched me.

I kept my eyes on hers, my tongue flicking her clit, and in one thrust, I pushed two fingers deep inside her.

She arched in a mixture of pleasure and pain, flying back down on the bed and gripping the sheets. She twisted them wildly as I curved my fingers inside her, holding back the screams I knew she wanted to let loose so we didn't wake Paige. Her hand pressing the back of my head more into her and her legs shaking around it told me what her screams couldn't, and I kept pace, flicking and flexing and pushing in and out until her entire body erupted into an earth-quake of trembles, her breaths short and loud, climax ripping through her.

She collapsed in a heap on the bed as I slowly withdrew my fingers, kissing my way up her body until I found her mouth. Sydney held my lips to hers, the kiss hard and desperate and appreciative, and then she bit my lower lip as I stifled a moan.

"Take these off," she whispered, tugging on my athletic pants, and I stood, eagerly answering her plea.

I peeled my long-sleeve shirt over my head, making quick work of my pants and briefs next, all while keeping my gaze locked on hers. Sydney tugged her sports bra over her head, too, and then crawled back until her head was on the pillows, and we both sighed in relief when I was on top of her, sliding between her legs, our bodies hot and slick where they met.

I was already lined up at her entrance, and all it would take was a flex of my hips to bury myself inside her. But we both paused, our breaths heavy and loud as Sydney ran her fingers back through my hair, and I held my weight on my elbows, balancing over her, our eyes searching each other's.

Everything that existed in the fundamental part of who I was screamed for me to tell her I loved her.

It echoed like my body was a chamber, like if each cell yelled loud enough, Sydney would hear it whether the actual words came or not.

And maybe she did.

Maybe she understood, as her brows bent together, and her lips parted, and she lifted her head off those pillows enough to connect her mouth to mine. Maybe she knew it all along, and that kiss was quieting me, as if to tell me I didn't need to speak it out loud at all.

Maybe she felt it, too, as her thighs tightened around me, and she pressed her forehead to mine, our breaths hot and heavy where they danced between our lips. Maybe our bodies and souls were having entire conversations without a single whisper as her heels gently dug into the back of my thighs, urging me on, begging me to push inside her.

And when I did, the rubber band of energy around us warped, stretching to its max before it snapped back with a pop that had us both letting out a shaky, longing sigh.

Sydney's hands pulled and gripped, her nails scratching and digging, as if she couldn't get me close enough, like any centimeter of distance was too much. And I worked between her legs, pulsing, in and out, my lips on her neck, her breasts, her chin and jaw before we were kissing again, the pressure crushing.

I came with my mouth fastened to hers, and she rolled her body in time with mine, taking my release inside her without either of us slowing. Even when I was spent, when every drop was spilled and my body ached to collapse, I continued, slowing my pace but staying inside her with our kiss just as demanding as before.

I love you.

I want you.

Be with me.

Those words were never spoken, but they rang loudly through that room as if the walls had come alive long enough to say them for us.

We were slick, fastened together from lips to chest to hips, and still, I moved, flexing in and out of her until I started to get hard again, and Sydney rolled me onto my back. She straddled me with her hands on my chest, and took control, easing us into round two before round one had even fully ended.

Until the night turned to morning and I had to sneak out of her house, we made love.

And for the first time in my life, I understood the meaning of that phrase.

Chapter Eighteen

Jordan

"I cannot believe *this* is what you wanted to do for your bachelor party," Logan said the next night, looking around the old treehouse our father built when we were kids. It was out in the middle of nowhere, in an oak tree by the creek. Each corner of it was decorated differently, reflecting what our interests were at those ages, and we sat in our respected areas. "I mean, it's your last night as a free man. Shouldn't we have taken you to Nashville? Hit up some live music bars and some strip clubs?"

Mikey stopped where he'd been strumming on his guitar, cutting out the sound with a thump of his hand on the shell. His corner of the treehouse had been filled with music, even though he was only around six when Dad built it. Even then, we all knew Mikey would be a musician.

"To be fair, I'm still underage. I'd bet it's my fault we aren't out at the clubs."

"Nah," Noah said, clapping our youngest brother on his shoulder before he kicked back on his bean bag again. He rested his hands behind his head, looking up at the makeshift constellations Dad had made him on the ceiling. His area was filled with maps and sailboats, a reflection of his dream at the time to sail around the world.

I wondered if it was still a dream, if maybe he and Ruby Grace would do it together one day.

"It's not you, Mikey," he continued, his eyes still on the ceiling. "I wanted something low key. I mean, to be honest, I don't consider this the last night of me being a *free man*. The truth is, my heart was taken off the market the moment I met Ruby Grace."

Logan smiled at that.

"If anything, this is my last night of a chapter I'm excited to end. I think my real freedom, my real life starts when I marry that woman tomorrow."

"Yeah, but still, you don't want to see some titties?" Mikey asked.

Noah looked at all of us with an unreadable expression. "Does it make me the biggest pansy in the world if I say the only titties I want to see for the rest of my life are hers?"

There was a chorus of soft laughter from each of us, but not much of an argument, which was a testament to what we'd been through in the last few years. There was no doubt in my mind that had this night happened five years ago, we *would* have been at a strip club — whether Noah wanted to go or not. We would have snuck Mikey in, if we had to. Back then, none of us were settled down, and it wasn't even on the radar.

Now, we were different men.

All thanks to women we never saw coming.

"I would tease you about it," Logan said. "But the truth is, I'm in the same boat."

"Me, too," Mikey chimed in.

"I'll *bet* you're in the same boat, Logan. Especially now that Mallory's boobs are getting baby-ready, if you know what I mean," Noah joked, waggling his brows.

Logan pointed a finger at him from his corner of the treehouse — which was filled with books — and narrowed his eyes. "Talk about my girl's baby-ready boobs again and we'll be fighting, brother."

Noah threw his hands up on a laugh. "I told you, I've got my own boobs."

"Can we change the subject?" Mikey interjected. "Now I'm thinking about *both* your girl's boobs and I don't like it."

There was another shuffle of laughter, and then Noah was refilling the whiskey in our glasses. We were drinking a bottle from one of the single-barrel releases last summer — on the rocks, of course, Noah's favorite way. And Mikey was indulging in *his* favorite drink, a rootbeer float, since he'd volunteered to be our designated driver.

The conversation flowed on, and I stayed mostly quiet — which no one questioned me about since it wasn't unusual, thankfully, even though tonight's silence had more weight than my norm. My chest was still tight from Thanksgiving, from the night I'd spent with Sydney, from the feelings for her that were growing and stirring in my gut with the need to tell her and to hear her reciprocate, too.

I knew when she opened up to me about Randy last night that it wasn't the time, but I hadn't seen her today, either, and Noah's wedding was tomorrow. She would be in our family photographs forever. She would be there for one of the most important days of my little brother's life. This wasn't a family dinner or a public date, it was more.

Having her there as my plus one *meant* something to me.

And it was driving me mad that I didn't know if she felt the same.

Part of my brain told me to shut up and relax, to take her actions as reassurance. She'd spent the entire day with my family yesterday, and then we'd spent the entire night wrapped up in each other after she came to me with something she didn't go to *anyone* else with. She trusted me, felt comfortable with me, opened up to me. And over the last two months, we'd explored each other, discovering just as much about one another as we did about ourselves in the process.

But this was new for me.

I'd never opened my heart to someone before, and I worried about what I was feeling, what *she* was feeling, and where we would go from here.

If we would go anywhere, at all.

I wondered if I read all the signs wrong, if I was in too deep when she was wading in the shallow end, if we would be able to survive working together if whatever this was between us didn't work out.

And I knew she was wondering how we would survive working together if whatever this was between us *did* work out.

I was worried about one thing, and she was concerned about another.

How could we meet in the middle with those two facts being true?

This was the constant whirl of my thoughts over the last twenty-four hours, and I couldn't shake loose from them, no matter how I tried.

"So, Jordan," Mikey said, snapping me back to the moment with my brothers. "You going to fill us in on the Sydney situation willingly or do we have to beat it out of you?"

I blinked, trying to think of the right words to assure them that there was nothing to talk about, but Logan rolled his eyes before I could speak.

"Oh, come on. Mikey told us that you kissed her earlier this season, and though he *also* told us she didn't want it to ever happen again, I think it's pretty clear after yesterday that it has."

"A lot, I'd wager," Noah added with a smirk.

I narrowed my eyes at Mikey, who threw his hands up. "Hey, we're brothers. Don't act like y'all didn't talk about me behind my back when I was going through my shit with Bailey and Kylie."

I sighed at that, because it was true, and because if my brothers didn't worry about me, *I'd* be worried. We were a family unit tied together with bonds as strong as steel, and we watched out for each other, ready to fight if necessary or be there as a shoulder to cry on.

And we *hated* to cry.

But we were never too proud to. It was one of the many things our father had instilled in us — that it was okay to have emotions, and it didn't make you less of a man.

"Come on, guys," I said on another sigh, looking through the binder of old football rookie cards I'd once collected. It felt good to keep my eyes there instead of meeting their gaze. "You know I'm not a man of many words."

"So just use a few of them," Mikey offered.

I scowled, but closed the binder with a heavy breath. "I don't know. Obviously, we're not just friends."

"Quite," Logan said, and I narrowed my eyes at him before continuing.

"We... were intimate, after the first home game win," I said, feeling a little uncomfortable airing our personal business like that. But it was my brothers, and I knew I could trust them. "And I thought that was it, you know? That we were going to cross over the friendship line. And we did, but... it was different for me than it was for her."

"Meaning?" Noah probed.

"Meaning we had a conversation the next day about how she didn't want to tell anyone, and she didn't want it to get too serious."

"Yikes," Logan said on a whistle. "And you said?"

I shrugged. "I was honest, told her I didn't do the *hook-up* thing. So, we made a kind of deal, I guess. That we'd keep it on the down low, not make a big deal of it, but that I wanted her to come to your wedding with me." I looked at Noah then. "And I basically implied that if we made it to this point, we would know if we were serious or not, if we should tell people, claim our relationship."

"And?" Noah asked.

"And..." I sighed. "I know how I feel, and I *think* I know how she feels, but I'm not sure. And I want to ask her, but I'm afraid to push, but I also can't wait much longer, because I think I'll go fucking crazy if I do."

They were all silent for a long moment, and finally, Noah asked, "What's the rush? I mean, would you be okay to not push it, to wait until she's ready to broach the subject with you?"

"I just don't like this game," I confessed. "Why are we not telling anyone, running around in secret, keeping it from our families and making it feel... dirty? You know?" I shifted uncomfortably. "This isn't how Dad taught us to be with women, and I don't like how it makes me feel."

"And you're scared."

I looked at Logan, who'd said the words I didn't want to admit.

I swallowed. "And I'm scared."

"I was the same way with Mallory," he said with a nod of understanding. "I understood our reasonings for needing to go slow and keep it to ourselves for a while, but after a certain point, I just... I needed to know I wasn't fooling myself."

"Exactly," I said on a breath, feeling understood. "And she's got her reasons — good ones — for us to keep it quiet. I mean, she's the only woman on a staff of men in a small town. People would talk if they found out we were together — and not about me, because that's not how it works."

"So shitty..." Mikey murmured.

"I know. And I couldn't protect her from that, though I could try. *She* has to be ready for it. She also has to be ready to tell Paige, who is just getting used to the idea of her parents being divorced, I'm sure."

"And then there's Randy," Logan said, his expression hard, and when his eyes met mine, I knew that *he* knew what Sydney had confessed to me last night.

"And then there's Randy," I echoed.

"What about him?" Mikey asked, confused. "So what, she was married before. They're divorced now. It's not like she's cheating."

"That's not it at all. It's more that Randy is a shithead," Logan said for me. "And he has been on a power trip since he first became an officer shortly after high school. I'd bet anything that he does whatever he can to constantly remind her of his power."

I hadn't thought of it that way, and I tilted my head to the side. "You think that's it? I mean, I figured she didn't want to upset him, because from what she's told me, he has anger issues and their relationship wasn't the healthiest. But... do you think she's afraid he'd do something to put her or Paige in jeopardy?"

"That's exactly what I think," Logan said.

We all fell silent, chewing on that, and finally I blew out a breath. "I don't know. I get that, but she knows I would be there for her through that. We could figure it out together. And honestly, I think I'll go crazy if I don't just *hear* it from her that she's feeling the same way I am. I know she's showing me with actions but... it's different."

I looked up at the stars above Noah's corner of the treehouse, trying to explain it.

"I'm already afraid of how I feel, like I'm an aerial artist that just flung off my hoop into the air and I have no idea if her hands are outstretched and ready to catch mine or if I'm going to freefall to my death. I'm more anxious than I've been my entire life, and I don't want to be stupid." My throat closed in on itself before I said my next sentence. "If she's not in it, I need to let her go."

There was another long pause, and we all sipped from our glasses, letting the whiskey settle in as if it could help us problem solve.

"I think you should tell her," Noah said. "Tomorrow. Just put it all out there."

"I agree," Mikey chimed in. "I mean, at this point, the possible gain is worth the possible risk. You just said it — if she's not where you are, then it's better to stop it now, before you both get in deeper."

I nodded, and Logan told me with his eyes that he agreed, too.

"Thanks, brothers."

They offered small smiles, and then the conversation was changed — blessedly — and they let me slip back into my quiet state.

Somewhere around midnight, as we were packing up and getting ready to leave, Mikey stopped in the middle of the treehouse, looking around at each of our corners.

"I wish Dad could be here tonight," he whispered. "And tomorrow, for you, Noah." He looked at our brother then, whose face crumpled a bit.

"I do, too," Logan said.

"He's here," I reminded them, clapping the two oldest ones on the shoulder. We all stood there, taking in what our father had built — not just with wood, but with his blood, sweat, and tears.

He'd built that treehouse.

And he'd built us, too.

My chest tightened, and I hooked an arm around each of them, reminding them that no matter what, we had each other. Then, I echoed the truest belief I had.

"He's always here."

• • •

Later that night — or rather, *very* early the next morning — I lay wide awake in my bed, one arm under the pillow behind my head, eyes on the ceiling.

I couldn't sleep, and I wasn't surprised.

Talking with my brothers had my thoughts running laps in my head again, and when I glanced at my phone screen where it lay on my bedside table and saw that it was nearly three in the morning, I huffed, tossing the covers off me and storming to the kitchen to get some water.

I needed to sleep. I was one of the groomsmen in the wedding tomorrow — or rather, *today*, and it would be a long day. I drank half a glass of cold water, looking around my little house and debating whether I should get in a quick twenty-minute, high-intensity workout and take a hot shower to see if those two things combined would make me pass out.

But then my eyes landed on my laptop where it sat on my coffee table, and on the external hard drive next to it.

Digging into Dad's journal this late was a bad idea. I was tired, and I needed to be focusing on sleeping, not on staring at a computer screen.

Then again, I knew even with a workout and a shower that sleep wasn't anywhere *near* within reach, so I refilled my glass and padded into the living room, pulling the computer onto my lap and plugging in the hard drive.

I scrubbed my hands over my face as the screen loaded, typing in Dad's password when the login page popped up. I had his journal open in the next minute, and then I lost myself in translating the Latin entries, in the boring day to day my father had experienced at the distillery.

I hadn't realized how long I'd been working.

I hadn't realized how much time I'd made up for, how much of his journal still remained when I dove into it that night.

I hadn't realized that after just ninety minutes, I'd be staring at the last entry.

It was marked at the top with the date of his death.

My stomach lurched — so violently that I shot up straight, gripping the edges of the laptop as my eyes scanned that date in the top right-hand corner over and over again.

It was the last entry.

And this one wasn't in Latin.

My heartrate accelerated, and the first thing I thought was *why didn't we think to scroll to the bottom, to start* here *instead of at the beginning?*

The next notion was more consuming, though, and I let it take me under — because these were my father's last private thoughts before his life was snuffed out like a match flame.

And I was about to read them.

Journal,

Ah, my old friend, I've enjoyed our secret conversations in the ancient language, but I'm afraid there's no time for me to practice that art today, for I have discovered something far too exciting to take my time in divulging.

As you know from previous entries, I recently discovered the Last Will and Testament of our founder — Mr. Robert J. Scooter. What I might have failed to mention before is that there was no record of this Will when he passed, and for that reason, I did something I'm afraid I should be ashamed of.

I read it.

For months, I have combed through each page — of which there were many — researching the legal terms I did not understand and making notes of my own, searching for something my father believed would have existed in Robert's Will — had there been one.

And he was right.

I needed to be sure, so even when I first discovered the pages that dictated how the company shares should be split in the event of Robert's death, I did not let my hope and excitement guide me. Instead, I read and re-read and made notes and researched until I was so certain that nothing could be refuted. And I discovered the missing piece to a puzzle my father never solved in his lifetime.

Robert left my father, and our family, fifty percent of the company stock.

Half.

Part-ownership.

Journal, even when I had the proof, I worried about whether or not to bring this information to Patrick Scooter. As you know, we haven't exactly been best friends throughout the years, which I attribute largely to his father's affection for me and how much he entrusted to me when it came to the distillery. I would also have to admit to Patrick that not only had I found the

Will, but that I had not come to him with it directly, but rather read it on my own without permission.

Nevertheless, I felt I had no other choice.

It was time to set things right.

Oh, I was nervous. My hands are still shaking as I type this, but now, from an exhilarating joy and anticipation rather than an uncertainty. To my utter amazement, Pat not only listened to me and agreed that I was correct in my interpretation of the Will — he insisted that we rectify the situation immediately.

He's going to name me as partner.

He's going to backpay my family for the years of income we should have been receiving, immediately include me on business decisions I was only a small voice for before, rewrite the staff organization chart, and for the first time since his father's death, he seemed open to hearing my ideas for the future of this distillery.

I guess now, he has no choice.

What's more, he wants me to move into his father's old office — the one I've been cleaning out for months. He insisted it was what his dad would have wanted, for me to follow in his footsteps, to "take my place at the table," so to speak.

As I write this, I have already gathered most of the belongings in my office to transfer over, and Patrick has asked me to meet him in his father's office after our four o'clock board meeting to discuss next steps.

Again, I am trembling with excitement and disbelief. I can't wait to get home to tell Laurelei and the boys.

This is it, Journal.

This is the day my father's legacy is revived.

This is the day my family's life changes forever.

There was no sign off, just those last nine words dangling at the end of the page, and I read them over and over again, heart pounding out of my chest with the dark truth that my father never could have understood they held.

Our lives *had* changed forever on that fateful day.

But not in the way they were supposed to.

Black invaded my vision as I stared at the screen, my head foggy, chest so tight I couldn't squeeze a breath out to save my life.

Half of the company was ours.

Half of the company had been left to my grandfather, to my father, to *us*.

There was never supposed to be a Will, and yet my father had found it. He'd brought it to Patrick. Patrick *knew* what was inside it.

And on the day of my father's death, he'd asked him to meet in the very office where he perished.

Every nerve in my body stood on end, my chest fluttering with the rapid beats of my heart, head pounding with questions and accusations circling like an F5 tornado. More and more questions popped into my head with every new re-read of the entry, and sweat gathered on my forehead, my gut churning, breaths shallow once I finally found them.

All the years we'd searched for answers, and now we had them.

And I knew sleep was the last thing I'd be able to do now.

Chapter Nineteen

Jordan

On the outside, everything was perfect.

It was perhaps the most beautiful November day Stratford, Tennessee, had ever seen. An unusual front of warm weather had swept in overnight, leaving us basked in a cloudless sky of sunshine and a comfortable sixty-seven degrees. It was just warm enough for women to not have to wear a jacket over their dresses, and just cool enough for the men in tuxedos to not sweat.

Perfect.

I stood by Noah's side at the altar, along with Mikey and Logan, and when the entire congregation turned to watch Ruby Grace float down the aisle in her floor-length, cream-colored lace dress — I watched him. His eyes welled with tears at the sight of her, and he bowed his head, trying to fight them off before he lifted his eyes to her once more and I watched two tears slip in parallel lines down each cheek. His smile was the size of his entire face, though he covered it with one hand, in utter disbelief that the stunning woman walking toward him was about to be his forever.

Perfect.

Ruby Grace's sister and best friend stood behind her, and I watched them get just as emotional as my brothers during the ceremony as we watched Noah and Ruby Grace pledge their undying love to one another. They held each other's hands as Pastor Morris spoke of eternal love and sacrifice and compromise and I knew without a doubt that they barely heard a word of it, because they were lost in each other's eyes, in the dreams they had built together, in the ones yet to come.

Perfect.

It all seemed to come and go in both slow motion and the quickest hour of my entire life. I was wrapped up in every moment, until Pastor Morris declared that they were now husband and wife and Noah could kiss his bride. When he did, the church roared with applause, and Noah turned to the crowd, thrusting his hand holding Ruby's into the air while he yanked his opposite fist into his side in a victorious pump. He'd landed the girl. She was his, and he was hers, and their new life together started now.

Perfect.

On the outside, at least.

Because on the *inside*, under the rib cage that held my lungs and heart in place, and under the skull that protected my brain, and inside the deepest part of my gut?

It was total and complete chaos.

As I'd predicted, sleep hadn't come for me the night before — not after what I'd discovered. I hadn't been able to eat this morning, either, because the mere thought of food made my entire body heave in protest. Every nerve, every cell that made up the man I was was focused on that journal entry, on what I'd read, on what my father had left behind as the final clue to solve the mystery of his death.

And the worst part was that I knew I couldn't tell anyone.

Not yet.

It was Noah's wedding day — a day he'd been planning for and looking forward to for months. It was a day Mom had dreamed of for his entire life. It was a day to celebrate love and union, not to make my entire family sick with the knowledge that Robert J. Scooter had a Will, and we were in it, and Dad had found it, and Patrick knew about it, too.

And the last request he'd made was for Dad to meet him in the office he'd taken his last breath in.

All of it compounded right on top of the feelings that had been stirring inside me over Sydney — the *original* reason I couldn't sleep last night. So, while I forced my best smile for my brother and did everything in my power to be present, to celebrate, to let it all go until the day was over, I was powerless to fight the wave of anxiety that took me under over and over again.

After the ceremony, Ruby Grace and Noah stood near the doors to speak with all the guests in the receiving line. Mom stood on one side while Ruby Grace's parents — Mayor Barnett and his wife — stood on the other, each of them greeting the guests with a handshake or a hug and a *thank you so much for being here.*

My brothers and I stood off to the side, waiting for the time when our next job duties would kick in. We each had our role to play in the day, and the next step was transporting the bride and groom to the outdoor reception that would be hosted at the Mayor's mansion.

I had my hands in my pockets, watching Noah's genuine grin, wondering how the hell I would tell him and my other brothers what I'd found when Sydney stepped into view.

"You know, as much as you look at home in Stratford High colors, I *really* like you in a navy tux," she said, her hand finding the flax yellow daisy boutonniere fixed to my lapel. She adjusted the pin to stabilize it, pressing both hands to my chest before her cheeks flushed and she folded them together at her waist, instead.

She wore a long-sleeve, vermilion floor-length dress with a V-cut neck and an open back that exposed her lean muscles. Intricate lace details covered the bodice, the sleeves made entirely of the same lace, and the long, flowing skirt was a crepe fabric that had a slit up to her left thigh, showing her toned legs beneath. When I let my eyes wander over each inch of her face, noting the light and delicate makeup she wore, my stomach took flight on the wings of a dozen hummingbirds. Her eyes were highlighted with golds and pinks and slanted into the shape of a cat's with liner, and the way she'd braided her hair over one shoulder left the delicate slope of her neck begging for my lips to graze it. The longer I stared at her, the more my chest ached with the yearning urge to reach for her and pull her into me.

Perfect.

I knew I still wore that forced smile I'd put on that morning along with my tuxedo and bow tie, because when our eyes met, Sydney frowned.

"You look beautiful," I told her on a whisper, and my heart burned in my chest with the truth of it. "So, so beautiful, Sydney."

She smiled, but her eyebrows were still bent together, her eyes searching mine.

I wondered if she could sense it, my heart breaking — both from my feelings for her and from the discovery of my father's last entry early this morning. I wondered if just by looking at her, she could feel my pain.

She didn't ask if I was okay, but as my mother signaled that it was time to make our way outside for the bride and groom's exit, Sydney looped her arm through mine, holding my bicep as she snuggled in close.

"I'm right here."

Her words were softer than a whisper, but they brought me my first steady breath of the day, one that pushed out all the stiff air in my lungs and made room for a new, fresh, clean inhale of assurance.

And with her on my arm, I somehow found the strength to walk through the church doors and continue the celebrations, all the while holding the biggest secret I'd ever had buried where no one could see.

• • •

Sydney

I hadn't been to a wedding since my own, which had been small, and private, and far from glamorous. It was just me, Randy, and our families — including Paige, who was already growing in my belly at the time.

It was *nothing* like this.

While the church ceremony had been modest and simple, the reception at Mayor Barnett's home was nothing short of extravagant. Their home was something out of *Better Home & Gardens* magazine, the classic, all-American southern house — complete with a porch that wrapped all the way around. I couldn't say for sure how many acres they had as part of their land, but it was at least three, and a giant portion of it had been transformed into the nicest event space I'd ever seen.

At the center of it all was a dance floor, planks of wood fitted together in the middle of their yard as if it had always existed there. It was framed by gold and all around it were round tables with lavish floral centerpieces, candles of all sizes, and photos of Noah and Ruby Grace throughout their relationship.

While the tables surrounded the dance floor, at the head of it stood a small stage with a full string band — one that was currently playing the sweetest, most beautiful rendition of "From The Ground Up" by Dan+Shay while Ruby Grace and Noah shared their first dance in the center of the floor. He held her tight, her eyes cast up toward his as they swayed, both of them whispering softly to each other so no one else could hear.

Strings of gold and white twinkle lights criss-crossed above it all, casting the cool November night in a warm evening glow. There were pyramid flame heaters surrounding the tables and placed strategically between them, so that there was plenty of space to move around but also that no guest could ever possibly get cold.

Every detail was thoughtful and refined.

My eyes found Jordan's where he sat beside me, and he offered a wink before his gaze was on his brother and Ruby Grace again. The smile he'd been trying to hold all night fell once more, along with my gut, because I knew something was off — thought I didn't know exactly what it was.

Throughout the evening, as we listened to Logan and Ruby Grace's sister, Mary Anne, give their speeches, and as dinner was served, and as the band played soft music as we all conversed at his family's table — I held his hand in mine under the table. He felt so distant that I'd squeeze that hand from time to time, and he'd squeeze in return, letting me know he was still there, when for all intents and purposes he seemed universes away.

And I knew I was the reason.

Here we were, two months from the morning he'd sat at my patio table and told me that he would agree to keep our relationship between us if I agreed to be his wedding date this evening. And while I had followed through on my end just as he had his, I knew that to him, me being here meant more than just *me being here*.

He wanted all of me.

And what I'd realized this weekend was that I felt the same.

Maybe it was walking with his mother in her garden, listening to her tell stories of Jordan growing up. Maybe it was watching his brothers with Paige, the wide smile on her face and the stars in her eyes. Maybe it was that night, when I'd come to him with my deepest shame, and he'd accepted me fully, holding me and kissing me and making love to me until the morning light slipped through my guest room window.

But I knew it was more than that, too.

It was the way he was with Paige, the way he already cared for her as if she were his own. It was the way he saw all my scars and kissed them with reverence, as if they were what made me beautiful. It was quiet nights on his couch and lively afternoons in my backyard and secret kisses stolen in the locker room at work when no one was looking.

Somewhere, in the middle of all that, my fear and anxiety over what would happen if we were ever publicly together had faded. Somehow, the sense of knowing no matter what, we'd get through it together had taken its place. And some way, I'd fallen in love with the last possible man on Earth who I should have.

My stomach still tightened and rolled at the thought of what the town would say, the gossip that would fly. I still worried over Paige, though part of me knew she'd likely be excited about us being together, about Jordan being a part of our lives.

But the biggest hesitance still grew from the knowledge that my ex-husband was an angry, powerful man.

And I knew he wasn't ready to let me go yet.

I squeezed Jordan's hand, and he squeezed me back, his eyes catching mine just as Ruby Grace and Noah finished their last dance. The string lights above us seemed to fill his gray-blue sky eyes with stars, and my throat tightened, heart nearly pounding out of my chest with the need to tell him how I felt.

And I decided, right then and there, that tonight was the night I would turn my back on my fears, on what was holding me back, and I would finally break free of the chains my ex-husband had shackled around my wrists.

Jordan seemed to sense the erratic beats of my heart, because he leaned in close, whispering, "Take a walk with me?"

I nodded, and we politely excused ourselves from the table as the band picked up the mood, launching into a popular, upbeat country song that had the floor already flooded with guests ready to line dance.

Jordan didn't hold my hand as we weaved our way through the tables, the music softly fading out the farther we made our way across the yard. There was an extravagant garden and gazebo between the wedding reception and the Mayor's home, and we strolled through it quietly — him with his hands in his pockets, me with mine clasped behind my back.

For a while, we were silent but for the sound of our shoes on the stones lining the garden path. The vines and trees and bushes stretched so tall and wide that we were eventually hidden completely, the reception like another world altogether.

It was then that Jordan stopped mid-stride, and I turned, finding a mixture of pain and fear in his icy eyes.

My heart sank. "Jordan..."

"I know you can tell I've been off today," he said.

I bit my lip, but nodded, moving toward him. My hands tentatively reached for where his were in the pockets of his slacks, and he withdrew them, threading them with mine. My heart picked up its pace, the beat of it loud in my ears as I shook with the words I wanted to say.

I love you.

They were on the tip of my tongue when Jordan looked around us, as if he were afraid we'd been followed, before lowering his voice to a hushed whisper. "I found something last night." He shook his head. "This morning. Whatever four AM is considered."

My mouth was already open, ready to speak my truth, but I closed it slowly at his words.

"Found something?" I asked, confused, and suddenly, I was tracing back through my memory of the day, wondering if I'd read everything wrong.

Jordan nodded, looking around again before he pulled me over to the beautifully carved marble bench by the rose bushes. When we were both sitting, he let out a shaky breath, his eyes on mine.

"I've been sitting on this all day, but it's eating me alive, and I just have to tell someone. I *can't* tell my brothers — not yet. And, well..." He shrugged. "You're the only other person I trust."

My heart swelled, and I squeezed his hands, letting him know he *could* trust me — and that I trusted him, too.

"You know how I showed you my father's journal? The one I'd been going through?"

I nodded, and at the mention of his father, my pulse ticked up another notch.

"I couldn't sleep last night, I... I just had a lot on my mind," he added quickly, dismissing that part of his story. "So I started working on the journal to tire myself out. But before I knew it, an hour and a half had gone by, and suddenly, I was on the last entry."

I blinked. "Like, the last entry in his journal... ever?"

Jordan's expression tightened as he nodded. "Yes. Written on the day of his death."

A violent chill shot through me, so powerful I trembled where Jordan held me.

"And," he added. "This one wasn't in Latin. It was in English."

I shook my head, confused. "But... I don't understand. Wasn't that the whole point of him writing in the journal? Like... he wanted to learn the Latin language, I thought?"

"He did, at least... that's what we think. And I didn't understand it either, not at first." He swallowed. "Not until I read it."

His energy was flowing off him in tidal waves, and I was wrecked by each and every one of them, my body reacting like I was in danger of falling off a cliff at any moment. "What did it say?"

Again, Jordan looked around us, then he lowered his voice so much I had to bend in closer to hear him. "Dad read the Will he found, Sydney. The one Robert J. Scooter left behind. And we were in it. My grandfather, my dad, all of us. We were supposed to get fifty percent of the company shares when Robert passed."

My jaw hinged open, and my eyes found his, mirroring the terror I saw reflected in them.

"Patrick knew," he continued. "My dad wrote in that last entry that he'd gone to him, that he'd told him and showed him the Will and everything."

"So Patrick *knows* about it?"

"He knows," Jordan confirmed. "And he told my dad he wanted to rectify it immediately, make him partner, announce it to the whole board and the company and pay our family what we were owed. All of that."

I shook my head, so confused that I ached all over trying to reach for understanding. "I don't get it. If he knew, if it was all right there in the Will—"

"He told my father he was giving him Robert's old office," Jordan continued.

"The one he'd been cleaning out, right? Where he found the Will?"

Jordan nodded. "Exactly. He said that it's what his father would have wanted, and he told my dad to meet him there after their four o'clock board meeting to discuss next steps." Jordan's face went ashen. "He wrote in the entry that he'd already packed up some of his things to move over, that he couldn't wait to get home to tell Mom." He swallowed. "To tell all of us."

My hands ripped from where they were holding Jordan's, and I shook my head in disbelief. "No..."

"Yes," Jordan said, and he spoke the words out loud that I knew we were both thinking, but I was too afraid to breathe to life. "Sydney, I think Patrick Scooter murdered my father."

Those words hung between us like the razor-sharp blades of a thousand knives, like if either of us moved a single centimeter, we'd be sliced to ribbons.

I couldn't be sure how long the silence stretched between us with my vision fading in and out of blackness before I leaned back, letting out a long, cooling breath and pressing a hand to my forehead.

"I know," he said. "It's a lot. I think this is why Dad was writing his entries in Latin. I think he was covering his tracks, in case someone found his files and tried to read them."

I shook my head, speechless.

"And I need to tell my brothers," he continued. "But... I couldn't tell them yet. Not today. Not when we're celebrating Noah and Ruby Grace."

"When will you tell them?"

"Tomorrow," he said, definitively. "At least, I think. I mean, I don't know how I could sit on this any longer. It's not proof, by any means," he admitted. "But... it's *something*, right? It's written evidence that Patrick knew about the Will, that he has never told us about it even though he knew, and that he'd asked my father to meet him in that office on the evening of his death." He shook his head. "I'm no lawyer, but I'd say there's a leg to stand on there somewhere."

My gut twisted, and I sat upright, facing Jordan again as I steeled myself. "Jordan, there's something I need to tell you. Something that... oh, God," I said, tears flooding my eyes as I pressed my hand to my forehead again. "Something I can't be entirely sure of, but that I feel like I have to tell you."

His brows bent together, and he pulled my hands into his again. "What is it?"

I blew out a breath, holding onto the next. "That night... the night of the fire. I... I was pregnant, and Randy came home late, and he was talking on the phone to someone in the kitchen, and... I don't remember everything, okay? And it's all a little fuzzy and I don't know if this even *means* anything, and—"

"What did you hear, Sydney?"

I swallowed. "He was just... he was so *angry* when I asked him questions. I wanted to know how that was the only room in the whole distillery that burned, how your dad was the only one who died. And I didn't understand it being caused by a cigarette, you know? I mean, was he sleeping? Or so focused on something that he didn't see it catch fire? And when it did, wouldn't he have fled the room? Like... was it *locked*?"

"These are all the questions my family and I have plagued ourselves with for *years*. For an entire decade."

"I know," I said, and my voice was strangled with emotion. "And... Jordan, I swear I heard him on that phone call... I heard him say something about *homicide*."

Jordan's face washed over, all emotion gone before his nostrils flared and he scowled hard. "You *heard* that?"

"I think... No, I mean, I *know* I did. Yes."

For a long moment, he was quiet, and I wondered if he was angry with me. But then, he smiled, shaking his head as he released my hands to run his back through his hair.

"Sydney... do you know what this means? We *have* something. We have my dad's entry, and now, your testimony. This is it. We can get a lawyer, we can—"

"Testimony?" I echoed, already shaking my head. "Jordan, I can't... I can't testify against Randy."

Jordan's frown grew. "Why the hell not?"

"You *know* why," I told him. "You know how he is, how he's controlled me, the hell he's put me through even *after* our divorce."

"He doesn't own you."

"He might as well!" I argued back, fear crippling me in a completely new way now. "Look, I told you what I told you so you can have reassurance, so you and your family can hold onto that and... and... I don't know, work with a lawyer to find out more. But, I can't testify."

"But, it's the right thing to do. You have to!"

"I *can't!*" We both looked around, lowering our voices again. "What about Paige, huh? You *know* she comes first in my life. How could you even ask me to do this?" I shook my head. "He is a white male in a position of power, Jordan. The goddamn *Chief of Police*," I reminded him. "Do you not see how at his mercy I am? How he could turn this story around on me in a snap, make it look like I'm crazy, like I'm an unfit mother and take my daughter from me forever?"

Jordan opened his mouth to argue but I stopped him.

"And even *if* it somehow works, we go to court and I testify and the judge rules in our favor. Then what? Randy goes to jail for life, and Paige has no father?"

Jordan's mouth closed again at that.

"Don't you see how complicated this is?"

"If he goes to jail, it's because he deserves to. And Paige is strong enough to understand what's right and what's wrong."

I scoff. "That's a very naïvely simple way to put this situation."

He gawked at me incredulously. "It *is* simple — right or wrong. There is no in-between."

My bottom lip trembled as I tore my gaze from him, crossing my arms over my racing heart. He didn't understand. He didn't feel every motherly warning going off in my body, every cell of my existence flying into self-preservation and survival mode at the thought of confronting Randy with this.

"You know, I don't know why I'm surprised," Jordan said, standing and turning his back to me. "If there's any risk involved, you're out, right? Just like with us. We can be a team in secret, fuck in secret, *love* in secret, but when I need you to be my teammate for real, it's too much, isn't it?"

He turned on me then, and I shrank under his hard gaze.

"It's okay for me to sacrifice, for me to give, for *me* to put my values on hold in order to be what you need. But when *I* need you, and *you* have something to lose, suddenly, you don't want to play?"

My nose stung, and tears blurred the details of his face. "That's not fair."

"Maybe not, but it's the truth."

I shook my head, and Jordan dropped back to the bench, grabbing both of my hands in his and pulling me forward desperately — into him, into us.

"I *need* you right now, Sydney." His eyes flicked back and forth between mine as a tear slipped free and rolled down my hot cheek. "Please."

Moments before, I'd been ready to look into those eyes watching me and tell this man I loved him. It was all I could think about all day long.

Now, my body warned me of a threat, of danger for myself and my daughter, too.

And those two emotions went to battle inside me, breaking down everything in their path to fight for who would win out.

It was too much — the discovery Jordan had made, the confession I'd told him thinking he would understand, the demand he was making of me, the guilt I felt that I couldn't give it to him, the island I was stranded on as the only one between us who understood my choices, who knew what it was like to give *everything* to protect Paige.

I couldn't make the decision in this state — not now, not tonight.

"I'm sorry," I croaked, and I pulled my hands from his, covering my mouth as my eyes squeezed shut and released another flood of tears. I was already up and off the bench, flying through the garden and across the lawn to where I'd parked my car, and I didn't look back to see if Jordan was following me.

Maybe because I knew he wouldn't.

I'd gone into that evening with the intention to hold his heart in my hands, to promise to keep it safe, to tell him I wanted him — *all* of him — and I wanted him to take all of me, too.

I was supposed to tell him I loved him.

I was supposed to claim his heart as my own.

Instead, I'd left it shattered on the stony path of a cold, dark garden.

And I'd never hated myself more.

Chapter Twenty

Jordan

The next evening after Sunday dinner at Mom's, I sat at the firepit in her backyard surrounded by all my brothers, and I told them what I'd found.

I felt numb going through the story, telling them what I'd already told Sydney the night before and feeling my heart split open a little more with every thought of her. I wished she was there with me, telling *her* side of the story, but I kept that to myself.

Even if I didn't understand her choice, I respected it.

I wouldn't tell anyone what she'd told me.

Still, *I* knew now, and the fact that she'd overheard Randy on the phone that night talking to *someone* about homicide only fueled my justice fire.

We were going to take someone down for my father's death, though I wasn't sure who yet.

But we had to be smart about it.

We had to have a plan.

"We can't tell anyone else about this," I told my brothers after their initial outbursts at the news and the silence that had followed. I waited until each of them were looking at me to continue. "Least of all Mom. She'll kill him."

"Are you kidding me? *I* might fucking kill him," Noah seethed, fuming like a dragon.

"That would solve nothing," I reminded him, bluntly but as gently as I could. "The biggest mistake we could make right now is letting our emotions get the best of us. We have to be smart."

There were quiet nods, though I could tell by the way my brothers wore identical scowls and flat-lined lips that no one was happy about the agreement.

"And I want to tell Mom just as badly as you guys do, but it wouldn't serve her any good right now. Until we have someone in handcuffs or substantial proof, she doesn't need to know."

"I just don't understand," Mikey said, shaking his head. "How could Patrick *murder* someone like that? A father, just like him — and someone who grew up with him in that distillery? Someone his own father loved?"

"Maybe that's just it," Logan said. "I mean, you heard what Jordan found in Dad's last entry. Patrick never really liked Dad. He saw him as a threat."

"And look at all the illegal shit Patrick Scooter does without blinking an eye. His underground casino has gotten half this town into debt they'll never see the other side of — Ruby Grace's dad included. I mean, he found a way to pay it off, but he's the *mayor*. What about everyone else?" Noah shook his head. "I think, in his eyes, he owns this town and everyone in it, and he can do whatever he damn well pleases."

"He *had* to have known that Will existed," Mikey chimed in.

"I don't know," I volleyed. "If he did, why would he have had Dad working in that office *knowing* there was a Will hidden somewhere in there? And besides, we don't know that Patrick is the root of this. All we know is that he asked Dad to be in that office at the end of the day."

We all fell silent at that.

"Wouldn't Robert's lawyer have had the Will, too, though?" Logan asked after a while. "I mean, it has to be notarized. I imagine *someone* had a copy — a lawyer, a financial advisor, whoever. That one in his old office couldn't have been the only one."

"Money speaks, brother," Noah said quietly. "My gut tells me if Patrick didn't want that Will being read by anyone, he'd pay just about anything to get agreement from all involved that it never existed."

Again, silence.

It was a tornado of emotions for each one of my brothers, one that had already ripped through me. I was on the other side of it, sitting calmly in the rubble, thinking of how to rebuild. But right now, they were in the thick of the storm, and I knew all too well how disconcerting that was.

"I think I need to tell Mallory," Logan said after a moment.

I frowned.

"It's her *father*, for Christ's sake," he pleaded with me. "I don't feel comfortable making a plan to confront him without her being in on it."

My chest tightened at the thought of someone outside of my brothers knowing what I'd found, but I understood what he was saying. Mallory's father was the main subject of the discovery. It was only fair that we told her what we found.

"Alright," I conceded. "But, I think right now, we need to all stay calm and quiet about this. I'm going to look into getting a lawyer, see what our options are."

"It has to be someone outside of town," Noah said. "I don't think we can trust anyone here."

"Definitely," I agreed, then I ticked through the list of what we each needed to be doing. "Logan, you fill Mallory in, maybe she'll know something more about that night, or at the very least know how we can get Patrick to admit to whatever happened. Mikey, I want you to comb through the last few journal entries, make sure I didn't miss anything. And Noah," I said, looking at him last. "You are going to go on your honeymoon and forget about this until you get back."

He scoffed, ready to argue, but I shook my head firmly.

"I mean it," I said. "You just married the love of your life. There's nothing to be done right now, not until we get a lawyer and make a plan — and we won't do that while you're gone. Okay? I know it's going to be hard to do, but you need to focus on Ruby Grace and enjoy your time with her." I exhaled long and slow. "I have the State Championship game on Friday night. You'll be back from your honeymoon on Sunday. Let's just agree to meet up then, and we can talk through the next steps. We've waited ten long years, guys... we can wait another week."

My brothers all exchanged looks, but in the end, they nodded in agreement. One thing I'd learned as the older brother was that it was my responsibility to help them see reason when all they wanted to see was red. It wasn't always an easy task, but they trusted me — and as long as that was true, I knew they'd listen, even if they didn't agree.

"I need to come up with a reason why Kylie and I can't go back to New York," Mikey said.

"No, don't do that. Go back. You have work and she does, too. We need to keep everything normal. But I'll book you a flight to come back home next Sunday, okay?"

He frowned, but nodded. "I want her to come, too."

"Okay," I said. "I'll get you both a ticket."

We were silent for a long while, each of us staring at the fire where its flames licked away at the evening settling in around us.

"Do you think we'll get what we need to take him down?" Logan asked after a long while. "I mean... do you think we'll actually get justice for Dad?"

No one answered, because none of us knew for sure.

All we *did* know was that we had to try.

• • •

I hadn't realized how much of my focus had been on what I'd found in my dad's journal until I'd finally told my brothers and relieved myself of being the only one who knew.

As soon as I did, every ache inside me turned its attention to the hole Sydney had left.

The week passed by in slow agony, with my days spent working with my athletes in weightlifting class, my afternoons spent at practice getting them ready for Friday, and my evenings spent on the phone with one or more of my brothers, trying to calm them and reassure them that everything would be alright. Before I knew it, it was Friday night, and I was on the field watching my team warm up in preparation to play the biggest game of their lives so far.

And while I should have been focused on *that*, I could only think of Sydney.

I could only feel numb.

The naïve part of me thought that if I kept busy all week — and I did — there wouldn't be time to be broken up over Sydney.

But she didn't need to be the center of my day to be present in every moment of it.

She was like a slow leak, forcing her way between all the crevices of my broken heart and slowly, centimeter by centimeter, wearing it down and causing it to rust so much so that I wondered if a stiff inhale would make it shatter altogether.

Seeing her at work killed me, but it wasn't as bad as it would have been if I couldn't see her at all.

Every afternoon when I walked into my office, she was already set up in hers, working away and getting our boys in top shape for the game on Friday. We didn't speak about what had happened Saturday night at the wedding. Hell, we didn't speak at *all* other than in staff meetings or in the locker room when everyone was present and she needed to update me on an injury.

We avoided each other at all costs.

But when our eyes *did* meet, it was like standing in a blue-flamed fire.

I knew she was hurting. I knew she couldn't have been sleeping or eating much more than I was managing to. I wanted to ask her a million questions. I wanted to hear her say a million things that would take what happened at my brother's wedding away and give us the chance to start over. I wanted to pull her into my office, pull her into *me*, hug her and kiss her and tell her everything would be okay.

But I couldn't, because *nothing* was okay right now.

We were both fucked up, but what mattered even more than that was that we were both set in our ways.

She believed she was right.

I believed I was right.

And there was no in-between, not for either one of us.

I struggled with understanding her, especially after everything she'd told me about what Randy had done to her over the years. Here was the perfect opportunity to get him to answer for his evil, and she was too coward to stand up and make him pay.

I knew Paige complicated things, and that she was worried his power was too much, that we could never win.

But Paige was smart. She was kind-hearted. *She* knew right from wrong, and I believed in my gut that if she knew the full story, if her mother explained it to her, she would be okay. Maybe not immediately — but eventually. She was a tough kid like that.

Then again, did I have a right to say that, to believe that, when I'd never been a father? How could I ever fully understand the position I'd asked Sydney to put herself and her child in? How could I know what it feels like to make a decision that affects not only you, but a growing child, who will likely grow up differently *because* of that decision?

The answer was that I couldn't.

And could I really say that we had nothing to worry about when it came to Randy, that the justice system would prevail and the bad guys would lose and the good guys would win?

Because, realistically, what proof of that did we have *anywhere*?

If anything, the daily news only supported *her* side of it — that right and wrong didn't always matter, and sometimes, good people got fucked over.

But, it wasn't her views on what the right thing to do in this situation was that upset me the most. That wasn't what drove the nail deeper and deeper into my splitting chest, making breathing damn near impossible.

It was that I came to her with something I hadn't told anyone. I trusted her. And when everything was said and done, I looked her in the eyes and told her that I needed her.

I need you, Sydney.

And she'd denied me.

My ribcage hollowed out at the reminder of it, but it was a stinging pain I was beginning to get used to — like chronic back ache after a sports injury. I subdued it as best I could, focusing on the clipboard of plays in my hand as I talked to Coach TK in a hushed voice, our eyes on the players on the field.

It didn't matter now, what had happened between Sydney and me.

It was over.

We were over.

And maybe what hurt the most was that we had never really begun, at all.

I wished so badly to live in this moment that — *before* Sydney — had been all I could dream about. I was at the State Championship game. My boys were warming up on the green turf of Tucker Stadium at Tennessee Tech. We were about to play the other top high school team in the state of Tennessee, to have the chance to prove that *we* were the best. The massive arena was filled with screaming football fans, with our entire town, everyone showing up to support us and cheer us on to another W.

This was all I'd wanted.

Until Sydney.

I felt her warmth even when she was on the complete opposite side of the benches from where I stood — which was where she aimed to be at all times, it seemed. She was keeping her head down, working on players, wrapping and taping and doing soft tissue work and ensuring we were ready to play.

"Time to get focused, Coach," Elijah Braxton said from behind me, clapping me on the shoulder with a knowing look, like he could see I was a mess.

We'd been allowed to bring more people onto the field than we needed, and he'd been one of the fans we'd invited to be on the sideline with us. He was helping in whatever ways he could, getting water for the guys and helping run warm-ups, but for the most part, he stayed out of the way, watching.

And when he looked at me, looked at Sydney, and then gave me a knowing, sympathetic smile — my heart burned like a dying star.

I glanced at Sydney then, and our eyes met for one brief second before I jogged out onto the field for the coin toss.

In that one moment, we seemed to say a thousand things.

But I couldn't understand a single one of them.

I heard Eli's words like bell tolls in my ears when the coin was tossed and our players lined the field for kickoff. And with all the effort I had left, I shoved everything out of my head that wasn't football. It was a skill I'd practiced and perfected when I was younger, when Dad had died and I was trying to figure out how to take care of Mom and be there for my brothers and somehow still get my career as a coach off the ground, too.

It was a numb state of mind, one that felt like I was floating underwater, or like being tethered to the Earth but suspended in outer space.

Somehow, I slipped back into that zone for the next hour and a half, and I didn't emerge from it again until we were jogging into the locker room at halftime.

We were down by a touchdown.

I had to figure out a way to get my boys back on track, to get them fired up, to get this win.

So, I put on my game face and walked into a silent locker room with all eyes on me, waiting.

It was when I locked gazes with a pair of almond brown ones that I found the strength to speak.

Chapter Twenty-One

Sydney

If I looked at the facts alone, I was still alive.

I was still breathing, inhaling oxygen and exhaling carbon dioxide, and it had been like that all week long. I was still waking up each morning — though I wasn't sure it counted as *waking up* if I hadn't ever fallen asleep — and I was still getting Paige ready for school, and going to work, and coming home, and making dinner, and hanging out with her until bedtime, and then climbing into bed myself just to do it all over again.

I was showing up.

I was holding it together.

I was alive.

Those were the facts.

But if I broke it down to the molecular level, it was all a lie.

No one saw the tears I drowned in every time I took a shower, but that didn't mean they didn't happen. No one saw the hollowness I felt in my chest, or the ache that ripped through me as my heart broke every time I laid eyes on Jordan — but they were there, regardless.

My past had trained me to put on a warrior face, to stand tall and strong no matter what, and I was doing just that.

But inside, I was crumbling.

The week I'd spent without Jordan since that wedding had been nothing but a numb blur of daily tasks and motions that convinced me I was going to be okay. I told myself that the more time that passed, the less it would hurt, and one day, it wouldn't hurt at all.

That felt like a lie, too.

To his credit, Jordan hadn't reached out to me. He hadn't texted me or called me or asked for anything from me at all. It was the right thing to do — a clean break.

But it was the last thing I wanted.

Every time he walked into his office, I wanted to walk in right behind him, shut the door, and leap into his arms. Every time I stood next to him on the field, I wanted to lace my fingers with his, tell him I was sorry, that I loved him, that I wanted to be with him. Every time our eyes caught, I looked away as fast as I could, but every cell inside me begged to keep his gaze.

I wanted him. I wanted us.

But I knew deep down that I couldn't give him what he needed.

It was more than just the fight we'd had in the garden Saturday night. It was true that I couldn't testify against my ex-husband, that I couldn't be what Jordan wanted me to be when it came to finding justice for his father. There was too much at stake — my daughter, my safety, our future.

And past that? Jordan was right about me.

I was a coward.

He'd held up on his end of our deal, and I'd failed on mine. The first time he asked me to be there for him, I bailed. I was ashamed, but I wouldn't hide from that truth, either.

I couldn't be the woman he deserved.

I had a child, and an ex-husband I was still tied to. It went so much deeper than my reputation on the team and in our small town.

In the most fundamental ways, we were wrong for each other.

And *that* was a fact I couldn't ignore.

The State Championship game had snuck up on me like a snake in long-leaved grass, but it was a distraction I welcomed. It was easy to lose myself in the excitement of the players, to focus on getting them ready to play and keeping them iced and bandaged and warm throughout the game. Even in the locker room at halftime, I'd been able to stay distracted, working on the players and tuning out the sound of Jordan's voice as he motivated them to go out there and get us the win in the second half.

But when the last seconds of the game ticked down, when their team had one last Hail Mary throw chance to come back and score a touchdown and take away our three-point lead, when they *missed* that chance and the crowd roared and our team exploded off the benches and flooded the field to celebrate our win, everything in me stopped.

And all I could do was find Jordan.

The level of noise that stadium erupted into was unlike anything I'd ever experienced. It was dizzying, the roaring cheers and the sea of people crashing onto the field and swallowing it up. In a matter of seconds, it went from where you could see every yard of green on the field to where you couldn't see a single square patch of it.

It was absolutely surreal.

We weren't in our little hometown. No, we were on a *college* team's field, in a stadium twenty-times the size of our small one back home, and we had the entire state watching.

Watching us win.

We won.

It sank in more and more as adrenaline coursed through me, and I searched the crowd frantically, trying to find Jordan. There were already swarms of players and reporters and fans on the field, but I looked toward the middle of it, knowing he would have jogged over to shake hands with the opposing coach before anything else.

There were too many people, and the more that flooded the field, the more my chest tightened. I wanted to find him, but why? What would I do? What would I say? *Congrats on the win, Coach*? Nothing was right, nothing was *enough*, and yet I couldn't stop myself from seeking him out. It was as if I didn't have a choice at all.

I was still searching for the right words to say once I *did* find him when there was a little clearing in the field, and there Jordan was, jogging back toward our sideline as reporters chased after him.

He kept his head down, speaking from the corner of his mouth to a few of them but focusing on getting back to where his team was. I imagined he was telling them he'd talk to them at the press conference, or that he just wanted a moment with his players. But they were relentless, all wanting a piece, and when he looked up and saw me staring at him from ten yards away, he slowed to a walk, and then to a complete stop.

It was only a few seconds, if even that.

It was just a small, microscopic moment.

He looked at me. And I looked at him. And all the noise, the chaos, the thrill of the win faded, along with the crowd around us. Time was like an elastic band between us, and I knew he felt it, too — like those few seconds were hours, instead. He just watched me, and I watched him, and we somehow said everything, but nothing at all.

The corner of my mouth lifted, and his did the same.

You did it, I told him with my eyes.

We did it, he told me with his.

I swallowed.

His jaw clenched.

Tears flooded my eyes.

His brows drew together.

Then, as fast as the moment had come, it was gone.

I saw it — the moment Jordan decided not to run to me. His right knee jerked forward automatically, his body leaning into the motion, but he stopped himself, and pulled back, and in his eyes I saw the truth I'd reminded myself of all week reflected back at me.

This was it for us.

We were over.

All of that happened in a matter of seconds, though it felt like an entire lifetime to me, and then all at once, the universe snapped back into action, and

Jordan was enveloped first by a few of the players giving him a Gatorade bath from our bright orange water cooler, and then by the sea of reporters.

They swallowed him whole, taking him out of my sight, and I turned before another tear had the chance to fall.

I couldn't be sure how much time passed on that field after that. I checked in on players, talked to reporters, high-fived the other members of the staff and accepted an emotional hug from Principal Hanley, who told me he *knew* he made the right decision hiring me.

He also said the job was mine as long as I wanted it, and he was happy to see that Jordan and I worked together so well.

I ignored the fire in my chest at his words, encouraging him to go talk to the other coaches while I found my daughter. And as soon as he shook my hand and made his way deeper onto the field, Paige slammed into me full speed, wrapping her arms around my waist and screaming while I tried to keep my balance.

"YOU DID IT! YOU WON! WE WON! WE WON!"

She was hysterical, jumping up and down and squeezing me and jumping up and down again and then running in circles around me. Seeing her excitement brought the first genuine smile I'd had all week, and it somehow hurt, as if my face had forgotten how to activate those muscles altogether.

"I can't believe it!" she said, panting, her hands on top of her head as she looked up at me with wide eyes. "I mean, we were down at halftime and I thought for *sure* that was it! And then you guys came back out and *wham*!" She made a one-two punch motion with her fists. "Sacks here, tackles there, *two* interceptions and a field goal kick to gain the lead. And they just crumbled! They couldn't catch us once we were on fire like that!"

I chuckled, rubbing the crazy hair on her head. "I bet it was because you were in those stands cheering."

"I mean, I *do* think I'm a good luck charm," she said with a crooked grin. "But, this time, it was the team. And Coach! Oh my gosh," she said, as if she'd only just realized she was on the field. Her eyes scanned it wildly. "Where is he? Can I go find him and congratulate him?" She looked up at me before I had the chance to answer and clapped her hands together. "Please, please, please, pleaseeeee."

My next breath was stolen by my rib cage squeezing in on itself, but I looked back, finding Jordan standing with Principal Hanley, the reporters talking to the players now and leaving him be.

"Alright," I said. "But hurry over there and then come right back. Stay where I can see you."

She'd barely acknowledged my rules before she sprinted into action, and I kept my eyes on her as Randy sidled up next to me.

The moment he did, I felt sick again.

"Congratulations," he murmured under his breath.

I knew he was being condescending and didn't actually mean it, but I thanked him anyway.

We stood next to each other in silence, both of our eyes on the field. My stomach rolled when the scent of his cologne caught on the breeze. It was a scent I used to love, one I used to find comfort and love in. Now, it just made me ill.

I watched Jordan smiling down at Paige as she jumped around in front of him, animatedly telling him all her thoughts on the game, no doubt, and my heart ached so fiercely in my chest I had to press a hand over it.

Randy watched me from the corner of his eyes, then he looked at Paige, at Jordan, and back at me.

"Is there something you need to tell me, Sydney?"

His voice sent a chill down my spine, though I wasn't sure why.

"I have literally had nothing to say to you since the day I left you, Randy."

"I don't know, sweetheart. I think you *do* have something to tell me."

"What are you getting at?" I asked, hoping the long sigh from my chest gave away that I was bored and not interested in fighting with him.

"I ran into Marty at Buck's the other night," he said. "You know Marty. Barrel-raiser down at the distillery."

"Yes. And?"

"Well, he was at Noah Becker's wedding last weekend," he said, and then my heart stopped at the same time a wicked grin climbed on his lips from my peripheral view. "But I guess you already know that, since he told me *you* were there, too."

It took every ounce of willpower I had left to calm my breathing in that moment, to not let him see that I was intimidated by his menacing gaze, by the threat that lay beneath the innocent words he'd said out loud.

"I'm not doing this with you," I finally said, and I took a step toward Paige, but before I could walk away, Randy grabbed my wrist and ripped me around to face him.

Pain shot up my arm, and panic zipped through me before I subdued it, meeting his eyes with fierce determination to not let him see me scared of him ever again.

"Paige is nine years old, Sydney. Do you think she hasn't been telling me that *Coach* has been over nearly every weekend?"

My heart raced, but I didn't say a word.

"First of all, I didn't agree to Paige playing football. I'm still her father, in case you forgot."

"Randy," I said as calmly as I could when he gripped me tighter. Every cell in my body was slipping into survival mode, and I used every ounce of strength I had to remain calm.

But before I could ask him to release me, Randy pulled me in closer, eyes dark and narrowed.

"Are you fucking Jordan Becker?"

His words were a slap to the face, but I didn't flinch.

"Randy," I said calmly again, glancing around to make sure no one was watching us. Everyone seemed to be distracted by the win, but my heart ricocheted within my ribcage regardless. I lowered my voice to just above a whisper. "Let go of me."

He blew out an angry breath through his nose, his grip tightening even more on my wrist as I winced. That seemed to wake him, and he blinked, like he'd been in a fog. His eyes caught somewhere behind me, and he released me immediately, smoothing his hands over his uniform — which he didn't need to be wearing, but I knew he did because he needed that power, always.

Randy's eyes caught at the same point behind me before he found my gaze again. "We'll talk later," he said, and then he turned and left without even saying goodbye to his daughter.

And I let out a shaky breath that I covered with both of my hands, squeezing my eyes shut and releasing two tears down my hot cheeks. I tried so hard not to let them fall, but my body was acting of its own accord, the relief and anxiety crashing into me all at once like a tsunami.

I didn't have time to get it together before Paige was at my side, and then I heard Jordan, too.

"Sydney?" he asked, touching my elbow, and I nearly broke at the contact — so gentle and calming and sure.

So unlike Randy's.

"Are you okay?"

I swiped the tears from my face, not looking at him as I reached for Paige's hand. I knew if I saw concern on his face, if I saw care in his eyes, I would break completely.

"I'm fine," I said as calmly as I could. "I'll see you at school on Monday. Come on, Paigey."

I put on my best smile for her, steering her toward the locker room. I needed to get my stuff. And then I needed to get the hell out of here.

I'd driven separately from the team for the two-hour road trip so that I could take Paige home with me after the game, and I was thankful for that fact as I packed up my athletic bag and slung it over one shoulder, listening to Paige go on excitedly about what she'd talked to Jordan about. She was still going as we made our way across the parking lot reserved for the players and coaches and their families, and when we climbed into the car, she buckled up with a giant smile.

"I'm so happy for you, Mama. You're an amazing trainer. You know that?"

I smiled as best I could, heart still racing. "Well, coming from you, that's a high honor. Thank you, sweetie."

"One day, I'm going to be a player on that field," she whispered, looking out the window. "Just wait and see."

I was still trying to hold it together as she smiled, finally quiet as I started up the car. But as soon as I backed out of the parking space, she was on again.

"We should have Jordan over tomorrow to celebrate. Oh! Mama!" Her mouth popped open, eyes wide as she looked at me in the rearview mirror from where she sat in the back seat. "We could make him a cake!"

I covered my mouth as another wave of emotion surfaced, threatening to take me under. But I inhaled a hot breath, holding it together as best I could and smiling back at Paige before I took my eyes to the front. "Maybe, sweetheart. I'm sure he wants to celebrate with his own family tomorrow."

"Well, we could invite them, too," she offered. "They had us over for Thanksgiving, after all. Or, if not tomorrow, then Sunday. Whenever works for him. But we *have* to celebrate. We won the State Championship!"

I reached back and squeezed her knee in lieu of an answer, then I plugged in my phone and turned on her favorite country song, blasting it so loudly she couldn't hear the first sob that choked through my façade.

• • •

Jordan

It was late as hell, but the two-hour bus drive back to Stratford was anything but sleepy or quiet.

The energy wafting between the players was palpable as they relived every moment of the game, sang our fight song loud and proud, and passed the trophy around to take pictures and rub it for good luck going into the next season. They were already posting all over social media, making phone calls to their girlfriends or their families they had to leave behind at the stadium, and to the ones who hadn't been at the game at all. And of course, I heard talkbragging about what the sports articles were already saying about the game in the online blogs.

I half-listened to their merriment, half-zoned out in the front seat, with my eyes losing focus on the yellow dots peppering the two-lane highway that led into our town.

Thankfully, none of the other coaches pestered me — likely because they knew after talking to reporters that I was absolutely spent — so I had silence amidst the chaos for the entire ride home.

I spent most of it thinking about Sydney.

Again, I wished for the focus I'd had before I met her. I imagined a completely different scenario for this night had I never known she existed, where I would be celebrating with the guys and taking silly pictures with the trophy and handing out accolades to those who deserved it.

As it stood, I was saving all that for Monday, when — hopefully — I'd be feeling more myself.

I wondered if it was partly everything going on with my father, knowing that the day after tomorrow, I'd be meeting up with my brothers to discuss where we'd go from here.

We'd all been sitting on what we'd found all week long, powerless to move forward without knowing what our options were, and now that I'd spoken with a lawyer in Nashville, I knew the odds weren't in our favor.

We had something, that was sure, but if it would hold up in court was another question entirely — one the lawyer couldn't answer without doing more research.

She said she'd get back to me, and to not do anything drastic in the meantime.

But she didn't know my brothers.

Still, even as my heart squeezed with the thoughts of my father, I knew my misery tonight was wrapped up in Sydney. It was in the way I wanted to run to her when we won, how I wanted to pick her up and spin her around and celebrate with *her* more than anyone else in the world. It was in the way we found each other on that field, in the long moment that passed between us, in the tears that flooded her eyes before we both turned away.

And it was in the way I'd seen Randy holding her wrist, the way she'd panicked and fled the field, the way she couldn't even look at me.

I hated the power Randy had over her, and the way he could make her feel like shit on what should have been one of the best nights of her career so far. He'd had enough sense to leave before I made my way over to where they'd been standing, but he also knew that I'd seen it.

If I had it my way, I'd take him down right along with Patrick Scooter.

With my mind racing the entire drive home, I had a feeling it would be another sleepless night as we pulled into the high school parking lot. There was a small crowd waiting for the bus — friends and family and students who had beat us back to the school and were now holding giant signs that welcomed us home as three-time champions — and I stood in the aisle when we parked, addressing the team.

"Before you leave, all the equipment needs to be off this bus and put away *correctly* in the locker room, understood?"

There were murmurs of acknowledgement, but most of the focus was on the crowd outside, and boys were already hanging out the windows and shouting down, starting the fight chant.

I smiled, standing aside and waving them off the bus. "Alright. Go have fun."

They were a boisterous wave of noise and body odor as they flew out the bus doors and down to where the crowd waited for them, and the coaches and I stood back and waited, chuckling to each other when we finally made our way off, too.

I kept to myself while everyone celebrated, having already hugged Mama and Logan at that stadium after the game. They were staying in a hotel overnight, not wanting to make the late drive back, and Mama had already insisted that we celebrate tomorrow.

She didn't realize there was so much more to do than celebrate.

I took my time in the locker room, taking the equipment from the guys as they dragged it in and sending them on their way. I didn't mind staying back to organize it all and make sure it was in the right place.

They needed to be out living it up.

I smiled as the last of them filtered out, remembering a time when high school football felt like everything to me. I couldn't dream of a day past graduation, of a season more important than the one I played my senior year.

Those boys would remember this night for the rest of their lives.

When I was finally ready to leave, it was nearly three in the morning, and I was the only one left on school property. At least, that's what I thought as I locked up the locker room behind me and made my way across the field to the staff parking lot.

But parked next to my Bronco was a Stratford Police squad car.

The lights weren't on, but it was idling quietly, and when I was just a few feet away, the engine cut off and Randy stepped out of the driver side.

He looked manic — his hair out of place, eyes red, a bottle of something concealed in a paper bag wrapped in one fist. He took another swig of it as I approached, and a shit-eating grin spread on his face.

"Congratulations, Coach," he slurred as I threw my athletic bag in the back of my truck. I leaned against it when I was empty-handed, crossing my arms over my chest.

"Thank you," I managed, doing my best to keep a level of calmness in my voice. "Something I can help you with tonight, Randy?"

"Oh, fuck off with your niceties, Becker," he spat, shaking his head. He pointed one of the fingers wrapped around the paper-bagged bottle straight at me, closing one eye as if he was aiming a gun. "You're fucking my wife, aren't you?"

It was an instant reaction, every nerve standing on end as my chest fluttered with the *fight or flight* adrenaline kicking into gear. The hair stood up on the back of my neck, but I remained where I was leaning against my truck, simply blinking when what I really wanted to do was ram my fist into his jaw.

"I didn't realize you were married."

He growled at that, running at me but stopping with a few feet between us, his finger now pointing in my face. "Don't try to be fucking smart with me. I'll arrest you right now and take your ass *all* the way down, you understand me?"

"What exactly would you arrest me for, Randy?"

"Anything I goddamn please," he spat with a smile. "Don't you see? *I* make the rules here, and if I say you were driving drunk, or resisting arrest, or carrying a gun that you tried to pull on me?" His smirk climbed. "Then you were. No one questions me. I'm the Chief of Police, you worthless motherfucker."

The urge to connect my fist with his face strengthened, but I crossed my arms over my chest tighter, willing myself to calm down. Hitting him would only give him fuel for all the fire he just threatened me with, and as fucked up as it was, I knew he wasn't bullshitting.

He *could* get away with any of the things he'd just listed.

It was my word against his, and as one of the few men of color in this town, I knew the odds weren't in my favor.

Suddenly — and all at once — everything Sydney had said to me at Noah's wedding clicked.

She wasn't a coward for being afraid of Randy and the power he possessed.

She was smart. She was aware.

And she was a mother doing what she could to protect Paige from the man standing in front of me.

My heart sank at the realization, and I reminded myself to stay calm, to not agitate him, to play by his rules until I was out of this situation.

So, I waited, knowing he had something he wanted to say — and I just hoped once he'd said it, he'd leave me alone.

"Now," Randy said, straightening. "Are you, or are you not fucking Sydney?"

My jaw clenched, because the way he spoke about her was as if *fucking her* was all she was good for. He had no idea what he'd lost when she left him, and he never deserved her in the first place.

"Not that it's any of your business, but yes, Sydney and I were dating," I confessed — mostly to see the look of incredulousness on his face. But I didn't have a smug smile to meet him with, because my heart was already breaking before the next words made their way out. "But, we're not anymore."

Randy narrowed his eyes, as if he didn't believe me. When he found no sign of a lie, he must have been satisfied, because he smiled again, taking a long swig from the bottle wrapped in that bag before he took a few steps back. "That's what I thought."

I cocked a brow.

"I don't know what happened between you two, but I hope you realized that you will *never* have her." He stopped walking backward, tilting his head to the side a little, his red eyes narrowed in on mine. "Sydney is *mine*, do you understand? She always has been, she always will be."

My fists clenched where they were tucked into my sides, but I held back, biding my time until he would be gone.

"Stay the fuck away from her, Becker, or I swear to God, I'll take you and your entire family down." His wicked grin split his face then. "And believe me when I say I *can*."

With another slug from the bottle, he opened his door, pointed at me one last time, and slipped inside the squad car, slamming the door shut behind him.

Then, he revved the engine to life, flicked on the blue and red lights and an ear-splitting siren, and peeled out of the parking lot, leaving me in his dust.

Chapter Twenty-Two

Sydney

Paige and I slept in the next morning, which was usually impossible with Paige, but all the excitement from the game had kept her up late and led to her passing out hard when I finally got her tucked in.

We woke around eleven, and then she insisted on making me chocolate chip pancakes — which always ended up being more work for me than for her. But, she was adamant that we celebrate, and I was in need of a distraction from the way my chest was slowly ripping open, so I obliged.

The kitchen was covered in flour and smudged chocolate and bits of batter when we finished. We ate in the living room, still in our PJs, leaving the mess in the kitchen while we watched College Game Day.

When we were done eating, Paige asked if she could drag all her art supplies into the living room to make a card for Jordan. And of course, I told her yes, because what else could I say? I didn't have the heart to tell her he likely wouldn't be by as much as he had been.

Would he?

I wondered if maybe there *could* be a friendship between us, one that was comfortable and safe and where no lines would be crossed. Would he want to still come over and work with Paige? To stay for dinner? To be with us?

The answer, I knew, was that he would love those things — but that now that we'd crossed the line into being more than friends, we could never just tiptoe back over it as if nothing had ever happened.

My chest was tight, tears pricking the corners of my eyes as I watched Paige sprawled out on her belly in the middle of the living room floor making a card for Jordan. Her little legs swung in the air, and she'd stop every now and then to look up at the TV before she'd get back to her task.

It was too much for me to bear, and so I slipped outside, dialing my sister's number as soon as the sliding glass door was shut.

"Well, if it isn't the State Champ!" she greeted enthusiastically. "Please tell me you're extremely hungover from all the celebrating you did last night."

She chuckled, but my eyes flooded with the tears I'd been trying to hold back, and a soft sob broke through my lips and the silence I'd met her with.

"Oh, Syd," she said sadly. "What happened?"

For the longest time, all I could do was cry while my older sister listened helplessly on the other end. But finally, I found my breath, and I told her everything — from our agreement and the amazing two months we'd spent together to Thanksgiving and the wedding and the last week. When I'd said all I could think to say, I quieted, sniffling, waiting for her response.

It was her turn to be silent.

"Please say something," I finally pleaded, wiping my nose on the back of my sleeve and tucking my legs under me. It was cold outside, and I'd wished I'd grabbed a blanket or a jacket.

"Do you want me to bullshit you, or be honest?"

I cringed. "Honest."

She sighed. "Sydney, you deserve to be happy. Do you realize that?"

Another wave of tears assaulted me, and I closed my eyes, resting my forehead on my knees and holding the phone tightly to my ear.

"First of all, Randy does not *own* you. I know it can feel like that, but he doesn't. Jordan would protect you if he tried anything, and I think the bigger part of you knows that." She was quiet for a long pause. "Did you... did you really hear him say something about homicide that night?"

I sniffed. "I think so. I mean, I was pregnant, there were a lot of hormones going on and I was tired and we fought and..." All the muscles in my body tightened. "And that was the first time he hit me..."

I knew without her saying a word that my sister had her fists tightened at that, because no one in my family knew of the abuse until I left Randy.

As it so often goes.

"So, I don't..." I continued, sobs still breaking up my sentences. I forced a calming breath as best I could. "I don't know, my memory is foggy. But... I really think I did."

"Then you have to testify."

My jaw dropped. "Gab... I *can't*. He'll make me look crazy. He'll turn it around on me. And even if somehow they *did* believe me over him, and let's say he goes to jail, then what? What do I tell Paige?"

"The truth," she said. "Being her mother doesn't always mean hiding the bad things from her, Sis. Sometimes, it means *showing* her the bad things — leading her to them and teaching her how to handle them. This world is a fucked-up place, and you know that more than I do." She paused. "I don't know what would happen if you did testify, if the Beckers took Randy and Patrick and whoever else to court to get to the bottom of all of this but... I *do* know that if you stood with them, you'd be doing the right thing. And I know that's what you *want* to do."

My stomach rolled so violently I nearly lost my breakfast, and I shook my head against the urge to throw up. "But..."

"I know," she said, and I knew I didn't need to finish my sentence. "It's terrifying. You've been in survival mode for so long that this goes against everything you stand for. But, Sydney, do you really think you'd be okay to just sit back, lose the first guy to ever truly care for you, and watch him fight for justice for his entire family without you there on his side, helping?"

My face warped with emotion, and I shook my head, laying my tear-stained cheek on my knee. "No," I whispered. "But, Paige..."

"Mama?"

My head shot up, and Paige stood in the doorway, her little face so sad it nearly broke my heart as she took in the sight of me crying.

"Hey, baby," I said, wiping my face. "I have to go, Sis. I'll call you later," I told Gabby, and I ended the call, forcing a smile and patting my lap — signaling for Paige to come join me.

She padded over slowly, crawling into my lap as I wrapped her up in a fierce hug.

"Everything's okay, sweetheart," I told her as I rocked her. "Mama's just having a bad week, that's all."

"Is it because you and Jordan broke up?"

Shock zipped through me, and I couldn't hide the expression on my face as I pulled back to look at my daughter.

"Come on, Mom," she said, rolling her eyes. "Did you really think I didn't know?"

I covered my smile with my hand, amused. "Know *what*, exactly?"

"That you and Jordan are boyfriend and girlfriend, but that you thought you were hiding it from me and everyone else. But, I'm smart, Mom. I see the way he looks at you."

"And what way is that?"

"Like he *loooooves* you," she said, drawing out the word and tapping my nose with her fingertip. We both giggled, and then she looked sad again. "But he hasn't been here all week, and you haven't been sleeping, and I knew something was wrong when you guys were acting weird at the game yesterday. You broke up, didn't you?"

I sighed, but nodded, deciding it was no use to hide it from her now.

"Why, Mama? I like Jordan. I like having him here with us. He's nice, and we play football, and he was nice to you, too, wasn't he?"

My heart squeezed in my chest, and I let out another breath, trying to find the words to explain it to her, all the while trying to digest the words my sister had said to *me*. But before I could figure it all out, there was a loud, pounding knock at the front door — so loud we heard it all the way through the house and out the back door.

Then, a muted voice from around the other side of the house.

"Open up, Syd. It's me."

"Daddy?" Paige looked at me, surprised, before she jumped off my lap and sprinted through the house to the front door.

When I caught up to her, my heart stopped altogether.

She was looking up at where Randy stood on the porch, telling him how we'd made pancakes that morning to celebrate the big win, but I couldn't take my eyes off my ex-husband. He was a complete disaster — his hair sweaty and matted to his forehead, eyes bloodshot, hands trembling where he patted our daughter's head with an affectionate smile.

He'd been drinking, or worse, and when his eyes met mine, I knew without a doubt that he'd come looking for a fight.

"Paigey, why don't you go make a pancake for your dad, huh?" I asked her, smiling and smoothing down her wild curls as she grinned up at me.

"Okay!" she said, and bounded past me and back into the kitchen.

I narrowed my eyes at Randy then, standing in the doorway so he knew he wasn't invited in. "You're not supposed to be here."

"It's my fucking house."

I ignored my urge to argue that point. "What do you want?"

"You know what I want," he seethed back, and then his eyes traveled the length of my body in my thin pajamas.

I crossed my arms over my chest in disgust.

"You're drunk," I whispered, careful as to not let Paige hear. "Go sleep it off."

"I talked to your boyfriend last night."

I stilled at that, and Randy's grin grew even more wicked where it grew on his ashen face.

"Oh yeah, we had a *great* little chat at the high school after he'd unloaded the bus. You see, when I saw the way you were looking at him on the field, when I started putting the pieces together from everything Paige had been saying about him, I knew something was up." He shook his head, as if he pitied me. "You were at his brother's *wedding*, Sydney. I'm not stupid."

"It's none of your business who I date."

"Funny," he said on a laugh. "That's what Jordan said, too. But he *also* said that you guys broke up." He tilted his head at that. "And you know, it got me thinking... what has our poor daughter been subjected to all this time that I've been gone? First, being allowed to play football — a dangerous sport, mind you — without her father's consent. And her mother bringing strange men around... sleeping with them in our home... going through toxic break-ups..."

I moved to slam the door in his face and dismiss him, but his hand caught it quickly, and he stepped a foot over the threshold, his nose inches from mine.

"I *know* you fucked him in this house, in *our* house," he spat. "How *dare* you?"

"Your daughter is inside," I reminded him, hushing my own voice while he raised his. "You're drunk, Randy. Go home."

"I'm reporting you to child services, you ungrateful bitch."

I gaped at him. "What is *wrong* with you?"

"I'll tell them you're an unfit mother, that you're fucking strange men in the house when Paige is awake and can hear it all, doing drugs, partying all night."

"Literally *none* of that is true and you know it."

"It doesn't matter if it's true or not," he seethed. "Now, you can make this all go away if you just agree to have dinner with me."

At that, his eyes softened, and I struggled with not letting my jaw drop farther at his audacity.

"You know me," he said quietly. "You know how I grew up with nothing, how I worked so hard to get everything I have now. And you..." He shook his head, looking at me with reverence. "You were my crowning jewel. You were the best part of my life. I don't want to live without you anymore."

It was the same shit he'd pull on me after he hit me or we had a fight. He'd bring up his childhood, blame his parents or his abusive older brother for his behavior. He'd tell me I was his everything, that I was the one thing that kept him going, that made everything okay.

But I saw through the lies, eventually.

I was nothing but a prize to him, a toy he could control and play with when he pleased.

One dinner, Syd," he begged. "Give me a chance to remind you what we had. We can try again. We can—"

He was reaching out for me to caress my cheek, but I backed away, trying again to shut the door on him. "Randy. Stop."

"Come on, sweetheart."

I cringed, backing away from his touch again. "Randy, you need to leave. I mean it. If you don't, I'll—"

"You'll *what*?" he challenged, his eyes wild now that he hadn't gotten his way. The stench of whiskey rolled off of him in plumes thick enough to fog the entire town as he latched onto me, his hand wrapping around my wrist and crushing it the way he had last night at the game. "Call the cops? I *am* the cops, sweetheart."

"Daddy?"

We both ripped around in time to see Paige's bottom lip protrude, tears flooding her eyes as the pancake she'd just made slipped off the plate she was holding and flopped onto the floor.

"It's okay, sweetie," I assured her. "Just go up to your bedroom and—"

"Daddy, let go of Mama," she said through her tears, and then she had her hands wrapped around my arm, trying to pull me away from Randy.

"It's okay, honey," I told her again before I narrowed my eyes at Randy and whispered. "Let. Me. *Go*."

"Not until you agree!"

Paige was crying harder now, and Randy's grip tightened on me so hard that I winced and crumbled forward at the pain shooting up my arm.

Suddenly, Paige let out a scream, and then she wrapped her little hands around Randy's arm, instead, and with all her might — she bit him.

Randy yelped, yanking his arm back and holding it in shock. It was just enough time for me to shove him backward as hard as I could manage, and I didn't wait to see if he fell or regained his balance before I slammed the door shut and locked it. I ran to the sliding glass door next, making sure it was locked, too, and then I rushed back to where Paige was at the front door.

She had giant tears rolling down her cheeks and more building in her eyes when I pulled her into me, and I sank down to the floor, my back against the front door as my daughter sobbed into my chest.

From the other side came a cynical laugh. "This isn't over, Sydney," Randy sang. "You belong to *me*."

I squeezed my eyes shut, and Paige held me tighter, shaking and crying in my arms. I couldn't be sure how much time passed before I heard the car door to his cruiser slam shut, and then the squealing of tires as he pulled away.

I let out a gasp, my hands frantic where I smoothed Paige's hair and held her to me and assured her everything was alright. But I knew it was a lie. Things were *not* okay, and they hadn't been for a long time.

Through the beats of my heart pumping loudly in my ears, I heard Mallory's voice from Thanksgiving night.

We are fighters, Sydney. We are warriors. Survivors. You never have to apologize to me, okay? You just have to keep fighting. That is what you owe me — not an apology, but a fight.

Because if we don't fight? Then he wins.

The truth of her words cut me like the hot blade of the sharpest knife, taking my next breath with it. But when I did inhale again, it was calmer, deeper, more resolved as I felt my battle gear slip over me like the armor of a knight.

She was right. Jordan was right. My sister was right.

The Becker family needed me.

Jordan needed me.

And I needed him, too.

I'd run before. I'd been scared, and manipulated by the power I felt Randy still held over me. I worried for my daughter, but now I could see plainly that it was *him* who was putting her in danger — not me.

I had to make things right with Jordan.

I had to apologize, to tell him and his family everything I knew, to link arms with all of them and charge into battle — *together*.

We had to fight.

And more than that — we had to *win*.

· · ·

Jordan

I forced the biggest smile I had as Mom aimed her ancient digital camera at me, and Logan smirked from his side of the table, knowing I was hating every moment of this.

"Hold the cake a little higher so we can read it," Mom said, waiting until I did so before she lifted the camera to her eye again. She didn't even need to — it had a digital screen. "Okay, say *champions!*"

"Champions," I murmured through my smile, and Logan covered his laugh, which earned him a poke in the side from Mallory.

"Thanks, Mallory," I told her, narrowing my eyes at my brother. "At least *someone* has my back."

"Oh, come on, Bro," Logan said, hopping up from his chair and wrapping my head under his arm. He rubbed his fist into my skull before I shoved him off. "You're a three-time State Champ! Lighten up a little."

I smiled, but shoved him off again until he was sitting next to Mallory again. It was just the three of us and Mom tonight, a small celebration with Mom's famous barbecue ribs and a giant cake that we'd likely take to Betty at the nursing home after, because there was no way four people alone could eat it.

Mallory eyed me from the other side of the table, and when our gazes met, she nodded with a slight smile and understanding. I knew then that Logan had told her what we'd discovered, and I wondered if she was just as anxious as I was for my brothers' arrivals tomorrow. Noah and Ruby Grace would be home from their honeymoon in the Exumas, and Mikey and Kylie were flying in around noon.

Mom thought they were all coming back to celebrate the win, and that was the way I wanted to keep it.

Mallory held the small of her back as she waddled into the kitchen, returning moments later with a knife and serving set. She began cutting into the cake when I heard the wheels of a car on the gravel drive that led to Mom's house. When I looked out the front door window and saw Sydney's car, I was up off my feet in seconds.

"Who's that?" Mom asked, but I was already out the door. I didn't even bother grabbing a jacket, just jogged down the front porch steps and stood there, waiting.

Sydney had barely parked before Paige was out of the car, and she bolted straight to me, crashing into me with a force I never would have expected from the size of her. She wrapped her arms full around my waist and hugged me tight, burying her face in my shirt.

"Hey," I said, and I knew instantly that something was wrong, because Paige wasn't spouting off something silly or sarcastic.

She was crying.

She hugged me tighter as her little shoulders shook, and I looked up at Sydney just as she got out of the car.

Her red, blotchy face told me she'd been crying, too.

"Hey," I said again, softer now, holding Paige tight. "It's okay. Everything's okay."

I heard the screen door open behind me, and I looked up, meeting Mom's worried gaze. I didn't have to say anything for her to understand, and she made her way down the steps to join us.

"Hey, sweetie," she said to Paige, running her fingers through Paige's wild curls before she reached out her hand. Paige looked at it, and then up at Mom. "Why don't you come inside with me. We just cut some cake, and I saw an *especially* big slice with your name on it."

Paige sniffed, rubbing her nose with the back of her sleeve before she looked up at me. I nodded, encouraging her with a confident smile, and she took Mom's hand, who gave Sydney a soft nod of acknowledgement and me a sympathetic smile before she led Paige inside.

I watched them walk all the way inside, and as soon as Mom shut the wooden door inside the screen one and gave us privacy, I turned back to Sydney.

The sight of her made my knees buckle.

Her hair was tied into a messy nest on top of her head, and her eyes were swollen, bloodshot, the stains of tears still marring her cheeks. She looked so small and meek, so sad and defeated, and her eyes welled with more tears the longer we stood there — which just broke me even more.

"I'm so sorry," she whispered as the first tear slipped from her left eye and down her cheek. Another one followed it as her face crumpled. "To just show up here, after everything... I'm so sorry."

I shook my head, crossing the distance between us and pulling her into me without another word. She choked on a sob once she was in my arms, and every cell in my body stood at attention, like I'd have to fight to defend her at any moment.

"Don't apologize," I told her, holding her so tight in my arms I worried I'd crush her. My lips were right by her ear, and I resisted the urge to kiss the skin beneath it. Instead, I cradled the back of her head and wrapped my other arm full around her, holding her to my chest. "You never have to apologize for coming to me. I will always be here."

"But, I was so awful to you last weekend," she cried into my shirt, and her shoulders shook violently before she could speak again. "I was wrong, Jordan. You were right. I *was* a coward."

"Shhh," I tried to tell her, but she shook her head, pulling back from my embrace to swipe the tears from her face and look me in the eyes.

"I was," she instead again. "It was all just so overwhelming, so sudden, and the last thing I expected. I thought when we went on that walk…" Another wave of emotion flashed on her face, but she rolled her lips together, fighting against it before she whispered, "I wanted to steal you away to tell you that I loved you."

My shoulders deflated, but my heart swelled with hope.

"And then you told me what you found, and then we were talking about lawyers and testimonies and…" She shook her head again. "It just got so big and real *so* fast and I didn't know what to do and I ran," she confessed on a breath. "And I'm so sorry. But I *do*, Jordan. I do love you. And I'm not running anymore. I want to fight. I *need* to fight. With you, with your family, with *my* family. I'm done with this town and its corrupt powers. And I won't let you fight them without me."

I pulled her into me again, this time not fighting it when my heart urged me to kiss her hair. I held my lips there, closing my eyes and breathing her in.

"Sydney, I understand now," I told her. "Randy… he was waiting for me when I left the field last night. He threatened me, threatened *you*, and Paige. I understand now why you were scared." I swallowed. "It scared *me*, too. He has a lot of power, there's no denying that. And I don't want you to put you and your daughter in jeopardy just to—"

"No," she said loudly, pressing her hands into my chest and looking up at me. "He does *not* have power — not over me, or over Paige — not anymore. I decided that, and I will do whatever it takes to ensure it's true."

I searched her eyes, riddled with pain and terror, as I swept her hair back from her face. "What happened?"

Her bottom lip trembled. "He came to the house today, drunk or hungover or both. And angry. He was *so* angry," she whispered, shaking her head. "And he threatened me, said he would convince child services that I was an unfit mother, doing drugs and bringing random men home."

My jaw clenched. "That's fucking bullshit."

"I know, and *he* knows that, too — but as he liked to remind me today, *he is the cops*," she said, mimicking his voice. "And he has every powerful man in this town wrapped around his finger, waiting to do what he asks — whether to pay back a debt or to keep their *own* dirty laundry from being exposed."

"That motherfucker…"

"And he grabbed me," she continued on a sob, showing me her arm that was already bruising. "And said I could make it all go away if I gave him another chance, and then Paige saw us, and she was crying and screaming at him to let me go but he wouldn't." She closed her eyes, crying, shaking her head like she couldn't believe the story she was telling me was real. "And then she was pulling at me, and she *bit him*, Jordan." Her eyes met mine. "She bit him, and I pushed him out, and then he was still going on from the other side of the door." She sniffed, scowling. "He said he *owns* me. And I decided right then and there that this all has to end. I don't know how, but I know I would rather die trying than to give in to his bullshit even one more day."

My chest was on fire with rage, and it was nearly impossible to cool it down, to remain calm after hearing her story. I forced a long, slow exhale, closing my eyes for a while before I opened them and found her staring back at me again.

"I'm supposed to trade off with him on Tuesday," she said softly. "I can't… I *won't* hand my daughter back to that monster."

I nodded, pulling her into me once more and hugging her tight. When she looked up at me again, our lips were just inches apart, our breaths warm where they met between us.

"I'm in love with you, too, Sydney," I whispered, and with the words, more tears glossed her brown eyes. "Do you know that? I love you with everything that I am, and I give you my word that he will *never* hurt you or Paige again. Ever. You hear me?"

She nodded, and when she pressed onto her toes to kiss me, I tasted her salty tears on those sweet lips.

We held each other tight, kissing like the world was ending and this was our final moment together. It *felt* that way — like we were on the precipice of the biggest storm, one we weren't sure we would live through.

"We have to take him down," she said, definitively. "Him, and Patrick, and whoever else is responsible for your father's death. We have to get justice, Jordan. We must."

I nodded, framing her face with my hands. "My brothers will be here tomorrow. I've been trying to get a lawyer but…" I sighed. "I think Patrick knows we're onto him, or *someone* knows, because every time I get a lawyer willing to talk to us, they pull out the next day or even hours later, saying there's a conflict of interest."

She frowned. "He can't *possibly* have that much power over that many lawyers. Did you go to people outside of Stratford?"

I nodded. "I even talked to two in Nashville. I don't know, Sydney… I think we're in deeper than we realize."

Her eyebrows tugged together, a defeated sigh leaving her chest as she watched me. "What do we do?"

A breeze rolled in over my mother's front yard, whipping Sydney's hair about and stirring up something deep inside me. It felt like the heavens were taking up arms with us, like my father had just dropped down and landed beside me, ready to fight.

"Tomorrow, when Noah and Mikey are here, we assemble the troops. We make a plan," I said.

My chest caught fire again, puffing out, my heart racing loud and heavy in my ears as Sydney watched me. I saw the same fierce determination reflected in her eyes, and another gust of wind blew through the trees and through my soul, too.

"Then, we go to war."

Chapter Twenty-Three

Jordan

On Monday evening, after the workday was done and the sun had already set over our small, sleepy town, Patrick Scooter walked us back through his immaculate home and into his office.

It was a dark and royal room, with deep mahogany bookshelves that lined three of the walls, and the only one *not* lined with books boasted a floor-to-ceiling glass window that I imagined had an impressive view when the sun was shining.

I was glad you couldn't see anything out of it now.

Patrick was annoyed we were there — that much was clear. His annoyance seemed to grow when Mallory opened the blinds that covered the large window, and cranked a wooden handle to the right of it, which opened the bottom at a small angle to let a cool breeze in.

"There, that's better," she said. "It's always so stuffy in here."

"It's cold outside," her father argued. "And close the blinds, I don't want anyone being able to spy in on us."

Mallory rolled her eyes, sitting across from her father in one of the chairs opposite his side of the desk. "No one is *watching* us, Dad. It's Stratford, Tennessee, for Christ's sake, and dinner time on a Monday."

Patrick grunted, but didn't argue further, and my heart raced in my ears as I kept my eyes on him and away from the window Mallory had opened.

Noah and Logan were with us, and Logan sat in the chair next to Mallory, while Noah and I stood behind them. We were all quiet, letting Mallory do all the talking for now — as we planned.

If we knew anything right now, it was that we *had* to stick to the plan.

Patrick Scooter hadn't changed much in the years since my father had passed. He had an old western feel about him, almost never seen without one of his many cowboy hats donning his head of white hair. His face was long and lean, but hard at the edges, and the wrinkles in his tan skin were deep and severe. Mallory told us that he used to be nothing but kind to her when he spoke, a farce that she began to see through as a teenager.

It didn't seem to be that way now.

I wondered how *she* felt — being in the same room with her father for the first time in almost a year. After she told him she was with Logan and she turned down the job he tried to give *her* first, inviting that it go to Logan. Instead, he'd ripped away the small art gallery in town that he'd bought for her and exiled her from the family. Everything had changed then, as she'd told us, and he stopped putting effort into the charade of pretending he and his daughter had a good relationship.

He hadn't even wanted anything to do with them when he found out Mallory was pregnant.

What was possibly even worse was that Patrick seemed to control his wife, Mary, who had watched me carefully when we first arrived at the house. She looked worried that I'd mention how I'd seen her at Mom's earlier in the season, but I'd made a promise to my mom that I'd never say anything, and I'd kept it.

Still, I could see the pain in Mallory's eyes, and the longing in Mary's, like she wanted to hug her daughter and kill all the drama that had separated them.

But one look from her husband, and it was clear who was calling the shots.

It made me even more sick when Patrick sat back in his chair and steepled his fingers, waiting. Because he hadn't asked to see his daughter when he found out she was pregnant, but when she fed him the lie we'd come up with that pertained to Scooter Whiskey Distillery business — of course, he found the time.

He was a piece of shit.

And by the end of this night, we'd prove he was a murderer, too.

"Thanks for agreeing to meet with us," Mallory started, all business as she rested her hands on her baby bump.

Her father eyed her stomach with distaste before letting out a long, bored sigh. "Well, you tell me you've discovered something that could cost the distillery millions unless it's handled, and you've got my attention." He pointed at Noah and Logan. "Now, I can understand why you two are here — you both work for me, and I imagine you have knowledge on whatever this *thing* is that Mallory has found. But *you*," he said next, pointing his nubby finger at me. "I'm a little confused as to why you're here, being that you've never worked at the distillery, nor have you ever wanted anything to do with it from what I can gather."

I didn't have time to answer before Mallory spoke again. "You'll understand why soon. Now, should we get down to it?"

Patrick's mouth pulled to the side, and he watched me a moment longer before he finally waved his hands over the desktop as if to say *please, let's get this over with.*

And Mallory must have agreed, because she wasted no time with baiting him, she just reached into her messenger bag and pulled out the charred remains of my father's laptop that she and Logan had found last year.

My heart immediately accelerated to a gallop, but I held a steady expression.

Mallory sat the laptop gently on the desk between her and her father, and instantly, the color drained from his face.

Noah smiled beside me, and I had to fight to keep that same smirk from showing up on my face, too.

We got you, you bastard.

"So," Mallory began. "As you know, you and Uncle Mac thought it would be hilarious punishment for me and Logan to clean out the old storage closet last year. And, oh, Dad..." she said, shaking her head. "I'm a little disappointed in you, that you didn't think about *what* could be hiding in those old, dusty bins and boxes — especially when you had something this big to hide."

Patrick's eyes were wide, and I could see him searching the corners of his mind for a reasonable excuse.

When he finally tore his gaze away from the laptop and looked at Mallory, it was with feigned ignorance. "What is this piece of junk?"

"Don't play dumb," Logan said. "It's my father's laptop — or, what's left of it. We found it along with a box of his belongings. Funny," he said, tonguing his cheek. "You told my mother that the box you gave *her* was everything you had of his."

Patrick scoffed. "So, you found this and *took it* without telling anyone?" He shook his head, reaching for the cord phone on his desk that I wanted to roll my eyes at because it felt like a prop in an old sixties' movie that he'd wanted in his office just for show. "That's stealing. I'm calling the cops."

"You might want to hear us out before you get law enforcement involved," Mallory said, placing a hand over her dad's on the receiver. "Unless you want to be in handcuffs."

"*Me* in handcuffs?" Patrick repeated, laughing incredulously.

"You murdered our father," I said.

For the first time since we entered that office, Patrick Scooter looked at me — *really* looked at me.

"You killed him. And we demand to know why."

Patrick opened his mouth, ready to deny it by the looks of his features — as if he pitied me — but Noah stopped him.

"We were able to recover the hard drive in the laptop," he said. "And we broke into that, too."

"Great," Patrick said with a dismissive wave of his hand. "Even more evidence to slap you with in court. That's confidential information."

"Oh, we agree," I said. "In fact, I'd say the journal my father kept at work was *extremely* confidential — especially after what we found written inside it."

Patrick's face went white, and I took notice of the slight tremble in his hands as he folded them over his stomach again, leaning back in his chair. He was pretending like he knew about the journal, like we had nothing on him, like he was still in control.

But his body was betraying his façade.

"You know, I remember when *your* father died," I said. "I was young, but I remember. And even though I didn't quite understand what a Will was, I knew it must have been a big deal, because this entire town was shaken up that your father didn't have one." I paused. "But he *did* have one. Didn't he?"

Patrick's lips were sealed together, and he watched me — emotionless.

"Yeah... see, it seems my father *found* that Will when he was cleaning out your father's old office. But," I said, smiling as I pointed at him. "You already knew that, too, didn't you? Because my father *told you* he found it."

Patrick shifted in his chair, eyeing the phone like he would reach for it at any second to make a magic phone call to save his ass.

But it was too late for that now.

"He also told you that he read it," I continued. "And that *in* that Will, your father left half of the company to... well, I don't need to finish that sentence, do I? Should I let *you* tell us what was said in that Will?"

Patrick stood abruptly, slamming his fists on the table as he shook with anger, his face red, eyes bulging where he leaned over the desk and pointed at me. "You don't have *shit*, little boy — and that's what you are. You're nothing but a scared little boy messing around in matters you don't understand."

"We have our dad's journal," Logan reminded him. "And his last entry says that *you* asked him to meet you in your father's old office. After business hours. After the board meeting." Logan sat calmly looking up at him. "And in case you forgot, that was where he died."

"You think a *journal* is going to hold up in a court of law?" Patrick asked, laughing. "You could have written it. You could have faked it to frame me. There is no Will, and your little *discovery* is flaccid, at best. You have *nothing.*"

"How was the fire contained to only *that* room?" Noah fired back at him. "Started by a cigarette that everyone in this town *knows* my father never smoked? And even if it *was* a cigarette, how was he unable to get out of the room once the fire started?"

Patrick straightened, wiping his hands over his chest as if he'd just spotted some dirt there before he sat back down calmly. "Your family has been told this time and time again, Noah. The fire department thinks he might have dozed off after a long day at work."

"And he didn't wake up when the room was on *fire*?" I shot.

"Look, we all have questions about that day, okay?" Patrick said. "But this... *CSI* game you're playing at here is silly, and childish, and frankly, a waste of my time. I think we're done here."

"You are so predictable, father," Mallory said, and it wasn't a biting or sarcastic remark. It was quiet, sad, like she truly was disappointed that he was still the same man who had hurt her, too.

She shook her head before she stood, and then she left the room abruptly.

Patrick looked between me and my brothers, as if to ask what we were still doing there. But then, Mallory came back in and shut the door behind her again.

This time, she wasn't alone.

Sydney stood beside her, tall as she could, with her eyes set in a narrow line focused on Patrick Scooter.

Patrick pinched the bridge of his nose. "Jesus Christ, what *now*?" He looked at Sydney, thrusting an open palm toward her. "What could you possibly have to add to this? Oh, wait, let me guess." He snapped his fingers. "You found something buried in your ex-husband's files! An old diary, right? Or a Magic 8-Ball!"

He was toying with us, and Noah surged forward, but I planted my hand flat in the middle of his chest to stop him.

"Calm down," I told him under my breath, and Patrick chuckled at the outburst, amused.

"On the night of John Becker's death, I heard my husband talking on the phone in our kitchen. He was whispering about something, and for the longest time, I had blocked out that memory, that entire night, because..." Sydney swallowed. "Because that was the first night my husband struck me, and I wanted to forget it ever happened."

Patrick looked bored as he listened to her, and I clenched my jaw, wondering how someone could ever become so callous.

"But, the fog has cleared since our divorce, sir. And I know what I heard that night. I know he was in our kitchen, talking on the phone in hushed whispers. Talking on the phone with *you*," she clarified. "And I heard him saying that you needed to trust him, that you needed to keep your mouth shut, and that he didn't need to remind you that it wouldn't be easy to cover up a homicide."

Silence fell over that little study, and for a moment, as I watched Patrick, I thought that maybe we'd struck a chord.

But then, he laughed.

"Seriously?" he asked, pointing a thumb at her as he looked around the room, like it was some sort of prank being pulled on him. "*This* is the so-called *evidence* you have that you think will win the case?"

That was it.

I couldn't remain calm any longer — not with that snide son-of-a-bitch making jokes like my father's death was funny.

I slammed my fist on his desk, then reached forward, gripping him by the neck of his button-up and yanking him out of his chair. His face was inches from mine when I roared, "ADMIT IT, YOU BASTARD. YOU MURDERED OUR FATHER."

Patrick laughed, and I reared back to punch him square in the jaw before Logan and Noah yanked me back, freeing Patrick from my grasp as they contained me.

He was still laughing as my brothers tried to calm me, but then he dusted off his shirt where I'd held him, and smiled at us. "You know what? You're right."

Everyone went still.

Everything went silent.

"I *did* kill your father. Is that what you want to hear?" He shook his head, looking me and both of my brothers in the eye — boldly, unapologetically. "I killed John Becker. There. There's the answer you've been looking for. Does it make you feel *any* better? Because no matter what you do, no matter what *proof* you think you have, it doesn't matter," he said, exasperated. "The case is ten years old. It's already been solved. It's closed. It's over. The journal you found, this..." He gestured toward Sydney. "*Scorned* ex-wife of our Chief of Police testifying? It's nothing. It won't hold. I have lawyers, and police officers, and board members and firefighters who were there that night, and all signed witness accounts and official reports of what happened. Randy *did* help me cover it up," he confessed, more like a brag. "And he was damn good at it, too."

He pressed his palms on top of his desk, leaning over it with a sympathetic expression, like he felt *sorry* for us.

I surged forward again, but my brothers held me still.

"While I expect this sort of behavior from *you* lot," he said to me and my brothers before turning to Mallory. "I'm disappointed in you. I raised you to be smarter than this. And regardless of how you feel about me, I expected better."

To her credit, Mallory didn't react to his insult. Her gaze was steady while I felt completely unhinged.

He turned back to us, standing tall, voice booming. "I am Patrick fucking Scooter, you dimwits. I own this town and everyone in it. You won't win. Do you hear me? You will *never* win."

He stood even straighter, somehow, before sniffing as if he'd just realized he'd let himself get a little carried away during a board meeting.

"Now," he said. "If it will make you feel better, I can write you a check for two-hundred-thousand dollars. That's more than just a little something to help your mom, and we can put this all behind us."

I roared, and my brothers no longer held me back.

"You heartless sonofabitch!" I yelled first. "How dare you! That's our *father*. He was your friend!"

"You have the nerve to offer us *money* for his death?" Noah barked.

Logan was right behind us, and being that he was the peacekeeper of our family, I was shocked when he lunged at Patrick and I had to hold him back. "He *trusted* you," he screamed, his eyes glossing with tears. I knew he was angry they were showing. "He came to you with what he found and you betrayed him, betrayed your own father and his dying wishes!"

Mallory grabbed his arm, and her tender touch seemed to rein him in just enough not to kill her father, but it was still complete and total chaos. We were all flying toward him, screaming, asking him how he could live with himself, how he could do this to us, to his daughter, to someone who used to be his friend. It was like a tornado unleashed in that study until an unfamiliar voice broke through it with a high-pitched scream.

We all fell quiet, turning to find Mary Scooter standing in the office doorway.

"That's enough," she said, chest heaving as she looked at her husband and then at the rest of us.

"Mama…" Mallory said, standing.

It was quiet as her mother looked at her — *really* looked at her, not the way she had when we first got to the house, but as her daughter. Her eyes took in Mallory's swelling belly, and then she covered her mouth as tears flooded her eyes.

"This is business, Mary," Patrick said to her dismissively. "We'll be done soon, I assure you."

"No."

It was one, simple word, but when it came from that little woman's lips, it felt like an earthquake.

Mary looked so much like Mallory, or maybe it was Mallory who looked like her. The angle of their eyes, the slope of their noses, the pinch between their eyebrows as they watched each other in that room. Mary was shorter than Mallory, and her hair was a dark brown where Mallory's was naturally a dirty blonde. But it was there, the resemblance, and it was almost like they'd just noticed it in that moment, too.

I'd rarely heard Mary speak in all the years I'd known her. She was soft and quiet, always standing behind her husband and smiling, playing her part.

But in that moment, she stood on her own — for maybe the first time.

I felt it.

Everyone in that room did.

"Enough," she repeated, shaking her head. "I've had enough. Of your lies, your corruption, your… *power trips*. This is our *daughter*, Patrick." She pointed at Mallory like her husband must have forgotten that fact. "She's pregnant. We're going to be grandparents. And whether you like it or not, Logan is the father, and that means the Beckers are our family, too."

"They most certainly are *not*," Patrick argued.

"We have to make this right!" she screamed back at him, shaking her head. "I never knew… not for sure. I always wondered, but I never questioned you about that night." She looked as if she'd seen a ghost. "That's me, right? Always content to sit back and let you run the show, to tell me what part to play. But… I heard everything just now," she confessed. "Everything, Pat. And I swear to God that *I* will testify against you if you do not make this right."

Patrick's mask crumbled a little at that, and he seemed genuinely surprised and hurt as he stared back at his wife. "Mary…"

"No, don't even try," she said, holding up her finger. "I love you, Patrick Scooter, but I will *not* watch anyone suffer any longer, paying the price of a *scorned man* who never got over his first love rejecting him."

Patrick's face drained at her words, and the rest of us exchanged confused looks.

"Oh, they don't know that side of the story, do they, sweetheart?" Mary asked, and she seemed to be growing a bit of a backbone right before our eyes.

"That's enough," he warned her, but she was on a roll now.

"He was in love with your mother," she said to Noah, to Logan, but her eyes avoided mine. "All through high school."

"Mary," Patrick warned again, his voice climbing.

"But Laurelei saw Patrick as a friend. She always had. And when she and your father fell in love, it drove Patrick mad."

Mallory watched her dad like she didn't know him at all. "Is that true?"

He didn't answer. His eyes were murderous as he watched his wife betray him.

"Oh, it's true," Mary answered for him. "Believe me. As the woman who loved *him*, watching him love *her* was a heartbreak I'll never forget. Laurelei was my best friend," she said, her eyes blurring with tears, and I thought back to the night she was on my mom's porch. "I knew he liked her, but I didn't realize how bad it was until she rejected him."

"That's why I saw all those pictures of you with Laurelei when you were younger," Mallory whispered, shaking her head. "You weren't just *friends*. You loved her."

"He wouldn't let it go when she turned him down," Mary continued. "Why? Because of all the men she could have fell in love with, she fell for John Becker — the sacred little barrel boy Patrick's father loved more than his own sons."

"He was a liar, and a brat, and a disrespectful little shit and he didn't deserve her!" Patrick cried out, slamming his fist on the table. "He didn't deserve her," he echoed again. "And he *damn sure* didn't deserve half of my grandfather's company."

"Which is exactly why you told our family lawyer to never speak of your father's Will, isn't it? Because he had one, and you knew what was in it, and you paid everyone off who you needed to in order to keep that a secret."

Mary was fuming, and the rest of us could only watch, wide-eyed.

"I wouldn't have done what I did if it hadn't been for *you*, you lying bitch, and you know it!" Patrick fired back, and then to everyone's shock, he pointed a finger at me. "Because of *him*."

The silence that fell over us was sticky and wet, but it lasted only a split second before his finger was on his wife, again.

"I told you to *get rid of him*, but you couldn't do that, could you? No. You couldn't part with your bastard child, so you took him to Laurelei. To *my* Laurelei. And to *him*, to John fucking Becker, to the one man you knew I hated. You told them our biggest secret and left me forever in debt to him. It's because of *you* that I hated him so much. It's because of *you* that I did what I did to get rid of him."

Mary's bottom lip was trembling, a tear staining her cheek, but she held her head high, returning her husband's gaze before she finally looked at me for the first time that night.

When she did, my heart leapt into my throat.

"What is he talking about?" I asked. At least, I thought I did. The voice that came from me didn't sound like my own. It sounded distant, like it was in another universe altogether.

"Jordan, I am so sorry you had to find out like this. I never intended to tell you at all," she said, her voice shaking, face crumbling. I swore she shrunk seven inches in that single moment.

"Tell me what?"

Sydney reached for my hand, grabbing it in hers with a squeeze, but I couldn't look away from Mary as my pulse continued to race.

"I'm your mother, Jordan."

She whispered the words, or else the beating of my heart in my ears was so loud I *registered* it as a whisper. Either way, I said nothing in return, but I felt my brothers watching me closely with bent brows.

"I... God, I am so sorry to tell you this way," she said, sniffing back the tears pooling in her eyes. "I was lonely, upset, betrayed by Patrick and his undying love for Laurelei. And I am as ashamed to admit it today as I was ashamed to engage in it then, but... I cheated on Pat."

Mallory's jaw dropped along with my stomach.

"I did it because I was sad, or maybe to get his attention, to..." She sniffed, shaking her head. "To *feel* something. I was so numb. And then there was this sweet, caring, funny, kind, *amazing* man making me feel so special."

She shook her head with glossed eyes, as if she was remembering another version of who she used to be.

Who she could have been.

"But," she continued. "When I got pregnant, he sent me away, and no one knew. They all thought I was at rehab, that I'd been drinking too heavily and admitted to Patrick that I needed help and he'd sent me away. And when I came back, I was better than ever, and everyone congratulated me and suddenly I was being asked to speak and to run events and I found purpose again. And the baby." She stopped, correcting herself. "*You.* You were the wake-up call I needed. I know it doesn't make sense but... I came back to me and Patrick being stronger than ever before."

She shook her head, as if none of that mattered — and in this moment, it didn't.

"But, he was adamant that this all remain just between us. So, when I returned, I told him that I gave you to a family in Idaho." She rolled her lips together, her voice soft again "But... I couldn't part from you. I couldn't bear the thought of never being able to see my son grow up. So, I went to my old best friend, and I asked her for the biggest favor of a lifetime."

I could feel Noah and Logan watching me, but all I could do was stare back at this woman — this *stranger* — who suddenly, I realized, had features that were reflected in me. I saw the freckles on her nose, and the curve of her eyes, and the wrinkle between her furrowed brows.

They were all things I saw in myself, too.

My throat was tight the more she spoke, and Sydney squeezed my hand, reminding me she was there.

"Laurelei and John were having trouble getting pregnant at the time," Mary explained. "And I knew she wanted to be a mother so badly, and I knew she would help *anyone* — no matter what — because that's the kind of woman she has always been." Mary sniffed. "So, she did. She helped me. And she helped you."

My head was swimming, and Mallory and I exchanged a glance that held just as many questions as we'd walked into this room with at the beginning of the night.

We were brother and sister.

That was *my* mother standing on the other side of her.

But who was my father?

I didn't have time to ask, not before Mary brought our attention back to the matter at hand. "I'm sorry you had to find out this way, and I know you must have many questions. But right now," she said, turning back to her husband. "I don't care what your reasoning was for what you did, you need to make this right."

"*Fine,*" he seethed, looking at all of us then. "What do you want? You want money? Name your price."

"We don't want your *fucking* money," Logan said. "We want you to rot in prison for killing our father."

"You and everyone who helped you," Noah chimed in. "We want names."

"And we want the shares of the company that we are rightfully owed," I added, though my chest was tight, because now I wasn't sure which *we* I fit into.

I'd wondered for so long who my biological mother was. I never would have imagined that once I found out, I'd feel an invisible tear from the family I'd known my entire life.

Patrick laughed, shaking his head at us. "You're delusional if you think I would *ever* give you *any* part of my company. You're lucky I even let you pieces of shit *work* for me. And I promise you this," he added, thumbing his chest. "I will *never* go to prison — especially not for your worthless father and the end of his worthless life. Like I said before, you don't have any proof — none that would matter. None that would stand up against what *I* have built. Did you forget what I said earlier?" He sneered. "You. Will. *Not*. Win."

"Wow, that's a *good* one," a female voice said from outside the office window, and Patrick jumped, shock falling over him.

Noah and Logan exchanged a smirk, though I couldn't quite find it in me to join them.

"Who is that?" Patrick asked quickly, running over to the window. Just as he did, the light of a giant camera blasted in at him, and he shielded his eyes.

"Can I quote you on that? It would really add a menacing, *evil bad guy* tone to the piece."

The light disappeared, and Patrick was searching in the yard, wild-eyed and confused. He looked back at us, panicking. "Who was that? What's going on?"

Then, the door behind Mary opened wider, and Mikey stepped through it. Along with Miranda Hollis.

Miranda was a writer for our local newspaper — *The Stratford Gazette* — and thanks to Mallory helping us make a plan, we knew if we got her involved, we'd be able to slam the door on this case once and for all. She was famous for writing scathing articles about Patrick Scooter and she had for years — though, admittedly, none of them held much weight.

This one, however, would be a home run for her.

Mallory had blackmailed her father with Miranda before, telling him that if he didn't give Logan the position he was owed at the distillery, she would go to Miranda and tell her everything that happened when she was fourteen years old and Randy Kelly sexually harassed her in the basement of Patrick's underground casino.

With Miranda's father in politics and a place of power even *Patrick* couldn't touch, he would do anything to keep Miranda out of his business.

But that time was over now.

Patrick's face went sheet white at the sight of her, and he looked around the room like a cornered animal, trying to find a gap in our legs to escape.

"Hi there, Patrick," Miranda cooed, holding up the digital recorder in her hands. She had short brown hair and glasses too big for her face, the frames of which lifted a bit as she grinned at Patrick.

A burly man holding the large video camera that had blinded Patrick through the window came in behind her, and she pointed at him over her shoulder.

"Have you met my friend, Shadow? He works in Nashville for Channel 2 News. As you know, we don't have a video crew for our little newspaper here in town, but when Sydney came to me with this juicy story? Well, I just *had* to be prepared. And we've been listening outside this *entire* time, my dear."

Patrick just shook his head, over and over, his eyes scanning the room in disbelief.

"Oh yeah, buddy," Miranda said. "You're going *down*."

For a moment, Patrick just stood there, stricken, with everyone's eyes on him. Then, he laughed, though the worry slipped through every crack in his façade. "This is absurd. I didn't agree to you recording me," he pointed out. "You can't air this, let alone use it in a court of law."

"You *would* think that, wouldn't you?" Miranda asked. "But, you see, Tennessee is a one-party consent state, and everyone in this room consented to me recording them other than you. Therefore, this video and audio is protected, and *yes*, it can be used in a court of law."

Patrick looked to Mary, and Miranda nodded.

"Yes, even your wife — which solidifies this more than anything."

Patrick eyed Miranda, and then the deepest, most primal growl ripped from his throat. He was like a cornered animal, and in a flash, he crossed the room, ripping open the top drawer of his desk and whipping out a pistol.

His eyes were wild and murderous as he raised it. Sydney gasped, and Mary reached for Mallory, holding her close as if to protect her and the baby. But Patrick didn't have time to pull the trigger before Logan and Noah pounced on him, sending him flying to the floor and the gun spiraling away from him. I grabbed it, emptied the chamber, and held both the bullets and the gun in my hands as Patrick writhed in my brothers' grips.

"Oh, please say you got that, too," Miranda said, giddy as she turned to Shadow. "That will look just *perfect* on the evening news. Oh, by the way, Patrick," she said to him next. "The cops are already on their way. And not your shady Stratford cops either — who, by the way, we've been investigating undercover for years now. We already have a case building against Randy Kelly, and this is just the icing on the cake." She smiled victoriously. "You're all going to pay for what you've done."

Noah and Logan looked at each other, at Mikey, at me, and in that moment, the weight we'd carried on our chests for a decade was lifted, and I swore I felt our father in that room with us.

Noah smiled, still holding Patrick firmly, and Logan looked up at me with tears in his eyes.

"We did it," he said, shaking his head. "We did it, brothers."

Mikey made his way over to me then, and I wrapped him in a bear hug as chaos ensued.

First it was the sound of sirens, and then Patrick being hauled away while more cameras and reporters showed up at the Scooter residence. It would have been comical, watching him struggle against the officers, throwing a fit in their grips and saying, "*Do you know who I am?*" over and over again, had

I not been in shock. He even tried to throw a punch at one of them when they finally shoved his head into the squad car, the rest of him following suit, and then they slammed the door shut.

My brothers and I were clinging to each other in the front yard when our mother showed up, wide-eyed and riddled with worry, until we told her everything.

It was over.

It was all over.

And *finally*, we had justice for Dad.

A quiet, calm kind of numbness settled over me as we talked to police officers and reporters and filed statements. It wasn't the relief I thought we'd find, because as much as we'd finally found answers, we still didn't have our father.

He'd still died a horrible death, at the hands of a monstrous group of men.

I didn't know how late it was when the yard finally started to clear, and Sydney slipped her arms around my waist, and I held her against my chest, resting my cheek on the crown of her head.

"You okay?" I asked her.

She nodded, hands fisting in my shirt. "I'm shaken up," she admitted. "And confused. And heartbroken. And I still have no idea what I'll tell Paige, but... I'm relieved that it's over. I'm relieved that we can finally all find peace."

I kissed her forehead as my chest tightened, because peace seemed so far from my grasp.

"Are *you* okay?" she asked, and I knew she could feel my anxiety.

I just held her tighter in response, willing her without words to not let me go.

Because I *wasn't* okay.

I was far from it.

One weight had been lifted, but another had crashed down in its place, and while I was filled with exhaustion and joy and relief at the solving of my father's mysterious death, I was plagued with questions and betrayal at the discovery of my biological mother.

A million questions had been answered.

A million more had taken their place.

And as I locked eyes with my mother's — my *real* mother, not the biological one I'd just discovered — I had a feeling the answers I would find would be just as hard to hear as the ones we'd found tonight were.

"I'm right here," Sydney whispered, hugging me tight, and I tore my eyes from Mom's and closed them, instead. "No matter what happens next, you have me, okay? And we'll get through it. Together."

My throat tightened, and I held her even tighter, surrounding my aching heart with her words.

If I had her, I could face anything.

That much, at least, I was sure of.

Chapter Twenty-Four

Sydney

The week that followed that emotional Monday night was the longest of my entire life.

So much happened that it felt like being in the middle of the Daytona 500 raceway track while cars zipped by, but at the same time, it all seemed to somehow move in slow motion.

Neither Jordan nor I went to work — which was not contested by anyone, least of all Principal Hanley. The entire town was abuzz once the story broke, and we all had eyes on us — eyes of pity, eyes of sympathy, eyes of suspicion. Everyone had their thoughts, and everyone wanted to see what we'd do next.

Randy was locked up that Monday night along with Patrick, and then slowly, each day, more and more men were silently taken into custody for questioning. There were lawyers, police officers, firemen, prominent men on the Scooter Whiskey Distillery board. And as more and more information came out, more and more people being tied to the heinous crime, it felt like our entire town was a live wire, buzzing and zapping and tense.

Jordan and I were handling our own personal matters while also trying to be there for each other, and we'd found the task difficult. There was just *so* much going on. It seemed that we were away from each other every day, and when we finally came together at night, all we could do was hold each other, and be silent, and listen to each other's heartbeat as if that steady rhythm was the only thing keeping us holding on.

I had to sit Paige down that very next day — *before* anyone else had the chance to tell her what happened. It was perhaps the most difficult thing I'd ever done as a mother, to have a real discussion with her about her father, about what he'd done, about what would happen to him next.

She took the news better than I imagined, which I attributed to her seeing her father's true colors that day he showed up at our door drunk and belligerent. Still, she cried, and held me, and said she missed him and she didn't want him to go to jail. I knew it wouldn't be an overnight thing to get her to understand, nor would this be something she would ever fully let go of.

It would be a part of *her* story just as much as it would be a part of mine. It was my job now as her mother to help her through it, each step of the way, from now until forever.

Thankfully, when my sister heard what had happened, she flew in to take care of Paige while I dealt with everything else. If I was being honest, I don't think anyone wanted to see Randy rot in prison more than Gabby did. And I was thankful for her help, for her presence, for her love — especially when I had a hundred things to take care of.

Like making sure Jordan was okay.

I knew he wasn't — not after everything that came to light that night at the Scooter's house. Sure, he'd landed the justice his family had been seeking for his father for a decade, but in the process, he discovered a dark past he didn't know he had.

His biological mother was Mary Scooter.

Laurelei and John had hid that from him his entire life.

And, the latest development which had knocked him breathless... Mary had told him who his father was.

So, on Friday night, I sat next to Jordan on Elijah Braxton's back porch with my hand in his, squeezing it every now and then for comfort, as he told his biological father everything.

It was a cold December night, but Eli had a fire going, and we sat around it with our coats and scarves and blankets over our laps. Eli and Jordan were sharing a bottle of whiskey and trying to share a lifetime of what they'd missed, too.

It turned out that Mary had never even told Eli about Jordan.

He had no idea he was a father.

He had no idea that he'd been watching his *son* coach the high school team all this time.

For hours, they swapped stories, and asked questions, and looked at each other in a way that I could never describe in words. I was quiet for most of the night, just there for support, witnessing a beautiful moment I was sure Jordan never thought he'd have.

"I can't believe she never told you about me," Jordan mused as the fire died down, shaking his head with his eyes on the weakening flames. "I mean, I guess I *can* now that I've discovered the other secrets that family has been hoarding but... I'm just so lost as to how she could have lived with herself, knowing what she'd done, what she'd hidden."

Eli adjusted his beanie over his ears, tossing another log onto the fire and poking at it before he sat back in his chair. "Mary was a complicated girl," he said. "I knew it when we were in high school, and I knew it when she gave me that first look when I went over to her place to work on the plumbing in their housing extension. That was when it all started. She was bored, or felt mistreated, or maybe both. But... she was also lovely, and kind, and innocent in her own way. She just wanted to be loved," he said with a shrug, as if it was obvious. "And she's not the only guilty one here, either," he pointed out. "I knew she was married, and I fell into temptation with her, anyway."

"The affair is one thing," Jordan said. "But, not telling you that you had a child?"

"I know," he said, letting out a slow breath. "Trust me, it pains me as much as I imagine it pains you. But, something I've learned in my years is not to spend time or energy being angry about the past, or letting someone else's actions dictate how I handle my own life." He looked at Jordan then with a small smile. "We didn't know about each other before, but we know now. And I bet we still have a lot of life yet to spend together as father and son." At that, his smile fell, and he swallowed. "That is, if you want to."

"Of course, I want to," Jordan answered, frowning. "I've been wondering who you were my entire life. I just... I don't know how to handle knowing Mary is my mother." He made a face, one that passed over him every time the subject came up. "I'm... I don't know. I feel a little lost, if I'm being honest."

"I think anyone would be, if they were in your shoes," Eli offered, and I squeezed Jordan's hand where I held it under the blanket over my lap, letting him know I agreed.

"It's funny," Jordan mused. "I always thought if I found out who my real parents were, I'd feel complete, whole, like a missing puzzle piece had finally been found. But... I feel the exact opposite. I feel like an imposter in the family I've always known, and like I don't know where I belong."

My heart broke with his admission, and I squeezed his hand again, leaning my head on his shoulder.

Eli leaned toward him, too, balancing his elbows on his knees as he locked eyes with his son. "You listen to me. That family — Laurelei, your brothers — they are still your family. They always have been, and they always will be. You hear me?" He paused. "And furthermore, John will always be your father. And I can tell you with absolute certainty that if he were here, he'd tell you right now how proud he is of you, and how much he loves you."

Jordan's eyes filled with tears, but not a single one fell.

"You and I, we got some time to make up for. And our relationship will not be like the relationship that other sons and fathers have. It won't be *anything* like the one you had with John. And that's okay, Son. What we have will be different, but it will be our own. And I know it feels impossible right now, but you might even find a relationship with Mary one day, too. And *that* will be different. It will be nothing like your relationship with Laurelei." He leaned down until Jordan's eyes met his again. "And that's okay, too."

Jordan nodded, but he still seemed so torn up, and I wished I could take away all the confusion and pain. I wondered if he was thinking about Mallory, too — about his half-sister. With all the chaos since Monday night, I knew they hadn't had a moment together yet, either.

"You know, I think a part of me must have known," Eli said. "I mean, obviously I couldn't have known that you were my son, but I've always felt tied to you. I watched you grow up as a kid, and watched you play football in high school, watched you take over as coach. I never felt so invested in anyone else in this town, but there was something about you that I was drawn to."

Jordan smiled. "I felt the same way. The gang of moms at every practice and game drove me crazy, and I didn't like to talk about football with anyone else in town — at the barbershop, the post office, none of it. But with you?" He shrugged. "I don't know. I just felt comfortable."

"Sounds like God was going to make sure we were in each other's life in some way, whether we knew why or not."

They shared a smile, and then Eli stood, squeezing Jordan's shoulder before excusing himself inside to use the restroom.

When he returned, it was with more wood for the fire, and we spent hours in that backyard with Eli, talking and laughing and crying a little, too. It was too much to try to talk about everything in one night, but I could tell on the ride back to Jordan's house that he already felt a little lighter.

When we finally crawled into bed that night, Jordan opened his arms for me to slide in and rest my head on his chest, and we held each other tightly, silent for a long time.

"This has been the wildest week of my life," he said on a breath after a while.

I chuckled. "Yeah... to say the least."

"Are you doing okay?"

I sighed, considering his question — one that we'd continued asking each other all week long. It wasn't so much of a demand to *be* okay, but rather a reminder that someone cared, that the other wasn't alone.

"Yeah," I finally answered. "Yeah, I think I really am. I mean, I'm worried about Paige, but... like you said. She's tougher than I give her credit for a lot of the time."

"She is. And she has you," he reminded me, kissing my forehead. "Which means she can get through anything."

"I guess I'm kind of in shock," I admitted. "I mean... who knows what will happen with Randy and Patrick and everyone. I'm glad we have lawyers, because I don't know about you, but I don't understand any of it."

"No, I don't either," he said with a deep exhale. "The only comfort I'm taking in any of it is that with Miranda's story being out there, there's no way Patrick or Randy can use their power or their money to get out of it this time."

"What do you think will happen?" I asked, leaning up on my elbow to look down at him in the soft moonlight streaming in from the blinds.

He thought for a moment. "I think Patrick will be charged with murder. Randy and the board members and the firemen who were in on it, the lawyers... I imagine they'll be charged with either being accomplices or at the very least, covering up the crime. At least, from what the lawyers are saying."

My heart jumped. "Do you think Randy will get out of doing time?"

"No," he answered quickly, smoothing his hand over where mine was on his chest. "He knew about it. He helped cover it up. They burned my father alive, for God's sake," he said, and we both shivered. "I don't think any judge would let them get away without doing life in prison. If everyone else gets off with lesser sentences, that would make sense. But... Randy is an accomplice. He might as well have lit the fire."

I nodded, resting my head on his chest again. "This is all so much... I can't digest it all."

"Me, either."

"How's your mom?"

He sighed. "She's shaken up, too. I mean, of course she's relieved we found out what happened, we got proof for what we'd known all along, but... it's also her worst nightmare, you know? Now she *knows* the love of her life was murdered, and all because of a jealous man who loved her and wanted her to love him, in return."

I shook my head. "I don't know how he can live with himself."

"Me either."

"Do you think they'll give you half of the company now? I mean, your family?"

"I'm not sure," he confessed. "Mary said she wants to talk to Mom about that this week, but... to be honest, it's the last thing on my mind right now."

"I get that. Are your brothers okay?"

"For the most part. I mean, they're all worried about Mom, mostly. And about me."

I leaned up again. "And are *you* okay?"

Jordan kept his eyes on the ceiling, thinking for a while before he answered with a small smile. "Yeah... I am."

"You are?"

He nodded, sweeping my bed hair out of my face and holding my cheek as I leaned into the touch. "I still have a lot of questions, and a lot of feelings — especially regarding my biological parents. But... mostly, I feel at peace. I feel like my dad can finally rest, that my family can finally heal, that we can finally have justice and resolution that we have wanted for so long." He paused, tapping my nose. "And I have you," he whispered. "Which, honestly, is what makes me feel the best right now."

I smiled. "Yeah?"

"Yeah," he said on a nod, leaning up to kiss me gently before he rolled us so he was nestled between my legs, and my head was flush against the pillow. "I know we still have a lot to figure out, but... hearing that you love me? I think that gave me the sense that nothing else matters."

My heart squeezed. "I wanted to tell you before all of this. You know that, right?"

"I wanted to tell you, too. At Thanksgiving, actually. But then everything happened with Mallory, and you were so upset, and I didn't want to put any pressure on you."

"I seem to remember you putting a *lot* of pressure on me that night," I teased, rolling my hips up to meet where he rested between my thighs.

He groaned, pinning me with a kiss before he pulled back and smiled. "It's just crazy. My entire life, I watched Mom and Dad love each other and wondered if I'd ever find someone like that. And honestly, I'd given up. My brothers found their girls, and I watched from the background, just imagining that I would never be able to open myself up like that, or to have someone who would open up to *me* like that, either."

"And then I came along."

"Yep. And you put my ass in place."

"Someone had to."

He chuckled. "Well, you were perfect for the job."

"I knew I was in trouble after that first game," I confessed. "When we fought in my office, and you were all up in my space, and you looked at my mouth like you wanted to kiss me."

"I *did* want to kiss you," Jordan groaned, and he kissed up and down my neck like a feverish mad man as I laughed and shoved him off. "And I've wanted to kiss you every moment since, too."

"We broke all the rules."

"I'm sure we'll break a few more."

He hovered over me, eyes searching mine as I played with the hair at the back of his neck.

"I love you," I mouthed.

"I love you, too," he mouthed back.

Then, his head disappeared under the covers, his lips trailing a path down my navel to the band of my flannel pajama pants.

And we were done talking for the night.

· · ·

Jordan

The next day, Sydney and I gathered with the rest of my family at Mom's house before the parade.

It was tradition in Stratford — which I found pride in, seeing as how it could only be tradition if we *won*. The town had thrown one the past two years after we'd won the State Championship, with the team being the focal point.

I knew this one would hold more weight.

The entire town was buzzing with what had happened with Patrick Scooter and Randy Kelly, with more and more accomplices to my father's murder being outed each day.

And this would be the first time my family and I would make a public appearance.

Ruby Grace and Mallory made a giant breakfast for everyone at Mom's, and I sat at the table, mostly playing with my food and watching everyone who sat around it. Everyone was there — my brothers and their significant others, Mom, Betty, Sydney, Paige, and even Sydney's sister, Gabby, who was visiting from out of town to help with Paige.

She'd already pulled me to the side to threaten me within an inch of my life if I hurt her little sister.

But I know she believed me when I swore I never would.

"You look like you're about to *play* the championship game," she teased me. "Not go to a parade celebrating the fact that you already won it."

"Oh, that's just his permanent state of being," Betty chimed in. "He's the quiet type. Sydney didn't tell you?" Betty clucked her tongue. "Could be in a romance movie with all that broodiness."

Gabby laughed at that, and Betty steered the conversation away from me and onto Gabby's job, which Betty seemed to be interested in. She was *especially* interested in Gabby's hot doctor boss. And Betty winked at me as the conversation turned, as if she knew I just wanted to be alone.

I thanked her with a nod.

Gabby looked so much like Sydney, and I loved watching them together. They had that familiar comfort that I had with *my* brothers. It was in the way they spoke, the way there were so many things they didn't have to even speak out loud for the other to understand.

Sisters.

And when I glanced at Mallory from across the table, it hit me for the hundredth time that week that I now had one, too.

"Jordan," Mom said after breakfast, standing as Logan and Noah worked on clearing the dishes from the table. "Can we talk outside?"

Sydney and I exchanged glances, and she nodded encouragingly before I grabbed my coffee and made my way out onto the front porch with Mom. She sat in her favorite rocking chair, cupping her mug of tea between her hands, her favorite shawl wrapped tight around her shoulders as her eyes swept over the yard.

I took the seat next to her, and for a long time, we were both silent.

"Do you know why I named you Jordan?" she asked.

My stomach was in knots, because though we'd talked a lot since what happened at Patrick's home on Monday night, we hadn't been completely alone. And though she was still the same mom she'd always been to me, and I was still her son, there was a new, foreign cloud that hung between us — one with a lifetime of her hiding a secret from me that I found out in the worst way.

"I don't," I answered.

"In the *New Testament,* the River Palestine is where Jesus Christ is baptized by John the Baptist," she explained. "And *Jordan* comes from the Hebrew term, *Yarden*, which means to flow down. To descend."

I frowned, but Mom looked at me then with a soft smile.

"That's what you had done," she said. "You had flowed down to us from the heavens we were praying to every night to help us get pregnant. Descended, as if God himself had placed you in our arms. And we never could have known then that he would bless us later in life with three crazy, but amazing little boys to be your brothers," she said on a chuckle. "At the time, Jordan — you were it for us. You were our only one, and we thought that maybe you would *always* be our only one."

The corner of my mouth lifted, and I reached over to place my hand on hers for a moment before I held my coffee mug again.

Mom held my gaze. "I'm sorry, Son. I'm sorry it wasn't me who you learned your true past from." She looked grim. "I know it may not make sense to you, and I understand if you're angry with me. But... I made a promise to a woman who used to be one of my best friends. And, honestly, I swear, I didn't know who your father was," she added. "But, in my mind, as your mother, I was protecting you as much as I was protecting Mary by hiding the truth. In my eyes, you were never hers, anyway." Her eyes welled with tears. "You are, always have been, and always will be mine and John's son."

I set my coffee down and stood, extending a hand for Mom to do the same. She set her tea down, too, and then she was in my arms, and I hugged her tight as her little shoulders shook in my grasp.

"It's okay, Mom," I told her. "I understand. If Sydney has taught me anything, it's that parents sacrifice for their children, and they make tough decisions that affect their lives, too. But, I know you and Dad love me, and that everything you've done in your life has been with my best interests at heart."

"You don't hate us?"

I chuckled, hugging her tighter. "I could never."

She pulled back, looking up at me with a sniff.

"I was upset at first," I admitted. "Mostly because I was hurt by the truth, and confused, and I'll admit, a bit sad to know that I'm related to a family I've spent most of my life hating. But... I understand. Not just you and Dad, but Mary, too. And maybe one day we can have some sort of relationship," I offered. "Not now, but maybe one day."

"And what about Eli?"

I smiled. "I went over to his place last night and we talked about everything. He's in shock, of course, but said he kind of always knew, in a way. So... yeah, maybe I'll have a second father, too." I shrugged. "But, I feel the same way you do. You and Dad have always been and always will be my parents. This doesn't change that for me, either."

A few tears slipped free when she smiled, the edges of her eyes crinkling, and she hugged me tight again.

"Sydney is a good woman," she said when we finally pulled away. "I'm very glad you two found each other."

I smiled, glancing inside where I could see her, her sister, and Paige in the living room with my brothers. "Me, too, Mom."

"Don't mess it up," she warned, poking my chest.

I chuckled. "I'll do my best." Then, I held her arms in my hands for a moment, locking eyes with her. "Are *you* okay, Mom?"

She smiled. "I am. John is finally resting, and I think that means I can finally rest, too. I know we still have a long road ahead of us with all these lawyers and court dates and..." She paused, pressing a hand to her forehead as she looked back over the yard. "At least... we finally know the truth." She looked at me pointedly then. "And, as always, my sons have proven to me how stubborn and determined they can be."

"We should be detectives."

She laughed, and then I hooked an arm around her shoulder and led us both inside.

Before I could get all the way in, Mallory swung an arm through mine that wasn't holding Mom and turned me around.

"My turn, Brother."

Mom winked at me, letting me go, and I ignored the funny feeling in my stomach at Mallory calling me brother, letting her guide me back out onto the porch. When we were alone, she leaned against the railing, wrapping her long sweater around her tight as she appraised me.

"You going to just pretend forever like we aren't related?"

I sighed, tucking my hands in my pockets. "No, that wasn't the plan, but I'll admit, I've been trying to figure out what to say to you."

"How about we don't make a plan," she offered. "How about we just be us — the same us we've always been. Except now, maybe a little closer." She paused, smiling. "I'd like to get to know my oldest brother. Especially since the brother I've always *known* about isn't exactly my favorite human being."

I blanched at that, because for the first time, I realized that her brother, Malcolm, was also *my* brother now, too. He'd always been a huge pain in the ass for me and my brothers, and Noah had even nearly fought him in Buck's bar not too far back.

I ran a hand over my head, looking out over the yard. "It's so much to take in."

Mallory pushed off the railing. "Hey, one thing at a time, alright?" She patted my shoulder. "I just wanted to clear the air and tell you that I'm here when you're ready to talk more about it. Maybe we can sit down and go through family tree stuff." She shrugged. "You know, I'm not in the best place right now either, so I'm fine with us both taking a little time."

"It has to be hard for you," I said. "Your dad being locked away like that, and everything he admitted to."

She nodded, her gaze distant. "I knew he was a crooked man," she said quietly. "I found that out the hard way when I was in high school. But... I don't know. I guess I just never thought he could do something like *that*. And then Mom and Eli..." She paused, looking at me again. "And you."

"I know," I told her, and I didn't have to say much else. Because she knew I did.

"I will say, I'm glad to have Mom back in my life." She laughed to herself. "Maybe we'll actually have a real relationship now, one where Dad isn't running her like a puppet." Mallory's eyes were sincere when she found mine. "I think you'll like her, when you're ready to get to know her more. Something tells me my — er, *our* — mom has been through more than we give her credit for."

I frowned on a nod, but didn't reply. I wasn't ready to embrace Mary with open arms, but I did open them to Mallory, pulling her in for a long hug before we headed back inside.

Later, on the Main Street drag, I stood on top of a float with my team, all of us donned in our school colors and passing the State Championship trophy around as our town cheered in victory. We tossed out beads and candy, signed autographs as if we were the superstars we felt like, and slipped into that bittersweet mindset of knowing we accomplished our biggest goal, but also that the season was over.

It felt like that in my life, too.

One season had ended, a new one beginning, and I knew without a doubt I would not be the same man I was in the last one.

It was a new beginning, a new era — for me, for my brothers, for my mom, and for this entire town.

Sydney stood beside me at the top of the float, smiling and throwing out candy, until she realized I was staring at her.

"What?" she asked with a flushed smile.

The corner of my mouth ticked up, but I didn't answer her — not with words, anyway. Instead, I reached for her hips, turning her to face me as her face went ashen white. Then, I trailed my hands up over her arms, her neck, sliding them back to cradle her head. Her soft eyes were wide, searching mine, and in the next breath, I lowered my mouth to hers.

For what felt like a lifetime, everything slipped away. The crowd was gone, the parade in another universe, and it was just me and Sydney. I felt her like the piece of me that had always been missing had finally come home, or like *she* was my home, and now that I'd found her, I could finally find peace and meaning.

She was hesitant in my arms at first, but then she melted into me, kissing me back with purpose and pressing up onto her toes to deepen her affection. I could have stayed in that moment with her forever, but the roar of the crowd around us, and a few players knocking me on the back in congratulations, zapped me back to the moment.

When we broke the kiss, the cheers that met our ears were deafening. Sydney looked around with the fiercest blush I'd ever seen before she hid her face in my chest, and I chuckled, looking around at the town below us and my team on the float with a shit-eating grin.

Then, I lifted one fist into the air, as if I'd just won the girl and the battle of my life, too.

And in more ways than anyone there realized — I had.

Sydney leaned into my side, still blushing but taking up her post and throwing candy once again. And as the band played on in front of our float, I let my eyes wander the faces looking up at us from below.

I saw my brothers, with their loved ones tucked into their sides, their smiles knowing as our eyes met. We weren't just brothers in life, now, but brothers in war, too — and we had come out on the other side victorious, but not without the striking sadness of casualties. We were bonded together closer than ever, and I knew that though we'd lived such a long life together already, our new lives were only beginning.

And they would be even better than the last.

I saw my mother, too — her eyes shining with pride as she waved me past. I waved back, blowing her a kiss that she caught in the air and tucked into her heart for safe keeping. I hoped what she'd said to me on the porch was true, that she could finally rest, that she could finally find peace.

Mary Scooter didn't show at the parade — and I knew she was hurting in her own ways right now, too. I hoped one day to build a bridge of understanding between us, though I knew it would take time.

But I did see Eli on the sidewalk, who tipped his hat at me with his wide, crooked grin. I nodded back, and in my chest I felt a tug of both sadness and joy. I was sad for having missed the first three decades of my life with the man who gave it to me, but thankful for the chance to get to know him now, and to have him in whatever years we had left to come.

I saw Gabby and Paige — who was holding up a giant sign that read *Go Wild Cats!* — and I realized with a pinch of my heart that they were my family now, too. I would protect them just like I'd protected my mom and my brothers.

And still wrapped under my right arm was Sydney — the woman who barreled into my life like a shooting star, bright and breathtaking and completely unexpected.

She turned to look at me and smiled, making my heart pinch again, and her eyes reflected the emotion surging through me in that moment. When I'd given up hope, when I'd been nothing but a numb, shell of a man walking through life and trying to find meaning in it, she'd swung in and knocked me on my ass, away from everything I'd ever known before and into an era I never saw coming.

In the darkest hour of my life, I'd somehow managed to find love.

I marveled at how ironic this life could be.

As the confetti cannons blasted, shooting a river of color into the blue sky above us, I followed those little ribbons up, casting my face to the sun.

And I felt the warmth of it as an embrace from my father — his life finally avenged, his legacy finally bestowed.

I smiled up at him, my heart light for the first time since he'd left us, and he seemed to reach out for me as sun rays on my shoulders to let me know it was time to grab this life and live it fully.

Sydney watched me from where she stood at my side, and when I met her gaze, she smiled knowingly.

It turned out, our scarred hearts beat in the same rhythm. And without a word being exchanged, we both sighed — because we knew that now, they'd never have to beat alone.

In the confetti rain, and in front of everyone I loved, I kissed her again.

And we walked into our new life, hand in hand, heart in heart, soul in soul.

Together.

Epilogue

Jordan - Three Years Later

"In your dreams, sucker!" Paige yelled, juking my little brother before sprinting toward the opposite side of Mom's backyard. She paused when she was a few feet from the line we'd drawn in the grass to indicate the touchdown zone, and then she turned, walking backward in a kind of moonwalk dance with her tongue stuck out.

Mikey was in her dust, hands on his knees, panting.

I laughed, calling out from where I had just thrown her the ball. "Atta girl!"

"She's a freak of nature," Mikey panted.

"I told you she was the best one on her team."

"Yeah, but you didn't tell me she played like an NFL player instead of a twelve-year-old."

"Shouldn't sleep on me just because I'm a girl, Mikey," Paige said, patting him on the back as she jogged back over to me. "Need me to get you some water?"

He side-eyed her while I held back another laugh.

"You still getting your butt whooped over here, little brother?" Logan asked, balancing a smiling Tamara on his shoulders. His daughter, named after one of Mallory's favorite painters — Tamara De Lempicka — had giant green eyes and white-blonde hair, tied into a tiny ponytail on top of her head that looked more like one single feather than a gathering of hair. She was giggling as he bounced her — a deep belly laugh that made me smile, too.

"Sure is," Paige answered for Mikey, high fiving me as she passed. "Pouting about it, too."

Mikey laughed, finally standing straight and hanging his hands on his hips as he caught his breath. "I would argue with her, but she ain't wrong."

"Guess you should stick to playing guitar and leave the football to Paige, huh?" Logan teased.

Mikey flipped him off, but smiled as he passed, anyway, taking our niece from Logan's shoulders and putting her on his own before he outstretched her arms like an airplane and took off running across the yard to where Mom had set up multiple folding tables for dinner.

It was Thanksgiving Day, and we were all together for the first time in months. It seemed to be harder to get us all in the same place now that life was running full speed, so when we did get the chance, we made the most of it.

Paige paused long enough to stretch out her quads and hamstrings before jogging back across the yard, and she threw me the ball, a perfect spiral. We fell into an easy rhythm of catch, but I knew she could tell even from the distance that I was nervous.

"Mikey looks good," I said to Logan to distract my thoughts.

He nodded. "He does. I think he and Kylie have really found their groove in New York City."

"Especially now that he's in that band," I said. "I knew he wouldn't be able to go without music for very long."

"Well, as he so grossly reminds us, Kylie brought back the music in his life."

"Such a sap."

"I know, right?" Logan shook his head. "And he's the only one. The rest of us aren't hopeless romantics at *all*."

"No way," I agreed. "I don't know if we even have feelings."

We shared a grin, and Logan clapped me on the back before I heaved the ball back to Paige. "She really is good," he mused. "How's she doing on the team?"

"She's easily the best at any position she plays," I answered. "But, just like we imagined, she's met some opposition along the way."

"Coach?"

"A little," I said. "But mostly the other players. They don't like being out-performed by a girl, and sometimes they're rougher with her than they need to be. But, she's tough," I said with pride, like she was my own daughter. In many ways, it felt like she was. "And when she's out there practicing twice as long and working twice as hard as them, I don't think it leaves them with much room to talk shit."

"I wonder what will happen when she gets to high school."

"Oh, God," Sydney said, joining us with two bottles of water in her hands. She tossed me one before calling for her daughter to come get the other, then she turned back to Logan. "Please, don't even get my anxiety spiral going on that front. She's twelve. I still have two years of pre-teen bliss before she'll be too cool for me."

"I'm already too cool for you, Mom," Paige teased, but kissed her mother's cheek anyway before taking the water from her hands. "Besides, at least when I'm in high school, you and Jordan can watch over me."

"*She* can watch over you," I said, putting an arm around Sydney. "But *I* will be your coach, and I'll likely be harder on you than on any of the other players."

"I can handle it," she said, chin high.

"Oh, I don't doubt that for a minute." I held up my hand, and we did our secret handshake that lasted a full sixty seconds and ended with me throwing an imaginary ball to her and her throwing it down to the ground in a victorious touchdown dance.

Sydney rolled her eyes, ruffling her daughter's wild curls once she was upright again. "We're about ready to eat," she said to all of us, then she turned back to her daughter. "Go wash your hands and help me bring the food out of the kitchen."

Paige saluted, giving me a knowing smirk before she ran off toward the house.

My nerves came back at once.

It was a beautiful day for November — the sun high and warm, a few clouds floating by to give us brief moments of shade, and a cool breeze sweeping over the yard. It wasn't too cold to be outside, though — which was a blessing, considering we had grown so much that we wouldn't fit *inside* anymore.

I took a seat at one of the folding tables, pulling out the chair next to Eli. He was in the middle of a riveting story that had Noah and Ruby Grace wide-eyed and leaning over the table toward him, anxious to know more.

I'd learned over the last few years that *all* his stories felt like that.

It had been easy, getting to know Eli and falling into a relationship with him. We spent a lot of time together, eating dinner or hanging out at football practice or me spending days on the job with him. He was getting older and needed the help, and I loved to see him in his element, helping people no matter their circumstances.

We'd been building our relationship for three years, and though I felt closer to him than I ever imagined I could be, I also learned something new every day.

What I loved learning *most* was about his family, *my* family, our ancestors and more. Because in addition to discovering him, I'd found that I had two aunts and five cousins who lived in Virginia, ones who I'd met *last* Thanksgiving when we joined them. I was finally able to explore all the pieces of what and *who* made me the man I was today.

At the table behind us, chatting with Mom, was Mary Scooter — my *other* mom.

Our relationship was a little more rocky.

We were trying, though it was stickier with us. She struggled with how she had left me with my adopted parents, though I'd assured her time and time again that it was the best thing she ever did for me. I loved my family, and I was blessed to have them — no matter the circumstances that landed me in their arms.

Still, Mary was in a dark place for a long time after Patrick was arrested. Everything fell into her lap then — the distillery, the Will, the flurry of court dates that had her testifying against the man she had loved and had children with. She was torn, there was no doubt about it, and we'd had little time to talk about *us* when so much of our focus had been on Patrick and Randy and everyone else involved in my father's murder.

Slowly, things were getting better — especially since the case had finally been closed. Patrick, Randy, three firefighters, and four members of the distillery board were all serving prison sentences of varying lengths — Patrick for life, Randy for forty years which might as *well* have been life. And as much as it broke Mary's heart that Patrick had been put away, I knew it brought her peace, too.

Mallory and Logan having little Tamara had sewed Mary even tighter into our family, and she and Mom worked well together as grandmothers. There was no way to say that little girl was anything less than spoiled by those two women. And the more time they spent together, the more we all saw their old friendship blooming again — one that had been tainted by a man no longer in our lives.

As for the distillery, Mary had been given charge of it, and after the history she'd had with the place, she wanted little to do with it in the end. She kept ten percent of the shares to live on and to remain on the board, but she signed the other ninety percent of the shares over to my family.

It's what Robert would have wanted, she'd said.

Now, Mom sat on the board, too — along with Noah and Logan. Noah served as President, with Logan as Vice, Mom as Secretary, and Mary as Treasurer. Together, they named the other members of the board — those they could trust — and were steering Scooter Whiskey into a new direction, a new era, born of the Beckers.

"Mallory, are you ready for the big grand opening of your studio next week?" Ruby Grace asked as we all started to gather around the tables. Mom had lined them up into one long one that spread half the yard, and Paige and Sydney were delivering giant dishes of food from the kitchen. Mom and Mary had hopped up to help while the rest of us got settled.

"More than ready," Logan answered for her, squeezing her knee with pride in his eyes. "She can't shut up about it."

Mallory pinched his side, leaning into his embrace next as they looked lovingly at each other. They'd morphed since becoming parents, and somehow dadhood had softened my brother. He wasn't wound as tight as he used to be — probably because he realized no matter what he did, his daughter was going to get dirty and messy and probably mess up everything else in her wake, too.

As was the beauty of being a parent.

He and Mallory had just bought land on the west edge of town to build their first home together, and Mallory had also purchased the same spot on Main Street that her dad had once owned. It was where her first shop had been set up and then ripped away from her a month later, and it was where she would be re-opening again next week.

On her own, this time.

"He's right," Mallory admitted on a sigh. "I'm excited, to say the least. Although, it's been a bit more challenging to get everything set up and ready to go with that little girl keeping me busy." She nodded down the table to where Tamara sat on Kylie's lap, Mikey playing peek-a-boo with her.

"Want me to come help this week?" Ruby Grace offered, then she rubbed her extremely swollen belly. "Honestly, anything to be moving and keep my mind off the fact that I'm about to pop is welcome."

Mallory chuckled. "As long as you don't pop on my new studio floor."

"No promises. His due date is two weeks from now, but I have a high suspicion we won't make it that long."

Noah smirked, rubbing her belly, too, with a mixture of love and complete terror in his eyes. I knew he had to be shitting himself on the brink of being a father, but Logan squeezed his shoulder reassuringly, as if to say, *you're going to be great.*

"I'll help, too," Sydney chimed in when she delivered the sweet potato casserole.

"I'd love that," Mallory replied. They shared a smile, and my heart beamed at the relationship my sister and my girlfriend had formed over the last few years. I knew a big part of it was standing up and testifying against Randy together. It hadn't been easy for either one of them, but it had brought them closer together.

Once everyone was seated and the food was on the table, Mom had us all gather hands, and she said grace. We all went around the table saying what we were thankful for, and after dinner, before the pie was brought out, we lit a candle in Betty's honor.

The old woman who had become such an integral part of our family and our lives had passed away that summer, leaving peacefully in her sleep on the Fourth of July. Kylie had joked that she'd planned it, wanting to *go out with a bang.* The news had been especially hard on her and Ruby Grace, who were by far the closest with Betty, but Mom had suffered, too, as they had become close friends over the years.

Betty had lived a long and full life, which was one comfort we found in her passing. More than that, she had been a light in our lives, too — helping so many of us out of the dark when we couldn't see even a ray of light that promised a way out.

The truth was we *all* missed her dearly, but the impression she'd left on our hearts was one that could never be forgotten. And we all knew she was dancing with *Mr.* Collins in heaven now.

Kylie and Mikey told us over dessert about the trip they were planning to Asia for the following summer, but I could barely listen, because my heart was ticking up a notch faster with every passing moment, beating loud and hard in my ears as I rehearsed what I'd been practicing for months. Before the plates could be cleared, Paige found her way over to me, clamping her hands down hard on my shoulders.

"Let's play catch, Coach," she said.

I swallowed, standing on shaking legs as Sydney smiled up at us.

"Do you two *ever* get tired of football?" she asked, laughing.

"Never," Paige answered, and she was already shoving me back toward the open yard where we'd been playing earlier.

When we were safely out of earshot, she put her hands on my shoulders again — which had her standing on her toes — leveling her eyes with me as best she could. "Alright, Coach," she said, seriously. "This is the big game. Your big moment. The play of your lifetime. You gotta focus, alright? Don't mess this up."

My palms were sweating, but I managed a laugh. "Gee, thanks for reminding me that there's nothing to worry about."

"Always here for you," she said, clapping her hands down on my shoulders once more before she pointed at me and started jogging backward toward the tables. "You've got this."

She turned, taking off in a slow jog as I forced as steady of a breath as I could manage. Then, I looked down at the football in my hands, and I pulled a small, navy blue, velvet box out of my pocket, fastening it to the ball with the sports tape Paige and I had tested a hundred times.

When it was safely in place, I looked up, finding Paige waiting in her designated spot behind her mom. Everyone was in conversation, still, and oblivious to what we were doing.

At least, until I took a breath and launched the ball, and Paige cried out, "*Heads up, Mom!*"

Sydney looked up just in time to notice the ball spiraling toward her, and her hands went up instinctively, catching it before it hit her chest. She screamed, though, and then laughed, looking back at Paige before her eyes found me and she pointed. "That was on purpose, you jerk!" She laughed again. "You're lucky I caught that!"

"What exactly did you catch?" Paige baited behind her, and Sydney looked back, confused, before her eyes fell to the ball in her hands.

And the little box strapped to the side of it.

I jogged over with my heart still pounding in my ears, and everyone fell silent, Sydney's eyes widening as she fingered the box out of the tape hold and held it between two fingers. She looked at it, looked at me, looked at it again, looked at me.

I swallowed, rounding the table until I was next to her chair, and lowering down onto one, shaky knee.

"Sydney Clark," I said, taking the box from her trembling fingers and holding it in my own.

Her eyes found mine, wide with surprise, her lips slightly parted as she waited for me to continue. From somewhere behind her I heard Ruby Grace whisper, "*I can't believe Betty is missing this.*"

"All my life, I watched my dad and mom love each other, and I wondered if I'd ever find someone to share my life with the way they had," I said, and I heard my mom sniff from where she watched us at her end of the table. But my focus was on Sydney, and I grabbed her hand in mine, squeezing gently. "I decided at a pretty young age that I wouldn't, that it was rare and, in most ways, impossible. And I settled into a life alone, content to just be a brother, a son, and a football coach."

"A damn good one, too," Eli said, and a soft chuckle found the tables.

"And I was happy," I said. "I was. I didn't think anything was missing." I leveled my gaze with hers. "Not until you walked into my life, and my heart realized long before my brain did that I could never go back to life without you — not once I knew what it was like with you in it."

She smiled, her eyes glossing over with a sheen of tears.

"I know I'm not perfect," I started. "I know we will have mountains to climb. But if I've learned anything from the ones we've already overcome together, it's that there isn't one high enough to defeat us — and that there's no one I want to be standing with at the top more than you."

I fumbled, clumsily opening the box in my hand until the modest ring I'd bought her caught the sunlight. She gasped at the sight, covering her mouth as her eyes flooded even more.

"Sydney, I want to spend the rest of my life with you. I want to be a father to Paige, and a husband to you. I want to help you in the garden and watch you do yoga on the porch."

"Gross," Paige chimed in.

I laughed, and Sydney did, too, freeing two parallel tears down each cheek.

"I want to come home to you, every night, and I want to wake up to you every morning. I want to dream together, and accomplish together, and fight together, and *love* together. And I want to grow old with you, with the family we've built, with a love story only we could write."

Sydney was already nodding when I pulled the ring from its place in the box, lining it up with her ring finger on her left hand.

"Will you take me as the scarred, damaged, football-crazed man that I am and trust me to love you, to protect you, and to care for you, until our days on this Earth are done and we pass into our next life?" I asked, and I slipped the ring onto her finger, because I already knew the answer. "Sydney, will you marry me?"

She nodded more vigorously, wrapping her arms around my neck and lowering to kiss me as our family erupted into a burst of cheers around us. They clapped and whistled and my heart swelled to the size of a hot air balloon in my chest, relief finding me in a wave that nearly knocked me off balance where I was still on one knee.

"This calls for champagne!" Mary announced, and already she was up out of her chair and heading toward the house, Mom calling out to her where she could find some.

And when Sydney finally pulled back from our kiss, we were both swarmed, my brothers and family congratulating me while my mother and Mallory and Kylie and Ruby Grace surrounded Sydney, hugging her and begging to see the ring.

Paige high-fived me, pretending to be tough when she didn't know I'd seen the tears in her eyes, too.

"Nailed it, Coach," she said, proudly.

"Thanks for your help," I said back, then I opened my arms, and her eyes welled with tears again as she leaned in and let me wrap her in a hug.

"I'm so glad you found us," she whispered.

I nodded, holding her tight with a pang of something I only felt for that little girl tightening my chest. It was a longing to protect her, to fight for her, and to be a good man in her life — even if I wasn't her real dad.

Champagne was poured and toasts were made, and when the sun began to set, we made a fire in the pit and gathered around to listen to Mikey play guitar while we all sang the words to our favorite songs.

Surrounded by my family — *all* of my family — I held my fiancée's hand in mine and kissed her knuckles from time to time, both of us smiling at each other like a couple of love-sick loons. And for the first time in a long time, everything felt good and right and true.

From across the fire, I locked eyes with Noah, and we shared a nod, both of us smiling. We looked to Logan, then, who nodded to both of us, too — bouncing Tamara in his lap. Then, we all looked at Mikey, and he smiled at each of us, still keeping time on his guitar as he sang along to one of Betty's favorite country songs.

We made it, we all seemed to say.

And in my heart, I knew there was nothing the Becker brothers couldn't face together.

Slowly, Mikey changed the way he was strumming, slowly shifting until a soft, familiar melody met all of us. Mom's smile dropped, but only for a moment, and then she smiled, tears in her eyes as Mikey began singing the first words of "Wonderful Tonight."

I kissed Sydney's knuckles again before releasing them, and then I stood, walking over to where Mom sat and extending my hand down for hers. She took it with a knowing grin, and then she was in my arms, and we swayed like we had so many nights in the living room of that old house.

It wasn't long before Noah tapped my shoulder to cut in, and I danced with Sydney, instead — watching as one by one, each of my brothers took a turn with Mom on the makeshift dance floor.

"I think I'm marrying into the best family there is," Sydney whispered as we watched Mikey attempting to dance with Mom while still playing the guitar. They were laughing, even though Mom was crying, too — and the love and joy surrounding that fire was strong enough to be seen and felt, like a warm blanket or a perfect summer day.

"You'll make it even better," I whispered back, and Sydney smiled, her brown eyes shining in the firelight.

Then, I kissed my bride-to-be, whispering that she looked wonderful tonight as I pulled her closer, and knowing I'd be singing those words for years to come.

For an entire lifetime, if I was lucky.

And I swore I'd never blink, so as to never miss a single moment of it.

a tall Order

Chapter One

I can't remember my husband's drink order.

It's been years since he left this world, but I can still remember so much about him. I can remember the exact shade of his eyes — cobalt blue with flecks of turquoise. I can still remember the hard slope of his nose, the way his five o'clock shadow would race in almost immediately after he shaved it. I can remember the baritone of his laugh, the high-pitched scream he only let out when he saw a grasshopper, and the distinct ways he said my name, depending on what he wanted.

I can remember how he smelled after a long day of work at the distillery and the bodywash he used every shower. I can remember how he'd wake me every morning with a soft smattering of kisses along my shoulder.

So much of him still lives within me, little pieces that I don't even have to try to reach for. They float to me on gentle breezes, tiny memories delivered by a familiar sound or sight.

But I can't remember his drink order.

I woke up this morning, on Christmas Eve, with that same familiar longing in my chest. I was excited to prep and clean and cook all day in anticipation of having my children and grandchildren home on Christmas Day. I look forward to this holiday every year.

At least, I used to.

Things are different now. My kids are grown, starting families of their own, and that means I have to share them more than I ever used to before. It means the house I've tended for decades that was always loud and filled with love is empty more often than not.

It's quieter, too.

So, so quiet.

It was near silent this morning as I worked on various pies, other than my humming. I had a tendency to hum in the kitchen. John used to always say I was like permanent elevator music. Sometimes, he'd make a game out of trying to guess what I was humming before I hit the chorus.

In that quiet humming moment of baking, I thought about my late husband, specifically about the night he'd turned twenty-one and we'd gone to Buck's for him to order his first legal adult beverage.

And I couldn't remember what he ordered to drink.

I'd told the story a hundred times. Not that *what* he ordered was ever really a big part of the tale, but it was still a detail I remembered — even if I never made it part of the story.

But this morning, that piece of my memory didn't show up when I called it from the archival files of my mind.

And it stopped me like the hard pull of a bus brake.

Now, on an evening I used to spend wrangling my four boys into matching Christmas pajamas so we could bake cookies, I'm walking into the only bar in my small town of Stratford, Tennessee.

And I'm hell bent on calling that memory back home.

Buck's hasn't changed a bit — and considering I haven't been in this bar in at least ten years, that's saying something. I like that about this bar, though — about this *town*. It stays the same. It's constant and steady in a world obsessed with change and progress.

I've had enough unwanted change in my life. The least I can have is a home that didn't love to surprise me.

A soft smile finds my lips as I step inside, old neon lights playing with the shadows across all the dark wooden surfaces. The old jukebox has been updated, I notice, thanks to a Chris Stapleton song crooning through a fancy-looking touch screen near the pool tables. But the photos on the wall are worn with age, the cushions of the barstools cracked a bit from years of pressure.

I find one at the far-left corner of the bar, the same one I was sitting in the night John Becker waltzed into this bar like he owned it to order his first legal drink.

When I met John Becker in high school, he'd shot me one charming smile and melted me into a puddle at his feet. I'd never met a man so confident, one so sure about what he wanted.

I fell for him instantly.

The bar reminds me of my house tonight. It's usually a boisterous place, but given the holiday, I'm one of only about a dozen people in here. Of those dozen, there are a few themes — kids home from college looking for a break from their families, grumpy old men, grumpy old women, a couple recently married but with no children yet, two members of our local motorcycle club, as well as a few travelers passing through.

And me.

I settle into my seat at the bar and look around, placing my purse on the stool beside me. That little smile is still on my lips, but I feel it growing weaker by the moment.

How did I end up here?

How, on a holiday that used to fill me with such extreme joy I couldn't even fully appreciate what I had, was I now widowed and alone in a dusty old bar?

I know, come morning, all these feelings will pass. When I'm surrounded by my family, that joy comes rushing back in like a tidal wave.

It's just that I'm not with family as much anymore.

John and I were blessed with four boys — Jordan, Noah, Logan, and Michael. We adopted Jordan, and then gave him three rowdy little brothers to chase after.

Now, Jordan, Noah, and Logan are all married and starting families of their own, and Michael is getting married on New Year's Eve. Just one week from tonight.

My chest pinches, sorrow right on the heels of my joy. I love the women my sons have found, love the lives they've created.

I just miss when they were my little boys.

"Lorelei?"

The raspy voice shakes me from my thoughts, and I look up to find Buck himself watching me with one thick, caterpillar eyebrow hiked high on his forehead.

"Merry Christmas Eve, Buck," I say.

"And to you." He places a napkin and a coaster on the bar in front of me, a grin curling under that thick beard of his. "Gotta say, I can't remember the last time this old bar was graced with your presence. Feels good to have you here."

"Feels good to be here," I reply, and it only feels like half a lie. It *does*, strangely, feel a little nice to be back in this seat, in this bar. It makes me think of a different time in my life. But it also makes me long for a reason to not be here, makes me wish I still had kids to chase around that kept me out of places like this.

"What can I get you?"

I sigh. "Any chance in hell you remember what John used to drink?"

Buck's eyes soften. My late husband was a good friend of his, a good friend of everyone's here in Stratford. He essentially ran the distillery before he perished in the fire there, and that distillery counts for more than everything in this town other than church. He was like a mayor. Hell, he was *better* — since the mayor we had at that time was an evil son of a gun.

But I don't want to think about that tonight.

"I don't," Buck says, and he looks as if that bothers him as much as it bothers me that I can't remember, either.

"Well — maybe a taste test will refresh my memory. Let's start with an old fashioned. We know it had to be some sort of whiskey concoction."

"I'd say that's a pretty safe bet," Buck agrees with a smile. "Coming right up."

While Buck whips up the cocktail, I look around the bar, memories tickling the inside of my brain like a feather. They don't rush back over me, they just flirt with the edges of my peripheral.

I remember a night where I drank too much and ended up falling off of my barstool. I remember John laughing as he hauled me over his shoulder and carried me home. I remember dancing until the band's last song, remember laughing so hard I couldn't breathe with a group of friends one Thanksgiving when we all decided to blow off our families and hang out here, instead.

Every little corner I scan conjures up a new memory, a fresh smile.

I'm lost to those memories when I realize I'm staring at the darts corner a bit too long.

When I realize I'm staring at *him*.

There's a man I don't recognize, broad-shouldered and silver-haired. He's wearing tight-fitted Wranglers and a worn pair of Stetsons, his eyes trained on the dart board as he lets another one fly.

It hits the wide part of the twenty.

As he gears up to throw again, I notice the muscles in his arms, how they're still defined against the long-sleeve button up he's wearing even though I know he must be in his sixties. He looks as fit as a thirty-year-old bull rider, his waist tapered, pectoral muscles rounded. He's rolled the sleeves of his button-up to his elbows, and his forearms are tan and dusted with hair — a fact I'm surprised I notice.

Noticing him *at all* is a surprise.

I can't remember the last time I looked at a man and felt my stomach erupt with butterflies — probably because it hasn't happened since before my husband passed away. But this man, with his weathered skin and hard scowl and effortless dart-throwing and tight jeans...

He's doing something to me.

He throws another dart, this one hitting the bullseye.

Then, he turns.

And looks right at me.

I flush and tear my gaze away when I'm caught ogling him, but as soon as Buck slides the old fashioned into my hands, I take a sip... and look back at the man.

The corner of his mouth crooks up when I do, and he grabs his beer from the cocktail table next to him, tilting it toward me in a cheers.

My cheeks burn as I return the gesture, and then I focus on the bar in front of me, trying and failing to not peek over at him again.

On the third time, I watch as he grabs his cowboy hat from that same table, fits it carefully on his head, and then starts walking toward the door.

No.

Toward *me*.

I haven't cursed since long before I had young children running around desperate to repeat every word I said, but I nearly mutter one under my breath as I train my gaze on where my hands are glued to the tumbler of whiskey in my hands.

I'm still staring at my fingers that I can't remember looking this aged when he slides onto the barstool next to me.

"Good evening," he greets.

My neck is actually on fire.

"Good evening," I echo, briefly glancing at him with a smile before I'm staring at my glass again.

"I have to tell you," he says, his voice somehow reminding me of a strongly brewed hot coffee on a crisp fall morning. "I am not in the habit of approaching beautiful women at bars. In fact, I find myself quite out of practice," he adds with a chuckle. "But I would love to sit and have a drink with you, if that's alright."

My stomach flips, which makes my anxiety spike because I haven't felt anything remotely like this in so long, I've wondered if this part of me died along with my husband.

The awakening of it scares me as much as it lights me up with curiosity.

I swear, I can almost feel my husband, can almost *see* him grabbing my hand and squeezing it. I swear I can hear his voice telling me not to shut out life.

So, I take a long, slow inhale, and I look up to meet the man's gaze. "I'm out of practice, too," I admit. "But I think I'd like to change that."

The smile that spreads on this man's face nearly knocks me to my knees. He has the kind of smile that takes up the entirety of his face, skin crinkling at the edge of his lips and the corners of his eyes when he flashes it.

He reaches up for his cowboy hat and removes it with one hand, setting it to the side before he extends that hand for mine.

"Walker Jones," he says.

And when I slide my hand in to fit his, when I feel the warmth and the calloused palms and the firm grip of his fingers curling around mine, my entire body buzzes to life like I'm sixteen again.

"Lorelei Becker," I reply.

For a moment, we hold that handshake, his warm brown eyes searching mine. He seems almost reluctant to release me, and when he does, he holds up his almost-empty beer toward Buck to signal a fresh one.

The smile on Buck's face is like that of a man who knows every secret in the world, and I shoot him a warning glare before replacing it with a quick smile when Walker turns to face me again.

"I've been in this bar quite a few nights since my crew started work here," he says. "But I have definitely not seen you."

"Well, that would be because I haven't stepped foot in this bar in at least ten years."

He arches a brow. "Ah, so you're a local."

"Born and raised," I confirm. "And I take it from your mention of a crew that you're just passing through?"

"I'm a contractor, working on the expansion of the distillery."

I know the exact expansion he's talking about, the new building we're erecting to serve as a museum and tasting bar for our tours. I know because I'm a member of the board — have been ever since the will of the founder was discovered and my family was given our rightful share.

All thanks to the detective work of my four relentless sons.

But that's a story for another time.

"Better do a good job," I warn, taking a sip of my old fashioned just as Buck slides a fresh beer in front of Walker. "I happen to know the boss lady in charge, and she has pretty high standards."

There's that heart-stopping smile again.

"I've heard she's a sweetheart," he says knowingly. "I bet she wouldn't harm a fly."

"Mess with her family, her church, or her distillery, and you'll find out just how wrong you are about that."

His chuckle rumbles through his chest. "I don't intend to test that theory."

Something about the way he looks at me has my next breath a little harder to take. It's new and familiar all at once, curiosity mixed with desire.

There's no hiding it.

He wants me.

And there's no denying how good it feels to be wanted.

"Where are you from?" I ask.

"Here and there."

"A nomad, huh?"

"I like a life on the move," he says, pausing to take a long pull of his beer. "I spent far too long sitting still."

Those words knock against the inside of my rib cage, a sorrow I can't explain waking up when they do.

As if he can sense it, Walker flashes me a smile, and he stands.

Then, that calloused hand reaches out for mine.

"Dance with me, Lorelei."

Chapter Two

Who even *am* I?

Before I realize what I'm doing, my hand is in his, and then Walker is tugging me toward the dance floor in front of the stage where the band usually plays.

Except there's no band tonight, just an old George Straight song playing over the speakers. There's also not a single other person dancing, but that doesn't stop Walker from pulling me into his arms and beginning a gentle sway.

He doesn't move in too close. In fact, I find myself somewhat disappointed at how much of a gentleman he is with the space between us, and then promptly flush because I cannot *believe* I want to be close to a man.

That thought only lasts a moment before we start to dance, and I think of John.

I wish I could say I have fully moved on, that I eventually found peace in his death and the fact that I'd have to live a life without him. But it doesn't matter how many years have passed. I still miss him — and dancing makes me miss him more than anything else.

"I'm not *that* bad of a dancer, am I?" Walker asks, smirking a little before he moves us from a gentle sway into a slow two-step.

"What? No, of course not," I say quickly. "You're lovely. I mean, this is lovely. Not you. I mean you are, too, but not that I would say that. Not that I've noticed. Not that I *haven't* noticed. Oh, God."

I clamp my mouth shut, and Walker grins, twirling me out for a spin before he pulls me back to him. This time, he brings me a little closer, close enough that I feel the heat radiating off his skin and permeating my own.

"I just meant that you look a little lost in thought there," he comments.

I sigh. "I suppose I am."

"A pretty woman like yourself wanders into a bar like this on Christmas Eve, and I'm not surprised to hear it." His palm splays flat across my lower back, warm and expansive. "Care to share with the class?"

I peek up at him through my lashes, then look at where my hand fits in his. "I was just thinking I haven't danced with a man who wasn't my son in a long time." I swallow. "I was thinking that it feels nice."

"Were you also thinking that it doesn't feel right?"

I blink, my next breath hollowing out in my chest.

The corner of his mouth twitches up, but then falls quickly, and his eyes wash over mine with understanding.

"It felt weird for me, too," he confesses. "The first time I danced with someone who wasn't my wife. It was years later, and even though the woman in my arms was beautiful, all I could think was how her hands weren't the same, how she didn't spin quite right, how her head didn't fit perfectly in the crook of my neck when I brought her into me."

"Yes." The word is more of an exhale than anything else, and I shake my head, furrowing my brows as I assess Walker in a new light. "You're a widower."

He nods, just once, that same sad smile on his lips.

"How did you know?" I ask as the song changes. Thankfully, it's another slow one, and Walker adjusts us to match the pace before he responds.

"I see it in your eyes," he says, and then he searches those eyes he referenced like he's looking for more. "Has it been long?"

My throat is dry when I respond. "Fourteen years."

"And yet, it feels like you were with him just yesterday, doesn't it?"

My eyes water, and I look down at Walker's chest. "Time is a tricky little thing, isn't it?"

"My Karina has been gone for eight," he says, making me lift my eyes to his again. "I miss her every day. I thought there'd come a time when I'd stop thinking of her, but that hasn't happened. At least, not yet."

I nod. I know that exact feeling, know how strange grief can be. One moment, you're drowning in it. Then, you emerge on the other side of the intense wave, and you think maybe it's gone.

But it never fully leaves.

It's like a freckle after a long day in the sun. One day it wasn't there, but now it is, and it's with you forever. Even when you forget about it for a moment, it's still there.

"I came here tonight because of John," I confess. "That was his name. John Becker." I smile, letting Walker spin me again before I continue. "It hurts a little more on the holidays, I think."

"So you came to drink away the pain?"

"No, actually. I came because I cannot, for the life of me, remember his damned drink order."

Walker blinks, and then barks out a laugh. "So what's the plan?"

"Sit at that bar and order every whiskey combination I can until it clicks."

"Sounds like trouble."

"And you interrupted."

His thick silver eyebrows shoot up, and he lets out that delightful laugh again before we stop dancing. He still keeps one hand at the small of my back, though. And the other waves in front of us.

"Well, my deepest apologies, ma'am," he says, guiding us toward the bar.

I find myself savoring that rich voice of his again, even more so as I find the ways his drawl is different than my own. I can tell he's from the country, but not from Tennessee.

"I think I can make it up to you, though."

"Oh? How so?"

"I happen to know every whiskey drink there is. Perhaps God sent me here to help you in your quest tonight."

"You think God aligned our paths so we could drink hard liquor on a holy holiday, huh?"

He shrugs, helping me onto my barstool before he takes a seat in his.

"I don't presume to know what God has planned," he says, his eyes twinkling. "But I always trust Him to lead me right where I'm supposed to be."

Chapter Three

As Walker predicted, ordering multiple whiskey cocktails was trouble, indeed.

I am admittedly a lightweight. Always have been. And after the second drink, when I was already feeling tipsy, Walker suggested changing methods to a simple taste test.

Buck was either bored or invested, because he jumped right on board, whipping up tasting flights of every whiskey cocktail we could think of.

Manhattan. Mint Julep. Whiskey sour. Whiskey smash. Irish coffee. Whiskey highball. We even tried a whiskey mule.

In the end, nothing triggered a memory of John's tried and true drink order.

And now, I'm two sheets to the wind, giggling and trying to remember why I cared so much in the first place.

"You didn't actually jump, though, right?" I ask, rapt with the stories of Walker's travels all around the world. Currently, he's telling me about a time he worked on a project in Croatia and got caught kissing the daughter of the man who'd hired him. It was his first international job, and at the time, his most profitable one.

He was about to lose it all when the man said he could keep the contract if he jumped off the highest cliff in their seaside town.

Naked.

"Oh, of course, I did."

"You *did?!*" I gasp, jaw hinging open as I shake my head.

"I did," Walker confirms, taking a sip of his beer. He licks the foam off his lips and then adds, "I fell at an awkward angle, too. Landed on my side. Took the breath right out of me. It quite literally felt like the ocean was whooping my ass."

I cackle, leaning in and hanging on his every word. "So you got to keep the job?"

"Oh, no."

"No?!"

He shakes his head. "They stole my clothes and left me in the water to fend for myself. I had to swim to the nearest beach and then beg tourists for clothes and hike my way back up into town. When I got to the house they'd put me up in, my clothes were on the brick stairs leading up to the door, along with the rest of my belongings." He takes a long pull of his beer. "And that was how I learned the hard lesson of doing a job without an official contract."

"I hope you also learned not to kiss your clients' daughters."

"Still haven't learned that lesson."

He shoots me a wink over his glass, and I playfully shove at his arm, a yawn stretching my mouth when I straighten up on my barstool and crack my neck.

"Ready to try another one?" he asks.

I sigh. "I think it's water only for me at this point."

"Don't tell me you're already giving up," Walker teases, even though it was *him* who'd suggested I order a water. "We still have so many possibilities. Maybe John was a scotch man."

I wrinkle my nose. "Definitely not. He always made fun of scotch drinkers. Said they were pretentious."

"I think he and I would have been friends."

I grin up at Walker — not deterred at all by the fact that I now see two of him. In fact, I rather like that he's spawned a twin. I wouldn't mind if he spawned a few more. Maybe we could fill this entire room with copies of Walker Jones so I could stare at them all day long.

"I think you would have been, too," I muse, leaning my chin on my palm. My vision clears a bit, and when I'm back to seeing only one of him, I allow myself a moment to appreciate the view.

He's just so *sharp*.

There's something enticing about his silver hair, the deep lines in his tan skin, the roughness of his hands. Without more than a glance, you can tell he's a man who's worked hard his entire life. You can also infer he's a gentleman, a country boy. He was the kind who might get you lost on a long dirt road but would always have you back by curfew, who might steal a kiss but would bring your momma flowers and call your father *sir*.

"Why are you looking at me like that?" Walker asks, though the way those brown eyes of his are heating, I have a feeling he already knows the answer.

"You make me feel young."

His brows tug in a bit at that, but he smiles despite them. "You are young."

"Tell that to my arthritis."

He barks out that delectable laugh of his, and then finishes his beer and climbs off the stool. "Well, I think it's time we get you home."

I sigh, sliding off the barstool. Walker pays our tab before I can fight him on it, and truth be told, I don't want to. It's nice, having a man pay for my drinks and spin me around an empty dance floor.

It makes me feel like maybe I could still be a woman someone like Walker Jones desires.

"I can call my son to pick me up," I say, checking the time on my watch. "He's got two little girls. My bet is he's been up all night making a doll house that Santa will get the credit for."

"I'm happy to drive you, if you'd like."

I scoff. "You've had at least five beers just since I walked in."

Walker shares a look with Buck, which has me lifting a brow when they both turn back to me.

"Non-alcoholic," Walker explains. When I show my surprise, he shrugs. "I've been sober for more than twenty years now."

I study him for a moment. "Who *are* you, Walker Jones?"

"Oh, I'm just an old man being selfish with the time of a beautiful woman."

"I'm not sleeping with you."

That earns me a barrel of a laugh out of Buck, and Walker licks his lips on an amused smile before sliding his cowboy hat back on his head. He tilts it until it's just right, drapes my coat around my shoulders, and guides me toward the door.

"I'd just like to get you home safe."

"Uh-huh. I know what that means, mister." I wag my finger at him, but I also lean into his embrace, savoring the scent of his cologne.

He smells like raw bergamot and crisp sage, like smoked whiskey and rough-cut tobacco.

Like a man.

"I feel like a silly little girl," I whisper, mostly to myself, but Walker hears it. He pushes the door open for me and ushers me into the cold night before his arm is around my shoulder once more.

"Why's that?"

"Because I like looking at you," I say, peeking up at him with a smile. "And I like the way you look at me."

Chapter Four

True to his word, Walker Jones was the picture-perfect gentleman.

He opened the passenger side door to his truck for me, helping me inside before he climbed behind the wheel. He drove right at the speed limit, parked in front of my house, and then walked me to my door.

Now, we're standing in the cold, our breath puffing out in little clouds of white between us and our noses turning red.

And neither one of us wants to say goodnight.

I swear this man is like a light switch. I walked into that bar quietly and with a plan to stay invisible, melancholy dripping off me like rain.

But one look from him, and my night had shifted.

One dance with him, and I felt more seen than I had in years.

One night with him, and I want more.

It's as terrifying as it is exhilarating. After John passed, I couldn't *think* of ever being with another man. I thought eventually, that feeling would pass. I thought surely, *one day*, I'd be ready to move on. But that day never came.

At some point, I made peace with my new reality. My family was my focus. I didn't need a man in my life.

But tonight, I've been reminded of feelings I'd forgotten existed. I forgot how it felt to have my heart racing out of my chest, to have my skin flush with heat, to have my body hum in anticipation of a look, a caress...

A kiss.

"You never did tell me where you're from," I say, wrapping my arms around myself to stay warm.

"You never asked."

"I was a little too busy staring at your arms."

"My arms, huh?" he asks, and my cheeks flame at the fact that I said those words out loud.

But I don't take them back.

Something about this man makes me feel bold — and I don't want to run from that feeling, nor do I want to shy away from it.

"Here," he adds, peeling his Carhartt jacket off one arm. He held it up in a flex. "Wanna feel?"

I don't even pretend I don't. Instantly, my icy hands wrap around his bicep muscle, and I test the rigidity of that muscle with a squeeze.

"You're a freak of nature."

"Nah," he says with a chuckle, and I reluctantly free my grasp so he can put his coat back on. "Just built by a lifetime of construction."

"Don't you more so manage and oversee projects?"

"I never let my men work alone," he says quickly, his voice dropping an octave. "Ain't no one too good for a day's work."

I smile, tilting my head to the side as I assess him. I don't say it out loud, but what he said earlier tickles my mind.

He and John really would have been great friends.

"So, are you going to answer my question?"

"The one you asked or the one you haven't?"

I frown. "The one I asked."

Something glimmers in his eyes, like he knows I'm still turning over what he said about the question I *hadn't* asked, like he knows I won't be able to resist pestering him about that next.

"Texas," he says.

Instantly, it makes sense. Everything about him *screams* Texas, from his jeans to his boots to his hat.

"What do you think of Tennessee so far?"

His eyes dance over the length of me, the light from my porch playing with the shadows of the night on his face.

"I think I should have come sooner."

Butterflies fill my stomach, and I smile against a blush, looking down at our feet.

"What's this question you think I haven't asked yet?"

His winning grin tells me I played right into his hand, but I don't mind it. I like this game we're playing. I thought I'd forgotten how to play at all.

"You're wondering if I'm going to kiss you goodnight."

Suddenly, my throat is dry, my heartbeat present in my ears as I keep my eyes locked on his. "Is that so?"

I wanted the words to come out as a tease, but they're breathy and light. They're confirmation and a plea.

Walker reaches up for his hat, carefully removing it with one hand. When he takes a step, he eliminates what little space had existed between us, his warmth and heady scent pulling me into him like a magnet.

My heart is beating so loud and hard against my rib cage I can't believe it hasn't knocked me over. And when he bends, when his warmth invades me even more, I close my eyes, tilt my chin...

And promptly have a spike of anxiety.

I haven't kissed another man since John, and suddenly, the fact that I'm willing to — no, that I *want* to — socks me in the gut.

My eyes fly open, and I'm ready to press a hand to his chest and hold him back.

But then I realize the angle of his descent, and I blink just before he presses a feather-light kiss to my cheek.

"Merry Christmas, Lorelei," he says, his voice rumbling under the shell of my ear. When he stands straight again, he puts his hat back on, and I swear I melt into a puddle right there at his feet, all the anxiety gone in an instant.

"Wait," I blurt out when he turns toward his truck. He pauses, arching a brow when he's facing me again. "You're... you're just leaving?"

"Well, I do believe you made it quite clear that I was not invited to stay," he points out with a wry grin.

"But I mean, you didn't ask for my number. You..."

I quiet, swallowing my words and the sinking feeling in my stomach when I realize I'm being a fool.

I'm sure Walker will bolt, murmuring some excuse, but he spots my insecurity and steps right back in front of me, tilting my chin with his knuckles until I have no choice but to look him in the eyes.

"I want to see you again," he says, soothing my worry like a balm. "If it were up to me, this night wouldn't end — not now, maybe not ever. But you'll have a house full of family early in the morning, and my bet is you'll feel better with a good night's rest. I didn't ask for your number because I already have it."

I frown, then think about the contract, the expansion. Of course, he'd have my contact information. I wasn't his first point of contact, but I'd be on the list just in case.

Walker smiles, smoothing his thumb over my jaw line. "Come on, now. You really think I could walk away from you now?"

I'm pretty sure I swoon like a wilting flower, my body rushing with heat despite the fact that it's in the twenties tonight.

"And what about you?"

"What about me?"

"Where will you be tomorrow?"

He smiles. "I've got plans with the buffet in the next town over. Don't you worry about me."

"What?" I instantly shake my head. "Absolutely not. Please, come here in the morning. Come spend Christmas with me and my family."

Walker laughs. "I don't need to impose on—"

"I want you here."

The words shock me as much as they do him, and he swallows, his thumb running that same line across my jaw.

"If it's what you want."

"It is. I won't take no for an answer."

His eyebrow ticks up at that, and he releases his hold on my chin. "Oh, I think I gathered that already."

"Then it's settled. I'll see you in the morning."

He nods, backing up two steps. "It shall be the longest night."

"I didn't take you as a poetic man."

"Well, what can I say?" he asks, backing up a few more steps. "You're the kind of woman poetry demands to be written for."

And with those words swirling in my ears like the sweetest song, he tips his hat, trots down the stairs, and climbs in his truck.

He waits until I'm safely inside with the door locked behind me before he pulls out of the drive.

Chapter Five

I wake with a headache and a smile on my face.

I don't even care that I'm hungover. I groan as I swing my legs out of bed and pad barefoot into my bathroom. I groan even more when I see the atrocious monster staring back at me in the mirror. I'd been too exhausted to even wash my face last night — and it shows.

After a quick shower, I blow dry my hair and apply a touch of makeup, smiling a bit at myself in the mirror.

I used to be so afraid of aging.

I remember when I was in my early thirties, how I fretted over every wrinkle and sunspot, how my skin started showing me it wouldn't be tight and smooth forever and it felt like such a betrayal.

Somewhere along the way, I found appreciation for the wrinkles, for the gray hair and the achy bones. All of those things were proof that I'd lived and laughed and loved — just like the cheesy signs I saw in the home décor stores.

Now, I could even find beauty when I looked at my crow's feet around my hazel eyes, at my olive skin peppered with brown and red spots. I liked how my hazelnut hair had faded to an ashy gray. I liked that my body, that used to be leaner, had soft curves now.

I sigh on a smile, my eyes trailing from the mirror to the photo of my late husband I have next to my makeup. He's just twenty-eight in that photo, and I hate that I was robbed of seeing him grow old.

"Merry Christmas, John," I whisper, and then I kiss my fingers and press it to the photo before flittering out of the room.

It's time to get dressed. I have a Christmas to host.

I turn on the Bluetooth speaker Noah got me for my birthday a couple years ago, putting on my favorite holiday playlist before I get to work in the kitchen. I have the early hours of the morning to myself, knowing my boys will be opening gifts with their families. But at just past ten, the first of them pushes through the door.

And my favorite, personal brand of chaos begins.

"Merry Christmas, Nana!"

I wipe my hands on my apron just in time for Paige to launch herself into my arms, and I squeeze her tight, eyes watering already. I'm always such a mess on holidays. I can never keep my emotions in check — especially because I seem to be more aware of how much time has passed. Christmas was always a reminder that another year was gone, that my babies were another year older and their babies, too.

"Merry Christmas, my girl," I say, releasing her from the hug but holding her arms in my hands. I frown instantly at the sight of a ghastly scrape along her jaw. "Oh, my! What happened?"

She grins like she's proud of it. "Pretty cool, huh? One of the boys on the team made a comment about how I'm a kicker because I couldn't take being tackled. So, I put on pads and told them all to give me their best shot."

"Paige!"

"Trust me, Mom," a deep and familiar voice sings from the living room. Then, my oldest son swings in with presents balanced in his arms. "It's the boys you should feel sorry for. Half of them couldn't catch her, and the half that did struggled to ever bring her to the ground."

Jordan stopped by the tree long enough to deposit the gifts before he ruffled Paige's hair.

"You sound surprised, Coach." She beams up at him like he hung the moon, this man who isn't her father by blood but in all the ways that really matter.

He looks at her just the same.

"Little shit has me second-guessing if I should make her a receiver, instead."

"Language," I scold, but it's with a smile as I hold my arms open for Jordan next.

I sigh when he wraps me in his firm hug, and then his wife, Sydney, waddles in.

"Sorry, I had to run straight for the bathroom." She shakes her head and rubs her swollen belly. "Can't go more than twenty minutes anymore, it seems."

"I remember those days all too well. You look beautiful," I tell her when I pull her in for a hug, and we no sooner let go before the front door is kicked open again for the next crew to file in.

Logan and Mallory arrive, their daughter running inside and immediately showing me the toys they got from Santa. Tamara is five now and starting to show us more of her personality. She loves art, just like her mom. But she also has more fun cleaning up her toys than she does actually playing with them — just like her dad.

Michael and Kylie are next, the two of them glowing only the way an engaged couple can. They spent the night with Kylie's father, who stops by only long enough to say hello before he's off to spend his day at the nursing home. He picked that habit up from his daughter, and I love that it's a tradition he's kept alive.

Noah and Ruby Grace are last, Noah holding their two-year-old son, Bentley, in his arms and Ruby Grace sharing a commiserating look with Sydney. She's due with their second in February, and Sydney is due in just a couple of weeks.

In a matter of twenty minutes, my house goes from silence, other than the soft croon of holiday music, to a level of noise most people would find unbearable.

I, on the other hand, feel more at peace than ever.

For a while, it's a flurry of everyone getting settled — coats and scarves being shed, appetizers being set up, my oldest son chasing the youngest around while the middle two talk business. Kylie and Mallory help me in the kitchen while Sydney and Ruby Grace rest and chat. Paige plays with Tamara all while yelling for someone to turn the TV on and find the right channel for the first football game.

It's my favorite music — the voices and laughter of my children, their children, and the women who feel more like my best friends than daughters-in-law.

The knock on the door confuses everyone, not only because no one in this family knocks, but because everyone who is supposed to be at our Christmas celebration is already here.

Michael frowns at me from where he sits next to Kylie, one arm around her shoulder while she shows him something on her phone. "Who's that?"

My stomach does a little flip, and I pause my work on the stuffing, wiping my hands on my apron and heading for the door.

I don't know what I expected to see on the other side. Of course, I knew it was Walker, but I think a part of me wondered if the magic of last night was just that — magic. I wondered if maybe he wouldn't show up today. I wondered if maybe he *would*, but that when he did, I wouldn't feel anything other than the desire to show him the sort of kindness that you might show a stranger.

I thought maybe I would just feed him and introduce him to the family. Maybe we'd share a meal and a few stories, and we'd go about our merry ways.

But when I open the door and see Walker standing there, I know instantly that I was wrong.

He's wearing his cowboy hat again, and the stubble on his jaw is freshly shaven. I decide right then and there that no one wears jeans like this man does, and consider briefly if I should sneakily take a photo of him and submit it to Wrangler's marketing department before deciding I'm just selfish enough to want to keep the view for myself.

Under his jacket he wears a deep, forest green button-up shirt, tucked into those jeans I love, and punctuated with a large, gold belt buckle. That green sets off his eyes in a way the dimness of the bar last night couldn't, showing me the warm brown is actually full of colors — from gold to jade to coffee.

I realize then that the magic from last night wasn't the fictional kind. It was the kind that reminds you God is real, the kind that shifts your life in a way you can't ignore — even if you don't fully understand it, yet.

"Merry Christmas, Lorelei Becker," he says, that gravelly voice making chills sweep over my spine.

"Merry Christmas, Walker Jones," I echo.

He has a beautiful poinsettia in his hands, one I can't help but wonder when he found the time to pick up. He must have stopped by the corner store on the edge of town. It's the only thing open today, and only because Mrs. Lamar would never pass up a chance to make a buck.

Walker offers me the plant, which I accept with a smile before I open the door farther and usher him inside. He has to duck to make it through the doorway, and when he does, everyone in our chaotic house goes quiet, save for Tamara, who's making little doll noises, oblivious to the sudden hush.

Maybe I should be ashamed of how much fun I'm having watching my sons internally short circuit at the sight of my new Texan friend, but I can't help but bathe in it. It's been so many years of them looking at me with either respect or sympathy.

It's fun seeing that I can still surprise them.

"Walker Jones, this is my family. Family, this is Walker Jones. He's our guest for this Christmas. I would say treat him like he's family, but I don't want to scare him away. So let's treat him like a customer at the distillery."

It's still quiet when I shut the door, and then I loop my arm through Walker's and tug him toward the kitchen for just a moment of privacy.

I also figure I should give my family a moment to exchange their theories that I know must be burning in their minds.

'I'm so glad you came," I say as I set the poinsettia in the middle of our long dining table. I cast a curious glance to the living room where my sons and their wives are already whispering in a tizzy before I pull Walker into the kitchen and out of view. "Can I get you anything to drink?"

"I'll take a water on the rocks."

"Oh, be careful now. You do have to drive at the end of the night."

We share a smirk that has my cheeks tingeing pink, memories of last night making my chest flutter. I don't know how it's possible, but he's even more handsome in the daylight. Sure, the lines of his face were alluring beneath neon lights, but in the natural light coming through the back door and kitchen window? He's a vision.

I catalog everything that I missed the night before, like all those colors dancing in his eyes, and the scar just under the left side of his jaw that I hadn't noticed at all. When I meet his gaze again, I do so just in time to catch his eye roaming over me, too.

Our eyes lock, and we both smile a little wider.

"That plant isn't the only gift I brought you."

"No gifts necessary. The only one you'll get from me is a hot meal."

"I beg to differ," he argues quickly, his eyes perusing my body. "You in that dress and apron is the best present I've had in years."

I can't fight against the roll of my eyes, and his mischievous grin tells me he knows just how cheesy that sounded but he isn't the least bit ashamed.

Walker reaches inside his Carhartt jacket and pulls out a small paper bag. Our fingers brush when he hands it to me, and I feel my neck heating again. *God,* I love this feeling — the simple, sweet, consuming feeling of having a crush.

When I peek inside the bag, I let out a single laugh that I feel all the way down to my toes.

"Ibuprofen, Liquid IV, and... a donut?"

"That right there is the signature Walker Jones hangover kit. And I promise — if you do it in the exact order that you just described? You'll be feeling good as new."

I chuckle, which makes the headache I'd almost forgotten about vibrate my skull. "Well, with a sales pitch like that, how could I say no?"

I pop the ibuprofen, pour the Liquid IV into a bottle of water, shake it up, and promptly chug it all before taking a big bite of the donut. When I do, powder dusts my lips and falls down over my apron as I laugh.

Walker steps into me, that gorgeous little tilt of his lips making my laugh fade to nothing. All I can do is stare at the beautiful man as his thumb reaches out to brush over my bottom lip.

It's a sweet gesture.

That is, until he takes that thumb covered in powdered sugar from my lips and puts it to his own.

It's so quick I would have missed it if I blinked, but he licks that powdered sugar that was touching my skin, and then his smile grows into the charming, dazzling one that knocked the breath out of me last night. All I saw was one little flash of his tongue as he tasted the sugar, and yet it was as if I'd tasted it, instead.

A bolt of electricity strikes me in a place I thought was dormant, and I'm shocked speechless.

"I'm glad you invited me today, Lorelei," he says, his eyes a mixture of intention and amusement. "I'm very glad to be here. With you."

I'm so flustered, the donut falls from my fingers. And then, when I exclaim, "Oh!" and bend to pick it up, I don't realize that Walker is already on his way down, too.

We bump heads, not hard, but enough to make us both rub our skulls and laugh a little as we stand upright again.

And then Walker's eyes fall to my lips, and every fiber of my being hums with the desire for him to kiss me.

We're still staring at each other, my heart racing and Walker looking cool as a cucumber, when Logan rounds into the kitchen.

I clear my throat and fold my hands in front of my apron. "Hi, honey. Everything okay? You need anything?"

Logan is my most observant son, the one who can't help but make note of every detail most of us easily overlook. I can see his wheels turning as he looks at me, arches one brow into his hairline, and drags his gaze to Walker.

When he looks back at me, there are a thousand questions dancing in those eyes that look just like my own.

I just smile wider, not ready to answer a single one of them.

"Everything's fine," he says warily, narrowing his gaze at me as if to say we were going to have a conversation later. "We were just about to put the game on. Walker, you like football?"

"Come on now, I'm an American, ain't I?"

Logan likes that answer, and he nods his head toward the living room, clapping one hand hard on my new friend's shoulder as soon as he shrugs off his coat.

"So, Walker Jones — how do you know my mom?"

Walker looks over his shoulder at me with an amused smile, and I wonder if he's silently asking me if I'm feeding him to the wolves.

And maybe I am in a way.

I know my boys. I know they're protective of their mom, especially considering they've only seen their mom with one man — their father.

Their father who has been gone for so long now, and yet still lives fresh in all of our hearts and minds.

I know they'll have questions for this man. I know they'll likely be suspicious of him until they work through whatever tests they think he needs to pass.

But I also know those boys would do anything to see me happy.

And if they were looking close enough, then I know they already see that Walker Jones makes me happy.

I have faith that that alone will be enough for them.

Chapter Six

Just as I expected, each one of my sons puts Walker through some sort of test.

Logan is first, interviewing him through the first quarter of the football game. I think he would have been content to question the poor man all night long had Mallory not have gently pulled him out back for some fresh air.

Noah took his place as soon as he was gone, inviting Walker out for a stroll while Ruby Grace helped me get the last little bit of supper ready. I had more than a sneaky suspicion that Noah had taken Walker out to the old treehouse John had built for the boys, that he was asking the questions Logan hadn't thought to ask — the deeper ones.

Noah was a man of character, and he'd want to peel back layers I hadn't even had the chance to yet.

Walker got a brief break during dinner, when it was all laughs and mini food fights and me pestering Kylie for more details about the epic honeymoon trip she and Michael had planned. At one point while she was talking, I felt a strong hand fold over my knee under the table, and I covered it with my own and gave a little squeeze.

It felt so good, to have Walker there, to feed him and hear his stories and watch how easily he fit in with my family.

I was becoming jealous as the evening progressed. Michael played guitar for us around the fire, and when he asked Walker if he played, Walker had surprised us all with an affirmative. When he'd taken Mikey's guitar and strapped it on, I felt my heart leap out of my chest.

In so many ways, he was night and day different from my late husband.

And yet, in so many ways, he had the same soul.

He sang a rowdy Willie Nelson song that had us all laughing, and his eyes would catch mine with a wink when he thought no one was looking.

Of course, they always were, and just when I thought I'd be able to have some time with Walker for myself, Jordan pulled him back outside to toss the ball around with him and Paige.

It wasn't until after we'd opened gifts and dug into dessert that Walker and I finally got a moment alone. He joined me in the kitchen, nudging me aside so he could wash the dishes and I could rinse and dry.

"So, what's next on your list of adventures?" I ask as he hands me a casserole dish. He'd been regaling all of us with his worldly travels all evening, and I knew that project at the distillery was nearly complete.

"Oh, I don't know," he says, one shoulder inching up to his ears before it drops again. "Part of me is ready to slow down a bit. The other part of me worries if I stop moving, I'll croak."

I chuckle even though it isn't funny. I don't like to think about death. I suppose no one does. Then again, it's hard not to think about when your body keeps reminding you day in and day out that you're not getting any younger.

"I have a friend who lives in Florida," he adds thoughtfully, his eyes losing focus a bit as he scrubs a pan. "He has this old sailboat he's parting with. It'd need a bit of work, but... something about that calls to me."

"Owning a boat?"

"Living on one."

My eyebrows notch up. "Wow. I can't imagine that."

"Why not?"

I sigh. "Well, this old house has been my home for longer than I can remember," I say, looking around at the aging appliances, weathered floors, and cracked paint on the walls. "I've made so many memories here, and have so much... *stuff*." I shake my head, taking the pan from Walker and rinsing it. "Can't fit all this on a sailboat."

"No, probably not," Walker agrees, but then he turns off the water and wipes his hands with a dish towel, leaning a hip against the counter. "But have you ever wondered if you really need all this stuff you just referenced, or if you just hold onto it because you don't know what else to do?"

I turn those words over in my mind, wondering why they feel so heavy on my chest. I don't have time to answer the question though, not before an all-too-familiar melody spills in from the living room.

"Wonderful Tonight" by Eric Clapton.

I close my eyes on a smile, inhaling a deep breath that makes my heart ache. When my eyes open again, I find that Walker has stepped aside, and Jordan is in front of me with one hand extended for mine.

I let him guide me to the living room, but every step of the way, I'm hit with memories of my first dance with John at our wedding decades ago to this very song. We used to dance to it after dinner, every night, as a little renewal of vows between us. It didn't matter if one of us was mad, or if one of the boys was misbehaving and driving us crazy. No matter what, we danced after dinner.

It always seemed to solve all our problems.

Since John passed, my boys have taken up the tradition, dancing with me after every dinner I host with them here at the house.

They make me proud in so many ways, but none more so than this.

Jordan sways with me for the first bit of the song, smiling down at me with a mixture of understanding, joy, and heartbreaking sadness. It isn't long before Noah takes his place, and then Logan, and finally Michael.

My youngest son and I both get a bit emotional when he takes over, knowing he will be having his own first dance in less than a week with Kylie. They've been best friends since they were kids, and now, they'd be united in love under God forevermore.

I only let one tear fall, one I swipe away as Michael brings me in for a hug. There's still a little bit of the song left, but when Mikey returns to where Kylie is at the dining table, I move to turn it off.

I don't make it to the stereo before Walker is there in front of me, one hand behind his back and the other extended for mine in an offering.

I swear, I feel everyone in that house holding their breath as I stare at that hand, at that *man* who swung into my life so unexpectedly and reminded me what it feels like to flood with heat. I feel that heat now, bubbling up my spine and coloring my cheeks as I slide my hand into his.

He pulls me into him, keeping a respectful distance between us that he didn't bother with last night, and then he moves me into a waltz.

I nearly break down when he does.

Not because I'm thinking of John — at least, not in the way of comparison. But because in his arms, with his eyes on me the way they are now... I don't feel like the sad mom whom my boys have to take care of. I don't feel like the poor woman who never moved on from the passing of her husband.

I feel like a girl again, like I have a whole life ahead of me waiting to be lived.

And like Walker Jones is the key for me to start living it.

Chapter Seven

"**A**re you sure you don't need help cleaning up?" Logan asks for the fifth time, his wary eyes flicking to where Walker is sweeping the kitchen before they're on me again.

"Son, I love you, but if you don't get out of here and let your mother have some fun, I'm going to ground you."

That earns me a hearty laugh from Mallory, who promptly high-fives me before dragging my sulking son down the porch steps and toward their truck.

He wasn't alone in his concern for me. It had taken me quite literally shoving Noah off the porch to get him and Ruby Grace to leave. Michael had tried to pull the wedding card, saying they could use my help finalizing the seating chart. As for Jordan, he seemed to be the most understanding. He'd kissed my temple and told me to have fun.

But he'd also shaken Walker's hand in a firm grip and leaned close enough to mutter something I couldn't hear — something I would bet money on was a threat against his life, should he hurt me.

When everyone was finally gone and the house was quiet, I shut the front door on a sigh, turning to find Walker dusting his hands off and looking around to see if there was anything else to clean.

He found nothing.

And then, his eyes were on me.

"Well, you survived, and it doesn't *look* like you have any notable injuries," I joke, though my voice is laced with insecurity as I cross the living room toward where he stands next to the dining table. I fold my arms over my chest, eyes flicking between his. "Now the only question is, how fast do you want to run away?"

Walker chuckles, looking down at his boots. I wait for him to hit me with a witty joke, but instead, his eyes soften, the edges of them laced with sadness. "It was a wonderful day," he says quietly.

When he looks at me again, I see in his eyes what he must have seen in mine last night. It's a pain and a longing you can't understand unless you've felt it yourself. It's the kind of grief you wear like a tattoo only you know the meaning to.

"It made me miss a time in my life I haven't thought about in a while."

I nod, and without thinking, without wondering if it's too much, too soon, or if he will shy away from the touch, I open my arms and pull him into me, wrapping him up in a hug.

He's a little stiff at first, but then his arms wind around me, and he clutches me close to him as I wrap my arms around his neck. I have to push up onto my toes and he has to bend to make it work, but it's a hug.

And I realize it's the first hug I've had from a man who wasn't my son since John passed away.

The past twenty-four hours have been filled with so many firsts, it's almost dizzying. And yet, they're firsts that somehow feel comfortable and familiar.

How is it that this man whom I barely know at all feels like a long-lost friend finally coming home?

"What was Christmas like for you and Karina?" I ask when I pull back from the hug. While I wait for him to answer, I move into the kitchen, pouring myself a glass of red wine as I pour Walker a glass of eggnog.

There was a time I didn't drink at all. In fact, the first time I ever cared to drink was once I lost John. It started as a way to numb the pain, but somewhere along the way, I found an appreciation for a good finger of whiskey or a glass of wine.

I hand Walker the glass of eggnog, sweeping past him and into the living room to sit on the loveseat. He sinks into the cushion right next to me with a long sigh, sipping his eggnog before he answers.

"If I'm being honest, the holidays were usually quite torrential."

"Torrential," I ask on a surprised gasp that I can't mask. That was an adjective you used to describe a storm — not a holiday with your loved one. "How so? What do you mean?"

Walker wraps his hands around his glass, staring at his cup like he's lost in a memory. "When we both drank, we were no good to each other or anyone else around us. We loved each other hard, but we also fought like it was our job. We knew each other better than anyone else, but instead of using what we knew for good, we often pushed each other's buttons, and we knew *just* where to push, too. Just where to make it hurt."

He shakes his head.

"Eventually, I got tired of fighting and I sobered up. But my wife never did. She tried. But she had lived a tough life. And I think even though she loved me, there were demons she just couldn't outrun."

My heart was sinking more with every word he said.

John had been a drinker as long as I'd known him, but he was only a one or two drinks on a weekend night kind of man. On the rare occasion that he did get drunk, all it did was make him louder and sillier and more handsy.

Most times, I loved it when he got drunk. It usually led to a long, playful night under the sheets.

But the way Walker is looking at his cup now, I have a feeling his memories aren't so much the same.

"Don't get me wrong," he says, as if he can read the thoughts crossing my mind. "I love that woman with everything that I am, and I know she loved me just as fiercely until the very day she took her last breath. I still don't go a single day without thinking of her and missing her."

I nod, once again feeling a little piece of myself click back into place knowing I'm in the presence of someone who understands so acutely something that nobody else can.

"But sometimes, I wish I would have had the chance to love her sober, to know the version of us that could have existed in sobriety."

My heart cracks at his admission.

"Did you have any children together?" I ask after a moment.

"No," Walker says, and that line between his brows becomes more prominent. "We both wanted them, but it just never happened for us. Looking back now, I'm sure that all the drinking didn't help. But maybe it was a blessing. Any children we would have had would have lost their father on the same day they lost their mother." His eyes connect with mine. "I don't handle my grief quite as eloquently as you do."

That makes me laugh, and I shake my head, taking a long drink of wine before I look at him again.

"Well, I'm glad it seems eloquent now, but it wasn't always like this. I went through every stage of grief there is and made a couple of my own along the way. I was angry, I was devastated, I was numb, then I was angry again. What surprised me more than anything is that I always thought one day I would move on. I thought one day I would wake up and the pain wouldn't be there anymore."

Walker's chest rises with a little laugh. "But it always is."

"It always is."

"I think in a lot of ways, my job has been like a family to me," he says thoughtfully. "Not just the crew that I've kept over the years or the clients that I've worked for, but the actual projects themselves. I created them, you know? I have control, I have agency, and I have pride for each and every one of them. I know a lot of people like to give shit to those who love what they do for a living. There's a lot of talk around people who marry their jobs. But I think there's no better way. To have a passion for something that can also pay your bills is one of the greatest gifts in life."

I beam at him. "I think that's beautiful."

"I think *you* are beautiful."

His words suck out all the oxygen in the room, and suddenly I'm aware of how close we sit on the loveseat. I'm aware of how one hand still holds his glass, but how the other has found its way to my knee. I'm aware of how his thick, calloused fingers curl until they brush the top of the inside of my thigh. I'm aware of how his breathing has hitched a little in his throat, how his eyes are searching mine just before they drop to my lips.

Carefully, he sets his cup to the side. Then, he takes my glass of wine from my hands and does the same with it.

My heart picks up its pace when he takes my hands in his own, holding them tight and waiting until my eyes find his.

"I know you haven't even known me a full twenty-four hours yet," he says. "And I know we could probably spend a lifetime sharing everything there is to know about one another. But I also know that our lives are quite different, and I know that tonight, or maybe this week, or maybe the next two weeks — that might be all we get.

"I know your heart will always belong to another man. I'm alright with that. And I think you're alright knowing my heart was given away long ago, too."

I swallow, feeling where his thumbs brush my wrists like a searing line of electricity.

"But right now," he says, his voice low and melty like chocolate. "It's Christmas, and the lights from this tree you've decorated are reflecting in those lovely eyes of yours. Right now, your hands are warm and shaking, and my heart is about to beat right out of my chest."

He laughs a little at that, and I let out a relieved sigh of a laugh that I don't realize I need until my chest releases the pressure along with it.

"And the only thing I know," he continues. "Is that I want to kiss you."

I suck in a gasp of air at the words, at the insinuation, at the forceful desperation of a plea that wants to break from my lips.

"May I kiss you, Lorelei?"

"Yes."

I only whisper the word, but I feel it with a conviction I haven't felt in years.

As much as his speech made it feel like we're in a movie, our first kiss is nothing even close to cinematic. It's clumsy and awkward, hands fumbling to find the right place, both of us laughing a little when we can't quite get it right. Walker slides his hand into my hair and tilts my chin up, my mouth meeting his, but we meet a little too forcefully. Our teeth clang together and we laugh.

And then we kiss again.

And again, and again, slower and softer each time, both of us taking note of what the other responds to.

Before I know it, I am absolutely, wholly, completely and irrevocably caught up in a kiss with Walker Jones.

It's a first kiss with as much tenderness and passion as a last kiss.

It's a deep inhale and a sigh of an exhale and a sweep of a tongue that lights my body on fire.

It's a reawakening of my body, my heart, and my soul. It's a blatant disregard for what tomorrow brings and a desire to only live in this moment right here, *right now*, with this man I never saw coming.

The kiss is so precious to me, and I know it is for him, too, because he doesn't rush it.

There's no movement of his hands from where they cradle my face and hold me to him. There's no haste to take my clothes off or to move those hands to more forbidden areas.

Instead, it's a slow perusal of his mouth on mine, of his tongue tasting, his teeth nipping and exploring. The kisses grow longer and more needy, and his lips move from mine to travel across my jaw and up until he sucks the lobe of my ear between his teeth. Then, he leaves a trail of kisses down my neck to my collarbone before he's climbing back up again.

We kiss so long that I feel like a teenager again.

We kiss so long that my lips chap and I find myself desperate for a tall glass of water to cool me down and quench my thirst.

We kiss so long I can't begin to remember when we started kissing at all — and I can't fathom when we'll ever stop.

But somewhere in that lost span of time, I press my forehead to his, our breaths mingling in this space between us. And I ask the kind of question only an old woman feeling young again could.

"What are you doing New Year's Eve?"

"Can't say that I have a single plan."

I smile, smoothing my thumbs over the stubble on his jaw.

"How would you like to be my date to a wedding?"

Chapter Eight

Ten things I've learned about Walker Jones in the last week.

Number one: he is a good kisser.

No, this man is a *phenomenal* kisser.

I know that because in the last week, not a single day has gone by without me getting the privilege of having this man's mouth on mine. And in that week, I have learned that Walker Jones takes his time with every kiss he gives.

There's never a rush. There's never a feeling like he has his mind on anything or anyone other than me. I thought he made me feel like a girl again, but the truth is he makes me feel like a *muse*.

Like I'm all he wants.

Number two: Walker Jones is knowledgeable in the most bizarre array of subjects because he is the most curious man I have ever met.

Every evening, after we've returned from our little adventures around town and our voices are hoarse from talking too much, when we're content to let the quiet settle in around us — he always has a book in his hand.

If not a book, then a documentary pulled up on his iPad. And if neither of those, an article in a magazine or newspaper spread between his hands.

His thirst for knowledge is unquenchable.

And if there's anything more attractive than the way he looks when he kisses me, it's the way he looks when he discovers something new.

Number three: Walker Jones is an amazing contractor.

In this week between Christmas and New Year's, he has given his crew time off to visit their families and go back home. But for *him*, the work has not stopped.

Other than Christmas Day, which he spent with my family, he has been at the distillery, moving the expansion along and ensuring they don't fall behind schedule. And as much as I admire that hard work ethic and care for his employees, I admire the fact that he doesn't take life too seriously even more.

Because any afternoon that I wanted to pull him away, any morning that I wanted him to stay longer with me, any evening I wanted to keep him up far too late — he was more than happy to do so.

Life moves slower with Walker Jones in the most peaceful and soul-filling way.

Number four: Walker Jones is a great dancer.

Number five: Walker Jones drinks his coffee black and likes his eggs scrambled and piled with cheese.

Number six: Walker Jones likes to cuddle.

Number seven: Walker Jones likes to *only* cuddle.

He's a gentleman, through and through — something that has allowed me to feel more comfortable than I ever thought I could with a man who isn't John.

I have felt Walker's body pressed against mine, know the way he curls around me in the late evening and the early morning. But this man has never pushed me to do anything more than exist in his presence. More than that — it genuinely feels like, for him, that's enough.

Number eight: Walker Jones would have been a great father.

I know this because in the last week I have watched him interact with my family in a way only the best of fathers could. I've watched him throw the ball with my granddaughter and give advice to my sons who are running a multi-million-dollar distillery. I've watched him sit in patience with my youngest grandchild as if he has nowhere else to be, and I've watched him protectively dote on my two pregnant daughters-in-law as if they were his own daughters.

He has slipped into our family as if he's always been there, as if we've had a spot with his name on it just waiting for him to drop in.

Number nine: Walker Jones has the power to shift everything — as if he were magical or favored by God. And I know this because...

Number ten: Walker Jones is making me fall in love with him.

But to be honest, he hasn't had to try very hard.

Because I could list out one hundred different truths about this man, and it would never be enough to explain the feeling I have now that I know he exists, now that I get the chance to exist *with* him.

It's as if our souls have been dancing around each other all our lives, just waiting for the right time to come together.

Now that we have, it doesn't matter if everyone thinks we're crazy or doesn't understand. It doesn't matter that it's only been a week.

What matters is that I see myself in this man, and he sees himself in me, and all those aching, empty, hollow parts of us that we've been carrying with ourselves for years are suddenly starting to fill with the most glorious golden light.

It's exciting in a way nothing else can be, and it's also the most terrifying thing I've ever experienced.

Because Walker Jones is making me fall in love with him.

And I know that, one day, he will leave.

Chapter Nine

"Okay, no, you stop that right now," I warn, wagging a finger at my future daughter-in-law. I can barely see her through the bleariness of my watering eyes. "*I'm* allowed to cry, but you, my dear, are not!"

"But you look so *beautiful*," she blubbers, covering her mouth with her hands.

"That's supposed to be my line!"

We both laugh at that, and then I'm sweeping Kylie up in my arms before pulling back to get a good look at her.

She's stunning.

Her dark hair is pulled back into an elegant up-do, her delicate collarbones accented in the strapless mermaid dress she's donning. It's a cream satin, rouched at the hip and hugging her thighs all the way down to her knees before it drapes in a beautiful train. Pearls line the top edge of her sweetheart neckline, and they drape down over the bodice and flow over the skirt like starlight. On the chair behind her, a white, faux-fur shawl is draped and ready to keep her warm.

"Oh, honey," I say, thumbing the tear from her cheek when it falls. I'm careful not to smudge her makeup. "My boy is going to bawl his eyes out when he sees you walking down that aisle."

She laughs a little at that, but then her bottom lip is wobbling. "I wish Mama was here."

"Oh, sweetie. I know. I know." I grip her to me then, closing my eyes as emotion threatens to take me down.

Because I know my son is thinking the same thing about his father.

It was one of the things that brought these two together, the shared experiences of losing a parent far too young. I hate that they both had to endure that loss, but I'm thankful they could weather that storm together.

"Well, we better get into place," a friendly voice says, and I turn to find Kylie's father with evidence of his own tears on his worn face. I pass Kylie's hand to him, squeezing them both before I head to the opposite side of the house to meet Michael.

The wedding is taking place at a beautiful home in the country on the edge of town, one with a giant barn we've turned into the reception space, and a grand oak tree with a sprawling view of the mountains behind it where Michael and Kylie will exchange vows.

I find Michael right where I left him, wringing his hands and reciting his vows to himself in the groom's dressing room. He laughs a little when I join him, shaking his head.

"I'm a mess."

I don't say it out loud, but all I can think is *just wait until you see her.*

"Come here," I say instead, and I hug him tight. Then, I walk over to my purse and I pull out a slim box.

"What's this?" Michael asks when I hand it to him.

"Open it."

When he does, his eyes water, and he covers his mouth with a hand, shaking his head. "These are Dad's."

I nod, taking the cuff links from the box. I take one of his wrists, unfastening the links that he picked up on sale in New York and replacing them with the worn ones from the box.

"He wore these on our wedding day," I tell Michael, affixing the other one before I let him study them. "And on other special occasions, too. I know he would have wanted you to have them."

My youngest son's jaw is tight as he looks up at the ceiling, and he closes his eyes, shaking his head before his eyes open and find me again. "God, I miss him."

"I know, baby," I say, hugging him again. "I do, too. But he's here with us. I can feel it."

There's a gentle knock at the door, and then my breath hitches.

Because Walker Jones is on the other side of that door looking hotter than sin.

He's wearing an all-black suit, his dress shirt a light gray beneath it. It matches the gray of his hair and the scruff on his face. His cowboy hat is a bright cream with a black velvet strip of fabric around the rim, and when I realize he's wearing a sharp pair of cowboy boots with that suit, I swear I melt into a puddle of goop.

"You look like the taller, more fit, more handsome version of John Dutton."

I don't realize I say the words out loud until Walker chuffs a laugh with his neck reddening, and Michael groans.

"Mom," he chastises, but it's with a smile, and I pinch his side before making my way to Walker.

"And you look like an angel from heaven," he says, kissing the top of my hand.

For a moment, we just stand there staring at one another, and all I can think about is how I can't wait for this man to twirl me around the dance floor tonight.

There's another knock, and then the preacher sticks his head in. "It's time."

By the time I walk down the aisle with my arm looped through Michael's, my other sons are already at the oak tree altar with the preacher . I smile as they all fight back their emotions, their chins wobbling as they sniff and look up at the sky.

They're just like their father — rough around the edges, but soft as goo inside.

It's the most perfect golden hour I've ever seen, the sun streaming over the field and the barn with the shadowy mountains serving as a silhouetted background.

I kiss Michael's cheek when we reach the end, thumbing away the lipstick I leave there before I take a seat next to Walker.

As soon as I do, he wraps my hand in his, giving it a gentle squeeze and settling our clasped hands on my knee.

They stay there the entire ceremony.

And just like I predicted — Michael cries like a baby the second he sees Kylie.

Chapter Ten

The wedding reception is a Becker party — through and through.

Half the town is in attendance, and by the time the sun fully sets and gives way to the bright moon and stars, the barn is bumping.

The event staff clear dinner away and move tables aside, and the middle of the barn is transformed into a dance floor. Line dance after line dance has every guest sweating despite the cold night, and the drinks flow in a steady stream — mostly from small batch Scooter Whiskey barrels.

Walker keeps me on the dance floor all night long.

Whether we're two-stepping, line dancing, or just swaying gently side to side in a slow song, that man is insatiable when it comes to dancing with me. The only breaks we take are for the cake cutting, the speeches, and when Michael pulls out his guitar to play a song he wrote for Kylie.

He does have to share me, though.

Each of my sons take a turn dancing with me throughout the night. Noah teaches me some popular dance to a hip-hop song that I can't quite keep up with, but we both laugh as I try. Logan takes his turn with me in a two-step. And Jordan cuts in for a slow song, not saying a word as we sway, but his eyes tell me everything he doesn't say out loud.

He's happy for me.

My heart is so full by the time the night begins to slow. The last song is "Wonderful Tonight," which surprises absolutely no one. As soon as it starts to play, Michael takes me to the dance floor, and I sway with him for the first verse before Logan cuts in and Mikey dances with Kylie, instead.

One by one, my sons dance with me through the song that their father once did. I remember a time when hearing the familiar melody of that first guitar rift would make me burst into tears. Now, it's comforting in the way nothing else in my life is.

My boys did that for me.

Walker slides in for the very last part of the song, and just like he did on Christmas Day, he sways me under the lights with reverence in his eyes. I don't have to ask to know he's thinking about his Karina just as I'm thinking about my John.

But at the same time, our eyes are locked on each other.

How strange, to feel connected to someone through such a specific kind of loss, to know you never have to explain yourself.

You're always understood.

You're always safe to feel exactly what you need to feel.

When the wedding planner starts handing out sparklers for Michael and Kylie's exit, I can't help but look around at all our family and friends gathered together, and my eyes brim with tears yet again.

"You alright there, darling?"

I close my eyes at the endearment, at how nice it makes me feel. Then, I lean into Walker's chest, smiling up at him. "I'm the best I've been in decades."

He smiles knowingly at me, kissing my hair before pulling me tight under his arm.

We all cheer and hold our sparklers in a high arch for the newlyweds, holding the excitement all the way until they duck into an old vintage car and speed away into the night. They leave for their honeymoon bright and early in the morning, and once the car is gone, I look up to the stars sparkling in the dark sky above.

We did good, John. Our boys are okay.

A cool breeze whips through my hair then, and I smile, closing my eyes and soaking in the feel of it.

I can always feel him.

But tonight, I feel him a little more than usual.

Once the car is gone, the guests begin to gather their belongings and head out as the event staff takes care of the cleanup. The lights come on in the barn, the not-so-subtle sign that we don't have to go home — but we can't stay here.

Walker sweeps my hair behind my ear where it's fallen loose from the bun at the nape of my neck, and he smiles down at me, his eyes searching every inch of my face as if he's seeing me for the first time.

"Thank you for letting me share this night with you."

I lean into his warm, rough palm. "Care to share a bit more of it?"

His eyes flash with hunger, and he nods. "It would be my honor," he says, and then his eyes flick behind me, and he offers a rue smile. "I'll get our things from inside and let you say your goodnights."

He presses a soft kiss to my temple before releasing me, and I turn to find Logan, Noah, and Jordan approaching with wary gazes.

I hug each of them when they make it to me, squeezing their arms and looking up at them with pride beaming out of my chest.

"I'm so proud of you," I say to each of them. "Your father would be proud, too."

That gets Logan, who looks away from me to gather himself.

Then, Noah steps in, taking one of my hands in his and squeezing it. "We love you, Mom," he says, and then he looks at his brothers, who nod at him before he continues. "And we want you to know that you deserve to be happy."

I frown a little. "Well, thank you."

"*Walker* makes you happy, Mom," Jordan clarifies, his hands sliding into the pockets of his slacks. "We all see it. We saw it that very first day at Christmas. We've seen it all week. And tonight, I think it clicked for all of us that this is the happiest we've seen you since Dad passed."

My heart cracks with his words, but I'm smiling despite them, because it's true.

"He's a good man," I whisper.

"We agree," Logan says, and he takes Noah's place, pulling me in for a hug.

Jordan gets in a big hug next. "We love you."

"I love you all, too," I whisper back, squeezing him tight before I look at all three of them. "So, so much."

"Now," Noah says, clearing his throat as Walker joins us. "You two have fun tonight. But Mr. Jones," he adds, his voice stern, chest puffing as he stands a little taller. "The three of us want to have a talk with you about your intentions with our mother."

Logan and Jordan nod, brows furrowed and serious.

And I bust out laughing, the force of the laugh rattling through my chest in the sweetest way.

"I think my sons forgot just who the parent is here," I say, looping my arm through Walker's and giving them all a pointed look. "Good*night*, boys."

Walker tips his hat at them, winking down at me with a knowing grin.

And then he takes me home.

Chapter Eleven

My hands are shaking so badly, I fumble with my keys for what feels like an eternity before I finally unlock my front door.

It's dark inside the house until I flip the switch, which lights up only the Christmas tree. Its comforting glow soothes me a bit as I step inside.

As Walker follows behind.

"Sorry, I didn't get a chance to clean," I say when I drop my purse and keys on the small table by the door.

Walker drops his own keys and wallet next, removing his hat and placing it on a hook. "I'm not worried about a clean house, Lorelei."

My heart kicks up a notch.

"And it's so cold in here. Let me turn up the heat."

I move to the thermostat, and then immediately make my way to the kitchen.

"I'll make us some drinks," I offer, and then I open the fridge and see I don't have anything other than milk and orange juice. I'd intended to go shopping tomorrow, after the excitement wore down.

Walker joins me in the kitchen, standing behind where I'm still looking in the fridge.

"I'm not worried about a drink, either."

I shudder at the low rumble of his voice, and then my nerves kick in, and I shut the fridge door and rush to the fireplace.

"It's so *cold*," I say, unable to look at Walker as I fuss with the logs. "Let me start a fire."

I only get a couple loaded in before big, warm arms wrap around me from behind, and Walker pulls me flush to his chest.

"I'm not worried about a fire," he says, his breath hot on my neck. He presses a soft kiss there next, smiling against my skin. "Something tells me we can warm up all on our own."

My heart nearly bursts out of my chest, it gallops so fast.

I turn in his arms, looking up at him and praying he can't hear how ragged my breaths are.

But Walker just smiles more, his knuckles running the line of my jaw before he notches my chin up a bit. "You're nervous."

"Like I'm about to give the Inaugural Speech at the White House."

He barks out a laugh at that, and the sound releases some of the tension inside me. I chuckle, too, before burying my head in his chest.

"I'm sorry."

"Don't be," he says. He waits until I look up at him again before adding, "I'm nervous, too."

"Really?"

He nods, more serious then, and I note how his throat constricts with a swallow.

"But I want to," he clarifies quickly.

"I do, too," I confess, and electricity hums under my veins with the admission.

Walker tilts my chin again, and this time, he lowers his mouth to mine, making me melt with one long, slow, passionate kiss.

"You set the pace, darling," he whispers against my lips, and then he kisses me again, and a little more tension unravels when he does.

I sigh, threading my arms up and around his neck as I lean into his touch. For a while, we kiss softly and unhurriedly just like that.

But then, his tongue sweeps in, washing over mine as a low, needy groan rumbles through him.

The sound beckons my own need to the surface.

I moan, pressing up on my toes to deepen the kiss.

And just like Walker said — we don't need a damn fire to get warm.

I can hear my pulse in my ears as I kick out of my kitten heels, and then I grab Walker by the tie and begin walking backward toward my bedroom. He kisses me every step of the way, until the backs of my knees hit the edge of my bed and we both pause.

Forehead to forehead, our breaths mingling in-between us, we begin to undress.

I unfasten his tie, and he unzips my dress. He shrugs out of his suit jacket, and I shimmy my panty hose down to the floor. He kicks off his boots and unbuttons the top of his slacks, and I try not to completely freak out as I slide my dress down one shoulder and then the next.

Piece by piece, we bare ourselves — and yet, I feel like this isn't even the most naked we've been together.

Sure, I can see every inch of him now, from his silver hair-dusted chest to his long, thick erection. But this is nothing compared to when he's shown me his soul, to when he's shared stories of his past and laid out his scars for me to dissect.

And I've done the same for him.

So, I feel no shame when I unclasp my bra and let it fall to my feet. I don't shy away when I slide my panties down next.

I'm naked in front of a man for the first time in more than fourteen years.

But I also feel safer than I ever have before.

Walker swallows when I'm nude, and even in the dim lighting of my bedroom illuminated only by the Christmas tree lights making their way down the hall to us, I watch him taking in every inch of me.

He shakes his head, his eyes finding mine in the darkness. "You're beautiful."

He lays me down then, helping me under the sheets before he climbs in with me. Chills of anticipation race along my spine when he crawls between my legs, nestling himself on top of me and covering me with his warmth.

For a long, lovely moment, we exist just like that. We kiss and explore, my hands traveling over his back and down to his behind while he gently removes pins from my hair.

Then, I thread my hands in his hair and pull him to me, until our foreheads are touching again. I kiss him long and slow, and I whisper my only wish.

"Make love to me, Walker."

He closes his eyes on a long, slow exhale as if he's pained to hear those words. But then he's kissing me again, and our bodies are rolling together under the sheets, desperate for friction.

Walker kisses his way down my body, and when his lips close over each of my budding nipples, I gasp and bow off the bed.

It's overwhelming, the sensations throbbing through me at being touched again for the first time since my husband passed away. It feels different with Walker, of course — but not in a way that has me measuring them against one another.

He's all-consuming.

He owns me in this moment — mind, body, and spirit.

There is no one else.

His lips travel farther down, and I hitch in a stiff breath when I realize where he's heading. My heart thumps loud and fast in my chest as I lean up to watch him, and the moment he kisses between the apex of my thighs, I moan, dropping back into the pillows.

"Oh, my," I manage, but beyond that, I have no words.

I have no words for how Walker takes his time tasting me, how he explores every possible combination of his mouth with his hand until he finds what drives me wild.

I'm shocked silent still as he crawls back up to kiss me, and I taste myself on his tongue as he slides his length inside me.

We both groan when he does, him holding fast to me as my nails bite into the flesh of his shoulders.

Slowly, he works into a rhythm, carefully fitting himself inside me until we're both moving together.

I nearly cry, it feels so good. My body rejoices at the wave of pleasure already rushing through me, at how incredible it feels to be wanted, to be touched, to be desired in this manner.

We both move at a slow, steady pace for a long while, Walker planting kisses along my jaw and on my mouth as I feel him flex in and out. Then, my desire turns bolder, and I press on his chest until he climbs off and allows me to take the reins.

"Good God, woman," he says when I straddle him, reaching down to fit him inside me once more. His voice is a rumbling prayer as his hands fasten around my hips and help me ride. "You are sensational."

I beam under his praise, and then I ride him — slow at first, and then with more gusto.

And I count my lucky stars when Walker drops his hand between my legs, rubbing me in the perfect spot to help me find my climax.

This was the benefit of waiting for a real man — he knew just what to do to unravel me.

And unravel I do.

I roll and buck and ride out every last wave of my orgasm as it crashes over me, reveling in the release. And when I finish, Walker follows right behind me, groaning my name in a way that lights me up inside like nothing else.

I feel whole again.

I feel... *everything.*

We both laugh a little once we come down, and Walker pulls me to him for a bruising kiss. Then, he's helping me off him, and he takes my hand in his and pulls me into the shower.

He runs the water hot, ushering me inside and then stepping in after. I sigh happily as he runs a hot cloth over my skin, cleaning me, and then he reaches for my shampoo and lathers it in his hands before moving those hands to my skull.

I feel so pampered and loved as that hot water runs over my skin and his thick fingers massage my scalp.

When he's finished, I return the favor.

And when we're both clean, Walker kisses me as the water cascades down my back, and I smirk against his kiss when I feel him growing hard against my stomach.

"We're not twenty somethings," I warn him in a tease.

"Indeed, we are not," he agrees.

Then, he cuts the water, wraps me in a towel, and a surprised laugh rips from me when he manages to heave me into his arms and carry me back to bed.

"But we can act like we are tonight," he says.

And I'm tossed onto the mattress for another round.

Chapter Twelve

The next day, Walker helps me take down all the Christmas decorations.

I drink a mimosa and he drinks orange juice as we laugh and share stories, him taking care of the tree while I carefully box up lights and ornaments. We only get about an hour of work done before we're making love on the couch, and then we're back to it — until the house is void of Christmas cheer and ready for a new year to begin.

I always spend the first day of the year making a list of three things I want to accomplish. Walker, on the other hand, simply picks a word he wants to encompass.

My three goals are to travel to a new place, to finish the quilt I started in November, and to try something that scares me.

Walker's word is *passion*.

"Passion, huh?" I tease him when he tells me, waggling my brows as I thread my arms around his neck and kiss his chin.

"Passion," he echoes. "For life. For adventure." He smirks then, attacking my neck with aggressive kisses, his scruff tickling me into an unbidden fit of laughter. When I settle, his eyes search mine. "And for you."

The magic of the holidays carries over into the new year, even as Walker's crew comes back into town to work on the final needs of the expansion project. I go back to work, too, serving on the board for the distillery.

I may or may not find excuses to visit the construction site.

Someone's got to oversee it and make sure things are being done right.

A week fades, and then two, and then three, January ready to give way to February. Ruby Grace blesses our family with a new member, Sydney ready to pop any day now, and Michael and Kylie return to New York City to continue chasing their dreams.

Walker and I spend every day and night together.

At first, it was just how it was that week of the holidays. Either I would be with him at his hotel, or he would be with me at the house, or we'd be exploring around town. He would leave a change of clothes and a toothbrush at my place. Then, he'd leave a pair of boots and a coat, too.

Eventually, it just doesn't make sense for him to be in the hotel anymore. Eventually, he brings his suitcase, and checks out of that hotel altogether.

On the first of February, we have an uncharacteristically warm and sunny day sweep over Stratford. By the time noon hits, it's fifty-three degrees, and Walker and I decide to make the most of it.

Noah and Ruby Grace have a barn on the edge of town. One horse belongs to Noah, one to Ruby Grace, and several others to residents of the town who rent the space, food, and care Noah and his stable hands provide. One quick call has Noah in action, and by the time Walker and I get to the barn, Noah's groom has two horses saddled up and ready for us.

The sun beams down on us as we ride toward the river, the warmth of it welcome on my cheeks. Walker rides right beside me, his jacket open and letting in a bit of the cool air to combat the heat from the sun.

"Do you miss Texas?" I ask when we reach the riverbank and begin to ride alongside it.

"All the time."

"Really?"

He nods, the reins loose in his hands as he gives trust to the horse.

"What do you miss most?"

Walker lets out a long breath. "Oh, all sorts of things. The Tex-Mex. The heat. The way the plains look in the early morning light. The sound of the Gulf, the waves crashing softly on the shore."

"I think I'd miss that, too. Does it ever make you not want to leave?"

"No," he says, and the word is drawn out on a long, low laugh. "I'm too thirsty for adventure to stay put for too long. But missing Texas is part of the journey. We all get a little homesick sometimes, don't we?"

"I wouldn't know," I confess, letting go of the reins long enough to unwrap my scarf from around my neck and tie it to the saddle. "It's been so long since I've left Stratford. I mean, I helped Michael and Kylie get settled in New York when they first moved, but even that was overwhelming to me. I couldn't wait to get home." I pause. "Haven't left since."

Walker studies me for a moment. "I saw one of your goals for the new year is to travel to a new place."

I can't explain it, but fear spikes in my chest when he says those words.

"Oh, sure," I say, trying to laugh it off. "But I meant maybe a neighboring town, or maybe somewhere across the state. The aquarium in Chattanooga is supposed to be one of the best there is. I think I'd like to see that."

I smile, but when I look over to where Walker was riding beside me, I realize he's not there.

I pull my horse to a stop, turning us around to find that Walker has stopped a few yards behind us.

"That's not what you meant," he challenges.

My neck heats, but I don't deny it.

Walker hops down off the saddle, walking his horse away from the water until he finds a tree. He ties her up, and I follow suit, letting my horse rest right next to his.

Then, Walker takes my hand in his, and we stroll the beach.

"Lorelei, can I ask you something?"

I nod, though my heart is racing, my flight-or-fight instinct kicking in without me knowing why.

"What's holding you here in Stratford?"

I balk at the question. "What do you mean *holding me here*?" I shake my head. "I want to be here. Three of my boys live here. My *grandchildren* live here. My job is here."

"Do you like your job?"

I consider his question. "I like it well enough."

"What do you like about it?"

That it makes me feel connected to John.

The words don't make it out of my mouth, but they stop me in my tracks, my heart pounding with the realization that they're how I feel.

I was honored to take the rightful ownership our family had of the distillery once the truth about the late founder's will came out. But the truth was, I had never wanted to work — period. My kids have always been my life. Being home with them while they grew up meant everything to me.

It was John who loved the distillery.

Taking it over was *his* dream.

So, it felt like I was honoring him when I accepted the offer, when I decided to work alongside my sons and the mayor's ex-wife, Mary. She was one of my best friends once, before everything went sideways.

But again, that's a story for another time.

When I don't answer, Walker takes my hands in his, waiting until my eyes flick up to meet his before he says a word.

"My job is almost done here," he reminds me, as if that thought hasn't run across my mind a hundred times since we first met. "Just a couple more weeks, and I'll be out of here."

I nod, swallowing down the lump in my throat.

"I'm going back to Texas just long enough to get my affairs in order, and then I'm taking the bit of money I've saved up and I'm buying a sailboat."

My eyes widen.

"Passion," he reminds me. "For life, for adventure, for *you*. I've seen many things in this world. I've seen mountains and seas and deserts. But you know what I haven't seen yet?"

He pulls me closer, kissing my knuckles.

"I haven't seen the way you look when you wake up on a boat. I haven't seen the sea breeze play with your hair. I haven't seen your skin glowing under the sun with turquoise waters all around us."

"Walker," I warn.

"Come with me, Lorelei."

I close my eyes at the words, but he squeezes my hands until I look at him again.

"Sail around the world with me. Or, hell, not even around the world. We can go to the Bahamas. Or Mexico. We can go up north to the shores of Maine. We can go anywhere you want. I'll be the Captain, you'll be my First Mate."

I'm already shaking my head, and I see the desperation in Walker's eyes as he frames my face with his worn hands.

"God put us together in that bar on Christmas Eve for a reason," he says with conviction. "I think we have both been wandering through life like ghosts after losing our spouses. We've been floating by, letting time pass, but we haven't been living." He swallows, his eyes searching mine. "I want to change that. I want to start living, right here, right now. With you."

I close my eyes, and I don't realize they were welling with tears until I set them free with that blink.

There's a part of me, deep down, that wants to leap into his arms and say *yes*. That part of me is jumping up and down right now, screaming, throwing its hands in the air and waving for me to acknowledge it.

But the stronger part of me, the one I've trusted for far longer, is stubborn and still and digging its heels into the ground.

It's silencing everything else.

"I can't."

Walker's shoulders deflate at my words, and I pry my hands from his, sniffing and walking hastily over to my horse. I untie it from the tree, mounting it without help from Walker — which surprises even me.

"I can't leave," I clarify, my eyes meeting his. "And I can't believe you would ask me to."

"You can't believe I would want to spend the rest of my life, however long that may be, with you?"

Tears prick my eyes again, my heart bucking against my chest in a desperate plea for me to hear it out. "We knew when we met that this wouldn't last forever," I try to reason, but the argument sounds weak even to my own ears. "What if the shoe was on the other foot, Walker? What if I asked you to stay in Stratford with me?"

"Ask me," he says. There's not an ounce of hesitation, and he walks right up to my saddle, his gaze cast up toward me. "Ask me, Lorelei, and I'll give you my answer in a heartbeat."

But I don't have to ask. I see it in his eyes.

He would.

For reasons I can't explain yet, that makes panic slide down my spine like ice water.

My feet feel almost numb as I blink, shaking my head, and then the reins are pulled tight in my hands without me willing them to do so.

"I can't do this," I whisper.

Walker sees the panic in my eyes, and he softens, reaching up for me. "Lorelei, I'm sorry. Let's—"

"Please, don't follow me," I manage.

And then I dig my heels in just enough to make my horse start carrying me back toward the barn.

Chapter Thirteen

Mary Scooter sits across from me at the little café in town the next morning, her eyes sympathetic as she sips her coffee and mulls over everything I just told her.

She's the closest thing I have to a friend here in Stratford, other than my kids and their wives, of course. But our past is murky, years of darkness shadowing the bright ones. We used to be inseparable when we were younger, but a series of unfortunate events led to us growing apart, and then downright hating each other before we found an understanding and, eventually, a new kind of friendship.

I called her first thing this morning and asked her to meet, because as much as I love my boys, I need advice from someone who will give it to me straight, someone who won't make a face when I tell them about the more intimate details of mine and Walker's relationship.

"Well," she starts after a while. "I knew something was different about you, but I never would have guessed all this."

She smiles, setting her coffee down and leaning over the table between us.

"Why did you run, you silly thing?"

I blink at her. "You're joking, right?"

"Not in the slightest! Honey, this man is gorgeous. He's kind. He's generous. He gets along with your family. He cares about you. He wants to take you to the *Bahamas*, for goodness' sake!" She laughs a little, shaking her head as if I'm crazy not to see it. "What is there to run from?"

I bite my lip, the answer to that burning my chest and begging to be free. But I'm scared of saying it out loud.

I think I'm scared because I know how pitiful it will sound.

"I can't just leave Stratford," I say instead. "What about the distillery?"

"What *about* it?" she echoes back. "I sold my share of that thing last year, remember? And you know what? I'm glad I did. That gave me enough money to live on for the rest of my life, and now I'm free of a place that has had its dirty hands around my neck for far too long."

Given the history of her ex-husband, Patrick Scooter, and the awful crimes he committed in his desperation to own and direct that distillery the way his father had, I don't blame Mary for wanting nothing to do with it.

But it's different for me.

"John loved that place," I remind her softly. "I think he loved it more than everything, other than me and the boys."

"I want you to say that again, but re-arrange the words."

I frown, confused.

"John Becker loved you and your boys above everything else," she says, smiling as her hands wrap around mine on the table. "Honey, do you think he'd want you to tie yourself to the place where he perished? Do you think he wants you to relive that memory every time you go to work? Do you think he wants you to work *at all* when you could cash in and go live a little?"

My heart skips a beat before kicking into a chaotic pace.

"Sell your share to Noah and Logan," she says. "Let *them* run it. They love it. They belong there. They have made that distillery better than it's ever been. It's *their* passion, Lorelei. Not yours."

Passion.

The word makes every cell in my body hum and vibrate.

"The house," I murmur.

"Give it to the boys," she says without hesitation. "They can use it as a vacation rental or just keep it in good shape for when you visit."

"Paige," I say next, referencing my oldest granddaughter. "And Tamara, and Bentley, and—"

"All your grandbabies will be here when you come back to visit," Mary says firmly. "Which you will. All the time. And every time you do, you'll have new stories to tell, new adventures to share, new photos to pester them all with. They'll get excited and tell their friends when you come to town. They'll be like, 'Oh, here comes Nana Becker with her crazy stories again. I can't wait to hear where she's been since we last saw her. Do you think she brought us some gifts?'"

"Like I'd ever come back empty-handed."

"See!"

Mary laughs a little, and a smile finds my lips even as I shake my head, my heart threatening to break out of my ribcage.

"Just hearing you talk like that scares the living hell out of me, Mary."

"Because it's new, and exciting, and you have no idea what to expect," she says. "And because you know if John were right here in my place, if it were him sitting across from you?" Her eyes soften. "He'd tell you to go, too. In fact, he'd probably pack for you, if he could."

I chuckle at that, my eyes flooding with tears.

"He would, and you know it!" Mary smiles. "You have lived your whole life for other people, Lorelei Becker. You've been a great friend, an amazing wife, a *phenomenal* mother to four incredible boys who are doing just fine now. And the only thing you have left to do is show your grandkids that life doesn't stop when we go through grief. Show them that age doesn't mean a damn thing. Show them that we have a choice to live right up until we take our very last breath." She squeezes my hands. "Show *yourself* that you deserve to be happy, that you deserve a second chance at life, and that you deserve a man like Walker Jones to dote on you and take you to see the world."

The tears blurring my eyes well over and fall, and I sniff, batting them away.

"I know you're a woman of faith just like I am, Lorelei. And let me tell you something. If this isn't God talking? If this isn't John sending you a gift and a sign and a message?" She shakes her head. "Then I don't know what is."

My heart beats faster, but this time, it isn't being chased by panic.

It's lighting up with an excitement I haven't felt in years.

"The distillery will be fine. Your boys are *more* than fine. And this town will still be here whenever you need to feel it. But God is offering you the chance not to start over, but to take a different path, to walk a new road that he's been waiting for the right moment to reveal to you."

Mary rolls her lips together on a little shrug.

"The choice is yours, Lor," she says as she releases my hands and sits back in the booth, bringing her coffee to her lips. "Make sure you make it with love in your heart — not fear."

Chapter Fourteen

Two weeks later, I sit at the kitchen table with my boys.

Noah has his feet on the old, scratched wood, and Logan is lecturing him about all the ways that's disrespectful, not only to me, but to the furniture itself. Noah does nothing but goad his younger brother, even going so far as to move his feet closer to his brother, which makes Logan nearly crawl out of his skin in an attempt to get away.

Jordan mostly ignores him, his focus on his son resting peacefully in his arms. Sydney is taking a nap back at their place, savoring the quiet house that won't last long with a newborn.

Michael is smiling at his newest nephew through the screen of my laptop, his New York City apartment in the background. He has a show tonight, so he's freshly showered and shaved.

My heart nearly swells out of my chest at the sight of them all gathered at the table.

So many memories were born right here in this room. So many dinners, food fights, arguments and reconciliations. We've shared countless holidays, countless tears, countless laughs.

I close my eyes and smile, breathing all those memories in.

Then, I gather the binder and keys I've been hiding on the chair next to me and set them right in the middle of the table.

The boys quiet, sharing glances before Noah puts his feet on the floor and leans forward, grabbing the binder.

"What's this?"

"That," I say. "Is the deed to this home."

Logan takes the binder from Noah. "Okay…"

"And those are most of the spare keys — save for the ones I'll keep, of course."

Jordan's brows furrow. "I'm confused."

"This has our names on it," Logan says, flipping through the pages.

"It does. And, if it's alright with y'all, I'd like you to sign and accept it. Mary is a notary and I'll take it to her next to deal with the legal side of it all. But right now, I need a signature from all of you except Michael, whom I left off the deed only because I knew he wouldn't be able to fly in on such short notice. But he's just as much an owner as the rest of you, understand?"

"No," Noah barks, shaking his head and ripping the binder out of Logan's hand. "Mom, what the hell is going on?"

"Walker Jones is coming to pick me up," I say, checking the time on the clock behind his head. "Any minute now, actually. And we're skipping town."

"Skipping town," Michael echoes. "To go... where, exactly?"

I shrug. "Who knows!" That makes me laugh, and I sit back in my chair with a goofy schoolgirl grin. "The Bahamas, we think. But maybe farther south. Maybe north to Maine. All we know for now is that we'll be on a boat." I pause, taking a deep breath. "Together."

Silence falls over the house, and for a moment, I think Noah might blow a gasket.

But his older brother holds up one strong hand to silence him, the other still cradling his son to his chest.

"So, you're leaving," he says.

"I am."

"And you're signing the deed of the house over to us."

"I am," I repeat. "I know you'll take good care of it. Use it for your friends when they visit, or rent it out to tourists. Make it a distillery experience. I don't care, as long as you save room in it for me when I come home — or at one of your houses, should you decide to sell this one."

"All your stuff," Logan says, but doesn't quite finish the sentence. He just waves a hand around at all the furniture and knick-knacks and wall art and everything else I'm leaving behind.

"Yours," I say.

There's another long pause, and then Michael speaks up. "Are you... are you dying?"

"Oh, sweetie!" I laugh, reaching for the screen. "No. I am just fine. Well, I guess we're all *technically* dying, a little each day, really. But no. This isn't about me dying. This is about me *living*."

Jordan softens a bit at that. "You and Walker are going to see the world together."

"That's the plan."

"And the distillery?" Logan asks.

"I already spoke with the board. I've signed my shares over to you and Noah — split evenly between the two."

"Holy shit," Michael says.

"Language," I chastise, but it's on another little laugh. "Oh, boys. I love you. I'm sorry to spring this on you. It's taken the last two weeks to get everything in order, and I hoped to have more time to let it all settle in, but... well, adventure calls."

As if on cue, Walker pushes through the front door.

My heart leaps at the sight of him, a smile stretching my face as I hop up from the table and rush to him. He catches me in a warm embrace when I throw myself into his arms, but because he's ever the gentleman, he only presses a kiss to my hair since the boys are present.

"I see I'm a little early," he muses.

"We're just wrapping up."

Walker looks behind me with a wry grin, then he releases me and steps over to the table. One by one, he shakes my sons' hands.

"I want you all to know that I will care for and protect Lorelei with my life," he says. "You have my word."

"Yeah, well, your word better hold, or we'll have your ass," Noah says.

"*Language,*" I chime in.

Walker just nods, a good spirit through it all, and he claps Noah on the shoulder before making his way back to the bedroom. He comes out with two suitcases of mine, packed to the gills, and rolls them toward the front door.

"I'll be in the truck," he says.

"And I'll be right out."

Once he's gone again, I head back to the table, opening my arms on a sigh.

"Well," I say. "Can I get a hug from my boys before I go?"

"I can't believe this is happening," Michael says, but it's not with indignation or hurt. It's almost... *awe* in his voice. Respect. Admiration.

"Honestly, neither can I," I confess on a laugh.

Logan is the first up from the table, and he wraps me in a fierce hug. "I don't know what we're going to do without you here," he says. "But I know I'm happy to figure it out if it means *you* are happy."

I squeeze him. "Thank you."

Jordan steps in next, handing his son to Logan before he gives me a hug so big it lifts my feet off the floor.

"You deserve this," he says. "Don't worry about a thing here. We've got it covered. You just have fun."

"But be safe," Logan adds. "You still have that Mace I gave you?"

"In my purse, like always."

He nods, seemingly placated, and then Michael is beaming at me through the laptop screen.

"I hope these adventures of yours bring you to the city sometime," he says. "But if they don't, then we'll see you at home for the holidays."

"Always," I promise.

He blows me a kiss, and I catch it before blowing one back.

Noah still seems like he's grappling with it all, but to his credit, he stands anyway, heaving a sigh as he wraps me in a hug.

"I won't lie, I'm not entirely thrilled about this," he says. "But... I'm also well aware that you're a grown woman who can make her own decisions."

I pinch his side. "You're damn straight."

"Language!" Michael says, and everyone laughs.

"I love you," Noah says, serious now, his eyes searching mine as he frames my arms in his hands. "You could have given us a little more time, you know," he adds on a tease. "But maybe it's a good thing you didn't. I might have found a way to try to make you stay."

"I'll be back," I promised. "Often."

"We will be here," Jordan says. "And I think I speak on behalf of us all when I say... thanks, Mom."

His voice breaks a little, and he looks up at the sky before beaming down at the baby boy sleeping in his arms.

"Being a parent takes a lot of patience, a lot of sacrifice. I don't think any of us really understood that until recently. But just know we get it now. And we're thankful for everything you've done for us."

"Now, it's your turn to go out and be selfish for a while," Logan adds. "And if there's anything *we* can do for *you*, just name it."

"Take care of this house," I say instantly, pointing a finger at each of them. "And make room for one more at the table when we come home to visit." I look behind me at the front door. "Pretty sure I'm keeping this one."

With another round of hugs, I grab my purse and rush out the door before my emotions can catch up to me. My boys didn't know it until today, but I've already told their wives and kids about my trip, getting in all the hugs and kisses I could. I've bawled enough over the last two weeks to fill a river, and right now, I don't want to cry.

Right now, I want to kiss Walker Jones, and I want to start our new life together.

So I do just that.

I slide into the warm passenger seat, thanking Walker — who jumped out of the truck and opened my door for me, of course. Once he's seated beside me again, I plant a long, slow kiss to his lips, sighing as he thumbs my chin when we pull away.

"What do you say, Lorelei Becker?" he asks, hand on the gear shift, waiting. "You ready to see the world?"

I smile, emotion thick in my throat as I look away from him and out the passenger side window.

I never did remember what my late husband's drink order was, but I think I realized it didn't matter. That wasn't the reason I walked into that bar on Christmas Eve.

It was to find Walker.

And maybe that was my gift from John.

My eyes drift up to the clouds, to where there's a break in them, and a single ray of sunlight shines down on the town I've always called home.

My eyes flutter shut, and I feel him — in that ray of sun, in the house I'm leaving behind, in the town that built us, in this truck, in *me*.

A single tear slides down my cheek when I open my eyes, and I smile when I carefully thumb it away.

I will always love you.

The words fill my chest, and I send them to Heaven.

Or maybe, Heaven sends them down to me.

Then, I turn back to Walker, covering his hand on the gear shift with my own and kicking it to drive.

"Ready."

More from Kandi Steiner

The Kings of the Ice Series
Meet Your Match
One Month with Vince Tanev: Tampa's Hotshot Rookie – twenty-four-seven access on and off the ice. The headline says it all, and my bosses are over the moon when the opportunity of a lifetime lands in my lap. Of course, they aren't aware that they're forcing me into proximity with the one man who grates on my last nerve.

Watch Your Mouth
My brother's teammates know not to touch me — but that doesn't stop me from daring Jaxson Brittain to be the first to break the rule.

Learn Your Lesson
Single dad and grumpy goalie Will Perry finds himself wanting to break his own rules when it comes to his new sunshiney nanny.

The Red Zone Rivals Series
Fair Catch
As if being the only girl on the college football team wasn't hard enough, Coach had to go and assign my brother's best friend — and my number one enemy — as my roommate.

Blind Side
The hottest college football safety in the nation just asked me to be his fake girlfriend.
And I just asked him to take my virginity.

Quarterback Sneak
Quarterback Holden Moore can have any girl he wants.
Except me: the coach's daughter.

Hail Mary (an Amazon #1 Bestseller!)
Leo F*cking Hernandez.
North Boston University's star running back, notorious bachelor, and number one on my people I would murder if I could get away with it list.
And now?
My new roommate.

The Becker Brothers Series
On the Rocks (book 1)
Neat (book 2)
Manhattan (book 3)
Old Fashioned (book 4)
Four brothers finding love in a small Tennessee town that revolves around a whiskey distillery with a dark past — including the mysterious death of their father.

The Best Kept Secrets Series
(AN AMAZON TOP 10 BESTSELLER)
What He Doesn't Know (book 1)
What He Always Knew (book 2)
What He Never Knew (book 3)
Charlie's marriage is dying. She's perfectly content to go down in the flames, until her first love shows back up and reminds her the other way love can burn.

Close Quarters
A summer yachting the Mediterranean sounded like heaven to Jasmine after finishing her undergrad degree. But her boyfriend's billionaire boss always gets what he wants. And this time, he wants her.

Make Me Hate You
Jasmine has been avoiding her best friend's brother for years, but when they're both in the same house for a wedding, she can't resist him — no matter how she tries.

The Wrong Game
(AN AMAZON TOP 5 BESTSELLER)
Gemma's plan is simple: invite a new guy to each home game using her season tickets for the Chicago Bears. It's the perfect way to avoid getting emotionally attached and also get some action. But after Zach gets his chance to be her practice round, he decides one game just isn't enough. A sexy, fun sports romance.

The Right Player
She's avoiding love at all costs. He wants nothing more than to lock her down. Sexy, hilarious and swoon-worthy, The Right Player is the perfect read for sports romance lovers.

On the Way to You
It was only supposed to be a road trip, but when Cooper discovers the journal
of the boy driving the getaway car, everything changes. An emotional, angsty
road trip romance.

A Love Letter to Whiskey
(AN AMAZON TOP 10 BESTSELLER)
An angsty, emotional romance between two lovers fighting the curse of bad
timing.

Read Love, Whiskey – Jamie's side of the story and an extended epilogue – in
the new Fifth Anniversary Edition!

Weightless
Young Natalie finds self-love and romance with her personal trainer, along
with a slew of secrets that tie them together in ways she never thought possible.

Revelry
Recently divorced, Wren searches for clarity in a summer cabin outside of
Seattle, where she makes an unforgettable connection with the broody, small
town recluse next door.

Say Yes
Harley is studying art abroad in Florence, Italy. Trying to break free of her
perfectionism, she steps outside one night determined to Say Yes to anything
that comes her way. Of course, she didn't expect to run into Liam Benson...

Washed Up
Gregory Weston, the boy I once knew as my son's best friend, now a man I
don't know at all. No, not just a man. A doctor. And he wants me...

The Christmas Blanket
Stuck in a cabin with my ex-husband waiting out a blizzard? Not exactly what
I had pictured when I planned a surprise visit home for the holidays...

Black Number Four
A college, Greek-life romance of a hot young poker star and the boy sent to
take her down.

The Palm South University Series
Rush (book 1)
Anchor (book 2)
Pledge (book 3)
Legacy (book 4)
Ritual (book 5)
Hazed (book 6)
Greek (book 7)
#1 NYT Bestselling Author Rachel Van Dyken says, "If Gossip Girl and River-
dale had a love child, it would be PSU." This angsty college series will be your
next guilty addiction.

Tag Chaser
She made a bet that she could stop chasing military men, which seemed easy
— until her knight in shining armor and latest client at work showed up in
Army ACUs.

Song Chaser
Tanner and Kellee are perfect for each other. They frequent the same bars,
love the same music, and have the same desire to rip each other's clothes off.
Only problem? Tanner is still in love with his best friend.

About the Author

Kandi Steiner is a #1 Amazon Bestselling Author. Best known for writing "emotional rollercoaster" stories, she loves bringing flawed characters to life and writing about real, raw romance — in all its forms. No two Kandi Steiner books are the same, and if you're a lover of angsty, emotional, and inspirational reads, she's your gal.

An alumna of the University of Central Florida, Kandi graduated with a double major in Creative Writing and Advertising/PR with a minor in Women's Studies. Her love for writing started at the ripe age of 10, and in 6th grade, she wrote and edited her own newspaper and distributed to her classmates. Eventually, the principal caught on and the newspaper was quickly halted, though Kandi tried fighting for her "freedom of press."

She took particular interest in writing romance after college, as she has always been a die hard hopeless romantic, and likes to highlight all the challenges of love as well as the triumphs.

When Kandi isn't writing, you can find her reading books of all kinds, planning her next adventure, or pole dancing (yes, you read that right). She enjoys live music, traveling, hiking, yoga, playing with her fur babies and soaking up the sweetness of life.

CONNECT WITH KANDI:
NEWSLETTER: kandisteiner.com/newsletter
FACEBOOK: facebook.com/kandisteiner
FACEBOOK READER GROUP (Kandiland):
facebook.com/groups/kandilandks
INSTAGRAM: Instagram.com/kandisteiner
TIKTOK: tiktok.com/@authorkandisteiner
TWITTER: twitter.com/kandisteiner
PINTEREST: pinterest.com/authorkandisteiner
WEBSITE: www.kandisteiner.com

Kandi Steiner may be coming to a city near you! Check out her "events" tab
to see all the signings she's attending in the near future:
www.kandisteiner.com/events